Douglas Reeman joined the Navy in 1941. He did convoy duty in the Atlantic, the Arctic, and the North Sea, and later served in motor torpedo boats.

As he says, 'I am always asked to account for the perennial appeal of the sea story, and its enduring interest for the people of so many nationalities and cultures. It would seem that the eternal and sometimes elusive triangle of man, ship and ocean, particularly under the stress of war, produces the best qualities of courage and compassion, irrespective of the rights and wrongs of conflict . . . The sea has no understanding of righteous or unjust causes. It is the common enemy, respected by all who serve on it, ignored at their peril.'

Apart from the thirty novels he has written under his own name, he has also written twenty-four other historical novels featuring Richard and Adam Bolitho, under the pseudonym of Alexander Kent.

DOUGLAS REEMAN

BADGE OF GLORY

and

THE FIRST TO LAND

Badge of Glory

Douglas Reeman

ARROW

Published by Arrow Books in 1983

Reprinted 14 times

Copyright © High Seas Authors Ltd 1982

The right of Douglas Reeman to be identified as the author of this
work has been asserted by him in accordance with the Copyright,
Designs and Patents Act, 1988

First published in the United Kingdom in 1982 by Hutchinson

Arrow Books
The Random House Group Limited
20 Vauxhall Bridge Road, London SW1V 2SA

Random House Australia (Pty) Limited
20 Alfred Street, Milsons Point, Sydney
New South Wales 2061, Australia

Random House New Zealand Limited
18 Poland Road, Glenfield
Auckland 10, New Zealand

Random House (Pty) Limited
Endulini, 5a Jubilee Road, Parktown 2193, South Africa

The Random House Group Limited Reg. No. 954009

www.randomhouse.co.uk

A CIP catalogue record for this book
is available from the British Library

Papers used by Random House are natural,
recyclable products made from wood grown in
sustainable forests. The manufacturing processes conform to
the environmental regulations of the country of origin

ISBN 0 09 932100 9

Printed and bound in Germany by
Elsnerdruck, Berlin

For Winifred
with my love

Acknowledgement

I wish to thank all the Royal Marines, past and present, who gave me their help and encouragement, and especially the Director and Staff of the Royal Marines Museum, Eastney and the RM Commando Training Centre at Lympstone.

Contents

I

The Old Navy

It was said that the August of 1850 was one of the hottest and
finest anyone could remember. With only a few days left in
the month it showed no sign of breaking, and on this particular evening the fleet anchored at Spithead breathed and
quivered like molten gold. Only a certain mistiness around
the Isle of Wight and longer shadows beneath the towering
shapes of the assembled ships gave a hint that it was nearly
sunset.

Between the land and the anchorage many smaller craft
pulled busily back and forth, some connected with affairs of
the fleet, and others, less expertly handled, to carry their
untroubled passengers on sightseeing trips around the display of naval might.

One white-painted cutter thrust her way swiftly through
the local traffic with what appeared to be casual ease. For she
was one of the flagship's own boats, and woe betide anyone
who was foolhardy enough to delay her passage.

In the sternsheets, his scarlet coatee making a bright
contrast with the uniforms of the coxswain and the midshipman in charge, Captain Philip Blackwood looked around,
surprised that he had almost reached the flagship and had
barely noticed he had left the shore.

He searched his emotions for the hundredth time. Did he
feel resignation or apathy, resentment or excitement? There
seemed to be nothing at all. Like a clock which has stopped
for no recognizable reason.

He glanced at the biggest vessel which was anchored at the

head of the line. Her Majesty's Ship *Audacious* of ninety guns, the squadron's flagship, and somehow a symbol of Britain's unchallenged sea power. She was not old, but had been laid down and built to a design which had barely altered since Trafalgar, nearly half a century ago. She seemed to grow and expand as the cutter glided closer, and Blackwood saw a levelled telescope at the entry port as his approach was watched and reported.

Everything appeared to be exactly the same as when he had left two weeks ago to spend his leave with his father in Hampshire. During those weeks he had made up his mind, or thought he had. He had sent his marine attendant on ahead to deliver a letter to his lieutenant, the only other marine officer in the ship, and to pack his personal belongings in readiness to leave for the barracks. Blackwood had broken his own journey to face the colonel commandant at Forton Barracks. It had not been an easy interview, and in his mind Blackwood could still feel the dry stillness of the room, hear the distorted cries of a drill sergeant on the square as new recruits pounded up and down under musket and full pack.

Colonel Menzies had said in his calm, unemotional tone, 'Resign the Corps? *Bloody rubbish.*' One eyebrow had risen slightly. 'What did you *expect* me to say, man?'

Everything Blackwood had prepared, each carefully thought out reason had seemed to wither away like dead leaves under the colonel's unhurried appraisal.

'I served with your father. I respect him. And what of your grandfather? Another fine marine. A great man.'

At any other time Blackwood might have smiled. The colonel commandant's admiration for the Blackwood family had stopped there. All the others had been soldiers.

Colonel Menzies had pressed his fingertips together and stared up from his desk.

'You are twenty-six years old, and already a captain. You have proved your worth on active service, so one will aid the other. In these days of peace it is not easy to gain advancement, especially in the Corps. But there is no reason why you should not be an asset to us, and a link in your family's tradition.'

Looking back over the last hours Blackwood could remember little of his own voice in that quiet room.

Menzies had finished the interview in an almost matter of fact fashion.

'In any case, it is out of the question, at present. I have been told that the squadron will proceed to sea within the week. To replace the flagship's senior marine officer at this stage . . .' Even his austere face had cracked slightly. '. . . Twenty-six years old or not, would be unthinkable. I am required to send additional marines to the squadron, many of whom will be new recruits. Officers and NCOs with combat experience will be like gold nuggets.'

'My request is dismissed then, Colonel?' They were the only words he could recall.

'What request, Blackwood?' It was over.

'*Boat ahoy!*' A challenge from the flagship's gangway brought him back to earth with a jerk.

The coxswain cupped his hands. '*Aye, aye!*'

Perhaps that was it, Blackwood thought. The tradition before all else. The gangway staff knew this was one of the *Audacious*'s boats, and the duty officer would already have been told that Captain Blackwood, Royal Marines, was returning on board. He sighed and grasped his sword scabbard firmly in his left hand.

The playful enmity between seamen and marines was still there, another tradition. He was not going to stoke anyone's fire by tripping over his sword under the eyes of the side-party or by falling headlong into the Solent.

He pulled himself swiftly up the tumblehome and onto the gangway, conscious that he was no longer breathless in doing so. Two weeks ashore after the close confines of a crowded ship had worked wonders for him. Long walks around the estate, riding every day with his half-sister Georgina. It was already like part of a dream, made more so as the ship opened out as if to swallow him.

Blackwood touched his shako to the quarterdeck and nodded to the side-party. To his surprise, his lieutenant, Dick Cleveland, was not there to greet him, and instead the towering figure of Colour-Sergeant M'Crystal waited with obvious impatience for him to speak with the officer-of-the-watch.

The latter said quickly, 'There's been a change, Major.' He sounded harassed, on edge.

Blackwood waited. Once again tradition had spoken. Always the captain of marines was referred to as major, but had anyone, he wondered, ever in the past confused him with a ship's commanding officer?

'The Flag has shifted.'

Blackwood felt a tinge of warning. Menzies had said nothing about that. A new admiral for the squadron. It should have been worth mentioning, surely.

'The captain left word for you to see him as soon as you came off shore, sir.'

'And what about my lieutenant?'

The officer-of-the-watch stared at him as if that was of no importance at all compared with the awesome responsibility of receiving a new admiral.

'Mr Cleveland's broken his leg.' He flushed. 'There was a party aboard *Swiftsure*.'

Blackwood controlled his features with an effort. The lieutenant need say no more. Parties in other ships were always Cleveland's true weakness. After a few glasses he seemed to go wild. Now a broken leg had taken him from *Audacious* when he was really needed.

Blackwood said curtly, 'I'll see the captain.'

He nodded to Colour-Sergeant M'Crystal. Thank God he at least was here. To some people M'Crystal appeared frightening. He was tall and solidly built yet without an ounce of spare flesh on his frame. His scarlet coatee matching his face which, in spite of long service ashore and afloat, refused to tan and remained brick-red. Blackwood had known him since he had been commissioned at the age of eighteeen. M'Crystal had not always been a sergeant, and his stripes had gone up and down with his misfortunes and his hasty temper. But Blackwood had seen the real worth of the man. In New Zealand, just four years back during the Maori War, he had watched M'Crystal rally a handful of marines when they had been outnumbered by ten to one.

'What is it, Colour-Sergeant?'

M'Crystal ran his eyes over the youthful captain as if to reassure himself about something. It felt like an inspection.

He said in his thick voice, 'You heard about Mr Cleveland, sir, in Haslar Hospital. Took a fall, he did.' Without any change of expression he hurried on, 'New admiral's coming aboard tomorrow forenoon, sir. Full guard and ceremonial required, o' course. Twenty new privates have joined today and Sarnt Quintin is settling 'em into the barracks right now. Private Doak is under arrest for drunkenness.'

'I see.' Blackwood waited. There was more to come. Anything short of mutiny would be accepted as normal routine by M'Crystal and his crony, Sergeant Quintin.

'You've not seen the orders yet, sir?' He did not wait. 'The flag-officer to command this squadron is Sir James Ashley-Chute.'

'Come aft to my quarters.'

Blackwood fell in step with the towering sergeant and together they ducked their heads beneath the poop and made for the companion ladder. It was strange he had just been remembering M'Crystal's courage in New Zealand just four years ago. Vice-Admiral Sir James Ashley-Chute's appointment to command the squadron would have roused a few memories for him also. No wonder Colonel Menzies had made no mention of it. To be in the same squadron was bad enough. In the same ship was far worse.

Blackwood could picture the ferocious fighting on North Island as if it had just happened. Blazing sun, choking clouds of dust and musket smoke as the army had fought to overthrow the well-defended Maori stronghold at Ruapekapeka. A contingent of seamen had been landed earlier to relieve

pressure on the troops. Ashley-Chute had been in overall
charge of the operation, and had seemed determined that no
matter what the army attempted, his men could and would
do better. Things went badly wrong from the outset. Unused
to fighting ashore, the blue-jackets soon got themselves
separated from the soldiers and were hemmed in by hundreds
of the battle-crazed Maoris. Blackwood felt a chill at his spine
as he relived the sights and the terrifying yells of the attacking Maoris.

M'Crystal had been a corporal at the time, having lost his
sergeant's stripes after a brawl with a ship's cook.

The major in command of the marines had requested
permission to attack and relieve the beleaguered seamen.
Ashley-Chute had sent back a curt refusal. The major had
snapped angrily, 'At least I *asked* him, dammit!' Then,
drawing his sword, he had yelled above the din, 'Royal
Marines will advance! *Fix bayonets!*'

There had been less than fifty marines, and twenty-five had
fallen before the enemy had retreated and the stronghold had
been taken. The naval commander had been grateful enough,
but Ashley-Chute had sent an immediate summons for the
major to report to him with an explanation for his actions.

Seeing Blackwood, then a lieutenant, he had snapped. 'I
sent for your commanding officer! Has he not the courage to
face me?'

Blackwood had been shaking with fatigue and the delayed
shock of the short, savage fight. It had taken all his strength
to place his list of casualties on the admiral's table.

'The major is among the dead, sir.'

There had been no sign of remorse or pity, not even the
satisfaction of knowing that the marines' action had saved a
terrible loss of life and almost certain defeat.

He had said coldly, 'Just as well for him.'

M'Crystal was watching him grimly. 'There was talk of
you leaving the Corps, sir.'

Blackwood looked at him and smiled. There were no
secrets in any ship or barracks.

'It was *just* talk.'

M'Crystal beamed. 'Good. I'll pass the word, sir.'

Blackwood thrust open the door of his cabin and stepped into its familiar surroundings. There was no sign of a chest or case, and he could see his uniforms hanging in their canvas wardrobe, swaying very slowly as the great ship tugged at her cable.

Smithett, his personal attendant for two years, seemed to dominate the small cabin. He was almost as tall as M'Crystal, but whereas the colour-sergeant was fierce or joyful as the mood took him, Smithett was always the same. He was a dour, dull-faced man, with all his lines turning down. His eyes, his mouth, even his chin, seemed to be set in permanent disapproval. Fortunately, Blackwood had grown to understand him and to appreciate his many skills. Servant, orderly, Smithett could turn his hand to various things which were never mentioned in regulations. He had volunteered for the work of marine officer's attendant, and when Blackwood had asked him why, Smithett had given as near as he dared to a shrug and had replied, 'Knew yer father, sir.' And that, apparently, was that.

Blackwood sat down on the edge of his cot.

'You didn't pack my gear then.'

Their eyes met.

Smithett said, 'No point, sir. We're sailin' next week.'

Blackwood could feel his earlier resolve fading away. M'Crystal's anxious scrutiny, Smithett's positive belief that he would not quit the Corps and all that it stood for had a lot to do with it.

When he had faced his father on the first day of his leave he had expected a rebuke, even a show of contempt. Lieutenant-Colonel Eugene Blackwood would still be on active service if he had his way. But promotion was restricted, and in peacetime any officer who wanted an appointment was considered fortunate to gain one.

But his father had said, 'I know you, Philip. You want action. You think that is all there is to being a marine. Action and glory. There are many like you, men who forget that it is continuity of service and training which count. A month of war requires years of experience and leadership.'

Blackwood had tried to describe his feelings when he had seen his own commanding officer fall in the Maori War. It had seemed senseless for a man like him to die out there in a place nobody had ever heard of.

But as he had tried to explain he had felt the same inner uncertainty as when he had faced the colonel commandant. Perhaps his father was right. Action and glory, was that what he really wanted for himself?

He thought suddenly of his grandfather. What had Menzies said of him? *A great man*. Curiously, Blackwood had always felt closer to his grandfather than his father. As a boy he had grown up with the old man's memories, had seen the pale eyes above the white whiskers light up from within as he had told and retold the stories of places and ships he had known. Names painted in history. The Nile. Copenhagen. Trafalgar. In memory it was always the same, with no gaps of fear or boredom in between. The old man had died in the same house where Blackwood had tried to persuade his father to see his point of view.

It might have been different if his mother was still alive, he thought. But she had died after a short fever, and Blackwood's father had remarried the following year to a girl twenty years younger than himself.

Perhaps his father had been too worried about his own news to care much for his son's uncertainty over his future.

He had eventually dropped his announcement with the forthrightness of a thirty-two-pound shot.

'We're selling Hawks Hill, Philip. Your mother, er, Claudia intends we should move to London. It's her sort of world, y'see.'

Blackwood frowned as he thought about it. He felt Smithett running a brush over his shoulders, patting his coatee into place. Routine and order.

It was unthinkable to be leaving Hawks Hill and the estate

in Hampshire. His father obviously hated the idea but, as usual, would do anything for his wife. The colonel's lady, as they called her in the village. They had never really accepted her, but then she had done little to encourage the 'local bumpkins', as she called them.

Blackwood said, 'I am going to see the captain. Tomorrow we shall have to do something about getting another lieutenant sent to us.'

It was always easy to say 'we' and 'us' to Smithett. Rather as you might to a faithful dog. He never answered back, but could make his displeasure known in other ways when he felt like it.

He picked up his shako and left the cabin. For a moment longer he paused and glanced aft towards the great cabin and private quarters where the admiral would hold court. It would be even worse for the ship's officers, he thought, unless they knew Ashley-Chute's little ways.

With a sigh Blackwood ran lightly up the companion ladder and turned towards the shadowy confines of the poop. In the short while he had been in his cabin it had grown dark. Around and beneath him the great ship of the line groaned and murmured, her massive timbers and towering masts and rigging keeping up their constant chorus as they had since the day she had first slid into salt water.

The smells too were like part of himself. Paint and tar, cordage and damp canvas. The old navy. Blackwood stopped short within view of the scarlet-coated sentry outside the stern cabin. That too might be a reason. He did not *want* to stay with a navy which seemed content to remain old and unchanged. Young officers were volunteering to serve in the discomfort and dirt of the new steam vessels simply because they *were* new, and young like themselves.

The marine sentry's heels came together with a snap, and the level stare beneath the man's shako fixed on a point above Blackwood's left epaulette.

Blackwood gave a grave smile. 'Good evening, Rocke.'

'Sar!' Rocke shot a quick grin.

Blackwood rapped on the screen door, wondering if he would ever discover a way of knowing which of the Rocke twins he was speaking to. Even standing together in the same squad they were completely alike. Sergeant Quintin knew they changed duties to suit themselves, but had never been able to prove it. The twins came from Somerset, and their father had been a marine too.

It was so often like that. As one sergeant had said, 'In the Corps we don't recruit marines. We breeds 'em!'

The door opened and the captain's clerk ushered Blackwood inside.

Blackwood walked aft and saw the glittering lights of the anchored ships through the great stern windows, distorted like fairy lanterns by the thick glass.

He was back. Whatever it was he had tried to fight was far stronger than he had imagined.

Captain John Ackworthy half rose from his chair and sank down again. He was a heavy man, with shaggy grey eyebrows and a face like tooled leather, criss-crossed with hundreds of tiny lines. Ackworthy was old for his rank, and had been at sea all his life from the age of twelve. *Audacious* would be his last command, and was certainly the biggest vessel he had ever served. With the previous admiral, who had been old like himself, he had felt content, and had accepted that he would never bridge the gulf to flag rank. When *Audacious* paid off, Captain Ackworthy would join all the other ancient mariners on the beach.

The swift change of events and the appointment of a new flag-officer in command had unsettled him considerably. There were four ships of the line in the squadron, and Ackworthy would willingly have taken command of the oldest and smallest to avoid having a vice-admiral's flag flying at the fore, especially one with a reputation like Ashley-Chute's.

He regarded the marine officer thoughtfully. Blackwood looked strained, and his jaw was set just a bit too tightly. Ackworthy had never really understood marines, but he had liked Blackwood from their first meeting. He had removed his shako and his brown hair was surprisingly tousled, so that he looked even younger. He had clean-cut features and level grey-blue eyes. A reliable English face, but one you might never know in a thousand years, Ackworthy decided.

'Sit you down, Major. I want to talk about tomorrow.' He glanced meaningly at the deckhead as if he could pierce it with a glance and already see the vice-admiral's flag breaking at the foremast truck.

Blackwood listened as Ackworthy rambled on about the admiral's time of arrival at Portsmouth Point, the requirements for guard and band, the need for a perfect turn-out from captain to ship's boy.

Did Captain Ackworthy know about Ashley-Chute's nickname, he wondered? *Monkey*. Very apt too. Perhaps he had changed after four years. It seemed unlikely.

Blackwood had often wondered if there had been any official enquiry or action taken by the Admiralty over Ashley-Chute's failure to recognize the danger to his landing parties at North Island on that terrible day. If so, it had been kept very quiet. But Ashley-Chute was still of the same rank, and for someone so ambitious it might be possible he had been quietly laid aside like Ackworthy. In which case he would be doubly determined to force his stamp on the squadron without delay.

Ackworthy ruffled through some papers on his table. 'Almost forgot. Guard-boat brought a message from Forton Barracks. A marine second lieutenant will be joining the ship tomorrow. Sounds as if he may be straight from training. Don't even know his name yet. But all the same . . .' He did not finish.

Blackwood gauged the moment. They were alone except for Ackworthy's cabin servant, who was probably waiting in his pantry for the call to bring in some of the captain's claret.

He said, 'May I ask what orders we are under, sir?'

Ackworthy pouted his lower lip. 'We are assuming the duties of the West African Squadron. For how long and to what purpose I cannot say at present.' He frowned so that his eyes almost vanished. 'I'd be obliged if you would not mention anything about it.'

Blackwood nodded. 'Of course, sir.' *Poor old devil. You're scared of Monkey and he's not even here yet.*

The servant entered quietly and placed a tray and glasses on the table, then withdrew just as softly.

Ackworthy picked up a decanter and held it to the deck-head lantern. In his great fist it looked like a flask.

'I understand you served with Sir James Ashley-Chute before?' He poured two glasses with elaborate care. 'That affair in New Zealand, wasn't it?'

Blackwood sipped the wine. 'Yes, sir. In forty-six.' He waited, the wine moistening his throat, calming him.

'I have a new third lieutenant since you went on leave.' Ackworthy poured himself another glass and some of the wine slopped across his papers. He did not seem to notice. 'Thought you should know. He's Sir James's son.' He moved violently away from the table and stared through the stern windows. 'As if I don't have enough trouble on my plate!' He seemed to realize he had exposed his feelings too much in front of a subordinate and added harshly, 'Just make certain your marines put on a good display tomorrow.' He turned away from the windows. 'I expect you've got things to do.'

Blackwood stood up. 'Yes, sir. And thank you.'

Ackworthy shrugged. 'Glad you're staying under my command, by the way.'

Blackwood left the cabin and walked slowly towards the quarterdeck. *The West African Squadron. It was a long way to go. When he came home again there would be no house, no familiar places to walk and ride.*

He thought then of his half-sister Georgina. She was sixteen, with the wild beauty of a young foal. She had kissed him goodbye this morning, *was it only today?* She had not acted like a sister, nor had he felt like a brother towards her as she had pressed against him. *Perhaps West Africa was just about the right distance after all.*

Colour-Sergeant M'Crystal and his friend Sergeant Quintin stood motionless in the shadows as Blackwood approached the glowing rectangle of the companionway.

M'Crystal said in a hoarse whisper, 'There he goes, Joe. Cool as steel. Nothing to worry about.'

Quintin grunted. 'We'll see about that, Hamish. You just get this bloody commission over an' done with, *an'* with yer stripes still on yer arm, *then* I'll believe yer!'

As the first pale stars glittered above the gently spiralling mastheads, the ship and the eight hundred and fifty souls who served her settled down to wait for the new day which might change things for all of them.

'Got a good day for it, sir.' Smithett flicked a piece of invisible dust from Blackwood's coatee and regarded him unsmilingly.

Blackwood was used to him and knew that he would never have to worry about taking a parade with some fault in his uniform or equipment. He glanced at himself in the mirror above his small writing table and grimaced. Perhaps he was making too much of Ashley-Chute's arrival. Maybe they all were. He sighed and said, 'Keep a weather-eye open for the new second lieutenant.'

He climbed up the companion ladder knowing that Smithett would vanish until the ceremonial was over.

On deck the sunlight was bright and the reflections across the Solent harsh to the eyes. Since the hands had been roused and then piped to breakfast after the decks had been washed down, a sort of expectancy had fallen over the whole ship.

Blackwood tugged on his white gloves and glanced quickly along the upper deck.

Every line and halliard neatly flaked or turned on its belaying pin, each strand of rigging taut and stiff like black glass. On either side of the deck, partly hidden by the two gangways which linked forecastle to quarterdeck, the upper batteries of twelve-pounders looked as if they had been positioned with the aid of a carpenter's rule.

He shifted his glance to the marine guard and the smaller figures of the boy fifers who were being lectured by Corporal Bly.

Across the poop there were further ranks of marines, and he guessed that Sergeant Quintin had had the good sense to place the new recruits as far aft as he could manage so that they would not disgrace him.

He walked slowly towards the guard, his eyes automatically picking out the familiar faces, the expressions which disguised their owners' backgrounds which were as varied as their names.

That was one of the main differences between a marine and a seaman, he thought. Sailors usually came from ports and harbours, or very close to the sea, whereas marines were often recruited miles inland, or joined to follow a family tradition. Marines were trained ashore, and seamen had to learn from the moment they stepped aboard their ship, from the deck up, and from the deck down.

The marines were standing in loose lines, their long muskets at their sides, their ranks rolling slightly to the ship's motion.

Colour-Sergeant M'Crystal tapped the deck gently with his half-pike. 'Marines . . .'

He did not shout or raise his voice. It was more like a deep rumble. But Blackwood saw the ranks of scarlet coatees and white trousers stiffen, as if an invisible force had thrust rods right through each line of men.

M'Crystal reported, 'Ready for inspection, *sir*.'

Blackwood walked slowly along each rank. He could feel the officers watching from the quarterdeck, the seamen who were working aloft in the shrouds or on the yards pausing in their search for last-minute faults to stare down as the marines went through their ritual.

Beneath the peak of each Albert shako he caught a brief glimpse of a blank, expressionless face. Like the white cross-belts and gleaming bayonets, it was part of the whole, but to Blackwood every one was different. Corporal Jones who fancied himself as a prize-fighter. Private Callow who had dived overboard to rescue a seaman who had fallen from the main-yard. Private Frazier who had been with him in New Zealand, a superb shot, but a man who shied away from promotion as if it was poison. The Rocke twins, like mirror images. M'Crystal had said that if one cut himself shaving the other would do the same to sustain the confusion. Private Bulford who had run away from home to enlist. Later they had discovered it was because his father was in jail for robbery.

It was a good turn-out, as he had expected. How they managed it in their quarters, called as always the barracks, he could barely imagine. Especially with the extra marines who had been sent across from the shore. And why did they need additional men anyway? There should be enough aboard the four ships of the line and their two frigates for any normal activity.

The midshipman-of-the-watch called in a shrill voice, 'Barge has left the sallyport, sir!'

The quarterdeck stirred into life immediately. As another midshipman ran to inform the captain, boatswain's mates stood at the entry port, moistening their silver calls on their lips in readiness to greet the new lord and master.

Seamen vanished from the yards, and those still on deck were dressed in their best uniforms, their horny feet confined uncomfortably in shoes.

Blackwood glanced at the quarterdeck where the lieutenants and senior warrant officers were lined up in sweating discomfort. It was unusual to see them all together except for special parades. Cocked hats and gold lace, swords and gloves. His glance settled on a short, pale-faced lieutenant in the front rank. That had to be Ashley-Chute's son. The same short legs which made his arms dangle at his sides as if they were too heavy for him. He felt a tinge of sympathy even though he did not know him. Blackwood had always managed to avoid serving under his own father, he had heard too many tales about the rift it could cause. Like the teacher whose son attends the same school and must therefore be the brightest pupil, no matter what.

Captain Ackworthy, even bulkier and more impressive in his full dress uniform, appeared on deck. He had probably been standing in his cabin listening and waiting, Blackwood thought.

Blackwood turned his head slightly and looked across the glistening water. There were plenty of local craft about again, and he could see the upturned faces and the bright colours of women's clothing as they bobbed around the anchored ships. The guard-boat pulled warily amongst them, just in case one might try to get too close on this special day.

Eight bells chimed out from the forecastle, and from the corner of his eye Blackwood saw *Audacious*'s dark green barge turning in a neat arc for the final approach to the main-chains. Through the arched backs of the bargemen he could see the cocked hat of the passenger. Behind him, one of the ship's lieutenants stood with the coxswain as if he was carved out of wood.

'Stand by on the quarterdeck!'

The marine fifers raised their instruments or adjusted their drums, and Blackwood drew his sword, recalling with sudden clarity that day he had faced Ashley-Chute across the table, the day the major had drawn his sword and had died leading his men.

Colour-Sergeant M'Crystal hissed in a fierce whisper, 'God *Almighty*, sir!'

It was so unlike M'Crystal to lose his self-control during a ceremonial parade that it was somehow worse than if he had shouted a terrible obscenity.

Blackwood saw another boat pulling purposefully towards the *Audacious*. It must have come around the stern when everyone was watching the opposite direction. It was a small boat, probably from Gosport, not that it mattered now. It had only one passenger, and Blackwood could well appreciate the strength of M'Crystal's feelings. There was no mistaking the uniform of a Royal Marines second lieutenant.

Captain Ackworthy opened and closed his mouth but no sound emerged.

It fell to Netten, *Audacious*'s first lieutenant, to yell, 'Stand away there!'

The guard-boat too had realized what was happening and increased speed to intercept the waterman. Unfortunately, one of her oarsmen lost the stroke and vanished into the bottom, legs kicking wildly, to the delight of the boy fifers. They were too young to realize the enormity of the disaster.

The barge hooked onto the chains, the oars rising like white bones as the side-boys steadied the gunwale against *Audacious*'s fat hull.

Then all was drowned by the shrill of calls, the stamp and crack of muskets being brought to the present and the fifers' rendering of 'Heart of Oak'.

Blackwood brought his sword down with a flourish and watched narrowly beneath the shadow of his peak as the cocked hat and epaulettes of Vice-Admiral Sir James Ashley-Chute, KCB, appeared at the top of the ladder.

He looked much the same, but older. He still wore his cocked hat at a rakish angle. If his subordinates had dared to wear their hats in anything but a fore and aft position they would have imagined the heavens had fallen on them.

A broad, puggy nose and large iron-grey sideburns, and the disdainful stare which Blackwood remembered so well. His mouth was set in a thin line, as if he had no lips at all. He was carrying a pair of white gloves and he flicked his hat with them, more like a dismissal than a salute.

As Ackworthy hurried to meet him he made the vice-admiral look even smaller. But only in stature, Blackwood thought. Somehow Ashley-Chute's tightly packed belligerence seemed to reduce the captain to shambling awkwardness.

'Welcome aboard, Sir James.'

The admiral's eyes moved across the guard of honour and rested just for a second on M'Crystal. They shifted to the ship, the neatly furled sails, the assembled lieutenants and the blue press of seamen on the upper deck.

'Quite so, Captain Ackworthy.' He slapped his palm with his gloves in time with his words. 'A fine looking ship.' Ackworthy's smile vanished as the little admiral added crisply, 'But then I have the right to insist on excellence, hmm?'

For the first time his eyes settled on Blackwood. 'You may fall out the guard. Very smart. As I would expect on such an occasion and with ample notice, hmm?'

'Would you care to meet the officers, sir?' Ackworthy sounded already lost.

'Later. I would like to see my quarters. My flag-lieutenant is arriving shortly with further stores for my use. You may however make a signal to the squadron for all captains to repair on board in two hours time.'

Ackworthy lowered his voice. 'I think Captain Boyd of the *Argyll* may be ashore, sir.'

Ashley-Chute glanced up at him curiously. 'I said *all* captains. Please see to it.'

He turned towards the poop and then hesitated. Without turning his head he said, 'There appeared to be a marine officer of sorts attempting to approach my flagship in a fashion more suited to a Spanish fisherman. See that he is disciplined. Or get rid of him, please attend to that also.'

As Ackworthy followed the admiral into the shadow of the poop the first lieutenant breathed out very slowly.

To Blackwood he said softly, 'Well, Major, a fine beginning, eh?'

The dismissed guard tramped past to make their way below, but M'Crystal waited behind, fuming as if he would burst into flames. Beneath his shako his ginger hair added to his appearance of barely controlled fury.

'I'll get that officer's name for you, sir!'

Blackwood eyed him gravely. 'No need, Colour-Sergeant. His name is the same as mine.'

As Lieutenant Netten had just remarked, it was a fine beginning.

2

Of One Company

Philip Blackwood sat at his small writing table and glanced over the duty roster which M'Crystal and Quintin had prepared. He noticed that the new recruits had been carefully spread amongst the more experienced sections, and knew his NCOs would be quick to make further changes if the need arose.

He thought of the days since Vice-Admiral Sir James Ashley-Chute's flag had broken at the masthead. After the brisk scrutiny of the assembled officers and marine guard they had barely seen anything of him. Nothing had changed, Blackwood thought, not even that old idiosyncrasy which had stamped him like a hallmark. On the New Zealand station he had been notorious for his aloofness. He was rarely seen to speak to junior officers, let alone common seamen, but made his wrath felt through his captains. It was odd, but Blackwood could not recall Ashley-Chute ever being known for awarding a word of praise about anything.

The captains of the squadron had come aboard the flagship regularly each forenoon and had entered the admiral's quarters like men going to the scaffold. They had left in their various boats, with no word being exchanged but for the necessity of ceremony.

Blackwood leaned back in his chair and listened to the great ship around him. Ashley-Chute was like a force within the hull. The ship felt heavy with it.

He thought too of the army of carpenters and working parties which had converged on the admiral's quarters almost within an hour of his arrival. Officers had been moved from their cabins and made to share with others on the deck below. Screens had been extended, fresh furniture brought from the shore, and many of the guns withdrawn from the cabin ports and replaced by cut down Quakers or wooden replicas to give more space in Ashley-Chute's quarters. His flag-lieutenant, a nervous, stiff-faced man named Pelham, was frequently seen dashing ashore in the duty boat or rushing back again with some important message for his master.

But apart from a rare glimpse of the great man on the poop perhaps at sunset, or looking from the stern gallery of his cabin, the admiral remained withdrawn from his ship and her company.

Blackwood took up a pen and hesitated as he saw the name of his junior officer at the top of the list. H. Blackwood, RM2L.

As they had faced each other on the day of the admiral's displeasure, Blackwood could remember his feelings of annoyance, and something else perhaps, shame?

Harry Blackwood, his eighteen-year-old half-brother, was too like Georgina for comfort. The same recklessness in the eyes, the way of being serious and mocking at the same time.

It was not easy to be angry with him because of his eagerness to join his first ship, even at the expense of infuriating the admiral and of course Colour-Sergeant M'Crystal.

Calls trilled overhead, and he heard the muffled cries of boatswain's mates as they yelled at the working parties on deck to stand easy and prepare for the midday meal.

It would be good to get away from England, Blackwood thought suddenly. He was sick of all the uncertainties about his father's proposed move to London, about his own feeble attempts to resign his commission, about so many things.

He signed the list with an angry flourish and wished he could go ashore for one last walk through the untroubled crowds who were taking advantage of the late summer. But he knew it would be too risky to leave his young second-in-command to deal with the affairs of the flagship and a crowd of new recruits as well. He must stay aboard and keep an eye on him without his knowing it.

But to face one more lunch in the wardroom with all the unspoken questions, the sense of uneasiness which pervaded it like an extension of the admiral's moods, was unbearable.

They had all received a surprise this morning, those who did not yet know of Ashley-Chute's habits. There was to be a 'grand reception' on board before sailing. In the afternoon there would be a squadron race for the fastest boat's crew. The ship's company would provide entertainment with hornpipes and other dances, and *then*, Vice-Admiral Ashley-Chute would entertain his own personal guests to dinner in his quarters.

A handful of the squadron's officers would also attend the dinner. The captains, the flag-lieutenant, Ashley-Chute's son and, to Blackwood's amazement, himself.

He walked to an open gunport and leaned out to look at the Solent. Calm and with barely a breeze to ruffle its surface. It was to be hoped it remained so until after the admiral's guests had come and gone.

There were plenty of boats still clustered along the ship's side. Food and stores, equipment and spare rigging, everything a ship-of-war might need on a passage to the shores of Africa.

Blackwood thought of his grandfather. It was as if he could still hear the old man's voice as he had retold the stories of great campaigns, the horror and comradeship of battles long past.

Now, when *Audacious* broke out her anchor and led the squadron away from her home port, she would meet nothing but servile foreign traders who would willingly dip their ensigns to Victoria's unchallenged might on the oceans. Routine, ceremonial, drills and more routine.

There was a tap at the door and he turned to see Second Lieutenant Harry Blackwood standing stiffly in the entrance.

'Come in.'

The youthful officer closed the screen door behind him and took up the same stance of eager attention.

Blackwood gestured to the other chair. 'Sit down, for God's sake, Harry.'

The lieutenant sat and crossed his legs, his eyes fixed on his half-brother with a mixture of innocence and amusement.

'I want you to go round the ship with one of the lieutenants and learn all you can while we've got the time.' Blackwood felt irritated with himself that he should sound on the defensive. He added shortly, 'Colour-Sergeant M'Crystal will put you right about the duties for our people. *Listen* to him, and do not try to be clever. He has little confidence in junior officers.' He smiled in spite of the tension between them. 'I certainly had to earn *my* spurs from him!'

Harry Blackwood asked quietly, 'We are to sail on the day after tomorrow, sir? To Africa.' His tongue lingered on the word like a caress. 'I am so *lucky* to be coming with you.'

Blackwood studied him warily. There was a certain softness to Harry's mouth. A gentleness, like his sister's.

He asked abruptly, 'How *did* you get a last moment transfer to *Audacious*, by the way? You were at Woolwich. I'd have thought a replacement could have been more easily sent from Portsmouth.' It came out like an accusation.

The lieutenant shrugged. 'It was mostly coincidence, sir. I had been told I was to join a Portsmouth ship very shortly, but when I heard about the squadron needing more marines, I made enquiries about vacancies for officers.' He dropped his eyes beneath Blackwood's gaze. 'Then, er, Mother spoke to someone and hastened things.'

Blackwood nodded slowly. 'Did she indeed?'

So there it was. Whether this squadron's duties were to be important or not was open to question, but in times of peace any activity outside ceremonial visits to foreign harbours was a rare opportunity for a young officer embarking on a new career, sailor or marine.

And the colonel's lady would be the first to recognize such a chance, he thought grimly.

He relented and said, 'You may not be as lucky as you

think, my lad. I am no favourite of the admiral's, but I expect you already know that?'

Harry Blackwood eyed him mildly. 'Really, sir?'

'So keep on your toes. For the sake of the men, if not for me. They're a reliable lot of fellows. Rough and ready, but they'll give as good as they get. So stand up for them. No matter what.'

Harry's eyes followed him across the small cabin. 'Even if they're in the wrong?'

Blackwood looked down at him. 'Yes, if need be. We'll deal with our own, in our own way, understood?'

He wondered why he was speaking like this. Did he resent sharing it with a member of his family? Or was he really so protective of something he had so recently tried to leave?

Harry Blackwood was at the door again, his shako balanced in the crook of his arm.

Blackwood waited. 'Well?'

'What's it like, sir?' He kept his gaze fixed on Blackwood's face. 'I've never really had the chance to know you in recent years. Either you've been at sea or I've been away somewhere.' He shrugged, the gesture making him look even younger and more vulnerable. 'But to *kill* someone. In battle. What is it really like?'

Blackwood turned away. The question had hit him like a fist. Maybe because at one time he had asked it so often himself.

'You don't think about it, Harry. You put your shoulder against that of a friend and you keep going. No matter what is happening or how bad it looks. Afterwards . . .' He glanced down at the deck. 'Well, maybe you remember pieces of the whole, I'm not sure even now.' He met his gaze steadily, knowing it was important. 'But to kill a man is just a part of it. Like loading and firing a gun. You do it right, or you *go* under.'

Corporal Bly hovered in the passageway, and as the lieutenant withdrew he reported, 'Gangway sentries ready for inspection, *sir*.'

The young lieutenant tugged the shako down across his forehead and followed Bly towards the companion ladder.

Blackwood saw Smithett waiting to tidy the cabin after he had gone to lunch. Nothing seemed to matter to the taciturn marine, Blackwood thought. If the squadron completed a full three year commission on that inhospitable African coast he would not care. But if they were away that long Blackwood would be nearly thirty when he returned, whereas Harry would still only be twenty-one with his whole life ahead of him.

'Damn and bloody hell!'

Smithett paused in brushing one of Blackwood's tunics. 'Sir?'

'Nothing.' He smiled ruefully. 'The usual feeling, I suppose.'

Smithett hung the jacket carefully on a rail. 'There's nothin' ashore for me, sir.' He glanced around the cabin as if it were his own. 'This is the life. In me ship. With me mates.'

It was the longest sentence Blackwood had ever heard him make, and he was strangely moved by his sincerity.

He left the cabin, still thinking about Smithett. Perhaps it was better to be like him. No thought for the impossible or the improbable. Just one day at a time. He chuckled to himself. 'With me mates.'

'By God, Captain Ackworthy, I do declare that *Audacious*'s cutter is in the lead!' Ashley-Chute moved his telescope slightly to watch the other boats in the race and added, 'Just as well, hmm?'

Ackworthy said nothing, and Blackwood, who was standing nearby on the quarterdeck, saw the captain's hands opening and closing as if to restrain his feelings. Only a week, and yet Ackworthy seemed to have aged even further.

And yet on the face of it everything was going well. The weather was clear and warm, although the evening would have a nip in it, and the snaking currents of the Solent looked harder and more silvery.

From the forenoon onwards the ship had steadily filled with visitors, some important, some less so. Local dignitaries and their wives, the port admiral and the senior captains from around the harbour. The marine fifers played lively jigs, and a small orchestra which had been brought specially from Southampton was ready to fill any gaps in the entertainment.

There was one very important visitor who was also a personal guest of the admiral. Sir Geoffrey Slade was known to be a top-ranking government adviser on overseas development, a man who was said to be equally at home in Court and in Parliament.

He seemed a quiet, unassuming man, quite at odds with his formidable reputation, and Blackwood wondered what he and Ashley-Chute could have in common.

But the eyes of everyone, from midshipman to first lieutenant, had been on the girl who had come aboard with Sir Geoffrey Slade. Young but sure of herself, Blackwood decided, with dark, almost black hair and a face which could make your head swim. She was Slade's niece, and that was all he knew about her. Yet.

There were plenty of other lady guests, and their presence swept aside the pre-sailing uncertainty and added a gaiety which the Navy always seemed to encourage.

Somewhere a cannon banged dully, and Ackworthy said, 'The races are finished, Sir James.'

'Good. Capital.' Ashley-Chute's puggy face surveyed the jostling visitors, the bright gowns and bare shoulders mingling amongst the epaulettes and gold lace. 'A keg of rum for the winners, hmm?'

It was incredible. Nobody who did not know Ashley-Chute would realize there was any other side to his nature. Short in stature he might be, but people seemed to look up to him as he swaggered amongst the guests and visitors, kissing a hand here, pinching a cheek there as he murmured something under his breath which was guaranteed to bring out a blush of pleasure. Any other man taking similar liberties would probably have ended up with a bloody nose or worse.

Only twice did he show his other self, and Blackwood would have missed both had he not been watching.

To cope with the numbers of visitors, members of the ship's company, mostly seamen, had been pressed into service as mess servants and stewards. One man, overawed perhaps by so many women around him, dropped a full tray of glasses to the deck, splashing wine on a few gowns and the feet of several officers.

Ashley-Chute had frozen in the middle of a conversation and had given the man a glance which should have killed him stone dead.

Then an elderly captain from the dockyard had gestured towards Portsmouth Point. The sun was going down rapidly, and some of the ladies had sent for their shawls to protect their shoulders against the evening breeze. Etched against the fortifications and huddled dwellings around the Point was a long drifting smoke cloud. It was probably a paddle-wheeled tug, or one of the brand-new steam gunboats which had been vividly portrayed in the *Gazette* just a few weeks ago.

The old captain had said gruffly, 'Well, Sir James, what d'you think of the new Navy? I fear your squadron and its like may never be seen again.'

Ashley-Chute's eyes had fixed on him like needles.

'*Damn your impertinence!* You should stay ashore with the women, blast you!'

The captain had wilted. 'I beg of you sir – I – I did not infer that . . .'

Ashley-Chute had not even heard him. He had stared at the drifting cloud of black smoke with something like loathing.

'There is some small future for the steam vessel, but not in any true sense as a fighting ship. Beyond doubt, and entirely to my satisfaction, I believe that the fleet in being will remain under canvas and not be a victim of dirt and unreliability!'

He had turned on his heel and approached a young lieutenant who was holding hands with the mayor's daughter.

'Ah, my dear!' He had taken the girl's elbow and guided her aft towards the poop. 'Come and talk with me.' He had ignored the lieutenant completely.

Blackwood felt his half-brother move up beside him.

He asked, 'Is everything all right, Harry?'

'Yes, sir.' The lieutenant's eyes were searching among the crowd. 'Did you see that girl?'

'Which one?' Again Blackwood sensed his own stupid resentment. He knew well enough which one.

Harry Blackwood replied, 'The dark-haired beauty. Sir Geoffrey Slade's niece.' He rubbed his gloved hands together. 'She never smiles, but I'd lay odds I could make her.'

Blackwood saw Ackworthy beckoning to him. 'She'd have you for breakfast, you young ass!'

He heard Harry call after him, 'Her name's Davern Seymour, sir.' He could almost hear him stifling a laugh as he added, '*Miss*.'

Ackworthy said, 'The boats are leaving now, Major.' He glanced at the sky and at the dark tracery of rigging and spars overhead. 'Went well, I thought.'

It was a question, not a statement.

Blackwood watched the first of the visitors being assisted down into the various boats. There had been a plentiful supply of wine for everyone, and the *Audacious*'s own brand of punch had grown steadily stronger with each topping up by the admiral's steward. One or two of the guests looked as if they might have fallen into the sea and barely noticed it.

He said, 'They all enjoyed themselves, sir. By the time some of them sleep it off we'll be aweigh on the tide.'

He glanced across the nettings towards the other ships of the squadron. Their reflections glittered on the water as the sunlight faded, with coloured lights and the long lines of open gunports to make this last night a memorable one. Some would despair at seeing their husbands and sons depart on one more commission. Others would be secretly grateful and pray that the next reunion might be delayed. Grief, happiness, ambition and ignorance, none meant anything to the ships themselves.

Blackwood realized with a start that Ackworthy was speaking again.

'I never thought that I should be off on another campaign like this, Major.' He was talking almost to himself. 'I thought I should end up like the dockyard captain, the one who . . .' He did not finish it.

So Ackworthy had also seen the admiral vent his anger on the man.

He continued, 'But maybe when we get some sea-room things will seem different.'

Blackwood felt suddenly sorry for Ackworthy. Of all the officers in his ship he probably felt safe to speak his mind only with a marine who shared yet was quite apart from his chain of command.

Blackwood tried to draw him from his gloom. 'Sir Geoffrey Slade. Is he sailing with the squadron, sir?'

The captain shook his head, his mind already elsewhere. 'No, he's going ahead in a fast mail-packet. Don't like the smell of it. The Service and politics don't mix, not in my book.'

Some violins struck up, and the remaining guests moved aft towards the poop and the beckoning music.

Most of the screens in the admiral's quarters had either been removed or hoisted up to the deckhead to give as much space as possible. Tables of glasses and yet more punch to fill them lined the sides, and right aft in the great cabin itself Ashley-Chute's table had been fully extended to seat his guests in lavish comfort. Silver candlesticks were placed at measured intervals, and there was hardly an inch of its polished surface which was not filled with food, gleaming cutlery and flowers.

Ashley-Chute stood with his friend Slade and watched his guests' reactions with barely concealed satisfaction.

Pelham, the flag-lieutenant, glanced nervously around the

laughing, chattering throng and consulted his list of names and where each guest would be seated.

Blackwood took a glass from one of the temporary cabin servants and tried to remember how many drinks he had taken. This was no time to get drunk. The thought made him smile to himself. Ashley-Chute would probably put him ashore and Harry would be made to take over command of the marines in his place. 'Mother' would be pleased.

'Something amuses you, Captain Blackwood?'

He turned, startled, and saw her looking directly at him. She was even more striking close to, with the candlelight and deckhead lanterns making her dark ringlets shine against her bare shoulders.

'I – I'm sorry. Just something which might have spoiled an otherwise happy occasion.'

He watched for some break in her guard. Harry was right, she did not smile. But she had lovely skin, like cream in the reflected lights, and her eyes were dark, possibly violet, he thought.

He asked, 'How did you know my name?'

'Does it matter?'

Her directness took him off balance.

'Not really. I know yours, Miss Seymour.'

She looked away, but made no attempt to move. 'I hate these gatherings. So much talk. Too much.' She looked at him again. 'Actually, my uncle pointed you out to me. You were involved in the Maori War, I believe.'

Blackwood was getting out of his depth. There must be a great deal more to Slade than he had realized if he had kept note of the marines' part in the Maori War, especially that of a lowly lieutenant. Unless Ashley-Chute had said something. A warning clicked in his mind like a pistol hammer.

'I was there, yes.' When she said nothing he added, 'Straightforward landing operations. What we're trained for. It had to be done.'

'You don't sound so sure, Captain Blackwood.' She

watched him gravely, her gown rising and falling to her breathing.

Blackwood shrugged. 'I'm sure.' It was like listening to Harry all over again. *What is it really like?*

He looked down at her. God, she was lovely. He could smell her perfume. Like a part of her.

He added, 'We go where we're ordered, Miss Seymour. No country can survive without strength, but you must know that, surely?'

She shook her head, the dark ringlets barely touching her shoulder.

'I think it's wrong to oppress people. No matter who they are. Some folk seem to take a delight in power, at any cost. Greed and power usually go hand in hand.'

Blackwood retorted, 'I wouldn't know about that.' He had spoken sharply but could not help himself. She had got under his skin and he felt confused by her candour and her confidence. 'I do my – '

She nodded very slowly. 'Your duty, were you going to say?'

Lieutenant Pelham called in his reedy voice, 'Ladies and gentlemen! Dinner is about to be served!'

Blackwood found himself alone as the others moved eagerly to their allotted places. She had been laughing at him, had made him feel a fool, like a common foot soldier.

Pelham brushed his elbow. 'There, sir. Next to the lady mayoress.'

He was almost grateful to be submerged in a torrent of conversation and the din of eating and drinking.

The candles flickered across the bright gowns and the officers' epaulettes, and beneath the laden table Blackwood felt the ship stir as if made uneasy like himself.

The girl named Davern Seymour was seated at the head of the table with Ashley-Chute and her uncle. Occasionally he heard her laugh, but it was a controlled sound, and not once did she look in his direction.

The lady mayoress had had a great deal to drink and was leaning against him by the time the table was rearranged for a special pudding which had been prepared by the admiral's cook.

She said huskily, 'My father was a sailor, y'know.'

She had difficulty in focusing her eyes on Blackwood's face, but none at all in pressing her knee against his under the table.

Blackwood regarded her despairingly. She was sixty if she was a day. It would serve her right. He took another swallow of wine and dabbed his face with a napkin. What was the matter with him? Had that girl unsettled him so badly?

The lady mayoress seemed to take his silence for encouragement and he felt a hand on his thigh.

There was a sharp tap from the head of the table, and Blackwood thought for an instant that someone had seen what was happening.

Vice-Admiral Sir James Ashley-Chute rose to his feet and stared at the table until he had their full attention.

'Before the ladies retire, God bless 'em,' his eyes moved restlessly along their faces, 'I would like to say a few words on behalf of the squadron, *my* squadron, which is soon to quit these shores.' He tucked one hand inside his coat and continued, 'We are all living in stirring times. An age of discovery, the founding of trade and colonies the length and breadth of the globe. There will soon be no land worthwhile where the Union flag does not fly with authority. Our mother country will surely benefit and continue to do so.' Some of the gravity was thrust aside as he added, 'But I am a simple sailor. I leave such matters to others. Unlike some . . .' he paused and glanced coldly at Captain Boyd of the *Argyll* who was said to have a woman in Southsea, '. . . I am content to serve my country and take the ocean as *my* mistress.'

Somebody gave a nervous laugh.

The admiral stared into the distance, the lights shining on his iron-grey sideburns.

'We have a young queen on the throne, a fleet to be proud

of, and a future that holds no fears for those resourceful enough to *seek* and *win*!'

Captain Boyd of the *Argyll*, still flushed with anger at the admiral's pointed comment, muttered, 'God, you'd think we were going to fight a war!'

The lady mayoress slumped back, and Blackwood saw the girl watching him from the end of the table.

Ashley-Chute was saying, 'Loyalty and duty are the foundations of my faith.'

Blackwood watched the girl's mouth quiver very slightly. She was laughing at him. Goading him.

The admiral broke off and snapped, 'Well, what *is* it, Pelham?' He seemed irritated by his flag-lieutenant's sudden gestures. 'I am still *speaking*, man!'

But he listened none the less and then motioned for Pelham to relay his news to Captain Ackworthy.

Strangely ill at ease in his own ship, Ackworthy rose to his feet, his hair almost brushing the deckhead.

'I beg your pardon, ladies and gentlemen, but the master has sent his respects and apologies and insists that a squall is rising from the sou'-east. Under the circumstances, it might be in the interests of safety for visitors to return to the shore without delay.'

Ashley-Chute gave a fierce grin. 'Any lady still aboard will *remain* so, hmm?' He walked briskly to the cabin door to bid his guests farewell.

Blackwood said to the flag-lieutenant, 'A bit sudden, surely?'

The man shook his head wretchedly, probably visualizing all those hundreds of miles to Africa.

'Sir James is bored or tired, I'm never certain which. He *ordered* me to pass that message to him. There's no squall. It's an old trick of his.' He glanced at the long-armed lieutenant who was the admiral's son. 'I feel sorry for *him*. For all of us.'

'Come along, Pelham.' Ashley-Chute's voice was like a father speaking to a backward child. 'See that the ladies are escorted to the gangway.' He glanced at Blackwood and nodded curtly. 'So your brother is aboard, eh? A bit of string-pulling at the Admiralty, hmm?'

He turned aside to speak with his special guest.

The girl was waiting for him, her body concealed from her throat to her toes in a boat-cloak.

'Good night, Captain Blackwood.' She eyed him thoughtfully. 'I hope you are not *too* troubled by duty.' She did not offer her hand from the protection of her cloak.

Blackwood bowed from the waist. 'I look forward to our next meeting, Miss Seymour.'

She gave a brief smile. 'I fear that may be a long way off.'

She curtsied to the admiral, the movement taking her through the door and into the shadows like a trained dancer.

Blackwood walked out into the cool damp air and drew deeply on the tang of salt. Boats were already thrusting away from the ship's side, and he could hear laughter and muffled cheers as the occupants waved to the watching seamen on the gangway.

'How did you get on, sir?'

Blackwood swung on the scarlet blur of Harry's coatee in the gloom.

Then he shrugged. What had he expected anyway? That a girl like her would swoon into his arms merely because he was going overseas?

He said wearily, 'I survived, Harry.' He touched the lieutenant's sleeve, suddenly glad of his company. 'Come below and take a glass before you turn in.'

The admiral's quarters were already quiet, the screens replaced, a sentry planted beneath a lantern like a toy soldier.

Then, as Blackwood thrust open his cabin door they both heard Ashley-Chute's voice cutting through the screens and all else like a saw.

'What the *hell* were you thinking of, Ackworthy? Some of those servants were like ploughmen, more used to the dung in the fields than to civilized people!'

Ackworthy must have mumbled something and the admiral's voice rose even higher.

'It was a bloody shambles! I was humiliated by it! By God, Captain Ackworthy, you'll live to regret it if you repeat such incompetence!'

Harry Blackwood stared at his half-brother with aston-. ishment.

'What was *that*?'

Blackwood glanced at the quiet cabin, the bottle and goblets where Smithett had placed them in readiness. He never needed to be told anything.

'I fear, Harry, that the party has just ended.'

3

A Man of Authority

'Begin the salute.'

The crash of the first cannon shattered the afternoon silence and drove a cloud of gulls soaring into the sky in screaming protest.

Moving very slowly at the head of the squadron, the flagship *Audacious* headed purposefully towards the anchorage, beyond which the impressive slab of Gibraltar loomed up in the mist.

The sea was set in a flat calm, with only an occasional flurry of breeze to stir the ship's topsails and jib.

The squadron must make a fine if familiar picture from the shore, Blackwood thought. Like part of a great painting, or one of his grandfather's memories.

Audacious in the lead, with the three two-deckers, *Swiftsure*, *Valiant* and *Argyll* following obediently in her wake. Only the hulls were changed from those which had shaken to the roar of cannon fire at Trafalgar. White and black stripes instead of Nelson's black and buff. Otherwise there was little outward difference.

Gun for gun the salute to the governor on the Rock crashed out, to be returned with equal precision. Probably the only ones they would hear on this voyage, Blackwood thought.

He glanced forward from the quarterdeck at the assembled seamen who were waiting to wear ship in readiness to drop anchor. Others with their petty officers and lieutenants in their various parts of ship. To sway out the boats, to rig awnings and windsails, to man the side for visitors from the shore, and all within minutes of the great anchor splashing down.

The marines were paraded in three neat formations, Colour-Sergeant M'Crystal on the flank, Sergeant Quintin in the rear.

Second Lieutenant Harry Blackwood stood in front of the first platoon, his sword drawn and resting between his feet, his eyes slitted against the misty glare from the bay. Sea-haze mingled with the departing gunsmoke, and in the humid air the marines were getting the worst of it in their high-collared coatees.

'Ready, sir!'

Ackworthy nodded. 'Helm a'lee!'

Slowly and ponderously *Audacious* turned towards the wind. Sails flapped against the rigging in meek protest. There was barely enough air to carry her to the idling guard-boat with the bright pendant hoisted to mark where she should anchor.

Blackwood glanced across to the group by the quarterdeck rail. The misshapen figure of Ashley-Chute, his hands linked across his buttocks by a pair of white gloves which he had been tugging in time to the gun salute. Ackworthy and his first lieutenant, the signals midshipmen ready to make signals and acknowledge them, their assistants standing amongst the coloured bunting, very aware of the need for haste with their admiral barely yards away.

'Let go!'

As the anchor hurled spray high above the beakhead, the ship's sailing master glanced at his quartermaster and helmsman and gave a quick grimace. Blackwood could guess what he was thinking. It had taken fourteen of the longest days he could recall to reach Gibraltar from Spithead. With each dragging hour the ships of the squadron had gone through their paces in response to Ashley-Chute's endless procession of signals.

Three ships of the squadron had been spared. The little frigate *Peregrine* had been sent on ahead to Gibraltar, but even she had taken two days to draw away from her heavy consorts. The other frigate, the forty-four-gun *Laertes*, had held up to windward, a spectator as the ships of the line had formed up ahead or astern of their admiral, opened or closed distances as demanded, while the limp sails had been changed and reset until the various companies were worn out.

Only the squadron store-ship, *Amelia*, a very elderly vessel which had once been used for transporting convicts, had been allowed to make her own way south.

Even Biscay had been cruelly calm, with not the usual urgency of shortening sail and changing tack to keep the men's minds occupied. Around the north-west tip of Spain and still further south with the coast of Portugal just visible to the masthead lookouts.

Gun drill in blazing sunlight, the crews panting and cursing as they had hauled the great muzzles up to their ports, timed by the first lieutenant's watch, and with Ashley-Chute's small figure never far away from poop or quarterdeck.

Pelham stayed at his side like a lean shadow, a pad rarely absent from his hand, as the admiral's thin mouth opened occasionally to make a criticism or to ask who was responsible for a delay or a mistake.

It was a far, far cry from the eloquent host at the Spithead reception, the man who could describe the beauty of sail and dismiss the benefits of steam and leave no room for doubt among his listeners.

The slow passage had played its part. There had hardly been a day when the squadron had not been passed or, worse, overhauled by some packet or coaster.

In the Bay itself they had sighted a tell-tale plume of black smoke far astern, and Blackwood had heard the admiral say, 'Damn rattle-box! What did I tell you, Pelham? *Bloody useless!*'

But the little paddle-steamer had grown sharper in the telescope lens none the less, and when the hands had been piped to their midday meal she had been overtaking the

squadron in fine style. Her master must have done it deliberately, for his after-deck was almost awash from the paddles'
surging throw back. Smoke and sparks had belched from the
spindly funnel, and the vessel had churned up a bow wave
like a giant's moustache.

When the *Audacious*'s hands had been piped back to their
various tasks once more the little paddle-steamer had been
passing *Argyll*'s quarter at the rear of the line.

Ashley-Chute had snatched a telescope from a terrified
midshipman and had shouted, 'Captain Boyd's people are
cheering that filthy object!' He had hurled the glass at the
midshipman. 'God damn it, Ackworthy, must I be served by
fools?' He had swung away adding, 'Make a signal to the
squadron. *Make more sail and close on the flagship.*'

Ackworthy had seen the protest in the sailing master's eyes
and had pleaded, 'In these light airs, sir, it will do no use.'

Ashley-Chute had had to climb on to a bollard to seek out
the paddle-steamer.

'Just do as I say! *More sail!*'

Like monkeys the seamen had swarmed up the ratlines in a
living tide to set the topgallants and then the royals in an
effort to draw ahead. It was pointless, and the great main-
course could barely lift its belly, so weak was the wind.

The other vessel had steamed past, dipping her ensign as
she did so.

As the first lieutenant had said later, 'Not only that, but
she was a bloody Frenchie!'

Harry Blackwood brought the hilt of his sword to his
mouth with a flourish.

'Permission to fall out the marines, *sir!*'

From one corner of his eye Blackwood saw M'Crystal nod
with approval. He did not know the half of it. Harry should
have been an actor, not a marine.

He said calmly, 'Carry on, Mr Blackwood. Tell Sergeant
Quintin to detail a shore picket, just in case our people are
allowed off the ship.'

He shaded his eyes and looked up to watch the last of the

big sails being furled neatly to its yard. All down the squadron it would be the same. Another passage completed. A landfall made. At least they didn't have to put up with the admiral.

Blackwood walked on to the larboard gangway as the first of the boats was swayed up and over the side to a clatter of blocks and bellowed commands.

There were several steam vessels lying in the Rock's shadow. It must be marvellous to be able to manoeuvre at will and tell the wind to act as it pleased. To cut across an enemy's stern without the need to stand and receive a bellyful of iron because you have lost your sails in a broadside.

'Is this your first time here, Major?'

Blackwood turned and looked down at Ashley-Chute's son. He had barely spoken to the third lieutenant since he had joined the ship at Spithead. Their duties never seemed to meet, and he had thought him to be either aloof like his father or merely shy.

'No, I've been this way before.'

Blackwood watched him curiously. About his own age, and yet he seemed much older, or from another period altogether. He would not have looked out of place with Raleigh or Drake, he thought. He had deep lines at his mouth and nose, and his eyes were restless and heavy lidded. He gave the added impression of great physical strength, as if it was all gathered in his shoulders and long, ungainly arms.

Lieutenant Ashley-Chute pointed towards the shore. 'See that mast beyond the anchored store-ship?'

Blackwood shaded his eyes again. The lieutenant must have damn good vision as well.

Then he saw it. A raked mast, almost bare of spars and rigging, and a thin black funnel.

The young Ashley-Chute was saying, 'She's the *Satyr*. A new steam-frigate.' He could not contain the excitement he felt. It was like a secret pride. 'I was supposed to be joining her. I've completed the new gunnery course, everything.' His arms dropped to his sides as if they were too heavy. 'But I'm third lieutenant in *Audacious* instead.'

Blackwood did not need to ask why. 'Maybe you can transfer later on.'

'Later on?' He did not hide the bitterness in his voice. 'He'd never allow it. He wanted me here, to make certain I'd follow the "tradition".' He spat out each word. 'I love the Navy. I really do. And he's almost made me hate it!'

A petty officer hurried towards him and he thrust himself away from the side.

'Sorry about that, Major.'

Blackwood smiled. 'I think I understand how you feel.' He turned and stared again at the raked mast. Lithe, modern power; no wonder a young officer could dream of serving and maybe commanding such a vessel. 'Perhaps we could go over and look at her while we're here?' But when he twisted round Lieutenant Ashley-Chute had vanished.

The first lieutenant strolled across to join him. 'The captain wants a full quarter-guard mounted this evening, Major.' He removed his hat and wiped the inside rim with his handkerchief. 'More visitors to drink up our mess bills, I expect!'

But Netten, the first lieutenant, was wrong. The only important visitor to arrive aboard the flagship was Sir Geoffrey Slade, as neat and composed as ever, dressed all in white and removing his hat as he received full honours from the side-party.

Later, after dining with the admiral in his cabin, he came on deck where Blackwood was watching his marines mounting guard and listening to their night orders from Corporal Jones, the man who had wanted to be a prize-fighter.

He nodded companionably. 'Good to see you again, Blackwood.'

He seemed so relaxed and at ease that Blackwood asked, 'Are you remaining here at Gibraltar, Sir Geoffrey?'

Sir Geoffrey Slade shook his head and leaned out to watch some local trading boats idling as near as they dared to the ship's side. From the lower gunports there would be some brisk bartering between these boatmen and the sailors until the master-at-arms discovered what was happening.

'No. I shall continue in the mail-packet to Freetown and then, if everything is properly arranged, take a steam vessel on to Fernando Po. How the African coasts are opening up with these new craft, eh?' He gave an amused smile. 'I'm afraid I do not share Sir James's views on maritime progress!'

Blackwood hesitated. 'Er, your niece, sir . . .'

Slade regarded him calmly. 'She came with me, of course.' He saw Blackwood's surprise and added, 'But she's not here now. Left yesterday. Wouldn't wait, and I could not very well keep her company. My business here and in Africa is pressing.'

Blackwood had imagined the girl back in England. But she had been here and had already gone. It was making no sense.

Slade said, 'She wanted to join her father. She's a headstrong young woman. I've done all I can for her since her mother died. I can understand how she feels.' He waited and then said gently, 'You seem very interested in my niece.'

'I think she found me rather stupid, sir.' He shrugged. 'I thought she was fascinating, as it happens.'

'I see. Well, her father's a doctor. Could have been a great man in his profession, but he chose tropical medicine. It's what killed his wife, as a matter of fact. Now he's down there working his heart out in some wretched mission or other. I've sent word to our people in Freetown to help my niece as much as they can, but I'm not sure any more. The area where he was last known to be is in a state of turmoil. Which is why I am on my way there, and where you will eventually be required to make a show of strength, and I hope that is *all* that will be needed!'

He looked dreamily towards the Rock's great shadow. 'It's all there in Africa, y'know, Blackwood. The picklock of empire. People don't count for much when something's true value is realized.' He turned aft towards the poop. 'A game of cards with Sir James before I go ashore, I think.' He gave a casual wave. 'Remember what I said.'

Blackwood gripped the nettings with both hands and stared at the glittering lights on the water.

She had known when she had spoken to him. *I think it's wrong to oppress people.* Now she was on her way to Africa, to a part which Slade had made clear was about to erupt for one of a hundred reasons.

He walked quickly along the gangway, only partly aware of the watching side-party and boatswain's mate, a marine sentry who stiffened as he passed.

She might think differently of him if he could see her again.

In his mind's eye he seemed to see Africa spreading like a vast jungle, engulfing her and dragging her down into oblivion.

He thought of the screaming horde of Maoris as they had charged towards the single line of marines, the jarring pain in his arm as he had hacked one of them down, their faces almost touching.

Blackwood stopped short at the forecastle. There was a solitary marine sentry there on a little platform above the beakhead. To watch over the cable, to ensure no unlawful visitors used the great rope to pull themselves aboard. Likewise, he was useful to deter anyone from deserting.

The sentry stamped his heels to attention. Blackwood peered through the gloom but could not put a name to the stiff, youthful face.

'You're one of the new recruits?'

'*Sir!* Private Oldcastle, sixth company, sir!' He had a Yorkshire dialect you could carry in a spoon.

'Have you settled in, Oldcastle?'

The sentry's eyes gleamed in the lantern light as they moved across Blackwood's shoulder-belt and epaulettes. *Something to tell the others later on.*

'Aye, sir.'

Blackwood nodded. 'How old are you?'

'Six . . .' He swallowed hard. 'I— I mean, seventeen, sir.'

Blackwood smiled gravely. He made him feel like an old man.

'Why did you enlist, Oldcastle?'

'My dad were a marine, sir. But 'e died last year, so I thought I'd take on like.'

Blackwood looked at him. 'Good. Learn all you can and do your . . .' he hesitated, remembering her eyes watching him along the table, '. . . er, duty.' He touched his shako and walked towards the stern again.

Suddenly things did not seem so ordinary after all.

The nightmare rose to a whirling climax, the carved Maori club, jagged and bloody, swinging overhead, ready to smash down. Somehow the image on the club had become alive, with staring eyes and tongue extended, like the warrior who held it.

Here it came. With a gasp Blackwood rolled on his side, his legs kicking at his sheet as he tried to escape the death blow.

He opened his eyes and raised himself on his elbows. The cabin was barely visible from a shuttered lantern, and he saw the startled eyes of a midshipman peering at him over the side of the cot.

Blackwood licked his lips. His body was wet with sweat and yet his throat was like a kiln. Reluctantly his memory came back. The talk with Slade, the mistake of pausing with the purser to have a few drinks before turning in. It had been the purser's birthday. It was always fatal to drink with a man who held the keys to a limitless supply of brandy.

'What is it?' It came out a croak.

The midshipman stammered, 'Beg pardon, sir, but the captain sends his compliments, and would you join him aft — ?'

Blackwood was out of his cot in a bound, his mind clearing as he peered at his watch on its stand. It was barely three in the morning.

'What the hell is happening?'

The midshipman's eyes followed Blackwood's nakedness around the cabin, his earlier nervousness giving way to curiosity.

'Don't know, sir. Guard-boat came off with the gentleman who was here earlier.'

'Slade?'

'I – I think so, sir.'

Blackwood tugged on his trousers and groped for a shirt. Folded and neat where Smithett had placed it.

'Rouse Mr Blackwood.' He snatched up a brush and glared at his dim reflection in the mirror. 'And don't take no for an answer.'

It was surprisingly cold on deck after the heat of the day. There were plenty of stars, with a black triangular gap in their array to betray the Rock's brooding presence.

The watch on deck shuffled their feet, and Blackwood heard the guard-boat squeaking alongside, the oarsmen murmuring together and clinking mugs of tea.

Ackworthy filled his stern cabin as he waited for Blackwood to sit down. Netten, the first lieutenant, was present, red-eyed and jaded, Pelham too, and in a chair by the stern windows Slade sat with one leg crossed negligently over the other, a cup and saucer balanced on his knee. He was still wearing the same white clothes, as if he had never left the ship.

Ackworthy said thickly, 'Courier-brig anchored two hours ago.' He did not seem to know how to continue.

There was a clink as Sir Geoffrey Slade handed his cup to the cabin servant.

'Despatches for me. Serious news, I'm afraid. There's been an uprising north of Freetown. Mdlaka, a local king I had hoped to meet, may have been butchered with many of his warriors. It could create a very dangerous situation to the trade missions, to the stability of the whole coast area – '

He paused as the door was flung open and Ashley-Chute, dressed in a full-length robe of plum-coloured silk, strode into the cabin, both hands crammed with papers which he slammed down on to Ackworthy's table.

'I read your despatches, Geoffrey, while I was being shaved.' He seemed to realize the presence of the others for the first time. 'Full muster of brains, hmm?'

Slade gave a faint smile. 'You agree it is serious?'

Ashley-Chute thrust his hands into his pockets. 'Serious? Of course. I've always maintained that damn coastline, all of it from Freetown to the Slave Coast, is a tinder-box. Slavery is forbidden, the great nations *agreed* upon that!' There was an edge to his tone as he added, 'After Britain had used a little "persuasion" on the more avaricious nations. And yet the traffic in African slaves seems as strong as ever. I have no personal objections to a settler or plantation owner using such labour. I expect that most of the so-called slaves are better off under ordered circumstances. But the law says otherwise, and I intend to enforce that law.' He calmed himself with an effort. 'When my squadron is on its proper station I shall be very firm in whatever methods I use.' He looked at Slade as if expecting him to argue.

Slade said quietly, 'The courier-brig made a record passage to reach me. Even so it took far too long. The whole situation may have worsened by now, lives lost, Her Majesty's subjects put in jeopardy.' He pressed his neat fingertips together and watched Ashley-Chute across the cabin. 'How *long* would it take you to reach the area?'

Ackworthy said bluntly, 'Month at least, sir. Even with favourable winds, I don't think — '

Ashley-Chute snapped, 'I will speak with you later, Captain Ackworthy!'

Slade persisted, 'This is very important. Her Majesty's Government has ordered me to investigate certain matters on the Slave Coast, which is why I am going to Fernando Po. Eventually.'

Ashley-Chute plucked at his sideburns and prowled about the cabin as if he were trapped.

Slade persisted, 'A month is too long.' He spoke gently, as

if he shared Ashley-Chute's inability to move his ships where they were most needed. At the same time he left no room for doubt as to his authority.

The deck moved very slightly as the ship swung to her cable. Hundreds of men slept throughout the squadron while a mere handful kept watch over them, all unaware of the tension here in this one cabin.

The first lieutenant broke the silence. 'I understand that there is a permanent patrol in the area you mention, sir.'

'Was.' Slade's eyes had not moved from the admiral. 'She is reported missing, and the remainder of our patrols are much further south.'

Ashley-Chute stopped his pacing. 'I don't see what I can be expected to do.'

It must have been what Slade was waiting for.

'There is a steam-frigate here at Gibraltar, Sir James.'

'What?' His eyes shone in the lantern light like stones. 'Yes, of course, I know. The *Satyr*. She is eventually to be with, if not *of*, my squadron.'

'I have spoken to the governor and will send word to London by the next packet. The *Satyr*, which I understand can reach the destination in fourteen days, perhaps less, is ready for sea. Every minute we wait here talking is a minute wasted.'

Blackwood watched, fascinated. There was nothing calm and gentle about Slade now. He was like steel, a rapier.

'I see.' Ashley-Chute walked to the windows and stooped down to peer at the sky. 'All decided, hmm?'

Slade did not reply but looked at Blackwood. '*Satyr* carries twenty marines. It may not be sufficient if the worst has happened. And there will be nobody to ask for aid.' He let his words sink in. 'I am certain that Sir James will be willing to transfer you to the *Satyr* with a force of your own men, to take overall command.' He gave a wry smile. 'Under *Satyr*'s captain, naturally.'

'Yes, sir.' Blackwood darted a quick glance at the admiral, waiting for the explosion.

Instead the little admiral appeared very calm and even. 'Of course. If you *insist* on this method, Geoffrey, then of course I shall do my utmost to support you. And if any marines must be sent, those from *my* flagship are the obvious choice.'

Slade kept his face immobile. Honour was satisfied. Almost.

Ashley-Chute could not resist adding, 'I have no doubt that *Satyr* will break down or run out of coal long before she reaches the Guinea Coast. I shall put to sea with the squadron tomorrow to provide the ultimate show of force.'

'I am grateful.' Slade stood up and straightened his coat. 'I suggest we leave at once.'

Blackwood asked, 'Are you sailing too, sir?'

'Yes. Parliament is always weeping and wailing about the costs of maintaining a powerful fleet. Perhaps this time they will be satisfied that some of the money at least is well spent!'

Blackwood left the cabin and walked out into the shadows. It was an effort to keep his mind steady on the details of the task in hand. In spite of his training and experience he could not control the surge of excitement, something he might have expected in a first-year recruit.

Colour-Sergeant M'Crystal loomed from the shadows. He was fully turned-out in uniform and equipment, ready for anything. The old sweat.

'I want thirty men, Colour-Sergeant. Full equipment and ammunition for work afloat or ashore.' He forced a smile. 'Not all the experienced men. Mix a few of the newcomers into the pudding.'

M'Crystal cleared his throat noisily. 'Right away, sir.' He bellowed, 'Corporal Bly! First sections as ordered! Ten minutes, not a second more!'

As was often the case, Blackwood wanted to praise M'Crystal for his resourcefulness. A plan for everything. A man for each task. But he knew M'Crystal would be embarrassed, even hurt, to think his efficiency could not be taken for granted.

Harry Blackwood, yawning and rubbing his eyes, blundered against M'Crystal, who did not even quiver.

Blackwood said, 'You will remain here in charge, with Sergeant Quintin.'

The lieutenant nodded vaguely. 'Remain here? Sergeant Quintin? Why, what is happening?'

'No time now.'

He saw Smithett carrying his personal pack and weapons, supervising the lowering of his captain's kit into a boat alongside.

Smithett marched over to him and snapped, 'All done, sir. Put a couple of bottles in the bag too, might be a long job.'

Blackwood felt his attendant clipping his belt around his waist and adjusting his sword so that it hung directly in line with his hip. If he ordered Smithett to take on the king of the Zulus single-handed, he had no doubt he would be smartly turned-out for it.

His half-brother was pounding after him as he strode over to watch the first section of marines clambering down into the boats.

'Look, sir, can't I come too?' He was actually pleading.

'No.' Blackwood turned and looked at him. 'You are *in charge* here. Sergeant Quintin has years of service behind him, but he expects an officer to give him his orders. So do it.' He gripped his wrist impetuously. 'You asked what it was like. This is all part of it. They expect you to lead them, though God knows most of them could manage well enough if all their officers fell dead.' He shook him gently. 'I shall ask Sergeant Quintin how you managed when we meet up again.'

The lieutenant nodded, his face lost in the darkness. 'Take care, sir. Philip.'

'Ready in the boat, sir!'

It was time to go.

Blackwood glanced up at the tapering masts, the creepers of shrouds and rigging which seemed to climb to the stars. He might never see *Audacious* again.

He added, 'And keep out of the admiral's way.'

Then he was scrambling into the boat, while others, loaded down with marines and equipment, shoved away from the chains and began to pull towards the inner anchorage.

Colour-Sergeant M'Crystal sat very upright in the stern-sheets, the oilskin cover of his flag standing between his knees like an umbrella.

He said hoarsely, 'More like it, sir. Bit o' soldiering for a change!' He twisted round and sniffed the air. 'What's that, sir?'

Blackwood felt a shiver of excitement again. Coal and oil, smoke and damp iron.

'*That*, Colour-Sergeant, is a steam-frigate.'

M'Crystal considered it. 'Och, sir, the sooner we get there, the quicker we can stretch our legs.'

Blackwood watched the bowsprit of the anchored frigate rising like a lance above the boat. Like the warrior's club in the nightmare. He blinked. That had been just two hours ago.

He saw sparks drifting above where the funnel must be, the unfamiliar swish and creak of machinery, voices calling and the clatter of a chain cable. It was another world. He felt a complete amateur, like a sailor trying to ride bareback.

The bowman hooked on, and faces peered and bobbed along the *Satyr*'s black bulwark. Smithett stood ready to steady him if he lost his step, and then he was up and over the rail on to the frigate's deck. Strange shadows and shapes stood around him, and he had little sense of being in a ship at all.

A figure detached itself from the side-party and a voice said, 'Lieutenant Lascelles, sir!'

Blackwood took his hand. Lascelles was supposed to be the Royal Marines officer aboard, but he was dressed in blue like a member of the RMA.

He sensed Blackwood's curiosity and said apologetically, 'Sorry about my rig, sir. But the red coat doesn't take too kindly to the smut and sparks here!'

Blackwood smiled. 'I'll remember that.'

He heard Slade's voice in the distance, probably speaking with *Satyr*'s captain. It was all so different, so new.

Lascelles saw M'Crystal. 'My sergeant has arranged berths for your men in the barracks and on the orlop. Bit cramped, I'm afraid. But in this ship the engines come first.' He jumped as a siren shrieked wildly overhead, the echoes banging around the bay like an insane chorus.

'Captain Blackwood?'

A broad-shouldered, sturdy officer in a watch-coat came out of the darkness.

'Yes, sir.'

'I'm Tobin. I command here.' The handshake was firm and rough. 'I hope you'll be happy with us while you're in *Satyr*.' His voice was deep and resonant, and he made no attempt to conceal his pride for his command. As an afterthought he said, 'I'll probably see you at breakfast.' Then he too was swallowed up in the drifting vapours of steam and funnel smoke.

Blackwood allowed himself to be led rather than guided down a companion ladder and eventually to a square panelled cabin.

Lascelles said, 'It's yours, sir. I'm bunking in with the third lieutenant.' He picked up a bag from the deck. 'It's the next cabin, if you need me.' Then he stepped outside and closed the door.

Smithett had somehow been here already. Probably even forced Lascelles to vacate the cabin in his favour.

The stand was there, ready for his watch. A clean shirt nearby.

Blackwood sat down on the bunk and felt the hull shaking impatiently. What pleasure it must have given *Satyr*'s captain to shatter the night watches with his siren before he quit the harbour. It had been for Ashley-Chute's benefit.

He lay back and thrust his hands behind his head. *Monkey*.

He would not sleep, he was certain of it. The ship echoed and rattled all around him, and he heard a whirring sound like a fan. And she was not even moving yet.

Poor Harry. He would probably be on deck as they steamed past the anchored flagship. That was the last conscious thought of Captain Philip Blackwood. Even as the first iron link of *Satyr*'s cable clanked through the fair-leads he fell fast asleep.

4

First to Land

Private Smithett wedged himself in one corner of the cabin and muttered between his teeth, 'Is it *always* like this, sir?'

Blackwood pressed his body against a locker and peered at his reflection in a mirror. Each time he brought the razor to his face he could sense Smithett's quick intake of breath, as if he expected to see him cut his throat. It was not surprising. When he had been awakened by the ship noises around him he had been unable to recall where he was. Then, as his memory had returned, he had been startled by the unfamiliar clatter and growl of engines, and when he had tried to leave his bunk he had been hurled across the cabin and almost knocked senseless.

He answered tightly, 'I expect so.'

He laid down the razor and dabbed his skin with a towel. His body felt clammy, and he knew he was near to being sick. Smithett had already told him that several of the marines were 'spewin' fit to bust', but even he had lost his usual relish for disaster.

Blackwood thought of breakfast and clung to a stanchion for support as the deck rocked violently and the whole hull seemed to try and shake itself apart. Down and down, and then he heard the thunder of water alongside and saw a wave crest lift casually above the cabin scuttle. Breakfast? Not yet anyway.

He allowed Smithett to assist him with his coat and then struggled out into the cabin passageway which was also trying to roll on to its side.

Blackwood had been at sea in every sort of vessel from a line of battle ship like *Audacious* to a tiny brig, and had seen storms which had almost torn the masts from the decks. But never could he recall anything like this.

Staggering and gasping, he reached the foot of a companion ladder and looked up with surprise at a blue rectangle of sky. He had imagined they were entering a storm. Taking his time he climbed to the upper deck and clung to a handrail to get his bearings before stepping out into the open.

The *Satyr* was bigger than he had imagined her to be and totally unlike any warship he had seen. She had two masts and what appeared to be a brigantine rig, although all her sails were neatly furled, and his attention was immediately taken by the two giant paddle-boxes, one on either side, which were linked together by an unprotected catwalk like a bridge. Abaft the two paddles was a tall funnel, the smoke streaming towards the quarter in an unbroken trail. Just forward of the mizzen mast was a big double-wheel, but to his surprise Blackwood saw there was only one helmsman. The officer of the watch, a quartermaster and a red-cheeked midshipman completed the group near the compass.

'Morning, Major.'

Blackwood released his grip and almost fell. Captain Tobin had appeared from aft and was watching his reactions with some amusement.

'Sleep well?'

'Aye, sir.' Blackwood looked around again, the captain's obvious pride in his ship was giving him a kind of strength. 'I thought we were in a gale.'

'I should have warned you.'

Tobin had his hands jammed deeply in his watch-coat, and his salt-stained sea-going cap was tugged tightly down level with his eyes. He was a sturdy, ruddy-faced man in his mid-thirties, Blackwood guessed. You would know him as a sailor no matter what he was wearing.

Tobin added, 'You're used to carrying a lot of canvas, the same as I was. Steadies the hull, no matter how steep the angle. Here,' he waved his fist before replacing it in his pocket, 'we ride the sea.'

He rocked back on his heels and waited for the hull to plunge down into a deep Atlantic trough. The starboard paddle lifted slightly and Blackwood felt the same vibration as the blades churned up to the surface. Tobin's resonant voice carried easily above the regular thump of machinery and he spoke for several minutes about his ship, what she could do, if given half a chance.

Without bitterness he said, 'We are the scavengers of the fleet. We take any mission, any job so as not to give their lordships the chance to get rid of us.' He gave a crooked smile. 'But Sir James Ashley-Chute will have drilled *that* into you, eh? No place for steam, the majesty of sail and all that rot?'

Satyr was two hundred and forty-nine feet from her graceful stem to her taffrail, and was of nearly two thousand tons burden.

Blackwood listened without interruption. He had rarely heard a ship's captain speak with such understanding of every aspect of his command and the individual tasks of her company. It was something akin to love.

Tobin said, 'It's a long haul to our rendezvous, so I'll try and make your stay a pleasant one.' He grinned. 'Might even convert you too.'

Blackwood had noticed the apparent lack of guns. In any other ship you were always aware of the vessel's main purpose for being. On every deck, be she frigate or first rate, the guns pointed towards each broadside port. The seamen lived, ate and slept between them in their tiny messes. The guns were there when they were piped on deck. They were waiting when they were piped below.

Tobin saw his uncertainty and gestured with his chin towards the midships deck.

'Up forrard I've got two rifled ten-inch chasers, and abaft the paddle-boxes there are four-inchers divided on either broadside.' He pivoted easily on the deck and looked at him searchingly. 'Just six guns, compared with your average frigate's forty or so! Yet with my armament I can outshoot and outmanoeuvre anything else afloat.' He nodded to the lieutenant by the wheel. 'I'm going down to breakfast, Mr Spalding.' He looked at Blackwood. 'Well?'

Blackwood took a deep breath. His lurking sea-sickness had vanished completely.

'Thank you, sir.'

The captain's quarters were right aft, following the usual custom. There was little other similarity.

The dining space was panelled and unmarred by gunports. There was a proper carpet on the deck instead of painted canvas, and the place had a feeling of privacy and comfort. The captain's sword rested in its rack on the bulkhead, and nearby Blackwood saw a painting of a woman and a little girl by a stream.

Tobin had handed his cap to the cabin steward and sat at the table where Sir Geoffrey Slade was reading a sheaf of papers and sipping coffee, apparently oblivious to the ship's irregular plunges.

Tobin got down to a large breakfast, and Blackwood lost himself in his own thoughts. Steam and sail had one thing in common. Officers never spoke at breakfast unless absolutely essential. The wardroom was only yards away, and that too was silent.

Slade got up suddenly. He looked less at ease in the reflected sunlight.

'Are we making good time, Captain?' He smiled despite his inner worries. 'I know we have only been at sea for a matter of hours, however . . .'

Tobin watched him calmly. 'My officers are well aware of the importance of this passage, Sir Geoffrey. The chief engineer is confident enough. We shall put into Tenerife for more coal, although I *can* manage without it. But we might hear something useful.'

Slade nodded slowly, his mind moving on again. 'I hope so.' He moved to the door. 'I shall go and discover if my secretary has managed to overcome his nausea. He's here to work, not lie abed!'

As the door closed Tobin gave a slow grin. 'He seems worried. I'm damn grateful to him all the same. I'd still be anchored at Gib but for his insistence.'

'Why do you think so many senior officers object to steam, sir?'

Tobin gestured to the steward to refill his cup. 'They've never learned to handle it, to understand it. Lines of ships, thousands of men, those they do understand. But God help us when we go to war again, unless we've a steam-minded Nelson somewhere!'

Blackwood made to leave the table but Tobin waved him down again.

'A moment, Major. I asked you to mess with me and Sir Geoffrey and not join my wardroom officers, for several reasons. I think we might learn from each other. In my heart I have little doubt that we are set on something dangerous. Sir Geoffrey would not be here otherwise. And neither would you.'

He stood up and walked to a scuttle, his broad shoulders balanced to his ship's persistent motion.

Almost dreamily he said, 'I worked the West African coast for five years. On anti-slavery patrols mostly. I once commanded a little sloop down in the Gulf of Guinea when I was very young and raw. God, what days! Most of the slavers were better armed than we were, and they could show us a clean pair of heels if they got the chance. If I'd had *Satyr* then it would have been a different story.'

Blackwood waited. He could feel the man's powerful restlessness. Something like his own.

Tobin said, 'Ever seen a slave-ship?' He did not wait for an answer. 'If there is really a hell that must be it. Men and young girls, babies even, chained like animals to lie in their own filth until they reach a suitable market. And it's still going on, believe me, even though their lordships look the other way when it suits 'em. But now it's something worse. As our patrols draw the net tighter the rush for quick cargoes of black ivory, as they call them, are amounting. The whole coast will be in flames unless we can do something. All the trading missions we used to protect will have to be withdrawn. It will turn the clock back fifty years.' He pounded his palms together forcefully. 'We must act now, or a lot of people are going to get massacred.'

Blackwood tried not to think of the girl's face, or picture her going to search for her father. Perhaps one of Slade's subordinates would prevent her, but in his heart he knew she would get her way.

He said, 'And you think this new uprising is a part of it?'

'I do. I used to know Mdlaka, the king Sir Geoffrey was speaking about when he came aboard. Bloody pirate, cannibal too, I've heard, but loyal to the Crown? *Bought* might be a better word.'

When Blackwood grinned he said, 'Testing you, Major. You're my sort of man, I think!'

Calls trilled overhead and Tobin made to leave.

'Both watches of the hands to exercise. I like them to know I'm about.' He hesitated by the door. 'What makes this ship special is that she is new, and I don't just mean in timber and iron. Here, everyone has to learn something extra. It gives him pride, in the ship and himself. The Navy's no longer a place for felons and pressed men. It's become something they *want* to join and to put their skills into.' He grinned. 'I'm just saying this before Mr Lascelles tells you, Major. Because when we get to Tenerife and coal ship, everyone turns to and lends a hand.' His grin broadened. 'Even the marines. Understood?'

Blackwood smiled. 'Officers included?'

'*Everyone*.' The door had almost closed as he added, 'Except the captain.'

Deacon, *Satyr*'s lean first lieutenant, handed his telescope to Blackwood as he joined him at the quarterdeck rail.

'There it is, Major. We made landfall at first light.' Like
Tobin, he did not conceal his pride.

Blackwood levelled the glass and studied the great sprawl
of coastline. Tobin had promised Slade a fourteen-day passage. They had stayed for one day in Tenerife and had thrust
out of port with the decks covered in black dust. Despite
that, Tobin had made his landfall in only thirteen days.
What an unhappy-looking coast, he thought. Humps of
clay-coloured rock and steep hills, with a hint of high
ridges further inland. A shimmering mist and probably
blown sand made the picture in the lens vague and without
substance.

The steam frigate had reduced speed and her decks were
crammed with seamen and a sprinkling of marines, the old
hands telling the new ones what it was like. The stories never
changed. Only the tellers.

The great twenty-six-foot paddles were thrashing almost
quietly at the blue water, a far cry from the din and bedlam of
the past days.

Blackwood glanced along the upper deck and picked out
some of his own men among the rest. It was hard to believe
that some two hundred men could vanish into so crowded a
hull. Almost a third of the ship was taken up by engines and
boilers, and the warrant officers and the bulk of the complement had to fit in as best they could forward of the paddles.
Aft, in comparative comfort, the officers, and of course the
captain, had greater space, while below them on the orlop the
odds and ends of the ship's company lived like owls with
never a glimpse of natural light.

And yet, in spite of the overcrowding, machinery and coal
before human beings, there was a real sense of camaraderie
which Blackwood knew he would be loath to lose. During the
discomfort of coaling ship he had seen it at work. In blazing
sunlight, choking in clouds of grit and dust, the men had
toiled back and forth to the bunkers with baskets of coal until
Hamilton, the chief engineer, was satisfied. There had not
been a uniform to be seen, and the blackened, almost naked

figures had bumped against one another with a total disregard for rank and authority.

Even at sea, with the decks once more washed clean and the brasswork on the narrow bridge all agleam, it felt different. Not a cocked hat or epaulette in sight, and with Tobin usually in view somewhere on deck, Blackwood had shared the sailors' respect for a true seaman.

Blackwood had seen little of Slade after leaving Tenerife. He had been ashore during their short stay and had returned grim and unsmiling.

There was still no news of the missing patrol vessel. She was an armed schooner named *Kingsmill* and commanded by a young lieutenant. His first commission on the Slave Coast, so almost anything might have happened.

The first lieutenant tensed slightly and Blackwood knew that Tobin had joined them. For such a powerful man he could move like a cat.

'Well, there it is, damn it. That round-shouldered hill is the headland. The river winds inland to the south'rd of it. At this time of year it's too risky to head far up-river. But I'll close the land and anchor as near as I can.' Without turning his head he said, 'Alter course four points, Mr Oliver. Steer east by south.'

Blackwood turned to watch the order relayed by voice-pipe to the engine-room, and as the helm went over he saw the sudden increase of power on the nearest paddle-wheel. It was hot on the open quarterdeck. What it must be like down there as coal was shovelled into the hungry furnaces was hard to imagine.

'South by east, sir!'

'Steady as she goes, Mr Oliver.'

Tobin rubbed his chin. 'I'll bet a million bloody eyes are watching us already.' He looked at Blackwood. 'Have you got it fixed in your mind?'

Blackwood thought of the many hours he had spent with Tobin in his cabin. The captain had taken him over charts and sketches, had read him scraps from some of his old note-books until he felt he knew this place from memory. During each forenoon before the sun had become too hot he had exercised the marines again and again until they too knew what was expected of them once they had left the safety of *Satyr*'s hull.

'Aye, sir, thanks to you.'

Tobin regarded him gravely. 'I'll not risk lives for nothing.' Again a brief command. 'Dead slow, Mr Oliver.'

Somewhere a gong jangled and the great paddles rose and fell to a quieter beat.

Slade strode from the companion-way, his face shaded by a straw hat.

'Anything?'

'No, Sir Geoffrey. Not even a local fisherman. Like the grave.'

Slade looked past him, his eyes cold. 'Very apt, I shouldn't wonder.'

Suddenly he drew Blackwood aside. 'I did not intend this should happen. The fact is, I must know what is happening here, as it could have a vital effect on what action we must take later on. The only people who can help are at the mission. They were under Mdlaka's protection and able to do much as they pleased. However . . .' The word hung in the air like a threat. 'But if this uprising is no accidental affair to settle old scores, someone's behind it, fanning the flames.' Impetuously he touched Blackwood's arm. 'I'm sorry to ask you to do this. But I *must* know.'

Blackwood said, 'I'm ready, sir.' He forced a smile. 'Do my men good to stretch their legs.'

Slade did not smile. 'As quickly as you can. In and out before nightfall.' He fixed his eyes on Blackwood's features as if to try and memorize them. 'Right?'

'Right, sir.' Blackwood walked to the rail. 'Be ready, Colour-Sergeant! As soon as we anchor!'

Lascelles stood beside him. He had changed into his scarlet coatee.

Blackwood said, 'We'll take two boats, Mr Lascelles, that

way we shall divide the target.' He saw the lieutenant's eyes widen as if he had only just realized what was happening. 'I think we are in for some trouble, so check their weapons, and make certain each man carries an extra pouch of ammunition.'

Along the frigate's main-deck the marines dashed back and forth to prepare their equipment and weapons for loading into the boats. No longer the passengers, they made the rest of the ship's company look like mere spectators.

Lascelles would be quite useless. It hit Blackwood like a fist. Outwardly a good officer and popular with his own men, he would crack wide open in a real battle. But it was too late now.

Blackwood clapped him on the shoulder and felt the stiffness beneath the scarlet cloth. There was no nice, easy way.

'You draw your pay, Mr Lascelles. Now bloody well earn it!'

He watched the lieutenant march away, his face tight with humiliation.

Then he said quietly, 'Go with Mr Lascelles, Colour-Sergeant.' He saw all the arguments building up on M'Crystal's red face. 'I shall take his sergeant with me.'

M'Crystal nodded. 'Aye, sir. I understand.'

Tobin came out of the companion-way and said, 'I heard most of that, Major. You've an old head for one so young. Try and keep it on its shoulders. I think we're going to need you again before long.'

Lascelles came aft again and touched his shako. 'Landing party ready for inspection.' He did not look directly at Blackwood's face.

'Very well.' What was it his grandfather had told him? In the Corps it was always the same. *The first to land. The last to leave.* He glanced towards the bare line of hills and fallen rocks. And that meant anywhere.

When he spoke he was surprised his voice sounded so flat and unemotional. 'Once round that first bend and we shall be on our own. So remember, see to the men, no matter what.'

Much as he had said to young Harry. He would have loved this, hazards and all.

He paused by the second marine in the front rank. It was the young recruit he had spoken to aboard *Audacious* at Gibraltar.

'Eager to go, Oldcastle?' It was so cruelly simple to win the youth's heart merely by remembering his name.

'Yessir.' He could barely stand still as M'Crystal checked his weapons, pouches, bayonet and all the rest. 'Wh-where are we, sir?'

Blackwood looked at M'Crystal who snorted indignantly. 'That doesn't matter, boy, not now anyway!'

Half an hour later *Satyr* dropped anchor and swung to the current from around the headland.

At the last moment Blackwood glanced aft and saw Tobin watching him. He did not take his hands from his pockets but gave a slight nod.

Blackwood climbed out and down into one of the frigate's boats. Deacon, the first lieutenant, was already in the boat, and the marines were packed among the oarsmen like hammocks in the nettings.

'Shove off forrard! Out oars!' The boats sidled clear of the ship's shadow. 'Give way together!'

Blackwood gripped his chin strap with his teeth and tried not to blink in the glare. It was so quiet after the ship. Just the steady creak of oars, the occasional boom of waves somewhere around another hump of land. The water was deep and sluggish, and he could smell the shore, just as he could feel the stillness and the air of menace.

Deacon said quietly, 'We're going to look bloody silly if everything's normal here!'

Blackwood saw the stroke oarsman's eyes moving slightly, and when he turned saw that the headland had crept out like a great door to shut off the anchored frigate. How fine she looked above her own reflection, her ensign barely moving in the offshore breeze. The boat turned into the first bend and *Satyr* was hidden from view.

Blackwood noticed that the stroke oarsman had shifted his eyes to him. What are my chances with you? they were asking. Will you be any good if hell breaks loose?

He shut the man from his thoughts and tried to concentrate on what Tobin had taught him.

The river would widen in a moment. The trading mission would be to starboard. What sort of madmen would want to work in a place like this? He gritted his teeth on the chin strap. Stop wandering. You are on your own. No brave but foolhardy major to lead you this time.

He said, 'Next bend. If it's coming, that's where it will be. Private Frazier!'

But the sharpshooter was already crouched in the bows beside two seamen with a swivel gun, his long musket poking over the gunwale like a feeler.

He glanced at the other boat and was sickened to see Lascelles staring at him instead of watching over his men.

Deacon was examining his pistol and remarked, 'And to think I had the chance to go ashore and take a safe appointment in the dockyard!'

He looked up at Blackwood and they smiled at each other like conspirators.

The man at the stroke oar heaved back on his loom and let his limbs relax. The officers wouldn't joke about it if there was any real danger.

Along either side of the river the vegetation was thick and tangled. Blackwood watched it as it glided past, his mind darting from one possible eventuality to the next.

A seaman in the bows called, 'Comin' up now, sir!' He hushed his voice, as if he too was conscious of the unnatural stillness. Not a bird, not even a breeze here to make the bushes come alive.

Corporal Jones exclaimed, 'Flash from the top o' the hill, sir! Larboard quarter!'

Lascelles' sergeant muttered, 'Silly bugger!'

But Blackwood said, 'What was it, Jones?' He gestured to the boat's coxswain, and as the oars stilled the silence crowded in like a living force.

Of all the men in the boat, Corporal Jones had probably seen the most action. He had originally been a soldier in a line regiment stationed in India. If only half his barrack-room yarns were true, he had tackled every kind of situation a soldier on the Indian frontier could expect.

Jones said without hesitation, 'Light from a mirror, sir. A signal of some kind. Bloody Afghans used to do it.'

Blackwood looked across at the other boat and motioned with his hand. He waited for Lascelles to tell his men what to expect and prayed he had not forgotten everything at the first scent of danger.

Smithett stirred uneasily on the thwart. ' 'Ere, sir.' He handed Blackwood a loaded pistol. 'The other one's ready when you needs it.'

Blackwood looked at Deacon. 'Let's get it over.' As the boat moved forward again he added, 'Still think we're going to look bloody silly?'

Deacon did not answer.

Blackwood rose to his feet and stared across the heads of the seamen and marines. It was hard to hold his concentration after what Jones had seen. He could feel a tingling sensation at the nape of his neck, as if it was already fixed in a sharpshooter's sights.

The boat swept round the next bend and the river opened out immediately to a width of about a quarter mile. To larboard it was still steep and rocky, but to starboard the land fell away to a long stony beach with a fragile looking pier or jetty giving the first hint of human life. A twisting swirl of current betrayed the presence of a sand-bar in the centre of the stream. No wonder Tobin was loath to venture this far.

Deacon whispered, 'There's the mission!'

It was more like a low fort. It was well sited at the far end of the beach, its stout walls built of stones and layers of sand pounded rock-hard inside outer palisades of timber. Ugly, but safe against anything but trained artillery.

Deacon stood up beside him and grimaced. 'No sign of life.' Some of his confidence returned. 'It was probably all a rumour.'

Blackwood ignored him and said to the *Satyr*'s sergeant, 'If you were putting men ashore. Where is the most dangerous place?'

The sergeant hesitated, unused to being asked for an opinion.

Blackwood felt the sweat trickling down his spine and soaking his shirt around his waist. The distance was falling away, but the sergeant had to understand. In minutes, seconds even, he might be in sole command.

'That pier thing, sir. No cover. Long run up the beach.'

Blackwood reached down and touched his shoulder but did not take his eyes from the land.

'Good man. I agree.'

He made himself fold his arms. Someone with a glass might be watching for a sign of alarm. On open water they would stand no chance, no matter what any marksmen ashore might believe.

'Steer for the pier, cox'n. Nice, easy stroke. No fuss.' He even forced a grin as he glanced above the crowded hull. 'But when I give the word pull like hell for the end of the beach. Get the boat ashore and use it for cover.'

His voice was hoarse yet he was afraid to clear his throat. Here and there a hand moved to loosen a bayonet in its scabbard or a finger beat a nervous tattoo on a musket stock.

Blackwood measured the distance. If they could reach the beach it was fifty yards to the nearest cover, some broken rocks below the mission. It would be up to Lascelles to give them covering fire. If he failed . . . he thought of M'Crystal's red face and took comfort. He at least would give the order.

Deacon said hoarsely, 'I wonder where the bloody door is on that place?'

Blackwood replied, 'Facing inland, I expect.'

He was speaking to hold his thoughts in check. There was no sign of movement. No smoke, not even a moored boat.

The pier glided towards them, the current gurgling gently through the rough piles. This was where the fort would receive its stores to trade with the local tribes, and from where their gains could be collected. Slade had described it as the 'picklock of empire'. It looked like a place of the dead.

Jones hissed, 'Saw something move, sir! Bushes to the right of the mission! By the split rock.'

Blackwood turned slightly and said, 'Easy, lads. Not long now.' My God, but for Corporal Jones they might all be dead on that pier.

He said, 'Stand by. Swivel gun at the first sign of attack. Have you got the bearing?'

The two seamen in the bows bobbed their heads like puppets.

'*Now!*'

It only needed one seaman to catch a crab with his oar like that day at Spithead and it would end in chaos. But to the manner born the boat's crew threw themselves back on their looms, and as the tiller bar went hard over the rickety pier seemed to fall away as they swept past, the blades churning like *Satyr*'s paddles.

For just a moment longer Blackwood imagined he had made a stupid mistake, and then as shadows moved beyond the line of thick scrub he heard the sharp crack of a musket. A seamen yelped in alarm as a bullet struck the gunwale and left a neat hole above his knee before striking the opposite side. A very powerful weapon, and certainly not handled by an ignorant savage.

'Pull, lads! *Faster!*'

Another shot cracked out and whined above the sweating oarsmen.

In the bows, Frazier, the expert marksman, took slow and deliberate aim and then squeezed the trigger. Even at that range, and firing from a moving boat, he did not miss. Blackwood had never known him to lose a target.

A figure burst from the scrub and staggered against the split rock before pitching headlong down the slope. It could be anyone, Blackwood thought. Dressed in robes, more like an Arab than a local tribesman.

He drew his sword and pointed at the shore. *'Fire!'*

The swivel, training hard round until it was pointing abeam, spat out a long orange tongue, the crash of the shot echoing around the river like a thunder-clap. The tightly packed charge of canister exploded amongst the bushes and coarse scrub barely feet from where the figure had fallen.

From this distance it was like seeing a freak wind hitting the side of the hill. Stones and branches were hurled in all directions, and Blackwood imagined he saw someone crawling into deeper cover, wounded perhaps from the murderous charge of the 'daisy-cutter' as it was termed.

There was no more time to wonder about that. The beach was suddenly right here, and as the oars stilled seamen and marines tumbled over the gunwales to wade alongside and guide the boat firmly ashore.

Blackwood did not even remember getting his feet wet. One second he was steadying himself against the grounding, the next he was on the hot beach, his eyes everywhere as the marines ran and staggered into two sections, their eyes slitted as they peered around for another sign of an enemy.

Blackwood looked across the slowly moving water. God in heaven, Lascelles was in direct line with this boat. He would be unable to offer covering fire without killing and wounding half of the landing party. He saw the oars come to life again and breathed out noisily. Either Lascelles or M'Crystal had seen the danger in time.

Blackwood shouted, 'Take cover in those rocks! First section, *go*!'

The marines and the sergeant trotted up the beach, while the others knelt down and aimed their muskets at the place where the swivel had carved its path.

Lieutenant Deacon called, 'Shall I call in the second boat, Major?'

'Not yet.'

Blackwood wiped his eyes quickly with the back of his sleeve. The first section was there. Like fallen red plums dotted among the rocks. He gritted his teeth. His fingers were so slippery he could barely grip his sword. Where was courage now? *What does it feel like?*

Corporal Jones peered up at him, his homely Welsh features anxious. 'Sir?'

It steadied Blackwood. *Sir.* He must have spoken aloud without knowing it.

He bared his teeth in a grin but his face felt frozen. 'Second section, *advance!*'

What must it look like, he wondered, had there been anyone to see? A line of marines walking up the beach towards the mission. He glanced quickly to left and right. A mere handful of men, faces grim beneath their black shakos, muskets held at the ready as they trudged across the open ground.

Doak, who had been under arrest for drunkenness when he had returned from leave. Frazier, who could shoot an acorn out of a tree but would do anything to avoid promotion. Oldcastle, not even seventeen and already facing possible death.

To think I nearly left them and others like them.

He could see the other section amongst the rocks watching their progress, ready to fire if there was any sort of challenge.

His heart was beating against his ribs loud enough for Jones or the others to hear. Soon now. The crashing impact. Hopefully quickly done. Not the agony of *Satyr*'s surgeon, the humiliation of returning home a cripple.

They reached the rough wall and halted. Blackwood looked up and listened. The enemy, whoever they were, would know that the only way into the compound was through the gate, which was on the other side where they would be unprotected and shot down before they could get inside.

Corporal Jones said, 'Grapnel, sir?'

Blackwood nodded. Suppose the first attack had been a ruse to get them this far? The real menace might be inside the wall, waiting for them to enter or attempt to climb over.

Private Doak slung his musket and stood back from the wall, a grapnel swinging gently from one hand. A solitary man, in spite of his calling, with a secret sorrow, Blackwood had decided. Whatever it was, he did his best to lose it with rum whenever he got the chance.

He made up his mind and unclipped his scabbard and handed it and his sword to Smithett. His shako too, while the nearest marines watched him with tense expectancy.

Corporal Jones said cautiously, 'Won't do at all, sir, begging your pardon. I'll go.'

Blackwood watched as the grapnel soared up to the parapet and caught fast. Then he took the line and tested it, his eyes on the rough horizon between wall and sky. 'If I fall, Corporal Jones, retreat back to the boat.' He took a firm grip on the line and hoped his palms would not slip. It would take too long to explain to Jones.

He leaned back and pressed his foot against the wall. What had his father said of him? *Honour and glory*. He cursed aloud and began to haul himself up the line. He had been ready enough to give Lascelles advice. Now it was his turn to earn his pay.

Once he paused to gather his strength, aware of the silence again, the upturned faces below him. By his hand he saw an ant probing into a hole in the crude stonework. How many people had died to build this place? he wondered.

With a start he realized his head was level with the top. Holding his breath he reached out for a fingerhold, his mind throbbing with strain and concentration.

As his eyes rose higher he saw a burned-out roof and some fallen timber on the far side of a mud compound. But the gates were there right enough, and heavily barred with a massive timber. His nostrils twitched and he felt his body contract with fear. Death. He knew the smell of that all right.

'Anything, sir?' Jones was getting worried again.

Blackwood did not answer but very gingerly hauled his body up and up until he was lying prone on the top of the wall. He heard a bang and flinched as a ball slammed into a piece of timber supporting an inner parapet. There was an instant rattle of musket fire, then the bang of a swivel as the challenge was met from the boats.

Blackwood threw himself over the wall and dropped on his knees. As he tugged the pistol from his belt he saw a face peering at him over the edge of the same parapet. Bearded and filthy, with eyes ablaze with despair and worse, the creature shouted, 'In God's name! *Who are you?*'

Blackwood moved towards him, knowing the next seconds were vital. The man was armed, although his weapon was hidden beneath the parapet's planking. He was also on the verge of madness. One false move and he would get a full charge straight in his belly.

He said slowly, 'The marines are here.' He deliberately thrust the pistol back into his belt as he watched the man's eyes trying to translate what they saw. Faded eyes like his grandfather's.

It was unbearable to see the ragged creature as he began to weep. There was no sound at all, which made it worse, and all the time those eyes stared at Blackwood as if unable to accept what was happening.

A white leg came over the parapet and Corporal Jones crouched beside him.

'Hell's teeth, sir!' He sniffed. 'Corpses too!'

Blackwood lowered himself on to the ladder and stared at the ragged defender.

'How many of you?'

'F-four, I think.' He shook his head dazedly. 'Bin here for days fighting them off.' He waved vaguely with his musket. 'The devils are out there still.' He reached out and felt Blackwood's tunic with a filthy hand. *'Marines*, y'say?' His eyes were pleading. 'Come to help *us*?'

Blackwood stood up slowly, his mind rebelling as he saw

the corpses littered by the gate and sprawled in careless attitudes where they had fallen. It must have been a pitched battle. He listened to the dull buzz of flies but heard only the screams and yells which must have filled this terrible place.

He saw Smithett clambering over the parapet, ducking without any change of expression as a ball shrieked over his head.

'I think we need one of those bottles, Smithett.' To Jones he said, 'Call up the others and get them in position.' He thought suddenly of the boy Oldcastle. What would he think of the horrors here? Black men and white, staring eyes and gaping wounds. 'When you've done that, signal the first section to join us at the double.'

He turned towards the old man with the musket. 'Yes, we are here to help you.' He made himself smile when he felt like weeping. 'But first I want you to help me.'

5

Battle Fury

Captain George Tobin stood with his shoulders set against the stern windows of his day cabin, his face grim as he listened to the first lieutenant's report. It was early evening, and although the wind had completely died *Satyr* rolled continuously in an offshore swell.

Sir Geoffrey Slade was sitting in one of Tobin's leather chairs, and huddled in a corner as if to be invisible. Barrow, the private secretary, peered at his papers, his pen scribbling at irregular intervals.

Lieutenant Deacon looked exhausted and had one wrist tied in a crude bandage as he completed his description of what they had found at the trading mission.

He said, 'The old man, Thomas Fenwick by name, says there were thirty-two white men in the fort.' He dropped his eyes as he remembered the gaping corpses, the swarming flies. 'Another died shortly after we scaled the wall. I brought the remaining three aboard for the surgeon.' He shrugged heavily as if it was all beyond imagination. 'Old Thomas Fenwick refused to leave, sir.'

Slade gave a wry smile. 'He would. He's been trading these coasts for as long as anyone can remember.' He stood up and crossed to the table and peered over his secretary's shoulder. 'If it's all true, Captain Tobin, I was wrong about Mdlaka. We were all wrong. The old king was not overthrown, he obviously planned the massacre himself, with outside aid.' He glanced up sharply, 'Rifled weapons, you say?'

Deacon nodded. 'Yes, sir. Captain Blackwood told me to

be sure I reported that. Not many of them, maybe only three or four. One shot went clean through the boat's side. No ordinary smooth-bore did that.'

Slade rubbed his chin thoughtfully. 'You waited all day and nothing else happened. Interesting. Our unexpected arrival in *Satyr* upset their plans, no doubt. They intended to kill the last of the defenders and make it look like a raid by somebody else.'

Tobin said, 'Any small vessel would have entered the estuary and moored at the pier as usual. Those few muskets would have cut down any attempt to make sail and escape. You're right, Sir Geoffrey, they'd not be expecting a steam-frigate.' There was no pride in his voice this time, only disgust.

Slade said, 'Wait outside, Mr Deacon, if you please.' As soon as the door was closed he said crisply, 'I cannot order you about, Captain Tobin. I can only *advise*, there is a subtle difference.'

Tobin smiled. 'I know, sir. I've been in the Navy long enough to learn that. I am the senior officer present, and until we reach higher authority at Freetown I must act as I think proper.'

Slade added, 'What you mean is that if you act wisely others will receive the praise, but if you make a mistake you alone will carry the blame?'

'Something like that, sir.'

'Then let me *advise* you. Mdlaka is just one of many African kings or chiefs who have kept an uneasy peace at our bidding. They grew rich on slavery, and now on a growing export of palm oil. Although most European countries have done their best to restrain slavery, if only in words, there are individuals who still see it as rich profit. Cuba, Brazil, even in the Indies there are ready markets for those who will run the risk of seizure. To compensate slave-owners was not enough. The sources must be stamped out. If an old king like Mdlaka can be bought with a few modern guns and induced to commit mass murder, there is no saying what will happen further south in the Gulf.'

Tobin sat down. 'Funny thing, sir, I was recently telling Captain Blackwood about *my* days in the Gulf.' He looked up, his eyes direct and hard. 'You're going to leave him there, aren't you?'

'You like him?' Slade walked to a scuttle and studied the golden sunlight on the water. It would soon be dusk. 'Yes, I must. If the fort had been taken and everyone killed, the bodies and evidence burnt, I might have left it at that.' His voice was cold as he continued, 'But Mdlaka knows me and will realize that I understand what he has done. If we leave now, the word will spread like a forest fire. The white man has fled from Mdlaka. There would be a stampede to copy his example.'

'And your advice, sir?'

'As soon as it is dark send the remaining marines across, and any stores you think Captain Blackwood might need.'

Tobin remained expressionless. There was no point in telling Slade there were only six marines still aboard. He was a landsman, a man of politics.

Slade said, 'I must reach Freetown without delay. There I shall discover the latest and, I trust, more accurate intelligence about what is happening.' He eyed the captain sadly. 'Do not fret too much about young Blackwood. He takes after his father, though I doubt he would admit to it. He is as resourceful as he is brave.' He shrugged. 'And like you, he is the only one who is available.'

Tobin moved from the chair. 'I'll tell my first lieutenant. The boats can go in as soon as it's dark.' He watched the other man and added, 'With respect, sir, you should have been an admiral yourself.'

Slade watched the door close and said, 'Have you written all that down, Barrow? I want no misinterpretation later on because you've omitted something.'

He peered through the scuttle again. Some people were frightened of Africa merely because it looked vast on a map. It just needed courage, the urge to explore and create a new way of life here. Already there was a steady stream of missionaries, religious and medical, some in the most feared and previously hostile territories. They were the true vanguard, whether they knew it or not. His mouth tightened. Not a thousand Mdlakas were going to ruin a dream of empire, there was far too much at stake.

Tobin came back and said, 'I've passed the word, sir.' He shook his head. 'A rum lot, these marines. The last six I had on board began to cheer when Mr Deacon told them they were being sent over.'

Slade smiled. 'You worry too much, Captain. Who knows, together we may be making a small part of history?'

Tobin cocked his head to listen to a boat being pulled around the stern. Stuck out there in the middle of nowhere. He considered how he would have felt under the same circumstances. Without a ship. Helpless.

He said, 'I've told the Chief to get under way as soon as the boats return, sir.'

Anything but sit here with this composed, practical man who seemed to consider any sort of sentiment as weakness.

It was completely dark when the boats returned and were hoisted smartly inboard.

Tobin was waiting to meet his first lieutenant on the quarterdeck, his mind for once uninterested in the coursing rumble of the engines and the gushing plume of smoke.

Deacon looked around the bustling seamen and listened to the clank of the capstan as if it was beautiful and inspiring music.

'How was it?' Tobin asked.

Deacon licked his lips. 'Terrible, sir. The stench, everything.' He tried to smile. 'Captain Blackwood sent you his best wishes, by the way. Cool as an ice-floe, that one.'

Tobin looked away. Shadows hovered around him, waiting for orders, ready to move, to prove once more what they could do. Deacon was a good man, but he didn't understand half of it.

He said harshly, 'I'll send him a message too. From us. The ship.'

Moments later, as the anchor rose dripping to the cathead and the frigate turned in a welter of froth and spray, her siren rent the sky apart with its piercing squawk.

Tobin climbed on to his unprotected bridge and examined the extra compass there. Then he looked astern where only the frothing wake left by paddles and rudder broke the darkness.

He said, 'I'll be back. Be certain of it.'

Captain Philip Blackwood walked slowly along the parapet, his eyes straining through the darkness which reached out from the barred gates like a black wall.

The marines had been hard at work all day with barely a break for rations and a gulp of fresh water. It was a marvel that any of them could even contemplate food, Blackwood thought. As it was, several of the marines had staggered retching from the grisly work of hauling the corpses to the parapets to fling them clear of the fort. Although the stench still lingered over the compound, the sights of horror were gone. The dead white men had been buried on part of the compound, while the food and stores sent across from *Satyr* had been stacked inside the communal building at the seaward end of the fort. The whole place measured about eighty yards by fifty, and from the size of the store huts, now burned to the ground, it must have been a thriving post until disaster had struck.

Brogan, *Satyr*'s marine sergeant, seemed very competent, and was outside the fort at this moment with a patrol of five men to make sure there were none of the attackers still in the undergrowth.

Blackwood paused and looked over the wall as he thought of his long talk with the remaining trader, Tom Fenwick. He was like something from a boy's story-book. Fenwick had been everywhere in his search for a fortune, which so far had eluded him. He had been at the fort for two years and knew the local tribes better than most.

As Sergeant Brogan had prepared to lead his patrol clear of

the gates he had said in his quavery voice, 'No point in it, Captain. Them buggers 'as gone. They'll be dancin' and jiggin' to their 'eathen rites right now, an' after they've filled their bellies with drink they'll be samplin' the local girls to make 'em feel like warriors again!'

Blackwood stared at the darkness, recalling his feelings when the *Satyr*'s siren had echoed along the river to signal her departure. It was typical of Tobin, of the man behind the uniform and the authority. He had seen the effect it had made on the others. The younger ones had gazed at each other as if only just aware that they had been left to fend for themselves. The older men had gone about their various tasks in silence. They knew what to expect, or thought they did.

Blackwood heard footsteps moving cautiously along the parapet and saw Lascelles peering towards him.

'Sentries mounted, sir. The rest are settling down as ordered.'

It was strange, Blackwood thought, but the lieutenant seemed more at a loss even than the recruits. Too long with a small detachment of marines in a modern vessel like *Satyr*, perhaps that was it. It would become easy to be a passenger under those circumstances.

He wrenched his mind away from vague uncertainties and said, 'We've got food and water for three weeks.' He saw him flinch. 'If need be. The water must be rationed, for although there is a stream, old Fenwick thinks it might have been poisoned. I've warned the men, but keep at them.' He felt drained and unreasonably angry that Lascelles seemed able to let him make all the decisions and offer nothing. 'Marines are taught to be clean and tidy at all times from the moment they enlist. They must unlearn that lesson immediately. I want all uniforms stowed away, and each man to stain his shirt so that it will not make him a target. Colour-Sergeant M'Crystal is dealing with that. Under protest.'

He pictured M'Crystal's red face, the look of horror when he had ordered him to use tea or coffee for staining the men's shirts. It must have sounded like blasphemy to him.

Blackwood added, 'We are trained to fight, but not to deal with this kind of enemy. I'll not have our men marked down by some bloody sharpshooter just because of the drill book.'

Lascelles rested his palms on the rough wall. 'You believe they'll come back?'

'Yes.'

He thought of old Tom Fenwick, the way he had somehow gained in stature after being on the threshold of hell itself. He had said that the king, Mdlaka, must have promised someone a clear passage down-river with an important cargo. It had to make sense. With the armed schooner *Kingsmill* missing, probably wrecked, it was a chance in a thousand to run a shipment to the coast for collection. Only the trading post stood in the way, and Mdlaka had had no intention of allowing a single soul here to survive. He had even sent men to steal the fort's two boats before the real attack had been started.

Fenwick had described it with little emotion. As if he had been somewhere else, or a mere spectator.

They had rushed the gates when they had been open for any would-be barter from the nearest villages, and the battle had surged back and forth, hand to hand and without quarter. Somehow they had driven the first attack clear of the compound long enough to bar the gates. After that it had been a slower, more terrifying process. Burning wads had been thrown over the walls to set fire to the huts, and several of the defenders had been shot down by marksmen concealed on the hillsides.

Two of the traders had decided to leave the fort and look for one of the missing boats. The next morning one of them had been found outside the gates horribly mutilated and apparently skinned alive. The next day the second man had been sighted tied to a tree directly opposite the gates but too far away for rescue. Even Fenwick, who had seen what savage torture could do, had said he did not know what had made the man stay alive for a whole day. 'They must've give 'im to the women to do that to 'im,' he had said harshly.

Blackwood said, 'They may try a mock attack to test our strength. But it's those rifled muskets I'm worried about.'

Lascelles said vaguely, 'The Corps will be getting them next year, sir, like the army.'

'That won't help us!' He relented, knowing it was fatigue and strain which were giving his tongue an edge. 'Fenwick has drawn a map for me.' He pointed across the wall into the blackness. 'There's a shallow dip in the ground beyond the ridge, and then a pointed hill, like a loaf. Perfect place for a spotting post. We'll have it manned as soon as we know the enemy are keeping their distance.'

Lascelles nodded and swallowed hard. 'I see, sir.'

Blackwood said, 'I know it sounds bad, but it's all we have. Whoever the enemy is, they're going to fight in their own way, and that is what we must do. This fort is an important key and it must be held. Now go around the sentries and I'll relieve you in an hour.' He groped his way to a ladder and lowered himself to the compound.

A fire was burning cheerfully behind a wall, all that was left of a store-room. Several marines, unfamiliar without their red coats and cross-belts, crouched around it, and Blackwood waved them down as they made to stand in his presence. He noticed that their weapons were in easy reach, the pouches of ammunition and percussion caps ready to be snatched up in seconds.

'Carry on, Corporal Jones.'

He walked to the shadows again and tried not to think of the *Satyr* as she pounded her way further and further to the south.

He found a blanket and rolled greatcoat propped by another wall, and a metal cup of brandy covered with a piece of wood to keep out any insects. He sat down carefully and sipped at the brandy. Thank God for Smithett.

Blackwood tried to free his mind from tomorrow, of Fenwick's horrific description of the mutilated traders.

He wondered if his father had taken any further steps to sell the estate and move to London. Compared with his own predicament, his father had led a very full life. Two wives, an eventful career in the Corps, with sons to carry on the tradition.

A creature shrilled beyond the palisade, and Blackwood rolled on to his side and pressed his eyes tightly shut. Harry stood a good chance of being the only one left.

He tried to think of the dark-haired girl named Davern, but her picture was blurred and indistinct. It made him suddenly apprehensive and sick, and when Lieutenant Lascelles came to rouse him he found him still wide awake, his chin resting on his knees as he stared at the leaping shadows from the marines' fire.

It was nearly dawn by the time he felt he could sleep, and by then it was too late.

He watched the men stirring and finding their bearings, glancing at each other for reassurance, to convince themselves it was really happening.

Beyond the wall and vigilant sentries the land was coming to life. Unusual bird cries, unlike yesterday's eerie silence, and a glint of sunlight on the ridged hillside.

Sergeant Brogan had reported finding dried blood where the swivel gun had blasted through the undergrowth, but the corpse had been spirited away, or as Fenwick had commented curtly, 'Probably eaten by some poxy hyena.' It made your flesh creep.

Blackwood surveyed his temporary command without enthusiasm. It looked like a forgotten place. It had even changed the marines. In their shirts and white trousers, unwashed and unshaven, they already had the appearance of renegades. It was a far cry from drilling on the barrack square at Forton, the stamp and swagger which even the foot guards envied.

Lascelles watched him anxiously. 'Both watches have eaten, sir. Weapons inspected.'

Blackwood glanced at the marines' shirts. The staining had only partly worked, but would certainly help to break up a man's outline, especially at night.

Old Fenwick was at the far side of the compound, his jaw

working on a piece of dried beef as he stared moodily at the line of graves. How well had he known them? How much did he miss them? Or was it like soldiering, Blackwood wondered, where survival was the only real consideration?

Fenwick turned as if he had felt him watching, but said, 'They're comin'!'

Lascelles stared at him. 'How can you be – ?'

Blackwood snapped, '*Stand to!*'

In total silence the marines seized their muskets and pouches and ran to the ladders as if it was all part of a regular drill. But Blackwood could recognize a pattern even here. Friends of long standing kept together. An old hand cast a cautious glance at a younger companion as he stood up to the parapet, his face like a mask.

Blackwood climbed to the parapet above the gates. He could hear it now for himself. A throbbing murmur of sound, like a giant bird beating its wings.

Fenwick wheezed up to join him and remarked, 'Gettin' up their courage, blast 'em!'

Blackwood bit on his chin strap until the pain steadied his tumbling thoughts. A cloud of dust was spreading over the side of the hill and the din was growing every minute.

He darted a glance at the nearest marines. Shakos tilted to shield their eyes from the sun, muskets at their sides and shoulders back. They must have been the same sort of men at the Nile or Trafalgar. Except that this was no fleet action, no field of honour.

'Here they come!' Sergeant Brogan pointed over the wall.

Lascelles whispered, 'Oh, my God!'

It was impossible to estimate the numbers or how far the advancing army extended. The swirling cloud of dust could not hide the black bodies which shone with sweat or the precision of the drum-like beat as they pounded their shields with spear hafts. Just ahead of the packed ranks a few individuals stood out as they capered in complicated steps, striking at the air with stabbing spears as they led their cohorts into battle.

Blackwood said, 'Mark those men down.'

He heard Private Frazier mutter a reply. He had doubtless already selected his first target.

Fenwick said, 'Mdlaka must've called in reinforcements. 'E means business right enough, God rot 'im!'

Blackwood stared at the oncoming, bobbing tide until his eyes were raw. This was no North Island, he thought grimly. No ships behind you to carry you off if things went against you. No soldiers and blue-jackets to give support.

The wall seemed to shiver as a great roar of voices came down the hillside like a roll of thunder. There must be hundreds and hundreds of them.

Then they started to run. It was not a controlled movement like their slow advance, but a mad rush, as if it was a matter of honour to be the first one at the gates.

Spears flew towards the fort and were trampled underfoot by the charging mass of figures.

Blackwood yelled, 'Face your front! Take aim!'

Along the parapet the muskets lifted and settled as one.

Blackwood tried to swallow but it was no use. He felt as if his throat was choked with that dust.

'Fire!'

The volley crashed out along the parapet, and as the first line of marines fell back to reload the second line stepped forward to the parapet wall and took aim.

'Present! Fire!'

Surely every shot must have found its mark, they could not miss, but it had as much effect on the mass of charging bodies as a pike against an elephant.

The first of them hit the gates and the wall on either side like something solid, and above the bark of commands and the sporadic bang of muskets the yells and screams were joined in one terrible chorus.

Loading and reloading, the marines kept up a steady fire, and as Blackwood emptied his pistol into the attackers directly below the parapet he saw heavy logs being rushed through the throng to be used as battering-rams against the gates.

A marine beside him fell gasping with a short spear embedded in his shoulder. Another was holding his face, his fingers running with blood.

'Load . . . present . . . *fire!*'

Sergeant Brogan was beating out the time as the ramrods rose and fell and the men stepped up once more to the parapet wall.

Someone yelled, 'They're attacking from the river, sir!'

Blackwood swung round. 'Mr Lascelles, take a section to support them!' He saw him nod jerkily, his eyes glazed like glass in the sunlight.

A marine whirled round and fired his musket from the hip as a black, screaming face appeared above the wall. They were handling logs and branches with the same skill as grenadiers would use scaling ladders.

The savage's face exploded in a scarlet blur as he dropped out of sight.

Blackwood tugged out his sword, remembering the dead major as he shouted hoarsely, 'Marines! *Fix bayonets!*'

The hiss of steel ran along the parapet, and as more struggling figures tried to pull themselves over the wall the blades rose and fell with desperate precision.

One attacker, his powerful body naked but for a twist of feathers, threw his leg over the wall and smashed down a marine with a knob-headed club. It all happened in a second. Blackwood saw the young recruit, Oldcastle, staring at the savage, his bayonet shaking, his face transfixed with horror. Then he was almost knocked down by Private Bulford as he thrust his bayonet into the man's belly. As he wrenched it free he swung the butt of his musket into the contorted features and set him crashing to the ground below.

He stared at Oldcastle. 'Don't *play* with it, sonny! The bugger'll do for you else!'

Colour-Sergeant M'Crystal, massive even in his stained shirt, shouted, 'They're running, sir!'

'*Cease firing!*'

Sergeant Brogan had to forcibly pull a musket from one marine's grip as the attack turned just as swiftly into a retreat. Bodies lay everywhere, some still, others writhing and groaning where they had dropped.

Blackwood removed his shako and wiped his face with a rag. *A near thing*. His heart was pounding faster than he had ever known, and he felt as if his stomach was filling with bile. He tugged on his hat again and gritted his jaws together. *Must not show it*.

He heard some of the injured marines whimpering like sick animals as they were carried into the shelter of the remaining building.

He heard himself say, 'Check the ammunition, Sergeant. Corporal Jones, how many wounded?'

Colour-Sergeant M'Crystal was wiping his sword very carefully on some dried grass. The blood looked black in the sunlight.

Old Fenwick chewed on his meat. 'They'll come again. Mdlaka will be watchin', the cunnin' bastard, weighin' up your strength. 'E'll try to pare it away if 'e can.'

Jones reported, 'Seven men wounded, sir. Private Simcoe's pretty bad. Lung, I think, sir.'

'Thank you.'

Blackwood stared at the hillside. It must be important for Mdlaka to risk so many lives. If some traders could defend the fort, the marines were a much tougher proposition. And yet there had been a madness, a fervour in the attack which made a mockery of numbers and experience.

What was the choice? Stay behind the walls and lose men with each ferocious attack, or get out and fight them in the open? There seemed no choice at all.

He raised his small telescope and examined the bare hill beyond the ridge. From its summit you would be able to see for miles.

Crack! A piece of stonework flew from the parapet and fanned past his face.

He stepped behind one of the supporting timbers as

M'Crystal said angrily, 'One of those new guns, sir. Och, I'd like to get my hands on that bugger!'

Blackwood deliberately turned his back towards the unseen marksman and said, 'I think we'll issue a tot of rum per man, Colour-Sergeant. This is thirsty work, eh?'

He felt his shoulder-blades throbbing as he waited for the pain. He saw some of the smoke-grimed marines peering at him, even grinning at his apparent contempt for the danger. It was working. They could still respond to his stupid bravado.

Sergeant Brogan came back again and said, 'Most of the men used up their extra ammunition. But they've got sixty rounds each, and the others which *Satyr* sent over for us. Course, it all depends how long we're 'ere, sir.'

Blackwood nodded. *They want reassurance.* They needed to know that things would be all right, that somehow their officer would think of a plan.

'Here they come again!'

'*Stand to!* Controlled firing this time!'

Another shot from the concealed marksman ripped into the wall and flung fragments over their heads.

If the marines were prevented from manning the parapet while the attackers smashed through the gates, it would all be over in minutes. He stared at the drifting dust cloud and the tangled barricade of scrub until he was blinded by it.

'*Fire!*'

The flashes of muskets rippled along the parapet and several charging figures pitched among those killed previously.

The marksman must have fired at the same time, for Blackwood saw a marine fall from the parapet to the compound below.

Corporal Jones ran to help him but looked up and shook his head before hurrying back to his section.

Blackwood's eyes smarted with hatred and despair.

Their first death.

He pushed forward to the wall and fired at a man directly below him. Smithett thrust a loaded pistol into his hand and he fired again, seeing a man fall and be trampled down by the writhing press of shining bodies and shields.

M'Crystal had taken up a musket from a wounded marine and stood like a bear at bay as he fired and reloaded more with rage than accuracy.

'Come on then, you black bastards!' M'Crystal had always seen himself dying gloriously in battle like one of the paintings at the marine barracks; the red coats, the impassive stares of the tightly formed square as they confronted their country's enemies.

To die here in squalor was unthinkable, and his fury seemed to transmit itself to the men near him so that they yelled and cheered like lunatics as they fired, reloaded and fired again.

Blackwood stood back and lowered his arm as the attackers waned and then scattered away from the fort.

'Cease firing!'

How many wounded this time? Blackwood was almost fearful to ask. He saw the dead marine being carried towards the other graves. One of the recruits. He could not even remember his name, his brain was pounding so badly.

He looked at Fenwick. 'What do you think?'

The old man plucked at his beard. ' 'E knows 'ow many men you've got now. 'E'll keep tryin'. Otherwise 'e'll lose face, an' 'e's an old man.' He showed his few teeth in a grimace. 'They'd soon get rid of 'im.'

Keep trying. Blackwood peered down at the scattered corpses and the few which still twitched in agony.

Sergeant Brogan looked up from the compound. 'We got fifteen wounded all told, sir. Private Carson 'as been killed, an' Private Simcoe's sinking fast, if you ask me, sir.'

Blackwood nodded. He did not trust himself to speak. Sixteen killed and wounded altogether. It was a third of their total strength, and all in one day!

Lascelles joined him and after a moment said, 'About that spotting post on the hill, sir.' He looked tight-lipped and desperate. Like a stranger.

'Yes?'

'I could reach it. If you think it will help, sir.'

Blackwood studied him gravely. 'If they keep attacking, and Fenwick knows them better than we do, we'll be down to a dozen men in a week, probably less. Mdlaka is running out of time. He's trying to swamp our defences.' He saw Lascelles' eyes watching a wounded man being assisted into shelter, his face running with blood. 'Fenwick believes that slavers are behind it, that they've put pressure on Mdlaka to destroy the fort. It makes sense to me. The use of a mirror for signals, the accuracy of that rifled weapon tells me there's another brain behind Mdlaka.' He was speaking his thoughts aloud. 'Those marksmen, no matter how few, can shoot down our men with each frontal attack. We either die piecemeal or get butchered when the others force the gates.' He faced Lascelles again and said quietly, 'I won't order you to go to the hill. You know the odds against survival, what might happen if you get captured.'

Lascelles swallowed hard, his eyes very bright in the sunlight. 'I'll go. I *want* to.'

'Very well.' He looked away, unable to watch Lascelles' fear, his fight to overcome it. 'At dusk, take Corporal Jones and Frazier and all the rations you need and make for the hill. When they rush the fort tomorrow, try and discover the sharpshooters.' He thrust his small telescope into Lascelles' limp hand. 'Jones and Frazier will do the rest.'

'What will *you* do, sir?'

Blackwood smiled. 'I'm not waiting here to die.' He gripped his arm and felt the strain Lascelles was enduring. 'If we fail, try and work your way to the headland and wait for *Satyr*. Someone should tell them what happened.'

Colour-Sergeant M'Crystal marched over the dried mud compound and waited, breathing heavily.

'Orders, sir?'

'Mr Lascelles is taking out a patrol as soon as it's dark. See that he gets all he needs.'

Blackwood looked around at the marines along the parapets, leaning on their weapons or the rough palisades, their eyes dark from fatigue and the fury of battle. The spirit was going out of them. They were not to blame. Perhaps it had been decreed from the beginning.

He came to a decision and added abruptly, 'After that, I want every fit man paraded for inspection. I want them washed and shaved and turned out like marines.'

He could feel the sudden apprehension around him. They imagined he had gone raving mad.

'The wounded men will be moved to the parapets before dawn, and I want every spare musket and pistol ready to fire. There may be no time to reload.'

Sergeant Brogan asked warily 'We goin' to fight 'em in the open, sir?'

Blackwood saw Smithett unrolling his kit below the wall. He must have ears like a fox.

Then he turned and looked at Lascelles again. 'Let me know when you're ready and I'll tell you what I intend.'

To Brogan he added, 'You will command the fort. If we fail tomorrow, I shall expect you to fight to the finish and not leave the wounded to suffer at the hands of those savages.'

Brogan nodded, his face pale. Now he understood.

Blackwood walked towards the wall, hoping that his light-headedness would not make him stumble.

Right or wrong, he had made a decision. Tomorrow would show if it was the right one.

6

One of the Best

'Everything quiet, Sergeant?' Blackwood peered over the parapet for what felt like the thousandth time.

'Aye, sir.' Brogan, still dressed in his filthy shirt, made a sharp contrast with Blackwood's coatee and white shoulder-belt.

Three hours since they had left.

When Lascelles' party had lowered themselves over the rear wall which faced the river, Blackwood had expected a challenge or some terrible cry to show they had been captured. But there had been no sound at all. That might mean nothing. Fenwick had described only too clearly how his two companions had vanished without even a whimper.

'You know what to do?'

Brogan bit his lip. 'I'd rather be with you, sir.'

Blackwood thought of the wounded marines who had said much the same as Brogan. It had not been a stupid gesture of loyalty or courage. They were used to being together. The thought of being separated now in the face of almost certain death was too much for them.

Twelve wounded men might be able to defend the front wall for a short while. It would be up to Sergeant Brogan and old Fenwick to make as much noise and to fire as many weapons as they could to support the deception.

He looked at the sky. They would need plenty of time to get into position. In spite of all that Fenwick had told him, there was still a possibility that a few of Mdlaka's men were watching the fort. But why should they? There was no way of escape without boats, and Mdlaka knew it. If they attempted to force their way inland they would be tracked down and killed like wild animals.

He said, 'I shall inspect the men.'

Down in the compound, lit only by a flickering fire, the marines were paraded in two ranks as if aboard ship.

Blackwood, followed by M'Crystal, moved slowly along each rank, conscious of the silence, the strange air of resignation which seemed to hang over them.

No packs or unnecessary equipment this time. Muskets, bayonets and ammunition pouches were all they carried. In the dancing reflections from the fire their cross-belts and red coats added a final unreality. Dressed to kill, or be killed.

'Stand easy.' Blackwood did not raise his voice. He did not have to. 'We shall be leaving the fort very soon. No sound, no talking. We must be on the hillside before first light.' He glanced down the front rank. 'Private Ackland, don't forget your bugle. Suck a pebble if you must, but I don't want your mouth too dry to blow when I give the order!'

Some of them actually chuckled as if it was all a great joke.

Blackwood continued, 'When they attack the gates they will see only what they expect to see, our men shooting down at them.' *Provided*, a nagging voice seemed to whisper, Lascelles is not already dead or screaming out his life under torture, and provided the marksmen were not there when he made his move. 'The last thing they will expect is to be attacked from the rear, and by marines in proper kit, unlike Sergeant Brogan's scarecrows!'

A few even laughed outright this time.

Blackwood waited until they had quietened again and said, 'We did not ask to be here, and this might be the last day for all of us.' He let his words sink in and there was absolute silence now. 'But we are Royal Marines, and we shall act as such.'

He turned away, unwilling to watch their faces. In the strange, shadowy light they already looked like spectres from a battlefield.

Colour-Sergeant M'Crystal joined him by the wall. 'That was well said, sir. They'll not let you down.' He jerked his belt into place. 'Wait till Sarnt Quintin hears about this. He'd not have missed it for anything.'

Blackwood froze as a chilling scream rent the night air.

But M'Crystal said, 'No, sir. That was only an animal of some sort.'

Blackwood breathed out slowly. He could not take much more of it. Concealing the fear was squeezing his insides like giant claws, and hiding the uncertainty made every thought distorted.

'I hope so.' He saw Smithett pouring brandy into a cup for him. It was almost time. 'I'm just sorry it had to be here, in this wretched place.'

M'Crystal showed his teeth in a grin. 'My dad died fighting two sailors in a street in Naples, sir. If I've a choice, I'll do it this way.'

M'Crystal moved away into the shadows. He would pour some of his rough confidence into the recruits, although after this nobody could be termed an amateur, Blackwood thought.

The brandy was hot and strong, and he handed the cup to Smithett, who had already packed up everything which was not immediately needed. The perfect attendant. Now Smithett was adjusting his belt and bayonet. Soon he would be an equally perfect marine.

Lascelles lay prone in a narrow depression at the top of the hill, his body aching from a dozen cuts and bruises, after finding this place in the darkness. He could hear Frazier nearby, moving some scrub to cover his position, his musket already trained and resting on some loose stones.

It had been the most terrible journey Lascelles could remember. Every sound had been like approaching death, and even the rustle of dry leaves had been an invisible army. He had seen himself captured before he could turn his pistol on his temple. Pleading and whimpering while they had tormented him before burning and cutting the life from his body.

Reaching the hill was only a postponement, it had to be. But it felt like a triumph all the same. He looked fearfully at the sky. Surely it was already brighter? He wondered where Corporal Jones was at this moment. A few yards further down the hill where he would be better placed to see the marksmen, if and when they appeared.

Lascelles felt his eyes sting at the thought of the shipboard life he had come to enjoy so much. The smell of the sea was keener on the hill and he imagined a dozen vessels out there in the darkness, sailing too far out to see or realize what was happening here.

He hissed, 'Can you see Corporal Jones?'

Frazier took his time answering. Jones was the old campaigner and knew what he was doing. The lieutenant just had to say something. He snorted. Bloody officers.

'Down an' to the left,' he hesitated, 'sir.'

'Yes. Yes, I see.'

Lascelles groped for his flask and sipped some water. It was warm and made him feel sick. God, the waiting. *Waiting*.

He thought of Blackwood, his calm assurance and quick flashes of impatience. A captain at twenty-six, a real-life hero by all accounts. Now he was there at that damnable fort waiting to lead his remaining men to oblivion. Lascelles rubbed his eyes with his knuckles. It was *unfair*, wrong that they should be here. He thought of his cabin aboard the *Satyr*, his books, the portrait of his mother, of his married sister in England, and how her children had admired his uniform on his last leave.

A cold shiver ran through him as Frazier whispered, 'Somebody's about already. I 'eard a cough.'

Lascelles could barely breathe. A cough. As close as that? He felt for his pistols, suddenly petrified. He blinked rapidly to clear his vision and saw the slope below him, and further still a small black square. That must be the fort. Beyond it the river, and beyond that the sea. Safety. If only . . .

Frazier had sensed his lieutenant's fear. He had once seen an officer stand as stiff as a ramrod as if on parade, too stricken to move, to avoid the blade which had hacked him down.

He said tersely, 'Easy, sir. We're safe enough for the moment.' He turned his head a few inches and added, 'Here comes the corporal.'

Lascelles made a great effort to control his shaking limbs. He had neither heard nor seen Jones' stealthy approach, and he was a large man.

Jones knelt beside the little hiding-place and plucked at his torn shirt. Without taking his eyes from the hillside he said softly, 'One of the buggers is right below us by the rocks. I heard him talking with his mate. Dagoes, by the sound of 'em. The other one's further to the right. Can't see him now.'

Lascelles peered up at him, searching for comfort in the corporal's words.

'Well? What will we do?'

Jones did not glance at him then. Blackwood, even the boozy lieutenant Cleveland would have told *him* what to do.

'The first one's easy, sir. I'll take him myself. The other bugger is too far away. Won't see him until he starts firing.' He looked at the shadows. 'Up to you, Frazier.'

Lascelles nodded jerkily. 'Yes. That's right.'

Jones laid his musket down very carefully and drew out a broad-bladed knife.

Lascelles stared, horrified. 'With that?'

Jones shrugged. 'Took it off a Dago. Might as well give it back, so to speak.' His gentle Welsh voice made the words all the more horrific.

Frazier moved again very slightly and gripped his musket. 'Here we are then.'

Lascelles saw the first light making a small shadow below his out-thrust arm. He turned to speak to Jones but he had vanished, as if he had never been.

*

Sergeant Brogan watched the sky brightening above the ridged hills and knew that the sun would be showing itself at any moment.

Someone called, 'Simcoe's dead, Sarnt!'

'Very well. Leave him an' take up your post.'

Another voice muttered, 'He's better off out of it, if you ask me!'

Brogan snapped, 'We're *not* asking, so shut it!'

He looked along the fort's puny defences and wondered why he felt no fear. Maybe it was what he had always expected since he had first seen his father in a marine's red coat. Unlike some of the others, Brogan had never had any doubts. He had been born within sight and sound of the barracks, had got to know the routines and drills before he could write his own name.

God, what a mess they all looked, he thought bitterly. Wounded men propped along the parapet at intervals like a line of cripples, their stained shirts and rough bandages adding the final touch to their suffering. One sat with his legs out-thrust, his back to the wall. His eyes were tightly shut against the pain of a deep wound in his chest, but he was surrounded by pouches of shot and percussion caps and gripped a ramrod in his fingers like a talisman.

Brogan eyed him grimly. He did not look as if he would last much longer. But even with his eyes closed he could still reload the spare muskets until his strength finally gave out. Brogan knew his men well. They could clean or load their weapons in pitch-darkness if need be.

He saw the old, long-bearded trader, Fenwick, at the far corner, a great musket cradled across his chest. It looked as if it could knock down six men at once. What sort of fools would want to stay in this hell? To trade with a bunch of treacherous natives? Fenwick's mates had paid dearly for it, others would soon follow.

The man nearest him asked, 'Do you think we can 'old them, Sergeant?'

Brogan shrugged. 'Can't say, Oastler.' He tried not to

think of Lieutenant Lascelles and what use he might be if Captain Blackwood fell. Brogan had carried the lieutenant during their time together in *Satyr*, and they both knew it. He added, 'If we get rushed and the gates bust open, we'll re-form at the river end, right?'

They both turned, their eyes gleaming in the first red glow of sunlight as it painted the top of the hill.

Private Oastler gritted his teeth against the pain in his leg and said, 'They're comin' already, the bastards!'

Brogan glanced at his handful of men and then at the loaded weapons by his side.

He heard Fenwick call in his shaky voice, 'They'll 'ave the sun behind 'em.'

Brogan gripped a musket and stared at the departing shadows with quiet desperation. Why didn't the old bugger shut up? Most of the men knew what was happening, and the others, well, they were better off in ignorance.

The dust looked thicker this time, but the swish and thud against the shields sounded the same.

'Stand to.' He did not raise his voice. They were all as ready as they could be.

The sun lifted more rapidly, and Brogan tried to shade his eyes as he peered at the distorted shapes of rocks and dark undergrowth. For the first time he felt his chest tighten with anxiety. They were coming. How long before it was over, and how would he behave when it happened? He glanced again at his men, at their tight faces and pain-filled eyes. He had seen some of them reeling drunk, or taking part in fleet regattas with the best of them. He had heard them cursing his name when he had turned them out on deck for a kit inspection or for drill. He had seen their comradeship grow with the rough but reliable humour of the lower deck.

Brogan thought suddenly of Blackwood when he had outlined his impossible plan. God Almighty, it had been only yesterday, just hours ago. But he remembered even more clearly what he had said. 'Fight to the finish.' It seemed to pull him together, as if he had just heard him speak.

'*Face your front!*'

He ran a musket through his hands and rested it on the wall. One of the hidden marksmen might already see him, but it was more important that his men should think he was unafraid.

The drumming beat was louder, and Brogan saw the glint of light on naked backs and brandished weapons. They were heading straight for the fort but more spread out than before, as if to divide the marines' fire.

'*Ready!*'

Brogan heard his men trying to shout, some with their voices so cracked with pain they sounded like pensioners. Even Fenwick was yelling unintelligible commands, anything which might make the attackers believe there was the same number of men behind the walls.

Brogan squinted along the barrel and moved it in time with one of the running figures. It wouldn't take them long to realize the truth after the first volley.

'*Take aim!*'

Something hit the wall by the gates, a spear or a rock, Brogan did not know.

He heard the marine named Oastler gasping as if in further pain, while the man with his eyes shut who gripped the ramrod so tightly called, 'What was that, Tom? Tell me, mate!'

But Oastler could barely speak. All he managed was, 'It's the lads.'

Brogan could understand his emotion. He was hard put not to show it himself. At first he had imagined his own resolve had cracked.

Then, as the shadows rolled back even further, he heard it again, the blaring call of a bugle, as clear and as firm as he had first heard it as a young boy.

The charging mass of figures seemed to lose direction and swung round in a haphazard confusion as they realized what was happening.

Brogan said tightly, 'If I live to be a hundred I'll not forget it.'

As if rising out of the ground itself the line of scarlet-coated marines marched unhurriedly down the slope towards the fort. Their bayonets shone and caught the sun's early redness like blood, their muskets at the high port across each man's body. In the centre and slightly ahead of the slow-moving line Brogan saw the slim figure of the captain, and at the rear the heavier bulk of the colour-sergeant, his sword already drawn across his shoulder.

Brogan had to wrench himself from his trance.

'Ready! Fire!'

He snatched up the next musket almost before the aimed volley had swept among the mass of figures below.

Everyone was yelling like a madman, and two of the marines were standing up on the wall itself, regardless of the risk, as they reloaded and fired again.

But some of the attackers were still coming on and Brogan yelled, 'Fix bayonets!'

The last time? He no longer cared.

'There's the fort, sir.' M'Crystal kept his voice low as he watched the early sunlight give an outline to the wall and parapet.

Blackwood nodded and examined the lay of the land. How different it all seemed in daylight and from this angle. He could see the charred beams of the burned-out store-house above the parapet, the litter of black shapes around the gates, like dead leaves until the sun uncovered them too.

He saw a glint of light from the left of the wall as the strengthening rays touched a marine's badge like a tiny mirror.

'Listen?' M'Crystal turned his head as if to smell out the danger. 'They're early, sir.'

Blackwood crawled away, his mind grappling with what might happen. The marines were in a long line, kneeling or sitting among the high dried grass which was thicker than he had imagined. He tried not to think about Lascelles, or if the marksmen had been taken. Once they began to move it would be too late, each white cross-belt would make a perfect target.

He wiped one hand on his sleeve and then pulled on his white gloves. At least he would be able to retain a grip on his weapons, he thought.

'Get ready!'

His words were repeated and whispered along the line of concealed figures. Blackwood bit tightly on his chin strap as he tried to shut out the mounting din from around the hill.

He leaned forward, his sword blade slithering through the grass as he craned up to watch the first running figures as they charged into view. Not so many this time. Perhaps Fenwick had been right and some of the warriors had already deserted Mdlaka?

He glanced along his own men, or what he could see of them. They were still outnumbered by at least four to one. He closed his mind against it and called, 'Ready, Ackland?'

The freckle-faced marine nodded and spat out a pebble before he moistened the bugle with his tongue.

Blackwood found that he was looking into the eyes of Private Oldcastle. Just a boy, who but for a twist of fate would be settling down to a routine life aboard the *Audacious*.

'Are you all right?'

The boy licked his lips, but his tongue seemed to stick to them.

'Y-yes, sir.'

'Good. Keep together, remember it.'

What was the point? The full mass of the charging mob was visible now, heading towards the gates in a human tide. There was no time to worry about anyone's feelings.

He stood up and pointed towards the fort. Without looking he could feel his men rising up on either side of him.

Blackwood walked through the rank, his arm brushing against Oldcastle's musket as he did so.

He looked at him again. Of *course* there was a point, and it *did* matter.

'Stay near me.' He saw him nod, then he strode forward and shouted, '*Sound the Advance*!'

The bugle echoed up the hillside and across the lower flat ground where they would confront their fate.

Lieutenant Lascelles lurched to his knees and pointed wildly. 'Look at them! Just *look* at them!'

He felt Corporal Jones grip his arm and drag him down without bothering about dignity as he exclaimed, 'Watch out, sir!'

Lascelles stared past him, his breathing wheezing like an old man's as he watched the red line of figures march out of cover and on to the flat ground which faced the fort.

He saw the ripple of stabbing flames as the men on the parapet fired into the attackers, and two marines who had climbed up in full view as they reloaded to fire again. It was an awful madness, and yet the most inspiring thing Lascelles had ever seen or heard. The bugle's strident call, the marines advancing as if they had all the time in the world.

Frazier ignored the lieutenant's excitement and pressed his cheek against his musket with deliberate care. He too had seen the two madmen on the wall, he had also seen Jones wipe his knife on some grass as he had emerged from his hiding-place. One dead, another to go.

He held his breath as a shot echoed from the hillside, magnified by the fallen slabs of rock where the other marksman had been concealed. Frazier did not watch as one of the small figures pitched from the wall where it was immediately engulfed by a hacking, stabbing mob. Frazier concentrated on the drifting feather of smoke from the rocks, his eyes unblinking as he waited.

A head rose very slightly, and Frazier imagined he could see the man reloading. He was wasting his time, he thought, and squeezed the trigger, letting out his breath as the marksman leapt into the air and then rolled down the slope like a bundle of rags.

Jones said harshly, 'That's it, sir. We can join the others now.'

He watched as Lascelles half rose to his feet, his face empty as the air crackled with shots and another blare on the bugle.

Frazier fired again and saw one of the running figures fall spread-eagled even as he waved to some of his warriors to change direction towards the marines.

Lascelles licked his lips. 'I – I'm not sure.'

Frazier stood up and snapped his bayonet on his musket. 'I am.' He started to lope down the slope without another glance.

Corporal Jones said, 'Come along, sir. Captain Blackwood may expect it. You've done what he asked.'

He watched the officer's emotions with angry resignation. *Me and Frazier did all the work*. He could still feel his arm around the marksman's neck, his terrible gurgle as he had thrust the blade up and through his ribs.

But above all else Jones was a trained marine, and would no more leave his officer than fly. Frazier would probably be disciplined if any of them survived, but he was used to that.

He persisted, 'Now, sir.'

Lascelles nodded and picked up his pistols. Then together they walked down the slope.

'Halt! Prepare to fire!'

Blackwood did not turn his head as the odd numbers in the single line stepped forward and knelt on one knee while the others remained standing.

He hardly dared to draw breath, and was certain that every muscle and limb in his body was shaking beyond control.

But in spite of everything *they had remembered*. In the face of death, even the most junior recruit among them had recalled the drills aboard *Satyr*.

Blackwood looked at the oncoming tide of painted shields and glittering spears. The first surprise was over and the bulk of the attackers were now heading for the motionless marines. Blackwood had seen the man fall from the wall and guessed he had been shot by one of the marksmen. There had been no further shots from the rear as far as he could tell. He flinched as another crack made his hope a lie, but instead of a marine, one of the leading savages was flung to the ground by the force of a ball.

'*Present!*'

Blackwood raised his sword, his eyes fixed on the leading runners. Thirty yards, twenty, now less . . . he felt a spear thud into the ground nearby.

'*Fire!*'

The fusilade of shots ploughed through the advancing crowd like an invisible scythe.

There was not time to reload or for anything else. They were out in the open. No way back, and no help other than they could give each other.

'*Again*, Ackland!'

How he could blow his bugle after all the din and frenzy which confronted him was a miracle.

The front rank rose together, and as the others moved up to re-form the line Blackwood shouted, 'At 'em, lads!'

Keeping together they charged headlong towards the nearest shields. Every man was shouting and cursing, and the pace seemed to quicken as the attackers wavered, those behind colliding with their companions in a momentary tangle of limbs and weapons.

The marines hit the front ranks like a battering-ram, the bayonets knocking aside spears and clubs alike as their despair gave way to a desperate ferocity.

Blackwood vaguely heard a ragged volley of shots from the fort as Brogan did what he could to cause confusion from another direction. He saw a pair of bulging eyes above the rim of a shield and fired his pistol through the painted hide, seeing the man collapse even as he jumped over him and slashed another across the chest with his sword. He could hear Smithett at his side, saw his bloodied bayonet stabbing forward like a tongue, his boot thrusting the corpse free as he guarded his face from a club.

From one corner of his eye Blackwood saw a red coat fall among the stamping feet and stabbing bayonets. Another marine pitched amongst his attackers, his screams cut short by a single blow from an axe.

Blackwood trampled on more sprawled bodies and realized, as if in a daze, that they were advancing, that the enemy was reeling back and causing panic in their rear.

'Halt!'

Breathless and lurching, their eyes wild, the marines heard and obeyed.

Blackwood watched, his heart pounding like a hammer as he waited for the attack to begin again. But the gap was widening and there were no longer any battle cries to urge them on.

'Reload!'

He saw a figure dart from the stamping, gesturing mob and run headlong for the marines. One of their leaders making a last challenge which could so easily end everything.

Blackwood heard a solitary shot and saw the running man fall. Frazier was back with his comrades.

'Ready, sir!'

Blackwood looked down and saw blood on his leg. Yet he had felt nothing until now.

'Present!'

The muskets lifted again. Not so steadily this time, some of the men were finding it hard to breathe after their short, crazy charge.

'Fire!'

They did not even try to run. The volley hit the packed bodies and hurled several to the ground. But the others stayed where they were. More like beasts at the slaughter than the warriors they had been.

Surely it was enough? It had to be. Blackwood felt sick of the sights and the stench of death, but knew it was not yet finished.

Very deliberately he walked towards Mdlaka's warriors, praying that his leg would not give way as the pain came up to his thigh like a hot iron.

At any second one of them might lunge forward. Not even Frazier could do anything to save him.

Just ten paces clear he sheathed his sword, feeling its resistance as the blood caught on its scabbard.

He could smell them, feel their strength, temporarily lost for the lack of a leader.

Then they parted to allow a small figure to approach. Tiny, wrinkled, he was more monkey than man. The thought almost unnerved Blackwood as he thought of Ashley-Chute safe in his flagship, in another world. *Monkey*.

The old man must have taken his silence for dissatisfaction, for with surprising dignity he waved his arm towards his men and without hesitation they dropped their weapons and shields beside the corpses.

Blackwood looked at him, his mind cringing from all the senseless, brutal slaughter this place had seen.

Slade had spoken of meeting this man, who was obviously Mdlaka. Two of a kind perhaps. Dedicated to conquest.

Blackwood shook himself angrily. What the hell did it matter? Any of it?

He snapped, 'You are under arrest.' He saw emotion for the first time in the reddened eyes. Fear or contempt, he was not certain. He thought of what would be happening here if his tactics had failed and added coldly, 'Tell your people to go home. *Now!*' He motioned to the line of marines behind him. '*Present!*'

It was only a gesture, for he knew the marines had not even reloaded. Every eye had been fixed on him as he had strode to meet the enemy. But it was enough. Slowly at first, backing away as if suspecting some further trap, the crowd of warriors broke into a stampede.

Colour-Sergeant M'Crystal marched through the corpses and said thickly, 'God in heaven, that was a wild thing to do, begging your pardon, sir.' He glared at the king. 'What'll I do with *him*?'

Blackwood looked back at the men who had followed him without question to attempt the impossible. Three were obviously dead, several others crouched or hobbled among the motionless line of fixed bayonets.

Smithett joined him and exclaimed, 'Gawd, yer leg's done in, sir!' It sounded like an accusation.

But Blackwood ignored him. He stared instead at one sprawled figure with out-thrust legs, a musket still gripped in his hands as he stared unseeingly at the sky.

A sixteen-year-old boy from Yorkshire who had signed on when his father had died.

He said quietly, 'Put the prisoner in irons and see he is guarded.'

He tore his eyes from the dead marine, the boy who had been so frightened but who had trusted him.

'I want Mdlaka to share the shame of what he has done.' He could barely keep his voice under control. 'And I want to see him hanged.'

He looked at M'Crystal. 'Return to the fort. You know what to do.'

M'Crystal nodded, his face troubled. 'Aye, sir. We'll not leave any of our own out here.' He followed Blackwood's glance towards Oldcastle's body. 'Especially him.'

Blackwood turned on his heel and limped towards the gates. As if in a misty dream he saw they were open, that the handful of defenders were waving and cheering.

He knew he would collapse. The pain was worse, but it acted like a spur to drive him on and through those gates.

Sergeant Brogan ran to assist him, but from somewhere in the blur Smithett said fiercely, 'I can deal with 'im, Sarnt!'

Brogan stood aside as M'Crystal and the first section of marines tramped wearily through the gates.

'Close thing, Colour-Sergeant.'

M'Crystal watched Blackwood being lowered to a blanket by the wall, his face stiff against the pain.

To nobody in particular he murmured, 'He'll do me, and that's a fact. One o' the best.'

7

Pride

'Starboard your helm, *steady*, steer east-nor'-east.'

Captain George Tobin watched narrowly as the frigate's bows began to swing towards the headland and then settle in direct line with the swirling current.

'Ring down dead slow.'

He would have smiled but for the anxiety in his mind. The engine-room responded to the order instantly, as if Hamilton, the Chief, had been sweating it out as he waited for the signal on his telegraph. They had steamed along the coast from Freetown with all the power the engine could offer, and Tobin had been forced to overrule Hamilton on a dozen occasions when he had pleaded with him to reduce speed.

Deacon touched his cap. 'Cleared for action, sir.'

Tobin grunted and took a telescope from his signals midshipman. The same bleak coast, the rocks and shoals he remembered so vividly from his days on the anti-slavery patrols.

No sign of life anywhere. Just a pall of drifting smoke which they had sighted soon after dawn as the great paddles had driven *Satyr* towards the land like an avenging demon.

He looked along his command, the men at the guns, Spalding, the third lieutenant, up forward by the two ten-inchers, his arms folded and with one foot on a flaked rope as he watched the shore with the others.

Tobin swore beneath his breath. One of the most powerful, modern ships afloat, but what use were *Satyr*'s big rifled guns against spears and poisoned arrows?

'I am going under the headland, Mr Deacon.'

Tobin tried not to think of what they might discover and concentrated instead on his ship's safety.

'Put the best leadsmen in the chains. I don't trust the charts hereabouts. Sand-bars come and go like smoke in these rivers.'

'Starboard two points.'

The slow-moving paddles threshed noisily as the first of the inshore current surged around the hull.

Tobin added, 'Be ready to lower boats and take the landing party ashore.'

Deacon nodded, his eyes on the top of the headland searching for a possible lookout.

How trivial they had tried to make it sound in Freetown, Tobin thought savagely. They were all too busy with their trade and lofty ideas of expanding it along the African mainland to take Blackwood's position seriously.

The senior naval officer, a commodore, had snapped testily, 'It could happen to any of us. It's what we're here for, dammit!' Perhaps he had just been told that Ashley-Chute would be relieving him of his command and could think of nothing else.

Even Slade, who had dashed ashore with his secretary within minutes of mooring, had said, 'He'll know what to do. He'd better.'

Very gingerly, the helm moving this way and that to compensate for the current, *Satyr* nosed her way into the shallows, the leadsman's cry making the master and his assistants tense with apprehension.

Tobin levelled his glass as the fort's low outline moved into view. He heard the clank of metal as the starboard ten-inch gun moved slightly on its slide, the black snout already trained on the fort.

It was still early morning, and a mist hovered along the shore to merge with the smoke from inland.

Lieutenant Deacon watched him curiously. If the captain ran this ship aground it would be the finish of his career. He saw a muscle jerk at the side of Tobin's jaw as a whistle shrilled and the signals midshipman called, 'Chief engineer, sir!'

Tobin strode to the big bell-mouthed voice-pipe and barked, 'Don't bother me now, Chief! I don't care if your dog-clutch *has* burst apart!' He paused and then said, 'My apologies, Chief,' and replaced the whistle in the pipe.

Then he glanced at Deacon and grimaced. 'Just wanted me to know I can have all the steam I want! And I almost tore his head off!'

They forgot Hamilton and his crashing, roaring world below decks as a lookout yelled, 'The fort, sir!'

Tobin stared as something moved on the wall. It was occupied. By whom and with what intent he did not know.

'Stand by, all guns!' Tobin glared at the master. 'Be ready to come about and keep an eye open for that bloody sand-spit!'

Deacon was so overwhelmed he touched his captain's arm with excitement. 'They're running up the Colours, sir!'

Tobin trained his glass again and watched the familiar flag jerking up to a crude pole above the wall. He saw red coats too, and somebody waving his hat in the air, his shouts lost in distance but no less moving in the telescope's lens.

'Larboard helm! *Steady*, man! Stand by on the fo'c'sle, Mr Spalding! Look alive there!'

Men dashed forward with rope fenders while others climbed out on to the cathead in readiness to leap on to the rickety pier.

Tobin snapped, 'Stop engine. Take over, Mr Deacon. I'm going ashore myself.'

Tobin knew now that his earlier fears had been false. He had expected them all to have been killed, wiped away like some of the other outposts he had heard about at Freetown. Normally he would have waited for the engine's last dying quiver before he relaxed, and then only until the next demand of duty. He was like that, even though he believed he could hide it from his subordinates.

But the sight of that flag, the one which he knew M'Crystal had carried ashore with him, had driven all caution aside like steam in the wind.

Lines snaked across the pier, and as men leapt down to secure the bow and stern ropes, *Satyr* ground against the sagging piles and came to rest.

Tobin beckoned to his midshipman. 'Come with me, Mr Allison!' Ignoring the glances of the second lieutenant and his armed landing party who were already mustered amidships, Tobin clambered out and down by the great paddle-box, the midshipman hurrying behind him.

He was only halfway up the beach when he stopped and said quietly, 'We'll wait a while, Mr Allison. Just a moment longer.'

He watched the file of marines as they appeared around the side of the fort, their fixed bayonets shining brightly in the early sunlight.

'Marines halt! R-i-g-h-t turn!'

Tobin said softly, 'Watch this, Mr Allison, and mark it well.'

Colour-Sergeant M'Crystal marched down the slope and saluted stiffly. Only near to could you see the stains on his trousers and coatee, the stubble around his chin.

Tobin returned his salute and asked, 'Was it bad?'

M'Crystal stared past him at the ship. 'Seven dead all told, sir. Not too bad when you consider the odds. We've got fifteen wounded too.' Only then did his eyes return to Tobin. 'Including Captain Blackwood, sir.'

Tobin said, 'Fetch the surgeon, Mr Allison, and tell Mr Oliver to take his landing party to the fort, at the double.'

Tobin walked up the slope with M'Crystal at his side. It was all so clear, as if he had taken part in it himself. The piled-up earth and stones where the corpses had been buried, the thousands of footmarks where a savage army had attacked this place again and again. As he got closer to the fort he saw the scars on the wall, the dark bloodstains both at the top and at the foot of the rough palisades where men had died.

'Will they attack again?'

M'Crystal glanced at him, seemingly surprised at the question.

'We fought 'em in the open, sir. Up there, by those rocks. Blade to blade.'

Feet pounded up the beach and seamen bustled past towards the fort, but Tobin did not see them. He saw only the small detachment of marines, fighting in the open, the only way they knew.

M'Crystal added firmly, 'No, sir, them buggers won't try it again.'

'What is the smoke?'

'Captain Blackwood insisted we pushed inland, in spite of his wound, sir. The day after the battle he took half of us and marched round that hill. We found several barracoons and burned them, big enough for two hundred slaves apiece they were. Empty when we got there, o' course. Just a couple o' dead ones and some shackles.' He added bitterly, 'For souvenirs.'

So that was it. The slavers had brought their live cargoes here to be collected by a ship of some kind. The fort, and then a handful of marines, had stopped them. They were probably fleeing through the bush right now with the slaves' own people in hot pursuit.

'I must see Captain Blackwood at once. How badly is he hurt?'

But M'Crystal stood his ground. 'With respect, sir, we've been waiting here for two weeks. Captain Blackwood would not thank me if I did not have you inspect the guard.'

Tobin had seen many sights on his various commissions around the African shores, but to inspect a single squad of gaunt and shabby marines who stood like ramrods as he looked at each unshaven face was one he would put above most of them.

Godby, the frigate's surgeon, met him inside the gates. 'Bad gash in his left leg, sir. Poison of some kind. Maybe it was on the weapon which made the wound. Can't do much here.' He darted a glance as the marine guard marched back into the fort. 'He might lose the leg anyway.'

Tobin followed him to a screened-off corner of the fort. Blackwood lay propped on some rolled blankets, his eyes closed as Smithett lathered his face and prepared to shave him. He did not seem to notice as the surgeon lifted a blanket and the dressing he had just cut from the wound.

Godby said softly, 'I can't smell anything putrid in it. Not yet.'

Tobin saw Blackwood's eyes staring at him. They were very bright and feverish.

Blackwood said, 'Good to see you again, sir.' He winced as Godby lifted his out-thrust leg to examine it again. '*Bloody* good. Things were a bit difficult here.'

'I've heard. Don't wear yourself out. You worked miracles.'

Blackwood murmured, 'Lost some good men. A few others will never do a parade again either. And for what? Some greedy, murderous chief and a couple of dead slaves.' He gave a crooked grin. 'The rest of the slaves scattered, so we won't even get the bounty money!'

He was delirious from the pain and the poison in his leg.

Tobin glanced at M'Crystal and asked, 'Where is Lieutenant Lascelles? Is he . . . ?'

The colour-sergeant shook his head. 'No, he's alive, sir. Out at the village with a patrol and old Fenwick. Making certain those devils don't have any more weapons hidden away. He'll burn the place to the ground if he finds 'em.'

Tobin looked away. It did not sound like the amiable Lascelles he knew. Then he glanced down at Blackwood again and guessed what must have changed him.

'Have the wounded carried to the ship right away. Mr Lascelles will take command here with one squad of marines.' He looked meaningly at M'Crystal's red face. '*Volunteers.* I shall leave a landing party and two six-pounders to give them some more authority – ' He broke off as Blackwood struggled up on his elbows.

'They are *my* men, sir!'

Tobin smiled sadly. 'You rest and finish your shave. I'm taking you to Freetown. No arguments. Have no fear about this bloody fort. I've seen what you did. A steam gunboat will be here tonight. She couldn't keep up with *Satyr*!'

The surgeon was signalling to some men with a stretcher but made himself wait until Smithett had completed the shave to his own satisfaction. Then Smithett eased Blackwood's arms into his coatee and made an attempt to adjust his shirt for him.

It was then that Blackwood realized how weak he had become, that Lascelles and the others had somehow managed to hide it from him.

Feet pounded across the compound and Lascelles appeared, gasping for breath.

'Don't worry, sir. Everything will be all right.' Their eyes met and he added quietly, 'Now.'

Blackwood was lifted on to the stretcher and faces swam around him like balloons.

Here and there a hand reached out to touch his shoulder or just the stretcher as he was carried from the fort. Beneath the gate he saw the marks of battle, the stains where one marine had been hacked down. Now it was his turn. He felt his eyes smarting as he tried to hide his despair. He would lose a leg. It was better to die like Simcoe, Oldcastle and the others.

At the pier he was able to open his eyes as a shadow spread over him. It was M'Crystal, as he knew it would be.

'I shall stay with Mr Lascelles, sir. But he's thriving on it now.' He was too used to duty and the stern demands of discipline and was unable to say what he really felt. Instead he said, 'I'll see you again soon, sir. When they come back for us.' He managed a grin. 'Last to leave, that's us.'

Blackwood twisted his head to answer him but he had already gone.

'Worth fifty men, is M'Crystal.' He even sounded as if he was dying, and his voice lacked any message of hope.

Tobin watched him being carried carefully up the frigate's

side and said to himself, 'You're worth a few yourself, my friend.'

Later, as he lay in the same cabin he had used after joining the ship at Gibraltar, Blackwood felt the hull begin to shake and quiver to the power of her engine. He peered up desperately at the scuttle and tried to picture the scene as *Satyr* cast off and thrashed violently clear of the piles. The surgeon must have given him something because he could feel no pain, and for a terrifying instant he imagined his leg had already been taken off.

The door opened and Smithett padded to the scuttle and opened it slightly. He did not speak but turned to watch his officer's reaction as the sound of distant cheering penetrated the cabin.

Blackwood tried to move higher but his strength failed him.

'What are they cheering? Tell me, *please!*'

Smithett winced as the ship's siren blasted raucously along the shore and to the hidden village whose king was now a prisoner on the orlop deck.

He closed the scuttle tightly and replied, 'Cheerin', sir? It's fer you, that's wot.'

Smithett picked up Blackwood's coatee and curled his lip. Take a week to get it back into shape. Work, work, bloody work, there's no end to it.

He glanced at Blackwood and waited until he was back in a drugged sleep then left the cabin.

A petty officer was coming along the passageway and paused to say, 'Glad you got out of it in one piece! You deserve a bloody medal, to all accounts!' He hurried away to his allotted station.

Smithett stood quite still, the coatee dangling from his hand, as the ship began to surge ahead.

It was then, and only then, that he understood the true significance of the petty officer's words. *He had survived.*

*

Tobin entered the cabin and studied Blackwood thoughtfully. He was required everywhere. Move to another anchorage. Take on more coal. Report to the senior officer at Freetown for orders. But this moment was important too.

'How are you feeling?'

Blackwood raised himself on his elbows and winced as the pain came back. As if it had been lurking there. Lulling his defences.

'What's going to happen now?'

He felt rotten and knew that Tobin had already read the surgeon's report so knew better than he did about his condition. The wound had been deep and badly infected. But for his stubborn insistence on following up their victory with a march on Mdlaka's village, he might be on his feet right now.

Tobin shrugged. 'You are being taken ashore. A surgeon there will be better placed to help you. After that . . .' He shrugged again. 'Back to England probably.' He attempted to smile. 'I did hear a rumour that you wanted to resign from the Corps anyway?' But he regretted it instantly as Blackwood's expression changed to one of dismay and loss.

Two seamen were in the passageway with a stretcher, and Smithett had already packed up their gear. The cabin looked empty and alien. Waiting for Lascelles to reclaim it.

Blackwood said quietly, 'I'm all right. No worse than some of the others, and better than the dead ones!'

He beckoned to Smithett who was standing behind the seamen.

'Here, help me up!'

Smithett stood fast and said dourly, 'Don't seem right to me, sir.'

'Do as you're told, damn you.' Blackwood was almost sobbing with pain and humiliation. 'Fetch my coat!'

Tobin's midshipman hovered in the passageway until the captain saw him.

'Mr Deacon's respects, sir, and *Audacious* is approaching the anchorage.'

He was careful not to stare at Blackwood.

'Thank you, Mr Allison.' Tobin carefully closed the door and shut out the others. 'So he finally got here.'

But Blackwood scarcely heard him. All the while he had been in *Satyr*, then at the fort, Ashley-Chute's squadron had been sailing ponderously for this same destination. The terrible sights and sounds, the feel of a man's last breath as he had hacked him down on that stretch of hard-fought land had meant nothing to the squadron as they had gone about their daily affairs. Now Monkey was here. Ready to take over command of operations from a mere commodore. It was a strange sort of promotion, but at this moment it was all Blackwood could think about, all he had left. If he went ashore he would be put aboard a home-bound ship. Marine captains, young or otherwise, carried little weight, and he knew he would be discharged without room for argument.

He knew too that it was desperately important he should hold on, and the *Audacious*, slow and outdated as she might be, was his only chance.

'I'd like to return to my ship, sir.'

Tobin stared at him. 'The admiral may think otherwise.'

'Let me *try*, sir.' He was pleading.

Tobin listened to the dull thud of a gun salute as the squadron flagship tacked towards the anchorage.

With any luck *Satyr* might be ordered to sea again within a day or so. Reports and despatches took time to pass from hand to hand, especially here at the Freetown naval base. He was probably doing Blackwood no favour, and he might end up a cripple if he rejected proper care. But Tobin could not forget his own feelings when he had seen the mission fort, the flag, the ragged defiance of M'Crystal's guard of honour. Nor would he ever lose the picture of these same men as they had watched Blackwood carried down to the ship. If they had held on to their strength, then Blackwood had certainly given it to them, and it had shown on their faces.

He made up his mind. 'Call away my gig for Captain Blackwood!'

He did not open the door but feet hurried away to do his

bidding. He did not want his men to see Blackwood's face.

Blackwood held out his hand. 'Thank you, *very* much.'

'It's worth a try.' Tobin opened the door for Smithett. 'I'll be waiting to hear. Perhaps you'll come back to *Satyr* one day.'

Very carefully Blackwood lowered himself to the deck while Smithett encircled his waist with a grip of steel. He could smell the rum on the marine's breath and guessed that he too had been saying his farewells in his own way. He gasped as the pain came again. *To me mates.*

It seemed to take an hour to reach the quarterdeck where he was almost blinded by the sunlight. There seemed to be ships everywhere, every class of war vessel, colourful native craft with huge lateen sails, even a stately East Indiaman unloading cargo into a mass of bobbing lighters.

But Blackwood had eyes only for the slow-moving flagship, her black and white hull shining like glass on the clear water, the receding gun smoke still clinging to her rigging and yards like muslin.

It was like a pain in his heart, and he wanted to tell Tobin how he felt.

Tobin gave a slow smile. 'I wish you luck.' Then he stood aside and saluted as Blackwood was carried bodily down to the gig alongside.

The first lieutenant joined him by the rail, eager to get on with the day's work. They were short-handed without the landing party.

Tobin watched the gig until it was swallowed up amidst the bustle of local craft and bat-like sails.

'If he lives long enough, that young man will do great things.'

'About coaling ship, sir?'

Tobin glanced at him and they both smiled. Deacon was not that good at hiding his feelings. Yet. He had been there when the attack had been made on the boats. He had memories of his own now.

'Yes, Mr Deacon, now what *about* coaling ship?'

*

The flagship's side and tumblehome looked like a great cliff from the gig. Blackwood gritted his teeth as the bowman hooked on to the main chains and faces lined the gangway to peer down at him.

God, he must look a mess. The other marines had already been sent across from *Satyr*, except the badly wounded ones, so the story would be all over the ship.

Smithett muttered, 'Don't like it at all, I don't, an' that's a fact, sir.' He squinted up at the thick stairs to the entry port and then to a ladder which dangled from the gangway itself. Either way was asking for a fall.

Blackwood got into a more comfortable position on one leg, his arm around Smithett's shoulders. The gig's crew sat at attention as they watched his every move, and the midshipman in charge seemed at a total loss as to what to do next.

If only the pain would stay away. Blackwood could barely see through the mist as he fought to contain the rising fire in his leg. At any moment the wound would burst open. Why had he imagined he could do the impossible?

Smithett was watching him worriedly. 'I'll 'ave a bosun's chair sent down, sir!'

Feet clattered on the steps and Blackwood looked up into the eyes of his half-brother.

'Come along, sir.' He reached down and slipped his hand through Blackwood's arm. 'Easy now. Together.'

A seaman had also climbed down, and as they waited for the boat to lift and then settle again, Blackwood took his first step on to the tumblehome.

He nodded and tried to speak but nothing came.

Harry guided him carefully so that he could make use of the handholds. Blackwood could feel the protective strength of his arm, the care he was taking to help him. It was as if the whole ship was holding her breath, urging him to make the climb without failing.

His whole body was running with sweat, and from the wetness on his leg he guessed that some of his dressing had come loose.

'Never mind, Harry!' He peered up at the outstretched hands and concerned faces. 'Never bloody well mind, eh?' He was half gasping and half laughing as the senses of shock and pain joined against him.

Harry whispered against his ear, 'Oh, Philip, you crazy, wonderful idiot!' He did not seem to care if Blackwood heard him or not. All that mattered was the entry port, the bright blue sky above.

Blackwood felt more hands gripping his arms to lift him to the quarterdeck.

The sight of the assembled side-party, the officer of the watch and all the rest of this ordered world was too much for him.

What chance had he now of staying aboard? He had been stupid, too full of his own pride to accept the inevitable.

As if through a mist he saw Captain Ackworthy's great bulk striding towards him, and Sergeant Quintin coming aft from the main-deck. What a sight he must make.

Everybody froze as if suddenly bewitched, even their expressions of anxiety, surprise or merely curiosity remained fixed and set.

Only one small figure moved at the poop rail, head jutting forward, his voice cutting through the shipboard noises like a saw.

'It would appear that my captain of marines has decided that a life in coal dust and filth is not for him! He has shown some sense. I shall see him aft when he has collected himself, hmm?' He vanished.

Blackwood looked around him. Monkey neither could nor would bid him welcome, it was not his style. But at this moment it was the closest thing to it Blackwood had ever heard.

Slowly and carefully he straighted his back and balanced himself on one foot while he gauged the ship's gentle motion.

Then he looked at Ackworthy's strained face and touched his hat.

'I am rejoining the ship, sir.'

Ackworthy glanced from Blackwood's pale features to the bright spot of blood which had fallen to the deck by his feet where it gleamed like a malevolent red eye.

He needed to find the right words to convey what he felt, but all he could feel was envy. Not that it mattered, for at that moment Blackwood fainted.

8

Temptation

For two whole weeks after he had boarded *Audacious* in such an undignified fashion, Blackwood lived in a state of mounting frustration. His relief at being allowed to return soon gave way to a feeling of reprieve, a momentary delay after which he would be sent packing to England. He had plenty of visitors, but noticed they were wary about discussing the daily routine, as if that might only make it harder when the axe fell.

Dalrymple, the senior surgeon, was not very encouraging and almost as gloomy as Smithett. *Too early to say. Wait and see* seemed to be the corner-stone of his diagnosis.

Confined to his cabin, Blackwood was very aware of his isolation. When he was not in a drugged sleep he lay in his cot putting faces and names to the sounds above and around him. There were several receptions and parties given on board, apparently to mark Ashley-Chute's taking command of the West Coast Squadron. As the temperature in his cabin rose to stifling humidity, Blackwood was forced to listen to muffled music, the clink of glasses and the carefree comings and goings of boats alongside.

He thought a great deal about the fort, and especially of the men who had fallen there. Of Oldcastle with his fear and determination, and Lascelles who had been prepared to throw his life away rather than let him down. What would become of Old Fenwick? he wondered. Stay there until the next traders joined him at the mission fort, or try his luck elsewhere in his hunt for riches?

At night, when the ship was quiet, Harry would come to the cabin and sit with him until he dozed off in his cot. Blackwood had got to know his eighteen-year-old half-brother better than he had ever done before, and together they had spoken about their futures, what would become of Hawks Hill and the estate after it had all been auctioned.

Harry had been more than candid about his mother. 'Far too young for the gov'nor. Still, but for her I suppose the Corps would be missing the services of a *superb* second lieutenant!'

Ashley-Chute's son had also visited him on a couple of occasions, but mostly it seemed to speak about *Satyr* and her performance rather than what lay ahead.

One late afternoon as Blackwood climbed from his cot to stand naked before Dalrymple and his assistant surgeon, he somehow knew it was the moment of decision. For several days he had heard stores being hoisted inboard from lighters, the familiar squeak of tackles punctuated by the twitter of boatswain's calls. A ship preparing to leave port.

He fixed his eyes on the mirror above his table and made himself stand quite still as Dalrymple's hard fingers probed at his leg. In the mirror he looked older, with deep lines at his mouth to reveal the strain he had been under.

Dalrymple said casually, 'Your other marines returned aboard today. They were brought from that fort by a gunboat. Full of bounce, they are. Fighting seems to agree with 'em.'

The assistant surgeon chuckled and wrote in his notebook as Dalrymple murmured something to him as an aside.

Blackwood felt a bead of sweat run from his hairline and drop on to his bare shoulder. They were back, apart from the ones who would never return.

Think of them and stop being so bloody selfish. You lived. They did not.

He could stand it no longer. 'Can I stay?'

Dalrymple looked up and a basin of water appeared as if by magic as Smithett eased his way round the cabin.

'Of course I shall make a report to the captain.' The surgeon's eyes settled on Blackwood. 'What do *you* think? Could you do your work under the same circumstances which gave you this wound?'

Smithett's voice broke the sudden uncertainty. 'Cap'n's comin', sir.'

The cabin seemed to shrink as Ackworthy stepped inside, his head lowered still further beneath the deckhead beams. He looked at Blackwood for several seconds, his eyes even more troubled than usual.

Blackwood guessed that Ashley-Chute had driven them all very hard on the passage from Gibraltar. Ackworthy more than anyone.

Ackworthy said abruptly, 'The squadron will weigh tomorrow morning.' He could not resist adding, 'Wind or no wind, apparently. How do you feel?'

Blackwood was very aware of the watching eyes, the two surgeons, and Smithett trying to be invisible in the background. He was more conscious of Ackworthy's tone than he was of standing naked in front of them.

The surgeon murmured, 'In my opinion, sir – '

Blackwood replied, 'I'm all right, sir. Bit stiff.' He had meant it to come out like an adjutant's report on the barrack square. Brief and firm. Instead he had sounded like a guilty schoolboy.

'Can you get dressed?' Ackworthy glanced round the cabin, probably remembering other ships, other times.

When Blackwood nodded he added, 'We are proceeding to Fernando Po. Sir Geoffrey Slade has already taken passage there in *Satyr*. Left yesterday.' He glanced at Blackwood's pale face. 'He didn't come and see you, did he?'

Blackwood shook his head, surprised he could still feel hurt about it after he had invented so many excuses for Slade's behaviour.

'By the time we've picked up the right winds it'll be close on two thousand miles to Fernando Po.' Ackworthy let his words sink in. 'It's a foul coast down there, all the way from

Lagos to Benin there's nothing but fever and trouble. There are some powerful slavers pushing the local kings into using their territory for the trade. Your experience with Mdlaka was just a tip of the iceberg.' He mopped his jowls with a handkerchief. 'Hardly apt, eh?'

Blackwood understood well enough. 'Then I must decide now. After tomorrow there'll be no turning back.' His leg throbbed as if to mock him.

'Correct. I have spoken with the admiral. He wants a report.' He managed a smile. 'Which means an hour ago.'

'I *want* to remain in *Audacious*, sir.'

The surgeon made one last attempt. 'I've not really decided . . .'

Ackworthy said bluntly, 'I have. He stays.' He tugged out his watch and examined it. 'I'll expect you aft in an hour.' He studied him questioningly. 'Can you get there?'

Blackwood grinned, the years falling from his face in spite of the pain.

'If I have to crawl.'

As Ackworthy made to leave Blackwood asked, 'The king, Mdlaka, has he been taken to a prison sir?' He could picture him without difficulty, old maybe, but with all the cunning of his ancestors.

Captain Ackworthy did not turn. 'He's been sent back to his village where he will be under British protection. He needs it now to survive. Sir Geoffrey Slade wrote the order himself. Better the devil you know . . . that kind of thing. Now you understand why Sir Geoffrey chose not to visit you.' The door closed with a bang.

The surgeons picked up their bags and Dalrymple said severely, 'I think it's madness.' He sensed Blackwood's sudden anger and added, 'Don't expect miracles, that's all I ask.' Then like ghouls they both withdrew.

Blackwood slumped on the cot and stared fixedly at the bulkhead.

'Well, Smithett, what did you make of that?'

Smithett unfolded a clean shirt and shook it out. ' 'Ow d'yer mean, sir?'

'We lost some *good men*.' He thought of Oldcastle, the way his arms had hung out like broken wings as he had been carried up to the fort for burial. 'For bloody nothing! I wish I'd shot that little bastard while I had the chance!'

Smithett regarded him calmly. 'Might 'ave 'ad someone worse to take 'is place like? We did wot we was *sent* to do, sir. It's all there is to it.'

Blackwood ran his fingers through his hair. *All there is to it.*

'Come on then, help me get into that shirt.' There was no getting the better of Smithett.

Vice-Admiral Sir James Ashley-Chute crossed one leg over the other and regarded Blackwood unsmilingly.

'I understand you consider yourself fit for active duty?' His lipless mouth opened and closed to ration each word. 'Another day and I would have had to discharge you from my command. However . . .' his cold stare dropped to Blackwood's leg, 'that would have meant transferring an officer from *Valiant* or *Argyll*. Untidy, and in any case you have been in this ship long enough to know your men and what they can do.' He indicated a pile of papers on his table. 'Interesting reading. It seems you were very *active* in the defence of the fort.'

Blackwood could sense Ackworthy's sweating discomfort somewhere behind him, the pain in his leg and the fact Ashley-Chute had pointedly not asked him to sit down.

Blackwood replied, 'Had I known what was intended, sir, I would have acted differently.'

'Indeed?' Ashley-Chute plucked at one of his grey side-burns. 'I think not. But I have to confess I did feel some irritation at the way that damned native was allowed to go about his business.' His eyes hardened. 'I'd have had him dancing at the main-yard in double quick time, politicians or no damned politicians, hmm?'

Audacious swung slightly on her cable, and through the cabin windows Blackwood saw the misty panorama of lush green hills and clusters of pale buildings along the shore.

Ashley-Chute continued in a more relaxed tone, 'However, everything will be changed from now on, as I explained to the commodore before he *left*.'

Blackwood tried to concentrate and ignore the ache and its attendant nausea. Ashley-Chute was testing him with no less dedication than the surgeon. There was still ample time for him to be put ashore.

The vice-admiral said, 'For years now we have been contending with fleets of slavers who have grown rich on their profits. Our patrols have taken a prize here and there and the guilty shipmasters have been punished. But the trade goes on, and will continue to do so while we play games instead of destroying it at its roots. Britannia rules the waves, so they say. But it has its disadvantages. Other nations who are supposed to be allies in stamping out slavery are content to let us get on with it. France is less cautious than our government in colonizing parts of Africa, she is careful to avoid antagonizing the local chiefs and traders. America is too slow to support our patrols and has sometimes accused us of hitting too hard.' His eyes settled on Blackwood's again. 'We shall hit harder, believe me!'

Ackworthy said, 'I think Captain Blackwood should be seated, Sir James.'

'Oh, really?' Ashley-Chute gave a thin smile. 'A chair, Blackwood.'

Blackwood sat down, almost hating Ackworthy for his genuine concern.

'Well, we've nearly three weeks to prepare ourselves.' Ashley-Chute stood up and walked to the stern windows, his hands grasped tightly behind him. 'I was given this station to *put things right*. Had I been appointed a year ago . . .' He shrugged. 'But there's no point in fretting over spilt milk, hmm?'

Blackwood was more confused than before. Why had

Ashley-Chute sent for him? Of all his captains and advisers, why pick on a junior marine officer?

Ashley-Chute continued, 'I intend to attack the slave trade in its own territory. No more chasing ships around the ocean only to discover they have already dropped their victims overboard at the first sight of danger. You may think that your skirmish at the fort was a waste of time, Blackwood. By God, I wish there were more such opportunities to show them we mean what we say, dammit!' He changed tack in a second. 'Any suggestions, by the way?'

Blackwood said, 'We're using old methods, sir.' He saw the warning light in Ashley-Chute's eyes but persisted. 'My father spoke of the same tactics in his day.'

Ashley-Chute said dryly, 'You talk of him as if he were deceased.'

Blackwood flushed. 'I'm sorry, sir. It's not that. But in the big ships of the line we drill and exercise as we have always done. On land we march and fight like infantry, form squares, and die if so ordered.'

He expected to be cut short but the admiral remained silent, his eyes boring into him, while Ackworthy's breathing got steadily heavier by the second.

He added, 'This is a different enemy, sir. They can fall back and regroup, while we must hang on with minimum rations and await the next attack. They *know* their territory, we do not.'

'Good. Capital. What I hoped you would say.' Ashley-Chute's thin lips split into a wide smile. 'I wanted to hear it from you. Somebody who has seen these conditions at close quarters, not from some shoe-licking staff officer who will tell me anything to gain favour.' He glanced past him towards Ackworthy. '*Fighting* men, that's what I want!'

Blackwood forgot the pain and discomfort in his leg. Ashley-Chute spoke as if he was embarking on a personal vendetta which only he could inspire. Perhaps it was true about him, that after the confusion in New Zealand he had been quietly censured. What was this appointment to him?

A chance to redeem himself, or was he to be a scapegoat if everything failed? Slade had said he was genuinely concerned with the expansion of an empire. He had left little doubt that he would use anyone to achieve that end. Blackwood bit his lip. *Even me.*

Ashley-Chute cocked his head as the bell chimed out from the forecastle. It was the moment to leave. The audience was over.

Blackwood got to his feet and hesitated. 'I should like to say something, sir.'

There was a brief spark of irritation. 'Well?'

'The rivers are the main channels for the slave-ships, sir. It will take time to get our people into position even without opposition from the shore.'

Ashley-Chute sounded almost relieved. As if he had been expecting something different.

'You are about to suggest I demand more steam vessels for this operation, am I right?' He shook his head. 'I am disappointed, Blackwood, and must put it down to the strain you have been under. This will be a perfect example of seamanship and discipline ashore and afloat. We are fighting slavers, Spanish and Portuguese for the most part, and ignorant, bloody savages! What would the world think if I ordered a fleet to do what any well trained flotilla should be capable of achieving, hmm?'

Ackworthy mumbled, 'I, er, I think – '

'I am delighted to hear *that*!' Ashley-Chute glanced at the pantry door. It was time for his glass of claret.

'Steam-powered ships are a novelty, Captain Blackwood, but they are not yet reliable under testing conditions.' His smile was almost gentle. 'Do I make myself clear?'

Blackwood left the admiral's quarters and tried not to limp until he was well clear of those probing eyes.

Ackworthy said thickly, 'In *your* place, Major, I'd have gone home, and that's a fact.'

'I doubt that, sir.'

He saw the huge captain wince as a midshipman scuttled

into view and gasped, 'Flag-lieutenant's respects, sir, and would you rejoin the admiral.' He swallowed miserably. 'Immediately, sir.'

Ackworthy turned heavily, his hands opening and closing like that day at Spithead. 'He'll be the death of me, I'm certain of it.' He seemed to be speaking to his ship.

Blackwood continued towards the filtered sunlight and saw M'Crystal waiting by the companion ladder. It was the first time they had met since he had been carried from the fort.

'Good to see you again, Colour-sergeant.'

M'Crystal's eyes flicked over Blackwood's uniform and injured leg. The inspection completed he said, 'Not sorry to be back either, sir.' He gestured with his head. 'The lads are having a sale of goods in the barracks, sir. The kit of the ones who didn't come through.'

Blackwood thrust his hand into his pocket for some coins. The custom was probably older than the Corps itself. The money might be some comfort to the widows and sweethearts in England. Once again he thought of Oldcastle. His mother had nobody at all now.

M'Crystal put the money in a bag and shook it. 'Och, it's not much, sir, but . . .'

'I know.'

M'Crystal turned to go and then said cheerfully, 'We're going into action again then, sir?'

There were no secrets.

'How does it suit, Colour-Sergeant?'

M'Crystal put one big foot on the ladder and replied, 'It's what I do best, sir.'

For him the fears of death or mutilation were in the past. Already he was looking forward to the next challenge.

Blackwood smiled to himself. Perhaps it was the best way to be.

The next day the squadron weighed and put to sea. It was a

slow, demanding business to get the ships into line, and *Audacious*'s yards were alive with signals for several hours until Ashley-Chute's captains had satisfied his demands.

After a few days it was as if nothing had ever happened and nothing would ever change. The curiosity shown by the ship's company whenever Blackwood had appeared on deck soon gave way to routine acceptance. Even when the surgeon examined and dressed his wound Blackwood found it hard to hold things in the right perspective; the fury of the fighting, the wild need to kill rather than be cut down by the attackers.

It was even difficult to recall the noisy, bounding excitement of Tobin's *Satyr*. This was the other navy again, slow, majestic, monotonous.

The squadron eventually altered course towards the east to steer deeper and deeper into the Gulf of Benin, where the coast of Africa was occasionally in view of the masthead lookouts.

Some said that Ashley-Chute was keeping well to seaward to give secrecy to his movements. Others, less charitable, insisted it was because he was making sure he would not meet with any steam vessels which could cruise close inshore in comparative safety.

Ten days after leaving Freetown the morning watch was roused by the mutter of distant gunfire.

Men swarmed up the ratlines and on to the yards in hopes of sighting something, and when the general signal was hoisted to make more sail they went to work with a will. Anything to break the boredom.

Eventually the lookouts reported that a sail had been sighted, the squadron's own frigate *Peregrine* which had been cruising well ahead of her massive consorts. Now she was coming about, and just beyond her, partly concealed in the morning mist, was a brigantine.

Netten, the first lieutenant, closed his telescope with a click.

'A bloody slaver. *Peregrine* must have run right down on her, the lucky devils.'

Ackworthy stood at the quarterdeck rail, his cap tugged
down over his eyes.

'Alter course two points to larboard, Mr Tompkins.' He
did not sound enthusiastic about this unexpected encounter.
'My compliments to the flag-lieutenant, and – '

'No need, Captain!' Ashley-Chute had appeared on deck,
his eyes everywhere as he strode with his loping gait to the
rail. 'Signal the squadron to proceed. *We* shall close with
Peregrine and investigate.' He saw Blackwood on the lee side.
'Ah, Blackwood, I shall want you to go across and see what
you can discover.' His pale eyes flickered in the glare. 'Not
squeamish, I trust?' Again the barb, never far away. 'Not like
some, hmm?'

Netten whispered, 'There'll be murder done if he doesn't
stop goading the captain.'

It took most of the forenoon to reach the two drifting
vessels. Blackwood could not help wondering if the little
admiral had considered how speedily *Satyr* or one of her class
would have executed the task.

As they drew nearer Blackwood could sense the mood
around him. Seamen who had been cheerfully making bets on
prize-money had fallen silent as the brigantine rolled heavily
in the swell, her filthy hull in stark contrast with the little
twenty-six-gun frigate.

'Heave to! All hands wear ship!'

Audacious responded slowly, her canvas in disarray as she
turned into the wind. It was if she too was reluctant to stand
close to the slaver.

Ashley-Chute crossed the deck and snapped, 'Thorough
search, Blackwood. Bring the master back with you.' He
rubbed his palms together. 'Nice little surprise.'

Sergeant Quintin tramped aft and saluted. 'Boat's in the
water, sir.'

Netten followed Blackwood to the entry port. 'Even a
slaver will be a change from the flagship,' was his only
comment as they both climbed down to the waiting launch.

Close to, the brigantine looked like a hard-worked vessel.

Blackwood saw several armed seamen from the frigate placed
at intervals around the deck, and a young lieutenant gesturing to somebody by the wheel.

The launch hooked on and Blackwood hauled himself
bodily up the side, his leg moving clear of any bolt or
protruding timber. He was getting good at it.

The lieutenant approached them and asked, 'Can I help
you?'

Netten replied bluntly, 'We are from the admiral.' It was
all he needed to say.

The young lieutenant pointed along the dirty, littered
deck. 'Most of the crew are negroes, would you believe, sir.
The master's a Spaniard, and his mates are Dutch half-castes.'

Blackwood glanced at some swivel guns which were depressed towards the hold and hatch covers. It was unbelievable to accept that the hull was crammed with people. He
could smell brandy. The brigantine's after-guard must have
been celebrating their transactions. They had certainly not
been alert enough to see the frigate running down on them.

Netten asked, 'Want a look? I've seen it before many
times.'

Blackwood walked to the nearest hatchway with Quintin
close on his heels.

'Open it.'

Two seamen hauled aside the heavy iron staples and
together pulled the doors apart. Blackwood had often heard
old sailors speak of the stench in a slave-ship but he was
unprepared for it nonetheless. Even though the brigantine
carried a fresh batch of slaves, he doubted if the vessel had
been cleaned for years. Decay, misery and death were all
combined into something inhuman.

A petty officer said, 'Watch out, sir. If you fall amongst
that lot we'll never be able to get you free in time.'

Blackwood stared down for a long moment until he saw
the heaving mass of black bodies beneath him. While the
vessel rolled into the troughs as she lay hove to, the sunlight
spilled down the hatchway, and Blackwood saw it playing

across hundreds of upturned eyes. It was unnerving, perhaps because of the total silence. As if all the packed bodies had died and only the eyes held on to life.

'Open all the hatches.'

They could not escape or try their fury on the newcomers. Blackwood had no doubt they would, given the opportunity. British seamen, Spanish slavers, they all looked the same to them.

He saw the shackles, the cruel way that all the slaves were linked to longer chains which ran from forward to aft through each hold and cargo space.

There must be two or three hundred of them.

Netten said offhandedly, 'I want to know his destination and the last anchorage.'

The young lieutenant grimaced. 'He threw his charts overboard.'

'That's not what I asked. Tell him I want the truth, and quickly.'

The petty officer murmured, 'There's a whole bunch o' women up forrard, sir.'

Blackwood glanced at him. He could sense it in the man's voice. Slaves were one thing, girls were different.

The sailors removed the canvas from the forward hold and lifted a hatch for Blackwood and his sergeant.

This time there was no mute silence. They had probably been expecting some of the slaver's crew to drag them on deck for their sexual pleasures, and the sight of Blackwood's red tunic brought a chorus of terrified voices.

Blackwood found himself staring at them. Young, small-breasted bodies, white teeth and pleading eyes. He knew he should be disgusted. Instead he was reacting no better than the petty officer.

He strode aft again. 'Do the prisoners understand what you say?'

The lieutenant shrugged. 'I – I'm not certain.'

Blackwood looked at the three prisoners. The master was as thin as a stick, the two half-castes just the reverse in their filthy duck trousers and straw hats. There were enough weapons on the deck where they had been dropped to arm a vessel twice her size.

'Take them across to the flaghip. I'm going to look further.'

As he lowered himself through a small companion-way by the wheel, Netten said to the *Peregrine*'s boarding officer, 'Marines. What can you do with them, eh?'

The young lieutenant frowned. 'But isn't he the one who . . .'

Netten watched the prisoners being pushed down to the launch. 'Yes. He's the one. That's what a *hero* looks like.'

Blackwood groped his way to the master's cabin, his body bent in the low confines of the hull. A skylight was wide open and he heard Netten's words with some surprise. Blackwood had not realized that his exploits had created a barrier between them. He had always liked Netten, but now he had changed. Surely not envious of nearly being killed? He wished suddenly he had not heard him.

He forced the door open and then tensed as he saw a pair of eyes watching him from a low bunk.

Behind him he heard Quintin exclaim, 'Gawd, the pick o' the bunch!'

She was blacker than most of the others, but even here amidst the squalor she had an arrogance to match her primitive beauty. She was naked with a gold chain around her neck which betrayed her breathing as she watched his uncertainty.

As she moved closer her body rolled towards him and her eyes never left his face. She touched her lips with her tongue and ran it along her teeth. It was very pink, like a tempting serpent.

And what the hell would it matter? They had saved all these people from slavery, and worse. No one would care. Quintin would keep his mouth shut, and even if he didn't the marines would make a joke of it.

He gripped her shoulder and felt her thrust towards him,

her lips parted like a trap. He touched her breast and squeezed it, thinking of that last time so long ago.

It was like releasing a spring, and she pulled herself up against him, her hand tightening on his groin.

'Look under the bunk!' He had to shout for his own sake as well as Quintin's. '*Now!*'

The sergeant dropped to the deck and flailed about under the bunk with his hands although his eyes were still on the girl's out-thrust leg.

Quintin lurched to his feet and stared at Blackwood with astonishment. ''Ow did you *know*, sir?'

Blackwood pushed the girl down on the bunk and took the gleaming weapon from Quintin's grip. Like the ones which had been used against the fort. New, rifled, and deadly.

Almost to himself he said, 'She's the slaver's mistress. That gold chain is worth a few guineas, he'd not waste it on a slut. She's too at home here. I guessed there must be a reason.'

She seemed to understand what was happening and flung herself from the bunk like an enraged puma, screaming and slashing at him with her fingers.

Quintin twisted her arms until she became quiet again. It had been a close thing.

Blackwood said, 'Watch her. I'm taking this over to Monk . . . I mean the admiral.'

Quintin grinned. 'Right, sir.'

He watched Blackwood leave. She had really got the young captain going. He pressed the girl's shoulders down on the bunk. There was no time now. But it was still a long way to Fernando Po.

His grin widened. 'Now you be a good lass an' the nice sergeant will look after you!'

On deck Blackwood handed the rifle to Smithett.

Netten whistled softly. 'Well now, that's a find. How was it missed?'

Blackwood glanced at the *Peregrine*'s lieutenant who looked at the deck and blushed.

'Easily done.' He saw Netten's surprise and realized his

voice must have betrayed his feelings. 'A marine was killed by one of those rifles. He was a hero too.'

He could feel Netten staring after him as he climbed down into the boat which had returned from *Audacious*.

Was it really the first lieutenant who had inflamed his anger? Or the sensuous girl in the cabin?

She would have killed him if she had got the chance. But to take her by force if necessary, to sink into her and forget everything, would have been worth the risk. Sergeant Quintin was probably laughing his head off.

'Wind's gettin' up a bit, sir.'

Smithett had seen the gleam in Blackwood's eyes and felt relieved. Nothing was changed. The captain was just as moody as before the battle at the fort. A real fire-brand he had picked for his officer.

Blackwood nodded. 'Good. The sooner we get this over and done with the better for all of us.'

Smithett had no idea what he was talking about and did not much care. They were all back together again, and that was what counted.

Captain John Ackworthy trod heavily around his day cabin, his head moving from side to side as he listened to the occasional shouted commands from the quarterdeck.

As Smithett had observed an hour earlier, the wind was freshening, and *Audacious* lay over on the larboard tack, her spars and shrouds rejoicing to the unusual turn of speed.

Ackworthy touched his sword on its rack and glanced at the seated officers who waited like actors unsure of their lines.

Pelham, the flag-lieutenant, blank-faced but watchful, too afraid of his master to miss even a tit-bit of information. Netten, who lounged in a chair, his shoes still stained from the slaver's filth.

In a chair on the opposite side of the cabin Blackwood watched Netten and wondered why he had not noticed the flaw before. Casual and relaxed, always ready with a quip when things got heated. That was not him at all. He was tensed like a spring, expectant, wary.

Ackworthy said, 'With luck we shall lop off a few days to Fernando Po with this wind.' He looked at them gravely. 'As you know, we have a consul there who is solely responsible for the rights of all traders of any nationality in the Bights of Benin and Biafra. Sir Geoffrey Slade will be with him now, and upon their decision will rest our part in future operations. The capture of the brigantine by *Peregrine* was a piece of good fortune as it turned out.' His gaze paused on Blackwood. 'The slaves were taken from Dahomey and on passage to Brazil. It is proof, if it was needed, that the trade is still flourishing.'

Blackwood thought of the packed, shining bodies and wondered if many would have reached their final destination. Probably half would have died. It was cruel, inhuman madness to throw lives away.

Ackworthy said in the same heavy tone, 'The discovery of the rifle in the master's cabin was something I did not expect. A new French rifle, part payment, part bribe for these scum.'

Blackwood could recall without effort Lascelles blurting out about the new Delvigne-Minie rifle as he had fought to overcome his own fear. What the British army were already being issued with and the marines would be getting next year. Maybe. So if anyone with the right money could obtain them, they could not lay the blame of arms smuggling at the French door.

'I am instructed to tell you that a private despatch is being sent to each captain in the squadron. Sir James Ashley-Chute,' he all but spat out his name, and Blackwood saw the flag-lieutenant stiffen in his chair, 'intends that we should attack the main supply route from Lagos as soon as we get the affirmative.' He looked at their faces and added, 'You are here because you will be in the leading flotilla.' He looked at Blackwood. 'Your experience will be important, even though you will not be in overall command of the marines taking part.'

Blackwood had guessed that already. *Argyll*'s marine officer was senior to him in both age and service. A major named Fynmore, he was known to be something of a perfectionist. He saw Netten watching him, waiting for a reaction.

Blackwood said, 'I understand.'

Ackworthy moved on. 'Mr Netten, I am to inform you that as of tomorrow you will assume the rank of commander. It is the admiral's wish that the promotion be advanced.'

Netten compressed his lips and then said, 'I never expected *that*, sir.'

Ackworthy regarded him coldly. 'Really?'

Blackwood shifted in his chair as he weighed up the admiral's tactics. Any captain in the squadron could have been put in direct command of a landing operation. But no, it had to be under Ashley-Chute's own hand. A major would lead the marines, but Netten would be in overall charge.

Ackworthy turned towards the stern windows where *Valiant* followed obediently some two cables astern.

'I did suggest that we act independently.' He measured each word as if he already saw them on a brief at his own court martial. 'We have captured a slaver with a full cargo. The master confessed to everything once he was confronted with the rifle. Slavery is one thing, but when Sir James had done with him he was almost convicted for piracy! I advised the admiral,' he turned to look at Pelham, 'that we should send a force ashore without further delay.'

Pelham fiddled with some papers. 'It is necessary for the squadron to proceed to Fernando Po, sir.' He was like a boy repeating a lesson. 'Sir Geoffrey Slade's instruction was — '

Ackworthy waved him aside. 'I *know* all that, Flags.'

Blackwood knew that the captain had said as much as he dared. By the time the squadron reached Fernando Po the news would have spread up and down the coast like a brush fire. If they did attempt to land and seek out the slavers' main base they would have no surprise on their side and might find a hot reception.

No wonder Ackworthy was worried. He was a sailor to his finger-tips, one of the old school, but no match for his admiral. Surely Ashley-Chute did not want a bloody confrontation? Or was it Slade, moving his pawns with quiet dedication while he hoped for just that?

Old Fenwick had spoken of it at the fort one night when they had walked the parapet together, waiting for the dawn and dreading it.

He had explained in his quavery voice, 'They let some well-intentioned missionary chance his luck with the tribes. If 'e keeps 'is 'ead on 'is 'houlders, they allows a few traders to set up a post, then mebbe a fort to exchange their wares for somethin' better. When they get attacked or murdered, the soldiers arrives to restore order.' He wagged his unlit pipe like a sage. 'The difference is, Cap'n, that even if the priests and the traders go away, the military don't.' He had given his eerie chuckle, delighted by Blackwood's doubt. 'That's wot they calls empire, y'see?'

Fenwick, Slade and Mdlaka knew the rules. It was to be hoped that Ashley-Chute did too and did not merely see the operation as another North Island affray.

'So, gentlemen, you may carry on to your duties. Perhaps when we anchor we will receive contrary orders.' He did not sound as if he believed it.

As they left the cabin Netten said, 'We'll get a chance to do something useful after all.' He glanced at Blackwood. 'You all right?'

'Thank you, sir, yes.'

Netten grinned uneasily. 'Come along now. Not so much of the sir. We're between decks, not at divisions!'

Blackwood saw Harry waiting by the poop ladder, his features carefully composed.

'Tell me, sir, have you ever taken part in an operation like the one our admiral has in mind?' He saw a momentary uncertainty and added, 'It's not like a Spithead regatta, with a keg of rum for the winner!'

Netten's jaw tightened. 'To tell you the truth, I'm just

about sick of having your name jammed down my throat! You did your job, nothing more, now I'll do mine!' He strode away and brushed past the marine lieutenant without seeing him.

Blackwood sighed. It was better out in the open no matter what consequences it might bring.

'Storm-clouds, sir?' His voice was innocent.

'Shut up, Harry, and come down for a drink. I've got some thinking to do.'

In his cabin again Blackwood threw his tunic on the cot and massaged his leg while Harry poured two generous glasses of brandy. It was strange, but this was the first day he had not thought about his wound. Not until now.

Harry said, 'I hear that Major Fynmore is taking charge of our little war?'

Blackwood grinned. It was refreshing to have Harry with him even though he had first reacted against it.

The youthful lieutenant held up his glass to the light. 'Everyone's talking about it.' He shot him a direct glance. 'You two don't exactly hit it off, do you?'

Blackwood let the brandy run over his tongue. He could still feel the smoothness of her body, the animal heat as she had thrust herself at him.

'No, Harry. We don't. His father served with *our* father and they heartily disliked each other.'

He tossed back the brandy and gasped. What with Netten and Fynmore things would get very lively before long.

Harry did not look at him as he poured two more drinks. Even his hand shook as he said quietly, '*I can't wait.* Thank *God* I was able to get this appointment before you weighed anchor.'

Blackwood said nothing. He was eight years older than Harry. It might have been a hundred. But he remembered when he had felt like him, had itched for the chance to serve and fight rather than inspect some barrack guard.

It made him feel both protective and uneasy, as he had

about Oldcastle when he had looked at him on that dreadful
day when Ackland had sounded the Advance.

'God? I thought it was your mother?'

Harry laughed. 'Same thing!'

Suddenly the worst was over and it was so good to be alive.

9

Officers and Men

It was no great distance from the waterfront to the low-roofed buildings of the British Consulate of Fernando Po, but by the time he had forced his way through an endless throng of people Blackwood had cause to remember Ackworthy's warning. The heat was unbearable, so that his face felt as if it had been in a desert sandstorm. Noise, colour and a variety of smells and stenches made Blackwood wish more than once that he had remained in the flagship.

M'Crystal marched at his side, like a massive plough as he forced a passage for his captain. Without him Blackwood doubted if he would have been able to leave the waterfront.

The squadron had anchored in the early morning before the sun had gained its true power. Now, shimmering above their separate images, the four ships of the line, the frigates and their captured brigantine made an impressive array. Blackwood had often wondered why Britain had chosen a Spanish island like Fernando Po to set up this consulate which in fact controlled all the traders in the Bights of Benin and Biafra, which in turn affected the coastal shipping throughout the whole Gulf. But if the Spanish flag flew above the citadel, the impressive might of Ashley-Chute's squadron left no doubt as to where the real power lay.

It would be impossible to keep Ashley-Chute's intentions secret for long, he thought. The waterfront and anchorage were packed with vessels of every kind and nationality. Arab dhows and local coasters, Spanish scooners and American brigs. Ashore and afloat the place was a melting-pot of humanity.

M'Crystal said wearily, 'Och, there's the gate, sir.' He pushed a jabbering street vendor aside and guided Blackwood through the consulate's entrance and past the two sweating British sentries.

The wall acted like a shutter, so that as the street noises faded Blackwood felt a tinge of uncertainty. Harry had hinted that he was wasting his time when he had told him he intended to see Slade. Ashley-Chute would tear him limb from limb if he upset his old friend.

A robed servant appeared at a doorway and bowed smoothly. 'This way, sir.'

M'Crystal grunted. 'I'll be waiting, sir. Just in case.'

Blackwood glanced at him. The colour-sergeant had obviously seen through him as well. That thought and the sweating discomfort of this place made him unreasonably angry, and without a word he followed the servant into the shady entrance, which compared with the street was almost cool.

The servant gestured politely for him to wait and disappeared into one of the many doors which opened off the entrance hall. It was a plain, spartan building, with little to show of its true purpose.

A few minutes later Barrow, Slade's private secretary, came from one of the rooms and regarded him warily. When told of Blackwood's wish to see his master, Barrow pursed his lips and said, 'Sir Geoffrey is with the consul. However . . .' He sighed. 'I'll see what I can do.'

Blackwood tried to relax. Barrow had put him in his place with no trouble at all. He would leave it a few more minutes and then reappear to say that Slade was engaged, and anyway . . .

The door opened and Barrow said in his dry voice, 'Sir Geoffrey will see you now.'

Blackwood licked his lips and followed the private secretary through the door. He noticed that poor Barrow was wearing a heavy frock-coat, no doubt very suitable for London but certainly not here. The realization made him start. It would be December in a few more days. Perhaps there might even be snow over Hawks Hill, thoughts of Christmas in the cottages, decorations at the little church.

Through another door and there was Slade, standing behind a great marble-topped table as if he had been expecting him. There were papers and despatches all over the table, and two empty glasses. The consul must have made a discreet departure by another door.

Slade eyed him calmly. 'Unexpected visit.' He studied him for several seconds. 'You look recovered. I'm pleased.' Surprisingly, he smiled. 'Well, Captain Blackwood, since you seem to have forgotten what you intended to say, may I suggest you be seated.' He did not wait for a reply but rang a small bell and when a servant appeared said, 'Some hock.'

Blackwood sat down. He was out of his depth. What had he really expected? He looked at the one picture on the wall behind Slade's table. A portrait of the Queen. It must have been done soon after her wedding to Albert when she was twenty-one. A face which was both strong and sensitive. Now she was ten years older, and Blackwood wondered how she saw her expanding empire.

He blurted out, 'I wanted to ask you about Mdlaka, sir.'

'I thought you might. Naturally I was kept informed about what you did, the men you lost. But you must see that you and those like you are small though vital parts of the whole. I do my work as best I can, but even I cannot know the complete pattern. In war it is the same. There are always the lonely men who are never heard. The one on the prongs of a charge, or the first up the scaling ladders, men with little hope of survival.' He shrugged as if remembering something or someone. 'And others who out of necessity must be left behind to cover the retreat of their comrades. Peace too has such men.' He waited for the servant to place the glasses on the table and added, 'Mdlaka was a fool, but his weakness increased our influence over him. Mdlaka, alive and back with his own people, is unpredictable. But Mdlaka dead or in chains would leave a dangerous space which would soon be filled.'

Blackwood raised the glass to his lips. The hock was perfect, and he marvelled that it was so cold.

He said quietly, 'I wanted to kill him and burn his village to the ground.' He looked up, his eyes steady. 'But for my injured leg . . .'

Slade smiled gently and refilled his glass. 'You might act because of different reasons, but for revenge? I think not.' He seemed amused at Blackwood's surprise. 'I told you weeks ago. I take an interest in your affairs. Without officers like you, where would Her Majesty's ministers turn for aid?'

'You are laughing at me, sir.' He made to rise but Slade waved him down.

Slade said gravely, 'No. After what you have done, the courage you inspired in your men, only a fool would laugh, and that I am not.'

Barrow's head poked round a door. 'It is nearly time, Sir Geoffrey.' He pointedly did not look at Blackwood.

Slade nodded. 'Very well.' Then he turned to Blackwood and said, 'Sir James Ashley-Chute intends to mount an attack on an area which is known to be a main artery for the slavers. You know about it, of course, so I will not interfere. I guide the Navy and the military, I try not to impose my will.' Again the briefest of smiles. 'Not too obviously anyway.' He became serious once more. 'I must confess that I do not fully understand the ways of the Navy, but Sir James commands the forces in this theatre. He is a man of experience, of considerable determination.'

Blackwood waited, his earlier confusion forgotten. Slade seemed to be ticking off certain points in his mind, as if he expected each one to be challenged.

'If he insists on his present strategy, I am not the one to disagree.'

He hesitated, and for a second Blackwood imagined he saw anxiety on his features.

Then he said, 'You once asked about my niece.'

He turned, his eyes suddenly cold and fixed on Blackwood's reaction.

'Yes, sir. Is something wrong?'

'I have found out where she is. It is a mission some ten miles inland from where you may have to land your men.' He did not hide his concern now. 'Ten miles? In Africa that can be like a hundred!'

'Is she safe, sir?'

'At present, I believe so. But if Sir James's first approach fails, she and every other mission in the area will be in mortal peril. I must try not to think too much about it. I have to be above personal involvement. Results are the same as intentions where I am concerned. He walked round the table and grasped Blackwood's hand. 'But if you can, *bring her out.*'

Blackwood's head was awhirl. An argument, an eventual reprimand and worse, these he might have expected. In a few words Slade had dropped his guard, had revealed the agony he was enduring because of his headstrong niece.

Blackwood returned his grasp. 'You may rely on it, sir.'

Barrow entered the room, a warning frown on his urbane features.

Blackwood watched the change as Slade stepped easily into his other role.

'Don't fuss, Barrow. The wine was too good to hurry, eh, Blackwood?'

Alone with the Queen's portrait, Blackwood considered his discovery. That Slade, the instrument of government and empire, was just a man after all.

Major Rupert Fynmore leaned his hands on the sill of Ackworthy's cabin windows and peered at the shimmering jumble of passing craft.

Blackwood waited, wondering why he disliked the lean, sunburned major.

Fynmore straightened his back and turned towards him. He was forty years old but took every care not to show it. His coatee fitted his erect figure without a crease. His boots were like black glass, and his neat sandy hair looked as if it had just been trimmed by the company barber.

'Captain Ackworthy is ashore. He has allowed me the use of his day cabin while I prepare my orders.' He had a way of smiling with one side of his mouth, as if the lips were being turned upwards from within. The smile never quite reached his eyes. 'I was expecting to see you somewhat earlier.'

Blackwood said, 'I'm sorry, sir. I was not told of your intended visit.'

Visit?' The mouth lifted again. 'Hardly that. I am taking charge of the landing operations, eventually.'

Blackwood said quietly, 'Under Commander Netten, I believe, sir.'

'True.' Fynmore regarded him calmly. 'Funny how things turn out, don't you think? Meeting again like this, I mean?'

Blackwood remained silent. Fynmore was enjoying his new command. There was no sense in putting men's lives at risk by creating a wider rift between them.

Fynmore was saying in a level, matter of fact tone, 'My father served under yours at Lake Erie and at Navarino. Bit of a hard man in those days, I understand.'

Blackwood said, 'He never discussed it, I'm afraid, sir.' It was a lie but he saw the major's eyes spark with anger.

Fynmore snapped, 'No matter. I just want to get things straight before we go to work. I know about you, your ideas, your death or glory escapades. Well, I'll have no blind heroics on this mission. The job will be done. My way. Understood?'

'I think so, sir.' He was surprised how calm he felt. *Death or glory*. His father would have approved of this Fynmore.

Fynmore said sharply, 'You were at the consulate.'

'Sir.'

'By whose orders?'

'It was a friendly visit, sir.'

The lip lifted slightly and hovered as if uncertain what to do.

'Sir Geoffrey Slade?'

'Yes, sir.'

'Oh well, in that case . . .'

Fynmore walked to Ackworthy's table and opened his despatch bag.

Blackwood had heard a great deal about Fynmore. He was old for his rank and would use anything which might boost him to lieutenant-colonel and higher. And why not? Why should he be so unlikeable, Blackwood wondered? His old commanding officer at North Island who had died leading his men had been wild to a point of madness if an occasion offered itself. He had been a Scot like M'Crystal, and had been known to play the bagpipes while marching on the table at the end of a mess dinner. But the men had worshipped him, and in the face of death had followed him without hesitation.

Fynmore dragged some papers on to the table. 'Straightforward, seems to me.' He tried to relax. 'Sit down, won't you?' He smiled. 'We'll be the only two officers with field experience, how about that, eh?'

He hurried on, 'Won't come to anything probably. Flags of truce, while Commander Netten speaks with the local king.' He squinted at the top page of his notes. 'King Zwide, by all accounts. He should be no trouble.'

Blackwood watched the major's hawklike profile with sudden apprehension. It must be another of Fynmore's vanities that he was pretending he could read without effort when in fact his sight was obviously failing. Things were getting worse by the minute.

'May I suggest something, sir?'

'Well?' Fynmore looked at him warily.

'As senior marine officer could you not advise the admiral that we make use of some, if not all, of the steam vessels here?'

Fynmore chuckled. 'Thought of that already. I saw the admiral myself about it. He's made his own plans, of course, but only the flagship and the frigate *Peregrine* will be taking part in the operation. He did agree to one small steam gunboat, the *Norseman*, coming with us, more for use as a tug than as a warship, I suspect.' His chest shook with laughter, but no sound emerged.

Blackwood nodded. The bulk of the squadron would stay at anchor. They could do nothing anyway against the maze of rivers used by the slavers. By remaining at Fernando Po they might also put any spies off the scent.

'One steam vessel is better than nothing, from my experience.'

Fynmore faced him and said, 'Of course, you were in the *Satyr*. So you know all about that kind of thing, eh?'

Blackwood asked, 'Is that what it sounded like, sir?'

'I'm afraid it did. You know what your trouble is, Blackwood?' He gave his quick smile. 'Pride, that's what. Except that in your case it changes too quickly to arrogance.'

Blackwood stood up slowly. *He wants to provoke me.*

He said, 'You have the advantage of me, sir.' He watched Fynmore's eagerness fade. 'In rank, that is.'

Fynmore glared at him. 'You are dismissed. I shall let you know when I need you.' As Blackwood turned to leave he asked, 'Is your brother still aboard?'

Blackwood felt his throat go dry. Like that night on the wall of the fort. Fear. But not for himself this time. Fynmore's casual question was a threat. He knew well enough the name and seniority of every marine officer in the squadron. Men like Fynmore, who hungered for promotion and dreaded the prospect of being discharged from the Corps, always knew such things.

'He *is*.'

'Good. We must see he is suitably employed, what?'

Blackwood left the cabin and banged the screen door behind him.

Private Callow, who had once rescued a man from drowning, was the cabin sentry, but Blackwood did not even notice him.

Too proud, arrogant, hungry for glory? Blackwood had had just about enough for one day.

He thought suddenly of the girl with violet eyes, Davern

Seymour. What would Major bloody Fynmore say about her when he discovered what Slade intended?

By the time he had reached the quarterdeck he had regained his composure, outwardly at least.

As he stood by the nettings and took full advantage of the spread awnings he saw a boat approaching the main chains, and a boatswain's chair being lowered towards it.

He noticed several of the seamen who were working on deck grinning and nudging each other, and when he looked into the boat he saw Harry sitting in the sternsheets beside an African woman who was swathed from chin to toe in a long green robe. Blackwood stared as two seamen steadied the chair for her to climb into while the youthful marine lieutenant took her hand to help her.

The last time he had seen her she had been naked, like a wild animal as she had pressed herself against him. He found himself bunching his fingers into a tight fist as he remembered the feel of her breast under his hand, the way she had looked at him.

As the bosun's chair squeaked up towards the gangway she sensed him watching her. She held her robe up around her mouth and nose so that only her eyes remained visible, and they never moved from his face until she was lowered again and lost from view.

Harry appeared by his side and touched his hat, some of his jauntiness fading as he saw his expression.

'What is *she* doing aboard?'

Harry eyed him curiously. 'Apparently she's a princess. Daughter of a king near Benin. I received an order to fetch her from the slaver.'

Blackwood looked away. Slade's hand was doubtless behind this too. A bargaining point, a hostage, or a viper in their midst. It was not difficult to imagine the black princess selling her own people into slavery.

A huge woman in a brightly striped gown was now being hoisted aboard to the accompaniment of yells of encouragement from the sailors.

Harry was still watching him. 'A servant and guardian for the princess. She'll probably need one in a ship full of lusting tars!'

Blackwood glanced at him and smiled. 'The other way round.'

There was a quick step on the deck and Major Fynmore snapped irritably, 'I cannot have my officers setting a bad example by idling and gossiping, eh? We have extra marines coming aboard from the squadron, and I shall want a *full* inspection this afternoon, orders in the first dog watch, right?' He gave Harry the benefit of his crooked smile. 'No passengers here, what?'

Harry said softly as Fynmore bustled away, 'I wonder if he knows about the princess?'

Captain Ackworthy lowered his telescope and growled, 'Bad stretch of coast.'

With all sails furled to her yards, *Audacious* swung heavily to her cable, oblivious to the activity on the upper deck as boats were swayed out from their tier and dropped alongside. Slightly closer to the lush green coastline the small frigate *Peregrine* had also anchored, and was no doubt awaiting the next signal from the Flag.

Ashley-Chute stood by the nettings, well apart from his officers, hands gripped across his buttocks as he stared fixedly at the land.

Blackwood watched him. It was hard to tell what the admiral was thinking. If he was impatient at the delay in leaving Fernando Po, at the further irritations of failing wind and a snail's-pace to reach this point on the chart, he did not show it. He had given vent to some feeling on the first day at sea when, after gushing dense smoke high into the air, the little gunboat *Norseman* signalled that she had broken down and was unable to proceed.

Ashley-Chute had almost crowed with delight. 'What did I say, eh, eh?' He had darted his piercing stare from one officer to the next. 'No damn use! Bundle of bloody iron scrap, that's what *that* is!'

The officer of the watch approached Ackworthy and touched his hat.

'All boats lowered, sir.'

'Very well.'

Once again Blackwood noticed Ackworthy's hesitation. As if he was unwilling or unable to make the next decision. Or as if he had not been allowed to share his admiral's plans.

In that he could sympathize with the massive captain. Since Major Fynmore had come aboard, he and Commander Netten had been as thick as thieves, and had told him little beyond the needs of routine and preparation.

Fynmore seemed to revel in his new command. For the three days it had taken to reach this place, some fifty miles to the north-west of the Niger Delta, Fynmore had behaved as if the marines were to be employed on ceremonial parades rather than possible action. Every day they had been kept busy polishing and cleaning, painting their packs until they gleamed like black leather. Several marines had been awarded punishment for allegedly having grit in their muskets, although Blackwood had the nagging feeling it was Fynmore's way of covering up his poor eyesight when he inspected the weapons.

He looked at the shore and restrained a shudder as he recalled the last time. No birds, no tell-tale smoke, but he sensed that the two ships had been watched since first light as they had completed their slow approach.

It was a pity about the *Norseman*, he thought. She would have made the crossing to the shore easier and safer. It was four cables, at a guess, to the nearest wedge of green land, a long pull for the oarsmen with boats loaded with men and weapons. The marine landing party would consist of ninety men, with three lieutenants selected from other ships in the squadron. Blackwood glanced down to the main-deck where Harry was speaking with M'Crystal. He was coming too, for liaison work, as Fynmore had vaguely described it.

Netten would have a party of armed seamen from *Auda-cious*, and each boat would be under the command of a lieutenant or midshipman.

Blackwood looked again towards the shore. It was like something impenetrable, the overlapping layers of thickly wooded slopes completely hiding the rivers which twisted inland. He gripped the nettings until the pain steadied his nerves. They must not be outfoxed a second time.

Then he saw Fynmore, who had been called across to speak with the admiral. How pleased he looked.

He thought of Slade, two hundred miles away at the consulate. He was probably regretting that he had not joined them in the flagship, no matter what he said to his subordinates about responsibility which excluded all else. Or perhaps he realized that Ashley-Chute might see his presence here as a lack of confidence. But he had sent one of his aides, a mild-looking man named Patterson, whose knowledge of Africa in general and the slave trade in particular had astounded the whole wardroom.

One night he had walked the deck with Blackwood and had told him how Slade had tried over the years to tempt the African kings and chiefs away from their wretched trade by offering the lure of other profits. The greatest of these had been palm oil, which was always in growing demand in Europe. But the more powerful kings, and Zwide was one of them, had burned thousands of new trees to the ground to force their people back on the cruellest but most rewarding trade of all.

Slade must think very highly of Patterson to send him on such an important mission.

The officer of the watch coughed politely. 'Would you join the admiral, sir?'

Blackwood walked across the quarterdeck which was already half in shadow as the boatswain's party set to work rigging awnings above it.

Ashley-Chute regarded the small group of officers, his face expressionless. Netten would be in overall charge, Fynmore would command the landing force, and his own son was apparently taking control of the boats.

His eyes settled on Blackwood. 'All present. Capital. The sooner we begin, the better.' He looked at his son without any hint of recognition. 'Pass the order to start loading the boats.' He turned away, dismissing him. 'Questions?'

Netten leaned forward. 'If the king's people have left the area, sir, what – '

Ashley-Chute's wide mouth snapped open and shut like a trap. He said scornfully, *'Left?* Why should they? It is their reason for being, man. But Mr Patterson intends to speak with this Zwide fellow. After that it's up to him. But no damned arguments, hmm? I cannot abide upstart natives, and never have.' His cold stare swivelled to Blackwood. 'That's right, isn't it?'

'Yes, sir.'

Blackwood saw Fynmore's resentment. Something from the past which he did not share. Perhaps the little admiral had said it deliberately.

In the distance he heard Sergeant Quintin's rough voice yell, 'First section! Into the boats! Lively there! Private Shadbolt, 'old yer 'ead up, yer like a bloody whore on the mornin' after!'

Blackwood could picture them all grinning as if he were down there with them. Quintin's comments were always coarse and usually repeated until his men knew them word-perfect.

Ackworthy, who was standing a little apart from the group, said, 'Lookout has just sighted smoke to the sou'-east, sir. Must be the *Norseman.*'

Ashley-Chute scowled at the interruption. 'I'm not waiting for that madman! He'll likely blow up anyway!'

Netten laughed but Fynmore fiddled with his belt. Even he obviously disliked the way the admiral treated his flag-captain.

Patterson appeared below the poop yawning hugely as if he had just risen from his cot. He smiled gently. 'I'm ready, Sir James.'

To everyone's surprise, Ashley-Chute clapped him on his shoulder and exclaimed, 'Very good! Now go and tell that savage about our Queen's displeasure, or whatever you do in these circumstances!'

Several people laughed. It was rare for Ashley-Chute to be in such high spirits.

Then he turned on his heel and with a curt nod added, 'Carry on, gentlemen.'

Blackwood paused by the starboard gangway and stared along the upper deck. How empty it seemed after the squads of scarlet coats and piled weapons. He touched his shako to the quarterdeck and then scrambled quickly down into the nearest boat. Smithett was already in the sternsheets with his bag, and doubtless a bottle of something.

As he got his bearings the heat covered the boat like a heavy blanket. The marines were pressed together anyway to allow the oarsmen some room, and it was just the same in all the other boats as they idled clear of the ship's side.

Familiar faces leapt out of the crowd as he ran his eyes over them. Half smiles or carefully blank, he knew them all, as they did him. Some, like those who had been at the fort, knew him even better now.

He saw Harry sitting with Major Fynmore and Netten in the big launch, ready to perform his liaison duties, no doubt. He thought of the black princess who had remained in a carefully guarded cabin on the orlop deck forward of the sick-bay. This would be her first time in the open since she had been transferred from the brigantine. Her name was Nandi. Harry had told him after inspecting the sentries who had been posted to prevent any amorous seaman or marine from intruding on her privacy. From what he had heard, she had more to fear from Sergeant Quintin, who had protested at being taken off guard duty for the first time in living memory.

He saw Smithett's eyes flicker, and when he looked up he saw a midshipman and the mild Mr Patterson assisting the princess down the tumblehome towards the cutter.

Colour-Sergeant M'Crystal watched Blackwood's expression and wondered. Quintin had told him some of it, but there was more to come by the look of things.

In the next boat, Corporal Jones, wedged against Frazier the expert marksman, watched the second lieutenant who was aft with Major Fynmore. He grinned to himself. Cocky young buck. He had seen Second Lieutenant Blackwood, cool as you please, talking with the black girl in her makeshift cabin. Bloody good luck to him.

Private Ackland sat hunched over his pack and weapons, his lips pursed in a silent whistle as he stared unseeingly towards the shore. He was one of six brothers, all of whom worked on the land. Like a lot of farm labourers, he was a bit slower than those who lived by their wits. It had taken the Corps and several sergeants to sharpen him up. How his brothers had laughed at him when he had enlisted. It had happened almost by accident on market day in Tavistock. A recruiting party had been returning to camp, weary after a fruitless day trying to obtain volunteers for the Colours. The sergeant in charge had paused in front of Ackland and had said, 'Join us, lad. You'll not regret it.'

Ackland was a simple soul and his eyes pricked with pride as he thought of the day Captain Blackwood had just stood there and looked at him. A whole screaming mob lusting for blood, and he had spoken to him as if they were doing rounds between decks. *Sound the Advance*. If only his stupid brothers could have seen *that*.

The Rocke twins sat side by side, like peas in a pod, as they watched Private Doak trying to conceal a bottle of rum in his folded blanket. Nearby Private Bulford eased his cross-belt and watched the girl being helped into the other boat. Try as he might, he could not help thinking about his father. Shut up in jail for the rest of his natural life, they said. Some said he was lucky not have hanged for killing a man in a brawl. Bulford looked at the clear blue sky and felt the comforting jostle of his companions around him and was grateful. Lucky? To be shut up like a beast? Not for him.

Patterson thumped into the boat and fanned his thin face
with his hat.

'*Exhausting*, Captain Blackwood!'

But Blackwood was looking at the princess.

She said suddenly, 'It is you.'

Her English was fractured but clear. In the reflected glare
she looked graceful despite the all-enveloping robe, with the
grace of a puma.

He said, 'We are taking you to your father.'

She spat out the words, '*The King*.'

Blackwood retorted sharply, 'Just sit down and behave
yourself.' He could feel the eyes and grins around him.

She sat down at once and folded her hands in her lap, her
eyes turned to the shore.

Blackwood nodded to the bowman. 'Cast off.'

He tried to fix the picture of the chart in his mind. The
river with the sharp bend like a dog's hind leg. But instead he
kept looking at the girl on the thwart, now so aloof and
demure, a princess. It was hard to think of her as the nude
savage in that filthy cabin.

The midshipman by the tiller waited for the other boats to
form into line and then directed the cutter astern of the
leading one with the White Ensign curling from the stern-
post.

Patterson touched his arm. 'Join me, Captain.'

Blackwood half turned and sat, seeing the eyes dropping or
looking away as the crowded occupants pretended they had
noticed nothing.

Patterson said quietly, 'Sir Geoffrey explained things to
you?'

Their eyes met.

'Yes.'

'Good. I spoke to your admiral. If it can be done, then it
will be up to you.' He hesitated. '*If*.'

Blackwood felt the pressure of the princess's hip against his
side as the cutter rolled in the first inshore swell.

What would his father have done? His grandfather would

have made the best of it, he decided. Even in his last year alive at Hawks Hill his faded eyes could still twinkle as he had retold stories of the women he had met and 'served', as he always put it.

He shook himself angrily. He must be mad to let his dreams run riot. He looked at the green barrier which tilted across the bows like a curtain, and then astern towards the horizon. There, far away, was the tell-tale smudge of smoke. Monkey's pet hate. She was too late now.

When he looked again he saw the gleam of trapped water around the nearest headland and knew it was the entrance to the river. Zwide's kingdom, which lay across the slave trails like a treacherous snare. He glanced at the girl's hands in her lap, but they were relaxed, and he could feel no tension in her hip against his side.

He saw Lieutenant Ashley-Chute climb up in the leading boat and raise his speaking trumpet. How deformed he looked as he stood framed against the lush green slope at his back.

'*Take station!*' His voice sounded hollow in the trumpet.

Obedient to the order the boats changed formation until they were in two matching lines, which once inside the river would move out to opposite banks.

Blackwood waited until the midshipman by the tiller had increased the stroke to bring the cutter to the head of the starboard line, directly abeam of Netten's big launch.

It was all too casual, too easy. He could feel the warning ringing in his mind like a bell.

He stood up and looked along the boat. 'Ready, lads.'

It was all he said, and in the next boat astern he saw M'Crystal gesturing to his own party. He did not need telling, any more than when he had taken charge when Lascelles had lost his grip. Here and there a musket moved across a gunwale, or a man shaded his eyes to watch the land as it opened up to swallow them.

Blackwood looked at the midshipman. He was a popular youth and aged about sixteen. He looked as if he was enjoying all this enormously. Like a boy in a toy-shop.

'Mr Ward.' He saw the midshipman start. 'Leave the tiller to the cox'n and come here.' He waited for the midshipman to join him and then lowered his voice. 'If we come under fire I want you to take hold of the princess and *put her* on the bottom boards, right?'

The youth nodded jerkily. 'I – I think so, sir.'

'Good. I'm placing you in charge of her safety.' He forced a grin. 'Not every day we mix with royalty.'

Smithett muttered, 'I wish that bloomin' gunboat was 'ere.'

Blackwood glanced over at Fynmore. He was sitting bolt upright as if he was riding down The Mall in a carriage.

He saw Harry look towards him, his quick wave as if to reassure him he would be all right.

He touched the girl's shoulder and waited for her eyes to lift towards him.

'Your father. The *King*. When will he come?'

She did not even blink. 'He will come.'

Blackwood saw her nostrils dilate, like someone watching a terrible ritual. Seeing them all killed perhaps?

He turned to Patterson. 'Are we in danger yet?'

Patterson shrugged. 'Little is known about this place. Zwide is well protected on two flanks by the river. There is a ridge on the right, very soon now. Once past there we should be better placed.'

'Did you tell Major Fynmore about it?' Somehow he already knew the answer.

Patterson gave his shy smile. 'I did. He said it was best to leave such matters to professionals.'

'He would.'

No wonder they had given him a separate boat, he thought bitterly.

Patterson was watching him, reading his thoughts.

'Which is why I chose to accompany *you*, Captain.'

'Thank you for that.'

Midshipman Ward called, 'They've put up the white flag, sir!'

Blackwood bit his lip as he watched Netten's launch thrusting ahead under its two flags. It was so quiet, the boats had no substance, no reality.

He ran his finger round his collar. His skin felt like fire.

The bowman stood up and pointed excitedly. '*Here they come!*'

IO

Sudden Death

Harry Blackwood plucked his clothes away from his body which was running with sweat. Protected from any sort of breeze by the river banks and rising slopes of thick vegetation, the inside of the launch was like a furnace. He could feel Lieutenant Ashley-Chute moving behind him, speaking with the coxswain as he directed the slow procession of boats. There were ten in all, and when he looked across at the cutter which led the other line he gave his half-brother a quick wave without really knowing why.

Perhaps because of Fynmore, he thought. He had heard him speaking with the commander and had realized they were talking about Philip.

Netten had said something about Mdlaka and the admiral's reaction to the report on what had happened.

'Captain Blackwood as good as told Sir James he thought our methods were out-of-date. The admiral actually *listened* to him to all accounts. Any other time he'd have exploded!'

Fynmore had replied, 'That young chap is too damned intolerant with authority in my book. Needs taking down.'

They had changed the subject at that point.

Harry thought about England. It would be his birthday soon. He had always hated having it so close to Christmas. As a child he had loved opening his presents, but as he grew older some people seemed to think one gift would suit for both celebrations. He had thought a good deal about Hawks Hill and what would happen there. He enjoyed going to London but, like his childhood presents, he wanted to hoard those visits for something special.

He had always been a bit in awe of the old house where he had been born. It had been built originally as a fortified Tudor farmhouse with a moat all around it. Down over the years the house had spread and been added to until it stood as it did today, a great rambling cavern of rooms, hallways and little doors which led to the roof or down to the depths of the cellars. As a boy Harry had pretended the latter were dungeons and had almost frightened himself to death when he had become locked in a cupboard there.

Now the moat had all but gone, with just one strip preserved for the benefit of visiting swans and geese.

Hawks Hill had been bought from one of the previous owners by his great-grandfather, Major-General Samuel Blackwood, who, if his portraits were to be believed, was always employed in one war or another. He had served with Wolfe at Quebec, and had fought his way right through the American Revolution, after which he had retired from the army to settle in Hampshire.

It was strange to think that he had been the last soldier in the Blackwood family, and Harry had often wondered what had made his grandfather begin the new tradition with the Regiment of the Sea.

He heard Lieutenant Ashley-Chute say, 'The first bend is about half a mile ahead, sir.'

Netten grunted and raised his telescope to examine the nearest bank. The current was quite strong and the oarsmen were showing the strain.

Harry Blackwood dabbed his face yet again. The handkerchief was little more than a wet rag. He longed for the cool of the evening or the chance of a swim. He grimaced. It was doubtful if it was safe to paddle here, let alone swim.

He shaded his eyes to look at the cutter, at the girl in the green robe who was sitting with, yet somehow quite apart from his brother.

It was really strange, he thought, that his half-brother never seemed to understand women or that he was attractive to them. He had seen that attraction several times with a mixture of amusement and envy. Philip had a stiffness about him, a hint of experience far greater than his years, and yet he was totally unaware of it.

Harry had never met a black girl before, let alone one like the Princess Nandi. Even as he had tried to talk with her on *Audacious*'s orlop he had felt an urge to touch her, to make her want him.

He thought suddenly of the cellar where he had accidentally locked himself in a cupboard. His dungeon. When he was sixteen he had enticed one of the housemaids down there with him. She had been older than he, a friendly, buxom girl with a ready giggle.

By the light of a candle he had told her she was his prisoner, that she would be put to the rack and torture if she did not submit.

Her response had been astounding and immediate.

She had taken his hands and pulled them to her bosom, her eyes shut as she had murmured, '*I submit*, Master Harry. Take me.'

Afterwards, full of frightened excitement and guilt, he had tortured himself by remembering every breathless, tantalizing moment of their embraces. Things which he had never known and now would never forget.

Her tongue in his mouth, their skin chilled in the cellar's dampness rising to passionate heat as they had come together while she had instructed and guided him until they were both completely spent.

He dragged at his tunic again. He was feeling it now in this heat.

Fynmore snapped, '*There!* They've sighted something!'

Netten raised his hand to silence the chatter in the boat. 'About time.'

Harry Blackwood peered between his two superiors and saw a boat coming from around a bend in the river.

It was not a crude dug-out canoe, but another long-boat, larger if anything than this launch. The oarsmen were black, but in the stern he could see two, maybe three white faces.

Netten exclaimed angrily, 'Dammit, they've dropped a stream-anchor!'

Harry watched as the other boat's oars rose and halted like frayed wings while the current surged around the hull as if it was going astern.

Netten twisted round. 'Signal the boats to anchor!' He gestured towards the boat directly abeam, and after a moment's hesitation the cutter began to pull towards them.

Fynmore shifted on the thwart and asked, 'What do you intend to do?'

Netten was watching the anchored long-boat. 'Patterson will speak with them. He'll probably know the white men. Slavers perhaps, but it'll not be like dealing with bloody savages.'

Harry was only eighteen but he recognized alarm when he heard it.

The cutter closed to within a few yards and Patterson called, 'The king is not with them. One of those men is called Lessard. The last time we met was in Senegal.' There was nothing mild about him now.

He nodded to himself. 'I think we should stand off and let him make the first move.'

Netten exploded, 'I've run up the white flag, he must know we've come to parley.'

Patterson shrugged. 'If King Zwide was here we could let him see his daughter. Without him we cannot bargain. Lessard has little regard for life, other people's that is.'

Netten glared at him. 'I'm not here to *bargain*, as you put it. I have come in the Queen's name, and you would do well to remember it!'

Fynmore looked across at Blackwood. 'What are your views?'

Harry watched his half-brother, fascinated as he replied without hesitation, 'We should fall back and land our people on the right hand bank, sir. It looked safer there, easy to defend. The gunboat *Norseman* will come up in support before dusk. Once she's here, Lessard and his friends will not dare to move against us.'

Fynmore let him finish. 'Is that *all*, Captain Blackwood? No fire and blood? We just *retreat*, is that it?'

Blackwood replied flatly, 'There is a ridge over there, sir. Not more than a cable distant. If they have marksmen placed in cover they can fire down into the boats. The oarsmen are tired. It's not worth the risk.'

Fynmore swallowed hard. 'I shall speak with you later.' To Netten he said, 'I say we should call his bluff. Now.'

Netten nodded. 'I agree.'

Fynmore turned towards the cutter once more. 'You anchor and take charge of the flotilla, Captain Blackwood. *And* the women, of course.'

Harry watched his brother's features, sickened at Fynmore's jibe.

Netten looked aft. 'Give way together, Cox'n.' But his eyes lingered on the other boats which were dragging on their anchors or grapnels, the oarsmen drooping over their looms while they regained their breath.

As the launch started to move ahead Blackwood stood in the cutter, his heart pounding against his ribs as he tried to contain his anger. He did not even remember getting to his feet, but was aware of the watching eyes of his men. Indifferent, critical, hostile, they were all lost in a haze of disbelief.

Patterson said softly, 'You spoke correctly. I know that for a professional fighting man it must go against the grain. But even as a civilian I think you are right.' He peered after the launch. 'I know Lessard. He has estates in America, in Georgia. He has others in Brazil and Cuba, and has grown rich beyond measure from slavery. And never once have we been able to prove it.'

Blackwood tried not to look towards the launch which was now almost blocking the view of Lessard's boat.

'Why should this Lessard be here?'

'It will be important.' Patterson looked briefly at the black princess. 'Too important to be frightened off by a few redcoats.'

Midshipman Ward asked huskily, 'Shall I anchor, sir?'

Blackwood looked at him. The boy was ashamed, for him and of him. In his eyes he had failed, had chosen caution when he should not have hesitated.

'No, Mr Ward.' He heard an edge in his tone as he spoke over their heads. 'Be ready to pull with all your might. I don't give a damn if your arms come out of their sockets. Corporal Bly, get up forrard with two of the best marksmen.'

It was like a cold wind blowing through the boat. Hands jerked at weapons and pouches, others tugged down shakos as their owners responded to the hint of danger.

'Remain in midstream.'

Blackwood heard Smithett checking his pistols.

Midshipman Ward said suddenly, 'There must have been a waggon over there, sir!' He pointed abeam at the first slope of the ridge.

Patterson remarked, 'Unlikely.'

Blackwood leaned over the seated girl and felt her tense away from him.

'Waggon be damned! They're cannon tracks!' He straightened up and shouted, 'Pull, lads! *Together!*' He felt the bottom boards shiver beneath his feet as the oarsmen flung themselves back on the looms. 'Signal the next boat to – '

The rest of his words and thoughts were scattered by a shattering explosion which echoed above the river like a clap of thunder.

A tall waterspout shot up beside the launch, so close that several of the oars were flung into the river. As the current took control the launch began to swing round, the seamen in confusion as they struggled to back water with the remaining oars.

Blackwood saw a puff of smoke from the ridge and felt sick as another ball slammed through the forepart of the boat and something which a second earlier had been a sailor was flung over the side like a piece of meat.

Thank God Netten had not had time to anchor within speaking distance of the other boat. Now the launch was drifting with the current while somebody was frantically trying to bale out the inrush of water from that last shot.

'Stand by in the bows!' Blackwood saw Ward staring at him, his eyes wide with shock. '*Keep down*, the rest of you!'

He heard the familiar crackle of firing from the ridge, saw feather-like splashes as shots pattered around the other boat or smacked into her planking.

Blackwood bit on his chin strap. *Our turn next*. God Almighty. 'Keep pulling!'

Midshipman Ward gave a yelp as a shot whipped his cap away like an invisible hand.

Blackwood felt his mouth set in an insane grin. 'You are not doing your duty, Mr Ward!' He seized his shoulder. 'Join the princess!'

The midshipman lowered himself until his body all but covered the girl on the bottom boards.

Across the boy's shoulder she stared up at Blackwood with neither fear nor hatred.

Blackwood saw the bowman getting ready to hurl his grapnel into the drifting launch. He could see Harry trying to drag an injured seaman aft away from the incoming water, and Fynmore standing up in the sternsheets, pointing at something, while one of the few marines in the launch opened fire on the river bank.

Shots cracked against the cutter now, and others whimpered overhead. A seaman gasped and fell across his oar, blood pouring from his skull, and another was hugging his chest and sobbing with agony.

Down-river a bugle wailed mournfully, and Blackwood guessed that the other boats were heading towards the shore. With three lieutenants who had never been in action before, it might fall once again on M'Crystal to drag the hot coals out of the fire.

The cutter lurched against the other boat and there was a stampede to drag the injured into an already overcrowded hull.

Blackwood stood on a thwart and ignored the deadly whisper of shots as they passed dangerously close. The launch was obviously sinking fast. There was blood everywhere, even splashed up on to the pathetic flag of truce.

Fynmore stared at him, his eyes wild as he shouted, 'They've got artillery, for God's sake!'

As if to taunt him another bang echoed across the river and they fell back gasping and spluttering in a cascade of stinking water.

Blackwood grabbed a wounded seaman's arm and hauled him bodily over the gunwale and shut his ears to his screams.

'What are the orders now, sir?'

Fynmore lurched aside. 'No good asking him.'

Commander Netten was still seated aft, his telescope grasped in his hands like a baton.

His chin and most of his face had been shot away, and yet above the torn flesh his eyes remained staring ahead, frozen at the moment of impact.

With the launch drifting clear, its dead occupants lolling deeper and deeper in water, Blackwood's boat turned and thrust towards the lower bank.

A few more shots struck the side, and near the bows an unconscious seaman was hit again but died feeling nothing.

Blackwood felt for his shako, but, like Ward's cap, it had been knocked from his head and he had not noticed.

He looked at Harry, his throat raw from shouting.

'Close thing.' He wanted to smile for both their sakes but nothing came. He kept thinking of Netten, how they had avoided each other after that day aboard the brigantine.

Then he glanced down as someone touched his foot and saw the girl staring at him. He dropped on one knee as he saw blood on her face, but as he reached out she shook her head, and then with unexplained tenderness put her arms around Midshipman Ward.

She said, 'His blood, not mine.'

Very gently they lifted the midshipman from the girl's body. A shaft of sunlight shone on his tightly closed eyes. It came through a neat hole in the planking where the bullet had found its mark.

Harry bent over his shoulder. 'Is he dead?'

Blackwood covered the midshipman's face with some canvas. *The boy in the toy-shop.*

He could barely speak and was afraid his voice would betray him.

'Yes, Harry. He was obeying orders, you see. *Protecting the women.*' He looked at Fynmore's stricken face. 'So you command, sir.'

Fynmore seemed to jerk himself from his trance.

'Yes. Get the men ashore.' His eyes followed the sinking launch as it drifted past, the terrible figure sitting upright in the sternsheets as if to seek out his killer.

Of the long-boat and the mysterious Lessard there was no sign.

Smithett let out his breath very slowly. 'Now fer a spot o' soldierin', I suppose.'

Blackwood looked at the river, the marines tumbling ashore and forming into squads like parts of a machine.

It was the same nightmare about to begin all over again.

Dust and gunsmoke mingled in a low cloud above the ridge as the hidden cannon kept up a measured bombardment of the river.

Blackwood watched the marines fanning out on either flank, their movements jerky as they responded to a hundred drills ashore and afloat. No more men had fallen, and the boats were huddled together as if for comfort below the nearest bank.

'What sort of guns, d'you reckon, Colour-Sergeant?'

M'Crystal's eyes vanished in concentration. 'Big enough, sir. Twelve-pounders, is my guess. Two, mebbe three o' them.'

Major Fynmore marched down the slope, his attendant trotting behind him carrying his sword and pistol like a native bearer.

He snapped, 'Where's the bloody gunboat, eh?'

Blackwood glanced at the tall colour-sergeant and said, 'She's very small, sir. Only mounts a six-pounder and a couple of mortars.'

Fynmore's eyes swivelled on him hotly. 'Not like the *Satyr*, eh?'

Blackwood watched the puffs of smoke from the scrub as Quartermain, one of the lieutenants, put his marksmen to work. Fynmore was beginning to sound just like Netten.

He said evenly, 'I meant that if we can drive those sharp-shooters off the ridge, *Norseman* can get inshore and use her mortars to better effect. If the cannon straddle her before she can bring her weapons into action, she'll stand no chance at all.'

Fynmore massaged his chin vigorously. 'I was thinking much the same.' He gestured to the nearest lieutenant. 'Mr Heighway! First platoon, prepare to advance!' He watched the officer hurry away, his face pale but determined. 'Young idiot.' He beckoned to his runner. 'Pass the word to both flanks. Covering fire.'

Patterson winced as a stray bullet smacked among some rocks. 'I think you're taking one hell of a risk, Major.'

'You stay out of this!' Fynmore swung on him. 'Get back with the wounded. I'll need you in a minute when that bloody slaver sees sense!'

A bugle blared, and all firing ceased along the ridge as if the hidden enemy had stopped to listen.

Fynmore eyed the deployment of his men with obvious impatience.

Harry said quietly. 'There go the skirmishers, sir.'

Fynmore raised his small telescope and studied the centre platoon of marines as they formed into two long lines.

'God damn his eyes! What is that fool Quartermain doing?' He looked at Blackwood. 'Get up there. I want that ridge cleared before they can move those cannon and lay them on *us*!'

Blackwood drew his sword and saw Harry's eyes following the blade, mesmerized as he laid it across his right shoulder, the steel warm against his neck.

Then he strode quickly up the slope, his boots crunching on sand and stones, and he stared unwinkingly at the lines of marines as they began to move forward.

He barely knew the lieutenant in charge, but guessed he was probably too stunned by the swift change of fortunes to have much else in his head.

Blackwood shouted, 'From the centre, *extend*!'

He hurried past the rear line of marines and caught up with the lieutenant.

'Keep them well spread out!' He saw the lieutenant staring at him, his expression a mixture of gratitude and confusion. 'And fix bayonets, *now*!'

Quartermain's head bobbed. 'Platoon, fix – '

The order was drowned by the sporadic rattle of musket and rifle fire. Shots whipped past and through the slowly advancing lines, but by a miracle nobody fell. Most of the marines were too busy dragging out their bayonets and snapping them to their muskets and did not even falter.

Blackwood licked his lips. A long line of heads had risen above the ridge. Not some blood-maddened natives, but men in robes, and others dressed much like Patterson. There were hundreds of them. An army. The mysterious Lessard must have banked everything on driving any British expedition from his territory with enough force to discourage further interference.

'Halt! Ready!' Blackwood saw the bayoneted muskets rise in a wavering line. '*Fire!*'

The mass of figures along the ridge swayed back and then forward again like corn in the wind.

'*Retire!*'

Blackwood watched the front line of marines fall back through the second rank and begin to reload as a corporal barked out the time as if on a firing range.

'Ready!'

Before the marines could fire another volley of shots lashed down from the hill, and here and there a marine fell or rolled gasping down the slope.

Somewhere a bugle sounded the Advance, and Blackwood knew that Fynmore was rushing up support. If only they could top the ridge and find some cover.

'*Fire!*' Quartermain was waving his sword, his face split into a madman's grin, as fear drove away caution.

Blackwood darted a glance down the slope and saw Lieutenant Heighway's platoon charging after them, the front line already passing one of the men who had fallen to the second fusilade of bullets.

He also saw Smithett close on his heels, his musket across his body as he loped easily over the rough ground.

The marines' refusal to fall back had obviously caught the enemy off guard. Perhaps they had imagined the destruction of Netten's launch and the presence of their heavy guns would be enough.

Blackwood saw them darting about among the scrub which lined the ridge like the ruff on a wild boar's back. They were shooting and dropping into cover to reload with practised ease. As they must have done so often when they had surprised a sleeping village to kill the old and carry the young away as slaves.

More red coats lay on the ground. It was taking too long, and, like the oarsmen, the marines were getting worn out by the uphill attack and the relentless heat.

Blackwood yelled, 'At 'em, lads!' It was the same madness. '*Charge!*'

Shouting and cheering like demons, the marines pounded up the steeper ground of the ridge, some firing as they ran, others breaking from their ranks to overtake their exhausted companions.

Blackwood slithered and almost fell as his foot caught in some brush, and he realized they had almost reached the top. A figure rose from the ground just yards away, teeth bared as he threw up his rifle and aimed straight at him.

There was a slapping sound and the man fell back, a bayonet, complete with its musket, impaling him like a lance. The marine who had hurled it cheered and ran forward, jerked it free and dashed on after other figures who were breaking from cover, unable to face such a fierce attack.

'Extend from the centre! Right section, covering fire!'

Blackwood saw stones jumping around him as bullets hammered into the ground. Some marksmen were keeping their heads and had already marked him down as a leader.

His face felt like a mask of dust and sweat, and without his shako to protect his eyes from the glare he had to mop his face repeatedly with his sleeve.

'Cease firing!'

Blackwood peered round for a bugler but saw him lying face down, blood pouring from his neck.

'Sergeant!' He waited until the man reached him. He did not know his name. 'Send your skirmishers along the other side. No risks. See if you can find where they've gone.' He was shouting, and yet with all firing stopped by both sides it was as quiet as a grave.

The sergeant blinked the sweat from his eyes. '*Sah!*' Then he was off again, calling names, whipping up their energy like hounds who had lost the scent.

Blackwood dropped on one kneee and dragged his telescope from his belt. Beyond the ridge there was another, and then another. Where were those guns?

He turned and looked towards the river as it swung away towards the sea and wondered if they had heard the shooting aboard *Audacious*.

A runner dropped panting beside him, his eyes fixed on the dead bugler.

'Sir! Major Fynmore's compliments and will you rejoin him?'

Blackwood touched the runner's arm. He was young but would learn quickly if he survived this.

'Steady down, my lad.' He made himself smile. 'Tell the major I'll be with him as soon as I have deployed the men here.'

He beckoned to Lieutenant Quartermain and together they watched the runner scamper down the slope, zigzagging amongst the dead and wounded as if he was afraid of them.

Quartermain was still grinning with disbelief. 'There were *hundreds* of 'em, sir! Thirty of us, and they *ran*!'

Blackwood listened to the cries of the skirmishers as they called to each other among the scrub. He hoped the sergeant would remember to collect the new rifles if any had been left behind.

'They'll be back.'

What was the matter with Fynmore? Why didn't he come up here and show some encouragement to his men? It was not fear in his case. Fynmore had walked through the whole affair from the firing of the first cannon without any change of demeanour at all.

Quartermain took his silence for interest and added, 'I've had a look at some of the men we shot. Every race under the sun, I'd say, but mostly Spaniards and Portuguese by the cut of them. Bunch of bloody pirates.'

Blackwood stood up and tensed as if expecting a shot. 'Take over here.' He saw Smithett waiting for him, his face as mournful as ever. 'You did well.'

Quartermain beamed. 'Thank you, sir.'

Blackwood walked swiftly down from the ridge, his mind grappling with what they should do. Without support from *Norseman* they could achieve very little.

He saw a marine on his knees beside another who had fallen earlier in the fierce exchange of shots. He was trying to shield his friend's face from the sun with his body, and turned as Blackwood approached, his voice desperate.

'It's me mate, sir! Can't leave 'im like this!'

Smithett hurried forward and stooped beside them, his water flask held to the wounded man's lips. As Blackwood's shadow joined with the other marine's Smithett glanced up and gave a brief shake of his head.

Blackwood looked at the wounded man. His face was like parchment and there were flecks of blood on his lips. He was dying while he watched him, shot once, possibly twice in the stomach. It was amazing he had lasted this long.

His friend said, 'He'll be all right if we can get 'im back aboard ship, sir!'

Blackwood watched the dying man. 'Did you hear that?'

He seemed to realize for the first time Blackwood was there and whispered hoarsely, 'It ain't true, sir. Them bastards 'ave done for me.' He reached out to hold his friend's arm to console him but he had no more strength and his hand fell in the coarse grass as if its life had already gone.

'You go with the officer, Tim. I'll be all right 'ere. You see.'

Smithett said roughly, 'Do as 'e says. I'll stay with 'im.'

Blackwood walked away, his mind holding the picture of the dying man and his friend like an engraving. Behind him he could hear the other marine's dragging steps as he repeatedly stopped to look back up the ridge where Smithett crouched like some ancient warrior. He would not have to wait long.

Fynmore greeted him testily. 'Took your time.'

Blackwood ran his fingers through his dishevelled hair. It was filled with sand.

'We've taken the ridge, sir. There's less chance of being outflanked now.'

'Outflanked? Oh yes, I see.' Fynmore's lips twitched in a smile. 'A touch of steel. That did the trick. Knew it would. Damned barbarians!'

Sergeant Quintin crunched over the loose stones. 'Casualties, sir. Ten killed, includin' Commander Netten and Mr Ward. Twelve wounded.'

Blackwood saw Smithett coming from the slope, his shadow lengthening as he approached.

'Make that eleven killed, Sergeant.' He turned to the major. 'Will you move the third platoon to the ridge, sir?'

Fynmore rubbed his chin busily. 'I think not. We're better off here. I've already sent one of the boats back to *Audacious* with the first group of wounded, and my report to the admiral. It'll be an hour or two before we get fresh instructions. I suspect that Sir James will order us to return on board.' When Blackwood said nothing he snapped, *'Well?'*

'I think we should hold the high ground, at least until the gunboat arrives.'

Patterson had materialized from out of the rocks. 'And there's the matter of the *mission*, Major.' His eyes were calm but his tone was like a knife.

Slade chose his aides with great care, Blackwood thought. He could almost feel sorry for Fynmore as Patterson dropped this extra complication into his lap.

Patterson looked at Blackwood. 'You'd better get started. If you're not there by dawn, my guess is that you'll be too late. If we're not already.'

Fynmore exclaimed, 'I'll trouble you to stop giving orders to my officers.'

Patterson was unrepentant. 'Only Captain Blackwood knows what Sir Geoffrey's niece looks like, Major. Apart from Mr Blackwood junior that is. Dead or alive, Sir Geoffrey will insist on knowing and expect an answer.' He let his words sink in. 'Or I could go, of course.'

Fynmore looked trapped. 'No. I shall need you here, in case Lessard sues for peace.'

The idea of offending Slade had changed everything.

Patterson said, 'Well, Captain Blackwood, I wish you luck. At least by your going inland there's no possibility of a complete retreat.'

Blackwood glanced at Fynmore but he had moved away and had not heard the bitterness in Patterson's voice.

He saw Harry waiting to speak. 'Yes?'

'I've just been speaking with the Princess Nandi, sir.' He flushed under their combined stares. 'She will agree to guide us to the mission by a quicker route.'

Patterson pouted. 'Makes sense. She would know all the tracks around here. She could also be used as a hostage if need arose.'

Blackwood thought of it warily. The black princess might betray them as soon as they were away from the river, although she had certainly shown some dismay when her father had failed to meet her under the flag of truce. It was only this morning. The two lines of boats, Netten's hideous injuries, Midshipman Ward and the marine who had died on the hillside, unwilling to embarrass his friend with his final suffering.

Fynmore returned, his back erect and showing no sign of fatigue.

'That's settled then. Take eight men and Second Lieutenant Blackwood and leave as soon as you can.'

They watched one another like adversaries. Blackwood had already selected the men he would take, as if this had been decreed for a long while. Perhaps this was how it would end?

Fynmore added, 'As soon as you've gone I shall withdraw the men from the ridge.' It sounded like some sort of triumph.

'I think you're wrong, sir.'

Fynmore gave his twisted smile. 'Your privilege.' He turned on his heel, already searching for his runner. 'And I'll see that you eat your words, believe me!'

Patterson smiled wryly. 'He's a strange one, but I'll not deny his courage.' He knew Blackwood wanted to go and thrust out his hand. 'Good luck. And watch the black princess night and day.'

Later, as Blackwood and his small party moved away from the river and the long ridge where men had died, he heard the mournful call of the bugle once more.

He thought of Quartermain and wondered how he would accept retreat after overcoming his fear to lead his men to victory.

He saw two marines moving away ahead, scouting for any kind of danger as the bush and scrub thickened around them. *Eight good men and true*.

Blackwood turned and saw Harry following up in the rear, the black princess moving with easy grace just ahead of him. Had she really suggested she should lead them, or had Harry dreamed up the idea as some extra excitement?

By afternoon the river, and even the smell of the sea, had left them to their own devices.

A Bargain Kept

Blackwood tensed and was instantly awake as he felt a gentle pressure on his shoulder. Thoughts crowded through his mind as the realization of where he was drove away all ideas of sleep.

Smithett whispered, 'All still quiet, sir.'

Blackwood sat up slowly and gingerly, his body aching from the forced march through the bush, his face and skin pricking from countless insect bites and stings.

He felt Smithett put a cup in his hand and heard him pouring water from a flask.

Smithett said, 'I can give yer somethin' stronger if you want, sir.'

Blackwood sipped the water, it was lukewarm. 'Save it for later.'

He thrust his hand through his open shirt and rubbed his skin to drive away the itches. How quiet it was. Not like the first part of their uncomfortable march or when dusk had fallen and the air had been rent apart by strange animal shrieks and barks, like an insane asylum.

Only the princess had made light of it. She had never faltered or complained, and her feet had found a path when others had stumbled or cursed their way through clinging thorns and creeper.

Around him patches of deeper shadow showed where his men were sleeping, their weapons in easy reach. Sergeant Quintin would be out there in the darkness, making sure their sentries stayed awake.

He thought of the princess, the way she had looked at Quintin, goading him.

Blackwood smiled in the darkness. *As she did me*. But there had been no sign that she had betrayed them . . . yet. He had seen several places where an ambush could have been easily sited.

The mission was not far away now. Two miles at the most. It would have been folly to continue in the dark, and the men needed to rest. It was hardly what they had enlisted for, to fight slavers who were obviously better armed and prepared than they were themselves.

He looked at the sky, held like a small blue lake in a circle of trees. It was already lighter and the few stars had lost their brilliance. The realization stirred him and made him uneasy.

With an effort he got to his feet and crossed the clearing where they had made camp and eaten their meagre rations. Once again the black princess had shown her strength, had refused to share their food and had sat apart from them, missing nothing.

He would give his final instructions to Harry. If something was about to go wrong it would be soon.

Blackwood stopped dead as he saw his half-brother's shape, pale in the darkness. For a moment he could not speak or breathe. Harry was sprawled across a blanket, one arm outflung, his face pressed into the ground. Of the girl there was no sign.

Blackwood threw himself down and grasped Harry's arm. He had been guarding her. Sharing the duty with Corporal Jones. She must have had a knife or some other weapon concealed in her robe and . . .

Harry rolled on to his back and peered at him. 'What is it?'

Blackwood stood up violently. 'You bloody young fool, she's got away!'

Harry scrambled to his feet and they faced each other like strangers.

'She gave her word — '

Blackwood exclaimed angrily, 'Is that *all* she gave you?'

'You thought she'd murdered me, that's right, isn't it?'

'What the hell does it matter what I think! She's gone, and is probably getting her father's warriors on their way here right now!'

'Look, sir.' Harry's sudden formality made it even more unreal. 'It wasn't like that. She said that if her people saw her as our captive they would kill us, we'd have no chance. But once freed she *promised* to help us.'

Blackwood saw Jones groping through the scrub and beckoned to him. 'Rouse the men.' To Harry he added fiercely, 'If we get out of this alive I'll see you court-martialled, damn you, family or not!'

Sergeant Quintin stood aside as Blackwood pushed past him. 'Trouble, sir?'

Harry tried to smile but nothing happened. 'I seem to have put my foot in it, Sergeant.'

Quintin was glad the second lieutenant could not see his face. It wasn't only his foot he had put in it. Quintin had paused in his patrol around the clearing and had heard them, had seen Mr Blackwood's buttocks framed by the girl's black thighs. Going at it like a fiddler's elbow, he was. Lucky young bugger.

He said as calmly as he could, 'I s'pect it'll be all right, sir. I probably know 'im better than you do, in a manner o' speakin'.'

Harry said quietly, 'You're fond of him, aren't you?'

'Fond, sir? That's too strong a word fer the likes o' me. But as an officer 'e's the best I've served with. That'll do.' He could not restrain a grin. 'But then, sir, I'm not *family*!'

A few moments later Blackwood gathered the others around him. Sergeant Quintin and Corporal Jones, while his half-brother tried to stay invisible between them. In the clearing the marines were buckling on their belts and pouches, taking a last look at their weapons. Nobody said a word about the black princess. Blackwood was beginning to suspect he had been the only one not to know what was happening.

He said, 'We'll leave now. According to Mr Patterson's map and instructions the mission is about two miles distant. A short climb and then downhill all the way to another river.' He glanced at the sky again. But for the princess's unerring sense of direction he doubted if they would even have got halfway, let alone by dawn as Patterson had suggested. 'If the worst has happened we'll make our way back to where we landed.' He glanced at each one in turn. 'Tell the men that.' He had known it happen in the past. Marines were half-sailors at heart, and if the mission had been destroyed and the occupants butchered they would very likely continue down to the next river. To seamen and marines alike, water was not an enemy or a barrier, but a way out. Not this time, he thought grimly. 'Questions?'

Quintin said, 'Them slavers wot fired on the boats will be too busy to come this way, won't they, sir?'

Blackwood had already considered it. Lessard and others who used the local tribal chiefs like a private army must have some method of maintaining contact along hundreds of miles of coastline. They had seemed to know what Ashley-Chute had in mind before he did.

'We can't take that for granted. We are passing through King Zwide's territory. He may have other ideas about our progress.' He saw them glance at Harry and added shortly, 'But what's done is done. We'll have to take the chance. Once we reach the river,' He looked at Harry, 'you'll go with Corporal Jones and Private Frazier to a point above the mission while the rest of us move in to investigate.'

Harry remarked as lightly as he could, 'Rather like being an umpire, sir!'

Blackwood eyed him calmly. 'You'll be the bloody burial party if you don't watch out!'

He turned away, angry with himself and with Harry's inability to take things seriously.

'Corporal Jones, lead off. If you see or hear *anything*, I want to know instantly.'

He could feel his heart beating faster. And they had not

even started yet. He wished suddenly he had accepted
Smithett's offer of something stronger than water.

As the marines waded into the clinging grass and bush
Harry said quietly, 'Take my shako, sir.' He held it out to
him and added simply, 'It might give them a bit of
confidence at the mission.'

Blackwood bit back an angry retort and jammed the shako
on his head.

'Thanks.'

Then he swung on his heel and followed the others into the
remaining shadows.

Harry Blackwood paused only to look at the small,
flattened patch of grass where the blanket had been. His legs
still felt like jelly, and he could feel the scent of her body like
something physical.

He saw the Rocke twins trudge past, muskets at the ready
as they watched the scrub on either side. He was getting to
know all of them, their ways and their attitudes. He thought
of the sergeant's comment. *Too strong a word.* Perhaps it was
trust which Philip offered them and in return they gave him
an instant loyalty.

He sighed and fell in behind the twins, his pistol drawn
and resting in the crook of his arm.

His mother and father would be proud of him, but in his
heart he knew that the one man he needed to share it with was
up there in the lead, wearing *his* shako.

Harry smiled, the mood past. After today nothing might
matter any more.

The last part of the journey took longer than expected, and by
the time Blackwood was satisfied they were close enough, the
sky seemed too bright for any hope of surprise. With
Sergeant Quintin breathing heavily behind him, he crawled
through the treacherous gorse and dried grass to make sure
each of his men was in position.

'What d'you think, Sergeant?'

Quintin had already discarded his shako and leaned on his

elbows as he scanned the river below their hiding-place. In the weak daylight it looked dirty yellow, the sluggish current moving idly through long reeds and around sand-bars as it continued towards the sea. In the protective arm of a bend stood the mission. A collection of crude huts and one central building which was larger but no less spartan than the others.

Blackwood waited while Quintin, the old campaigner, took stock of the situation. There was no sign of movement, nor of smoke from cooking fires. He shivered and felt the hair rise on his neck. Maybe they had already been seen and were surrounded, and at any second a spear might plunge into his back. He recalled with stark clarity what old Tom Fenwick had told him about the mutilation which had been done to his companions and felt the bile rise in his throat.

Quintin said slowly, 'There should be some natives at the mission, sir. But there's nobody, as far as I can make out.'

Blackwood swallowed. 'Very well. Two men with me. You stay here with the others.' Their eyes met and he added, 'If it's a trap, get out while you can. Lieutenant Blackwood and his two marksmen will cover you.'

He looked at the tangle of trees and creeper. Harry would be up there by now. Did he realize he had been sent with Jones and Frazier to keep him safe if things went wrong? Safe? Even the word was a mockery here.

Blackwood listened to the disturbed squawking of birds, or were they humans signalling to one another, preparing an ambush.

He got to his knees and examined his pistol. Smithett was ready to go with him, his face grim and strained. Another private, named Bell, a man almost legendary for his skills in brawls and hand to hand fighting alike, was the second one.

Quintin whispered, 'Pass the word. Be ready to fire.'

Blackwood nodded to Bell. 'To your left.'

Then, very slowly, crouching and hopping like frogs, they moved down the slope towards the huts. As they drew closer Blackwood felt a sense of apprehension and dread. They were too late. It was a dead place.

Bell dropped on one knee and held up his hand while he gripped his musket and bayonet firmly with the other.

Blackwood wormed his way among the scrub, unaware of the scrapes and cuts on his hands and face.

Bell whispered, 'Here, sir.' He did not need to explain further.

A man sat propped against some kindling wood, a floppy straw hat over his forehead as if to protect his face from the sun. A musket lay across his legs, and there was a wine bottle at his side.

Bell grasped the man's head and levered it back so that Blackwood could see the terrible slash across his throat which ran almost from ear to ear. It must have been swift and instant, for the man's eyes were wide and bulging, brought from his doze to meet an agonizing death.

He had certainly not been a member of the mission. Doubtless one of Lessard's men. Blackwood wiped his mouth with the back of his hand. Whoever had done it had left the musket behind, something more precious in Africa than gold itself. Somebody? He thought of his brother's explanation and wondered. Maybe he had been right, and the black princess had kept her word and had helped in the only way she understood.

Bell hissed, 'Someone's about, sir!'

Blackwood cocked his pistol with great care. He had heard nothing.

Then feet scraped on sand and a figure emerged from the main hut, ducking through the low entrance and then stretching up his arms and emitting a huge yawn. The yawn and the stretch froze as he saw Blackwood and the others. It was a matter of seconds, and yet they all seemed to stand stock still like statues for an eternity.

Blackwood bounded forward and fired, seeing the ball smash through the man's forehead and hurl him against the hut. He was dead before he touched the ground.

He shouted, '*Now!*' and charged for the low entrance, tossing his empty pistol aside as he dragged out his sword and ducked under the crude thatch.

The world exploded in his face in a livid flash and he was momentarily blinded, but aware the shot had missed him and had hit Bell who was immediately behind him.

Vague shadows swayed about him and he felt the pain in his wrist and arm as his blade cut through muscle and bone and then slashed hard against another.

A figure blotted out the light from the entrance but fell back inside gasping, propelled by the thrust of Smithett's bayonet which had taken him in the stomach.

Smithett finished it with a second lunge and then loped across to join Blackwood in the centre of the mud floor.

Blackwood ignored the two men he had just cut down and hurried to the hut's one other occupant. The girl lay against some old bedding and broken cases, her hands and ankles pinioned, her mouth cruelly gagged with a neckerchief. Her clothing had been ripped open almost to the waist, so that her bared breasts shone in the filtered daylight, moving painfully as she stared up at him in a mixture of terror and shocked disbelief.

Blackwood dropped down beside her and pulled her torn dress together across her breasts, feeling her eyes watching his every move.

'Fetch Sergeant Quintin and help Bell.'

Smithett glanced at the two groaning figures by the wall. 'Bell's done for, sir.' Then he hurried away.

Blackwood removed the gag with great care and held her shoulders as she gasped and choked, ashamed in spite of her suffering that he should watch her vomit on to the floor.

He had to use a knife to cut her bonds, and he felt her cringe as he massaged the bruised skin where they had bitten into her. They must have made her suffer. It was a wonder she was not driven mad by what she had seen and endured here.

She fell, breathing fast, against him, her eyes hidden by the cascade of hair across her face.

Outside the hut there was the sound of order and discipline as Quintin and the others arrived. It would not last for long, but the moment was precious to Blackwood as he held her, saying nothing, while he waited for her breathing to recover.

Then she said in a small voice, 'I can't believe it. You of all people.'

One hand moved up to touch her throat and breast and she turned away as some terrible memory was reborn.

He said, 'We came as fast as we could.' He could feel her sobbing, each beat driving against him as if he was sharing her pain. 'Now we must leave.'

He glanced up as Quintin stooped through the door. 'Two natives dead round the back, sir. Nobody else except . . .' He looked at the girl.

She said huskily, 'They took my father. He's done so much for the people here.'

Blackwood said, 'Smithett, come here. Look after this lady.' He released her shoulders and saw the tears making lines on her dusty face. 'Don't leave her.'

Outside the sunlight was brighter but seemed without warmth.

Quintin said heavily, 'They'd pegged 'im out by the river while 'e was still alive. There must be crocodiles round 'ere. There ain't much of 'im to bury.'

Blackwood leaned on his sword and closed his eyes tightly for several seconds.

'Must have happened recently.'

Quintin nodded. 'They came by boat. I found marks on the sand. The people at the mission must 'ave known 'em, or seen no reason to be afraid. There's no sign of a fight. It must 'ave bin over in minutes.' He spat out the words, 'The murderin' bastards!'

'That girl is in no state to walk. Make a litter. We must get away from here before any of Zwide's people find us.'

He ducked into the hut and waited for Smithett to move away.

He said, 'It's time to go, Miss Seymour. We've a hard march to reach the others. Then you'll be safe.' He looked around the hut at the upended boxes and chests. 'Is there anything you need?'

She shook her head violently. 'Nothing. I don't want to

touch any of it, ever.' Then in an almost level voice she said, 'My father knew there was trouble. He'd been warned often enough. All his helpers had left. He said he had to stay, *had to*. It was his purpose for being, especially after Mother died. Then a ship came.' She glanced at the low door. She did not seem to see the corpse which had been forced back on Smithett's bayonet. It was as if she saw the ship in the river.

Blackwood held her tightly, knowing the sudden calm could not last.

'I can remember what Father said.' Her voice shook. ' "It's the Navy, Davern. That young lieutenant who is always coming here to warn me." ' She turned and looked at Blackwood, her eyes in deep shadow. 'But it was not the Navy. It was men like those over there, like the ones who killed the house-boys, and then . . .' She pressed her face into Blackwood's shoulder, '. . . they took my father away . . . I could hear what they were doing to him . . .'

Blackwood tightened his grip around her as the sobs returned until it felt as if her body would break.

The vessel must have been the missing armed schooner *Kingsmill* which Slade had spoken of a million years ago. A young lieutenant and probably a couple of master's mates. The crew would likely have been made up of recruited natives, a lot of local vessels used Kroo seamen, usually reliable, but no match for this kind of thing.

'Now I'm going to ask you to stand.' Blackwood got to his feet but kept a firm hold of her hand. She shook her head and tried to pull away but he insisted, 'Please. For me. Will you try?'

Very slowly and carefully Blackwood helped her to rise and then steadied her until she was able to face him again.

She said in a voice so small he could barely hear, 'The last time we met I was rude and hurtful to you.' Then she began to weep uncontrollably and did not resist as he held her against his body as if to shield her from her suffering.

Sergeant Quintin re-entered the hut and said, 'Ready, sir.'

Blackwood looked at him across the girl's head. Quintin was carrying a shovel.

'Very well, we're coming.'

Quintin glanced coldly at the two moaning figures. 'Shall I do for 'em, sir?' He might have been discussing chickens for the pot.

Blackwood felt the girl go rigid against him as some part of her listened to what was happening.

'No. Leave them. A doctor could have helped. They can think about that.'

He guided the girl out into the sunlight where the handful of marines waited and watched in silence. Blackwood noticed a mound of sand and rocks by some trees, a crude cross with Bell's shako on the top of it. Another familiar face and voice wiped away.

One of the Rocke twins helped to break the tension. 'Litter's roight 'ere, Missy.' Whichever twin it was, his round Somerset dialect seemed to help.

Smithett and Quintin lifted the girl on to the litter as if she was a piece of delicate porcelain, and as she tried to hold her torn dress together her eyes remained fixed on the pathetic mound they were leaving behind.

Quintin said roughly, 'I took care of yer dad meself, Miss. 'E's safe enough now.'

Blackwood accepted a reloaded pistol from Smithett and sheathed his sword.

What a sight we must look. Not a bit like the fierce-eyed veterans in his grandfather's paintings at Hawks Hill. The lines of scarlet coats, the streaming flags, and not even a whisker out of place.

'Ackland, take the point.'

In single file, with the litter in the middle of their little force, they trudged back into the cover of the bush. At the prescribed place, Harry, with Jones and Frazier, joined them, and together they continued towards the other river.

When they were well clear of the mission Harry dropped back to walk beside his half-brother. He had not asked about the doctor who had been left for the crocodiles, nor even about Private Bell. The faces of the others and the presence of the exhausted girl on the litter spoke more than words.

He said, 'You were being watched, sir, did you know that?'

Blackwood looked at him. '*Watched?*'

'A hundred or so warriors were on the next hill to ours. Armed to the teeth. But they did nothing. They just stood and waited.'

Blackwood removed his borrowed shako and returned it to Harry. 'It seems you were right about the princess and I was wrong. She kept to the bargain, otherwise we'd all be dead.'

Harry glanced back at the litter. 'I'm really glad about her.' He looked at his half-brother's strained profile. 'For your sake too.'

Blackwood quickened his pace. 'Don't talk such damned rubbish, and get up front with Ackland.'

But in his heart he was pleased. It was hopeless, just as it was dangerous to fantasize at moments like these. They were to all intents and purposes fighting a war. Small, local and unheard of in Britain, but just as deadly as the grander fields of battle.

He turned to look at the girl as if to reassure himself it was not a dream and saw her watching him as the litter swayed between the two tall brothers.

Could she ever forget what had happened to her? Would she find some small part in her life which he might somehow share?

He heard Quintin rasp, 'Watch where yer walkin', Private Frazier! Yer a *marine*, remember?'

Blackwood sighed. That just about summed it up.

12

'Up the Royals!'

Major Rupert Fynmore sat on an upturned ration box and nodded impatiently.

'What shape is Sir Geoffrey's niece in? Must have been a terrible ordeal for her.'

Blackwood wiped his face with a filthy handkerchief. After the return march through the bush and the constant threat of being attacked, even Fynmore's brusque manner seemed like a relief.

As his small, weary party had scrambled down to this same river-bank he had left just three days earlier he had seen their step smarten, the air of defiance and something akin to pride as they had carried the crude litter to the boats.

Nothing had changed as far as he could see. A few marines were scattered among the rocks and others sat or lay in the shelter of the bank while they waited for orders.

Some more seamen had joined the landing party, and he saw Lieutenant Ashley-Chute moving among them as they loaded their weapons under the watchful eyes of their petty officers.

Blackwood said, 'Miss Seymour was wonderful. I can't imagine what she's been through!'

Fynmore's sharp eyes watched him curiously. 'Raped, d'you suppose?'

Blackwood looked away, his thoughts laid bare by Fynmore's brutal reality.

'No. I think Lessard had given his men certain instructions.'

Fynmore's mind had already moved on. It was no longer his responsibility.

'And you believe the schooner *Kingsmill* was responsible. That, more to the point, she's up there round the bend in the river?'

'Yes, sir. I think she must have entered the river just ahead of us.'

He watched his words sink in, but he was thinking of the moment when Lessard's long-boat had rounded the bend and confronted Netten's launch bows on. King Zwide's territory had been Lessard's haven. Now it could be a trap, provided Fynmore acted without any more delay.

Blackwood asked, 'Is there any word from the admiral?'

Again he felt Fynmore's cool scrutiny. It made him feel unclean and dishevelled. In contrast, the neat, sandy-haired major could have just come from a parade-ground.

'He ordered me to wait your return, until tomorrow anyway.' He gave his lopsided smile. 'I sent word to *Audacious* as soon as our pickets reported your approach. We'll just have to be patient.' He flinched as a crack echoed across the hillside and a bullet kicked into hard ground. He said irritably, 'We've had a few casualties because of those bloody sharpshooters!'

Blackwood looked at the ridge where Quartermain's platoon had charged among the enemy, where one marine had told his friend to leave him before he had died. Fynmore had kept his word and had withdrawn all his men from the high ground. A good marksman like Frazier could mark down an army from there.

But now it did not seem to matter. He tried to put it down to exhaustion, to the relief of getting his men safely back here. But in his mind he could see the girl being carried swiftly to one of the boats with Slade's agent, Mr Patterson, watching over her like a guard dog.

She was probably already aboard the flagship and would remember little of their flight through the bush. She had been barely conscious for most of the time and seemingly unaware of what was happening.

Fynmore remarked, 'The gunboat is here, by the way.' He regarded Blackwood calmly. 'The admiral will send her up to us shortly.' He compressed his lips into a tight smile. 'Not much choice really. The wind has veered. Nothing else can stand inshore.' It seemed to amuse him greatly.

Crack. Another shot echoed among the rocks and a sailor shouted angrily at the invisible marksman.

Fynmore said, 'And that black woman, the er, princess, you believe she called off the hounds?'

'Yes. No doubt about it. We were tracked all the way. They could have swamped us any time had they wanted to.'

Fynmore looked up as one of the lieutenants hurried towards him.

'Well, Mr Shephard?'

The lieutenant swallowed hard. 'Mr Heighway's pickets have sighted the gunboat, sir.'

But Fynmore glanced at him accusingly. 'Do up that button, sir! You are supposed to set an example to the men!' He calmed himself with an effort. 'Send a runner to Mr Quartermain's section. He knows what to do.'

Blackwood saw the neat major in another light. He was about to mount an attack, the method and the outcome of which were doubtful to say the least. And yet he could still find strength from petty detail, if only to cover his poor eyesight.

A finely-pitched whistle floated up the river and several birds rose flapping and screeching from among some reeds. The gunboat's siren was no match for Tobin's *Satyr*.

Minutes dragged by and eventually the small, shallow-draft gunboat, gushing smoke from a stick-like funnel, nosed around the first bend where everything had first started to go wrong.

After *Satyr*'s impressive size and raked bow, the *Norseman* seemed little more than a platform suspended between two thrashing paddles. Blackwood watched her approach, thinking of her two mortars and solitary six-pounder, hardly a match for those well-sited cannon. Unless she could get into a suitable position before she was severely mauled.

Several of the marines raised an ironic cheer as the gun-boat's anchor cable rattled into the swirling water and she came to rest beneath a cloud of dense black smoke.

Fynmore snapped, 'My compliments to *Norseman*'s commander, and would he join me with alacrity.'

As a runner scampered away he turned to Blackwood again.

'This is the plan. *Norseman* will proceed up river followed by six boats to carry *Audacious*'s landing party. Mr Ashley-Chute will command the boats. As soon as action is joined I want you to lead a platoon ashore from the gunboat to harass the enemy's rear. The enemy can do one of two things, fall back to avoid being cut off from Zwide's stronghold or try to come this way, in which case the remaining marines will advance on them from here.'

He tugged down his impeccable coatee but was obviously awaiting Blackwood's reaction.

Blackwood said slowly, 'Unless we can get them to withdraw and take their cannon with them we shall be in for a hard fight.'

What was the point of reminding this infuriating man that had he left Quartermain's men on the ridge they could have attacked the battery from both sides at once. If he did not realize the fact, he soon would.

Lieutenant Heighway came panting up the slope, his face wet from hurrying between the sections of hidden marines.

'Sir!' He halted, gasping for breath.

Shipboard life had taken a hard toll on one so young, Blackwood thought. Heighway was not much older than Harry.

Fynmore scowled, 'Yes?'

'The admiral is here, sir!'

'*What?*' Fynmore jerked to his feet and adjusted his chin strap carefully. 'In a *steam* vessel?'

Round the side of the hill, accompanied by a sunburned officer who was obviously the gunboat's commander, the familiar shape of Sir James Ashley-Chute marched towards

Fynmore's command post, his hands behind him, his hat tilted at a rakish angle. Following at a discreet distance was Pelham, his flag-lieutenant.

'God in heaven, Major, what is going on here, a damned blood-bath?' He glanced briefly at Blackwood. 'You are untidy, sir, a spectacle!'

Fynmore stammered, ' 'Pon my word, Sir James, I didn't expect you . . .'

'I don't want a guard of honour, or one of your damned ceremonials, Major, I want *action*! I'll not have my squadron made a laughing-stock, tied down by a handful of bandits!'

Blackwood watched him as he worked himself into a white-hot rage. It was an act, and Blackwood had seen it many times, but it was always impressive. This tiny, deformed figure, long-armed and fierce-eyed, seemed to have the power of ten men. As his bright epaulettes bounced up and down in time with his words Fynmore seemed to wilt under the admiral's wrath.

Ashley-Chute shouted, 'Otherwise d'you imagine for a single second that I'd have set foot on that scruffy, *miserable object*?'

The *Norseman*'s commander said, 'She's a fine little ship, sir.'

'Hold your impertinence, sir!' The admiral was enjoying his anger. 'Begin the attack at once!'

Fynmore looked uncomfortably at Blackwood. 'Carry on, if you please. Signal when you are ready.'

Blackwood turned away and then heard Ashley-Chute shriek, '*What* did you say, Major? The *Kingsmill*?'

Blackwood glanced at Colour-Sergeant M'Crystal who had appeared as if by magic. Like Fynmore, he seemed able to remain clean and smart no matter what was happening.

He grinned broadly, 'We were all right glad to see you safely back with the poor lass, sir. Do you have orders for me?'

Blackwood shaded his eyes to look at the ridge. It would all depend on the gunboat, and the admiral knew it even if he would never admit such a thing.

He turned as the sunburned officer strode after him and said, 'I'm told I am to take a platoon aboard.' He could not restrain himself. 'She's a *fine* ship. I had to tell him, blast his eyes!'

His hurt pride made Blackwood smile. 'I'm Blackwood.' He held out his hand. 'I'm coming with you.'

The lieutenant grinned ruefully, 'I'm Ridley, acting-commander.'

M'Crystal was back again, his red face calm and reassuring. 'All taken care of, sir.' He cast a quick glance as the marines tramped past towards the boats.

Blackwood said, 'But the men who went to the mission with me are among them, Colour-Sergeant, they must still be tired from two forced marches.'

M'Crystal's eyes did not even flicker. 'Exactly what I told Sergeant Quintin. He said, begging your pardon, sir, that if you could do it, so too would they.'

Ridley fell in step beside Blackwood and together they walked down to the water. There had been no more firing for some time, and Blackwood guessed that Lessard's men had observed the gunboat's arrival and were now waiting to see what they intended to do.

Ridley watched the marines scrambling into the boats. 'A lot of men could die if things go wrong.'

Blackwood wiped his eyes and throat. 'A lot have already. So let's get started, shall we?'

Smithett, who was close behind him, bared his teeth in a mournful grin. The captain had put *him* in his place and no mistake.

'Shove off forrard!' The boat's coxswain held up his fist. 'As you were! Belay that order!' He watched despairingly as the marine second lieutenant ran the last few feet and vaulted into the boat.

Blackwood regarded his half-brother and waited for an explanation.

Harry took a deep breath as the boat gathered way. 'Major Fynmore ordered me to liaise between both detachments once we have landed, sir.' He beamed under Blackwood's gaze. 'And of course, sir, you may need the use of my hat again?'

Blackwood looked at the bustling activity in the other boats as the blue-jackets swarmed aboard with their weapons and prepared to follow astern. Each boat mounted a bow-gun, and there was a lieutenant in command of each craft. Both flagship and frigate must have been stripped of everyone except for midshipmen and ancient warrant officers, he thought. As well they might. It was not merely impatience which had brought Monkey ashore in a hated steam vessel. He knew better than anyone that his reputation was at stake. He wondered how Captain Ackworthy was feeling about it. Sir Geoffrey's shocked and terrified niece in his care, the flagship denuded of lieutenants and a large part of her complement, all might be compensated in his eyes just by getting rid of his admiral for a few hours.

It was barely a few feet to climb aboard the gunboat and in no time the restricted upper deck seemed filled with marines and their weapons.

Blackwood joined the *Norseman*'s commander by the wheel and then he turned to face his brother.

'Report to Mr Quartermain, he is second in command. Then join M'Crystal down aft.'

Harry faced him stubbornly. 'Out of danger, you mean? Like the hill at the mission. I'm not a child, Philip, not any more.'

Blackwood smiled grimly. 'Just do as I tell you.'

Harry touched his hat. 'Yes, *sir*.'

Clank . . . clank . . . clank . . . the anchor cable was already hove short. Somewhere below his feet a bell clanged and the two motionless paddles began to revolve, slowly at first, and then as the anchor rose dripping from the river with ever increasing power. Coal dust gritted between his teeth, and he could feel the hot air from the boiler-room like wind off a desert.

Commander Ridley was calling orders to his helmsmen and quartermaster as the gunboat forged out into deeper water, and Blackwood saw the two mortars were already manned and pointing their fat snouts towards the shore. Quartermain seemed to have forgotten his first nervousness and with the prospect of more action was giving separate instructions to the sergeants and corporals who would lead the attack.

'Mr Pooley! Slow ahead, if you please, or we shall leave the boats too far astern!'

Blackwood watched the paddles thrashing at the water. They were not massively heavy like *Satyr*'s, but appeared to tread delicately on the surface like the legs of a gnat.

But to Ridley, her young commander, she was everything, greater possibly even than *Audacious* was to Ackworthy.

There was a new crispness in Ridley's tone as he called to his second in command, 'She moves well, Mr Pooley.' Their eyes met. 'Hoist battle ensigns, if you please.'

The gunboat's wash disturbed some thick reeds and Blackwood saw part of a shattered boat, mercifully capsized among them. Perhaps Netten and his terrible face was still trapped inside, or maybe, like the girl's dead father, had already been devoured by crocodiles.

He raised his eyes as the White Ensigns broke from *Norseman*'s two small masts, and tried to recognize his own feelings at this particular moment. Death or glory, Fynmore had said, too much pride.

He looked again at his men as they took their positions beneath the gunboat's bulwark.

I am proud of them at least.

Smithett leaned forward. 'Sir?'

'Nothing.' Blackwood smiled tightly. He had not realized he had spoken aloud.

Then he thought of the girl who was aboard the flagship, protected now and yet more vulnerable to the eyes and unspoken questions. She would soon forget him, perhaps she had erased him already from her tortured mind, if only to save her sanity. Sir Geoffrey Slade would do his best to shield her, she . . . his thoughts came to a dead stop as a seaman shouted, '*Hill*, starboard bow, sir! *Enemy in sight!*'

*

'Bring her round two points to starboard, Mr Pooley!' Ridley had to shout as two of the concealed cannon banged out from the far end of the ridge. 'Keep as close to the shore as you can.'

He turned, squinting in the noon sunlight as twin waterspouts shot skywards on the far bank. He knew the cannon had no chance of hitting the gunboat as yet. They were too high on the ridge and probably protected by earthworks to make them invisible.

Blackwood also watched the fall of shot. The river was deep and powerful for the most part with occasional sand-bars and swaying reeds to betray the other dangers. It must have taken hundreds of King Zwide's people to haul and manhandle those massive guns up to the ridge. Was he there too, watching the approaching gunboat perhaps, or with his daughter who had spared their lives, even traded her own for Davern Seymour's?

The gunners would know they could not depress their muzzles enough to straddle *Norseman*'s bustling approach. They were probably firing to build up their own morale and to warn off the attackers at the same time.

There was a solitary explosion and a great gout of flame and blasted bushes from the opposite bank. M'Crystal had been right the first time. Three large cannon backed up an army of killers who had nothing to lose but their lives. In battle or on Her Majesty's gibbets, it would make no odds to them.

He glanced along the crouching section of marines, their muskets protruding over the bulwarks and some makeshift sandbags like uneven teeth. Lieutenant Quartermain, his sword unsheathed, a bugler, a mere child, beside him. Sergeant Quintin, chewing on his chin strap as he watched his men and the nearest paddle as it thrashed up the spray like rain.

Blackwood said, 'That's where the launch was hit. Right on the bend.'

Ridley lowered his telescope and grunted. 'Mr Pooley, pass the word to engage the moment we are up to that cairn of rocks!' To Blackwood he added, 'I have two boats towing astern for your men. I'll do what I can to give you covering fire.'

Two more bangs heralded another fall of shot. Water rose and fell languidly, clear of the other bank this time.

A midshipman wrote busily on a slate and hung it near the wheel. Would anyone ever read what he had recorded, Blackwood wondered? He thought of Midshipman Ward who had died trying to protect the black princess, the way she had held him with apparent tenderness as his blood had fallen on her.

Ridley said abruptly, 'The other boats can act on their own for a while. Mr Pooley, tell the Chief to give me full speed ahead!'

The slender paddles churned at the river and a long wash rolled away to rock the nearest boats and break across the bank like a small wave.

It was a tense yet exciting moment, the low hull shaking as if to fall apart, the officers and seamen standing about their weapons more like spectators than people about to fight.

Blackwood heard a solitary bang and waited as the shot fanned above the foremast and burst in the water well abeam. He could picture the gunners on the ridge, working with crude tackle and handspikes to train their weapons towards the small, thrashing vessel below them.

Some of the seamen were waving their hats and cheering, it was the madness which no one seemed able to control.

Both mortars were squatting on their mountings, and Blackwood saw *Norseman*'s gunner gesturing to his men to adjust their elevation so that they would not be caught out when the order to fire was given.

Blackwood tried to ignore the preparations on the crowded deck, and looked instead at the oncoming bend in the river where Lessard's long-boat had dropped a stream-anchor.

Soon now. Very soon. He glanced astern and saw the flotilla of boats pulling strongly up river, their work made even harder by the armed blue-jackets who were packed in the hulls like beans in a box.

Bang! Blackwood flinched as the sunlight shimmered in a haze of pale smoke and a massive shot ripped across the water like a sounding dolphin. They had the range, and their guns would bear.

Ridley snapped, 'Closer inshore, Quartermaster! Boatswain's mate! Put a leadsman in the chains immediately!' He blinked as two shots roared down from the ridge and hurled shredded water high over the forecastle.

A seaman with a lead and line scampered forward to begin sounding as *Norseman* edged even closer to the land. He ducked violently as another shot hammered into the river, the shock of the explosion hitting the hull like a muffled fist.

'Open fire with the mortars!'

The gunner must have been watching his captain like a hawk. Each heavy mortar fired separately, the deck jolting as smoke drifted aft from the black muzzles.

Blackwood thought he saw where the charges exploded, and counted seconds while he tried to gauge the effect of the shots. But the hidden battery crashed out again, the pair first, and moments later the third one. The latter was more to the left, he thought, directly above the bend where the river narrowed.

The gunboat's little six-pounder fired sharply, and some of the younger marines who were peering over their defences at the ridge gasped with alarm and probably imagined they had been hit. Several grinned sheepishly as M'Crystal bellowed, 'Och, who'd want to shoot at *you* then, Private Morrison!'

Around the bend it was another cable or so before the river divided into twin forks. In the centre of one fork Zwide's village was sited perfectly, with only the easterly approach undefended by water. Lessard had chosen well.

Suddenly Blackwood knew that the next shot was going to strike. Sixth sense, fear or instinct, he did not know or care.

'Keep down!'

The crash when it came was violent and terrible and must have hit the hull just forward of the starboard paddle. Blackwood heard it smashing through the deck below as if it would never stop, the splintering destruction of wood and metal which would kill or maim anyone between decks. He realized with a start that he had not even heard the gun which had fired.

'Mortars, Mr Pooley! Mark that one down!'

The starboard mortar recoiled and belched fire like a crouching dragon, the shot tearing through a line of trees and flinging up fronds and stones as it exploded.

Ridley snapped, 'Report damage!'

From forward the leadsman yelled, 'By the mark *two*!'

'Starboard your helm, Quartermaster!' Ridley glanced at Blackwood, his eyes glazed with concentration. 'I know she's shallow, but I don't want her to drive aground!'

Blackwood saw reeds and sand spewing from the paddle nearest the land, and heard someone give a sigh as the gunboat moved out a few more yards.

'By the mark three!'

Blackwood wiped the dust from his eyes and studied the shore. Time to go soon.

He sought out the lieutenant and shouted, 'First section aft, Mr Quartermain!'

The marines hurried towards the quarterdeck, their bodies bent almost double as they made their way to the boats which were towing astern.

Ridley said between his teeth, 'That overhang will offer some cover. I'll reduce to dead slow.' He raised his telescope again as both mortars fired together. 'I wish you luck.'

Blackwood nodded to Sergeant Quintin and another section came pounding aft, eyes averted as a shot tore overhead and brought down some signal halliards like broken creeper.

'First boat loaded, sir!'

Blackwood turned and saw Harry staring at him through the drifting smoke. His eyes were wide with excitement and strain, but his voice was steady.

'Very well, I want – '

He cringed down, pulling Harry with him, as the deck bucked wildly and threw splintered planks and gratings like crude arrows.

As the smoke funnelled through a gaping hole in the deck Blackwood imagined he saw the glint of water, but his ears were still ringing from the explosion and he could barely think. Several men had fallen to the hail of deadly splinters, and only the quartermaster still clung to the gunboat's double-wheel, his chest heaving in and out as if he had just been saved from drowning. Pooley, the first lieutenant, sat drooping against the bulwarks, his bloodied fingers grasping a great jagged splinter in his chest, his eyes misting over as his life ran into the scuppers.

One of the mortars had been upended, pinning down one of its crew, and Blackwood saw a man's body picked up by the whirling paddle and then smashed down into the frothing water. Blackwood saw a line snaking after the crushed corpse and guessed it was the leadsman.

As his hearing came back he heard shouted commands, screams and pitiful whimpers as the wounded groped at the legs of Ridley's men as they ran to repair the damage.

The foremast had gone and trailed over the side like a sea-anchor until axes hacked it free.

Ridley rose from the deck and shook himself like an angry dog.

'Slow ahead, Mr Poo . . .' He saw his dead lieutenant and yelled, 'Mr Thomas, take charge there!'

The remaining mortar continued to fire, the gunner unaware that he was splashed with blood from the other crew.

The paddles slowed reluctantly and Blackwood said, 'Come on, Harry. Our turn.' He watched him searchingly. 'All right?'

The young second lieutenant stared past him at the carnage, the strange patterns of blood which seemed to writhe with a life of their own as the churning paddles carried the gunboat forward.

He nodded and said in a forced whisper, 'I – I never thought it would be like this!'

Blackwood gripped his arm. He understood exactly how Harry felt. But there was no more time.

He heard himself explain, 'You wanted to know what it was like! Now *get down aft* with the other boat!' He pushed him roughly. 'They'll be looking to you today!'

He tore his eyes away as Harry lurched after the other marines. He wanted to keep him at his side, to make him understand. The thoughts surged through his mind in distorted confusion.

It was no use. Blackwood looked at Ridley. 'We'll do our best!'

He remembered the burly able seaman grinning at him and shouting, '*Up the Royals!*' The next instant he was staring at the deck, his cheek bleeding on the planking where he had been hurled by an explosion he had not heard. Wreckage and splinters were falling across the deck and splashing outboard to add to the turmoil. There were more cries and yells, and the hull seemed to be tilting right over so that for a moment he imagined they were sinking. A crazy thought shone through his cringing mind so that he wanted to laugh. They would sink in the shallows anyway, the dead leadsman had proved as much. His body convulsed violently and he thought he was going to vomit. He could barely move, as if he was pinioned to the deck.

Slowly and fearfully he tested each limb in turn, but apart from the raw pain of his wounded leg he felt nothing. He tried to lever himself up, his lungs rebelling against the smoke and stench of burned powder.

'Damn you, Fynmore!' The words were torn from him. '*Damn you to bloody hell!*'

He felt someone gripping his shoulder and when he twisted his head saw that it was Harry.

'Help me, Harry!'

His half-brother tore at some smoking timber which had tumbled across the deck like a trap.

'I – I thought you were dead! When you fell, I . . .' He could not continue.

Blackwood staggered to his feet and together they swayed about like a pair of drunks returning to barracks.

The motion was far worse, and there was a grating sound and deep crashes in the hull. There seemed to be blood everywhere, and men and pieces of men were flung about the deck in grisly profusion.

But all Blackwood could think of was Harry's face, the pale lines of tears which were cutting through the grime, like the terrified girl at the mission. It did more to steady him than any other thing, and he knew it.

Smithett rose from the chaos and groped for his musket and his precious bag.

Ridley knelt near the wheel, hands clasped as if in prayer. Even as he saw him, *Norseman*'s commander fell forward on his face and lay still.

Blackwood gasped and retched, and then heard the sound of a pump. Someone was alive and working to save the ship. Blurred figures were groping through the dead and dying, and then Blackwood heard a youthful voice ask, 'What are your orders, sir?'

It was the midshipman who had written a part of history on a slate just before the game had become stark reality.

Blackwood saw the starboard paddle spinning wildly, most of it broken and useless, while the other wheel continued to drive the hull in a wild arc towards the shore.

Through the smoke he could see the boats, the blurred red coats of the landing party which he was supposed to be leading.

Smithett said helpfully, 'There are six of th' lads still aboard, sir.'

'Fetch them.'

He looked at the midshipman. Like Harry, he was near to breaking. *As I was.* 'Now, Mr?'

The youth said huskily, 'Sampson, sir.'

'Well, Mr Sampson, you are in command of this vessel now.' He saw the midshipman's eyes widen. 'Stop the engine, and do what you can to anchor. We shall be wrecked if we are not careful.'

Corporal Jones and the remaining marines pounded past to

help the seamen and a solitary petty officer who were trying to put out a blaze on the forecastle.

The gunfire had stopped as the cannon could no longer be depressed enough to hit them.

Blackwood stared at the destruction and the gruesome litter of death. Instead of success it would be a disaster. The survivors of the attack would be lucky to get back to the original landing-place.

The broken paddle jerked noisily and then fell still, and Blackwood felt the keel quiver as the hull lurched on to a sandy bottom.

Harry was tearing at his collar as if it was choking him.

Blackwood eyed him gravely. 'Ready?'

'For what?'

'Lessard, or whatever his bloody name is, will know by now that his guns have done for *Norseman*.' It was like talking to yourself. There was no understanding on Harry's features. 'If *Kingsmill* is up river, this is the moment she'll break out. She's an agile vessel and has the wind's favour, the same one which is keeping our admiral's ships useless and too far off shore to help.' *Why am I telling him this?* Maybe to convince myself it is worth dying for. 'The *Kingsmill* will carve through our boats and kill every man-jack aboard, unless we act now.'

Harry stared at him. 'What can *we* do?'

Blackwood brushed some splinters and dust from his jacket. He was thinking aloud as he said, 'We can wade ashore here. Fetch Corporal Jones and the others.'

He touched Harry's arm impetuously. 'Of course, you never knew your grandfather, I was forgetting.' He smiled at his incomprehension. 'I know what *he'd* have done. Finish what he had started.'

He gestured to the handful of marines as they mustered by the listing bulwark.

'So then, Master Harry, shall we.'

13

Remember This Day . . .

'Come on, at the double!' M'Crystal's voice carried above the floundering marines better than any bugle. He seized a man who had sprawled headlong within feet of dry land and dragged him bodily from the water. 'Pick up your musket, you silly wee man!'

A few stray shots whined overhead and splashed into the river.

Lieutenant Quartermain dropped to one knee and tugged his telescope from his belt.

It was hard to believe that minutes earlier they had been on *Norseman*'s deck, that they were abandoned now to their own resources.

Blackwood watched the last of the platoon scrambling ashore. The enemy must be surprised at their own success, he thought bitterly. The smoke from the stranded gunboat was swirling across the water in a protective screen. But for it, the marksmen along the ridge would already be shooting down at his men.

'Spread out! Take cover!'

He saw sand spurt from the bank and guessed that someone was already in position and testing the range. He gritted his teeth. They would have to get much nearer to have any chance of success.

Quartermain called, 'There's a deep fold in the land to our left, sir.' He grimaced as a shot smacked down beside him as if to answer him back.

'I see it.'

Blackwood made himself stare up at the ridge as a solitary cannon fired. It was the one which had been sited above the bend. He saw a brief puff of smoke before it was quenched by the gun's crew and sponged out to hide their position.

'Did you mark that, Mr Quartermain?'

The lieutenant wriggled amongst the brush and scattered stones. 'Aye, sir.'

Blackwood lay on his side and peered around at his men. Colour-Sergeant M'Crystal on the flank. Quintin with the fifer, Doak, Frazier and all the rest of them, hunched like animals facing a trap. They would fight well enough, but pinned down and killed piecemeal they would soon lose the will to move forward.

'Stand to!' Blackwood got to his feet, his eyes like slits in the dusty glare. '*Advance!*' He waited for the scattered groups to hurry into some semblance of order. 'Third section, *fire!*'

The muskets crackled as the leading lines of marines charged forward.

Quartermain yelled, 'Second section . . . ! Prepare to fire!'

Blackwood shut the lieutenant from his mind as he ran up the steep incline, his heart pounding as if it would burst from his body.

Shots cracked and whimpered around him and he heard one smack into flesh and bone, a terrible gasp as a marine was hurled on to his back.

Another man, just to his left, spun round and dropped his musket, his hands tearing the air as if to seize the invisible attacker.

Blackwood saw the astonishment in the marine's eyes, as if he was incapable of accepting what was happening to him. He rolled out of sight, and the man nearest to him hesitated, his bayonet drooping as he stared after his dying companion.

'*Forward!* Get up there, damn you!' Blackwood shook his sword at him and the line lurched forward again.

The third section had reloaded, and with M'Crystal bellowing like an enraged bull, charged up the slope, yelling and cheering while they passed through the motionless marines who had just fired, their ramrods rising and falling. Routine, discipline, tradition.

Two more were hit, their cries lost in the crack and hiss of musket fire.

Blackwood blinked the sweat from his eyes. Merciful God, they had reached the fold in the ground. It was very shallow, but as they threw themselves along the far side it felt like a fortress.

'Take aim!'

Blackwood stared at the ridge and thought he saw a figure dart from cover to cover.

'Independent!'

He sensed the aim steadying as they regained their breath. '*Fire!*'

The next section bounced into the depression in a flounder of weapons and limbs.

Quartermain darted him a glance and grinned fiercely. 'Bloody *hell*!'

Blackwood drew a pistol and got to his feet. 'Covering fire!' He gestured with the pistol. 'Second section! *Advance!*'

As they struggled up again a volley of shots raked over the depression and two men were hit simultaneously. The little fifer stared horrified at the nearest one, he had been hit in the face and was making terrible gurgling noises as he drowned in his own blood.

Blackwood shouted, 'Sound the *Charge!*' He punched the boy's arm. '*Now!*'

The bugle responded, and Blackwood marvelled that he had managed to make any sound at all.

Up and running again. Here and there a man fell or crouched down while the next section bounded up in support.

There were fewer shots from the ridge, and Blackwood guessed that Frazier and his companions were keeping the enemy's marksmen pinned down.

'Mr Quartermain's hit!'

Blackwood saw a shadow move from a clump of trees and felt a shot whip past his cheek as one of the marines knelt and fired. The shadow merged with the grass and lay still.

In those brief seconds Blackwood saw Quartermain lying on his back, his teeth bared in agony while he gripped his left shoulder, his clenched fingers the same colour as his uniform.

Harry was running with a mere handful of men on the flank, but they were not in any sort of panic. They wheeled and zigzagged, fired and ran on again, and if anyone was foolish enough to break cover to try and shoot them down he would expose himself to Frazier or one of the others.

They burst into scrub and among trees, the shadows blinding them after the relentless glare. More shots whined through the bars of smoky sunlight and ricocheted from the trees like hornets.

'Take cover!'

Blackwood threw himself down and stared at another darting shape beyond the trees. The pistol jerked in his grasp but the shot went wide.

He heard his men crashing down and reloading, while others attempted to drag their wounded companions into some kind of shelter, no matter how flimsy.

He heard M'Crystal's deep voice calling the roll of survivors and pictured the individual face of each man who answered.

A wounded marine gasped, 'For God's sake shut yer bloody mouth, can't yer?'

M'Crystal's voice found him too. 'I heard that, you miserable man!' He seemed to relent slightly. 'See to him, Corporal Bly!'

Then M'Crystal called, 'Nineteen men fit for duty, sir. I think we've lost six dead.'

Blackwood rolled over and crawled to join Harry who was helping Smithett to cut away the lieutenant's sleeve.

Smithett remarked gloomily, 'Lost a lot er blood, sir.'

Blackwood leaned across the lieutenant and looked at the wound. It had missed the bone, but he was in great pain.

'I – I'm all right, sir.' His eyes flickered and tried to focus on Blackwood's face. 'Not too bad at all really.'

He fainted away and Blackwood said, 'Put a dressing on it.'

He stared round. Already his men were quietening down. The worst sign of all. Accepting it. Waiting for the inevitable.

Quintin said, 'I reckon that cannon is less'n fifty yards over yonder, sir.' He tugged his shako over his eyes. 'Them buggers is waitin' for our boats to appear.'

Blackwood stared at him. Surely Ashley-Chute's son would not continue with the attack now that the gunboat was run ashore and unable to assist? The thought of the little admiral's rage answered the question for him. He would never dare to retreat and face Monkey, not after all this.

Harry said in a whisper, 'Where is the major?'

Blackwood glanced at him, but he was not speaking to anyone. It sounded more like a prayer.

'Makes sense, Sergeant.' He clapped him on the arm. 'A diversion is what we need.'

Quintin sucked at his chin strap. 'I'll go.'

M'Crystal growled, 'Like hell you will, *Sergeant!*'

Blackwood wriggled between them and peered through some entangled thorns. He had not realized they were so near to the end of the ridge. The river was now on his left, he could even see a spiral of smoke from the stranded gunboat below the overhang. *Norseman* with her child-captain was safe only until Lessard's men had driven the marines back to the water again.

He looked down at his hands, filthy and cut in a dozen places. A tiny insect, smaller than a pin's-head, crawled across his fingers and he winced. It had a sting like a wasp. It had been a fatal mistake to bring his men here with no hope of retreat. When the gunboat had been put out of action and her commander killed, he should have broken off the attack altogether. It had been his decision. Pride again? It had cost his men dearly and worse was to come.

He dug his fingers into the hot ground until they were like claws.

Quintin said, 'Funny thing, sir. Them blacks 'ave kept out of it. Far as I can fathom it's only the slavers.' He sucked his teeth as a single shot brought down some leaves from overhead. 'But they're more 'n enough.'

Blackwood stared at him. Trust Quintin to notice what should have been obvious. The bully sergeant, feared, admired and seldom loved, but a real campaigner. Not for Quintin the complications of blame or final responsibility. He was the true professional and thought only of winning if there was still a way out.

Harry whispered, 'It's true.'

Blackwood took his telescope out and thrust it between the thorns. King Zwide was far cleverer than Mdlaka, it seemed. He was determined to see who was going to win before he threw in his weight of warriors.

They must move soon, and before dusk. Fynmore was obviously waiting for more support from the ships anchored off shore. What did he feel at this moment? Despair, or shame for what he had begun without thought for the consequences?

He heard a marine yell at someone to keep his head down and saw a seaman crawling anxiously through the scrub, his head swivelling from left to right as he searched for an officer.

M'Crystal groaned. 'All we need is Jolly Jack, I don't think.'

The seaman fell panting between Blackwood and his half-brother. He gasped, 'I've been sent from the boats, sir. Lieutenant Ashley-Chute's respects, an' 'e intends to refloat *Noreseman* an' tow 'er clear.' He fell silent, his job done, the responsibility safely handed over.

Blackwood looked away to hide his concern. The misshapen lieutenant was already beneath the overhang. *Save the ship*, every sailor's unspoken prayer. The solitary cannon had not fired for some time. He felt the hair rise on his neck.

Lessard's men must already be moving it where it could depress directly on the boats and the stranded *Norseman*.

He looked at the seaman. A plain, homely face you might see any day in a man-of-war or a barracks. He had a round Yorkshire voice. Like Oldcastle.

'My compliments to Mr Ashley-Chute. Tell him he is likely to be attacked at any moment, from above and from upstream.' It would take too long to explain all the dangers, and it was important that this seaman should get it right.

The seaman nodded. 'An' what shall I tell 'im about you, sir?'

'Tell him we are going to attack.'

The seaman hesitated. 'Aye, sir. I'll do that.' He started to crawl away and added, 'Good luck, sir.'

Quintin murmured, 'We'll need all er that, matey!'

Blackwood beckoned to the others. 'We'll attack in two halves. We can't afford anything grander. But it's now or never. I think . . .' he forced out each word, '. . . they're moving the gun. God knows where the other two are, but my guess is they'll be kept in case Major Fynmore's contingent arrives.' He watched their mixed emotions. Quintin's doubt, M'Crystal's grim acceptance and Harry's too-steady stare. He undersood now what it all meant. 'Share out the ammunition between the men. Leave everything else here.'

There was no more time for any of them. And yet it was important they should not leave without a word more.

He said quietly, 'This is a bad place to die, if die we must. But there's more at stake than just us.'

M'Crystal sighed. 'Och, I'm no bothered, sir.' He glanced at his friend. 'Sarnt Quintin will look after me!'

They crawled away and Blackwood felt as if a line had been cut.

Harry asked, 'Ready?'

'Attack from the right when I give the signal. If we fail, you must press on with the attack.' He touched his arm, hating each word. '*Must!*'

Muffled by the overhang he heard the sullen bang of

Norseman's remaining mortar. It could hit nothing from there, but Lieutenant Ashley-Chute was showing that he understood the gamble which the marines were about to take.

Harry was saying, 'Attack from the right.' It was as if he was afraid he might forget at the last moment.

Then he said, 'I'll go and prepare the others.' His voice was quite calm again. 'I shan't let you down, Philip.'

Blackwood smiled. 'Never imagined you would.'

Then he turned and crawled into the dense thicket where the wounded had been dragged for safety. *Safety?*

Blackwood saw the small fifer watching him fearfully and said, 'You'll remain here with the wounded. Private Ackland has a bugle.'

He watched the boy's desperation give way to pitiful relief.

He added, 'If we lose today, you must get back to Major Fynmore.' He stumbled deeper into the thicket, grateful to be spared the boy's gratitude.

A wounded marine peered up at him and tried to wriggle into a sitting position. Blackwood noticed his musket was beside him, his bullets and caps within easy reach.

'All right, Collins?'

The man tried again to sit up. He had been shot in the side, how badly nobody had found time to discover.

'Yew'm not leavin' us, sir?'

More time was running out like sand from a glass. Blackwood patted his arm.

'No. We're going in to the attack. You rest easy.'

The man fell back and stared at the sky through the overhanging trees.

'Wish I was with you . . .' He peered round wildly, all his pain and despair seemingly gone as he yelled, 'Come on, lads! *Load! Present! Fire!*' His voice trailed away as he sank again into unconsciousness.

Corporal Bly looked down at him. 'Beggin' yer pardon, sir, but we're ready to move off.' He bent over and felt the other marine's chest. 'God's teeth, another good one gone.'

He looked at Blackwood, his eyes bleak. 'We'll take a few of them buggers with us, eh, sir?'

Blackwood nodded. 'I'll just speak with Mr Quartermain.'

Bly stared at him. 'Didn't you know, sir? The lieutenant's already gone!'

'*Gone?*' The picture of Quartermain's agonized face, the jagged wound in his shoulder, put a new sharpness to his voice. 'What the hell d'you mean?'

Bly said, 'Clipped on 'is sword and marched out bright as paint, sir.'

Blackwood left the thicket and hurried to find the others.

M'Crystal watched him warily. 'Aye, we know, sir. The lieutenant's gone.'

Blackwood drew his sword and took a pistol from Smithett, glad he had something to grip and so stop his hands from shaking.

Quartermain, a man he barely knew. Driven almost mad by his wound, and yet like the marine who had just died had held on to that one final spark of determination and courage.

He crawled to the last barrier of thorns and rough scrub, his eyes stinging in the glare as he stared straight at the spot where he had seen that tell-tale puff of smoke. Quartermain had realized what they were doing and had offered his own life when he knew he was most needed.

'Frazier! Corporal Jones!'

But they were already kneeling in position, as if they too had known. Even through his reeling thoughts Blackwood realized that Frazier had taken one of the captured rifles and was stroking it as if to pacify it.

'*Gawd!*'

Quintin's sharp exclamation made Blackwood turn towards the far side of the ridge. It was like some terrible dream, a nightmare coming alive even in the brightness of day. Lieutenant Quartermain was marching very stiffly up the slope, his drawn sword in hand, while his other arm hung motionless at his side. The dressing had burst open so in the

distance his bared arm matched his coatee as he headed
purposefully towards the summit.

There was the sudden crack of a musket and Quartermain
halted as if to listen before continuing on his way.

'On your feet!'

Blackwood kept his eyes on the erect lieutenant and knew
the tension around him was stretched like a taut cable.

'Ready, sir!' That was M'Crystal. Even he sounded different.

Crack! The musket's sharp bark echoed over the ground,
and Blackwood held his breath as he saw Quartermain
stagger and almost drop his sword.

Frazier watched only the ridge where the scrub and trees
ended, his eyes unblinking as he cradled the rifle against his
cheek.

The lieutenant had been hit. He could not take another.
And yet he was still marching up the slope, his mouth
opening and shutting as if he was shouting orders to his own
invisible platoon.

Frazier's finger tightened on the trigger. A man's head and
shoulders had appeared over the ridge, and another, then two
more. Frazier could barely stop himself from laughing. They
had their bodies turned away from the marines and were all
looking at the oncoming spectre with the glistening arm.

'Ready, Jonesy?'

Corporal Jones grunted and gripped his musket even
tighter. He heard the crack of muskets on the ridge and saw
Quartermain fall, only to struggle up again, his shako gone,
his head thrown back in torment as he staggered up towards
the group who had left cover to shoot at him. Jones was
sickened by what he saw, the pathetic figure as it fell and this
time did not rise. He hated Frazier in those brief seconds for his
callous acceptance, his interest only in the target and his aim.

Blackwood heard the muskets fire together, the sharper
crack of Frazier's rifle ringing in his ears as he yelled, *'Charge!'*

Then they were bounding up the slope, oblivious to everything but the figures silhouetted against the sky. Two had

fallen dead, and Frazier was already reloading. One of the men was standing by Quartermain, his body twisted round as he realized too late what was happening. Blackwood saw Quartermain's sword strike out at the man, as if it alone was trying to defend its owner.

He forgot everything else as they reached the top of the ridge and he saw the great gun directly below him in a shallow pit. It was surrounded by a litter of tackles and handspikes and there were more figures running from cover as the marines hurled themselves over the top.

Beyond the gun was the fork in the river, and he thought he could see the pointed huts of Zwide's kingdom on the far bank. There were two vessels at anchor, one he guessed was the captured *Kingsmill*. But none of it mattered any more. Blackwood saw a man in ragged white clothing running at him, a pike levelled at his stomach. He stepped aside and parried the pike with his sword and waited for the man to stumble before slashing the blade hard across his neck.

There was no time to reload now, and hand to hand, blade to blade the marines lunged and hacked their way remorselessly to the other side of the ridge. Here and there a red coat was down, and as Blackwood fired his pistol into a man's chest and slashed out at another with his sword he knew it could not last much longer.

Corporal Bly had lost his bayonet and was using his musket like a club. He swung round on loose sand, his mouth wide in a silent scream as a blade darted at his stomach like a steel tongue. Another figure leapt forward and drove a cutlass into his body again and again, until Quintin fought his way through and cut him down beside the dying corporal.

A great blaring bellow echoed and resounded against the ridge and far beyond to Zwide's kingdom.

Tiny pictures flitted through Blackwood's mind as he crossed blades with a tall, swarthy slaver and rocked back on his heels from the man's thrust.

Satyr was here.

Tobin, calm-faced and proud of ship, had come for them.

There was another blare from *Satyr*'s siren, followed immediately by the crash of one of her geat guns.

Blackwood saw the expression on the slaver's face change to apprehension and then hatred as some of the men around him threw down their weapons, the fight already gone out of them like blood.

He parried his blade and their hilts locked. Blackwood gasped as his wounded leg seemed to buckle under him and he felt himself falling.

The siren blared again and the slaver yelled, 'Too late for *you*!'

Blackwood lay on his back and stared at the other man's blade. No matter what happened, they had won. He tensed his body and prayed it would be quick.

There was a single shot and the shadow above him was flung aside like a curtain.

Corporal Jones ran the last few yards and lowered his smoking musket until the point of his bayonet touched the wounded slaver's throat.

Blackwood felt himself being hauled to his feet, the searing pain of his wound making him cry out. *I am alive*.

The wounded slaver gasped, '*Quarter!* In th' name of God!'

Corporal Jones looked around the dazed and bleeding figures and then saw Corporal Bly. They had served together for a long time. Had been made up to corporal together. Had made *Audacious*'s contingent of marines something special.

Jones was a gentle man for the most part and popular with everyone, even Frazier.

He looked straight into the slaver's eyes. 'Quarter, you bastard?'

Blackwood called thickly, 'Stop him, Sergeant!'

Jones leaned on the bayonet and watched the light in the slaver's eyes snuff out, as Bly's must have done.

Quintin pulled him roughly aside and said, 'I didn't see nothin', sir.'

Blackwood looked away and allowed Harry to guide him to the overhang above the *Norseman*. All the seamen on her

deck and in the boats which crowded around her were waving
and cheering, at him, and then at the great thrashing paddles
of Tobin's *Satyr* as she ploughed towards the bend of the
river.

Through a vague mist he saw patches of scarlet on the
frigate's deck and knew she had picked up Fynmore and his
rear-guard on her way up stream.

He said abruptly, 'Take charge of the prisoners, Harry.'
He no longer recognized his own voice. It was thick and
ragged, like his emotions. To Smithett he added, 'Help me
to the lieutenant.'

It was a hundred yards down the slope from the hidden gun
to where Quartermain lay staring at the sky.

Blackwood broke away from Smithett's hands and
stumbled the last few paces on his own. He did not care about
his reopened wound and the pain which grew with each foot of
the way. It was desperately important that Quartermain should
be alive, should know that he alone had carried the day.

Quartermain's eyes flickered and looked up at him.

Blackwood said, 'Get some water, Smithett.' Then he
knelt down and said, 'I just wanted you to know that we took
the battery. All because of you.'

Quartermain was smiling, but Blackwood sensed that he
could not see him.

'So, so glad . . .' He tried to find his sword which had
fallen beside him. 'W – wanted my son to wear this one day
– one day. Now I'll not have one.'

Smithett thrust his flask into Blackwood's hand. ' 'Ere,
sir.'

'Would you send it to my mother? Tell her . . .'

Blackwood held the flask to his lips but saw the water
trickle unheeded across the lieutenant's cheek.

Then he closed Quartermain's eyes and waited for Smithett
to help him to his feet.

I'll tell her, have no fear.

He limped away, resting on Smithett, the lieutenant's
sword under one arm.

Some armed blue-jackets had climbed up from the boats while they had been away and were already herding the prisoners into line and searching them for weapons.

M'Crystal was shouting at the dazed handful of marines as they stared at the chaos around them, as if they no longer understood where they were or what they had done.

'Who d'you think you are? You're more like a bunch of sea-cooks than Royal Marines! Smarten yourselves up, *d'you hear*!'

He realized that Blackwood had returned, and when he swung about to face him Blackwood was shocked to see the hurt and despair in his eyes. He did not recall ever before seeing M'Crystal's guard drop.

The towering colour-sergeant reported hoarsely, 'Ready to move off, *sir*!'

Blackwood released his hold on Smithett's arm. Just as he had needed to see Quartermain before he had died, it was suddenly necessary he should face his men, the survivors.

The fire in his leg was almost unbearable, but he made himself walk along the single rank of men, only vaguely aware of the watching sailors and prisoners, now silent without knowing why.

Blackwood paused at each familiar face. Here and there one tried to smile, others were too stunned to meet his gaze. Jones, Doak, Frazier, and even the Rocke twins were still together.

He saw Harry take half a pace forward and realized he had expected him to fall. Blackwood clenched his jaw. He would not faint. Not yet anyway.

'Stand them at ease, please.' It sounded so formal, so out of place in this arena of death and hate that he needed to blaspheme or weep.

'I just wanted you to know . . .' They were all watching him now, but nothing was coming out right. He tried again. 'There will be other days, some worse than this and for less reason.'

He rested on Quartermain's sword and recalled the man

Jones had killed. But for his swift action with the musket he would be lying dead like Quartermain.

Blackwood continued, 'When that happens, I want you to remember this day with pride, and the friends we left here.' He was getting confused and could not see their faces properly. 'I am proud of each and every one of you.'

M'Crystal hissed, 'The major's here, sir.'

Fynmore's neat figure appeared over the ridge and Blackwood turned in time to see his face stiffen in a mask of disbelief as he saw the corpses and the small group of victors.

Then he strode forward and snapped, 'Well done. I am sorry I did not get here earlier but—'

Harry Blackwood ran from the others and caught his half-brother before he hit the ground. Through his teeth he exclaimed, 'I am sure we all understand, *sir*!'

When he looked up he saw Fynmore's face had gone pale, as if he had just been struck. Without another word the major turned away and, followed by his attendant, vanished down the slope.

A lieutenant from one of the boats hurried across the scorched grass and said, 'I'll have my men do the burials.'

Harry shook his head. 'No. Just get Captain Blackwood to the surgeon, will you.' He picked up Quartermain's stained sword and handed it to the naval officer. 'Take this too.' He looked at M'Crystal's grim features. 'Burial party, if you please, Colour-Sergeant.'

He saw a brief flicker in M'Crystal's eyes. For once he had said the right thing. What Philip would have done. *We take care of our own.*

The pounding in his head was louder and more insistent, and Blackwood had to use something like physical strength to force his eyelids apart. There was a vile taste in his mouth and he guessed he had been sick. He felt sudden terror and groped frantically beneath the sheet for his leg. He sobbed aloud.

There was a cool dressing, not some obscene stump where a leg had once been.

As his senses returned he peered around fearfully as memory after memory flooded through his aching mind. He was in a ship. A steam vessel. Alone in a cabin, but it was too dark to recognize anything. He heard the rumble of machinery, the surge of water against the hull as it frothed astern from the paddles. He thought of the little *Norseman* stranded on the river-bank, men cheering, the cold claws of fear and the wildness of battle.

He tried to recall Fynmore's face, what he had intended to say to him before he had collapsed. But nothing came, and he wondered how long he had been unconscious.

He thought of the girl on the litter, the way she had looked at him, the feverish touch of her skin when he had tried to cover her breasts. He groaned. It was all behind, over.

The door opened and someone stepped carefully over the coaming. Blackwood knew it was Captain Tobin. How did he know?

Tobin said, 'How are you feeling?' He must have smiled in the darkness because his voice changed as he added, 'Yes, you're back in *Satyr*, the same cabin too.'

Blackwood stared at the man's sturdy shadow. 'How long?'

'A week or so. You gave my surgeon a few scares, but you're on the mend now. It will be up to more professional doctors to finish the job.'

'Where are we headed? Freetown?'

Tobin cocked his head as a voice-pipe shrilled in the depths of the hull.

'We're going home. England. You've more than earned it.'

The door closed just as silently as it had opened. Blackwood lay back and stared into the darkness. Home. Hawks Hill. A new beginning.

Once he was able to move about again he would write to Davern Seymour and tell her . . . He smiled ruefully. Tell her what?

He was still thinking of her when he fell into a deep sleep.

14

The Colonel's Lady

Philip Blackwood sat listlessly in a high-backed cane chair and stared at the snow-edged window. It was cold in spite of the stout walls, even for late January, and to Blackwood it felt like the nearness of death.

Instead of showing a steady improvement, Blackwood knew his health and his memory were faulty. Days and places overlapped, and the slow passing of time meant nothing.

He glanced around the room, practical and spartan like the place. The Royal Naval Hospital at Haslar. At night, if he was allowed up, he could see the lights of ships in the outlet to Portsmouth Harbour, the one remaining link with a life which seemed to have passed him by.

The surgeons had explained that his wound had been badly infected, that he had been fortunate not to lose the leg. He had suffered some kind of fever too, which in turn had blunted his memory. When Tobin had told him that *Satyr* was on passage to England, he had failed to mention that Blackwood had been desperately ill and the ship had in fact already been at Freetown. And he could remember nothing about it. Blurred images, pain, gentle hands, parts of a dream rather than reality.

In his eagerness to get Blackwood back to England without further delay, Tobin had driven his ship hard. *Satyr* had paid for his haste and was now out there in the dockyard having her engine overhauled and put to rights.

But it had given Blackwood his other link with the outside world. Lieutenant Lascelles had visited him at the hospital whenever he had been spared from his duties. Lascelles had been bursting with news, about the capture of Lessard's base, of the marines' victory against odds which had been far better armed and prepared.

Lessard was dead and would never stand trial after all. Perhaps someone had suspected he would still use his influence and wealth to evade punishment and had carried out his own judgement and execution. It seemed that Lessard had been ready to leave Zwide's anchorage and escape in the larger of the two vessels there. He had probably calculated that the Navy would be more intent on retaking the *Kingsmill* than in capturing the second vessel. The latter had been crammed to the deck beams with slaves, one last profitable cargo before he turned his attention elsewhere, Blackwood thought.

But *Satyr*'s sudden arrival firing her massive guns had put paid to escape. Lieutenant Ashley-Chute had sent a cutting-out party to board both vessels and in minutes it had ended.

Blackwood could vividly recall how a petty officer had warned him not to stand too close to a hold aboard the first slaver, the glittering pattern of white eyes from that stinking prison-ship.

Even as the slavers had flung down their weapons in surrender to the jubilant boarders, Lessard was said to have lost his balance and had fallen headlong into one of the tightly packed holds. Lascelles had described how Lessard had literally been torn to shreds.

Blackwood had had other visitors. The colonel from Forton Barracks who had somehow refrained from reminding him of their last meeting when Blackwood had tried to resign. He was very likely thinking that he would no longer need to resign. In his poor health he would more likely be discharged from the Corps.

Even the port admiral had paid him a visit and had brought a case of wine to mark the occasion. The case had been swiftly removed by a doctor after the admiral's departure.

Blackwood wondered why his father had not come immediately to see him. He had been told there had been regular enquiries from Hawks Hill, but always by courier. Perhaps his father was ill or unable to travel. It was only twenty miles from Hawks Hill to Portsmouth, but the whole country was under a blanket of snow, the worst anyone could remember. There was one good thing, Blackwood thought, they had not sold the old place. Not yet anyway.

The window shivered in a fresh squall and Blackwood turned to look at the framed painting above the bed. It was the Royal Marines crest, the globe and the laurel, and the famous Corps motto, *Per Mare per Terram*, underneath. Painted by a previous inmate, no doubt. How many had this and places like it seen, he wondered? Crippled, diseased, broken survivors of war.

'If I stay here much longer . . .' He stood up violently and prepared to meet the pain. He was sick of his own self-pity and anxiety. He did not have to think back as far as the unknown painter to recall faces he would never see again.

There was a discreet tap at the door and Smithett peered in at him.

Blackwood tried to stand without revealing the discomfort of his wound. Even Smithett had come to say good-bye. Off to serve another officer, or to make his own way in the ranks. With his mates.

Smithett regarded him mournfully. 'Jus' come from the company tailor, sir. You've lost so much weight I've 'ad to get some of yer tunics taken in like.' He tried to grin but all the lines remained pointing down. 'Can't 'ave the other MOAs sayin' I don't take proper care of me captain, can I?'

'You're *staying* with me?'

Smithett laid a tunic across the bed with great care.

'Course, sir. ' 'O else would want me?' He turned and looked at Blackwood's strained features. ' 'Sides, you got a visitor. She's wiv the 'ead sawbones right now.'

Blackwood stared. 'Visitor? She . . .'

Smithett looked round for somewhere to hang the other items of clothing.

'Yeh. That's right, sir. Yer mother.'

Blackwood sat down and allowed Smithett to prepare him for his visitor.

I am a bloody fool. Who had I expected?

Smithett waited for him to stand again and waited while Blackwood stepped carefully into his trousers. Not near enough to make the officer think he couldn't manage on his own, it was not Smithett's style.

'There, sir.'

Smithett nodded with approval as the red coatee slipped into place. That wily tailor had done a fair job, he concluded. Worth the rum he had 'won' for him.

'I never really thanked you for all you did . . .'

Smithett shrugged to hide his discomfort. Intolerant, impatient, bad-tempered officers he could accept. Blackwood's distress was something else.

He said, 'Somethin'll work out, sir. There'll be another war somewhere an' the Royals will be expected to put things shipshape again, you see, sir.'

'You're probably right. I wish to God we were with young Harry right now. Today's his birthday.'

Smithett flicked a brush across his shoulders and gave a secret smile. If the captain knew just half of what that young bugger had been up to he'd soon be his old self again.

He was very tempted, but at that moment the door was thrust open and the senior surgeon and his assistant entered the room.

But for once Blackwood was not looking at their faces to try and discover what would happen to him. Framed between them, his stepmother seemed to make the room empty, to reduce the surgeons to nothing. She had always been a beautiful woman, even though he had been unprepared to accept it. Now, set against the drab and austere surroundings, she was elegant, even regal.

Her hair was like rich chestnut and piled on top of her head to set off her perfect oval face and slender neck. Her skin was white, like marble, and she was completely composed, like an actress about to mount the stage.

In those few seconds Blackwood felt her steady gaze as it moved over him, missing nothing. *The colonel's lady.* How well it fitted her.

'Well, Philip, and what have you been up to?'

Her voice was exactly as he remembered it. Level and cool, like the woman, without any outward warmth. He doubted if she had reached her fortieth birthday but could not be sure, and was suddenly angry that he had not learned more about her.

He said, 'Sorry, I'm a bit of a mess.'

It came out like a complaining child. She did that to you.

The senior surgeon said breezily, 'Out of danger now, Ma'am! Captain Blackwood has inspired all of us.'

Her eyes, which were tawny brown like Harry's, turned towards him.

'In my opinion he would be better served in more suitable surroundings. My carriage is here.' She held up one hand and added in the same confident tone, '*You* must be Smithett.'

Smithett bobbed. 'Aye, Ma'am, that I am.'

'Fetch my groom and see to things, Smithett.'

Then she moved across the room and laid a gloved hand on Blackwood's arm.

He could smell her perfume and wanted to hold her, to hide his face on her perfect neck and tell her everything. What it had been like. About Harry and the others.

She said quietly, 'Just in time, I think.'

Blackwood looked at her and tried to smile. 'I'm so sorry. I was thinking only of myself. How are you and . . .'

But she had turned away and was giving curt instructions to her groom, a man Blackwood had not seen before.

To the senior surgeon she said, 'I will send news to you of my own doctor's opinion.'

Blackwood expected the surgeon to explode but the magic had already taken effect.

'Of course, Ma'am. My pleasure, Ma'am.'

She slipped her hand through Blackwood's arm, and when a hospital orderly hurried forward with a walking stick she said in the same calm voice, 'Captain Blackwood is a gallant officer. He is *not* an invalid.' She gave the surgeon a cool stare. 'Any more.'

Through the same corridors which Blackwood had seen so often in what felt like a century, along which he had been wheeled for examination, where he had been probed and prodded, discussed as if he were already dead, this too was like a dream.

Once he staggered and winced as the pain returned and he felt her grasp tighten on his arm.

'Just a few more steps, Philip. I'll not have you fall to suit their tiny brains.'

Outside the main entrance it was like pure ice, and yet it seemed to revive Blackwood. The crisp snow, the grey stones, the bracing wind from the Solent. In a moment he would wake up. The same room. The picture above the bed.

She said, 'Get inside, Philip, out of this wind.'

Blackwood stood beside the coach. Despite the thick patterns of slush on its side and door he saw it was a very elegant vehicle, and, like the groom, new.

He said, 'After you. I'm not an invalid now. You said so back there.'

She raised the hem of her gown and put a hand on his shoulder to steady herself before climbing into the coach.

'Well now, I almost forgot.' She lowered her head and waited for him to kiss her cheek. 'You may call me Marguerite if you wish.'

Blackwood followed her, his pain forgotten. Her cheek had been like ice too.

She tapped the window. 'Drive on, Lloyd. I'm not paying for horses to waste time and eat their heads off!'

Smithett climbed up beside the coachman and pulled a blanket around his knees.

'So that's the colonel's lady, eh?'

The coachman flicked his whip. 'Come on, Wizard! *Easy*,

Comet!' As he hauled on the reins he murmured between his teeth, 'You mind your words, soldier, she could take on your lot single-'anded.'

Smithett settled down and braced his legs against the savage motion. He even found time to wave a casual salute to a shivering group of hospital porters.

He had no idea where Hawks Hill was, nor did he care. Private Jack Smithett, who had drawn his first breath in a London slum, had become *somebody*.

It was getting dark by the time the carriage eventually turned off the road and through the familiar snow-capped gates.

With a start Blackwood realized he must have dozed off several times during the journey, but the sight of the tall, weathered pillars, the gatehouse banked with driven snow, drove the clinging weariness away like a cold wind.

His stepmother had replaced her elegant hat which she had tossed on to the opposite seat and was tying a ribbon beneath her chin while she studied herself in the mirror of her travelling case. She showed no sign of strain or the discomfort of the journey from Haslar, and was examining herself more with satisfaction than anxiety.

She glanced at him and closed the case with a snap.

'Home, Philip.'

Blackwood nodded and wiped one of the carriage windows as the banks of snow and grotesque shapes of trees and bushes rolled past.

He said, 'I'm glad you've decided to stay here.'

'For the present anyway. I've made some changes.' She watched him calmly. 'But they need not concern you. You need rest. You are tired out.'

The carriage swung round in a wide curve and Blackwood saw the broad façade of the main building loom through the snow flurries like a cliff. There were lights in several of the windows which painted yellow reflections on the driveway and churned slush.

Blackwood turned as she put one hand on his sleeve.

'I did not mention it earlier, Philip, but your father has been ill.' She studied his reaction impassively. 'He is over the worst of it. But I wanted to warn you. He had a stroke. He had been fretting about things.'

Blackwood said, 'I guessed as much. He was worried about leaving Hawks Hill. He told me.'

She gave a brief smile. 'Quite.'

The carriage lurched to a halt, and as the snow-covered groom clambered down from the rear and the coachman applied the brake, Smithett jumped on to the driveway and stood stiffly to attention.

She said, 'Help them with the bags, Smithett. The house-keeper has arranged a room for you.' She watched the tall marine curiously. 'Your *quarters*, as you will doubtless call them.'

The double doors at the top of the steps were opened and more light spilled across the mud-stained coach and its steaming horses.

Blackwood watched, fascinated, as his stepmother mounted the steps, her head erect as she entered the stone archway and gave a curt nod to the waiting servants.

They had kept Hawks Hill, but on her terms, Blackwood thought.

There were several unknown faces, and a smell of newness and fresh paint. He glanced into the great hall, which had looked more like an armoury with its collection of ancient weapons and militaria. There were still a few items on display, but they were high up and arranged around the minstrels' gallery in decorative patterns. He could not imagine his father giving permission to do that.

He realized she was watching him as she allowed a maid to remove her travelling cloak and take her hat.

She asked, 'Do you approve?'

Blackwood smiled. She sounded as if she did not really care what he thought, yet somehow he knew it was important to her.

'It's fine. Rather grand.' The heat from one of the blazing fires was making him dizzy again. 'Really.'

She pursed her lips. 'There were times when you did not expect to see it again.' It was a statement. 'There will be a lot of changes in future.'

'I was wondering.' He hesitated as he saw the sudden caution in her eyes. 'About Georgie?'

'Indeed?' She turned aside and examined herself in one of the long mirrors near the entrance. 'Miss Georgina, the little madam, is in Paris. It was decided to send her there to finish her education.' She faced him, composed once more. 'Do her good.'

'So very glad to see you back again, Captain.'

Blackwood turned and tried to hide his dismay as he saw a face which should have been very familiar. Oates, his father's old attendant, orderly, valet and friend. So much had happened since he had last seen him and yet it was barely six months ago. In that time Oates had become an old man, had lost his marine's bearing and was now bent over, his hair almost white.

Blackwood held out his hand. 'I'm grateful to be here, believe me.'

Oates seemed to hesitate and glanced quickly at his colonel's lady before returning Blackwood's handshake. As if he was seeking permission to do so.

Oates studied Blackwood sadly. 'The colonel asked to see you immediately you arrived, sir.'

Blackwood looked at his stepmother. So she had already decided to remove him from Haslar before she had left the house. That must have been early in the day, and yet she looked as if she had just dressed for dinner. Only some drying mud on the hem of her gown gave a hint she had been all the way to Gosport and back.

She met his gaze without flinching. 'Go to him. But don't tire yourself. We've a lot to talk about.'

She turned on her heel, and Blackwood saw the assembled servants part before her as she headed towards the drawing room, her maid hurrying behind her.

Blackwood said, 'Take me to my father. How is he?' He

thought he saw the old man's guard fall into place and persisted, 'I want to know.'

Oates fiddled with his white gloves. 'He's been taken all aback by his illness, sir. He'd been hoping, you see, hoping they'd ask him to return to the Colours.' It was obvious the faithful Oates hated to share his secret, to him it was like a betrayal. 'Now he knows there's no chance. He's finished.'

Oates led the way along the first landing and through a gallery where some of the family portraits had been rehung since his last visit. He caught an impression of watching faces and proud stances. Clouds of battle, ships of the line and prancing horses.

Then Oates opened the doors of the bedroom and Blackwood hurried past him, his mouth suddenly dry as he saw his father sitting by one of the tall windows, a small table and a decanter within easy reach.

He did not turn, and Blackwood guessed he could not do so unassisted.

Blackwood moved around the chair and looked down at him.

'Hello, Father.'

Lieutenant-Colonel Eugene Blackwood, the man who had once commanded Fynmore's father, raised his eyes and withdrew one hand from beneath a blanket.

'You're too thin, boy. Must tell cook to prepare one of your favourites, eh?'

Blackwood sat on a small stool and watched his father's efforts to be as he wanted to be remembered. But it was heartbreaking to see the way his face was set and twisted on one side, to feel the feebleness of his handshake which had been like steel.

'I'm glad you stayed here, Father.'

'Pour some madeira, Philip. Can't reach the damn thing myself.'

Blackwood filled two glasses. Like his father, they had been waiting here.

'Been reading all about your escapades, every deuced

word.' He lifted the glass and examined the wine carefully.
'In a skirmish like that you've always got to think and act
fast. You did damn well to all accounts.' He moved restlessly
in his chair. 'Though from what I've read in the *Gazette* and
The Times you'd imagine Ashley-Chute had done it all on his
own, blast his eyes!' He sank back again, even that small
outburst had weakened him.

Blackwood raised his glass. 'To us, Father.'

But his father looked past him at the snow-dappled window, his eyes sad as he said, 'To the Corps.'

Blackwood watched him and felt disturbed. At any other
time it would have been almost amusing to hear the past
months described as a 'skirmish'. His father saw everything
but a full-scale war as a necessary backwater and nothing
more.

His father added abruptly, 'The papers were full of it. If it
wasn't Ashley-Chute it was that other bloody upstart. Fynmore this and Fynmore that; I think if I see that name again
I'll – I'll . . .'

He broke off and for a few moments seemed barely able to
breathe.

The reports were much as Lascelles had told him in the
hospital, Blackwood thought. It had obviously not fooled his
father.

'Anyway . . .'

His father sounded drowsy, and Blackwood could sense
Oates hovering outside the door like a guardian.

'You've shown them, my boy. They'll never forget the
name of Blackwood in the Corps. Never.' He reached out and
took Blackwood's wrist in his hand. 'They don't need me any
more, but you have a real future. There'll be no more of those
damned "Blue Colonels" blocking promotion, thank God.
There'll be nothing to stop you after this. How was young
Harry?'

Blackwood replied gently, 'He was good, Father. We were
brought close together by what happened.' He watched the
strength going from his father, his head drooping.

'Nothing like a bit of campaigning to do that, boy.' He jerked upright in the chair again as Blackwood made to leave. 'I'll want to hear all about it, don't you forget now. Names, places, everything. It's something to look forward to.'

As he left the room Blackwood knew that his father slept here alone and wondered if it had always been so.

As he expected, Oates was by the door.

'You've taken good care of him, Oates. He's sleeping now.'

The man nodded, pleased and sad at the same time. Blackwood could feel him watching him until he had descended the stairs.

His stepmother was waiting for him by a fire in the elegant drawing room. He barely recognized it. The walls, the high ceiling, even the furniture was changed.

She watched him and said, 'Mostly from London. Paris too.'

Blackwood sat in a chair and massaged his leg.

She said, 'I'll have Doctor Sturges over to look at that after you've rested.' She changed tack without waiting for an answer and asked, 'What did you think of him?'

Blackwood looked at the fire, remembering his father as he had once been.

'Ill. Tired. Worse than I expected.'

'I suppose so. Well, the weather should improve soon. I'll have him taken to the coast. Somewhere he can see his marines marching up and down. He'll like that.'

Blackwood tried to accept what she was saying. She spoke of his father as if he were a child. The thought made him angry and bitter. Nothing was the same. Even Georgina had been sent away by this unreachable woman. No wonder Harry had made jokes about it, that she was a god in her own right.

She was still watching him. 'You can have a light supper in your room. I've spoken to cook about it. Nothing heavy just yet.'

Blackwood stood up carefully. 'That would never do, would it?'

She ignored his angry sarcasm, if she even noticed it. In a matter of fact tone she said, 'By the way, Philip, I had a letter from that girl.' She picked an invisible hair from her gown. 'What was she like, pretty?'

Blackwood stared at her with disbelief. 'D'you mean Miss Seymour?'

She gave him a gentle frown. 'Remember where you are, Philip, dear. This is not a man-of-war, there are servants about.'

Blackwood sat down again and tried to calm himself. She had actually written about him and his stepmother had not even thought it worth mentioning until now.

'Well, *was* she pretty?'

'Yes.' Without noticing he had clasped his fingers together. 'As a matter of fact she is.' He tried not to plead. 'What did she say? In her letter?'

She smiled. 'Just how brave you were. That you saved her life, and that she hoped you would soon be in good health again.'

She had known about his fever and his injuries. All the time he had been in *Satyr* and she had been carried to safety in some place selected by her uncle, she had remembered him.

'Is that all she wrote?'

'More praise, is that what you want?'

He stood up and crossed to her chair. 'Please. Tell me. Don't tease. It's important to me.'

She nodded gravely. 'I can see that. She merely wanted us to know.' She bit her lip in thought. 'And to wish you well.'

'I see.'

She looked up at him and took his hand playfully in hers. 'Don't look so tragic, Philip. She has her life now. You gave it back to her. She's luckier than some.'

Blackwood looked at her and wondered if she was holding something back.

'I'm glad she's all right. It was a terrible ordeal.'

'I'm sure it was. You must tell me about it one day. Now off you go to your room. I've told Oates to instruct your man in his duties here. A very *strange* fellow is your Smithett.'

Blackwood realized he was still holding her hand, and as he made to release his grip she said quietly, 'She said she was going to get married. I did not intend to tell you, but there, it's in the open now. Best forgotten.'

Blackwood moved away. *If only I had known before.*

It was absurd. What could he have done? He did not know where she was or anything about her. But she had cared enough to write.

'I shall come up later, Philip. Try and rest now.'

At the door he paused and looked back at her, but she was already leafing through some sort of diary. She had changed everything, had made it her world.

He found Smithett waiting for him, a bath filled. and ready.

Poor old Smithett, it must be worse for him. He might even see himself ending up like Oates.

He forced a smile. 'All settled in, Smithett? If anyone starts to chase you about, let me know at once.'

Smithett stared at him in surprise. 'Nothin' like that, sir. Easy as fallin' off a log, so to speak. When I've given 'em a bit er Colour-Sarnt M'Crystal's spit an' polish they'll be ready to enlist theirselves!'

Blackwood allowed Smithett to help him out of his clothes, the steam from the bath making him suddenly weary.

Smithett watched him warily and got ready to hold the wounded leg clear of the water.

'Bad, was 'e, sir?'

Blackwood tried to see his father as he had been before.

'I hope I never get like that, Smithett. When nobody wants you. When it's all gone.'

Smithett sighed as he remembered his own father. Usually fighting drunk and bashing his old woman about. Six kids too, all living in a place half the size of this one room. Officers? They didn't know they were born, most of them.

He said, 'All seem better in the mornin', sir.'

During the night the snow fell more heavily, and in the small cottages the families were thankful for warm beds and ample food for the days to come.

In the big house the staircases and alcoves, portraits and weapons shone only slightly from the light of a few candles. All the fires had burned low, but before dawn the maids would be up and about, cleaning out grates and laying new logs from the barn ready for another day.

There were very few people still awake on the first night of Captain Blackwood's return, and none of them saw the colonel's lady as she walked slowly along a gallery, a single candlestick held before her slender figure.

She looked into her husband's room and heard his breathing, uneven and heavy, his occasional meaningless words lost in his pillow.

Then she went to her stepson's room and stood for several minutes looking down at him in the small, flickering light. In sleep his face had lost its strain and its hurt and displayed nothing but youth. She bent over and touched his bare shoulder and held her hand there until he stirred in his sleep. She withdrew quickly, her heart pounding, ashamed and disgusted by her own thoughts and longings.

She had tried to win, to break free from Hawks Hill and its influence. She paused and looked down at the hall from the minstrels' gallery. A thousand shadows danced there. A masked ball perhaps?

Her own shadow moved on and, like the others, was soon swallowed up by the house.

15

Something Personal

The days and then the weeks of Philip Blackwood's convalescence seemed to get longer and longer. The weather had not improved, so that he was even denied the freedom of riding around the estate as he had once done with Georgina.

Whenever he ventured from the house he was made very aware of the bitter cold and what his fever had cost him.

He was back at Hawks Hill, and yet he felt it had rejected him in some way, as if he did not properly exist.

Servants came and went about their business, a table was always set for one, so that at each solitary meal Blackwood could sense their polite watchfulness and nothing more.

His stepmother, after arranging regular visits by her own doctor and making certain his comfort was carefully regulated, left for London. When he mentioned it to his father he merely commented, 'She's more in London than here most of the time.' Then his eyes came alive as he had said, 'Now, where did we get to? You were telling me about the steam gunboats, and what use you think they'll be in the future.' If he was vague about his wife's activities or chose not to discuss them, there was nothing wrong with his memory on naval and military matters.

Then one day a ruddy-faced man named John Rainbott came up to the house, and upon finding that Mrs Blackwood was away, introduced himself as the new steward of the estate. He seemed a bright and cheerful fellow, and spent over an hour discussing the affairs and the business of running the estate. A true countryman, he had come from a similar

position in the county of Surrey, once the home of the late
Lord Lapidge.

His lordship had died, with nobody left to succeed him,
and had arranged for his estate to be sold. Rainbott apparently knew Blackwood's stepmother very well, so his transfer
to Hawks Hill was no surprise, or so it seemed.

Later, as Blackwood sat alone in the library, he considered
what the steward had told him, although he had been less
than forthcoming when asked more direct questions. Rather
like old Oates, he thought, but who were they protecting and
of whom were they afraid?

One thing was clear. Marguerite Blackwood had not only
changed her mind about selling Hawks Hill, she had also
decided to take very firm grasp of the tiller. She sat at the
meetings for farmers and tenants, discussed repairs to buildings, and the purchase of stock and machinery. She was not
merely beautiful, she was also a very forceful lady when it
came to management.

Blackwood knew she had plenty of money of her own, far
more than his father, but he had never heard any mention
before of the late Lord Lapidge.

Thinking about the various possibilities and relationships
helped to pass the time, but not for long. Each day Blackwood read and reread the news reports of the West African
campaign, and pictured all the familiar faces and wondered
what they were doing. He yearned to be back with them, and
would have accepted any appointment in Ashley-Chute's
squadron rather than endure his isolation.

Encouraged by the successes against the slavers and their
armed camps, the Royal Navy was increasing its activities
and had several more steam vessels employed up and down
that wretched coast. The campaign must soon come to a
head, he thought, while he would still be sitting out the
hours and waiting for a reprieve. Around the world the Navy
was involved in actions against everything from Chinese
pirates to the growing illegal traffic in Irish emigrants to the
USA. It was part of the aftermath of the terrible potato

famine which had raged throughout Ireland just a few years before.

Now, families desperate for a chance to find a new life in America were buying their passages to be smuggled illegally, sometimes in vessels which were little better than the hulks.

In addition, many of these same people had been robbed of all their possessions and property in the process.

Blackwood felt he was being left behind by the speed of events. His mother, for instance, had not gone to London by coach as was her custom, but by train, something which would have been impossible not so long ago.

Trains had caused a certain amount of trouble in the countryside, the noisy engines and belching smoke having much the same effect on the farmers' cows as *Satyr*'s siren on African warriors.

Then his stepmother returned from her visit to London, and Blackwood was grateful for her company.

She rarely showed excitement about anything, but even as her maid had gathered up her parcels which had been brought in by Lloyd, the coachman, she exclaimed, 'I took tea with an old friend of mine, Lady Ballison.' She walked quickly to one of the mirrors and patted her hair into place, although to Blackwood it looked perfect. 'She was full of news, but then things are *always* happening in London.'

Blackwood looked over her shoulder and saw the sparkle in her eyes.

'I don't think I know her.'

Her gaze shifted to his reflection. 'You are silly sometimes. She's a lady-in-waiting to Her Majesty.' She offered him her cheek for a formal kiss. 'You're looking much better. I hope you have been properly attended to.' She hurried on, 'It seems that our Queen has been taking quite an interest in the East African campaign.'

Blackwood sighed. '*West* African.'

She pivoted round and glared at him. 'Well anyway, she has.'

Blackwood watched her as she moved across the floor, her

eyes everywhere as if to detect any idleness during her absence.

She said, 'It will be in the *Gazette* tomorrow. Darling Harry has been *promoted* to first lieutenant for leading an attack by boat and routing a force twice the size of his own!' This time she could not hide her elation. 'Isn't that wonderful, Philip? I knew he would do well, I just *knew* it, and my friend will ensure that Her Majesty is informed!'

Blackwood smiled. 'I'm glad.'

He looked at the snowflakes which ran slowly down the windows like tears. Was he glad? Or was he jealous and stupidly hurt by the news of Harry's success?

He added, 'I just wish . . .'

She crossed the floor and touched his lips with her fingers.

'Don't say it. It will make it harder for you. You *know* these things happen. You are lucky to be alive.'

He looked down at her and wondered. 'You think I shall be discharged, don't you?' He saw her smile fade and was suddenly angry. 'Well, I'm not giving in so easily!'

She moved away to a mirror again. 'Of course not, dear. But you must allow yourself time. And . . .' she darted a glance at his reflection, '. . . if the worst should happen, you could soon learn to manage things here.' She did not flinch under his stare. 'And eventually settle down.' She waited just a few seconds and added, 'Your poor father is a burden and will become more so. I cannot do *everything* on my own.'

Blackwood stared into the fire. He was beaten before even a skirmish, but knowing it did nothing to help.

He heard himself retort, 'You seem to do quite well, according to your Mr Rainbott.'

He looked up and was astonished to see the shocked disbelief on her face.

'When was he here? What did he tell you?'

Blackwood walked across the thick rug and grasped her hands in his.

'Forgive me. He came to see you about a farm matter. That was all. He had been in Winchester and did not know you

had gone to London. I – I suppose I was being stupid. I really
am sorry.'

She regarded him thoughtfully for a long moment. 'I have
already forgotten it.' She thrust her hand through his arm and
swung him round. 'Now come and see what I bought for
you.'

Her change of mood was unnerving. She had not once
asked about her husband's health, or his either for that
matter. The mention of the cheerful Mr Rainbott had been
uppermost in her thoughts.

A maid stood hovering by the door, a silver tray in one
hand.

Marguerite Blackwood asked, 'What is it, Horrocks?'

The maid held out the tray to Blackwood and blushed.

'Th' post-boy's just bin 'ere, Ma'am. 'Tis a letter for the
captain.'

Blackwood felt the grip tighten on his arm.

'Apparently someone else knows you're back.'

But Blackwood was looking at the envelope, the neat,
sloping handwriting. His stepmother had somehow mislaid
the other letter from Davern Seymour, but in his heart he
knew this one was from her too.

'Thank you.' He took the letter and stared at it.

'I think you'd better go and read it, Philip.' She released
his arm and turned towards the drawing room. 'Then come
and tell me all about it.'

In the privacy of his room Blackwood slit open the
envelope and sat quite still for several seconds. In that short
time he felt all the emotions of a fifteen-year-old youth and
not in the least like a man who had just escaped death.

The beginning was almost painful. *Dear Mr Blackwood* . . .

But after the opening formality he became lost in her
words, as if he was hearing her speak, feeling her near like
that terrible day at the mission, the stench of death and fear.

She was in London but only waiting for her uncle's return
to England. She did not say what she had been doing, or

where she was living, and Blackwood imagined it had taken a long time and a great deal of restraint to write as she had. She had come home in a fast packet, and 'people had been very kind'. Blackwood got up and strode to the window and held the letter to the dull light.

She would never forget what he had done or the way his men had acted to make things better for her.

Blackwood folded the letter carefully and placed it in his pocket. The last sentence was burned on his mind like a brand.

As you may know, I am getting married shortly. I shall think of you often. It was signed with equal formality, *Davern Seymour*.

Blackwood paced about the room and tried to find a glimmer of hope when he knew there was none. She was thanking him, and would probably want to forget him altogether. Any memory of him would link her immediately with her father's horrific death and everything which she had seen and suffered.

Eventually he went down to the drawing room and was surprised to see that his stepmother had changed her clothes. It seemed only minutes since he had gone to his room, but the curtains and shutters were closed and the place bright with the glow of lamps.

She looked up from some papers and watched him curiously.

'Good news?' She patted the sofa beside her. 'Sit down and tell me about it.'

Blackwood sat and stretched his hands towards the fire.

'It was nothing. Much the same as the one she wrote to you.' She remained silent and he added, 'Getting married.'

'That sounds like *everything*, the way you say it.' She put down the papers. 'How old is she?'

He tore his mind away from the girl's voice, the one he had heard in her letter, and replied, 'Twenty-four, I believe.'

'At that age she *should* be married. Not bustling around the world.' She softened her tone as she saw his face. 'No parents either?'

'None. Sir Geoffrey Slade, her uncle, told me that – '

She grasped his wrist. 'Slade? The man everyone's talking about?'

She shook his wrist chidingly. 'I had no idea.'

Blackwood looked at her and smiled. 'Perhaps you don't listen.'

She tossed her head. 'I would have remembered that. I know Lady Slade well enough to speak with. A rather grand lady, but I believe *he* is a nice little man.'

Blackwood thought of Slade's torn emotions. The concern for his niece, the need to hide his feelings from his subordinates.

He said, 'He's like stone when he feels like it.'

'Perhaps.' She was already miles away, her mind busy. 'But it will not hurt to make his acquaintance.'

Oates shambled into the room and looked at them patiently.

Blackwood said, 'Would you care for a drink before dinner?' He suddenly needed one very badly.

'If you like. Some sherry, I think.'

Oates glanced at Blackwood. 'And a glass of brandy for you, sir?' He moved away without awaiting an answer.

She said softly, 'I think you're drinking too much. Brandy before dinner indeed. I don't know what the Corps is coming to.'

Blackwood lay back on the sofa and replied, 'I'm going to London tomorrow.'

She took a finely cut glass from Oates' tray and remarked, 'I don't know what Doctor Sturges will say about it.' Then she smiled. 'But it might do you good. I'll give you an address, somewhere suitable.'

He barely heard her. 'I'll probably stay at the club.'

She tossed her head again and said disdainfully, 'You should be at home there. More like a barracks than a civilized place.'

Blackwood was surprised she had not probed more deeply or tried to prevent him from going. Perhaps, like Major

Fynmore, she was too impressed by Slade's reputation to care for other matters.

It was madness of course and he knew that he would suffer for it. But he had to know. She might not even be there, or refuse to see him. All at once he could not bear the waiting.

She asked wryly, 'Another drink, Philip?'

He started. The glass was empty and he had not remembered drinking anything.

'Sorry.'

There was the sound of a trolley being wheeled into the dining room, hushed voices as the evening ritual was begun.

She said, 'Be careful. That is all I ask. You are quite a catch, you know, for any young lady.'

They stood up together and she patted his cheek as if to reassure herself.

'We'll go in to dinner, Philip. I feel so proud to have a fine young man to escort me.'

Blackwood glanced at her but her face gave nothing away.

He had sensed she had been in his room the night he had arrived home. That she had been standing by the bed. He had told himself it was a dream, but now he knew differently, and the realization disturbed him. He thought of the rebellious Georgina who had been sent away to be 'finished'. Like mother like daughter.

He stared at the soup which had appeared before him. Perhaps his wound and the bloody fighting he had survived had also unhinged him in some way. He looked up and saw her watching him from the far end of the table. No, he was not mistaken. He could see it in her eyes like hunger.

He thought of his father upstairs in the large, silent room and the picture helped to steady him. Until the next time.

'Good afternoon, sir.' The butler was tall and impressive, like the house. 'May I be of assistance?'

Blackwood looked beyond the butler to the quiet elegance of Sir Geoffrey Slade's town house. The square in which it stood was subdued and totally apart from the London which Blackwood had seen on his way here. The noise of wheels and clattering hoofs, the smell of horses and damp clothing, a bedlam of haphazard crowds, vehicles and tall buildings.

Now he had finally reached the house he was suddenly apprehensive and less certain he had done the right thing. Even the hansom cab which had carried him from the club in St James's still idled at one corner of the square as if the cabby thought a young marine officer was out of place here.

He said, 'I was wondering if Sir Geoffrey Slade is at home.'

The butler stood firm, like a sergeant of the foot guards.

'Even if he were here, sir, I doubt he'd be free to entertain you without an appointment.'

Blackwood saw the man's gloved hand move the door very gently towards him.

'I will, of course, take a message, sir.'

Blackwood shrugged. It was hopeless. Perhaps he was really glad, that it was all better forgotten. Even as he thought it, he knew it was a lie.

The butler said persuasively, 'If you would care to leave your card, sir?' He was an old hand at this kind of thing.

Blackwood turned to look for the hansom cab but it had gone. Worse still, he was feeling slightly sick and dizzy. The journey by train had been exciting but taxing on his strength, and all the din and bustle of the London streets had not helped.

'Is anything wrong, sir?'

Blackwood licked his lips. 'No. This is the first time I've been outdoors for some while.' Why had he bothered to tell him that? 'But thank you.'

The butler seemed to loom over him. 'Good heavens, sir! It's Captain Blackwood, isn't it?' He held open the door. 'Please come in and wait by a fire. Her ladyship will be back directly. I'm *certain* she will wish to see you.'

Blackwood walked into the house, dimly aware of two small maids who were watching open-mouthed from a dark hallway. They were probably more used to visiting diplomats and ministers than a lowly captain, he thought.

The butler led the way to a snug little room which overlooked the square. He was saying, 'You must forgive me for
not realizing who you were, sir. Unpardonable!'

Blackwood allowed himself to be helped into a deep chair,
and wondered how to escape, what he would say when that
'rather grand lady', as his stepmother had described her,
returned.

He asked, 'Is Miss Seymour staying here?' He saw the
man's shoulders stiffen. 'I hoped I might see her.'

The butler plucked at one glove. 'We have had to be so
careful, sir. All the trouble she's had, the wedding coming
along.' Then he smiled and looked less formidable. 'But in
your case, of course, sir.'

He turned as a maid called softly, 'They're 'ere, Mr Tom-
kins.'

Blackwood stood up, alone and suddenly nervous, as the
butler left the room in three great strides. He heard the jangle
of harness, the murmur of voices, the formidable Mr Tom-
kins saying something in a stage-whisper.

Lady Slade swept into the room, magnificent in a broad
feathered hat and a long military-style coat.

She proffered her hand and said, 'So charming of you to
drop in, Captain Blackwood. Such a *surprise*.'

Blackwood took her hand and kissed it lightly. She was
certainly grand and more beside. She must be a head taller
than her husband. Her greeting was partly a rebuke for not
announcing his visit, but he did not care. His eyes were on
the girl who stood quite motionless in the doorway. She was
dressed in dark clothes, Blackwood did not know what, for he
saw only her violet eyes, her hands which had risen to her
breast as if she was remembering, and hating him for his
intrusion.

He said quietly, 'I – I just wanted to wish you well, Miss
Seymour. I apologize for coming in this fashion.'

Lady Slade sat down gracefully and folded her hands in her
lap.

'It is nothing unusual, Captain Blackwood. Young people

these days are always in too much of a hurry.' Her face softened slightly. 'Please be seated again. I was going to visit your, er, father after Sir Geoffrey returned home. But it was really you I wished to see, so all's well that ends well.' She settled back on the cushions and waited.

Blackwood held a chair so that the girl could sit near the fire. He could feel her warmth, the touch of her gown against his hand as she sat down, her eyes averted.

Then she said, 'I wrote to you . . .' She faltered. 'I don't know if you . . .'

'Yes. I got it yesterday. I came to London today, by train.'

She lifted her face and studied him, her eyes misty as she said, 'You look tired. I'm so sorry.' She moved her hand as if to touch his but withdrew it.

Lady Slade said, 'You came in some haste, Captain Blackwood.'

It sounded like an accusation, but when he looked at her, her eyes were warm and friendly.

She stood up before Blackwood could help and said, 'I must see to the arrangements for a reception. I shall not be long.' She looked at the girl and asked gently, 'Unless you wish me to stay, my dear?'

She shook her head, her eyes still on Blackwood.

'I shall be all right, Aunt Lydia.'

Lady Slade swept through the door but left it partly ajar, the requirements of etiquette satisfied.

He said, 'She's very nice.'

'Yes.' She watched him as if it was an effort not to flinch as he sat down beside her. 'How are you, *really*?'

'Well enough. My leg is a bit troublesome, but much better.' He smiled. 'But I am afraid I find the weather a bit demanding after Africa.'

She said, 'I read about your brother today. Your family must be pleased.' She looked at him imploringly. 'Why did you come? *Tell me!*'

He tried to take her hand but she pulled it away.

She recovered quickly and said, 'I'm so sorry. It's just that I can't . . . I don't know . . . I'm trying very hard. Please don't be offended.'

Blackwood let her talk, feeling her pain as the words tumbled out of her.

She said, 'I am going away. Start a new life. But I don't want to hurt you.' She looked at him, her gaze level. 'You of all people. After what you did. Everything.' Her hand hovered against her breast again and then fell to her lap like a dying bird.

'I had to come. Why must you leave again so soon? You need time. Most wounds heal when given the chance.'

She reached out and grasped his hand in both of her own.

Blackwood watched his hand imprisoned in her two small ones, felt the longing course through him as she traced invisible patterns on the palm. Perhaps she was remembering that same hand gripping the sword which had hacked down her captors. The one which had touched her naked breasts as he had tried to cover her.

She whispered, 'What are you saying?'

'I am saying that I want you for myself.'

The sudden desperation was making him awkward and clumsy, and he knew that at any second she would leave him or their stately chaperon would return. Either way it would be finished, once and for all.

'Forgive my blunt manners, Miss Seymour. I am too used to the ways of ships and men under arms. I am out of place in this kind of world.'

He tried again, his eyes fixed on her hands, the gentle movement of her fingers against his skin.

'When I first saw you aboard the flagship I knew then there could be nobody else. For me nothing has changed, you must believe that. Given time you could learn to like me, I would make you!'

More carriage wheels rattled to a halt outside the house and Blackwood heard voices again, the butler's resonant tones as he hurried to greet a visitor.

Blackwood persisted, 'Please say that you will consider it?'

He felt her bracing herself to leave and knew he had failed.

She said in a low voice, 'I shall never forget you. Perhaps it would have been better if you had not found my father's mission at all.' She stood up quickly and released his hand. 'Goodbye, Captain Blackwood. I do not think we shall meet again.'

Without another glance she almost ran from the room.

Blackwood stood by the fire, unable to move, unwilling to accept what had happened.

The door opened and Lady Slade stood watching him, her face sad.

'It was so good of you to call. My husband will be sorry to have missed you. He wrote to me of your valour. You are a very brave young man.' She watched his despair and said, 'Do not blame yourself. She imagines she is acting for the best.'

'May I ask, Lady Slade, what sort of man she is to marry?'

'A member of the medical profession, once a colleague of her late father. I barely know him, except by reputation. She intends to help him with his work, to cut free from society. But then I have said too much already. You will know that my husband is a man for offering advice. Then I shall do the same. Find a good, sensible girl and marry her. Someone who will complement your profession. Better still, marry one who can help you reach your goal in life. Otherwise, I warn you, you will end up with a broken heart.' She offered her hand and added gently, 'If at any time you feel my husband can help you, perhaps a transfer to London . . .' She smiled as he straightened up. 'No, I think not, Captain. You are too much the man of action. God bless you, and remember what I said.'

Blackwood found himself on the pavement again, the door closed behind him. It was all unreal, as if he had dreamt it.

He glanced at the house and thought he saw a curtain move slightly as someone looked down at him.

Then he turned on his heel and walked rapidly towards the park, oblivious to saluting guardsmen, nursemaids with their prams, even the fact that the snow had stopped and the trees were heavy with a thaw.

He reached the club, his leg throbbing from the exercise, his mind still going over what she had said, how she had held his hand.

It was almost obligatory for naval and military officers to be members of this respected club, but most of them used it as a refuge from the world outside, something more familiar, like wardroom or garrison.

Blackwood slumped down in a leather chair in the spacious smoking room and signalled to a waiter to bring him some brandy. His stepmother had been right. He was drinking too much, but unknown to her it had been going on for some time. A prop for courage, a shield against fear. He smiled at his own rambling thoughts.

He had seen a few left-over wrecks in various establishments and barracks. Put ashore to 'keep things going'; who drank their pay away until, like dead marines, they were quietly disposed of.

There were only two other people in the room and they were discussing the news.

One said irritably, 'Bloody country's going to the dogs. No spirit any more. This damn government is cutting down everything. They say that half of the fleet is laid up an' rottin' for the want of good hands. They should have been around when the press gangs were on the prowl, eh?' He gave a thick chuckle. 'Do some of today's youngsters a spot of good, what?'

Blackwood smiled wearily and signalled to the waiter for another drink. The anonymous member was like his father, he thought.

The second voice said, 'I was at Christie's the other day.'

'Oh yes? Didn't know you were interested in auctions, George.'

'I'm not really. But it was poor old Lord Lapidge's stuff. Furniture and that kind of thing. Went along out of curiosity, I suppose. Not nice to see such personal things under the hammer.'

Blackwood's glass froze in midair as the voice droned on.

'Thought of him when I read about the young marine who was mentioned in the *Gazette* today. His mother was the old boy's mistress, y'know.'

'You don't say! I didn't know that!'

The other man gave a fruity laugh. 'You're about the only one in London who didn't then!'

Blackwood left his drink and strode blindly from the room. No wonder she had changed her mind about leaving Hawks Hill and moving to London. Her mind had been changed for her. It was all horribly clear, the transformation of the house at any expense, the planned improvements to the estate, everything.

But when the source of her wealth had been revealed in Lord Lapidge's will the rest had followed swiftly.

Blackwood entered his small room and sat on the edge of the bed. He thought of his father, confined more than ever by his poor health, young Harry, now on the crest of a wave with his new-found fame. Georgina too would have to be protected, but how?

He stood up and began to pace about the room, his mind busy as he thought of how he would confront her. He would leave for Hawks Hill first thing in the morning and settle things once and for all.

Blackwood stared around the room and listened to the muffled murmur of carriage wheels beyond the heavy curtains. Coming to London had been a mistake. A double defeat which he had brought upon himself.

16

Last Farewell

It was late afternoon when Blackwood arrived back at Hawks Hill. It had been a slow and frustrating journey, and the final part he had shared with a local carrier who had offered him a ride in his little cart from the railway station.

He could barely recall what the talkative carrier had said as they had trotted down familiar lanes until the tall gate pillars had come in sight.

In spite of the time it had taken to reach Hawks Hill he felt angrier rather than calmer. He had filled a flask with brandy at the club and yet he had not touched it. That in itself had surprised him.

Blackwood hurried up the stone steps and pushed open the doors. He saw Mrs Purvis, the housekeeper, staring at him as if she had just seen a ghost and said, 'I came back early.' Something touched his mind like a warning. 'What is it? Has something happened?'

She exclaimed, ' 'Tis the colonel, sir. He's been taken bad again. The doctor's just gone.'

Blackwood removed his gloves and handed his heavy coat to one of the maids. It gave him time to think. To settle his mind. Like a moment in battle when the obvious has changed to something entirely different.

The housekeeper was watching him anxiously. 'Master Harry's here, sir. Arrived first thing.' She sounded close to breaking down. 'He looks a fine sight, bless him.'

'I'll go up.'

Blackwood mounted the stairs slowly and deliberately. He

had pictured his half-brother in Africa or patrolling the coast with Ashley-Chute's squadron. The unexpected news of his return made him feel even more out of touch and vulnerable.

At the end of the passageway he saw Oates slumped in a chair outside the door. He looked like death but got to his feet as he heard Blackwood's footsteps.

He said huskily, 'We found him lying on the floor, sir.' He dropped his eyes, again ashamed of revealing something secret. 'He was trying to put on his dress-uniform when it happened.'

'Who else was there, Oates?' He thought he already knew.

'The colonel's lady, sir. She sent your man for the doctor. Must have flown like the devil.'

Blackwood looked away. Poor Smithett had ridden nothing but a mule in his whole life as far as he knew. He was a man of many surprises.

He gripped the handle and said, 'Try and rest.'

He pushed open the door and saw the table with the decanter and glasses near the window. As if his father had been waiting for another detailed account of his exploits in Africa.

His stepmother came from the shadows near the bed and reached out to take both of his hands.

'I'm so glad you came, Philip. It was as if you knew.'

Blackwood kissed her cheek, searching for a sign, some hint of what had happened here. He was conscious of her perfume, the cool smoothness of her skin, and the fact that in spite of everything she was beautifullly dressed in a dove-grey gown and her hair was set in a crown which left her ears bare.

He said, 'Tell me!'

She moved to the end of the bed and looked at her husband. Blackwood joined her and saw that his father was in a deep sleep, his eyes screwed up as if to protect them from danger.

She said quietly, 'I could not rest. The house seemed empty with you away.'

She touched his arm and he watched her fingers on his sleeve, fascinated even as he tried to hate her.

'I often feel like that, Philip. I was walking in the gallery, watching the shadows in the moonlight. Then I heard him cry out.' She turned away as if to dismiss it from her thoughts. 'He was wearing his uniform, or part of it. Doctor Sturges says he is over the worst.' Then she faced Blackwood and held his eyes with her own. 'But any bad shock might bring on another stroke, and that would kill him.'

Blackwood returned to the bed and saw the dress-coat lying on a chair. What had made his father do it, he wondered? Like that dying marine perhaps, who had found the strength to yell commands and encouragement to his invisible comrades.

'Harry's here, by the way.'

Without turning he could see her expression. It was as if she knew, had been prepared for something like this. He recalled with sudden clarity how she had lost her composure for a few revealing seconds when he had told her about Rainbott's visit. The late Lord Lapidge's steward.

'I heard.'

She came round and gripped his arm. 'Something's happened. Was it that girl?'

That girl. 'I saw her.'

He could not bear to speak about her here. He felt trapped, outmanoeuvred.

'Well, perhaps it's better this way.'

He swung round, his voice shaking in a harsh whisper. 'What do you know about her? How can you possibly understand?' He saw her step back as if he had tried to strike her.

The door opened and Harry strolled into the room, his eyes moving between them as he said, 'Hello, Philip, I feel better now that you're here.'

Blackwood looked at him and crossed the room in quick strides. His half-brother was wearing his uniform trousers and his shirt which was open to the waist. He looked tousled and tired, and somehow even younger than ever.

Blackwood clapped his hands on his shoulders.

'Sorry I missed your birthday, Harry.' He knew he was not

making any sense, just as he knew he was already beaten.

'Why don't you two go downstairs and get Mrs Purvis to fetch you something. I'll stay here for a while.'

Blackwood looked at her. She was watching him steadily, her hands relaxed by her sides. She knew too.

Blackwood left the room and together with his half-brother walked along the gallery which was dappled in weak sunlight.

Harry asked quietly, 'What do you think about the old man? Did he have a shock or something?'

Blackwood paused by a window and in his mind's eye saw his stepmother walking through the silent house in the darkness. Something she often did. He felt the same sensation of warning. Perhaps his father had also found out about Lord Lapidge? He gripped his hands together until the pain calmed him.

'What's *wrong*, Philip?'

Blackwood shrugged. 'I went to see Miss Seymour.'

'Yes, Mother said. Bad luck, but it happens.'

Blackwood studied him. *You sound just like her.*

He said, 'It's me, I expect.'

Harry looked different in some way. More confident, and yet with the same old touch of recklessness.

He said, 'Congratulations on your promotion, by the way.'

Harry grinned. 'Yes. I'm catching you up.' Then he said, 'Seriously, I think it's terrible you've had no recognition for what you did. But for you there would have been no "afterwards".'

Harry's mood changed again. 'Anyway, things will be different now. The squadron's being split up. Some of the older ships are being paid off, and others are being ordered to the Mediterranean. I came home in a steam-frigate.' He sliced his hands through the air. '*Whoosh!* Like a streak of lightning. Well . . . almost!'

'What did Doctor Sturges say?'

Harry grimaced. 'Nothing much. He's arranging for a senior physician to come down from London. But he said that

Father will be better off here than in some damned hospital, and I agree.'

Blackwood thought of his quiet room at Haslar, the painting of the crest above the bed. His father would go out of his mind there.

One of the maids bustled past, her arms laden with towels. She saw them and blushed as Harry said, 'Why, Jenny, I do declare you're prettier than ever!' She tried to pass but he blocked her way and said, 'I shall have to do something about you one of these days, or nights, eh?'

Blackwood watched her as she fled down the passageway. Harry made him feel older than his years with his casual treatment of the local girls. Yet they seemed to love it.

He felt Harry watching him as he said, 'You had a bad time, Philip. After you'd been put aboard ship for passage home there were some who said you'd never recover.' He touched his arm with sudden affection. 'Not me though. I know you better than that. Now.'

Together they descended the stairs, and Blackwood asked, 'How were the others when you left?'

Harry toyed with the idea of teasing him and then blurted out, 'You'll see for yourself. They're all here, at Forton Barracks.' He watched the life returning to Blackwood's eyes. 'Two new companies are being formed. They need all the trained men they can get.'

Blackwood strode to a fire and held out his hands. 'When have things ever been otherwise?' He was strangely excited at the prospect of returning to duty, just as he was touched by Harry's genuine pleasure in seeing him.

Harry was saying dreamily, 'Someone in high places must have listened to your ideas about new methods of training for the Corps instead of the Waterloo mentality.'

Blackwood looked up quickly. 'How's Fynmore?' It was not difficult to recall his face that day when he had climbed up from the boats and had seen the carnage.

'Oh, didn't I say?' He was not that good an actor. 'He's *in command*. Been made up to half-colonel too for his brilliance!'

Blackwood smiled grimly. It was much as Lascelles had told him at the hospital. Fynmore had not allowed the grass to grow under his feet.

He asked, 'What about the new companies?'

Harry played with the front of his shirt. 'Ogilvie's got one, and a Major Brabazon's been given the other. He's also second in command.'

Blackwood nodded. He had no right to feel disappointed, but he did. He was lucky to be alive, and that had to be enough. But to think of Fynmore being given overall command of some crack contingent was laughable.

Harry changed the subject. 'Mother's a marvel, don't you think? All this worry and responsibility, yet she seems to ride right over it.'

Blackwood walked to a window, afraid Harry would see his expression. *She's a whore with no thought for anyone but herself and her greed.*

He said, 'I can see where *you* get it from.' But the joke went flat.

Smithett appeared silently and said, 'They're bringin' yer 'orse, sir.'

Harry nodded and began to fasten his shirt. 'Thanks.'

He sauntered away to dress himself, and Blackwood said, 'You remain at Hawks Hill, Smithett. I'm going to Forton to report for duty.'

Smithett watched him passively. 'Somethin' wrong, sir?'

'Probably not. But I'd like you here, just in case. Poor old Oates is getting shaky. It would please my father no end if there was a *real* marine nearby when he feels better.'

'I dunno about that, sir.' But Smithett was obviously pleased with the compliment.

Half an hour later they were both ready to leave.

Harry clasped his mother to his chest and hugged her. Blackwood saw that she was watching him instead of listening to her son, her eyes level and challenging.

He could do and say nothing now. It would only add to his father's suffering and provoke a family disgrace.

She moved towards him and touched his collar.

'You both look very splendid. I'm proud of you. We all are.'

Harry climbed carelessly into his saddle and looked down at them with amusement.

'You look more like lovers than respectable people.'

Only then did Blackwood see her start, her eyes spark with alarm. 'Don't be so *vulgar*, Harry!'

Blackwood stooped and kissed her cheek. It was as cold as ever. Then without another glance he mounted his horse and followed Harry away from the house.

Whatever happened after this, things would never be the same at Hawks Hill.

Lieutenant-Colonel Rupert Fynmore handed his hat and riding-crop to a clerk and marched through the outer office and into his own.

It was morning, and although the air was cold and damp the sky remained clear, as if the snow was just a bad memory.

Fynmore glanced briefly at his desk and the carefully arrayed papers which awaited his attention, then, as if for the first time, he looked at Blackwood.

'I hear you arrived back last night?' His eyes moved busily over Blackwood's appearance. 'You could have reported then. I am never too busy to receive one of my officers.' His mouth shot up in his twisted smile. 'Especially one of so gallant acquaintance, what? Delayed, were you?'

Blackwood nodded. 'My half – Mr Blackwood had to retrace his steps and leave some papers with somebody.'

It sounded so peculiar that he flinched under Fynmore's stare. It had been strange, he thought. They had been keeping up a good pace, talking about the African campaign, the squadron, filling in the gaps. Then Harry had reined up his horse and had pointed at a small inn nestled in a curve of the road.

'God, my memory! I was supposed to leave some letters at

a house back there. But for this inn I'd have forgotten completely. You wait there and have a glass. I'll not be long.'

Without waiting for an answer he had turned his horse and cantered back along the road. When he had eventually arrived at the inn about an hour later he had been reticent and apparently unwilling to elaborate on where he had been.

Fynmore snapped, 'No matter. You're here and that's the main thing. Mr Blackwood has told you about the formation of the new companies, right? We have to make a success of it. A step in the right direction. Half the trouble in the past has been the lack of coordination in a squadron. *Send the marines*, orders some admiral or other, and we all tumble into boats and storm ashore, most of us never having worked together before. Monstrous, in my opinion, asking for trouble.'

Blackwood watched him, fascinated. Fynmore seemed to have grown in stature with his new rank, and it was almost impossible to remember him as the cautious, hesitant commander in West Africa.

'I've read your reports, Blackwood. Fine as far as they go. But the medical men are all agreed. Your wound could weaken you again. Can't have that, what?'

Fynmore crossed to a window and raised some papers to his eyes. 'Now let me see. Your own Doctor Sturges says much the same.'

Blackwood stiffened as he saw an envelope pinned to the other papers. He would recognize his stepmother's writing anywhere. He felt trapped, or like a boy at school who is about to be expelled.

Fynmore replaced the papers on his desk and adjusted them until they were in an exact line with the others.

'Still, can't believe everything they say, can we?'

'I'd like to return to duty, sir.'

'Of course.' Fynmore studied him thoughtfully, his sandy hair perfect, his uniform looking as if he had been poured into it.

'I have spoken to the Colonel Commandant. He fully understands the need for experienced officers. The fleet is undermanned and cannot raise enough volunteers for any sudden emergency. The marines, on the other hand, are the *real force*. Like a well-forged weapon which, if properly used, can put a stop to local wars and uprisings before they know what's hit them.' He calmed himself with an effort. 'I got the Colonel Commandant to agree to your secondment on a temporary basis.' He watched his words go home and added smoothly, 'Do your duty, and make good use of your undoubted experience in the field, and I feel sure that this will only be a momentary setback.'

Beyond the room and the thick walls Blackwood heard the measured tramp of feet from the parade-ground, the shouted commands which came from every angle until they merged into a meaningless chorus.

One, probably the sergeant-major's, ebbed and flowed, chased and persuaded above all the rest.

'Advance in column from the left, A Company leading!' There were more shouts and then, '*Stand still, that man!* Wait for the order!'

Fynmore was enjoying this. Watching his disappointment, waiting for him to plead. Secondment on a temporary basis. It was better than nothing. But only just.

'Thank you, sir.'

'Anyway, there's a lot to do before we leave.' He sounded vaguely irritated. 'We are embarking in a troopship the week after next. For Malta.' He squared his shoulders and glared round the office. 'Not like this place, eh? Do some of the recruits good to see what an *old* barracks looks like.'

Blackwood considered it. That was unexpected. An immediate transfer to the Mediterranean. He had imagined that perhaps the new companies had been formed to support the campaign he had left behind in *Satyr*. For although the Navy was having plenty of successes against the remaining strongholds of slavery, the campaign was still dragging on, with fever taking a heavier toll of seamen and marines than anything else.

Fynmore said suddenly, 'I understand Sir Geoffrey Slade is back in England too.'

'Yes, sir. I visited his London house just two days ago.' There was no need to add that Slade had not been there. His so-called friendship with Slade must be about the only reason Fynmore had requested his secondment to the new command.

'Splendid. *He* thinks out every move. I *like* that.'

The door opened two inches and a clerk said nervously, 'The sergeant-major's here, sir.'

'Good. Punctual as usual.' Fynmore glanced around the office and added, 'Two men for field punishment this morning. I will not have slovenly behaviour and I want everyone to know it.'

Blackwood followed him through the outer office and into the pale sunshine.

Fynmore said over his shoulder, 'We are getting some of the new Minié rifles too. Mine is the first command to have that honour.'

The sergeant-major stood like a ramrod on the side of the parade-ground, his stick tucked beneath one arm. In the sunlight his brass shoulder-scales shone like gold, perfection, like the rest of his uniform.

His eyes flickered to Blackwood and his mouth opened and closed like a trap.

'Good to 'ave you back, if I may say so, sir.'

That was all he said, but Blackwood valued his bare welcome more than a full parade.

He watched the nearest marines marching past, their boots kicking up the dust, their eyes glazed with the constant changes of direction, the intricate movements with musket and bayonet which, if the sergeant-major had his way, would soon be as familiar as their own feet.

He saw Harry standing by a platoon which was being instructed in the use of the new Minié rifles. If he remembered the cruel accuracy of these rifles which had taken the lives of so many of their own men he did not show it. He was smiling and joking, and even at a distance Blackwood could sense the relaxed almost carefree atmosphere.

Fynmore said fiercely, 'Deal with *that*, Sergeant-Major.' As the giant strode towards the offending platoon Fynmore muttered, 'Sloppiness will not be tolerated.' He darted Blackwood a quick glance. 'From anybody.'

Harry hurried across the square and saluted.

Fynmore said coldly, 'Those men are raw recruits, Mr Blackwood. You may wish to appear popular in their eyes, but I warn you, they'll not respect you for it. Discipline is what they know and need.'

Harry flushed. 'I'm sorry, sir.'

'Report to the adjutant for extra duties, Mr Blackwood. But first attend to the punishment of two offenders. A dozen lashes each, I believe?'

The sergeant-major grunted. 'Sir.'

'Carry on then.'

Fynmore turned on his heel and strode away, an orderly trotting behind him.

Harry murmured softly, 'Pig.'

Blackwood said, 'You asked for that. *And* you know it.'

Harry grimaced. 'Extra duties too.' He glanced at the procession which had emerged from the guard-house. Two men stripped for punishment, an armed guard and a sergeant with the necessary papers in his hand. He said ruefully, 'I'll be glad to get back to sea.'

Blackwood saw the familiar shape of M'Crystal hurrying across the square.

'Stay out of trouble, Harry. I mean it.'

Harry watched his half-brother shake hands with the big colour-sergeant. What was the difference? The greeting was warm, and yet there was no lowering of the barrier between them. He kicked angrily at a stone.

Never mind. Fynmore would have cause to regret his outbursts. It had been sickening the way Fynmore had lost no time in passing off Philip's ideas to the admiral as his own. By so doing he had gained promotion beyond his dreams, a command which any officer would envy.

He smiled in spite of his resentment and wondered if there were any young women in Malta who might be of interest.

'So you're off again, Philip. Best thing, I suppose.'

Blackwood adjusted his father's pillows and watched him sadly. He had difficulty in forming his words, as if his mouth was frozen. But his voice seemed stronger and his mind had not wandered very much while they had been talking.

'Day after tomorrow, Father. We've not been told much, but it sounds as if they genuinely want an independent unit which can be sent anywhere.'

'Won't be the first time we've had to get the army out of trouble.'

Blackwood smiled. 'There's no war.'

'Will be soon. You mark my words. New weapons, bigger fleets, they're not being made to play with. Only Britain believes in letting things slip. God, these politicians make me sick.' He coughed and snatched a handkerchief from his side before Blackwood could help him. 'Get me a drink, will you?'

Blackwood poured a glass of claret. There was no point in denying him. Oates would fetch it once he had left.

'Don't forget what I told you, my boy. Watch that Fynmore. He'll try to hold you down. You could lose your position, seniority, everything, so keep your eyes on him.'

'I don't know why he asked for me anyway.'

'Then you're a fool. He *needs* you, don't you see that? He's promoted out of his depth. Just like his idiot of a father.' He sipped the wine and was suddenly quiet. Then he said, 'Wish I could be there when you sail. What ship, by the way?'

'The trooper *Liverpool*. She's steam driven, so the passage won't be too uncomfortable.'

His father was getting drowsy. 'I'd like to have seen her. Always a fine sight. Bands playing, people holding up their children as the red coats go past.'

Blackwood looked around the room. His father had always been a strong man. To see him cut down like this was pitiful.

From what the other officers had said, it seemed likely they would not return to England until completing a full commission. This was probably the last time he would see his father alive.

He bent over him and said, 'Send me a letter if you feel like it. Oates will write it if you feel too tired.'

His father glared at him. '*Tired?* I'm not a bloody invalid. This is just a setback, nothing more.'

He thrust out his hand and Blackwood grasped it between his own.

'Take care, Philip. Look after young Harry if you can. The name has to survive in the Corps, always remember that!'

He watched as Blackwood stood back from the bed and gave a fierce smile.

'You'll do, my boy.'

The door opened softly and Blackwood heard her say, 'The doctor's here.'

Blackwood walked towards the door and then paused to look back.

His father said, 'Tell your man Smithett from me. Good marine. Hope for this bloody country yet.'

The door closed as the doctor hurried inside. He barely glanced at Blackwood. He probably felt guilty for his part in the medical reports.

Blackwood forgot him and ran lightly down the stairs where Smithett was filling his bag with gifts from the kitchen.

His stepmother walked with him to the steps and said, 'You despise me, don't you?'

When he looked at her she appeared perfectly composed, but something in her tawny eyes made him hold back what he had intended to say.

'I know about Lord Lapidge, if that is what you mean.'

Her lip quivered slightly. 'Think what you like. Just remember this. But for me Hawks Hill would have been sold up long ago. When I married your father there were so many debts and outstanding claims it was a matter of weeks, not months.' She watched him impassively. 'But all your father thinks about is the Corps. He would never listen when I told him about the estate. I used a great deal of my own money, but I became lonely. You will discover, if your pride allows, that there is no price high enough to buy off loneliness.'

He stared at her, wanting to leave, knowing he could not go just yet.

'What of Harry and Georgina?'

'I did it for them, don't you see that?' She reached out and impetuously seized his arm. 'But you were the one I wanted to *impress*, to share my hopes with. Now it's too late.' Her hand fell to her side and she gave a small smile. 'So be off with you before the roads become dark.'

Blackwood heard the horses being led across the cobbles and noticed that some of the servants and stable-boys had come out to watch him leave. Perhaps to them he was a hero, something of their own, a symbol.

He held out his arms and she came to him without protest.

'Goodbye, Marguerite. Your secret is safe with me. It has to be.'

When he bent to kiss her cheek she put her lips against his and held him for several long seconds.

She exclaimed, 'I shall think of you.' Their eyes met. 'Often.'

Then she was gone and he could taste the salt of a tear on his mouth.

Smithett sat uncomfortably on his horse like a sack of potatoes. He was sorry to be leaving the comforts of Hawks Hill and the admiration of the servants here. But from what he had just witnessed it was not a moment too soon for the captain, he thought.

Not very far from the main coaching road where Blackwood and Smithett would pass, Harry stood by a window in the quiet house and watched the last of the dying sunlight.

His red coatee was draped over a chair, and he held a glass

of brandy balanced in one hand. He was genuinely pleased to
be leaving the country again so soon. He felt different, able to
think out each move, when in those first days in West Africa
he had been almost sick with fear.

He had believed it was Philip's example, but now he was not
so sure. Maybe it went deeper, something which was his alone.

'How do you like it, Harry?'

He turned from his thoughts as he saw the woman in the
opposite doorway. She was very pretty in a doll-like way,
with her hair in neat ringlets and a small, slender figure. She
was wearing a green silk robe which Harry had brought with
him from Freetown. In this quiet, Hampshire house it looked
crude and garish, but she was obviously pleased with it.

'You look lovely.'

'You *mean* that, don't you?'

Harry downed the brandy in a gulp, the sting making him
gasp as it burned through him.

'Of course I do.'

It was hard not to show irritation when she was like this.
He had first met her at a ball in Woolwich while he had been
completing his training. She had made him feel adult and
dashing, but he had never imagined it would come to this.
He was excited, in spite of their difference in ages. He was
nineteen, and she had admitted to being thirty. But she
looked much younger, childlike in her need to be reassured
about everything.

He put his arms around her and felt her stiffen. It had
never quite reached this stage before. Any moment now she
would slap his face or push him away, and then the next time
she might let him go a little bit further.

But there would be no next time. In two days they would
be standing down-channel to show the flag, as Fynmore had
put it.

She protested shakily, '*Please*, Harry.'

But he said nothing and pulled her closer to him. When he
reached around her and touched her neat buttucks she gasped
and almost fell against him.

Harry looked at her eyes, the dampness of her lips.

She said in a small voice, 'I think we'd better stop.'

Without a word Harry picked her up and carried her through the door and slammed it with his foot.

'I'm not stopping.'

He saw her eyes widen with alarm as he dropped her on the bed, and when she tried to pull away from him he gripped the robe and dragged her towards him. The robe was only cheap, he had bargained for it with a street trader. She gave a cry as it parted across one shoulder and then she began to fight him as he tore it further.

Harry barely knew what he was doing. She had been wearing nothing beneath the robe, and as he tore the last fragment aside she tried to cover herself with her hands until he slapped her hard across the cheek.

Then he knelt over her, her protests forgotten as he explored her body and touched her breasts while she lay quite still, her eyes watching his hands as if they belonged to someone else.

She whispered, 'Not like this, please.'

His fingers stroked her nipples and he sensed her anguish giving way to something else.

'One more thing.'

He reached out and turned a bedside photograph on to its face. Fynmore looked younger in the picture, he thought.

Then he thrust her last resistance aside and stifled her pain with his mouth.

When it was over she crawled across the bed, groping after him as he began to pull on his trousers and boots.

She gasped, 'You hurt me. You really did.'

Harry glanced quickly round to make certain he had not left anything. Then he bent over and kissed her, sorry for the red mark on her cheek.

'I'll bring you a better robe when I get back.'

Long after the sound of Harry's horse had been swallowed up in the dusk she lay on the bed, staring at the ceiling, her heart pounding as she relived each frightening, beautiful moment.

Then reluctantly she stood up, her knees like water. She straightened the bed and replaced the photograph on the table.

Only then did she realize what she had done.

17

New Arrivals

Philip Blackwood stepped from the shade of a partially collapsed wall and braced himself for the fierce heat. The sky seemed drained of colour, and the stony ground which surrounded the firing range was white, as if it too had been scorched beyond recognition.

Colour-Sergeant M'Crystal watched him curiously as if to determine his mood.

Eventually he said, 'Second platoon is ready to begin firing practice, sir.'

Blackwood nodded. It was almost too hot to think, let alone speak. And yet in Malta you were rarely out of sight of the Mediterranean. Deep, shimmering blue which made the heat ashore almost unendurable. He had imagined that compared to Africa this would have seemed easy. Yet after their arrival and the excitement of new surroundings, he knew that most of the marines were finding each day longer than the preceeding one.

'How are they shaping up?'

It was ridiculous to ask, he thought. They had been on the island for months, drilling and exercising, performing ceremonial parades and guards as requested by the admiral superintendent or whenever it took Fynmore's fancy. It seemed incredible they had been here so long, had accepted the regular routine and spartan living quarters as if they had known nothing else.

Some had settled down better than others, a few, and Harry was one of these, had grown frustrated and resentful about the total lack of purpose.

M'Crystal said, 'I sometimes think they miss the old muskets, sir. These rifles are *too* accurate.'

It was true. The new Minie rifle had a range of nearly a thousand yards and could outshoot any other infantry weapon. Even the excitement of using it on the range had lost its first glow and it had become just one more time-filling drill.

Blackwood had received several letters from his father, which was unusual. The handwriting was shaky, but his letters were full of news about Hawks Hill, of a new alliance with 'the old enemy' as his father still called France, and a genuine interest in what his two sons were doing in Malta.

M'Crystal asked, 'D'you think we'll be moving out soon, sir?' He waited for Blackwood to face him. 'It's not what some of the new recruits had in mind.'

'Having trouble with them?'

M'Crystal bristled. 'I'd not tolerate that, sir. I've a handful of gallow's-bait I'd like to lose, but even they'll do as they're told or I'll know the reason.'

Blackwood knew that the real cause for M'Crystal's annoyance was a small, tight group of new recruits who had all enlisted together. Liverpool-Irish, they had been in more brawls with the military, seamen and marines from ships in harbour than he would have thought possible. Field punishment, doubling round the square in the blazing heat in full kit and a pack filled with sand until they collapsed had done nothing to break their fighting spirit.

Only Lieutenant-Colonel Fynmore appeared satisfied and content. As the senior officer Royal Marines in Malta he had carte blanche to visit any ship or barracks he chose, and seemed to thrive on the monotony of the routine.

He heard the crack and echo of rifle fire and recalled the times in Africa when so few of the enemy had pinned down his own trained and disciplined men without effort. He found he could go over those days with less anguish, another memory already blurred and out of focus.

'I've heard nothing of a move, Colour-Sergeant. Not yet anyway.'

Each day as he looked at the proud array of warships as they shimmered beneath their awnings in the Grand Harbour he found himself longing to be back in one of them. Maybe all marines were the same. Always wanting the opposite, torn between land and sea.

M'Crystal said softly, 'Colonel's coming, sir.'

Blackwood was tempted to pull out his watch, but knew inwardly that Fynmore's daily punctuality would not have varied by more than a second.

He squinted his eyes against the glare and watched the small procession approaching across the white stones, Fynmore in the lead, very erect in his saddle, one arm down his side as if it was made of wood. The adjutant, First Lieutenant George Speer, and an orderly trotting close behind.

Fynmore halted and stared towards the range. 'Improving,' he remarked.

If we carry on like this the rifles will be worn smooth before they are ever used in action, Blackwood thought.

He said, 'I think we should change the drills, sir.'

'Really?' Fynmore brushed a speck of sand from his sleeve. 'I expect we shall receive orders if and when the Admiralty reveal their intentions.'

Blackwood watched him. There was something unusual about Fynmore today. Not quite so calm as he tried to appear.

'The fact is, Blackwood, I have been asked to attend a reception at the admiral superintendent's residence. I shall let you have a list of officers who should also be present.'

Blackwood sighed. Another reception. They seemed endless.

There were plenty of women present on these occasions. Usually wives of senior officers or officials, they must get equally bored at making small talk with an obedient band of junior lieutenants.

'As a matter of fact, my own wife will be joining me here. The mail-packet arrives at the end of the week and she will be aboard. I should like *you* to arrange for her to be escorted to my quarters.' He played with his sword-hilt. 'Make her feel at home.'

The small moment of warmth passed and he snapped, 'Get someone to chase up those damned buglers. I'll not tolerate them arriving at Troop like a bunch of silly old women!'

He wheeled his horse about, and followed by the perspiring adjutant clattered towards the Royal Marine Artillery battery which overlooked the Grand Harbour.

'You heard that, Colour-Sergeant?'

What sort of woman would be married to Fynmore, he wondered? It was strange he had never brought her to Forton. He thought suddenly of his stepmother and realized that his father had not mentioned her at all in his letters.

M'Crystal stamped the details on his memory. 'I'll lay it on, sir.'

He watched Blackwood walk back into the shade and shook his head. The captain was the one who needed a woman, a girl who would take him out of himself. Someone who cared enough to share his life. He thought of the captain's young brother. There would be plenty of trouble with that one if he didn't watch out. Women? He couldn't get enough of them, even here on Malta. If he brought some disgrace on the Marines it would put the colonel's head squarely on the block and things could become distinctly uncomfortable.

He saw his friend Sergeant Quintin tramping wearily over the sun-baked ground and grinned. At least he never changed.

An orchestra played without a break throughout the balmy evening, and while long fans swayed back and forth above the heads of the guests, messmen and servants struggled to supply everyone with drinks.

Blackwood stood near an open balcony and watched the glittering lights from the anchored men-of-war in the harbour. A complete record of the Royal Navy's progress since

Trafalgar, he thought. Majestic ships of the line, and two or three of the new first-rates which, although similar in appearance, were also equipped with engines and screws as additional power.

Steam gunboats and paddle-frigates, they all symbolized the unchallenged power of the Queen's Navy.

He ran one finger round his collar and felt his shirt sticking to his chest like another skin.

He saw the admiral superintendent and his wife by the stairs greeting their guests, the gold epaulettes and varied uniforms making a fine setting for the ladies' gowns and bared shoulders. Here and there a face stood out. George Speer, the adjutant, head lowered and face set in an interested mask as he listened to the wife of the dockyard superintendent. Poor Speer, he was known to have problems with his own marriage and was probably wondering what had happened at home since the contingent had sailed from Portsmouth all those months ago.

Blackwood saw Fynmore too, his wife standing nearby as the admiral greeted her with one of his set speeches. She was obviously a lot younger than Fynmore, a pretty little thing and outwardly very shy when he had met her at the landing-stage. She was very much in awe of her husband and impressed by the marines he had sent to welcome her and to transport her baggage to the colonel's quarters. In the reflected lights her shoulders looked cool and youthful, he thought. The sort of wife who might do Fynmore's future a lot of good.

Harry pushed through the crowd and stared at the throng with distaste.

'I shall steal away when I get the chance.'

Blackwood watched him with surprise. Harry's disappointment and impatience at the soul-destroying garrison duties had often found other outlets in his zest for women. Usually on these formal occasions he had managed to find someone's wife or daughter who would enjoy his company and some of his daring remarks.

'Don't let the colonel see you.' He smiled. 'Have you met his wife, by the way?'

Harry turned swiftly, his eyes searching. 'Once, yes. Why?'

Blackwood shrugged and signalled to one of the servants with a loaded tray.

'Seems a shy sort of person.'

He twisted round to pick up a glass. He must have had too much to drink without realizing it, but Harry sounded unusually guarded. He even looked guilty.

Blackwood said quietly, 'Well, pull yourself together, man, they're coming over.'

But when he looked round, Harry had been swallowed up in the crowd.

Fynmore said crisply, 'And of course you know my aide, Captain Blackwood.' He watched as Blackwood took her gloved fingers and kissed them lightly. 'My right arm, believe me.'

Blackwood asked, 'Have you settled down after your voyage, Ma'am?'

He saw a small pulse pumping in her throat, the nervous movement of her breasts beneath her silk gown. Like a child at her first party, he thought. But there was something else. An elation, an excitement which she was trying to control.

She said, 'I was grateful for your presence at the harbour, Captain. All that noise and confusion.' She flicked open her fan and waved it below her chin. 'I find this heat very taxing.'

Fynmore was peering round at the others and probably wanted all of them to see his young wife, Blackwood thought.

She said, 'Your brother, is he here?' She put her head on one side. 'You are not much like him.'

Fynmore asked, 'You *know* Lieutenant Blackwood?' He frowned and nodded. 'Yes, I remember vaguely. You met him at Woolwich, you told me.' He smiled, satisfied with his memory.

Blackwood cleared his throat. 'We have the same father, Ma'am, that is all.'

He looked around, his mind grappling with what he had unwittingly discovered. He must have been blind not to see Harry's alarm when Fynmore had announced that his wife was coming to Malta. He had been so wrapped up in his own worries he had even forgotten what the adjutant had said about Fynmore's house in Hampshire. It was suddenly stark and clear, so that even the orchestra seemed to fade as he recalled Harry's casual mention of the letters he had forgotten to deliver to that house near the inn. His reluctance to speak about it afterwards. *The bloody idiot.*

He calmed his thoughts with an effort and said, 'He is somewhere in the building.' He thought that Fynmore was watching him again. 'Shall I fetch him?'

Fynmore chuckled. 'Certainly not. Let the young devil enjoy his freedom, eh? I know he can be an irritation to me, but with instruction he may make a fine officer one day.'

It was the nearest thing to praise he had ever made, and yet Blackwood remained uneasy. Fynmore never said or did anything without a strong reason.

His wife tossed her ringlets as if it was all of little importance.

'I think I shall enjoy my stay here, Captain.'

'I sincerely hope – '

Blackwood stared transfixed as the admiral superintendent released the hand of another guest and turned to reveal the woman at his side.

Fynmore exclaimed, 'In God's name, isn't that the girl we saved, Blackwood?'

Blackwood did not even notice the 'we'. But for Fynmore he would have believed he was going insane or suffering another aftermath to his fever.

He nodded, unable and unwilling to take his eyes from her. 'It is, sir. Miss Seymour.'

Fynmore's wife turned and followed their glances. For a few seconds she showed irritation on her doll-like features, as if she resented the intrusion.

She said, 'Oh, that's not her name, Rupert. She was aboard

the packet too. With her husband, a doctor of some repute, I was told. Much older than she, but of course some of us prefer more experienced husbands.'

Fynmore either ignored or failed to notice her tone.

'Fine looking woman, in spite of everything, Blackwood.'

Blackwood said nothing. Instead of the girl with the shining dark hair and demure gown he saw the one in that squalid hut, cut and bruised, and almost naked to the waist.

In spite of everything. In those moments he hated Fynmore and his crude indifference.

He heard himself say, 'If you will excuse me . . .'

He saw their interest sharpen as he made his way among the perspiring, colourful crowd until he was near to the stairway.

If anything she was more beautiful than when he had seen her in London all that time ago. While her husband was speaking to the admiral she stood with and yet apart from them, her eyes downcast as if she was listening to what they were saying.

But Blackwood could remember when he had first seen her aboard *Audacious*, a lifetime ago. She had been the same then, it was her defence.

He heard the admiral say in his booming voice, 'I wish you every success, Doctor Hadley. It is high time that our sick and wounded were treated with greater professional care than in the past.' He chuckled and looked at the girl by his elbow. 'Begging you pardon, Mrs Hadley, but in my early days at sea the work could have been done as well by the ship's butcher!'

Blackwood bunched his fists. She was almost close enough to touch. He must leave now before she saw him and was humiliated by his attention. She and her husband were probably taking passage by another ship very shortly. *He would go right now.*

It was then that she looked up and stared directly into his eyes. As if she had felt him there, had known exactly where he would be.

The admiral pivoted round on his heels, his bushy eyebrows set in a protective frown.

'This is Captain Blackwood. One of our marine officers.'

His eyes said *go away*, but the doctor asked quickly, 'Aren't you the one who . . . ?'

He glanced at his wife and then back at Blackwood as she said quietly, 'He is the one who saved my life.'

The admiral beamed. 'Bless my soul! Then I take back all I said about the marines.' He sensed that he had spoken out of place and added, 'You must join me later, Blackwood. When the masses have departed, what?' He patted his scarlet sleeve. 'Splendid, didn't know about that.'

As the admiral turned to greet another arrival Blackwood found himself tongue-tied and helpless. All he wanted to do was look at her, to hear her voice again, even though there was no hope for more. Instead he was facing her husband, a serious-faced man aged about forty with a studious manner and voice.

'I have heard something of your exploits, er, Captain? My wife's aunt, Lady Slade, mentioned you to me of course. I am really delighted to meet you at long last. I hope to be able to speak with you, away from all this.' He seemed to dismiss the people around him. 'I would find it most interesting.'

She asked in the same level voice, 'Have you been well, Captain Blackwood? I heard of your father's illness, I was very distressed.' Her eyes were steady and yet too bright as she added, 'I never expected to see you here.'

Blackwood looked at her and tried to sound as calm as she had done. It was difficult not to study her from her dark hair to her clasped hands, to seek something lost, or which had never been.

He replied, 'I have been on Malta since my time in hospital, Ma'am. Sometimes I feel I have been here forever.'

Doctor Hadley nodded thoughtfully. 'A man of action, eh? In peacetime you must find life heavy on your hands.'

Blackwood glanced at him and tried not to dislike him. He spoke as if he was conducting an experiment with a patient. But she had married him and so . . .

She said, 'My husband is on a government commission to

look into the methods of after-care in military and naval hospitals.'

The doctor waved a tray aside and asked for a glass of fruit juice. He said absently, 'We shall be staying here at the medical inspector's house while I carry out some tests at the Hospital of St Angelo.'

Blackwood glanced quickly at her as the doctor's fruit drink arrived. She would be on Malta. For a short time perhaps, but *she would be here*.

He tried to sound matter of fact. 'Yes, I see. Most of our sick and injured people go there.'

He saw her hands gripping more tightly together and was suddenly disgusted with himself. She had made her choice and wanted only to forget her ordeal and avoid anyone who might bring it alive again.

He said, 'I should leave now.'

He saw her sudden tension, the appeal in her violet eyes, and felt his heart begin to pound a warning. She did not want him to go.

The doctor said, 'I have just seen the fleet surgeon yonder. I would be obliged if you would remain with my wife until I have spoken with him. He can be very elusive, I'm told, when it comes to inspections within his realm.'

The great hall could have been empty, the music and voices completely stilled.

Blackwood said, 'I have thought about you so much. Just now I imagined I was dreaming, even now I am not sure. You look so lovely . . .' The words were flooding out of him and he could do nothing to contain them. 'You have never been out of my thoughts.'

She held up a fan and clasped it with both hands. 'You must not speak like that! I implore you!' Even as she spoke she studied his face, her eyes tender as she added, 'Do not imagine I had forgotten *you*. But things have changed. You must see that? I cannot bear to see you hurt.'

'Hurt?' He touched her wrist and then held it, feeling her warmth, seeing the response in her eyes. 'I would risk far more than that. Anything.' He lowered his voice, 'May I see you again?'

She glanced away and he saw her breasts moving quickly as she tried to remain calm.

'Do you mean alone?'

'I have to see you. To talk. It may be the last chance.'

She faced him again but her composure was gone.

'This is madness. I do not know what to say, what you expect of me. I am a married woman.' She hesitated, as if aware of what she had just said. It had sounded like a defence, an admission. 'We go on to Cairo after this.'

He gripped her hands in his. 'Please. I will not be a nuisance, I promise.'

She looked up at him and smiled for the first time. 'You could never be that.' Her hands slipped away as she lowered her fan to her waist.

Doctor Hadley rejoined them and said, 'Another job done.' He glanced at each of them in turn. 'You must have a lot of memories to discuss, eh?' But he was humming quietly to himself as if the question was merely put out of politeness.

Blackwood gave a bow. 'I look forward to our meeting at the admiral's table later on.' He released her gloved hand and stepped back. 'Until then.'

He pushed into the crowd and walked halfway across the hall before he knew what he was doing.

She was so right. It was madness. But it was one which left him helpless. Like a ship without a rudder at the mercy of a relentless gale.

He realized he had reached one of the balconies again and stood by the balustrade, drawing deep breaths while he relived each precious second.

In one corner of the hall Fynmore watched Blackwood's behaviour and then said, 'I shall have to keep an eye on him. I'll not have the good name of my command jeopardized. He is one of my trusted officers, and *she's* a married woman. I had a feeling about those two before. It won't damn well do!'

She lowered her eyes and hid a smile. 'Of course not, dearest. If you say so.'

18

Gesture of Hope

The Hospital of St Angelo was a quiet, secluded place, in spite of the island's bustle which surrounded it. There were winding, tree-lined paths and a garden which was tended by convalescent soldiers and sailors under the eye of one of the resident nuns. It seemed to have a peaceful effect on the inmates, and as Blackwood walked along one of the paths he found it hard to picture some of them as roistering, hard-drinking servicemen.

She was waiting by a stone bench, a place which they had come to regard as their special meeting-place, even though Blackwood had only visited the hospital twice before.

They sat down in a deep patch of shade and looked directly in front of them as if ashamed of what they were doing.

She said quietly, 'It was good of you to come, Philip.'

The use of his name had come naturally and without reservation, as if they both knew it had been decreed by fate.

Blackwood watched one of the nuns sail past like a ship of the line in her head-dress and pale habit. What did they think about these meetings, he wondered?

He said, 'I wish we could see each other every day. All day.'

He felt her turn, and when he faced her he saw the sadness in her eyes.

'I must tell you. My husband has finished his work here. We sail for Cairo on Wednesday.'

He had been expecting it. But as the days had lengthened

into weeks and he had managed to meet her in spite of all the difficulties, he had somehow put the inevitable aside.

'I had hoped . . .' He took one of her hands and pressed it to his cheek. 'I was wrong to hope, and now I have hurt you.'

She shook her head and smiled. 'That you have not. I have got to know more about myself than I believed possible because of you. I cannot bear the thought of our parting.' Her lip quivered. 'Of losing you.'

When he tried to speak she squeezed his hand. 'No, you must hear me. I married Paul because I had known him for a long while, he was one of my father's protégés when I was still at school. After what happened in Africa, I did not know, did not dare to look for love in any man.' She lifted her eyes and made herself say, 'Now I know. You were really the one. But I could not risk destroying both of us.'

Blackwood thought suddenly of Lady Slade's voice in that quiet London house. *You will end up with a broken heart.*

'I thought that Paul would be different. He is much older than I am and the gap between us seemed more so then in other ways. I needed to lose myself, and to do that I thought I might help him in his work as I had once helped my father.'

The air shook to the sullen rumble of gunfire and she held his hand more tightly while her other hand touched her breast.

He watched her profile, the sudden alarm in her eyes.

'It is all right, Davern.'

He listened to the regular crash of a gun salute and recalled that a new man-of-war was due to arrive from England.

He asked, 'Is he a bad husband to you? If so . . .'

She stared at him and shook her head. 'He is neither bad nor good. He is *interested* in me.'

Blackwood thought of his manner at the admiral superintendent's reception. Cool and *interested*. She was right.

'Anyway.' She played with his hand, her skin warm against his fingers. 'It must not be your concern.' She looked away. 'I wish I had had your courage when I most needed it. I know now you might have understood, have helped me. But I dared not risk it after what you did to save my life.'

She tore her hand away and walked to a low wall and stared at the overlapping white buildings and towers.

Across her shoulder she said huskily, 'You never once asked, did you? You knew they'd raped me, but not once did your eyes ask *what was it like? What did they do to you?*'

She almost fell as he seized her and pulled her against him.

'Oh, how I *wish* I'd died that day!'

Blackwood held her without speaking. He let it pour out of her unchecked, knowing it might help, understanding at last what she had been enduring ever since he had freed her.

And all this time she had lived with her secret, and now that she had told him it was too late.

He raised her chin very gently and brushed some hair from her eyes.

'All I know is that I love you. To lose you now is unthinkable.'

He kept seeing her husband, questioning her, persisting about the details when he should have been helping her forget.

A nun, her hands thrust inside her wide sleeves, hurried along the path and then paused to peer at them.

'Your husband has just come from the admiral's residence, Mrs Hadley.' She bobbed and added, 'Good day to you, Captain Blackwood.'

Blackwood watched her as she vanished around the next bend.

'Bless her. Our guardian angel.'

But she gripped his arm and said fiercely, 'Go now. I have caused enough. I'll not see your reputation in ruins too.'

He held her again and felt her tremble as they came together. It was like hanging to a thread when your life depended on it. A rough word or thoughtless move and it would all change to ashes.

'Listen to me. I *want* you. Do you understand? I cannot face losing you.' He slipped his hand around her waist and pulled her more tightly against his body. 'We are meant for each other. Perhaps we were made to suffer before we could find this love.'

Very carefully and reluctantly he released her, watching her eyes, the way she was looking at him as she fought against her own reactions.

Then she said, 'Please kiss me, Philip.'

He felt her arms wrap around his neck as they touched mouths and then kissed. Blackwood had no idea how long they stayed embraced or if anyone passed by on the path. Her mouth told him without words that it was a gesture of desperate hope and nothing more. A realization of something wonderful which would soon slip away.

She put her hands on his chest and said breathlessly, 'You must go. Please.' She dabbed her cheek with the back of her hand. 'It can do no good.'

Blackwood had to force himself to stand away from her.

'I will write to you. Somehow I shall — '

But she had already turned away and was hurrying after the nun.

Blackwood left the hospital enclosure by a side gate and walked towards the harbour. There were more people than usual on the move, he thought vaguely, probably going to see the ship just arrived from England.

News from home, old friends, orders for the future.

He glanced up at the fortress on the hill where the flag flapped limply in the glare. It was all there waiting for him. Fynmore, Harry, the Corps, routine and duty.

He turned and looked back at the hospital with its domed roof and shady trees. But my life is there, with her, and soon she will be gone.

On the harbour wall he saw the people who had come to watch the display of armed might, and most of all the big three-decker which was moving very slowly towards her anchorage.

She looked much like any of the other large men-of-war, except that she was steering into the wind, her sails loosely furled and her yards manned by some of her company. But the tall thin funnel just abaft her foremast and the tell-tale froth beneath her counter from her screw-propeller showed that she was something different. An admiral's flag fluttered from her mainmast truck, riding above the drifting smoke from the gun salute like a lance pendant.

Blackwood tried to get interested in the ship's reason for coming and where she would go. But it eluded him, and he touched his mouth as if he expected to feel some trace of the girl still there.

They had shared a few precious moments together like conspirators. Could that really be an end to it?

He turned on his heel and strode quickly up the hill towards the battery, his step firm as if to mark his determination.

It was not over, nor would it be.

Harry Blackwood watched warily as Fynmore's wife moved eagerly across the cabin. It was a small, ornate schooner which belonged to a local chandler whom Harry had befriended, the only safe place he had managed to find.

It was unnerving how things had changed. Julia Fynmore was enjoying her power over him and seemed totally reckless about the risks they were taking.

He pulled the small curtains aside and peered across the anchorage. Mostly local craft, but you could never be certain on an overcrowded island like Malta.

She glanced into the adjoining cabin and he heard her give a murmur of satisfaction. She turned and faced him like an excited child.

'It's lovely, Harry. Come here and hold me.'

Harry knew now to his cost there was not much childlike about the colonel's wife.

He put his arms round her and felt her push herself against him. A far cry from the woman he had all but assaulted in Fynmore's house in England.

He said, 'We'll have to be careful, Julia.'

He tried to gauge her reaction, what mad thing she might do if he attempted to finish their affair. She actually enjoyed playing with his emotions.

'Oh, stuff!' She looked up at him and smiled. 'Nobody suspects anything. Rupert's too busy anyway.'

Harry started as the boat tilted slightly and then relaxed again. It was one of those blank-faced deck-hands who lived aboard. Even they might tell someone about their master's furtive visitors.

She began to unbutton his shirt and then kissed his chest.

'Come along, Harry.' She ran her hands over his skin and whispered, 'I can't wait.'

He tried again. '*Please*, Julia.' He saw her mouth pout. 'I'm not supposed to know, let alone tell anyone, but the whole Marine contingent is being taken aboard some of the ships here. God knows what we're going to do or where we're going.'

She shook her ringlets with impatience. 'Oh that. I know all about it. It's because of some silly rumour that the Russians are occupying Turkish territory. As if *that* matters!'

Harry stared at her. It had been only yesterday that he had learned about the new orders. The most surprising part had been that the powerful man-of-war which had dropped anchor in Grand Harbour had been wearing the flag of Admiral Sir James Ashley-Chute. Promoted at long last, and with a brand-new flagship, he was amongst them once more like a small typhoon.

Harry had never thought he would be glad to see the little admiral again. He did not care if the Russians, or even the Chinese, were the cause of the excitement. Anything was better than all the dreary months of inactivity and boredom. And with Fynmore's demanding wife constantly marking down his movements it was a double reprieve.

'Well, it can't be helped, I suppose.' He saw her growing impatience and added, 'But we must be careful all the same.'

He stripped off his shirt and followed her to the adjoining cabin. He hated it, the way it had all changed, the 'games' she invented whenever they had managed to meet.

She turned and looked at him, her slim body swaying to the hull's gentle motion.

'What shall it be, Harry?' Her tongue touched her upper lip. 'You are the pirate and I shall be your prisoner again!'

He pushed her roughly on to the wide bunk and when she pretended to struggle he seized her throat and squeezed it. She had ruined everything, had probably known this would happen from that first meeting when he had been little more than a youth.

He realized that she was choking and that he had almost strangled her in his sudden anger. But to her it was just a part of her game, and when he eventually threw himself on top of her she was more eager than ever to return his demands of her.

The thought of getting away to another place, to rid himself of her clinging attention, gave him new strength, and when they fell apart, exhausted and panting, he even managed to smile.

The flagship's spacious wardroom was packed with attentive officers as Admiral Sir James Ashley-Chute drew near to the end of his address.

On one side of the wardroom, and close to an open gun-port, Philip Blackwood listened to the misshapen little admiral and was fascinated by his vigour and his grasp of the newly arisen crisis in the Black Sea.

The admiral looked much older and if possible was even more bent, and yet showed the enthusiasm and keenness of a junior lieutenant.

Unaware of his half-brother's predicament, Blackwood was also eager to be part of the fleet again, to keep busy until he could find Davern. She had left the island with her husband and would be in Cairo by now. He had thought that the memory of her voice, the touch of her hands in his would make the parting too painful to bear. Strangely, it had given him a strength of purpose, a determination that somehow they would be together again, no matter how formidable the obstacles.

The admiral said crisply, 'The Russians are apparently determined to occupy more and more Turkish territory. The warnings have been all too clear, and if they are prepared to wage war because of their greed, then, gentlemen, so be it.'

He had all their attention now. The slow, unruffled existence of fleet or garrison seemed to fade with the admiral's words, and when Blackwood glanced quickly at some of the others he saw their excitement too. It was infectious, like the little man who dominated the wardroom.

The Navy was to send a small but impressive force into the Black Sea itself. The flag would be in *Tenacious*, the newest of her kind, and armed with one hundred and thirty-one guns. Blackwood had wondered since he had heard of Ashley-Chute's arrival how he had managed to accept the use of coal and all it represented to him. In addition to the flagship there would be three steam-frigates and six gunboats. The lioness and her cubs. They might not win a war but they might discourage the Russians from causing one.

Ashley-Chute's deep-set eyes moved over the assembled captains and senior officers until they came to rest on Fynmore.

He said, 'I expect you will all have noticed a preponderance of scarlet among our ranks.' That brought a few laughs, as he knew it would. 'The marines will be divided among the ships under my flag and if need be will be put ashore in battalion strength. An independent force of infantry, well trained, and better armed . . .' his gaze rested briefly on Blackwood, '. . . than they have been in the past.'

Major Brabazon, Fynmore's second-in-command, whispered, 'He almost sounds as if he likes us!'

But Fynmore's back and shoulders remained like a ramrod, and Brabazon glanced past him and gave a weary shrug.

Blackwood smiled. It was never easy to get the colonel to share a joke at a superior officer's expense. Always careful, never a loose word which might injure his prospects.

He liked Brabazon, a big, comfortable man, a marine's marine who had done more than anyone to mould the recruits and old hands into a single force.

'That will be all for the present, gentlemen.' The admiral

nodded curtly to his flag-lieutenant. 'Flags here will explain about appointments to the various ships and er, barracks.' There was another chuckle. 'Afterwards you will return to your commands and prepare the people for weighing on Thursday.' He made to leave as they all stood up and added, 'Captain Blackwood, come with me.'

Blackwood left his place, surprised at the curt order and aware of the watching eyes. Of Fynmore's suspicion more than anything.

Doors opened and closed behind him and then he was in the admiral's day-cabin, the anchored vessels shimmering in haze beyond the broad stern windows.

Ashley-Chute sat down on a bench seat and crossed his legs before saying, 'You will be aboard *Tenacious*, of course.'

Blackwood took a glass of sherry from the cabin servant and wondered why he was here.

Ashley-Chute sipped his glass and sniffed. 'God, what is the purser thinking of, hmm?' He looked at Blackwood and said calmly, 'I am sorry I could not do more for you. Had your wound been less serious I would have retained you under my command. But had it been worse you would not even be here, so you should be grateful.' He gave what might have been a smile. 'There's going to be a fight. I can smell it. You'll get your chance then, right enough.' He glanced around the gleaming, white-painted cabin with obvious satisfaction. 'I suppose one must make some concessions for progress, eh?'

Blackwood asked, 'Is your son well, sir?'

Ashley-Chute glared. 'I suppose so. He commands one of those stinking gunboats yonder. But it's what he wanted, blast him.'

Then the admiral said abruptly, 'Do you think your new contingent could fight ashore against trained troops? I want the truth now, not some sugary answer just to please me.'

'I'm certain of it, sir. In Africa it was different – '

'Africa was not *so* different, Blackwood. We were used as a means to an end. Perhaps that will be so in the Black Sea. To you the African campaign was a series of actions with no true understanding of the main purpose.' He did not conceal the bitterness in his voice. 'I'm an old man, and it's taken me a long while to understand the dishonesty of politicians.'

Blackwood said, 'Slavery was stamped out, sir.'

'Huh, that would have happened anyway. It was Lagos they wanted, but those politicians had to justify their reasons for taking it.' He spat out the words, 'The seeds of Empire! Bloody rubbish!' He gestured to the decanter. 'Pour some more sherry.'

Then Ashley-Chute said slowly, 'I wanted you to know that I appreciated your part in that campaign. You were the hinge in the door, so to speak, and but for you there could have been a severe setback. As it was, the campaign cost us two thousand officers and men.' He glared at his glass. 'For that stinking coast and all the trouble it will bring us.' He looked up again, his monkey face impassive. 'If you repeat a word of what I said I'll have you boiled in oil.'

'Of course, sir.'

So that was it. The little admiral's way of saying he was sorry that he was the only one who had gained nothing from the whole affair.

'Never try to discover a reason, Blackwood. Just do it. It's always been my way in the past and I have no intention of changing.' He looked around as if to find the right words. 'Not even for the Tsar of bloody Russia!'

Two days later the *Tenacious*, accompanied by her small flotilla of steam vessels, left the Grand Harbour and put to sea. The bands played from the battery and rockets were discharged over the darkening water until the winking lights finally disappeared.

It was a gala occasion, a display of pride and cheerful arrogance for the admiral and his latest command.

It was much the same aboard the flagship, although for different reasons. Colour-Sergeant M'Crystal was grateful to get his worst troublemakers contained where he could watch and control them. Private Frazier cared for his new rifle with something akin to love. He had practised on the range until he could hit a small target at three hundred yards, and could hardly wait to use his rifle in deadly earnest. Corporal Jones, as reliable and conscientious as ever, still nursed the grief for his dead friend, Corporal Bly. It was strange, he thought, that he had never got over it. He knew he was wrong, but he could not find anything to like in the new corporal, and that disturbed him deeply. The Rocke twins settled down again to shipboard life and to the business of tormenting Sergeant Quintin. The adjutant, Lieutenant Speer, grew gaunt with worry as he thought about his wife in England and the affair she had been having when he had last caught her. Lieutenant Harry Blackwood, on the other hand, was twice his old self, always cheerful and easy with his men, with nothing to show of the humiliating strain he had been under.

Lieutenant-Colonel Rupert Fynmore was very satisfied. He was the right age and held the right rank. New horizons stretched in every direction. He had already forgotten how he had dreaded being discharged from the Corps or dropped into some meaningless post which led nowhere. There had never been a general in his family. But now things would change.

It warmed his heart to realize he held the same rank as his late father, the same as Captain Blackwood's father also. He often congratulated himself on his choice of a young wife. She came from a respected military family, and that fact would do no harm at all when the time came.

The network of courier-brigs and fast packets kept the Mediterranean's flag-officers informed of world events, but the mass of seamen and marines remained in ignorance as to what was happening.

While Ashley-Chute's squadron moved eastward on its slow and unhurried cruise, news was received that Russian forces had invaded more Turkish territory, and in self-defence the Sultan had declared war. Later, when *Tenacious* lay at anchor and suffered the indignities of coaling ship, Ashley-Chute was informed that a strong Russian force had sailed from Sebastopol and had totally destroyed a Turkish squadron with great loss of life.

Throughout Ashley-Chute's command there seemed to be little sympathy for the Turks. Russia had, after all, been Britain's ally against them just twenty-six years earlier.

Philip Blackwood had noticed the arrival of several French men-of-war in the Eastern Mediterranean, and their captains had often been aboard to meet Ashley-Chute and presumably to discuss possible strategy.

But daily routine continued, sail and gun drills, coaling ship and washing-down again.

It was an ordinary day too when the flagship's company was piped aft to hear an announcement by the captain.

If Ashley-Chute resembled a monkey, then Captain Montagu Jervis was certainly everything a bulldog should be.

Short but heavily built, he looked older than his years because of his sweeping, 'heavy swell' side-whiskers. He was a stern, even severe captain, but seemed to be quite at ease with his admiral, and Blackwood often wondered what had become of Ackworthy, his original flag-captain.

On this particular morning, as the seamen swarmed aft, Captain Jervis stood with his commander, cap tugged over his eyes, his hands in his pockets until silence had eventually fallen over his ship.

Blackwood waited with the other officers and watched the captain's impressive side-whiskers blowing slightly in the breeze and wondered what was so important.

Jervis said in his hard voice, 'The Russians have shown no sign that they intend to release their hold on Turkish lands, and Her Majesty's Government have consequently ordered us to enter the Black Sea without further delay.'

That was all he said. But it was no longer an ordinary day. Britain was at war.

19

The Enemy

Harry Blackwood stared at the shore and grimaced. 'The Turkish Empire? If that is what the rest of it looks like, I think we must be fighting on the wrong side.'

Blackwood glanced at him curiously. His half-brother seemed to be constantly on edge, his original good humour had vanished.

It was true that the first excitement of being part of a war had somewhat disappeared after the squadron had passed through the Bosphorus and into the Black Sea. Nobody was quite sure what he had expected, but with the exception of a few patrols within sight of the Russian coast they had seen and done nothing.

Now, anchored off the Turkish port of Varna at the western end of the enclosed sea, the squadron swung to its anchors and gazed longingly at the low-roofed town.

'Is something wrong, Harry?'

Harry looked at him uncertainly. 'I'm sick of kicking my heels like this. I sometimes wish I'd cut with family tradition and gone for a line regiment. If I have to mount one more guard of honour for the French and Turkish High Command I really will go mad!'

Blackwood tried to put his half-brother's discontent from his mind. When they had last dropped anchor after a fruitless patrol in search of Russian ships there had been sacks of letters waiting for the squadron. Sweethearts and wives, news from home, the vital link with that other world.

There had been one for him posted in Cairo.

He had already written several times to the address she had given him but this was the first real news he had received in reply. It appeared that all his letters had arrived at once, and he was touched that she had taken the trouble to read them all in order and with great care. He was also surprised that it had been so easy to converse by letter. Perhaps he had half expected her to break with him as soon as she had left Malta.

She wrote with warmth and affection, as if they had been lovers instead of brief companions. Blackwood had read her letter so many times it was crumpled from constant handling. Harry, always so confident and assured about his lady friends, would have laughed at him if only he knew.

A midshipman saluted and said, 'Captain's compliments, sir, and would you muster a guard. The admiral is returning aboard directly.'

'Very well. Pipe for Sergeant Quintin, if you please.'

So the admiral was coming back. He had been across in the senior flagship for most of the day, probably giving vent to his own hatred for inaction with his immediate superior.

Harry tightened his sword-belt and stamped his feet on the deck. It had been a close thing that time. He had almost burst out to Philip about the letter he had received from Fynmore's wife in Malta. It had been devoid of love and mystery and had been filled with remorse and fear.

She had apparently met another officer after the squadron had sailed from Grand Harbour, and from the tone of her letter Harry guessed she had not been so successful in gaining the upper hand. She was with child and quite obviously terrified at the possible consequences when Fynmore found out about it.

Harry swallowed hard and stared at the anchored frigates and steam gunboats nearby browsing beneath their usual haze of dusty smoke. She may have had the child already. She had also hinted that she would plead her husband's forgiveness if only for the good of their reputations. If that failed she would do something terrible.

Harry looked forward as the first squad of marines tramped

up a companion ladder and moved to the entry port in readiness for the admiral.

Suppose it all came out about his own attentions to her? Fynmore was already jealous of the Blackwood family, no matter what he pretended. Something like this would ruin everything.

A barge moved from the other flagship's shadow, and with the oars rising and falling like wings turned towards the *Tenacious*.

Sergeant Quintin reported, 'Guard ready for inspection, *sir*.'

Blackwood watched his half-brother as he carried out a cursory inspection. No shared jokes with his men now. The marines resented his unexplained change. It showed on their stiff faces.

Captain Montagu Jervis strode heavily across the quarter-deck and looked grimly at the barge. He nodded to Blackwood and murmured, 'I hope that Sir James is in good humour. The frigates have reported a coal shortage in the port. It will be a week at least before fresh supplies arrive.' He glared up at the impeccably furled sails of his ship. 'How can you run a modern fleet with stone-age brains in control?'

But when Ashley-Chute's head and shoulders rose over the ship's side he appeared to be in an extremely affable mood.

He touched his hat casually to the guard and waited for the chorus of trilling calls to fall silent. Then to the quarterdeck at large he said cheerfully, 'Prepare for sea, gentlemen. It's *action* this time, so stir yourselves.'

Even Captain Jervis's gruff explanation about the coal supplies did not appear to dampen his humour.

'Well, what did you expect from a bunch of godless heathen, eh, Captain?' He rubbed his hands together and added, 'Just so long as the flagship is ready, hmm?'

With his flag-lieutenant trotting behind him he hurried below the poop towards his quarters.

Later at a hastily called conference Captain Jervis explained the cause of his admiral's excitement.

Just before the outbreak of war with Russia the battery at Odessa had fired on Her Majesty's Ship *Furious*, despite her flag of truce, as she was about to parley over bringing any British subjects away from the port. One of the first operations after the declaration of war had been for the fleet to bombard that same battery and to leave it and many of the harbour installations wrecked and burning.

Now it seemed there was a second large battery which had been sited just to the east of Odessa, which was being used to protect an assortment of Russian men-of-war lying at anchor there.

If a full scale invasion was eventually to be mounted against the Russians, the British and their allies had to hold command of all the sea routes which carried their troops and supplies.

Captain Jervis said in his usual severe manner, 'We will bring those ships to action and destroy them, the battery too if need be.'

It sounded simple enough, and the effect on the ship's company was immediate as the news spread from mess to mess.

As dusk closed over the anchorage *Tenacious*, accompanied by the steam-frigate *Sarpedon*, and the little paddle-gunboat *Rupert*, headed away from the land.

The other vessels watched in frustrated silence as the flagship's company manned the yards and cheered as if they had already won a resounding victory.

Aft in the great cabin Ashley-Chute cocked his head to listen and to share the moment.

During his long career he had been criticized and berated many times, and more than once had been replaced by another officer because of his ideas and tactics. But in each case he had known himself to be right, and when others had doubted he had stood firm. A hard challenge demanded a harder solution. He knew he would never end his days in the peace and security of Admiralty, but he no longer cared. Here was where he belonged. Unfettered by higher authority and with the power of right and justice on his side.

The deck tilted slightly to the thrust of a south-westerly
wind and he smiled wryly as he thought of his flag-captain's
eagerness to use his mechanical power. That could wait. In
his mind's eye he could picture *Tenacious* with all her canvas
spread and filling to the wind. There was no finer sight. No
wonder the sailors cheered. Ignorant and insubordinate they
might be, but they shared his pride in the ship and what she
stood for.

They all feared him, and the idea amused him. He recalled
Blackwood when they had first met all those years ago in New
Zealand. Pale and angry after the savage fight, and deter-
mined to defend his dead major's name.

Maybe that was why he had retained Captain Blackwood in
Audacious. He was the only one he could remember who had
ever stood up to him.

His servant tiptoed into the cabin and waited anxiously.

Ashley-Chute waved his hand. 'Some port, I think, Fisher.
One of the *special* ones, hmm?'

The servant hurried away, grateful that the sun was still
shining over his master's head.

Two days after weighing anchor at Varna the *Tenacious*'s
masthead lookout reported land fine on the larboard bow.

They had made very good time, with a strengthening
south-westerly under their coat-tails to give them an extra
thrust through the water. The frigate and the little gunboat had
mercifully avoided any sort of mechanical breakdown, and had
even used their sails to maintain station on the flagship.

Admiral Sir James Ashley-Chute appeared on deck within
minutes of the cry from the masthead. Blackwood, who had
been taking his customary exercise up and down the quarterdeck, moved to the opposite side as the small, monkey-like
figure strode to the nettings. Ashley-Chute might pretend
that he was calm and unruffled, but Blackwood knew him
well enough to see through his pretence.

Captain Jervis said, 'Wind's still rising, sir. I'd like the hands to shorten sail presently. We're in for a full gale, according to the Master, and I must say I agree.'

Ashley-Chute's hands found each other across his buttocks and clasped firmly together as if for support.

'You are the captain. Act as you think fit.' He glanced at the sea and then up at the low, fast-moving clouds. All day the sea had been lively and broken into cruising ranks of jagged whitecaps. Now it looked darker, like the sky. Summer was short in the Black Sea apparently.

Blackwood noticed that the admiral's narrow shoulders were already soaked in spray, and he could almost feel the little man's agitation as he watched the worsening weather.

The admiral remarked curtly, 'Nothing much we can do now anyway. It will be dark in two hours.' Nevertheless, he took a telescope from his flag-lieutenant and steadied it against the ship's slow plunging motion.

Jervis offered helpfully, 'The bay and the Russian battery lie nor'-nor'-west, sir.'

The telescope snapped shut. 'Signal the frigate *Sarpedon* to investigate.'

Blackwood could imagine the relief aboard the black-hulled frigate which had been their constant companion since leaving Malta all that time ago. Free of the admiral's watchful eye, if only for the moment. He saw the signal dash up the *Sarpedon*'s yards and break out to the wind in acknowledgement. Against the threatening clouds the flags looked unusually bright, like painted metal.

Ashley-Chute paced a few steps this way and that.

'Put a reliable officer at the masthead, Captain Jervis.' His deepset eyes settled suddenly on Blackwood. 'Or would *you* do me the honour, sir?'

Blackwood handed his hat to a seaman and unclipped his belt. He had guessed what Ashley-Chute wanted to know. It was not mere curiosity.

'Aye, sir.'

Ashley-Chute beckoned him over, his manner impatient again.

'The Russians will know what we are about, Blackwood. I need a good eye at the masthead and not merely a sailor's judgement, you catch my meaning?'

Blackwood hurried to the main shrouds and swung himself out on to the weather ratlines. He could feel the wind pushing him playfully against the tarred ropes, the soaking slap of spray against his tunic as he began to climb. It was exhilarating and something he had never really got used to. Up and up, past the fighting top and on to the topmast shrouds, the masts and spars shaking and creaking to the wind's power.

How they had managed in the old days he could never understand. Ordinary men dragged to sea by the hungry press gangs, boys even who were expected to climb aloft in all weathers to fight the hardened canvas, to reef or splice repairs in the drumming rigging, or face the consequences of the lash if they hesitated.

He found a burly seaman squatting on the cross-trees, seemingly oblivious to the pale deck so far below his dangling feet.

If he thought it strange to find a marine coming to join him, and an officer at that, he did not show it.

Blackwood asked, 'Where away?'

The seaman pointed towards the unbroken line of coast, slate-coloured in the failing light.

Blackwood waited for the mast to dip over again and then levelled his telescope on the bearing.

Angry wave crests leapt into focus while an offshore current writhed among them like a giant serpent. He saw the frigate end on, a thick trail of smoke gushing downwind as she forged into the bay, spindrift and spray flying from her bows and paddle-boxes in a wild dance.

He moved the glass very carefully and felt the tarred cordage biting at his skin as the ship plunged into a deep trough. Jervis would have to take in much more sail unless he wanted to lose some of it completely, he thought.

He tensed. There were ships at anchor, their overlapping shadows making them hard to recognize and distinguish.

The lookout called, 'Two, mebbe three men-o'-war, sir, an' a few merchantmen besides!'

He sounded cheerful at the prospect. He had probably already worked out his share of the prize-money if they were lucky.

Part of the coastline flickered briefly, like lightning on a hillside. Blackwood held his breath and counted the seconds. Then he heard the echoing boom of heavy gunfire and watched as several tall waterspouts shot from the water on either side of the frigate. The battery had not been taken by surprise. He saw the spray from the falling columns of water being ripped aside by the wind and pictured the Russian guns already being reloaded and run up for another salvo.

Boom . . . boom . . .

The fall of shot was even closer this time, and Blackwood was almost certain that at least one hit had been made on *Sarpedon*'s hull.

A metallic voice echoed from the deck. It was Jervis recalling him with the aid of a speaking-trumpet.

It would soon be dark. Blackwood climbed down the vibrating ratlines and wondered what Ashley-Chute would do. The Russians were in a very strong position. The wind too was in their favour and would soon deny *Tenacious* the sea-room she needed to close the range to any effect.

Ashley-Chute snapped, 'Did you see the battery?'

Blackwood regained his breath. 'I can mark it on the Master's chart, sir. They are heavy weapons.'

They both turned as the booming crash of gunfire sighed over the deck like a storm.

Someone called, '*Sarpedon*'s bin 'it, sir.'

Jervis exclaimed harshly, 'Damn their bloody eyes!'

Then the captain made up his mind. 'Pipe both watches, Mr Norman. Hands aloft and reef tops'ls. Then take in the main-course, lively now!'

Calls shrilled and bare feet pounded across the decks as the flagship's seamen ran to their stations before swarming up the ratlines in a human tide.

Blackwood watched the tiny, foreshortened figures scrambling out on the yards, some above the sea itself, as they began to fist the bulging canvas into submission. If a man fell now he was finished. To hit the sea and drown, or to drop on to the deck, it was all the same to the professional seaman.

Blackwood turned as he heard Fynmore's voice. Immaculate as ever, he was standing with Major Brabazon, the second-in-command, while they watched the bustle aloft.

He guessed that Fynmore hated sharing a cabin with the major, but with so many extra marines aboard, everyone had been made to double up. Blackwood had gone to see Brabazon about gunnery practice but had stumbled on Fynmore instead. It had been embarrassing to see the way he had torn some gold-rimmed glasses from his nose and had rammed them inside his tunic while he had pretended to read his papers unaided.

Ashley-Chute rasped, 'Make to *Sarpedon*. *Discontinue the action and close on the Flag.*'

The signals midshipman called, '*Sarpedon*'s acknowledged, sir.'

Ashley-Chute joined Jervis by the quarterdeck rail. 'Blackwood saw the fall of shot. A stronger battery than I expected. Must be a reason, hmm?'

Jervis watched his seamen sliding down the stays to the deck, their work done for the present. The ship felt sluggish but easier under her reduced sails, and he was relieved.

He answered, 'We shall be in trouble if we tack any closer, sir. We are on a lee shore as it is, and if the wind rises still further . . .' He left the rest unsaid.

The admiral stuck out his jaw. 'I do not intend that — ' He broke off angrily as the signals midshipman called from the shrouds.

'From *Sarpedon*, sir. *Have received two direct hits and am making water. Enemy shipping at anchor* — ' he blinked the spray from his eyes while his assistant, another midshipman, thumbed through his book to ensure that the signal was correct, '— *includes three men-of-war.*'

Jervis snapped, 'Acknowledge.' He bit his lip. '*Sarpedon* will be awash if the sea gets up.'

But Ashley-Chute ignored him. 'Signal her to confirm the size of warships.' He strode impatiently to the opposite side, his body leaning over to the sloping deck.

The soaked and dripping midshipman, who was very aware of the presence of so many superior officers, tried again, 'From *Sarpedon*, sir. *Enemy shipping at anchor. Two frigates and one ship of the line.*'

He gaped down from his perch with astonishment as the admiral shouted, '*Well done*, boy!'

Blackwood felt Harry slide across the spray covered deck to join him. 'I've never heard him praise anyone so junior before!'

Ashley-Chute banged a fist into his palm. 'Don't you *see*, Captain Jervis? The Russians are reported as having no more than fourteen sail of the line in the Black Sea. And one of them is *right here*! Dammit, Jervis, I'll ensure she never gets away. *Never!*'

The flag-lieutenant gave a nervous cough. 'I fear the light is going fast, sir. We shall lose visual contact with *Sarpedon* in minutes.'

Ashley-Chute regarded him coolly. 'I am aware of that.'

Jervis said, 'It is too lively to lower a boat, sir. But I could drift your despatches across to *Sarpedon* and then signal her to return to Varna.'

The admiral looked from one to the other. 'If *Sarpedon* sinks on passage we shall not know if my despatches have reached the admiral commanding at Varna or not. Tell her to lie to and execute repairs to the best of her ability.' He clasped his hands behind him again.

'I have no intention of waiting for support from anybody. There is a ship of the line over yonder, gentlemen, and at first light tomorrow I intend to engage her.' He nodded approvingly as the signals party bent on more hoists of flags and sent them soaring up the yards. 'And you may tell your, er, chief engineer, Captain Jervis, that he had best be ready to put his three hundred and fifty horsepower into motion at the first crowing of the cock, *right?*' He strode aft without waiting to watch the effect of his orders.

Jervis stared worriedly at the listing frigate and the clouds of smoke which appeared to be seeping through her starboard side.

'I never thought I'd live to hear him say *that*.'

Harry said quietly, 'Let's hope he knows what he's doing.'

Fynmore walked over and grasped the nettings to stop himself from falling.

He looked searchingly at the marine lieutenant and said, 'That could be said of many, Mr Blackwood.' He walked away without another glance.

Harry turned his face to the wind and gasped in the cold spray. Fynmore knew something. God Almighty, he *knew*.

Blackwood did not see his anxiety but remained by the nettings and listened to the faint clatter of the frigate's pumps as she fought her lonely battle with her constant enemy.

And tomorrow it will be our turn.

Blackwood had never been in a ship of the line when she had cleared for action in deadly earnest. Before it had been a necessary part of training and routine drill, and it was difficult to believe there could be such a difference.

All hands had been roused and piped to breakfast well before daylight, and even that had been different, and he doubted if many of the *Tenacious*'s eleven hundred officers and men had slept very much either. It was like remaking a part of history, or living something which might never occur again.

As the drums had rolled and the pipes had called from deck to deck, Blackwood had felt his own excitement rising to match the occasion. Like his grandfather's old pictures; the Nile, Copenhagen and Trafalgar.

Screens had been taken down and the ship cleared from

bow to stern. *Tenacious* mounted sixteen of the new eight-inch muzzle-loaders, but the bulk of her impressive armament consisted of thirty-two-pounders which had served the Navy for nearly a century. The 'Long Nine', as it was affectionately termed by the British sailor, was still the most reliable for accuracy and effectiveness, or so it was claimed.

When Keene, *Tenacious*'s commander, reported the ship cleared for action, Jervis had gone aft himself to inform the admiral.

The wind had eased and backed during the night, but not enough to lessen the dangers of being on a lee shore.

Blackwood had been with his lieutenants and sergeants since dawn, for with so many extra men it was not easy to place them to full advantage. Aft on poop and quarterdeck and aloft in the three fighting tops, while others were doubled up alongside gun crews with some biting comments from the seamen who manned the batteries on either beam.

Blackwood made his way to the quarterdeck and reported to Fynmore.

Fynmore pursed his lips and squinted above the packed hammocks in the nettings.

'This will not take long, I think.' He did not sound very convinced.

Blackwood took a telescope from the rack and climbed on to a shot garland.

The coast looked hostile and blurred in the grey light. There was drizzle among the pellets of spray and he felt it sting his cheek as he stared at the anchored ships which lay across the larboard bow in an untidy array.

He could see the first-rate quite clearly, a three-decker, she was standing bows-on as she swung to her cable, and he saw her loosely brailed canvas puffing against the yards, and antlike figures creeping about her rigging as they made their own preparations. One of the Russian frigates showed no sign of life, but the other was already shortening her cable and perhaps preparing to weigh if the enemy drew too close.

Weak sunlight glinted on something gold, and Black-wood shifted his glass on to the dome of an isolated church which had appeared between two overlapping hills like a giant sentinel.

Colour-Sergeant M'Crystal said, 'Admiral's on his way, sir.'

He too sounded strange and his Edinburgh dialect more pronounced than usual. Perhaps he was remembering something or feeling the same sense of history.

Ashley-Chute appeared on deck tugging on a pair of freshly laundered gloves. He glanced forward at the groups of men beside their guns and aloft to his flag at the mainmast truck.

He seemed satisfied and sniffed at the keen air as he remarked, 'Fine day for it.' He gave a brief scowl as the hull shivered, as if something heavy had fallen between decks.

Jervis watched him dourly. 'The Chief is warned and standing by, sir. Shall I give the order to raise the funnel and lower the screw?'

The admiral did not reply directly. He was examining his flagship and evidently enjoying what he saw. He took a telescope and looked first at the damaged *Sarpedon*. She had a severe list, and there were black scars on her upper deck to betray the damage which the Russian guns had caused.

Ashley-Chute crossed to another vantage point and studied the enemy. Like Blackwood, he watched the way she lay at anchor, and then gave a snort of disapproval as two additional ensigns broke from her fore and mainmasts, the white flags with their blue crosses strangely peaceful above so much artillery.

He snapped, 'Run up two more ensigns, Jervis. She's the *Rostislav*, by the way. Ran across her in Vigo some years back.'

Jervis had recognized the Russian three-decker from the moment he had come on deck, but knew it would have spoiled the admiral's mood had he told him.

Ashley-Chute said, 'This is what I intend. The shore

battery is obviously sited to protect the main anchorage, in this case the *Rostislav*, hmm?'

Jervis took his eyes from the extra ensigns as they broke stiffly to the wind.

'I suppose so, sir.'

'Be certain of it. So we shall run down on her using the wind to full advantage. Once across her bows we will come about and rake her.' His eyes glinted as he saw it happening in his mind. 'We shall lose the wind-gauge, but no matter. Our Russian friends will not know of our additional power, what you call *progress*, eh? So we shall pass 'twixt the enemy and the shore battery and *steam* sou'-east from the bay.'

Captain Jervis glanced at the commander and then at his admiral.

'Very well, sir.'

It was hard to tell if he was alarmed by the audacity of the plan or by the admiral's sudden reliance on the engine-room.

Ashley-Chute nodded as if to confirm his thoughts.

'Signal *Rupert* to stand by but to stand clear of those guns.'

He smiled at Fynmore. 'Not much for your fellows to do today, Colonel. But they may learn something.'

Captain Jervis took a deep breath. 'Carry on, Commander. Load and run out. Mr Irving, alter course two points to larboard, Mr Aldham, pipe the after-guard to the braces and trim the driver, we'll shorten sail again when the range is reduced.'

Like nerves from a human brain, Jervis's officers passed his orders, which were then relayed to each deck. When the last messenger and boatswain's mate had reported to the quarter-deck, Jervis faced the admiral again.

Ashley-Chute took his sword from his flag-lieutenant and clipped it to his belt. It only made him look shorter.

'So be it, Captain Jervis.'

At the shrill of a whistle the gunports opened along the flagship's side, and to a second blast the lines of black muzzles poked out into the poor light. Between decks the gun crews on one side would see their enemy for the first time, even though their admiral's strategy would remain a mystery.

Jervis licked his lips. 'Let her fall off another point, Mr Irving, I do not want the enemy to know our intentions.'

Blackwood watched the anchored ships and saw the Russian three-decker's ports open in response to *Tenacious*'s challenge.

Smoke eddied through a vent and passed swiftly downwind as the engineers fought to keep their boilers under control until the very last moment.

At the top of the main companionway a marine bugler moistened his lips and waited for the order. Blackwood caught his eye and smiled. But the youth did not even see him. He was living each precious second, nursing it for the time when he got home to his parents in Portsmouth.

Boom . . . Boom . . .

Blackwood saw the flashes along the dull coastline and waited for the waterspouts to appear. Towering columns of water burst from the sea between *Tenacious* and the Russian, the rigidity of the barrage bringing a chorus of derisive jeers from the waiting gun crews.

Jervis rasped, 'Keep those men silent! Master-at-Arms, I'll flog the next one who disregards my order.'

Blackwood glanced at the powerfully built captain. This day would mean a great deal to him. His ship, his future, even his hopes for a new Navy might depend on it.

The enemy battery crashed out again and more waterspouts towered above the ships before being scattered by the wind.

Jervis said, 'Pass the word to the carronade crew. They may get a chance to engage.'

Ashley-Chute looked at him and said dryly, 'I intend to *rake* her, not step aboard!'

Jervis frowned. 'Pipe the hands to the braces, Mr Norman! Send the topmen aloft and shake out all reefs. The enemy will imagine we've seen our danger and are coming about to beat clear of the bay.'

Men swarmed up the shrouds once more, and as the yards were hauled round and extra helmsmen took their places by the big double-wheel, Jervis shot a glance forward where the boatswain's party waited with tackles and halliards to hoist the long funnel. Below decks, when the order came, another party of men would throw their weight on the lowering gear and lower the shaft and screw into the water.

Ashley-Chute sauntered across the quarterdeck and stood with one foot on a coiled hawser. He glanced up at his flag and the whipping masthead pendant and then said to Blackwood, 'Tell your fellow to sound off, hmm?'

Blackwood raised his hand and dropped it to his side.

All eyes turned to watch as the minute bugler brought his heels together and raised the instrument to his lips.

They were about to become a part of history.

20

A Handful of Rifles

'One of the frigates has weighed, sir!'

Captain Jervis grunted and watched the nearest Russian man-of-war tilt over to the wind, her billowing canvas in violent disarray as she fought clear of her anchorage. She lay on *Tenacious*'s larboard bow some three cables clear, and her captain obviously knew his ship and the bay very well indeed. The frigate tacked hard round until she seemed to be skimming the wave crests with her main-yard, but slowly and deliberately she managed to steer close-hauled between the flagship and her anchored consorts.

Blackwood clung to a stay and watched intently. The frigate captain knew he was in a hopeless position to protect the other vessels in the bay unless he could gain some sea-room. With the wind to his advantage he might even manage to beat well clear and attack the disabled *Sarpedon*. Ashley-Chute would then be forced to discontinue his plan and go to *Sarpedon*'s aid. It would take a lot of time, and by then the enemy might have brought up more artillery or found some additional ships to deter the invaders.

'Man the braces! Hands wear ship.' Jervis's square jaw was set like a crag while his heavy-swell side-whiskers blew forward with the wind. 'Steer nor'-east, Mr Irving.'

With blocks and halliards squealing in protest and the seamen flinging their bodies on to the braces, *Tenacious* began to turn slowly to starboard, so that the enemy frigate seemed to hang across the opposite bow as if held there.

Blackwood saw the Russian ship setting more sails, the

blurred gleam of copper as she rolled over to expose her bilge.

The range was falling away as *Tenacious* and the frigate moved inexorably together. Jervis held the advantage and was using the wind to swing his great ship as if on a pivot so that very soon all his larboard guns would bear on the enemy.

The frigate was almost in line with the anchored *Rostislav*. Forbidden to shout or cheer, some of the British seamen and marines were nudging each other to contain their excitement while gun captains crouched and peered along their sights, hands on trigger lines, waiting for the order to fire.

It was as if someone had drawn an invisible track across the choppy water, Blackwood thought. *Tenacious* was bearing down from the seaward end while the frigate lay somewhere between her and her heavier consort. The other enemy frigate remained firmly at anchor, and even the shore battery held its fire, an unwilling spectator as their aim was blocked by their own vessels.

Ashley-Chute said calmly, 'The *Rostislav* is shortening her cable now.'

Fynmore gave his twisted grin. 'Too late for *him*, sir.'

His smile vanished as a long orange tongue flashed from the frigate's side. Several men on the quarterdeck ducked involuntarily as a ball shrieked overhead and brought down a trailing creeper of halliard from aloft.

'Stand by, the larboard battery!'

Deck above deck the lines of thirty-two-pounders pointed blindly towards the lithe, fast-moving frigate.

'*On the up-roll!*'

Captain Jervis blinked as another ball fanned overhead and punched a hole through the mizzen-topsail.

Blackwood could picture the gundecks, the shadowy shapes of the crews, their eyes gleaming in the light from the open ports. As on the upper deck where at regular intervals the lieutenants stood at their divisions, midshipmen and warrant officers between them like links of a chain.

'*Fire!*'

It was more like hitting a reef than firing a controlled

broadside. The deck bounded beneath their feet, and as the guns hurled themselves inboard on their tackles and the crews leapt forward with sponges and rammers, the smoke erupted over the deck in a solid, choking barrier.

Blackwood wiped his eyes and watched the terrible wave of destruction as it smashed along the frigate's side and rigging like an invisible scythe.

It was awful to see. One moment there was a taut pyramid of sails, a graceful hull leaning as close to the wind as she dared, and in just a few seconds she had been transformed into a wreck. Her foremast and main-topmast plunged over the side in a great mesh of spars and thrashing canvas, while lengths of her gangway and poop were flung high into the air before splashing around her to reveal the extent of the damage.

'Run out!'

Squealing on their trucks the larboard guns were hauled hastily to the ports. The dragging mass of wreckage on the enemy's hull was pulling her round like a cruel sea-anchor, so that eventually her stern would lie exposed to *Tenacious*'s broadside.

Jervis glanced at his admiral. 'Cease firing, sir?'

Ashley-Chute clasped his hands together more firmly.

'No.'

'Fire!'

The range was less than half a cable and Blackwood could hear the iron smashing through the enemy's hull, upending guns and roaring between decks with a hail of splinters and flying timbers.

Jervis called, 'Stand by to alter course.'

As the yards swung round once more and *Tenacious* turned this time towards the land her starboard guns waited impatiently for their chance of action.

The Russian three-decker's anchor broke from the ground, and as sails flapped and then hardened to the wind she began her own fight to escape from the bay which had changed from a haven into a trap.

'Stand by to starboard!'

The careering Russian three-decker would soon be directly across *Tenacious*'s bows. She was almost aback as the wind moaned into her, the same wind which the enemy had relied on for keeping the British attackers well clear and easy meat for the shore battery.

Ashley-Chute snapped, 'No point in any more deception, Captain Jervis.'

Jervis looked at him only briefly. Blackwood saw the glance. Relief that he could use his engine to protect his ship from further risk of running aground. Contempt too for the admiral who had ordered him to continue firing on a sinking, dismasted enemy and cause a terrible and unnecessary slaughter.

'*Raise the funnel!*'

The working party jerked into life and the tall funnel rose from the deck, its stays humming in the wind. Smoke began to gush from it even as the deck shook and settled down to a steady vibration as the lowered screw started to take effect.

An uneven crash of gunfire cut across the water and Blackwood felt some of the enemy's shots hit *Tenacious*'s hull like muted hammers.

'Starboard battery!' Commander Keene was crouched down as if he alone was sighting every gun. '*Fire!*'

Because she was almost bows-on the Russian ship received less than a quarter of the broadside, but as the sea boiled around her and great columns of water hemmed her in like pillars of ice, she was seen to rock as many of the balls smashed into her. Her sails were pock-marked with holes and lengths of broken cordage blew unchecked in the wind.

Ashley-Chute heard some of the gun crews cheering again and said, 'Let them cheer, Captain, and let those ruffians hear them!'

Grim-faced, Jervis turned away. 'Hands aloft, reef tops'ls! Stand by to come about.' He tried to gauge the engine's beat but it was drowned by the thunder of the guns as another broadside flashed along *Tenacious*'s ports.

The Russian captain had realized what was happening but could do little. Once again his enemy was close enough to prevent the shore battery from helping him in his plight. As *Tenacious*'s canvas was lashed smartly to the yards and the engine brought her further and further round into the wind she stood like a black and white cliff between the Russian and the land. By this time there was so much smoke in the bay that it would have been hard for the gunnery officer ashore to hit anything.

Blackwood ran to the poop ladder and joined Major Brabazon who was pointing down into the water as it lifted against the tumblehome like a tide.

Survivors from the Russian frigate were clinging to broken spars and an upended cutter. Others, torn and bloody, or blackened by powder burns, rolled in the swell like so much grisly flotsam.

Brabazon yelled above the din of gunfire and shouting, 'The frigate broke up, Philip! God, it must have been a terrible end!'

Blackwood winced as a musket-ball slapped into the packed hammocks. Were they that close? And who was brave or foolhardy enough to bother with a musket as the two giants drove towards each other?

Brabazon yelled, 'Look! There's her poop!'

The frigate's battered stern was riding above the water with over a dozen men clinging to its gilded scrollwork like seals on a rock. Others splashed and pleaded for help among the tossing wreckage, and Blackwood thought he saw a woman amongst them, probably the wife of one of the officers.

'Reload!'

One of the enemy shots had come through a forward port and yet aft on the quarterdeck they had not even seen it. A gun had been knocked away from the side and two men lay motionless on the planking. As the other guns roared out again Blackwood saw some blood run across the deck and quiver in the sunlight as if it still clung on to life.

Some of the marines growled angrily and thrust their rifles over the nettings and trained them on the swimmers.

Sergeant Quintin snarled, 'Belay that! Save yer 'ate fer later!'

'*Cease firing!*' Jervis stared round fiercely, his eyes red from smoke. 'Tell them to hold their fire, damn you!'

A whistle shrilled somewhere and voices intruded through the din of canvas and creaking spars as the order was repeated to the lower decks.

The masthead lookout, marooned and without hope if his perch was shot from under him, must have been calling for some time but his voice had gone unheard.

Blackwood snatched a telescope from one of the midshipmen and trained it towards the bows. Through the rigging and past the thin funnel and its thrusting smoke until he had found the sea directly ahead. It was like something from a nightmare. As Brabazon had surmised, the enemy frigate must have broken her back under the crushing weight of *Tenacious*'s bombardment and the forepart had plunged to the bottom. Perhaps the shock of hitting the sea bed had torn out her remaining mainmast so that it had risen to the surface again like a missile. Now, as it reared out of the waves it seemed as if the whole ship would follow it. What made it worse were the sodden corpses which still hung in the trails of torn rigging, their drowned mouths wide open as if to scream for vengeance.

Captain Jervis shouted, '*Helm amidships!* Pass the order to stop engine immediately!' He tried to remain calm, not to transmit his anxiety to his immediate subordinates.

There was a sudden and terrible silence as even the enemy stopped firing. The Russian had not understood the reason for *Tenacious*'s unexpected change of course, but used the delay to try and extricate his own ship from her menacing broadside.

The broken mast had fallen back in the water again, its drowned seamen watching intently as the *Tenacious*'s long jib-boom and bowsprit cast a shadow above them. When the mast hit the flagship's bows it was little more than a nudge to the men on her upper deck. She was a new ship, well-found and constructed of the best oak.

'Engine's stopped, sir!'

Jervis clenched his fists until the knuckles shone like bones. 'Raise the screw!'

Ashley-Chute stared at him. 'We'll lose command of her, man!' He looked up at the furled sails, the streaming flags pointing towards the land which was creeping out on either bow like giant jaws.

The broken mast reached the propeller shaft and hit it a smashing blow. This they did feel, and once again as it reeled and plunged beneath the rudder.

A breathless messenger gasped, 'Chief engineer's compliments, sir, an' to tell you the screw is out of action!' His face went even paler as he grasped the meaning of his own message.

Captain Jervis strode quickly to the quarterdeck rail.

'Mr Cuttler! Prepare to anchor!'

Men dashed to the forecastle and Blackwood heard the boatswain yelling at the anchor party to cut all the lashings rather than waste another second.

The admiral's voice was shrill as he shouted, '*Anchor?* Under those damned guns?'

Jervis jerked round. 'Hard over!' He saw the bows swing reluctantly in response to the rudder. The way had all but gone from the ship. She was too close inshore now to beat clear, and without an engine she would soon be hard and fast.

'*Let go!*' He waited only for the great anchor to splash down before he said, 'We've no choice, sir.'

The first lieutenant said quietly, 'The Russian ship is coming about, sir.' He sounded almost apologetic. 'I think she intends to engage us.'

Jervis nodded heavily. 'Very well, Mr Irving. Tell the Chief to do what he can with the shaft and let me know how serious it may be. In the meantime – '

But Ashley-Chute had recovered his composure. 'Colonel

Fynmore, your people will have their chance after all it seems.'

Fynmore seemed to grow in stature. 'Yessir.' He glared at Blackwood. 'Marines stand to, if you please.'

Blackwood beckoned to his half-brother. 'Sharpshooters aloft!'

He saw understanding and determination on Harry's face. Everything had happened so suddenly. Now bad luck or over-confidence had placed them in real danger. As the ship swung to her cable Blackwood could feel the despair transmitting along the gun crews who moments earlier had been cheering their victory.

He saw Jervis speaking with the commander and the sailing master. If the wind changed in their favour, if the screw could be got turning again, if more ships came to their aid . . . There were far too many ifs for any sort of confidence.

Alone and separate from his officers, Ashley-Chute stood and watched the Russian three-decker as she tacked round to begin a slow and careful approach. She would open fire at extreme range to give herself room to claw away if the wind turned her into another victim.

Colour-Sergeant M'Crystal joined Blackwood and said, 'They're all in position, sir. I sent two sections below to reduce casualties.' He watched the oncoming pyramid of tan-coloured sails. 'Don't like it much myself, sir. Sitting target we are.'

Blackwood saw Smithett hurrying towards him with his pistols.

Sarpedon was barely capable of staying afloat, and the small gunboat could do little against a powerful first-rate. And there was still one Russian frigate to contend with.

He took the pistols and said, 'So much for the age of steam.'

Admiral Sir James Ashley-Chute folded his arms and studied the oncoming three-decker impassively.

Blackwood stood near him, ready to order a detachment of marines to any part of the flagship where it would be most needed. He wondered if the admiral regretted his hasty action, his eagerness to win a victory without waiting for aid or superior guidance. The Russian *Rostislav* was approaching on almost the same course which *Tenacious* had used in her first sortie. She had brailed up all but her fighting sails, and even without a glass it was possible to see the gleam of metal in her tops as marksmen gathered in readiness for close action.

Ashley-Chute snapped, 'Make to *Sarpedon* and *Rupert*. *Attack and harass the enemy.*'

Blackwood saw the flag-lieutenant's apprehension as he hurried to the signals party. *Sarpedon* was in no fit state to fight, but she might provide a diversion. Anyway, she and the gunboat were all they had.

The *Rostislav* heeled heavily to the wind, her shape lengthening as she changed tack to cross *Tenacious*'s bows. The range was about half a mile, Blackwood thought. But time was more important than accuracy, and the Russians had all the time they needed.

The flag-lieutenant returned. 'Signal acknowledged, sir.'

The Russian fired a slow and deliberate broadside, the darting orange tongues flashing from bow to stern as gun by gun found its target.

Blackwood felt the hull stagger beneath him as the enemy's shots crashed into it or seared along the side like bolts of lightning.

Voices yelled orders, and men scampered below to assist the boatswain's party and to help those already working at the pumps.

Blackwood saw a marine corporal lift his cheek from his levelled rifle and stare along the deck as if to reassure himself. *Tenacious* was more than a magnificent ship of the line, to him she was home. It was not possible that they could be penned in and destroyed by one arrogant Russian.

Blackwood could see all of it on his face, the shock and the anger, when this corporal had moments before been cheering with the rest of them.

Captain Jervis raised his speaking-trumpet. 'Bow-chasers!'

The forward guns recoiled on their tackles and Blackwood saw two splashes close to the enemy's stern. It was not enough. She was already firing again even as her yards started to change direction in readiness for a different tack.

The shore battery too had reopened fire, and one shot smashed through *Tenacious*'s starboard quarter and exploded in a torrent of iron splinters.

'Sir! *Sarpedon*'s heading for the enemy!' The flag-lieutenant sounded as if he no longer believed anything.

Blackwood ran to the poop ladder and stared abeam. The steam-frigate was not making for the anchored ships or the motionless Russian frigate, but was pointing straight for the *Rostislav*.

Jervis shouted, 'Signal her to stand away, Flags!'

But the admiral's voice stopped the lieutenant in his tracks.

'Belay that!'

He folded his arms again and watched coldly as the *Sarpedon*'s forward guns opened fire. Like *Satyr*, she mounted two massive bow-chasers on her forecastle, but one had obviously been knocked out when she had been straddled by the shore battery.

A great gasp rose from the deck as the shot crashed down by the enemy's bow, the sea cascading over her beakhead and bowsprit in a solid sheet of water.

The Russian captain was already setting his foresail and trying to beat back into more open water. But his gun crews were too engrossed in their work to care for the listing, smoke-blackened *Sarpedon*. Flashes ripped along the gun-ports and *Tenacious* gave a great shiver as iron smashed into the hull and screamed through the rigging.

There was one great crack and the sound of cordage being torn apart, and faces stared wide-eyed as the whole mizzen-mast, complete with spars and furled sails, came staggering

through the smoke. It smashed over the side, the trailing
shrouds and stays tearing blocks and bolts from the woodwork as if they were nothing, entangling men where they
stood and carrying them bodily over the side, their screams
lost in the pandemonium and the roar of another enemy
salvo.

Smoke billowed from the poop and through open hatchways. Seamen hacked at the treacherous rigging with their
axes and tried to shut their ears to the cries from their
messmates who were being dragged into the sea or cut apart
by the remaining lines.

Jervis yelled, 'Mr Irving!' But the first lieutenant lay dead,
a speaking-trumpet still gripped in one hand.

Blackwood looked round for Fynmore but there was no
sign of him. Brabazon had already gone below with some
marines to help with the dead and wounded there.

More shots crashed and splintered into the side, and a
thirty-two-pounder lurched on to its side, pinning down two
of its crew, while the others tried to shift the massive gun
with handspikes.

Jervis looked at the admiral with desperation.

'We can do nothing, sir! In God's name, we'll lose every
man-jack!'

Ashley-Chute tore off a glove and dabbed a cut on his
cheek with it.

'Continue firing! That's an order! I'll not strike to a bloody
Russian!'

Jervis swung away and then stood stock still, his eyes
staring.

Blackwood hurried to his side. He had imagined that the
captain had been hit by a splinter.

But Jervis seized his arm and pointed wildly.

'Look at *that*!'

The *Sarpedon* was drifting downwind, signal flags making
a small bright pattern above her splintered deck. She must
have fired several shots from her big bow-chaser, but in the
chaos and horror aboard the flagship it was doubtful if anyone

had seen them. One shot must have smashed through the Russian's stern and destroyed the steering gear. She was out of command, her additional canvas already carrying her broadside-on towards *Tenacious*.

Jervis said harshly, '*Sarpedon*'s done it, by God.'

Those last shots must have opened up all the previous night's repairs, for with her engine stopped and her list even more pronounced the *Sarpedon* was little more than a hulk. Blackwood saw the gunboat *Rupert* thrashing towards her, to take her consort in tow or lift off the people – he did not know or care.

Ashley-Chute snapped, 'Captain Blackwood, the Russian will be down upon us very soon. The guns won't bear. You know what to do!'

Blackwood realized that the little admiral was right beside him, his eyes desperate as he watched the enemy getting nearer and nearer. It was no use looking for Fynmore now. There was no time left. Like those other days in New Zealand and Africa.

Blackwood touched his hat. 'Very well, sir.' He tugged out his whistle and blew on it.

Then, as several red-coated figures ran from the line of crouching marines by the nettings, he swung himself on to the main-shrouds and began to climb. Without the mizzen-mast the afterpart of the ship seemed exposed and vulnerable. He climbed faster, and saw Sergeant Quintin peering down from the maintop barricade, his face split into a grin.

'Come to join us, sir?'

Blackwood scrambled over the wooden barrier and glanced at the grim, familiar faces.

'Well, Frazier, now's your chance.'

He saw Harry clambering into the foretop, waved to him as their eyes met across the destruction and death below them.

He said, 'The Russian will foul our cable. She can still fire on us, but our broadside won't bear on her. Make every shot tell. It's up to you now.'

He handed his pistols to Smithett, who had followed him at a more leisurely pace, and picked up a spare rifle.

Once he peered down at the deck and saw the admiral's strange figure below him. Men bustled about him, and wounded were dragged sobbing and screaming to the hatchways, their progress marked by scarlet lines across the deck. In spite of all this, the admiral seemed to stand alone. Whatever happened now he was ruined, and he knew it.

Blackwood thought suddenly of the quiet garden at the Maltese hospital all those months ago. Where was she at this very moment? Would she ever know what had happened to him?

More shots hammered into the hull and he felt the mast sway violently.

Quintin said, ' 'Ere come the buggers! Take aim, me beauties! Glass o' grog for the winner!'

Private Bulford pressed his cheek against the warm wood and curled his finger around the trigger. This might be the day when it all ended, he thought. Even so, it was better than being in prison like his dad.

Private Frazier's mind was empty of everything but for a man he had never met. He was watching him now, a Russian officer, resplendent in epaulettes and frock-coat. *Him first*.

With a shuddering jerk the other ship crossed *Tenacious*'s cable and began to slew into her.

Blackwood pulled the trigger and felt the new rifle kick painfully into his shoulder.

Down there in the enclosed world of smoke and searing flashes men fought and died while the two ships remained locked together. But on the Russian's quarterdeck the captain had already fallen to a shot from *Tenacious*'s maintop, and many of the other officers near him had shared his fate. Russian marksmen fired blindly through the smoke and saw their comrades die as the new pointed bullets cut through their defences and marked them down.

Unnerved by their change of fortune, the Russians tried to work their ship clear. As the *Rostislav* swung drunkenly free of the anchor cable she exposed her quarter and rounded bilge just long enough for Jervis's second lieutenant to point his remaining guns and fire. This time there was no response, and as the Russian drifted down the *Tenacious*'s side she was battered and raked for every yard of the way until blood ran from her scuppers in shining red stripes. There was more smoke too, probably from a burning wad or an upended lantern below decks.

In *Tenacious*'s maintop the marines had risen to their feet to fire down on the enemy's deck. Nobody seemed to miss, and even when a few shots smacked into the barricade they cheered all the louder, like men already driven beyond human help.

A great shudder transmitted itself up the mast and shrouds and a marine yelled, 'God, we're bloody aground!'

But Blackwood felt Quintin grip his hand and wring it until it ached, his normal sense of discipline momentarily lost.

'It's the engine, sir! Gawd, the bloody black gang 'ave got us moving again!' He too was nearly beside himself.

Blackwood grinned and leaned over the barricade to peer at the foremast. He saw Harry looking towards him and then toss him a casual salute.

Up forward axes flashed and cut through the cable, and with her last obstacle thrown aside *Tenacious* forged very slowly ahead.

A few waterspouts burst alongside, but as Blackwood climbed wearily down to the deck he felt the pain of the ship which no amount of cheering could ease.

'*Cease firing!*'

Blackwood saw men being carried to the hatches, some badly wounded, others already dead. The damage was immense, but the engine's steady throb and a growing plume of smoke told the rest of the story.

Jervis studied him grimly and said, 'That was well done, Blackwood. But for your marksmen those Russians would have battered us into submission and then overrun us. It was the closest thing I'd ever wish to see.' He clapped him on the arm and then turned as one of his lieutenants ran to report on casualties and damage.

Major Brabazon met him by the quarterdeck rail and mopped his face with a piece of bunting.

He shook his head. 'Like a bloody slaughter-house on the middle gundeck.' He eyed him curiously. 'You all right, Philip?'

But Blackwood was staring at a small bundle by the poop ladder. It was covered by a White Ensign, but there was no mistaking the outflung, gloved hand and admiral's sword by its side.

Brabazon said quietly, 'They say he just stood there. Never moved the whole time. He was killed instantly.'

Blackwood turned away. Ashley-Chute was no longer part of his life. He had gone and taken so many others with him.

He said, 'He didn't want to live after this.' He glanced at the damage, the terrible stains on the scarred decks. 'I never thought I would, but I shall miss him.'

He was even more surprised to discover that he meant it.

Later, as *Tenacious* moved slowly away from the smoke which had completely hidden the bay like something solid, Captain Jervis sent his men aloft to loose the sails and prepare to tack clear of the land before the damaged shaft broke down again.

Close by, the battered frigate *Sarpedon* clung to the gunboat's towing hawser, unaware that their admiral had died, grateful only they had survived.

Blackwood remained on deck and watched the land fade into a smoky shadow. It had been a very close thing. A lucky shot and a handful of rifles had saved the day, but only just.

He thought a lot about Ashley-Chute and the lessons he had refused to learn. How would he be remembered?

Better to be a dead hero than a live scapegoat.

21

The Redoubt

Captain Philip Blackwood stood on a craggy spur of land and looked down at the crowded anchorage of Varna. Ships of every size and class, from stately three-deckers to puffing paddle-steamers, with more coming and going every day. The badly mauled *Tenacious* had left for England and the repair yard several months ago, and now, looking at this great array of allied shipping, it was hard to believe the raid had ever happened, that Ashley-Chute was dead.

Even the role of the marine battalion seemed to have lost its purpose since the death of the little admiral. They had all been landed and encamped at Varna, and while the reports had been wild with excitement about the great Anglo-French force of some sixty-five thousand troops which had smashed through the Russian defences to land on the Crimea itself, Fynmore's command had been held fretting in reserve. The Turkish resistance on the Danube had halted the enemy advance on Constantinople, and with the fleets in the Baltic and the Black Sea harrying their flanks and now actually putting an army on Russian soil, the enemy was on the defensive.

An attempt to capture the vital port of Sebastopol had been repulsed with heavy losses, but undeterred the British had landed elsewhere, had crossed the Alma and had by-passed the Russian stronghold. They had marched south to capture the harbour and town of Balaclava instead. But the casualties were mounting. There had been a steady stream of wounded from the Crimean Expedition, as it was now termed, and their daily arrival made the marines even more aware of their inaction.

Winter was almost upon them, and the optimistic suggestion that 'it would all be over by Christmas' had given way to the prospect of a stalemate until the better weather returned.

Blackwood had received one further letter from Davern. It had been short but intimate. She had heard of Ashley-Chute's death and prayed that Blackwood was safe and well. She had mentioned that her husband had accepted a supervisory appointment with the British Army which, in view of the war and his previous researches, would be of some importance to him.

He had also received a letter from his stepmother. Colonel Blackwood was poorly, his condition worsened by the news from the Crimea. He and his faithful Oates studied the daily reports like retired generals, and Blackwood was saddened to think of his father ending his days in such a manner.

Blackwood turned his back to the sea and began to walk down the track to the camp. He might just as well be at Hawks Hill with his father as here, he thought bitterly. The inaction and lack of direction was having its effect on everyone, Harry most of all. It was almost impossible to get a civil word from him, even on the subject of his father.

A private hurried towards him and saluted smartly.

'Beg pardon, sir, but the colonel's called an officers' conference. Hour's time.'

Blackwood nodded. 'Thank you, Keele.'

What would it be this time? Slackness at drill, or punishment to be awarded to marines who had broken out of camp to sample the doubtful pleasures of Varna?

Later, as he walked with Major Brabazon to the command tent, he said, 'If the men were divided up again amongst the ships they would have work to take them out of themselves, sir.'

Brabazon glanced at him and winked. 'Better than that, Philip. We're under orders. Just between ourselves, we're going across to the Crimea.'

Blackwood looked away to hide his feelings. He had been expecting it, if he was honest, hoping for it. Now that it had happened he felt strangely apprehensive.

Brabazon added cheerfully, 'The sector commander is a Major-General Richmond. Bit of a fire-eater. Must be getting hard for him if he has to call in the Marines!' He sounded confident enough.

Fynmore met his officers and waited for total silence. He was as neat as ever, but his narrow features were strained, as if he had not slept well for some time.

'Gentlemen, the battalion is being embarked this week for the Crimea.' He frowned slightly as several of the junior lieutenants raised a cheer. 'I think that will do, gentlemen!' He waved one hand towards a large map which he had hung on an easel. 'We shall land at Balaclava and await orders. Platoon commanders will ensure that our men are issued with one extra pair of boots, entrenching tools and additional ammunition as will be laid down in my standing orders.'

Blackwood watched him thoughtfully. Apart from matters of duty their paths had barely crossed, hard to believe in an overcrowded encampment. Was it because of the commendation which had been sent to *Tenacious* after her return to Varna? A special mention had been made by the commander-in-chief of the marines' part in the battle's final stages. He had left it in no doubt that but for the prompt action by the marine riflemen in the tops, *Tenacious* might now be an enemy prize and a humiliation to the allies for all time. Fynmore should have been pleased and proud. Unless . . . Always the doubt was there. Where was he when the two ships had come together? Brabazon had never mentioned seeing him, neither had the lieutenant on the middle gundeck.

He looked at Fynmore's curt gestures and wondered what was wrong with him.

Fynmore said, 'I will expect the very highest standards of discipline and determination from all ranks. We shall be with the Army, remember that, and under their overall command.'

He seemed suddenly at a loss, and Blackwood could feel the officers around him growing restless while they waited for him to continue.

Fynmore said vaguely, 'It is upon the Corps, and upon — ' He broke off abruptly and nodded at Brabazon. 'Carry on, please.'

Mystified, the junior officers hurried from the tent, and only Brabazon, Captain Ogilvie of B Company and Blackwood remained.

Fynmore gathered up some papers and let them fall on his trestle-table again.

'Something wrong, sir?' Brabazon watched him anxiously.

'*Wrong?* Why should there be, dammit?' Fynmore glared at him. 'Naturally I'm concerned about the behaviour of my command, but I am relying on you to produce the best results, right?'

'Right.'

Blackwood and the others left the tent.

Ogilvie, a pleasant if unimaginative man, remarked, 'Wife trouble, old chap. Stands out a bloody mile. Always the same when you marry a woman much younger than yourself, what?' He did not see Brabazon's warning glance. 'It needs a man to ride to hounds, that's what I say.' He sauntered towards his company lines, oblivious to Blackwood's feelings and everything else.

Blackwood thought of his father, what his young wife would do if his condition continued to deteriorate.

Brabazon grunted, 'Stupid clod. Sorry about that, Philip.'

Blackwood found that he could smile about it. His father was right, the Corps was a family in itself. It was impossible to keep any secret from anyone.

After an unexplained delay the marines broke camp and accompanied by an Army band marched down to the harbour to board their various ships.

To his surprise Blackwood found the frigate *Satyr* to be one of them. She looked older than the last time he had boarded her, scarred and well-used, but as he climbed aboard he received a further surprise. Tobin was aboard and stepped forward to greet him like an old friend.

'Who knows, Blackwood, we may really achieve something this time, eh?'

Blackwood was warmed and touched by their meeting. For Tobin no longer commanded his beloved *Satyr* but flew a broad-pendant of commodore from her masthead. Blackwood could think of no one who deserved it more.

As the assorted flotilla of vessels moved north-east into the Black Sea the weather worsened and the dust and sweat of Turkey were soon forgotten. There was a bite in the air, and a wind which cut through clothing like cold steel.

As in the rest of the ships the marines in *Satyr* were packed like herrings in a barrel, but they seemed good humoured and glad to be doing something, although M'Crystal still complained bitterly of his Irish trouble-makers even though he never seemed to catch them committing any offence, much to his disgust.

A patrolling brig met them while they were still out of sight of land, and after a brief exchange of signals Tobin ordered a change of course. They would make their final approach by night, Blackwood was told. It would be safer. It did not sound quite so straightforward as Fynmore had indicated.

Blackwood was in his shared cabin when he heard the murmur of voices on deck. He pulled on his greatcoat and hurried up the companion and saw that the deck seemed to be filled with marines and many of the ship's company.

He found Tobin with the captain by the compass, his powerful shape just one more shadow on the crowded deck.

'Shall I order my marines below, sir?'

Tobin was puffing at a massive pipe and shook his head. 'Let 'em watch. It might help later on.'

Blackwood saw the commodore's features light up, and as he turned saw the sky alive with flashes which seemed to stretch from bow to bow.

He heard the sullen boom of artillery fire, and that too was unbroken, like thunder at the height of a storm.

Tobin bit on his pipe. 'Poor devils. It's like this every night, bombardment and artillery duels, shot and shell, they get no rest.' He touched his face as some sleety rain splashed from his cap. 'Then in daylight it starts all over again.'

Blackwood moved among his men, feeling their uneasiness, their surprise at the war's intrusion.

He found the sergeants in a tight bunch by one of the paddle-boxes.

Quintin recognized him in spite of the shadows and said, 'Bit more soldierin', sir?' The others chuckled as if it was a private joke.

Blackwood smiled. 'They need us to show them how it's done.'

He felt someone touch his sleeve and saw Harry's face pale in the reflected flashes.

'Philip, we must talk.'

Blackwood pulled him from the crowd of jostling marines until they shared the warmth of the tall, sparking funnel.

'What is it?'

'It's Colonel Fynmore. His wife wrote to me. She's having a baby, had it by now, I'd think, unless something went wrong.'

The words just tumbled out of him, as if he could no longer bear to carry his secret. 'I think she's told him about it, that I used to . . .' He dropped his eyes and added brokenly, 'Well, you know.'

Blackwood exclaimed, 'But it can't be yours . . .' He nodded slowly. 'But the blame will rub off, I can see that.' He gripped his half-brother's arm, wanting to show anger but feeling only concern for him. 'You idiot, Harry. I should have guessed, I suppose. I was thinking too much of someone else.'

Harry whispered fiercely, 'It might bring disgrace on the whole family, you know what Fynmore's like.'

Blackwood felt his stomach tighten. Suppose Fynmore knew or guessed about Marguerite Blackwood's affair, he would be far more likely to use that against them.

He said, 'I'm glad you told me anyway. Perhaps nothing will happen.' He turned as an extra loud rumble thundered across the black water. It was no time to be worried about things like that. 'Try not to antagonize the colonel.'

Harry made a weak attempt to grin. 'That should be easy.'

He raised his head and ran his fingers through his hair. 'It's been driving me insane, Philip. I feel better now, telling you. My big brother. I think it must run in my side of the family.'

Blackwood started and asked sharply, 'What do you mean by that?'

Harry was still thinking of something else. 'Georgina, didn't Mother tell you? She sent her to Paris to keep her out of trouble with some fellow from the Foot Guards.' He sighed and gulped at the cold air. 'I'm going to turn in.' He hesitated. 'And thanks for putting up with me. I'll not let you down again.'

Blackwood waited by the guardrail until he realized he was half frozen and that the deck had quietly emptied.

It was getting worse, not better, he thought.

The eventual landing at Balaclava was completed almost without incident, and the last marine and piece of equipment was ashore before dawn finally opened up across the black terrain.

An army major met Fynmore and Brabazon while the other officers inspected their men and ensured that nothing had been left aboard ship.

Blackwood stood slightly apart while he waited for the lieutenants to report. In just a matter of hours the marines seemed to have changed in some way. They were on edge, unsettled by the constant murmur of gunfire, the scene of incredible desolation. Shell-scarred houses and fallen rubble, among which small areas of order and planning made a stark contrast. Army huts and tents, guns and limbers, supply waggons and great piles of crates and casks for an unseen army.

But the army was evident here too. Maybe that was the cause of the uneasiness among the marines. The soldiers looked tired out and gaunt, their uniforms stained and often ragged. Many wore beards, something unknown in the Corps. Even the major who was speaking intently with Fynmore and making grand gestures with a walking-stick was a far cry from any parade-ground.

Blackwood looked at his men. Uneven red lines beside the pitted road. Some were staring longingly at the anchored ships, others watched the sky, or tried not to listen to the guns. Each man seemed weighed down by his weapons and equipment. Apart from his Minie rifle and bayonet, every man carried a full knapsack which contained three days' rations, extra clothing, the additional pair of boots, plus blanket, greatcoat and sixty rounds of ammunition and caps which were tightly packed into a black leather pouch. When they finally moved off, each would be carrying nearly seventy pounds in weight on his back.

'A Company ready, sir!'

Sergeant Quintin grimaced as some soldiers shouted, 'Wot 'ave we got 'ere then? *Sea*-soldiers?'

Quintin muttered, 'Sea-soldiers indeed!'

'B Company ready, sir!'

An extra loud explosion shook the earth but the soldiers took no notice. It was a part of their lives.

Fynmore came over and snorted, 'Five miles march to the line. No horses for the officers either, would you believe?'

He glanced at the lines of marines. 'The army have scouts out to guide us. We will head north-west.' He handed his notes to his orderly. 'It will be night again before we can settle down.'

Captain Ogilvie asked mildly, 'May I ask what we are to do, Colonel?'

Fynmore's pale eyes followed Harry Blackwood's figure along the leading platoon. He pulled himself together and snapped, 'The enemy has a strong redoubt in that sector. Open ground. Heavy artillery.' Each phrase was short and terse. 'Lot of casualties.'

Brabazon pulled on his gloves and stamped his boots on the ground.

'What a way to begin. Like a blind man joining the cavalry.'

Nobody laughed.

Blackwood saw M'Crystal with his colour-party, the cased flag carefully laid over his massive shoulder. Sailor one day, infantryman the next.

The lieutenants took their places, the marines shouldered arms, and without further ceremony they marched away from the harbour.

There was little talking along the ranks even when they were marching at ease. It was like nothing Blackwood had ever seen, so he could imagine how much worse it was for the young recruits.

Craggy, broken hills, treeless and hostile, while along the rough, winding track they came across signs of the war they had come to join.

Great puddles which were already crusted with thin ice hid the holes where enemy shells had exploded. Broken and charred waggons, discarded tools and unfilled sandbags marked every yard of the advance. Here and there were little cairns of stones, some marked with a crude cross, others with a man's head-gear or sword. It was probably too hard to dig a grave here, Blackwood thought.

Then there were the wounded. As the guns grew louder and more personal the wounded seemed to grow in numbers. Arm in arm, hopping on sticks, or being carried on stretchers by bearers, they passed the marching marines with barely a glance.

Blackwood quickened his pace to join Harry at the head of the first platoon. He glanced at the men's faces as he strode by. Most were like stone, some looked afraid of what they might see next.

He asked, 'All right, Harry?'

Harry turned his head to stare at a man who lay on his back, his hands upheld like claws. Corporal Jones broke ranks but soon rejoined them as he cried, 'Dead, sir!' The soldier must have died even as he made his own lonely way to a dressing station.

Harry murmured, 'Did you see those soldiers back there? They're still in summer uniforms.' As if to emphasize his remark his feet crunched through some of the wafer-thin ice.

Blackwood had noticed. The marines might complain about their heavy packs, but at least they had greatcoats and blankets.

A runner scampered past. 'Halt the column!'

Fynmore strolled to the head of the marines and tapped the ground with his stick. 'Bloody army,' he muttered.

There was a clatter of hoofs and two field officers, followed by their orderlies, trotted around the next bend.

The senior officer, a grey-haired major-general, reined in his horse and studied the marines for what felt like an eternity.

' 'Tenant-Colonel Fynmore?' He had a thin, incisive voice. 'Your men are two days late.' He did not dismount. 'Arrangements have been made for you to support the line.'

Fynmore stood like a ramrod, his mouth twitching with barely contained fury.

'We were ordered to stand off because of a bombardment, sir.'

The major-general turned to his companion who was smiling hugely.

'D'you here that, Percy? *Bombardment!* Talk about the giddy limit, what?' He touched his hat with his riding crop and then spurred his horse into a gallop.

Brabazon bit on his chin strap and said, '*That* was General Richmond, God help us!'

'Royal Marines, by the right . . .' They were on the march again.

The closer they got to their allotted sector the flatter the ground became. Low hills with tracks and gullies, some man-made, which wound through them like a maze.

The army pickets knew their job well. They seemed able to

smell if a shell was about to crash down on the jagged rocks, even allowed the extra seconds for the marines to get accustomed to the need for instant movement. Down on their faces, then scrambling up again to continue towards the gunfire. Quick, nervous glances to seek out friends, to reassure, to hope.

Then they were crouching and scrabbling along endless zigzag trenches, ducking and waiting as shots crashed into the ground or murmured spitefully overhead.

They came into a cleared, saucer-shaped gun emplacement and somebody gave an ironic cheer as the first of the marines panted past.

Blackwood saw the familiar blue coats around the massive guns, the cheerful grins. It was like a home-coming, in spite of the danger. They were a detachment of the Royal Marine Artillery, and as he looked at their faces he saw a big lieutenant running, arms outstretched, towards him.

Fynmore rasped, 'Fall out the column, Sergeant Quintin. Ten minutes rest, no more.' He glared at the grinning lieutenant. 'And who are you, sir?'

Blackwood shook the man's hand. 'This is Lieutenant Dick Cleveland, sir. Used to be my second-in-command in *Audacious*.' He studied the lieutenant warmly. What a place and a way to meet after all these months and months. 'I see you've changed to the gunners, Dick.'

Cleveland chuckled. 'I thought it would be safer.' He looked round as the ground shook to another shell. 'Wrong again.'

Blackwood looked at his half-brother. How long was the arm of coincidence. It never lost its grip. But for Cleveland breaking his leg after a drunken party at Spithead, Harry would have been sent elsewhere. He might even be at Hawks Hill with their father.

He said, 'Dick is the chap who got you into this mess, Harry.'

Fynmore snapped, 'Enough of this time wasting. Rouse the men.' He tugged out his watch. 'It looks like snow.' He strode back towards Brabazon and the others.

Cleveland pursed his lips. 'I pity you, *sir*.' Then he said, 'This really is odd, meeting you like this.'

'I was thinking the same.' *Audacious*, the summer balls and regattas seemed like part of history.

'No, it's not that.' He had to raise his voice above the din of shouted commands and the clatter of weapons as the marines fell into line again. 'I've been here from the beginning. They couldn't have managed without our battery. But a week or so back we received a lot of new supplies and medical stores at the base camp. You could have knocked me down with a feather, Philip, er, *sir*. Women, out here in the bloody Crimea, well, I ask you.' He put his head on one side and smiled. 'The prettiest one of the lot came straight up to me and asked if I knew *you* of all people!'

The marines shuffled into single line for the next length of trench, but Blackwood could not move.

'Tell me, Dick, for God's sake!'

The lieutenant nodded. 'I should have realized how it was. Her name is Davern something-or-other. You must have marched right past her!'

'Captain Blackwood, sir!'

Sergeant Quintin's boots crunched towards them.

'The colonel wants you to take the lead.'

Blackwood grasped the lieutenant's hands. 'Thank you. Thank you *very much*.'

As the twisting line of marines entered the trench a second lieutenant clambered from a gun pit and joined Cleveland by the track.

'Who was that?'

'That was Blackwood. The best I ever met.' He stared bitterly at a far-off patch of smoke from an explosion. 'Still a captain. He should be in *command* of these bunglers!'

He swung round and thought of the dark haired woman by the harbour. Already they were being called angels of mercy by the wounded and sick from the battle-front. Another great boom of falling shells shook the emplacement and he tried not to think of Blackwood and what was waiting for him.

Two hundred troops had already died there in less than a fortnight.

'Prepare to fire. On the hour, by the hour, right?'

The second lieutenant nodded and hurried away.

The marines repeatedly took shelter as directed by the army scouts and pickets. Breathless and often dazed by the crashing roar of gunfire from both directions, they eventually arrived at their allotted sector. The soldiers had dug holes into the ground and along the side of the trenches and lined them with stout props and timbers. An army captain assured Fynmore that there were also deep caves in the nearest hills where a whole platoon could find shelter and prepare its rations. If they took shelter during each bombardment there was little risk unless someone got buried under falling rocks, he explained. Like the others, the captain looked worn out, his eyes ringed with dark circles to reveal the strain of daily survival.

Blackwood and Brabazon made notes while Ogilvie held up a map for the soldier to complete his explanation. There was a Scottish battalion to the right, a light infantry regiment to the left. He shifted nervously from foot to foot. He was eager to go.

The ground shook once more and some loose stones rolled over the lip of a heavily sandbagged parapet. Far beyond it, pale grey in the dull light, was another hill.

Ogilvie asked brightly, 'And what's directly to our front?'

The soldier glanced at him searchingly then tapped the map with a grimy finger.

'Sloping ground, then that hill. That's where they are. The enemy.'

Fynmore plucked at his lower lip and stared at a flake of snow as it melted on his tunic.

'Carry on, Blackwood. Section by section stand-to. I'll inspect them when you're ready.' He beckoned to his servant and orderly. 'Find my quarters and prepare things.' He walked away with Brabazon, his shoulders squared and straight.

The soldier let out a long breath. 'Thank God.' He waved to one of his sergeants, and at a shouted command the troops began to climb from their defences. 'I never thought . . .' He looked at Blackwood and tried to smile. 'Sorry about this. Can't take much more. Never been so glad to see anyone before.'

He made to leave but Blackwood said, 'If you see a Mrs Hadley at the base camp, she's a doctor's wife . . .' He did not know how to continue.

But the captain nodded firmly, his fear put aside.

'I'll remember. Blackwood. I shall tell her.' Then he was gone.

Tell her what? Blackwood winced as the ground quivered and more dust spewed over the sandbags. He remembered what Tobin had said about the nights, the constant bombardment. The defences looked strong enough, but no army gained ground by staying put.

He saw Harry sliding down a bank of shovelled earth and said, 'All ready?'

He nodded. 'They're fine, sir.' He smiled at their sudden formality. 'I've put the old hands among the green ones, although after *Tenacious* I should think most of them know what to expect.' He watched him and added, 'Something wrong?'

Blackwood looked at the dark clouds and felt snow on his face. So light and gentle, like a secret kiss. She was down there now. Just a few miles away. He had walked right past her. What was she doing among all the horror and the suffering?

He said simply, 'If I fall, Harry, tell her for me. Will you do that?'

Harry stared at him, his face shocked. 'You won't! What would I do?' He tried to shrug it off. 'You tell her yourself.'

'When you are quite *ready*, gentlemen.' Fynmore's voice was like the chill air. 'I will inspect the positions.'

Soon it was dark, and as the marines settled into holes and

dug-outs and wrapped themselves in their coats and blankets there was a lull in the firing.

Blackwood made his rounds along the defences and the zigzagging support trenches and visited the sentries who were posted at intervals along the sandbagged parapet.

It was too dark to see their faces, but he recognized many of the voices as each man made his report. Dialects from Yorkshire and Dorset, his own Hampshire, or from Scotland, like M'Crystal, and the harsh accent of the London slums, like Quintin's.

In the stillness he could hear bagpipes from far away and knew M'Crystal would have heard them too. The Scottish soldiers were relaxing. Just for the moment. There was a smell of cooking, the squeak of a ramrod as someone, probably Frazier, lovingly cleaned his rifle.

He felt the searing pain in his eyes as the skies lit up to great vivid flashes. The nightly barrage had begun. Whistles shrilled, and men dived for cover as the air shook and trembled to the onslaught. It came from the hill directly in front of their position. The Russian redoubt.

Blackwood pressed himself against the sandbags and gritted his teeth.

Crash . . . Crash . . . Crash . . .

That must be Dick Cleveland's battery firing in retaliation. It went on and on, the air cringing to the din until it was impossible to think clearly.

His grandfather would have been at home here. Would have retold the story better than anyone.

The ground shook again, and pieces of wood flew above the sandbags like shredded paper.

Blackwood continued slowly along the ramparts, touching a shoulder here or murmuring a quick word to another crouching shadow.

He reached a tiny dug-out which had been allotted to him. Smithett was there warming a pot on a small fire, and he had even found some old canvas to hang across the entrance to give an illusion of privacy.

Blackwood lowered himself on to a blanket and held his hands to the flames.

'You're a marvel, Smithett.'

The marine gave a mournful grin and poured some scalding coffee into a mug. He had found it in an adjoining trench which was occupied by a line regiment. Their high and mighty officers would never miss it.

He watched Blackwood's eyelids start to droop as he sipped the coffee. Like most of the old sweats, Smithett had heard all about the girl at the base camp. He could remember that day in Africa when he had helped the captain to carry her from the hut. The hut where they had raped her, where he had cut one of them down with his bayonet.

Rest easy, Captain. He listened to the rumble of guns, muffled now as the enemy shifted their sights. *We'll be needin' you tomorrer, I'm thinkin'*. He reached over and caught the mug as Blackwood's head lolled in sleep.

22

A Time For Action

Blackwood climbed on to a crudely carved step and raised his head above the parapet. The first day, he thought. He stared directly ahead at the gently curving hill. It looked more brown than grey in the early morning light. No sign of life. He licked his lips and tasted Smithett's coffee. Then he examined the open ground which separated the trench from the distant hill and concealed redoubt. It was hard to look at it without feeling dismayed. A scene of indescribable havoc. The whole area was strewn with remnants of military adornment. Shakos and lance caps, and here and there a once-proud brass helmet. Rusting weapons and the rotting carcasses of slaughtered horses. There was no sign of a dead soldier, which made it worse in some way. As if their disgust had taken them away from where they had been cut down.

On either side of him he heard the marines whispering to one another as they lined the firing-step and aimed their weapons across the deserted battle-field. Looking to right and left Blackwood could see nothing of the army positions but noticed that the marines' sector bulged slightly ahead of the others, a place which might attract the brunt of an enemy attack.

M'Crystal and Quintin had not wasted their time during the night and had been into the Scottish lines to find out what they could. The Russians, it seemed, had nothing to match the British fire power, especially when it came to their rifles. They still attacked en masse, impossible to miss, but hard to stop.

He heard Fitzclarence, one of the newest second lieutenants, speaking with Corporal Jones as he inspected the ready-use ammunition and a stock of grenades which had been provided by the army. Poor Fitzclarence, he was so keen it was painful. The marines called him Girlie behind his back because of his gentle, even frail appearance.

A runner came dashing down the trench and stopped when he saw Blackwood.

'Colonel's respects, sir an' would you join B Company immediately.'

He ran on without waiting for a reply.

Blackwood jumped down and nodded to Fitzclarence. 'I shall be with Captain Ogilvie if you need me.'

B Company was spread out on the extreme left of the sector. It had taken a pounding over the weeks, and much of the defensive parapet had been blown apart. The gaps had been filled with sandbags and huge bundles of lashed sticks which were laid horizontally and called fascines by the military, and which were said to be good protection against small-arms fire.

Captain Ogilvie stood on his firing-step and surveyed the enemy positions without enthusiasm.

'Deuced difficult to see a thing, Philip.' He grinned as Blackwood joined him. 'Colonel just sent word. The army is about to mount a big attack at Inkerman. It's all *I* can do to find the damn place on my map.' He shivered. 'Bloody cold too.'

Blackwood looked across the sandbags. The view was much the same here. There were a few haphazard sap-trenches which snaked away to the left which had been started by the army for some sort of advance position. The sappers had either given up or had been caught in the open during an attack.

'Give me a glass.'

He took the telescope from Ogilvie's orderly and rested it between two sandbags.

The battle-field immediately grew in size and he saw that

it was not totally deserted. Some of the tattered uniforms contained corpses or pieces of them. A Russian trooper lay pinned beneath the carcass of his mount, a sabre still grasped in one hand.

He moved the glass upwards and saw the pale line of the enemy's ramparts. If the army attacked at Inkerman the Russians might be forced to evacuate the redoubt. Perhaps they had already gone?

Blackwood noticed that Ogilvie had one of the new five-shot Adams revolvers which gave its owner a tremendous advantage over the ordinary pistol, which, even when you found time to reload it, would often misfire.

Ogilvie saw his glance and grinned. 'Bought it in London off a Yankee gentleman. Dying to use the thing.'

They both turned as a voice shouted, 'Here they come!'

The word ran along the trench like a fast fuse, and Blackwood marvelled that such a force of the enemy could rise up apparently from out of the ground like a living tide. They must have worked around the foot of the hill, and now advanced on the British lines in a solid mass.

Ogilvie scribbled on his pad and thrust a page into a runner's fist.

'Give it to the colonel, on the double!' He peered along the parapet and shouted, 'Hold your fire!'

Blackwood found that he could watch the advancing Russians without fear. It was like seeing it from a distance, or not being here at all. Long coats, glittering bayonets, here and there a mounted officer. A sea of people, they even rose and fell like waves as they tramped into ditches and over humps of rough ground.

The marines had levelled their rifles and were peering at the enemy, each man within his own thoughts. They could not miss.

Dull bangs and then the whine of shots passing overhead showed that the artillery were awake too. Blackwood watched, sickened, as great gaps were carved through the oncoming mass, gaping, bloody paths which were instantly filled by the press of men behind.

Somewhere a bugle blared, and Blackwood imagined the whole Allied force cocking its head to listen to this small part of the war.

The front of the advancing Russians was about four hundred yards away, and although the British artillery were hampered by the sloping ground and the fear of dropping shells on their own lines, they were doing terrible damage to the closely-packed soldiers.

Ogilvie remarked, 'Must be ten thousand of the buggers.'

Blackwood glanced at him. He sounded completely untroubled.

The sergeants moved behind their sections. 'Easy, lads. Rest your eyes, 'til the order.'

There were several violent explosions from the other sector, and Blackwood guessed that the Scots had come under artillery fire to discourage them from interfering.

It's us they want. They probably know we're new in the line. And yet how could that great faceless mass think or plan?

Blackwood steadied his racing thoughts and said, 'I'll leave you now.'

'Quite right too. Don't want our two best eggs in one basket, what?' Ogilvie shook with silent laughter.

'Sir! The trench!' The marine sounded as if he was hysterical.

Blackwood jumped back on to the step and stared with disbelief as the abandoned sap-trench which dwindled away to the left suddenly spewed men over the edge in a wild stampede towards the British line.

'Shift target! Hundred yards! Take aim!'

The enemy were already firing as they came, the flashes darting from the ranks and slamming shots into the sandbags. It acted as a signal to the main attacking force, and Blackwood saw the whole mass of them begin to charge, their officers in the lead, leaning forward in their saddles as if afraid they would be overtaken.

'Fire!'

Along the trench the marines took aim and pulled their

triggers. Every shot must have found a target, and the pointed bullets probably cut through the leading soldiers to hit the ones close behind.

Ogilvie pulled out his revolver and examined it briefly.

'Must drive 'em back,' he said, as if his remark was addressed to the revolver.

'*Rapid fire!*'

The marines were shooting and reloading as fast as they could, faces grimly intent as they rose to the pock-marked parapet and aimed for the leaders. Horses fell screaming and were overrun by the infantry. Blackwood could hear them yelling, their voices linked into one great roar of sound.

Ogilvie yelled, 'Christ, we're not stopping them!'

There was a terrible crack and Ogilvie's forehead exploded into a gaping red hole.

Blackwood snatched the revolver from his hand and stared wildly at the advancing Russians. Fifty yards, perhaps less. They had no time to reload, but were intent on swamping all resistance by sheer weight of numbers.

Some of the marines were fumbling with their weapons and pouches, others fired before they had found a target. It was all going to be over in seconds.

Blackwood pulled out his sword. There was no other way.

'Fix bayonets!' He hauled himself on to the sandbags and stared along the ramparts. '*Up, marines!*'

There was a hoarse cheer as the marines clambered out of the trench and faced their attackers from behind their bayonets.

Blackwood raised the revolver and squeezed the trigger. He saw a man stagger and fall, an officer turning his horse towards him and spurring it on.

The marines' unexpected challenge made the Russians falter, so that a last ragged volley smashed through the leading ranks before the bayonets lunged, and sabres clanged as both groups hurled themselves together.

The Russian officer had dismounted and was brandishing his sabre to urge his men forward. He was a huge, handsome man, and Blackwood saw him cut down a marine apparently without effort.

But his eyes were on Blackwood, and Ogilvie's senior sergeant leapt forward to join him and gasped, 'Watch that un, sir!'

The sergeant reeled back, a Russian bayonet jammed through his teeth and jaw as he was hurled bodily into the trench.

Blackwood parried the sabre aside. It was like hitting a plough with a broom-handle. He saw the officer's eyes harden as he raised the great sabre for another cut, then the astonishment as he fired Ogilvie's revolver directly into his chest.

The Russian attack waned, and as they began to run back towards their lines the marines knelt down on the rampart to speed their retreat.

There was a wave of wild cheering along the trench, and as a bugle blared the order to cease firing and fall back, Blackwood heard the additional commotion of light cavalry charging from the flank to catch some of the enemy stragglers.

He vaulted down on to the firing-step and stared breathlessly at the men nearest him. A few were down, several either killed or so badly wounded they would fight no more. He glanced at Ogilvie's bloody face and was grateful for his revolver. *Otherwise* . . .

'Stretcher bearers, quickly!'

Blackwood wiped his face and throat and saw blood on his wrist. He was almost afraid to move away from the rampart in case his legs gave way. He felt as if he was shaking all over, as if the old fever had returned.

Smithett was wiping his bayonet on a piece of rag.

He asked, 'They comin' back, sir?'

Blackwood looked at him while his senses recovered.

'I think not. Later, I expect.'

A rumble of gunfire shook the air and shots whined over the trench to burst on the support lines in the rear.

Blackwood took a quick glance across the battle-field and saw that the enemy had disappeared. Swallowed up.

He watched the smoking, blackened holes which marked their advance, the scattered bodies and some crawling wounded. A solitary horse cantered through the carnage to rejoin its army. Blackwood leaned over and saw the officer he had shot sprawled beside a dead marine. The horse would need a new owner.

He heard feet pounding along the trench and saw Harry running towards him.

'You're safe, *thank God*!'

Blackwood climbed from the step. Every muscle ached. He said, 'Ogilvie's dead. I'm not sure about the rest.'

Two marines with a stretcher hurried past and a pain-filled face stared at the officers as the wounded man was carried away.

A lieutenant, hatless, his sword still in his hand, came from the far end of the trench. He stared at Ogilvie's body as if he could not believe it.

Blackwood said, 'Take command here, Mr Frere. I must report to the colonel.'

Together they walked along the trench until they found Fynmore in his command post.

Brabazon looked at them and nodded gravely. 'Rotten about Ogilvie.' It was all he said.

Fynmore had spread his map on an upended crate.

'Just had word from General Richmond. The army is on the move. This sector is the only one under threat.' He looked up, his eyes red from strain. 'That redoubt must be taken.' He nodded firmly. 'No other way.'

The adjutant said, 'The army have already tried, sir, several times.' He seemed to shrink under Fynmore's stare.

'All the more reason!' He returned to his map. 'Anyway, it's an order from Richmond himself, damn him.'

Outside the guns roared and crashed and the sky was hidden in drifting smoke, and yet in spite of it Fynmore's concentration seemed to hold the war at bay.

He said suddenly, 'The Russians were expecting to break the line. We would have had to call for support, and that would have held up the army's advance. In view of the weather, the general might even have postponed it.'

Brabazon said, 'I expect the Russians were surprised at their hot reception.'

'*Exactly*, Major!' Fynmore smiled at him. 'Don't you see? They'll bide their time, sit it out.' He folded his map with delicate care. 'If we let them. They'll not expect an attack so soon, eh?'

The others exchanged glances.

'By us, sir?' Brabazon sounded doubtful.

But Fynmore was thinking ahead. 'Speak to me like that, would he? I'll show him what the Marines can do, blast his eyes!'

They were dismissed.

Outside the dug-out the air quaked from the gunfire, but it was directed on to another sector. There was a lot to do. Bury the dead. Repair the defences. Send the wounded down the line when it was safe to do so.

Brabazon took Blackwood aside and said quietly, 'I'm speaking out of turn. You may know anyway, Philip. But the colonel heard from his wife.'

'Yes.'

'He blames young Harry. He's eaten up with jealousy and anger. Richmond's rudeness didn't help much either. Just thought I'd let you know.'

He walked towards his own company, his face prepared for what he might find.

Blackwood went to his tiny dug-out and squatted on a box. Then he took a pad from Smithett's capacious bag and after a further hesitation began to write.

My very dear Davern . . .

It might be all that he could send. But at least she would know he was thinking of her.

Corporal Jones waited squatting on his haunches while Blackwood yawned and stretched himself awake.

'What's the weather like?'

Blackwood wiped his face with a damp cloth which Smithett had placed beside a mug of coffee and felt the chill in his bones. Beyond the rough curtain it was pitch-black. Another hour before dawn. He shivered.

Jones grunted. 'Snowing, sir.' Even in the frail glimmer from Smithett's candle he looked crumpled and unshaven.

We all look like that. Blackwood glanced round the tiny dug-out and tried not to compare it with a ship's ordered surroundings. A whole day had passed without incident after the Russian attack. Even the artillery had fallen quiet but for an occasional exchange between the two sides. Waiting. Holding their breath.

This was the day. They had gone over it a dozen or more times. It was risky, fatal if anything went wrong before they could cut down the distance from the enemy line. Blackwood patted his pockets and then picked up Ogilvie's fine percussion revolver. If he was to die he would take five of the enemy with him. He smiled grimly at his stupid reasoning.

'Time to go.'

Outside the dug-out the air was like a knife. Every man was wide awake and ready to begin the attack.

He found Fynmore and the adjutant in the command dug-out, the map folded and put away. If they had overlooked anything, it was too late now.

Fynmore looked at him dully. He seemed to have aged terribly in the last few days.

He said, 'If the enemy suspects you are using the sap-trench you must try to draw their fire. Major Brabazon will continue with the attack from the opposite side.' He tugged out his watch but put it away without examining it.

Blackwood nodded. He had hand-picked every man, knew each one of them either by sight or reputation. Curiously enough, the lieutenants were the only inexperienced ones. That too would soon be remedied. Except for Harry.

He looked round and asked, 'I thought Mr Blackwood was with you, sir?'

'He was.' Fynmore examined his pistol and held it to the light of a lantern. 'I've sent him on a special mission.' He looked up and added, 'He volunteered, of course.'

Blackwood stared at him and tried not to think of Brabazon's warning. Not here surely? Not today?

'May I ask what it entails?'

A sergeant peered round the curtain and said softly, 'All ready, sir.' He was whispering.

Fynmore remarked, 'He's gone ahead of your company.' He tried to appear casual. 'Grenade attack.'

Blackwood thought he had misheard. 'But he knows nothing about grenades, sir!'

Fynmore blew out the lantern and watched him through the sudden darkness. 'Good chance to learn then. Being related to you does not make him a special case.'

Blackwood felt strangely calm, even his voice sounded flat, unemotional.

'It's because of your wife, isn't it? You'd go to these lengths just to get your bloody revenge on my brother.'

Fynmore's voice sounded cracked with anger. 'How *dare* you! I'll have you court-martialled for this, stripped in front of the battalion, God help me, I will!'

There were many men waiting for the order to move, to discover if they would live or die, but Blackwood could only see Harry's face when he had told him about Fynmore's wife. Like the day when he had left him at the inn while he had gone to visit her at Fynmore's house.

'That can wait, Colonel. Ogilvie's dead and the major can't manage all on his own.' He turned away. 'What the hell did it matter anyway? She'd have done it whatever you said or did!'

Fynmore almost screamed, 'I've not finished with *you*! Stand still when I'm addressing you! You've gone too far this time — '

Blackwood stepped into the icy wind and felt the snow trying to cool his anger and despair.

'Go to hell, *sir*!'

The marines nearest the command post parted to let him through. Blackwood heard his boots squelching through the slush in the trench and waited for Fynmore to put him under arrest, but nothing happened.

It was a long walk to the other end of the sector, past where Ogilvie had died and on to a tumble-down heap of shattered rampart and torn sandbags, now almost serene beneath their layer of snow.

Two lieutenants, Frere and the willowy Fitzclarence, would be with him, and he saw M'Crystal and Quintin etched against the pale backdrop with the others.

Quintin said harshly, 'All mustered, sir. The packs an' spare gear 'as bin stowed away in a cave. Just weapons an' ammunition.'

The marines were not even wearing greatcoats. Nothing which would hamper their movements.

M'Crystal murmured, 'We heard about Mr Blackwood, sir.' He stared at the drifting flakes. 'He'll be out there by now.'

Blackwood did not answer. There was nothing anyone could do. Harry had Frazier and the new corporal, Fellowes, with him. Two good men. He thought of Harry's smile. No, three good men.

'Let's get on with it then.'

He clambered over the wrecked defences and slithered down a slope, his feet feeling for firm ground as he pictured the little pattern of sap-trenches.

It took all of twenty minutes to find the first trench. The marines flopped into it and began to crawl on their knees, their backs barely covered by the shallow sides.

The snow was a blessing, Blackwood thought. There was an awful stench, and he felt his hands fumble across things which were better unseen.

Once, where the trench was sheltered by some wooden planks, he felt his heart leap as he saw a solitary figure framed against the snow, watching their slow approach.

Quintin swore savagely and pushed the corpse aside with a

musket, and another marine retched as the weapon sank into rotten flesh.

'Pass the word. Absolute silence.'

They would not need telling, but someone might cough or sneeze.

Blackwood raised himself very slowly until his head and shoulders were above the trench. The hill was just to his right, and apparently quite close. He wanted to look back to see how far they had come but dared not move. He could smell burning, or charred wood, and his stomach rebelled as he heard rats squeaking as they did their nightly hunt on the battle-field.

The enemy did not have to rely on trenches here. The redoubt was somewhere on the hill-top, with plenty of natural cover for defending infantrymen.

He looked down and saw his hands on the edge of the trench, the sleeve of his uniform already showing a hint of colour. It would be dawn at any moment.

He wondered if Brabazon with the bulk of the marines was advancing from the other side. If they were all caught in the open they would not even get the chance to run. *Run?* Fynmore would never allow it. He would rather die. Or was he back in his empty command post? Missing, like that day aboard *Tenacious*?

Lieutenant Frere wriggled up beside him and whispered, 'Mr Blackwood's party have three grenades each, sir. I watched them leave. They will throw them all together in some nets which the adjutant found.'

Blackwood bit his lip. Grenades with their unpredictable, hazardous fuses were always a menace to those who handled them. Three in a net would be even more dangerous.

Where were they? Perhaps they had been captured and were tied up somewhere, helplessly waiting for the sound of their attack.

'Can't wait any more!'

He dragged himself out of the trench and gripped Ogilvie's revolver in his left hand. He heard the others preparing to follow him and strained his eyes to measure the last piece of open ground. Less than a hundred yards now. It seemed like ten miiles.

He darted a glance at the first men to join him. Quintin and Jones, Doak and Bulford. As Doak brushed past him he smelled the heady aroma of rum. Bayonets were already fixed, while their shakos and scabbards, and any other useless equipment, were piled in a cave like a memorial.

'Now!'

Blackwood moved away from the trench and, part walking, part trotting, the marines hurried after him, fanning out on either side, the sound of their feet growing as more and more clambered from the trench to follow.

They had been told what to do. Keep the pace down until the last moment. It was a hard order to obey or enforce without making more noise. They were moving quickly already, their eyes wide to pierce the shadows, their bayonets glinting occasionally while the snow eddied around them.

There was a startled cry and a figure seemed to rise straight out of the ground at their feet. Blackwood got a blurred vision of a levelled musket, then saw the man fade into the snow as someone drove him down with a bayonet.

There were more shouts and then the shrill of a whistle. The time had run out.

Blackwood yelled, '*Charge!*'

Then he was running with all his might, seeing nothing but the hill, while he swerved in and out of broken rocks and the remains of some abandoned gun-pits.

Flashes darted through the snow and lit up the nearest faces and pounding feet. Faster, faster.

More shots swept through and past them, and Blackwood heard someone scream and fall.

The firing was increasing from the hill-side and more marines were vanishing in the snow, their cries lost in the din of enemy muskets.

Suddenly there was one great explosion which painted the hill-side livid red, and as Blackwood's eyes throbbed to the sudden glare there was another, even higher, near the redoubt, it had to be.

To the breathless marines it was like a signal, a chance of survival when moments before they had expected to die.

Blackwood slipped and almost fell as he bounded over a fallen tree, heard M'Crystal's powerful voice controlling the charge, containing and driving his men like a shepherd with his sheep.

'Erin go bragh!'

The cry was wild like the moment as the Liverpool-Irish marines, the curse of the colour-sergeant's life, charged up the slope, the rest yelling meaningless words as the first group of Russian defenders broke from cover and tried to run for the redoubt. The snow swirled and danced as the figures rushed on, bayonets lunged and clashed, and as some of the Russians paused to fire several of the marines dropped dead or rolled away holding their wounds.

Blackwood saw a soldier running straight towards him, and knocked his musket aside with his sword. More were appearing from a hole in the ground, and he emptied the revolver into the tight group so that they fell back again and blocked the escape of the others.

A marine fell on to his face, and as Blackwood ran past he saw another hesitate and try to grope his way back through the wave of levelled bayonets.

Blackwood yelled, 'Advance, damn you!' He seized the marine by the belt and swung him round. 'Get on!'

He realized it was one of the Rocke twins.

The marine shouted frantically, 'It's me brother, sir! He's down!'

Blackwood forgot him as more shots hammered from the hill-top and the balls whined through the attackers.

A fire had broken out in the redoubt, probably caused by the last grenades. There had been just two explosions.

Blackwood saw a man crawling along the ground towards a discarded musket and slashed him across the shoulder before hurling himself up the last part of the slope. He clawed at buried timber and sandbags and saw Lieutenant Frere, who had managed to reach the enemy rampart before him, wheel round and fall from sight as a musket exploded almost in his face.

It was a scene from hell. Some kind of magazine or store was well ablaze, and against the leaping flames he suddenly saw Harry. The snow was swirling around him, the flakes like droplets of blood in the glow, so that he appeared to be floating.

Beyond him, shining dully through the smoke and snow, was one of the big Russian guns. Harry swung his net slowly round his head and threw it, then as he turned to run he saw Blackwood and waved.

The explosion was deafening, and while the marines flung themselves down and gasped for air in a wave of intense heat, Blackwood heard the nearest gun crash over on to its side.

He got to his feet and groped for his sword.

'Open fire!'

The marines dropped to their knees or remained standing while they fired for the first time since they had left their own lines.

Everything was made more confused by the din of exploding ammunition and the crack of rifles. Faces, wild with the fury of battle, loomed through the snow as the first daylight pushed the shadows aside.

Blackwood waved his sword.

'Again!'

His cry seemed to hang in the air like something quite apart from him. He saw his sword clattering across the overturned cannon, felt the jarring pain of his body hitting the ground. Voices were muffled as if calling through a blanket, and he tried to get to his feet, to rally them, but his mind rebelled and he fell down again.

Then came the agony, and when he put his hand to his side he felt the wetness and something jagged in his fingers. Someone was crying in terrible pain and he wondered vaguely if it was his own voice he heard.

He saw Harry, his face only inches away as he leaned over him. There was snow on his ruffled hair and he needed to reassure him. He had seen tears on Harry's cheeks, cutting through the grime of that last terrible explosion. But when he tried to raise his arm the pain smashed into him, like a white-hot axe driving into his body.

Beyond Harry there was cheering, *that* he could recognize. A bugle too.

Then just as suddenly there was nothing at all.

Philip Blackwood opened his eyes and kept them fixed on a point above his head. He had expected to see Harry, to tell him everything was all right, and the realization that there was nobody to see and total silence around him made him go stiff with terror.

I am dead.

When he tried to move he could feel nothing, and even the air around him seemed misty and warm, when it should have been touched with ice.

He saw a light spreading towards him, watched it fascinated as it played across the pattern of planks above him.

A face looked down and gave a slow nod. The man wore a white coat and there were little red dots on it. Blood.

The realization came through his drugged mind like a bullet.

'Where am I?' How strange he sounded.

The face said, 'Base hospital.' He nodded again. 'Welcome back to the living, Captain.'

He turned away and another face appeared to swim towards him. It was surrounded by a white robe of some kind. He struggled. If he lost her now she would vanish completely.

She rested her hand on his shoulder, her fingers cool against his burning body.

She said, 'I'm here, Philip. I'll never lose you again.'

Blackwood allowed the darkness to close over him once more. Nothing else mattered. They were together.

Epilogue

Philip Blackwood sat in an old wicker chair, his legs propped on a stool, and stared across the well-tended grass towards the gates of Hawks Hill. It was late afternoon, and he had been sitting here on the familiar stone-flagged terrace as if he was afraid to miss something. How quiet it was, the house and grounds could be empty. Only the far-off chorus of rooks and the sound of cattle in the nearby farm broke the stillness.

Here and there the trees were already tinged with red and gold. It was the start of autumn. It did not seem possible.

He twisted round in the chair and looked up at the house. It was still hard to accept that his father was dead. He should be at that window, waiting by his table to hear the latest news of the Royal Marines wherever they were in action.

As he moved in the chair he felt the tight pain in his side. They said it might never go. It was hardly surprising, he thought bitterly. The Russian shell splinter had destroyed one rib and had left a hole big enough to contain a man's fist.

His father had died even as the ship full of Crimean wounded had dropped anchor in the Downs. In his sleep, his stepmother had told him. As he would have wished. She had kissed him lightly, her lips as cold as he had remembered them. Then she had left Hawks Hill for Paris to join her daughter. She had taken a last look around the house and had spoken with the servants. She showed no emotion or sense of loss. It almost seemed as if she had felt a prisoner here.

She had said gravely, 'It's yours now, Philip. It was what the colonel wanted.' She had brushed aside his protests. 'You

will be well cared for. Make your own life as you want it.'
Then she had gone.

Blackwood saw old Oates wandering through the copse
towards his cottage. Completely lost. A survivor without any
goal in sight. They should have died together. The old
campaigners.

Blackwood felt a prick behind his eyes. Poor Oates, he had
probably known his father better than any of them.

He recalled the moment after his stepmother had left the
house. Oates had waited for Doctor Sturges and a military
surgeon to complete their examination of his wound and had
then carried the colonel's sword into the room. He must have
been guarding it. Saving it for the first Blackwood to return
home.

That had been three months ago. After all the surgical
treatment and pain, the uncertainty and those first steps
along the hospital corridor with the aid of two sticks.

He glanced at the stick by his side, hating it, wondering
what she would say when she saw him. If she came . . . He
felt something like panic. In that one precious letter after
their meeting in Balaclava she had told him that her husband
had decided to end their marriage. He had been offered a
highly important post in India where several military hospitals were to be built under his supervision. It was an amicable
parting. There had been no love, and yet in some strange way
each had needed the other at one moment in their lives.

I will never lose you, my darling, she had written. I shall
love you and take care of you.

But that had been then. The war continued, casualties
mounted. With pain Blackwood had read of the Marines'
exploits and what it had cost. Major Brabazon had lost an arm
during that last mad charge on the redoubt. Colour-Sergeant
M'Crystal, Corporal Jones, the willowy Second Lieutenant
Fitzclarence, even the hard man Frazier who had been killed
by one of his own grenades. They and many others had fallen
that day.

And weeks later, while he had been fighting against the

agony of his wound, others had followed. Like their Corps motto, *By Sea and By Land*. The tough campaigner Sergeant Quintin had died at the siege of Sebastopol, and the surviving Rocke twin had walked with fixed bayonet and had attacked a squad of Russians single-handed. Perhaps he had wanted to die after losing his brother. Blackwood wondered if Quintin ever discovered which was which before he too had been killed.

Harry had written him a strangely mature and subdued letter. It had been about Fynmore. With Brabazon in hospital, and most of his experienced officers dead or wounded, Fynmore had been forced to lead the final assault on a hill which overlooked the army's lines.

Harry had written simply. It was the bravest thing I ever saw. Fynmore was terrified and his nerve had cracked long ago, before you captured the redoubt, probably as far back as Africa. But he loved the Corps more than life itself, and he led his men to victory and died doing it. To be so terrified and to do what he did was real courage.

Blackwood had heard since that Fynmore had been mentioned as one of the first recipients of the Queen's new medal when it was eventually struck. Fynmore would have liked that.

He heard steps on the stones and saw Smithett crossing the terrace. *We shall be like my father and Oates*, he thought.

Smithett said, 'Time to get inside, sir. There's a nip in the air.'

In his sober black coat he looked every inch the perfect valet. He was that and far more. Sometimes, as Blackwood sat in the library for a last drink, Smithett would enter, gauge his mood and then bring out his endless tit-bits of memory. About so-and-so in the *Audacious*, or how they had rescued Private Doak from a brothel in Malta.

Blackwood watched the gates. Davern might not even have reached London. She had said in her letter that she would go first to Slade's house. She might have changed her mind. He could not blame her.

'Look, sir.' Smithett took the blanket from Blackwood's legs. 'Me old gran used to say, "A watched pot never boils." She'll come, you see if she don't.'

Blackwood smiled at him. Of course, he had almost forgotten Smithett's close link with both of them. The hut by the river, the smell of death, the look in her eyes as she had fallen against him.

He stared at the copse, the darkening shadows which made the trees look solid and invulnerable. It was all his now, and yet he felt like an interloper, as if at any moment he would see his father striding through the grounds giving orders to Woodstock, the head gardener, as if he were addressing his sergeant-major.

He heard carriage wheels beyond the gates and sighed.

'That bloody doctor again.'

Smithett folded the blanket over his arm, his mournful face giving the hint of a smile.

'Oh, I dunno about that, sir. Now, up we get, nice an' easy like.' He watched Blackwood's sudden anxiety. 'She didn't ferget us arter all, sir.'

Blackwood saw the fine carriage, the one with Slade's crest on the door, sweeping up the drive. Behind him he could hear the housekeeper's harsh voice as she held the servants at bay. Smithett must have spoken with her about this moment. Only he would have thought of it.

Blackwood took a step towards the drive and gasped as the pain shot through him. *Not now. Dear God, not now.*

Smithett snapped, 'Stick, sir!' He thrust it into his hand. 'She's seen more wounded than we have, I s'pect.'

But the stick flew clattering down the steps as Davern alighted from the coach and ran to meet him.

Blackwood felt her arms around his neck and tasted her tears, or were they his own?

Smithett watched for a few seconds and then picked up the stick.

Best leave 'em, he thought. The captain would not need a prop any more.

The First to Land

Douglas Reeman

ARROW

For Caroline Dawnay
With Love.
Tenax propositi.

Published by Arrow Books in 1985

Reprinted 12 times

Copyright © High Seas Authors Ltd 1984

The right of Douglas Reeman to be identified as the author of this
work has been asserted by him in accordance with the Copyright,
Designs and Patents Act, 1988

First published in the United Kingdom in 1984 by Hutchinson

Arrow Books
The Random House Group Limited
20 Vauxhall Bridge Road, London SW1V 2SA

Random House Australia (Pty) Limited
20 Alfred Street, Milsons Point, Sydney
New South Wales 2061, Australia

Random House New Zealand Limited
18 Poland Road, Glenfield
Auckland 10, New Zealand

Random House (Pty) Limited
Endulini, 5a Jubilee Road, Parktown 2193, South Africa

The Random House Group Limited Reg. No. 954009

www.randomhouse.co.uk

A CIP catalogue record for this book
is available from the British Library

Papers used by Random House are natural,
recyclable products made from wood grown in
sustainable forests. The manufacturing processes conform to
the environmental regulations of the country of origin

ISBN 0 09 942410 X

Printed and bound in Germany by
Elsnerdruck, Berlin

Contents

Acknowledgement

I wish to thank Major Tony Brown MBE, RM, and his staff at the Royal Marines Museum, Eastney, and all members of the Corps past and present who have willingly given me their help and encouragement in this series.

I

Old and New

The Hampshire countryside gleamed dully after a heavy overnight mist. The big house which dominated the Hawks Hill estate and outlying farm cottages felt damp despite the fires in each room which had been laid and lit long before dawn.

From a window in his study Major General Harry Blackwood gazed out at the grey clouds and frowned. November. At any other time he would have relished this month with its first meeting of the local hunt of which he was Master, but he could not dispel his apprehension, which both worried and irritated him. In a few weeks it was the birth not only of a new year but also of a new century. The thought disturbed him more than he would ever admit to Deirdre, his wife, or anyone else. When 1899 closed he knew his life would somehow lose its purpose. This might even be his last November. He swung away from the window and looked around the room with its dark panelled walls and cheerful log fire. The servants and visitors to Hawks Hill always referred to this as the General's Room. Indeed it contained innumerable relics and mementoes of his life and career in the Royal Marines. A portrait of his father hung on one wall. As he had lived, not as he had died here in this great house. Stern-faced and proud in his scarlet coatee, one hand resting on his sword. Even the sword was mounted in a glass case. Pictures, weapons, fox masks, a bugle with a hole punched through it. It was not difficult to see the expression of horror on the boy's face as he had been cut down by a bullet even as he was sounding the Charge.

Harry Blackwood was sixty-seven years old but in his immaculately cut frock coat he was as straight-backed and trim as the day he had won his majority in the Corps he loved so dearly. But his features told a different story. There were deep crowsfeet around his eyes caused by staring at sun and sky in so many ships, so many campaigns in all parts of the globe. His hair and neatly clipped moustache were white, in marked contrast with his skin, which was like tooled leather.

He crossed to the fire and lifted his coat tails to benefit from the blaze. He had been born here in this house which had been in the Blackwood family for four generations and purchased originally by old Samuel Blackwood: the last of a long line of soldiers. After him all the Blackwoods had been Royal Marines, although Harry had never been able to discover how the change had come about. The main house was a great rambling place which had begun as a fortified Tudor farmhouse. Added to over the years, it spread in several directions with cellars and tiny attics which had once delighted the Blackwood children like a magic castle. It even had a moat, although that was only half filled nowadays; a home for geese and swans.

He heard his wife speaking with one of the maids beyond the door and hoped she would not disturb him. A quiet, faded lady, it was difficult to recall her as the vibrant girl she had once been. She had given him three sons, all of whom were now in the Corps. The youngest, Jonathan, had joined his first ship at Portsmouth just two weeks ago.

Deirdre had been tearful about it but had made no protest when her husband had insisted that his sons should follow the family tradition.

The General had many fixed ideas, one being that women in any kind of authority could not be tolerated. Even the Queen whom he had served for the whole of his life irritated him. Still on the throne after sixty-one years. It did not seem possible. With the British Empire spreading to encompass the whole world you needed strong and decisive leadership, an example for those who had to defend it.

He smiled grimly, the years falling from his features as he did so. It was proclaimed that the sun never set on the Empire. Nor would it while there were still marines.

The door opened slightly but it was Briggs, once his trusted attendant and orderly, now his valet, his shadow.

'Well man?' His voice was sharp. He was not looking forward to the next moments. The thought of them had spoiled the morning, and Deirdre might just be inclined to argue with him.

'Young Mr Blackwood is 'ere, sir.' Briggs eyed him warily. He knew all the General's moods and had been at his side on blood-reddened decks with all hell breaking loose around them. In the desert, and the jungle, wherever the Royal Marines had been called to action.

'Give me a few minutes, Briggs.'

Briggs withdrew. He knew *this* mood. Keep a young officer waiting, even if he was one of the family. Make 'em sweat a while.

Alone again the General walked to the place of honour in his collection. A great painting depicting a battle which had raged in the Crimea, snow, flashing guns, grim-faced marines with fixed bayonets running and dying to the summit of that terrible redoubt. Framed against one fiery explosion was a solitary officer, sword high over his head as he urged his dwindling followers to drive the Russians away from their guns.

Philip Blackwood, Harry's half-brother, was that officer. Now as then he was a hero in the General's eyes. All those years ago when Harry had been a youthful lieutenant like the one he was about to receive in this room, Philip's life had been marked with pain. His wife Davern had died in childbirth, and Philip just ten years later from a fever he contracted in India.

The General had taken it upon himself to care for and raise Philip's only son Ralf. Maybe he and Deirdre had

spoiled him because of his background. He had never
known his mother, and seen little enough of Philip, who
like all serving officers had been more away from the
country than in it.

Ralf Blackwood was eighteen, the same age as Jonathan,
and was until recently at Woolwich, the Court Division as
it was nicknamed. There was no other similarity with the
General's youngest son. Ralf had some of his father's good
looks, but was resentful of discipline, and inclined to sulk if
admonished.

For although the General's military activities were now
confined to occasional ceremonials in London or twenty
miles away at the Royal Marines' barracks at Portsmouth he
retained a close link with the Corps and had plenty of
friends who were still serving.

He knew all about Ralf's heavy gambling in the mess.
His frequent outbursts of temper when he had been accused
of cheating. Being a bad loser usually led to something
worse. Had his weakness been women the General would
have understood and probably encouraged him. As a boy he
had had his first woman, one of the servant girls, right here
at Hawks Hill. There had been dozens since of every class
and colour.

Deirdre knew the General's record but like most things
she never mentioned it.

The door opened and Ralf Blackwood entered. He was in
uniform, the scarlet tunic bright in the poor light.

The General said, 'You look well.'

Ralf exclaimed, 'I've come from Portsmouth, Uncle.' He
sounded as if he could not believe it himself. 'I was sent to
the barracks yesterday. No notice. Nothing. The Colonel
must be mad!'

The General snapped, 'Don't be so bloody impertinent!
You were sent to Portsmouth to join a new detachment
which is going overseas.' He added dryly, 'I can see you
know that too. But *I* was the one who arranged the transfer.
For your own good and that of the Corps.'

Ralf stood his ground, his face pale and astonished.

'I want to resign, Uncle.'

'Say *sir* when you address me. You are my nephew, but today I am speaking as your superior. You have been gambling heavily. Again.'

'They all do it.' He flinched under the General's cold stare. 'Sir.'

'Three hundred pounds, I believe?' He saw it strike home like a bullet. 'And just *how* did you intend to repay the debt?'

'I – I'll borrow – '

The General ignored him and glanced again at the picture. In the flickering glow from the fire it seemed to be alive. In quieter moments he often relived it. The terrible crack of grenades as he had blown up the magazine on the redoubt, the shock of seeing his hero Philip fall wounded in the bloody snow.

'Your father should have got the Victoria Cross for what he did.' He touched his coat as if to seek the precious decoration. 'Instead I got it. With my eldest son David, that makes two VCs in the family, not a *bad* achievement, wouldn't you say?' It was all he could do to keep the bitterness from his voice as he thought of his mother, elegant and beautiful, but a whore for all that. Society had known of her relationship with the late Lord Cleveland and others like him. It was never mentioned, but like troops in battle society had closed ranks and excluded her. Harry blamed her for the harm she had done him. A major general, and awarded the most coveted decoration the country could bestow, but no knighthood like some of his contemporaries, most of whom had never attained such merit.

A knighthood would have rounded things off and Deirdre would have liked it. He thought of her mild tolerance for some of the things he had done in his life. More than that, she *deserved* it. He thought suddenly of his eldest son David, a captain and somewhere at sea on passage for Hong Kong under orders.

He frowned and did not notice Ralf's sudden apprehension. David had got his Victoria Cross at the capture of Benin. Now he was on his way to the Far East, eventually to China unless the situation there eased. The Chinese mandarins were becoming troublesome again and it was hinted that there might be actual attacks on British trade missions and foreign legations. So why was David being wasted there? With his record, and a captain at twenty-seven, he should have been sent to one of the new iron battleships for further experience and promotion. It seemed almost like a punishment after what he had done in Africa.

He said crisply, 'You will be going to the Far East by troopship. With luck you will be placed under David's command. I say with luck because there are those who would be quick to see your manners as insolence. I will not tolerate any more of this gambling. It will only drive you to something far more serious and bring disgrace on the family. Do I make myself clear?'

'Yes, sir.' He looked at the floor, the corners of his mouth turned down like a pouting child.

The General snorted, 'Resign indeed!' It was strange that Philip, his beloved half-brother, had once intended to resign from the Corps. Philip had imagined he liked action too much. Maybe David's experiences in Africa had hardened him too?

'I shall see Mother before I leave, sir.'

The General relented but only very slightly. There was more at stake than family affections. 'Do that and then return to the barracks. I wish you good luck.'

When he turned his head the room was empty again.

He sat down wearily. The brief interview had drained him. Getting old. Past it.

He would pay off young Ralf's debts. He gave a rueful smile. Could have been worse.

Briggs padded back into the room, a glass of sherry balanced on his small silver tray.

Harry stared. 'Sun's not over the yardarm yet, man!'

Briggs grinned. 'Can't be sure in this weather, sir.' He saw the General's hand shake slightly as he took the glass.

Harry said, 'I'd better see the steward this morning, I suppose.' It was the part of Hawks Hill and all its farm workers and smallholdings he hated. They were always complaining, asking for new roofs, more livestock, it never stopped. He had spent a fortune on the estate. The local hunt, the hounds, and a lavish fashion of entertaining which was the talk of the county.

Trent, the estate steward, was an old woman, he decided. Always hinting at bankruptcy, the need to sell off land to pay for what he had the gall to describe as extravagances.

He thought of Ralf's pale, defiant face and stood up abruptly.

'Maybe the boy'll have lunch before he leaves.'

Briggs looked away. ''E's gone already, sir.'

'*Damn!*' The General left the room and saw his wife watching him from the entrance hall. Reproachful, hurt, it was hard to tell.

'Had to put him right, m'dear.' It sounded defensive and that angered him too. 'Young idiot.'

'Quite so, dear.' She smiled gently. 'But you'll pay off his debts just the same, if I know you.'

The General straightened his back and touched his neat moustache, suddenly pleased with her remark.

He took her arm and led her into the big drawing room where the windows faced a stone-flagged terrace and a line of bare trees beyond. It looked cold and miserable outside these stout walls, he thought.

They sat down and Harry stretched his legs. 'Did I ever tell you how Philip and I chased some slavers halfway across Africa?'

She smiled. 'Remind me, dear.' A hundred times or more. But he obviously needed reassuring, to relive those moments which became more precious with each passing month.

The General leaned back. 'It was this way — '

Briggs walked away. The General sometimes got his facts mixed up when he told his stories. Only his longing to be back with the Corps remained the same.

Captain David Blackwood lay motionless on his vibrating bunk and stared at the slowly revolving fan overhead. He was completely naked, his tanned limbs spreadeagled to catch even the slightest coolness, but there seemed to be no relief.

Around and below him the little paddle-steamer *Cocatrice* squeaked and rattled as her hull deeped over the long undulating swell of the Indian Ocean.

Blackwood was beginning to wonder if he had made the right decision when he had decided to take passage in the small mail and passenger steamship.

When he had received his orders to proceed to Hong Kong he had been serving as acting major aboard the massive battleship *Royal Sovereign* in the Mediterranean. After all the land-fighting he had seen and shared at the capture and burning of Benin in the Niger Protectorate he had felt strangely out of place in a powerful man-of-war, a symbol of Britain's unchallenged might at sea.

Even in the Mediterranean there had been plenty of action when the Royal Navy had taken steps to evacuate Christians who had somehow escaped the terrible Turkish massacre the previous year.

He could have waited for passage in a warship, but the *Cocatrice* was faster if only because of her lack of armament.

He touched his bare skin with his fingers. It was almost dusk and yet he was still damp with sweat. It had been another long, hot day in the Indian Ocean, ninety degrees of blazing sunshine and not a breath of air.

He too had been thinking of Hawks Hill all those hundreds, thousands of miles away. The gardens, the terraces, the agelessness of the rooms with their great pictures and proud portraits.

His youngest brother, Jonathan, would be at sea by now unless there had been some delay. Neil, the middle brother who was twenty-three, was probably still serving as a lieutenant in a frigate in India. Communications might be far superior to those of his father's day, but it still took a long, long while to discover what was happening around the fleet.

He closed his eyes and half listened to the rumble of the great paddles. The passage seemed as if it would never end. They had spent a week at Trincomalee where he had been invited to several dances and receptions aboard ships there. Thank God for the Suez Canal, he thought. It did cut the monotonous journey by weeks.

It would be cold and frosty in Hampshire. Bare trees, sodden hedgerows. He felt his lips smile. Heaven.

Singapore next, then Hong Kong, and then? It was pointless to think further than that. The Chinese situation might have settled itself. He might easily be sent home to England, another ship.

He thought of the day he had joined the *Royal Sovereign* at Gibraltar. The glances in the mess, the way they looked from his Victoria Cross to his face as if to discover something. Even the battleship's captain had received him with something like awe.

'Two VCs in one family.' He had asked dryly, 'Have you finished now?'

And yet the only thing that had made that fight on the Niger River different for Blackwood had been its ferocity and the firm belief that he was going to be killed.

His captain had died within minutes, a sergeant major next, and two experienced marines before Lieutenant David Blackwood had been made to realize that it was upon himself and a small squad of marines that the whole flank depended.

His hand moved up to his shoulder and rested momentarily on a livid scar. The bullet had remained embedded in his body for a whole day before he could find a surgeon. In that climate and under such conditions it was a marvel the surgeon had not lopped of his arm. As it was he still felt pain on occasion. He smiled again, the shadows falling from his face, making him look younger than his twenty-seven years.

There was the girl in Trincomalee. The young wife of an army paymaster who had gone into the interior to visit some isolated infantry unit.

She had made the stay in Ceylon memorable with the fierceness of her passion, her need of him. Her husband was either a lot older than she, or unaware of the luck he should have enjoyed. She had knelt over him in that tall, cool room one night, her loosened hair touching his body until his eagerness for her was roused yet again. She had kissed the scar so that the shame he had felt over it seemed dispersed and forgotten.

He peered at his watch on its stand beside the bunk. It would be laughable but for the discomfort. For even in the little *Cocatrice* you dressed for dinner. Swan, his servant and attendant, would be here soon to arrange a bath and lay out a clean shirt and all the rest of it.

Then in the cramped saloon, with the captain at the head of the table, he would have to endure a hot curry, and some conversation which got more stilted with each league steamed.

There were ten passengers including two Catholic nuns who were intending to join a mission somewhere in China. One was old, the other quite young and pretty. The sailors had been ordered by the captain to mind their language as they worked the ship. He on the other hand, who was a model of good behaviour in the saloon, had a tongue like a lash when he was on his bridge.

Blackwood threw his legs over the side of his bunk and ruffled his dark hair. In the mirror above the small washstand and dressing case he saw his eyes watching himself. Tawny-brown like his mother's. An ordinary face, he told himself, with lines by his mouth as evidence of his suffering after being wounded.

He saw the door open in the mirror, Swan's head coming round it as it always did. The ritual was about to be repeated. .

Private Jack Swan of the RMLI had a round, homely face like a polished apple. Hampshire born and bred, he came from a family of marines. That was so common in the Corps it was barely ever mentioned except by exasperated drill-sergeants on the barracks square. 'Don't suppose *yew* 'ad a mother or father, did yer?'

Swan was the same age as Blackwood and the latter had given up trying to make him go for promotion to corporal. Swan was intelligent and quick, both at his duties and in the fury of a battle. He had been with him for three years and whenever Blackwood had mentioned the subject Swan had replied in his round Hampshire dialect, 'Better wait 'n' see, sir. Early days.' It was hopeless.

Swan reached into the canvas wardrobe and took out the mess jacket. Like everything else he supervised it was perfect, but it gave him time to glance at his master. Not the young captain with a VC but the man underneath.

Captain Blackwood had the look of recklessness which made him appeal to women. Swan knew that better than most. He was not one to drive his men when they were doing their best either. But get on the wrong side of him and you would soon know it. They said his father, the old Major General, had been like him once. Blood, guts and women.

Swan gave his secret smile. Promotion indeed. Just being with the young captain was worth all the stripes in the bloody Corps!

Africa, then the Med, next China. In the Corps you took it all for granted. Like their motto. By sea and land. Barracks or frigate, mud huts or stockade, you were still a marine.

The captain's next appointment bothered Swan a bit. He was a hero. Swan had felt quite proud when he had read it in the newspaper. It seemed to rub off on him in some way. He had been with him when those black bastards had tried to cut down the Royals. Swan had lost some good mates on that bloody awful day. He'd not forget that in a hurry.

Unbeknown to either of them, Swan and Captain Blackwood's father thought much the same about the proposed appointment.

The Chinks had learned their lesson back in the fifties in the *Arrow* War as it was called. In 1856 the Chinese had seized a British ship of that name and it had resulted in the bombardment of Canton and a considerable loss of life. In Swan's uncomplicated mind there seemed little likelihood that anything like that would be repeated.

Later at dinner in the *Cocatrice*'s saloon Blackwood had to use something like physical effort to prevent his eyelids from drooping.

The curry had been extra hot, and the captain's wine limp and warm.

The two nuns said nothing, their eyes hidden by their wimples. Only once did the young one glance up as Blackwood replied to the captain's comment about a Boer uprising in South Africa.

Blackwood had been thinking about something else. Of Hawks Hill, and what his brother Neil had written to him about their father's expensive tastes. The farmers did not like the hunt trampling over their fields but could do nothing about it. The labourers on the estate met nothing but rebuffs whenever they tried to have improvements made to their cottages. Trent, the estate steward, had told them to shut up or get out, and jobs were not so easy to find as winter closed in.

Something would have to be done, otherwise Hawks Hill would find itself in serious debt.

He had looked at the captain and had replied, 'If it comes to anything I expect we'll have to go in and finish the fight for the army!' Perhaps it had come out sharper than he had intended. Maybe he was just tired, but he saw the girl's eyes lift to his face. Her empty untroubled expression had made him feel clumsy and childish.

The captain laughed. 'Always spoiling for a battle, you lot are!'

One of the passengers, a rubber planter returning to Singapore with his newly found wife from England, leaned over the table and said loudly, 'I see you have the VC, er, Captain Blackwood. Would you care to tell us how you won it?'

Blackwood looked at him coldly. 'No.'

The planter grinned at his wife. 'Modest too.'

Blackwood stood up abruptly. 'Please excuse me.'

He heard the captain murmur, 'He's had a bad time, poor fellow. Must make allowances.' He also heard the planter's loud guffaw. He suddenly wanted to return to the saloon and tell them in straight, unvarnished words what it was like, *really* like, not just once when someone gave you a medal, but all the other occasions in places which most Britons had never heard of. What right had those nuns to look at him as if he was some sort of animal?

Always spoiling for a battle, the captain had said. He had only been joking, but it was probably true. Aboard *Royal Sovereign* with her endless drills and ceremonial Blackwood had thought of those other times, the fear and elation, the ready comradeship and rough humour which had made his men special. A walk on deck, then some brandy in the cabin. Another day nearer his destination.

There would be some familiar faces at Singapore, rumours to discuss.

He walked to the guardrails and watched the great frothing wash sweeping astern from one of the paddles. Ships such as this one were putting paid to sail. The steam engine and the opening of the Suez Canal through which the square-riggers could not navigate were making sure of it.

Blackwood had been in the Corps for nine years and had

served aboard a sailing frigate when he had first gone to sea. He remembered it clearly. The creaking spars and booming canvas, the sense of mystery which sailing vessels still retained. What was it some old tar had said? *Sail is a lady. Steam a bundle of iron.* He smiled and returned to the companion way.

Within minutes of his head touching the pillow Captain David Blackwood of the Royal Marines Light Infantry, Victoria Cross and Mentioned in Despatches, was fast asleep.

The Officer Commanding Troops of the big transport *Aurora* leaned back in his chair and pressed his fingertips together. All round the cabin the hull shook to the thump of booted feet, the clatter of tackles and shouted orders as the last of the military came on board.

The *Aurora* was very old and fitted with a single propellor which would probably break down before they reached the Bay of Biscay. He hoped it would not be the case, for the trooper was packed to the deck beams with soldiers, guns, supplies, even some mules and horses, many of which were destined for the latest trouble in South Africa. A whole company of Royal Marines had been the last to arrive on board. The OC Troops did not like the Royal Marines. They were neither one thing nor the other in his view.

Outside the stout hull he heard the muffled sound of a military band on Portsmouth Point as it ran through its repertoire of lively and patriotic tunes. A great crowd had gathered on the harbour wall and pier to watch the old ship put to sea. Mothers and children, wives and lovers. Troopships were only too common as they sailed to the ends of the Empire to restore peace and good order, to attack and destroy the Queen's enemies. But to the watching crowd each ship was different.

The rain was sheeting down. He would be glad to leave. But he had to see a junior second lieutenant of the Royal

Marines. He snapped, 'Enter!'

Ralf Blackwood marched through the door and halted smartly in front of the desk.

The OC Troops said coolly, 'You should see one of your own officers. I have a thousand things to deal with. However – '

He would have liked to have kicked him out of the cabin, but a friend had told him that this young marine came from an important family.

Ralf Blackwood was still not sure what he had been expecting when he had marched with a full company from the barracks to Portsmouth dockyard. Even here in harbour his stomach heaved from a mixture of smells. Horses and men, cabbage water, tar and sweat. Once at sea he would probably be sick.

'My quarters are inadequate, sir.'

'*What?*' He swallowed his anger. 'Four officers to a cabin. When I was your age, your rank, I was lucky to get a berth at all!'

Ralf hung his head. 'I'm not even sharing with a Royal Marine, sir.'

That did it. 'Not good enough, eh?' He flung some papers aside from his desk and stared furiously at a list of names and cabins. 'Three second lieutenants from the Rifles! They're the ones who should be objecting!'

Ralf Blackwood stared at a point above the other officer's left epaulette. Damn him to hell, and his uncle too for landing him in this slum. He thought of London, the bright-eyed girls, the music and the balls he so enjoyed.

He did not really know his cousin David but from what he had heard he was not one to take any misdemeanour lightly. It was all so damned unfair. He felt his eyes smart with despair. A warship would at least be tolerable. Where they were going sounded like the end of the earth.

The OC Troops winced as something very heavy crashed down on the upper desk and was followed by a stream of obscenities from one of the ship's petty officers. He could waste no more time.

'I have little to do with your Corps.' His tone was icy. 'But I can only advise you to think less of yourself and a bit more of your responsibility, *if* you have any!'

Ralf snapped his heels together and left the cabin, his face devoid of expression but inwardly seething.

The major in command of the marines saw him and shouted, 'And just where the bloody hell have you been?' Like the OC Troops, he was preoccupied with getting his own people settled in their overcrowded quarters. 'Report to the Adjutant at the double, sir!'

An artillery lieutenant touched Ralf's sleeve as the angry major strode away.

'Never mind him. I understand you're quite a hand at cards?'

Ralf was both surprised and flattered by the other officer's knowledge.

He thought of the General's Room, the great house which but for his parents' deaths might have been his.

They treated him like a child. Aunt Deirdre and her dreamy detachment from daily events. And his uncle, always on at him to remember the family, uphold the honour of the Corps. He was a fine one to lecture him. Ralf had heard things about the General's mother, about Harry Blackwood's own affairs with whores no better than she.

Ralf replied calmly, 'Any time.'

The artillery lieutenant grinned. 'As soon as we leave harbour.'

Ralf watched him go. This time his luck must change.

His sergeant found him and saluted.

'The men are waitin', sir.' He ran his eyes over the second lieutenant, critical and anxious. He would have to carry this one, he could see all the signs. Spoiled, arrogant, lazy. But if he let down the platoon and the adjutant became aware of it he knew who would get the blame.

'Let them wait, Sergeant. Can't you deal with them?'

The sergeant saw one of his corporals watching and

glared. His own wife was out there on the dockside. Two kids he might never see again.

Blackwood was a fine name in the Corps. The sergeant tightened his belt and grimaced. But there was usually a rotten apple in any barrel.

The *Aurora* slipped between Portsmouth Point and Fort Blockhouse just before dusk, her black and white hull shining in the steady rain like glass.

Her decks were crammed with scarlet and green, blue and khaki, the great anonymous mass of faces peering for someone dear or familiar as the band played its own farewell. Hundreds of troopships had sailed from here, and many more would follow. But it was a moment they would all remember.

2

The Letter

Private Swan took the sword and helmet and laid them carefully on a chest while he gauged his master's mood.

Outside the white-painted room the air still vibrated to the sorrowful drums and the slow marches of marines and soldiers, as dust swirled over the docks and parade ground and seemed to change colour in the sunshine.

David Blackwood allowed Swan to unfasten and remove his tunic. His shirt was plastered to his body like a second skin. After the marching and the drills the room felt almost cold.

No matter what was happening in other parts of the Queen's Empire the importance of ceremonial remained paramount. There had been several visits to Hong Kong by senior foreign dignitaries as well as senior British officers. It seemed as if almost overnight Hong Kong had become the hinge upon which the power in Whitehall extended to the Far East and beyond. In the spring it would be the ailing Queen's birthday, and that would mean even more drills and parades.

In South Africa what first had been scoffed at as a mere skirmish had changed into a full-scale and bloody war where British troops were too often getting the worst of it. That again was impossible to accept. Trained regular soldiers and marines against Boer farmers and renegades. More than once the enemy sharpshooters had proved a match for cavalry and tactics which had not altered since the Crimea.

Blackwood sighed and waited for Swan to tug off his

boots. It was now February 1900, and he had been in Hong
Kong with little to occupy his time since he had arrived in
the *Cocatrice*.

The harbour and dockyard were packed with men-of-war.
Gleaming white hulls or black and buff, they represented
the new iron navy. Here and there like reminders of a past
era were still some of the old 'wooden walls', now mostly
used as store and hospital ships.

Blackwood thought of his brother Neil who had been
sent to South Africa. He had received one letter from him
which had described the raids on Boer positions, the
unending sniping which had caused heavy casualties
amongst the British troops.

He had seemed extra bitter in that letter, scornful of the
generals who had no idea of modern fighting conditions. He
had described the perils of moving large numbers of men
across open country without breaking formation even under
fire.

David Blackwood could picture his father striding about
his room at Hawks Hill, laying down the law on what they
should be doing in the colony, demanding that he should be
sent to take command. No wonder there was news of more
trouble in China, he thought. The Empire seemed beset
from every side while the great powers of France and
Germany watched with unconcealed satisfaction. A real
uprising in China would at least cement the relationships
between these powers. But by the time they realized that
danger like prosperity could be shared, it might be too late.

He heard Swan whispering at the door of his room and
prayed that there was no further ceremonial for the day.
After the relaxed atmosphere of Singapore this place was
like an overcrowded beehive. Daily, men and guns moved
along Queen's Road while the anchorage became full of
vessels of every shape and class.

Swan returned, his round face disapproving.

'The major sends his compliments, sir, an' would you go
over an' see him.'

Blackwood stood up while his faithful attendant went into the adjoining room to lay out a fresh uniform and shirt. Orders at last? He did not dare to hope. Anything was better than sweating it out here in Hong Kong. It had almost doubled in size since his first visit as a youthful lieutenant. New docks, larger barracks, a cricket field, he barely recognized the place. Likewise the harbour was flanked by bigger buildings. Prosperous merchants, warehouses and offices as the Empire's trade flowed further and further eastwards.

Twenty minutes later he was ushered into his commanding officer's little house which stood beside the barracks and yet was so much apart from it.

Major James Blair was standing by a wide window watching the harbour as Blackwood was shown into the room by a Chinese servant. He turned and nodded. 'Ah, David. Have a drink.' He did not wait for a reply. 'Parade went off extremely well, I thought, what?'

'Yes, sir.' Blackwood liked the major although he did not really understand him. Blair was described as an *old China hand*. One who loved the place and dreaded the thought of being sent home. It was said that he had a beautiful Chinese mistress. Today he looked worried, and it was unusual for him to suggest a drink before noon.

Blair gestured to his servant and waited for the door to close. Then he said abruptly, 'No easy way, David.' He watched him steadily. 'Just heard and thought you'd take it better from me than some idiot from the base.'

David Blackwood felt his fingers crushing the glass almost to breaking point. 'It's my brother Neil, isn't it, sir?'

Blair nodded. 'Killed in action. In some bloody place I've never heard of. A sniper.'

Blackwood let out his breath very slowly. In his heart he had known about it all the time. He had been closer to Neil than anyone. A lively friendly person. Without an enemy in the world. It would destroy their mother. The General would go and stand by the painting in his room. Pay homage to the family's dead.

He heard himself murmur, 'I'm glad you told me. I'd like to ask for a transfer immediately.' His fingers relaxed slightly and he placed the empty glass on a table. It was all he could think of. All he wanted. Revenge against those murderous, savage Boers.

Blair eyed him sadly. 'Impossible. You're appointed to Peking as soon as the arrangements are finalized.'

'China?' He stared at him. 'But what use will I be there, sir? Wiping carriage seats for the ladies of our legation and mounting guard for foreign ambassadors, is that all I'm worth?'

Blair poured another glass of whisky and waited for the captain to recover his composure.

Blackwood said, 'I'm sorry, sir.'

'Don't be.' He looked up searchingly. 'You've had a few hard knocks in your time. We're all proud of you. I'd not want you to think you're being wasted or pushed into an unimportant backwater. I know there has been little trouble with the mandarins since the *Arrow* War in fifty-eight, but there have been many changes since then. European governments are pushing hard for more concessions, getting greedy in some people's eyes, but as they say, China is a sleeping tiger. You can step on her tail once too often. If there *is* real trouble there must be some professional, experienced officers ready and available. Not here or in England, but on the spot.' He tried to smile but it would not come. 'You in fact.'

As if from a thousand miles away Blackwood heard the steady tramp of marching feet as the marines drilled in the unbroken sunlight. He could see them in his mind, still wearing their ceremonial scarlet tunics and their newly designed helmets. Just like his own men in the Niger expedition. Ready targets for any hidden marksmen. Only their blood had been concealed.

He thought of Neil's letter, his anger at the way they

were being sacrificed by minds totally outdated in a new kind of war.

And there was his youngest brother. He felt his eyes prick with sudden emotion. Jonathan was his only brother now. How much worse it might seem to him at the very beginning of his career with the Corps.

He asked dully, 'How many men, sir?'

'Ninety. I could give you more but the other legations would kick up a fuss. Even ninety may be too many.'

Blair added, 'Go to your quarters, David. You are relieved until I hear something final. You never know . . .' He did not finish.

Outside the house Blackwood paused to recover himself. An hour ago he had been cursing his luck. The news about Neil made his own troubles seem infantile.

He thought of the girl Neil had brought home to Hawks Hill. Like him, laughing and happy. He had wanted to marry her and the General had said, 'When you've been made up to captain, m'boy.' But even he had sounded pleased.

Who would tell her? he wondered.

'*Sir!*'

He looked round and saw the tall, ramrod figure of Fox, the sergeant major, striding after him. With so many new recruits in the Corps veterans like Fox were worth more than their weight in gold. How could he put his mind to duty? What was it this time? Someone for promotion, a defaulter, orders for tomorrow? It all seemed trivial.

'What is it, Sergeant Major?'

Fox slammed to a halt and saluted. Nothing wasted, not a crease in his tunic to mark that he had been on the square for several hours during the gloomy ceremonial.

'Just wanted to say I'm sorry, sir.' He watched him calmly from beneath his helmet. 'Mr Neil, sir.'

Blackwood stared at him. Of course, Neil had served with the tall sergeant major. Second lieutenant and sergeant then. And Fox already knew. It was like that in the Corps.

In the family as they called it.

He said, 'Thank you.' He could not continue.

Fox fell in step beside him, his gloved fingers gripping his stick beneath one arm.

With unusual vehemence Fox said, 'I 'ates them bastards. We puts on a uniform. They shoots our lads in the back and then ˢpleads fer mercy when they're caught.' His fist tightened on the stick's silver knob. '*Mercy?* I'd give the poxy varmints mercy all right!'

They stood outside the officers' quarters not looking at each other.

Fox said, 'The old trooper *Aurora* is reported enterin' 'arbour, sir. I'd best get down there with a couple of sergeants and sort out the new arrivals.'

'I'll be there.'

Fox tightened his lips into a thin line. 'No, sir. I'll take young Mr Gravatt. Time 'e learned a thing or two.' He almost smiled. 'With respect, we'll be needin' *you* later on, sir.' His hand shot up to an immaculate salute and he marched away before Blackwood could protest.

Swan held the door open for him and he saw a glass and decanter already on the table.

Swan could not look at him either.

Blackwood sat down heavily. 'You've heard?'

'Aye, sir.' His hand shook as he poured a full measure of Scotch. 'Anything I can do, sir?'

'No!'

Swan paused at the door and saw the captain unfolding a letter. The one he had received from his brother in South Africa.

Blackwood did not hear the door shut but stared at the letter as a solitary tear splashed across his dead brother's writing. He swallowed the neat whisky and closed his eyes very tightly. What would those two nuns say if they could see him now?

'How was the family when you left England?'

David Blackwood offered his cousin a chair and watched him curiously. Ralf's arrival in Hong Kong had been a complete surprise, but his manner and attitude were even more astonishing.

He had not seen the youthful second lieutenant for a long time, since he had been a mere boy, but he had expected he would follow in the family mould, like the faces in the portraits at Hawks Hill.

He had grown a thin moustache on the passage from Portsmouth but it had made him look even younger and somehow vulnerable.

Ralf replied, 'I think they were all right, er, sir.' He was looking at him warily as if he expected a confrontation like the one he had had with his uncle.

Blackwood heard the other officers of his new detachment gathering in the mess nearby and decided that after this meeting he would treat the second lieutenant no differently from the rest. He wondered why his father had arranged Ralf's transfer. There must be a reason. He would soon discover what it was once they had worked properly together as a team.

But too many meetings like this would be seen as favouritism. Something he hated and which could disrupt any small unit.

Since the *Aurora*'s arrival in the harbour there had been many more signals and rumours about growing danger for the 'Foreign Devils' in Peking and around the various European and Japanese concessions along the coast. Major Blair had been correct. There would be trouble of vast proportions unless prompt action was taken.

For two weeks the new company had been drilling, marching and exercising together in the hills above Hong Kong, or from boats around Aberdeen harbour. It had already worked wonders, but there were too many new recruits amongst them to be certain of anything so soon.

Ralf Blackwood did not seem interested in anything. Of

Neil's terrible death he had muttered only a few words and then launched into his own list of complaints and requests for a transfer to one of the larger men-of-war in the harbour.

Major Blair had not even considered it. He had snapped, 'You *make* something of him, David. He might learn a bit about soldiering if he can set his mind to it.'

He tried again. 'How are you settling in, Ralf?'

The moustache turned down slightly. 'I don't think they like me.'

'Why not?' He was wrong even to ask. There was something not quite honest about this young man. Like a sulky child.

He shrugged. 'It's not my fault.' He looked up defiantly. 'I – I think it's because of the family. The name of Blackwood. They're jealous, I expect.'

Blackwood sat down and felt strangely satisfied that he had been right. Disappointed too for all their sakes.

'I don't want to hear that sort of trouble-making rubbish again, do you understand?'

He saw the sudden alarm in Ralf's eyes. And anger. That he had played his hand badly and too soon.

Blackwood tried again. He had always been sorry for the boy, and now that he was grown-up and an officer under his command he could appreciate what he must have suffered down the years.

'I never knew your father, Ralf. But he was a fine man, one to be proud of. Keep that memory alive.' He saw that he was making no impression. Ralf's eyes had the knack of becoming motionless and opaque. Like coloured glass. He said wearily, 'Dismiss. I'll see you when I speak to the others.'

Ralf marched from the room and shut the door as loudly as he dared.

Blackwood smiled gravely. He would have to watch that one very closely.

Later in the small private mess allotted to his newly formed company Blackwood ran his eyes over their expectant faces. The usual mixture, he thought. Excitement, anxiety, acceptance, it was all there. He could feel Ralf's eyes fixed on him as he ran briefly through his orders.

They would embark aboard the cruiser *Mediator* tomorrow and steam the thousand miles north-east along the coast of the mainland to Taku at the mouth of the Peiho river. There they would anchor and await instructions which would depend on the state of the emergency.

While he was speaking he was looking at his officers, the ones who would have to interpret them, to lead if he and others fell. The three lieutenants Gravatt, Bannatyre and de Courcy, the last from a very old marines family. Two second lieutenants, Ralf and a childlike youth named Earle. The three lieutenants had seen some action but on a very punitive and limited scale.

Blackwood continued, 'We shall be under the command of Captain Masterman of the *Mediator*. But *if* we are required to move inland to Peking we shall be taking orders from the military at the embassy.'

He saw a few grimaces. The Royal Marines tolerated being given orders by a ship's captain. There were plenty of second thoughts about the army.

Lieutenant Gravatt asked politely, 'How do we get to Peking, sir?'

It was a good question, Blackwood thought.

'Upriver as far as possible, then overland by train.' He had a stark picture of the armoured trains in South Africa. Neil had described them in his letter. He had probably been shot while he and his men were moving across country.

Gravatt, who was his second-in-command and acting adjutant, grinned. 'I shall sit with my back to the engine.'

They laughed. All except Ralf who barely seemed to blink.

'Just remember this.' His grave tone stilled the laughter like a closed door. 'We shall have to adapt to a new sort of warfare. Sentries and pickets in full marching order are perfect targets. Scarlet tunics have cost too many lives already. At sea we stand-to with the sailors. Ashore we will fight like the enemy. But on *our* terms.'

It was a beginning.

The *Mediator* was a second-class light cruiser of some three thousand tons. As the marines had climbed aboard with their piles of equipment and weapons Blackwood had found time to admire her sleek and graceful lines. She was less than a year old and a far cry from the old ironclads which had once been the backbone of the fleet.

Now as he lay in his comfortable bunk Blackwood wondered what had awakened him. He had been dreaming about Neil, and had seen him walking away, glancing back at him, his face incredibly sad.

Blackwood groaned and rolled over to find the bunk light. It was still pitch dark, not even dawn.

As he gripped the side of the bunk he felt the *Mediator* shivering under his touch, and as his mind pushed all thoughts of sleep aside he heard the swish and plunge of the light cruiser's hull as she increased speed.

They had been at sea for four days, but never exceeded ten knots. Captain Masterman believed in conserving his stocks of coal, just in case of some last-minute emergency.

Blackwood lowered himself to the deck and felt the tremble pulsing through the steel plates. She was doing a lot more than ten knots now.

As if to settle his uncertainty the whistle of a voice-pipe shrilled above the bunk.

Blackwood snapped on the light and blinked at the bulkhead clock. It was only four in the morning.

'Captain Blackwood.' He held the tube to his ear.

'Bridge, sir.' The sailor had a strong Cockney accent, like the sergeant major. 'Cap'n Masterman's compliments an' could you join 'im.'

'What's happening?' But the voice-pipe was dead again.

Blackwood scrambled into his uniform and smiled to

himself. He could not expect to hear any gossip with
Masterman on the bridge.

The cruiser's captain was tall and straight, as if every
ounce of unwanted fat and weight had been honed away. A
large beaked nose, dominated by deceptively mild blue eyes
and two sweeping sideburns iron grey against his sunburned
cheeks.

Blackwood had spoken to him only twice since he had
come aboard. Not a man to waste words. Like his coal. But
someone who would be like a rock in any kind of
emergency.

He climbed quickly to the upper bridge and soon saw
Masterman's tall outline framed against the white screen.
The bridge was full of people. Most of the ship's officers, the
yeoman of signals, lookouts, everyone.

Masterman glanced at him. 'Mornin', Soldier. Sorry to
get you up.'

'There, sir! Port bow!'

The lookout pointed above the screen with one arm.

Blackwood saw it. A rocket or flare, drifting lazily in the
far distance. Without any clouds to reflect the light it
looked puny, unreal.

Masterman breathed out very softly. To Blackwood he
remarked, 'Second one. Beginnin' to think the lookouts had
imagined it all.' He chuckled and some of the officers near
him visibly relaxed.

'Course to steer?'

The navigating officer was ready. He needed to be.

'North fifteen west, sir.'

'Alter course.'

Blackwood listened to the orders being passed down to
the quartermaster, the slight heel of the deck as the ship
changed course very slightly.

Masterman said offhandedly, 'Shanghai is about eighty
miles nor'-west of our present position. That ship is
somewhere in between.'

He made up his mind. 'Full ahead together. Close up

action stations.' He swivelled round as one of *Mediator*'s own Royal Marines stamped smartly to the rear of the bridge, moistening the mouth-piece of his bugle with his tongue.

'Not *that*, dammit!' He glared at the commander. 'I don't want the whole bloody world to hear us!'

The boatswains' mates scampered from the bridge and moments later seamen and marines poured up from below decks and ran to their stations while others manned the barbettes on either side.

Masterman said, 'She'll likely be the *Delhi Star*. Passengers and mail. She sailed two days before us.'

He did not attempt to hide the pride he had in his ship. Blackwood could picture her smashing through the water as she worked up to her impressive maximum of twenty knots. White hull and two buff funnels, she would look like a spectre in the pitch darkness. Light she might be but she carried six-inch guns as well as smaller weapons and could if required speak with authority.

Blackwood hesitated. Masterman did that to you. You felt obliged to honour his silence.

He asked, 'Shipwreck, sir?'

The captain shook his head. 'Unlikely. I know her master. A wily old chap.'

A voice called, 'Ship at action stations, sir!'

Masterman ignored him. 'My guess is pirates. This coast is rotten with 'em.'

The bridge was shaking so violently that it felt as if every rivet would burst loose. A great creaming wake carved a straight line astern and above it Blackwood could see the dense smoke belching low over the sea as evidence of the stokers' efforts far below the decks.

Pirates. They were in for a nasty surprise.

Masterman said abruptly, 'I want you to go with the boarding party, Blackwood. My people are pretty young and inexperienced.' He almost smiled but contained himself. 'Like *Mediator*. Do 'em good to have a real-life hero amongst 'em.'

Blackwood looked at him. There was neither sarcasm nor malice. He actually meant it.

He said awkwardly, 'I'll go below and change, sir.'

'Don't be too long. We'll be within range shortly. It will be first light by then. We'll need to bustle about a bit smartly. If there are any survivors aboard the *Delhi Star* they'll be in a bad way by now.'

Blackwood ran down a ladder and found Swan waiting beside the forward funnel.

'We goin' over, sir?'

'*I am.*' He relented immediately. To go without Swan would be like carrying an unloaded revolver. He grinned. 'Get our gear ready.'

It seemed unnaturally bright between decks. All the deadlights had been clamped shut across the scuttles and it was hard to imagine pirates so near. Masterman could be wrong, but that was even harder to believe.

The deck had been opened near the cabin flat and he saw some seamen by the tackles of a shell-hoist. He had not realized he had been sleeping directly above a magazine.

On the marines' messdeck Swan was dragging on his boots and buckling on belt and bayonet. He snatched his rifle from its rack and clattered up the ladder again to find the rest of the boarding party.

Blackwood dashed from his cabin and almost collided with Ralf. Like the rest of the new detachment he had no proper action station, and seemed at a loss.

'Is it true? About the pirates?'

Blackwood drew his heavy revolver and examined the chamber. There was no need. Swan had seen to that too.

'Yes, want to come?'

He had said it as a joke, something to steady his own nerves. But it was as if he had struck him.

'N-no, sir.'

A voice bellowed. 'A-way starboard whaler! Boardin' party to muster!'

Blackwood dashed by the men at the shell-hoist, oblivious to everything but Ralf's face.

He was terrified. And in a matter of weeks they might be fighting for their lives.

One of the light cruiser's lieutenants, pistol at his belt, saw him and grinned.

'Here we go, sir!'

The boat's crew were already in their places and there were more armed seamen in the sternsheets.

'Slip the gripes! Turns fer lowerin'!'

Blackwood climbed up and over the gunwale and saw the great seething wash begin to die away as *Mediator* reduced speed so that the boat could be dropped without danger of capsizing.

'Lower away, handsomely!' That was the commander. Masterman must have sent him to ensure there were no mistakes.

The boat dropped down the *Mediator*'s white plates, the sea lifting to meet them.

'Avast lowering!'

The pins were out and the boat swayed a foot or so above the water like an overloaded pod.

'Slip!' They were away, but as the oars dropped smartly into their crutches and the tiller was thrust hard over, all Blackwood could see was Ralf's terror.

3

Boarders Away!

Lieutenant Hudson, *Mediator*'s boarding officer, lurched to his feet to recover his bearings as the boat plunged and yawed in the short, choppy waves.

He rested one hand on Blackwood's shoulder, the only way he could remain upright, and shouted, 'I heard shots!'

Blackwood nodded. So there was still some resistance aboard the little steamer. How quickly the light was spreading down from the horizon, and how fast events were moving since the whaler had been lowered. He peered astern and saw that the ship had not moved and guessed that Captain Masterman was about to drop a second boat as additional support.

The lieutenant shouted, 'Watch the stroke, dammit!' But he sounded less confident without the *Mediator*'s authority at close quarters.

The boat seemed to fly across the water, spray rising from the oar blades as the seamen threw their weight on the looms, no easy task with the twenty-seven-foot hull packed with bodies and weapons.

Crack – crack – crack.

Blackwood licked his lips and unclipped the flap on his holster. He did it almost unconsciously, without even drawing the attention of the stroke oarsman.

The whaler's graceful hull lifted on an offshore roller and he saw the little steamer *Delhi Star* clearly for the first time. Masterman had been right about her too, he thought grimly.

And yet she was similar to dozens of an ever-growing fleet of such vessels. Small, single-screwed, able to carry passengers and light cargo for the benefit of the East's expanding trade and importance. He could see her white side glinting faintly in the early sunlight, her funnel smoke drifting downwind, and other smoke too, although whether from internal fires or explosions he could not say.

One of the seamen said hoarsely, 'Gawd! That'll please the Old Man, I don't think!'

Hudson snapped, 'Hold your tongue!' But he too stared astern where the second boat was in total confusion. She was the cruiser's cutter, and therefore double-banked for extra speed. But her oars were all mixed up and slashing at thin air, and Blackwood saw some men hanging over the boat's flat transom trying to re-ship the rudder which had obviously fallen off as the boat had been dropped from the davits.

The unknown sailor was correct. Masterman would be fuming.

He glanced at Hudson's tight profile. He looked scared to death. It was hard enough to board even a docile junk in these conditions. And there was fresh firing. Short and sharp. A last resistance. Perhaps the steamer's crew had sighted the light cruiser as sunlight swept over her like thin gold.

Blackwood turned his head towards the shore. He could not see the mainland, but there were several scattered groups of islets, some so small that they looked like basking whales, oblivious to the drama which was revealing itself more strongly every minute. There were fishing boats too amongst the islets, motionless like black sticks. Another hot day, he thought.

Hudson squatted down at his side, their faces an inch apart.

'Shall we wait for the cutter, d'you think?'

Blackwood could almost smell his fear. In a moment it would transmit itself through the boat with the speed of an arrow.

It was likely that the cutter was under the command of a midshipman, at best a sub-lieutenant. Hudson would still be in overall charge.

He replied, 'We'll go in as ordered.' He wished he knew the lieutenant's first name. It often helped in moments like these. He glanced at his attendant and knew that Swan was also recalling those other times. The fear changing to hate, the caution giving way to madness. Swan had already loosened his bayonet and as Blackwood nodded to him he jerked back the bolt of his rifle and slammed a bullet into the breech. It acted better than any bugle, and the oars seemed to blur as the boat surged forward. Blackwood peered over the swaying shoulders and saw the *Delhi Star*'s attacker rising above her opposite side like some nightmare bat.

Pirates and junks went together. The little steamer's master should know that. If not he was paying dearly for it.

A bullet hit the whaler's gunwale and threw a splinter at the stroke oarsman's feet. He barely blinked, but along the boat men were pulling in their heads as if that would help.

'Swan.'

Swan climbed deftly over the swaying looms and amongst the panting seamen until he was right in the bows.

He seemed to rise and fall like a figurehead, but Blackwood noted that the gleaming Lee-Metford rifle managed to remain steady.

There was a crack, and Swan remarked calmly, 'One down.'

'Keep firing, Swan. Drive them away from the rails!'

He did not need to be told but it would help to hold the discipline in the boat.

The air cringed as *Mediator*'s siren tore the morning apart with a raucous screech.

Birds rose flapping from the nearest islets, adding their protests to the din, and the whaler's coxswain exclaimed, 'She goin' to fire on the bastards, sir!'

There was a violent bang and from one of the light cruiser's long six-inch guns came a vivid orange flash.

They heard the shell rip overhead, like tearing a giant's canvas before exploding far beyond the fishing boats and islets in a solid tower of water.

Hudson said shakily, 'The junk's casting off!' He shook his fist in the air. 'We'll blow her sky-high!'

Blackwood kept his eyes on the steamer's hull, very aware of Hudson's relief, also that the junk's commander would use the *Delhi Star* as a shield until he was lost amongst the islets and the fishermen.

But it was too early for overconfidence. The junk must have cast off with such haste as the *Mediator* had announced her arrival that some of the pirates might still be aboard, and to all intents abandoned.

Hudson was yelling, 'Stand by bowman! Ready with grapnel!'

He looked elated, all his anxieties gone after the gun had fired.

The seamen boated their oars as best they could, and as the grapnel soared above the rails and held fast, they came alongside with a violent shudder.

'Boarders away!' Hudson had drawn his revolver and, with his men yelling and waving their cutlasses, scrambled up the ship's side. It was quite a low-hulled vessel, with just one line of scuttles before rising to a second deck beyond the bridge.

Blackwood darted a quick glance at the cutter; it was still a cable clear but pulling well, and there was a Maxim gun mounted above the stem.

He nodded to Swan and together they hauled themselves after the others.

The sudden silence was almost worse than a fusillade of shots.

Blackwood heard a man retching uncontrollably and saw a body by the scuppers so hacked about and mutilated that it was barely human. Blood filled the scuppers, surging this way and that as if to escape.

Hudson tore his eyes away. 'Bridge! Martin, take three men to the other side, lively now!'

From the corner of his eye Blackwood saw a movement by one of the companion-ways. He dragged out his sword, 'Swan, you come with me!'

It was useless to tell Hudson who was already charging towards a bridge ladder. It would delay things. Someone had run below. To do what? To blow up the whole ship perhaps?

He almost pitched down the ladder as he skidded on more blood.

He heard Swan gasp, *'Jesus Christ!'* It took a lot to impress Swan these days.

There was blood everywhere. Splashed on the sides of the long central passageway, up the sides, even on the deckhead. Corpses too, mutilated beyond belief, one even headless.

Blackwood said harshly, 'There's at least one of them down here!'

He almost ducked as *Mediator* fired again, the shell exploding in the sea with such force you could believe the ship had run aground.

A figure in white robes bounded from the cabin, a wide-bladed sword across his shoulder as he peered wildly at the two marines.

Blackwood felt Swan's bullet fan past his ear without remembering the sound of the shot. He heard it crack into the man's forehead, killing him instantly. But all Blackwood could recall was the blood pouring unheeded from the man's sword and down his arm before he dropped.

He kicked open the cabin door, his pistol held so tightly it hurt his fingers.

The contents of the drawers and luggage were all around but the cabin's occupants, a man, a woman and a small girl, were hacked to ribbons.

Blackwood looked meaningly at Swan. These people had

been butchered slowly. It was a scene from hell. But not by the man lying dead in the passageway. He had not had the time.

Swan said in a whisper, 'Reckon 'e was lookin' for a mate, sir.'

Blackwood pursed his lips. 'Another one then?'

Faintly overhead, from another world, they heard shouts and two shots. There was steel on steel as Hudson's men got busy with their cutlasses.

But this was here. Now. He could feel his heart thumping as if to break free, but when he glanced at his revolver his hand was as steady as Swan's rifle.

Two more cabins yet. Both doors shut. Not even a whimper.

Swan drew his bayonet deftly and snapped it into place.

He said almost casually, 'There's another of 'em in the shadows!' But as he lunged over a steel locker and swung the rifle down he gasped, 'This one's already done for.'

Blackwood pulled him backwards. There was a tiny hole in the cabin door where that one had fallen. A lucky shot perhaps but it had found its mark.

Swan gestured urgently to the other cabin. Its handle was moving very slowly. It would not even be noticed but for some blood which shone from the handle like cruel red eyes.

It was time to act. Blackwood pressed his back against the opposite side of the passageway and then hurled himself forward against the door just as it began to open.

He got a vague glimpse of another white-clad figure, the gleam of a swinging blade before he fell headlong into the cabin.

Swan fired from the hip, and using just his right hand parried the sword aside and drove his bayonet into the figure's chest almost to the hilt.

Blackwood peered at the body and then kicked the sword away.

They both looked up as feet stampeded across the deck above with sporadic firing coming from elsewhere, probably from the cutter.

There was a man sitting on the bunk, the body of a woman across his knees.

Blackwood murmured hoarsely. 'Take her from him and cover her up, for God's sake.' But the man tightened his grip, his whole body shaking to his grief. But no sound came from his lips as he held the dead woman in his arms.

Blackwood moved to the door, seeing it all in his mind. The last hope, then horror as the madman with the sword had burst in again.

'I'll be back!' But it made no impression.

Swan said tightly, 'Next door, sir. 'Eard a sound.'

'Right.' Blackwood felt hot and icy cold in turns. He looked at the cabin's door, the one with the small hole in it. Whoever had been in there might have killed one attacker but it could mean something else. More pirates. A last rally. After all they had nothing to lose. Once taken they would be hustled ashore and beheaded for their trade, and as a warning.

Blackwood had seen it before in China, could remember his own men standing around like uneasy spectators as a local mandarin's axeman had done his macabre works.

Blackwood heard himself say, 'I'm going in. These bloody doors are like cardboard.'

Swan grimaced, but kept his eyes on the door. 'Ready when you are, sir.' He brought his rifle to his waist. 'Good luck.'

Blackwood found a split second to look at him. The last time? Like it had been for Neil?

He drew aside and then flung himself at the door with Swan's bayonet almost brushing his shoulder as they burst through.

Light from the sun made a smoky beam across the cabin, and as Blackwood twisted round to get his back against a bulkhead he stared with astonishment at the woman who faced him. She stood absolutely motionless, her slim figure covered from neck to her bare feet by a dark blue dressing gown which shone in the sunlight like silk. Her hair was tangled across one shoulder and the gown had been badly torn; he could see the bare skin where a hand had tried to rip it from her.

A small Chinese girl crouched on her knees, her arms wrapped around the motionless figure. Blackwood noticed all and none of these things. He could only stare at the woman in blue, and at the tiny silver revolver she held in one hand, its muzzle levelled at his heart.

He said as steadily as he could, 'Don't be afraid. I am a British officer.' It sounded ridiculous, and he stared at her eyes which had not moved from his face.

There was a muffled crash as the cutter at last managed to get alongside, cheers and running feet, but somehow it meant nothing.

A body lay near the opposite end of the cabin, and for an instant he imagined it was a repeat of the terrible murders he had already seen.

Swan said, 'One of the pirates, sir.' He lowered his bayonet until it was aimed at the man in the white robe. 'Still alive.'

The woman slowly lowered the revolver and then, almost casually, tossed it on to the bunk.

'You were just in time.' She spoke with a foreign accent. 'I had but two bullets left. One for this foolish maid, Anna.' She seemed to realize he was looking at the bare skin below her shoulder. 'One for myself.'

Blackwood heard men charging through the ship, voices yelling orders, others vomiting as they discovered more butchered remains.

He took a step towards her, yet she seemed to get no nearer.

She said, 'I am the Countess von Heiser. I was – ' She hesitated and looked at the door as if expecting to see more attackers surging through. 'I *am* going to Shanghai to join my husband.'

Blackwood could feel himself shaking. It would not show

to others but it was there just the same. He slipped his
revolver into its holster and said, 'You are very brave,
Countess.' German. The name was familiar too. Her
husband was important. It explained why she had the best
cabin in the ship.

She waited for her quivering maid to release her hold and
then reached out one hand and said in the same level tone,
'Please. I think I am going to be sick.' She held his arm
with both hands, her nails biting through the tunic and
breaking his skin.

Close to she was not merely beautiful, she was entranc-
ing. Her hair was the colour of honey, her eyes, now tightly
closed, were violet.

Beside her Blackwood felt clumsy and unclean. He
wanted to hold her, to console her after what must have
been a terrible ordeal.

She said quietly, 'And your man is wrong. These are not
pirates. They are Boxers.' She made herself say it. 'The Big
Knife Society.'

He watched the pain moving from her face like a cloud.
She lifted her chin and looked at him curiously.

'I was in Hong Kong with my sister to buy some things.
I saw the British marines there. I know about the military,
you see.'

Figures loomed through the door and a petty officer said,
'Good God, sir. I thought you were done for!'

Blackwood replied, 'Carry on with the search. Any ship's
officers alive?'

'Two, sir.' The petty officer's eyes were fixed on the slim,
elegant woman as if he were mesmerized.

She said, 'The captain was a fool. He took on a deck cargo
of passengers. When the junk came near they rushed the
bridge. Only the mate had sense enough to hold the saloon
until he too was hacked to pieces.'

She slowly released her grip from his arm. 'In the next
cabin –' She looked at his eyes without flinching. 'Are they
killed?'

Somehow Blackwood knew the question was far more important than she had made it sound.

'I am afraid the lady is dead. The man with her is too stunned to move.'

She walked slowly to the scuttle and stared out at the clean, blue water.

'She is my sister.'

He saw her shoulders begin to shake, the pretence and the tenacity falling away like a loose robe.

He put his hands on her shoulders and said gently, 'I understand, Countess.'

She twisted round and stared up at him, her eyes brimming with tears.

'Do you? Do you indeed?'

He said, 'My brother was killed recently.'

She nodded and then reached up to touch his face. 'You are strong. Will you take me to her?'

Blackwood's mouth was dry like a kiln.

She saw his expression and laid her fingers flat on his mouth.

'I know what to expect, but I shall need your strength.'

Swan stood in the passageway and leaned on his rifle, one eye on the groaning figure inside the cabin.

Some seamen clattered along the bloodstained passageway and Swan jerked his head. 'In there. Wounded.' He thought of that tiny silver pistol. She had shot two of the bastards. They must have left her until last. There had to be a reason. The attack was no clumsy hit-or-miss affair. It had been managed like a military operation.

He saw one of the sailors pick up the fallen sword and felt a shiver at his spine.

Bloody hell. If all the Boxers were like these. He jerked to attention as Blackwood reappeared with his hand around the countess's arm.

Her face was ashen, but she had her chin lifted. She even tried to give Swan a smile as she passed.

Blackwood said, 'The boarding party has taken charge,

Countess. May I suggest that I have you carried across to the cruiser. It will take time to clean up this ship.'

She watched him thoughtfully. 'That is kind of you.' She beckoned to her tiny maid. 'Anna, lay out my things. Perhaps it would be possible to have a bath, yes?'

Blackwood looked at her with amazement. Her strength was returning even as he stood near her. One hand touched the torn gown, her fingers brushing over the bruise left on her skin.

Most women would have covered their faces and run through the horrific debris and not looked up until they were safely aboard the warship.

She felt his gaze on her and said, 'It would not do for your gallant captain to receive me looking like this, I think.'

He closed the door carefully and left Swan on guard outside. It would take an avalanche to shift Swan.

He found Hudson sitting on a bollard having his head bandaged by a young midshipman.

Hudson tried to grin but winced instead.

'Didn't lose a man. And *you* saved the German countess.'

Blackwood stared across at the ship. Of the junk there was no sign. Safe amongst the fishing boats and the crowded islets.

Masterman would not relish the prospect of risking his own ship's keel if he moved closer inshore. Anyway, he had done well. He watched a corpse being dragged across the deck. So they were Boxers. It explained the uniformity of their clothing. White robes and red turbans. Originally instituted as a powerful body-guard by Yu-Hsien, the Prefect of Tsau-Chaou, they now represented a force in their own right. Blackwood had heard from Major Blair of their fearful acts of barbarism, the inhuman killings of anyone who would not support their cause and their hatred for the 'Foreign Devils'.

Blair had said they were termed Boxers by the Europeans almost as a nickname because of their original title. *The Patriotic Harmony Fists*. He looked at the terrible pools of blood which were already drying in the sunlight. Big Knife Society seemed far the more suitable.

Hudson stiffened and stood up. 'Is that her?'

Blackwood turned and nodded. It was a picture he would never forget.

She was dressed in a cream, high-necked gown, her honey-coloured hair curled on the top of her head and shaded by a wide-brimmed hat which matched her gown perfectly.

It was like seeing an entirely different person from the one in the cabin with the pistol in her hand. Swan and the small Chinese maid followed her at a respectful distance, but Swan kept his eyes on his captain to watch the effect.

She walked slowly to the side where an accommodation ladder was already rigged, and Blackwood noticed that Masterman had even sent his steam pinnace to collect her. He felt suddenly shut out, and then angry with himself for his foolishness.

She paused and looked at him, her violet eyes almost hidden in shade.

She held out a white-gloved hand and he took it as she said gravely, 'Thank you, Captain Blackwood. We shall meet again.'

He raised her hand to his lips, seeing it as the one she had held out to him in that terrible cabin.

Around them the seamen and the engine-room crew who had survived the battle by sealing themselves in with the boilers stood motionless and spellbound.

She rested her hand on the midshipman's sleeve and he guided her carefully down the side to the swaying pinnace.

Blackwood watched the pinnace swing away from the ladder and searched for her but she had already been guided below to the cockpit.

She knew my name. She must have been speaking with Swan.

He removed his helmet and wiped his face with a crumpled handkerchief.

Swan joined him by the rails.

'Real lady, sir.' He nodded admiringly. ''Er 'usband must be proud to 'ave a lady like 'er, sir.' He watched the words go home like bullets.

Blackwood gave a great sigh and tried to return his mind to his immediate duties.

'Signal *Mediator* for a Royal Marines bugler. We shall have to bury all the remains before we can do anything else.'

He shaded his eyes to look for the pinnace but it had already vanished around the stern of the light cruiser.

He thought of her sister, and how the countess had held her until her husband had at last released his grip.

Courage was not the name for it.

Later as the two ships lay hove-to and the little marine bugler sounded the Last Post the pathetic bundles wrapped in canvas were dropped over the side.

Blackwood knew she would be watching and hoped she might find some comfort from the simple ceremony.

Then both ships got under way to leave the islets and the fishermen undisturbed.

4

A Bit of a Lark

Commander John Wilberforce, HMS *Mediator*'s second-in-command, handed Blackwood a glass of Scotch which he had taken from a passing steward and beamed at him.

'Exciting, eh, Soldier? I wish to God I'd been with you! When the Countess came up the side you could have heard a bloody pin drop on the quarterdeck!'

Blackwood smiled and glanced through one of the wardroom scuttles. Shanghai, crammed with ships, lighters, junks, even a few of the old trading schooners. The Waterfront of the World.

If Captain Masterman was annoyed at having to break his passage to the Peiho River in the north he had not shown it. There were some coal lighters being warped alongside already, so the captain was even using the occasion to replenish his supplies.

Blackwood could hear a petty officer bellowing threats at the coolies in the nearest lighter about standing away from the *Mediator*'s immaculate white paint.

Wilberforce was saying enthusiastically, 'What a lovely woman. God, no wonder they were after her.'

Blackwood asked, 'Her husband. Do you know about him?'

Wilberforce blinked as he tried to recover his train of thought.

'Count Manfred von Heiser. A sort of soldier-diplomat. Enormously rich, from an East Prussian family. Personal friend of the Kaiser. They say he is in China to decide which

German concessions and legations are worth keeping, and which should be bargained for.'

Once again Blackwood felt on the outside in his ignorance.

Across the big wardroom where the ship's officers were enjoying their first noon drinks since the anchor had splashed down, he saw some of his own subordinates, chatting and laughing like the rest. He tried not to consider how Ralf would have behaved if he had been with him and the boarding party.

Wilberforce said, 'The Old Man has been speaking with a couple of consulate officials for an hour at least. One German, the other one of our chaps. Not his line of country at all!'

Blackwood realized he had emptied his glass without noticing it.

We shall meet again, she had said. He imagined the feel of her gloved hand in his, the level gaze from those violet eyes. He shook himself. He must be more like his father than he had realized.

A messenger, cap in hand, hovered by the wardroom door.

Commander Wilberforce frowned. 'Here we go. They're all going ashore, I suppose.'

But the messenger's eyes rested on Blackwood.

'The Cap'n's compliments, sir, an' would you join 'im in 'is day cabin?'

The commander grinned but sounded disappointed. 'Lucky devil.'

Someone else shouted, 'Trust the Royals!'

Blackwood could sense the difference. That one brief action had broken down the barriers. They shared it with him, and wanted to show it.

The Royal Marines sentry stamped to attention at the door of Masterman's quarters. The sleeping and day cabins and the necessary offices filled a considerable part of the light cruiser's stern. As a steward opened the door for him

Blackwood realized he had only been in this place once since he had come aboard.

Blue curtains across the polished scuttles matched the furniture covers. *Mediator* was a new ship and the colours of some of the fittings had a woman's touch, he thought. Probably chosen by Masterman's wife after the commissioning ceremony. Strange, he had never thought of Masterman being married.

The man in question turned to face him, his tall figure impressive in white drill.

'Ah, Blackwood, may I introduce these gentlemen?' He gestured to a dispirited-looking man in a pale grey coat. 'Mr Pitt from the British consulate.' He waited for Blackwood to shake hands before adding, 'And Herr Westphal his German counterpart.'

Blackwood smiled and wanted to look at the countess who was standing right aft framed against the large open ports which were the captain's privilege.

She said quietly, 'Good-day, Captain Blackwood.'

He said, 'It is good to see you so well, Countess.'

They both sounded like total strangers.

Masterman grunted impatiently. 'There has been a lot of trouble along the coast as well as inland. Attacks on villages, even missionaries by these – ' He hesitated and cut back an adjective, ' – these *Boxers*.'

Blackwood waited. He sensed there had been some kind of argument.

Masterman continued, 'There is a steamship leaving for Hong Kong tomorrow. It is armed and able to beat off attack by such pirates, and I can think of them as nothing else.'

Mr Pitt said gently, 'The horse and stable door, er, Captain Blackwood, is it not?'

The German wiped his face and chin with his handkerchief, for in spite of an offshore breeze and the deckhead fans it felt like an oven.

He said, 'We have no ship of His Imperial Majesty's

Navy here.' He looked grimly at Masterman. 'Not yet. But a cruiser is to join your ship off Taku. There is only an Italian gunboat, a veritable relic, here in Shanghai which is available for the Countess.'

Her voice cut across the cabin unhurried but very definite.

'I am not setting foot on that thing!'

Blackwood could feel her watching him although she was in dark silhouette.

'They are concerned for my safety, Captain Blackwood. I should have met my husband here and accompanied him inland to the most recent trading mission.' She gave a shrug, as if it was of little importance. 'But he left without waiting for me. I am *expected* to be with him. It is my purpose for being.'

'Inland?' Blackwood could only think of her last sentence. What sort of man would leave his wife in a situation like this anyway?

Masterman explained, 'The mission is fortified, and there is a German river gunboat on regular patrol.' He hung on the words. 'In truth I would be happier if the Countess stayed aboard my ship, better still if she left the area altogether.'

She moved down the centre of the cabin and looked calmly at Blackwood.

'They are talking about me as if I were not here, as if I were a piece of cargo, yes?'

The German named Westphal mopped his face even harder. 'But, dear Countess, it is your safety which it is my duty, my *honour* to uphold!'

He said something more in German but she cut him short. 'In English if you please, Herr Westphal!'

She did not even raise her voice and yet Westphal seemed to cringe.

Masterman said heavily, 'It's the Hoshun River, about two hundred miles to the north-west of here. Impossible for a ship this size.'

Blackwood said, 'But if there is a German gunboat, sir.'

She smiled gently. 'You see, gentlemen, the gallant young captain has faith.' Her eyes suddenly flashed. 'I loved my sister very much. Do you imagine I would take unnecessary risks after what they did to her!'

Masterman bit his lip. He obviously hated the complications of the land. He turned to Pitt.

'If you can obtain a steam vessel suitable to carry Countess von Heiser and whatever staff she requires, I will escort her to the Hoshun River, or as close as I can.' He saw Pitt give a relieved nod. 'Furthermore, I can guarantee a naval escort aboard the steamship.' He looked meaningly at Blackwood. 'Your company can easily supply a suitable detachment, right?'

Blackwood swallowed. 'Yes, sir.'

God, he thought, Count von Heiser must be influential. The countess had turned away their ideas with barely concealed contempt. Westphal had all but hinted that relations between *Mediator* and the German cruiser which was also expected off Taku might be damaged without Masterman's co-operation, and Pitt appeared as if he would agree to almost anything which might shift the responsibility elsewhere.

'That is settled then.' She looked at Blackwood. 'I make just one small request, gentlemen.' They froze, not knowing what to expect.

'I would wish that Captain Blackwood should command my escort. I feel certain that the Emperor would be grateful.'

Masterman beckoned to his steward who was standing with an empty tray, as if turned to stone.

He said, 'I could send *Mediator*'s own senior Royal Marines officer.'

She moved towards Blackwood until they were almost touching.

'Has your officer been decorated for gallantry, Captain?'

She reached up and very gently touched the blue ribbon on Blackwood's tunic. 'I believe this is the highest award your country can give, yes?'

Masterman spread his hands and gave a grudging smile.

'I admit defeat, Countess. Captain Blackwood it shall be.' He nodded. 'Carry on, if you please.'

Blackwood backed away and then found himself outside the cabin beside the marine sentry.

'I must be mad!'

The sentry stiffened even more. 'Sir?'

Blackwood looked at him with surprise. He had not even realized he had spoken aloud.

He found Swan in his cabin gathering up shirts for the Chinese dhobyman. He looked neat and contented, and it was impossible to picture him with his rifle balanced under his forearm as he had lanced the screaming Boxer with his bayonet.

Swan watched him warily and said, 'Sounds more interestin', sir. More our sort o' style. Bit of a lark to go inland, so to speak.'

Blackwood dropped his head in his hands. What was the point of questioning Swan about anything? The whole ship probably knew by now.

He could still feel where her finger had touched the VC ribbon on his breast. If he opened his tunic he could almost expect to see a mark or a sign there.

A bit of a lark. It would be more than that. A whole lot more.

Swan left the cabin with his bundle humming gentle to himself. Just like old times.

Sergeant Major Arthur Fox stood very erect beside the small desk in the Royal Marines office and watched as Blackwood leafed through a list of names. Beneath his polished boots the deck swayed very gently as if even *Mediator* respected his presence.

Blackwood could sense Fox watching him and knew what he was going to ask. Eventually.

'Why the Second Platoon?'

'Well, sir, you'll be needin' Mr Gravatt to stay aboard with 'is men, seein' as 'ow 'e's in command durin' your absence. The Third Platoon, well, sir, Mr de Courcy is fairly experienced too. So I thought you'd wish to take the Second an' Mr Bannatyre.'

Blackwood leaned back and listened to the confident thump of engines, the whirr of fans as *Mediator* ploughed her way through the smooth water. Fox was right, of course; he usually was. Bannatyre was a very likeable lieutenant but the least experienced of his officers. So if things went wrong he would be the least missed.

He looked at Fox. Unbending, reliable in any situation and yet still something of a mystery. He had offered him a chair, but Fox had politely declined. Come to think of it, Blackwood realized he had never seen the sergeant major sitting down.

It was strange to think that the countess was aft in Masterman's quarters while the captain had retreated to his sea cabin on the bridge. He had not seen her since that brief meeting in Shanghai and yet he could always feel her presence in the ship.

Perhaps she was playing with him. A game to amuse herself while she waited to rejoin her husband. But that was impossible after what she had seen and endured. *I am deluding myself. If she uses me then I am willing.*

Fox watched him narrowly. 'There is another reason, sir.'

'Well?'

'The platoon sergeant, sir, Kirby.' He waited for Blackwood to pick the man from his thoughts before adding, ''E's bin actin' a bit strange. Used to be a very calm bloke, sir. Good NCO.'

'Comes from your part of London if I remember?'

Fox grinned. 'Right, sir. Sunny Shoreditch. Just three streets from my lot. 'E enlisted about a year after me. A real Marine.'

There was no higher praise from Fox.

Fox added, ''E's put two men up for punishment since we come aboard *Mediator*. Not like 'im. A good thump round the ear when no officers are about is more 'is style.'

Blackwood smiled. 'Anything else?'

Fox pouted. 'No, sir. I've detailed the men, an' inspected the weapons an' equipment. Little as possible, like you said.'

Blackwood looked at the map by his elbow. As *Mediator*'s navigating officer had pointed out, the Hoshun River was narrow and twisting, and very low at this time of the year. A small coasting paddle-steamer named *Bajamar* had sailed from Shanghai three days ago. With luck they could leave it until the final rendezvous at the Hoshun before transferring their passengers and Royal Marines detachment.

'Good. There'll be little enough water under the keel without taking extra stores and ammunition.' He frowned. 'It *should* be simple enough.' The river was nothing to the ones they had tackled in Africa. If the German gunboat was already downriver they could make the transfer of passengers at once. He knew immediately that he was praying it would not be so. That he would meet and speak with the countess again. I must be mad, he thought. A million miles separate us. She is married to a powerful and successful man. She had a castle and great estates, according to Commander Wilberforce. Blackwood gave a rueful smile. He had almost begun to hate Wilberforce because of his knowledge about her.

He said, 'I want one of the second lieutenants to come with my detachment. Good experience.'

Even Fox flinched. 'One 'as already volunteered.' He hesitated. 'Mr Earle.'

'I see. Thank you.' He could not conceal his disappointment. He had been hoping it would be Ralf.

'So be it. You can carry on, Mr Fox.'

'One last thing, sir.'

Blackwood looked at him gravely. Here it comes. Perfectly timed as usual.

'I should like to come with you, sir. Colour Sar'nt Chittock is due for promotion if 'e keeps 'is nose clean, so I'd not be missed if things get a bit lively.'

It was easily said but Blackwood knew it was very important to Fox. And why not? Neil had been killed by an unknown sniper but how long would he have been missed? It was not the way in the Corps. Not until it happened to you. He had wanted Ralf to volunteer, but for whose sake? His own or Ralf's dead father's?

Fox persisted, 'You'll 'ave some good blokes, sir, but you'll need someone with service. Just to be on the safe side like.'

Blackwood stared at him. It had never occurred to him that the ramrod, taciturn sergeant major wanted to go because of *him*. He was suddenly moved, like that day on the square at Hong Kong when neither of them had been able to face each other.

'*Thank* you, Mr Fox. It will be an honour.'

Fox marched out and Blackwood heard him speaking with his crony, the colour sergeant. As thick as thieves, and yet Fox always kept his position, just that step apart from his comrades.

He glanced around the ship's office and tried to think if he had forgotten anything.

The rendezvous would be during the forenoon tomorrow. After that it was anyone's guess. He thought suddenly of Hawks Hill, of his mother and the General. He had written to them, but it was strange, it might be months before his letter reached the old house. He felt himself shiver. The General might even have died and Hawks Hill would be without the guiding hand it needed. He stood up and walked to a scuttle to watch some small fishing boats bobbing abeam. Like an old watercolour. What would he do then? Resign the Corps and take his place at Hawks Hill. He felt his lips tighten. Leave the Corps? That he would never do, unless he was kicked out.

He left the office and almost collided with his cousin

Ralf. The latter had managed to avoid him since his return from the *Delhi Star* except for matters of duty. But now he seemed unusually eager and pleased with himself.

Blackwood asked, 'Where have you been?'

Ralf touched his thin moustache and smiled gently.

'I have been taking tea with the Countess Friedrike von Heiser, er, sir. It was most enjoyable.'

Blackwood nodded. Ralf was watching him. Taunting him.

And why not? He had asked for it.

Blackwood turned on his heel. 'Something it appears you are better suited to.'

It was a childish remark but he felt strangely hurt and that angered him even more.

Fox saw him stride past and glanced at the slim second lieutenant. He was actually laughing.

You'll laugh on the other side of your face one of these days, Fox thought. When that time comes I want to be there.

Captain Masterman walked out on to the bridge wing and peered down at the small paddle-vessel alongside. She was narrow-beamed and of such shallow draft that her paddle-boxes were built high on either side, as if she was hunching her shoulders.

Masterman looked down at the water. With the ship riding to her anchor the sea looked very clear and unhealthily shallow. It was safe enough for the paddle-steamer. As he had heard the yeoman of signals explaining earlier to a young seaman, 'She draws so little water she can float in spit!'

The marine detachment were already climbing down, watched by their comrades and the unemployed hands along the guardrails. Further abeam the land was misty blue, and the narrow entrance to the river marked only by a sluggish ripple on the surface. The mainland looked solid and lifeless

and yet Masterman felt that his ship had been watched since
first light when they had exchanged signals with the anchored
Bajamar. She was a real veteran of these waters. Commanded
by a massive, untidy Norwegian, and crewed by the worst
collection of rogues Masterman had ever laid eyes on, she was
hardly what Masterman would have chosen.

But Pitt, the consul in Shanghai, had spoken highly of
the vessel and her ability to drive off pirates on many
occasions. There were some ancient swivel guns mounted in
her bow and stern, probably loaded with rusty nails,
Masterman thought, but deadly at close quarters.

Wilberforce stepped into the sunlight and saluted.

'Detachment all aboard, sir. Passengers about to leave.'

The captain grunted. There was no sign of a German
gunboat, but there was no more time to wait. His ship
might already be needed to help reinforce the legations or to
evacuate refugees.

It was a great pity about the countess, he thought.
Women always complicated things.

He said, 'I shall go down.'

The last of the luggage had been lowered to the *Bajamar*
and had been taken below. Masterman walked slowly across
his quarterdeck to the accommodation ladder. The countess
was all in white, with another wide-brimmed hat with a
matching ostrich feather. She looked ready for a reception at
an embassy or Buckingham Palace rather than a cramped
passage upriver in the little steamer.

He touched his cap. 'I hope that everything goes well for
you, Countess.'

It was all wrong. The scruffy little vessel and the marines
in their white rig instead of scarlet and blue. Masterman
had definite standards no matter what the circumstances
might be. But he had left the arrangements to Blackwood.
He must know what he was doing.

She smiled. 'I thank you for your concern, Captain.' She
held out her gloved hand. 'It will not go unnoticed, I
think.'

She gestured to her maid. 'Go down, child.'

The maid looked at the smartly dressed side-party and the long-barrelled guns. Above it all the White Ensign rippled slightly in the offshore breeze. Security, power and safety. A stark contrast to the little hull alongside.

The man who had been married to the countess's sister was turning to leave. Masterman had learned that he was a commercial attaché to the German trade mission in Peking and had been sent to Hong Kong to attend a conference. But for that his wife, a good deal younger than himself, would still be alive. He had not spoken since Blackwood had brought him aboard. He seemed quite lost, as if unaware of what was happening about him.

Masterman brought her hand to his lips. He could smell a delicate perfume, and could sense her eyes watching him.

Suddenly he was glad he had agreed to send Blackwood. A gesture perhaps, but the right one.

He would get no thanks from the far-off Admiralty in London if he allowed any harm to come to the wife of someone so prominent. But then the Admiralty always laid the blame equally with the responsibility on the senior officer present. In this case, Captain Masterman.

Down on the *Bajamar*'s crowded deck Blackwood looked at the farewells on the light cruiser's quarterdeck.

He felt excited and yet apprehensive. The *Bajamar* might be of the right draught but there was little else in her favour once she was hemmed in by a narrow river. Most if not all her accommodation was above the waterline, even her engine, and her long boxlike superstructure with its thin black funnel was totally unprotected should they come under fire. It was unlikely that anything like that would occur, but if it did he would have to be ready.

He glanced at the *Bajamar*'s skipper, a great block of a man. He had skin like mahogany, and tufts of ginger hair which poked beneath his stained cap like spun yarn. It was doubtful if he had worn his gold-braided jacket for some while, Blackwood thought. The brass buttons were strained to bursting-point across the Norwegian's enormous belly.

He thought of Major Blair. Yet another *old China hand*.

His name was Lars Austad and Blackwood imagined he might look more at home in a longship and wearing a horned helmet.

Fox stood beside him and said, 'Comin' aboard now, sir.'

Blackwood watched her stepping carefully down the accommodation ladder, one hand on the rail, the other gripping a folded parasol.

Fox muttered, 'Strewth.'

Most of the marines had already been packed in sweating discomfort in the afterpart of the superstructure, their uniforms already crumpled in the humid air. Masterman might not approve, but Blackwood recalled hearing a story about his uncle in Africa, when he had made his men stain their shirts to conceal themselves when they were besieged in a trading post by both slavers and savage natives.

She allowed him to take her hand and guide her the last few paces on to the vessel's deck.

She smiled at the giant Norwegian and to Blackwood said, 'How quaint.'

He saw Swan's red apple-face split into a grin.

She nodded to the two Royal Marines officers, Lieutenant Bannatyre and Second Lieutenant Earle, and then paused by Fox who towered over her like a tree.

'I need have no fear with such as you to protect me, I think.'

She laughed, the sound fragile and out of place amongst the watching men and the neatly piled weapons.

Clank – clank – clank. *Mediator*'s cable was already jerking through the hawsepipe, and the accommodation ladder began to rise up her side even as her screws beat the placid water into a lively froth.

Blackwood looked at Austad. 'Get under way, Captain.'

The Norwegian's eyes were like saucers before he began to bellow orders at his ragged crew. It was doubtful if he had ever been addressed as captain before.

The deck swayed as *Mediator* moved slowly away, some of her people waving from the guardrails while Masterman's impressive figure stood on the bridge wing and saluted.

Austad cranked at a telegraph beside the wheel and the two paddles began to move, swinging the hull towards the shore.

Blackwood followed the countess to the cabin which had been prepared for her. It was not much larger than a cupboard. He watched her reaction, and expected her to explode.

He explained, 'I am sorry about this, Countess. But it is the safest one aboard in my opinion. Steel bulkhead at one end, and the storeroom just forrard. Your maid is in the adjoining cabin with your luggage.'

She turned and searched his face with her violet eyes. Then she tapped him gently on the shoulder with her parasol.

'You think of everything, Captain.'

Blackwood could feel her nearness and wanted to take hold of her. It was like physical pain. Worse, he knew that she understood exactly what he was thinking.

'A bath perhaps?'

Blackwood shrugged. 'I am afraid that is impossible, Countess.'

She watched him impassively. 'Two days in this craft and no bath? *That* is impossible.'

She touched her throat and dragged the high collar away from her skin. At any other time the gesture would have meant nothing, but Blackwood recalled with sudden clarity how she had looked in that other cabin, the blood on the deck, the tiny revolver in her hand. She had still had the strength, the will to take a bath after all that.

Feet thumped along the narrow side-decks. There was a lot to do before they reached the narrow river. The *Bajamar* might be quite at home in open waters. Once in the shallow river she would present an easy target.

She said, 'You may leave, Captain. Please send my maid to me.'

She waited until he had slid open the narrow door. 'I am grateful. You know that.' She was watching him without emotion, but her tone made her attitude a defence, a lie.

He replied, 'Thank you.' But he saw his cousin's face, the look of triumph and amusement. 'It is my duty.'

Outside the door he pressed his shoulders against the sun-heated metal and cursed himself for his stupidity.

Lieutenant Bannatyre hovered nearby. 'I have stationed the first section as ordered, sir.' He waited, suddenly alarmed by Blackwood's angry silence.

Blackwood clapped him on the shoulder. 'Very well, Ian, show me their positions, will you?'

He saw the little Chinese maid leave the cabin with her mistress's gown over one arm. It was the same one she had just been wearing when she had been plucking it from her skin.

He pictured her behind the door. Probably naked in the privacy of her cabin just a few yards away.

'Something wrong, sir?'

Blackwood sighed. 'It's the heat, I expect.'

Bannatyre nodded gravely. 'I see, sir.'

You don't, my lad. Blackwood turned to look for *Mediator* but she had already vanished around the headland leaving just a patch of funnel smoke to mark her passing.

Two days? It was going to seem a lifetime, he thought.

5

Just Ten Good Men

Blackwood stood by the starboard paddle-box and watched the night sky. The stars looked small and far away and added to the feeling of being shut in. Around and below him the *Bajamar* was very quiet after their first day crawling upriver. It was going to take longer than even the big Norwegian Austad had imagined. The river was extremely shallow and treacherous with uncharted sandbars and occasional clumps of rocks. Even a man of Austad's obvious experience and skill could not be expected to run his ship aground merely because he was under government orders.

Blackwood had just left him in his tiny chartroom. He had filled the space like a bear in a cave, the air thick with pungent smoke from a giant meerschaum pipe.

He had commented in his thick voice, 'You got your men posted, my ship is in dark, no more we can do.' It sounded final.

It was fortunate that such small craft should carry two boats, flat-bottomed sampans. Blackwood had sent one to either bank where the pickets would be crouching and listening to every creak and rustle.

Fox had made certain there was a fair sprinkling of old sweats amongst the recruits. All the same it must be nerve-racking to be landed in some unknown place with water at their backs. He nodded to the sentries, and continued right forward to where Lieutenant Bannatyre had sited the Maxim gun.

It would have been better to mount it amidships, but the

boxlike superstructure made that impossible unless you left it and its crew totally exposed on the upper deck.

He heard Sergeant Kirby mutter, 'All quiet, sir.'

'Good.' Blackwood stared at the black shoreline and wondered what had disturbed Fox about this stocky sergeant. He sounded normal enough. Blackwood had seen him in action when as a corporal he had rallied a handful of marines to charge a mob of savages and retrieve the flag from the grip of their dead colour sergeant.

'We'll relieve the pickets in half-an-hour. Men begin to imagine things after too long.' He touched the Maxim gun. Austad's cannon would be as much use in the dark.

He groped his way aft again and stared with surprise as he saw the countess standing by the guardrails, her figure shrouded in a long gown like a boatcloak.

'You should not be here, Countess!' He lowered his voice to a fierce whisper. 'It is not safe!'

She did not turn but stared intently at the shadows.

'China. The Tiger.' She spoke so softly Blackwood had to lower his head to hear.

She said, 'I could not sleep. I kept thinking – my sister – the sounds of those poor people screaming.'

Blackwood was afraid to move a muscle in case he broke the spell.

All the pent-up strain and outward poise were no longer enough. She was reliving it as she must have been ever since the attack on the *Delhi Star* had turned that night into an unforgettable horror.

Again he wanted to hold her but knew that her last reserves would turn her away from him.

He said quietly, 'And yet you risk this upriver passage, Countess. Must you go?' He sounded as if he was pleading, but he no longer cared.

She shrugged. 'You spoke of duty. I have mine also.'

She faced him through the gloom. 'That was unfair. Forgive me. But for you what would have happened to me?'

Blackwood listened to the soft footsteps of a native

crewman, the responding scrape of boots as a sentry came to the alert.

'You speak perfect English, Countess.' Why did he feel embarrassed?

She sounded as if she was smiling. 'I do travel a lot, Captain. My husband and I visit England whenever we can. He has relatives there. And there is Cowes, Henley and Ascot to enjoy, St James's too on occasions.'

Blackwood swallowed. It was another world, one controlled by the sort of people who decided where men like his marines, and like Neil and all who had gone before him, should be sent. Except that it would not show them as mere men on the plans. Units, ships, and the Flag. It was enough. Or was it? The thought of Neil could still wound him when he was unprepared.

She said, 'Was it wrong what I said?' She looked at him more closely. 'You are dismayed, hurt, yes?'

Blackwood shook his head. 'It was nothing. I thought of my brother. Just for a moment.'

'I understand. A comparison perhaps?' She saw him start. 'It is natural.' She seemed to sense danger in sharing her thoughts.

'This voyage is taking an eternity.'

Blackwood asked, 'Will you stay long at the trading mission?'

'I am not certain. Manfred will decide.' She sounded suddenly wistful. There was resentment too despite her outward calm.

'Do you have children, Countess? I expect you will be pleased – '

But she turned her face away and he could see her honey hair hanging down her spine in a long plait.

'No children.'

Just two words but they meant far more.

She said in a faraway voice. 'Naturally I wanted children. What woman does not?' She gave that same shrug again and the gesture touched Blackwood like a blade. 'It was not to be. But Manfred was generous. He accepts it.'

Blackwood tried to find the right words. 'There can be no blame.'

She swung round, the plait vanishing in the shadows.

'Blame? You astonish me, Captain. You act like a man. You speak like a child. *Blame!* I have just finished telling you, Manfred accepts it!'

Her words stung him like a blow to his face but he retorted hotly, 'You sound as if he had *forgiven* you, Countess! It might be his fault!' He had gone too far, and he could hear the regular thump of boots as the new pickets paraded for inspection.

He exclaimed, 'I – I am sorry, Countess. That was unpardonable. Please dismiss what I said – '

He looked down as she touched his forearm. In a small voice she said, 'There is nothing to forgive. What did you expect me to say?'

At any minute now Kirby would be coming to report to him.

He struggled with his words. 'I admire you so much, Countess. Your courage, everything about you – '

'You see, Captain? It is as I said. A childish dream.' But she did not remove her hand.

'Perhaps.' Blackwood covered her hand with his own. 'I suppose I am so involved with my profession. I have lost the ability to mix with civilized people.'

She smiled. 'Civilization counts for very little when a man sets his heart on personal gain.'

In the darkness Sergeant Kirby coughed politely and Blackwood hated him for it.

'I shall be there directly, Sergeant.'

She released her hand very gently. 'Go to him, Captain. He needs you.' She reached up impulsively and touched his face. In spite of the clinging humidity which enfolded the anchored vessel like a steam bath, her fingers were cool and very soft.

'We shall all need you soon.' Then she was gone,

swallowed up by the shadows like a phantom. He waited to hear her door slide and for his breathing to steady.

He found Second Lieutenant Earle and the next picket waiting to enter a sampan alongside.

'You know what to do?' Blackwood had to clear his throat. 'One sign of an attack and you will withdraw to the bank until we can give you covering fire with the Maxim. Stay together, and remove your helmets. You'll hear better that way.'

Earle nodded earnestly in time with his words as if memorizing every syllable.

'Yes, sir. I will, sir. You can trust me, sir.'

Kirby tore his mind away from his troubled thoughts and said harshly, 'I'll go with them, sir.'

Blackwood said, 'Very well.' He excluded the others as he added, 'No heroics, Charles.' He sensed the use of the youth's first name reaching its mark. 'I want this squad intact and ready for the next leg of the journey.'

Kirby groaned. It's all I need, he thought savagely. A second lieutenant who should still be in the bloody nursery, and a love-struck captain.

'Carry on, Mr Earle.' Blackwood watched the handful of men as they clambered down into the boat's paler outline. Then the sampan with its passengers merged with the river-bank and soon he thought he heard the returning marines climbing aboard. Thankful to be coming back. It was usually the way. The Royal Marines were soldiers and sailors too. But if there was a ship of any kind available he knew where their preference would lie.

Blackwood loosened his tunic and touched the bare skin beneath. Hot and sticky. Three hours yet to daybreak and then little relief as the *Bajamar* thrashed her way around the various obstacles and the sun pinned them down without mercy.

But he would speak with her again. He had to.

He sat down on a steel locker and stared hard across the rails. How did she see her husband? Respect, fear, admiration. There had been little hint of anything else, like the moments when she had spoken of her dead sister.

There was a sudden sharp crack, a momentary flash from the land and then a chilling silence.

Blackwood was on his feet as Lieutenant Bannatyre came running forward followed by the sergeant major.

Blackwood rapped, 'Silence on deck!' It was hopeless. The *Bajamar*'s crew were unused to discipline and voices called and echoed around the river in a mad chorus.

'Pistol shot, Ian.' Blackwood glanced at the lieutenant's motionless figure. '*Stand to, man!*'

Fox strode away, barely raising his voice and yet restoring instant order as his marines, some half-naked but grasping their rifles, bustled to their allotted positions on either side and up in the bows.

Blackwood strained his ears into the darkness but it was as if nothing had happened. It was on Earle's side of the river. He cursed himself for sending such an inexperienced officer. Maybe he had fired his pistol by accident. It was not unknown. He dismissed the idea instantly. He was looking for an easy way out. An explanation like the ones you heard at a court-martial. No. Earle was young and earnest but he was not a fool.

He felt the big Norwegian beside him.

'You want me go back?' He waited, the unlit pipe dragging at his jaw. 'Better going downstream.'

Blackwood swung on him, 'You have your orders. *Obey them!*' He realized with a start that the countess was on deck, her Chinese maid clinging to her arm.

'Please go to your cabin, Countess.'

She looked at him and said, 'Is it serious, Captain?'

Suddenly he wanted to throw his arms round her, to bury his face in her hair and tell her what it was like. Once the flood began he knew it would not stop. Faces flashed through his mind, his father the General, Neil and young Jonathan whom he barely knew. And all the other faces he had come to love. In the Corps you got to know people very well. Or you split wide open.

'Not bad, Countess.' He barely recognized his own voice. 'It will seem better when daylight comes. Try to – '

He heard the snap of a rifle-bolt and then Swan's round Hampshire voice. Its familiar tone did more to steady him than he could have believed.

'Boat's comin', sir.'

It was Sergeant Kirby. He dragged himself heavily over the guardrails and sought out Blackwood from the others.

Across that strip of dirty, sluggish current Sergeant Kirby's mind had stayed busy, ready for what was to come.

He said shortly, 'I've left Corporal Lyde in charge, sir.' Kirby had to grit his teeth together to control himself. Blackwood was like mustard and would see through any stupid lie. It was so bloody unfair on top of everything else. *But I should have known.* His own thoughts rang in his mind like an official reprimand. That stupid little bugger Earle. It was so *unfair*.

Blackwood asked quietly, 'In your own words, Sergeant. There may not be much time.'

Kirby fumbled inside his tunic and then dragged out a service revolver.

'Mr Earle's, sir.' He looked at the shadowy figures around him, quietly accusing. 'Weren't my fault! Must 'ave wandered off!'

Blackwood took the revolver and then handed it to Swan. He knew she was still there on deck watching him.

Swan said, 'It's 'is right enough, sir.'

Blackwood felt something like nausea as he recalled the mutilated gaping corpses, the great swinging swords and the blood.

He said, 'You go ashore, Ian.' He listened to his own voice and wondered how he could do it. 'Looks as if they've got him.'

The lieutenant nodded and hurried towards the boat.

To Fox he added, 'You take over here while I have a look at the map.' He gripped the nearest stanchion and murmured fiercely, 'Please God, let him be dead!'

The marines moved restlessly along either side as the news moved amongst them like an evil spectre.

Fox strode through the shadows and then paused by the slim figure with her maid.

'Would you please go to yer quarters, Ma'am.' He spoke very slowly and firmly as he always did when talking to foreigners. 'The Captain wants you to be safe. It's wot we're 'ere for, an' 'e's got enough on 'is plate at the moment without sweatin' about you, like.'

She only understood half of it but the man's genuine concern was clear in his rough voice.

'I shall do as you ask.' She hesitated, one hand on the door. 'You should be proud to serve him.'

Fox was taken aback. You did not discuss such things with women. 'I – I 'spect yer right, er, Countess.' He hurried away to look for Kirby and to force the truth out of him.

In the tiny, darkened chartroom Blackwood examined the map and compared it with a chart he had brought from *Mediator*. If nothing else happened in the next few hours they would up-anchor and proceed. He wiped his face with his sleeve. In the cramped space he could barely breathe. It was not helped by the stink of gin and stale pipesmoke.

Tomorrow. He blinked to clear his aching mind. *Today*. They would come to a great elbow-shaped bend in the river. High bank to starboard, a bit lower to port. If they got around that without incident they should be clear for a final run. The river was no deeper, but it was much wider. They could even anchor in midstream without the need to put pickets ashore.

But suppose this last terrible incident was a mere foretaste of what lay immediately ahead? He tried to keep his mind on an even keel, to shut out the pictures of what might be happening to Earle right at this moment. He *must* decide what to do. He tried again. If there was an attack or, worse, an ambush it would be there on the high ground.

The *Bajamar* would be too busy manoeuvring with her twin
paddles to take evasive action, and she could not attempt it
under cover of darkness.

They wanted the countess, whoever *they* were.

He measured the distances very carefully with some brass
dividers, the sweat from his forehead dropping on his hands
like hot rain. He thought of her cool fingers, the way she
had looked at him as he had rapped out his orders. She
would see him differently now. So would some of his men.
The cold ruthless officer who did not even care about one of
his own kind. Blackwood gripped the chart table until his
fingers cracked. What the hell did they expect?

His breathing steadied and he slowly straightened his
back. With unusual care he buttoned his tunic and adjusted
his holster.

And it was only just beginning.

They crowded around Blackwood at one end of the
Bajamar's saloon, a place normally used by the vessel's rare
passengers. Now it was littered with the marines' blankets
and packs and some spare boxes of ammunition.

Blackwood looked at them, at their grim faces under a
solitary deckhead oil lamp.

The sergeant major stooped even here between the
overhead beams. Lieutenant Bannatyre had just returned
from the shore. He had found Earle's white helmet tossed in
some bushes. As with the revolver it was as if they wanted
to be sure they knew they had captured the eighteen-year-
old officer. Sergeant Kirby, lips compressed in a thin line,
his eyes red from strain, and his two corporals, Lyde and
O'Neil, both old campaigners.

Austad stood with but a little apart from them, his heavy
face squinting through his own pipesmoke.

Blackwood said as evenly as he could manage, 'This is
what I intend.' He gestured to a rough drawing he had
made of the river bend they would have to pass. 'I believe an

attack will be made here. If they delay, we can reach the trading mission and have the protection of a German gunboat. Or if they hoped to frighten us into turning back,' he sensed Austad's resentment at his words, 'they could try another attack closer to the sea. They've had plenty of time to prepare if they are as well informed as I think they must be.'

Kirby said bitterly, 'Looks like we're in a trap either way, sir.'

Blackwood placed his finger on the crudely drawn map. 'We shall land a small party there. It will soon be daylight and if Captain Austad can make plenty of smoke any lookouts will know his ship is approaching.' Austad made no comment and Blackwood continued in the same even tone, 'We shall have to rely on surprise.' They watched his finger as it moved in a straight line, inland to a point behind the salient which guarded the bend in the river. 'By my reckoning it should take an hour. Forced march, weapons and ammunition only.' He glanced at their intent faces. They knew what he meant all right. Kill or be killed. 'We'll take them from the rear.' Then he did look at Austad. 'If we fail you will turn back and return to Shanghai. Do not try to proceed any further unsupported.'

Fox said sharply, 'You goin' with 'em, sir?' He sounded as if he had misheard.

Blackwood eyed him gravely. What else can I do? Aloud he said, 'Mr Bannatyre will take command here, and you will, I know, Sergeant Major, give him every support.' He shifted his glance from Fox's unspoken protest to the young lieutenant. Bannatyre seemed surprised, or was it just relief?

'Your only task is to protect the Countess and deliver her into safe hands, right?'

'Sir.' Bannatyre's head bobbed as if the neck had been broken. He was probably thinking about Earle. They all were.

Blackwood said, 'Sergeant Kirby and his two corporals

will come with me. I want the best marksmen you can find.
I am *not* asking for volunteers. Just ten good men.'

Surprisingly Corporal O'Neil gave a deep guffaw.
'What's a volunteer, sorr?'

Blackwood found that he could smile. 'A deaf Marine.'
He wanted to dash the sweat from his face but needed to
appear calm and in control.

Fox asked, 'How long, sir?'

Austad reluctantly removed the meerschaum from his
mouth.

'Give me a half-hour. Then, very slow, I move.'

'Thank you.' Blackwood saw the Norwegian giant sigh.
He had already accepted they were as good as killed.

They left the saloon and Blackwood doused the lamp.
Then he opened one of the steel shutters which covered a
square port and stared into the darkness. He could smell the
land, still hot from the previous day. If only it would rain.
Anything was better than this crushing silence.

He heard Swan say, 'Can I have your gun, sir?'

Blackwood drew it from its leather holster and handed it
to him without turning round. Swan would check everything. It seemed wrong to drag him into danger yet again.
It would be insulting to leave him behind.

'Shan't be sorry to stretch my legs, sir.' Swan was feeling
the revolver in the darkness, removing each bullet and
making sure it was a perfect one before he refilled the
chamber.

'I could be wrong.' It was easy to admit doubt to Swan,
when he could share nothing with his officers. Fear was
something. To show it to those he had to lead was different
entirely. He half smiled into the darkness. He even *sounded*
like the old General. Then with Swan beside him he walked
to the side-deck where Kirby was explaining to his landing
party what was expected of them.

Kirby had picked his men well. It was almost as if he had
expected something like this to happen.

Suppose there were eyes still watching from the river-bank, waiting to hack them down even as they climbed from the boat? Blackwood moved his shoulders briskly beneath his tunic. He was suddenly quite cold. It was always the same. A hazy plan, the need to act before you had time to think it through or to weigh up the chances of failure.

He could feel it. The decision right or wrong was made. Now all he wanted to do was to get on with it.

'Into the boat.'

Several of the shadowy figures nearby whispered farewells to their friends as they vanished into the little sampan.

Fox said, 'Good luck, sir. I just wish – '

Blackwood touched his arm and felt the power of the man. 'I *know*. But it has to be this way.'

Fox grunted. 'I know that too, sir.'

Then he was in the sampan and the paddles guided the box-shaped hull swiftly clear of the side and into the deeper shadows of the bank. They paused within feet of the land, the paddles motionless while the marines peered and listened for any sign of sudden danger.

Blackwood swung his leg over the gunwale. Once he glanced over his shoulder but the anchored paddle-steamer was little more than a pale blur against the opposite bank.

As he waded from the shallows he heard his feet crunching on coarse grass and scrub. Like everything else, tinder-dry and smelling vaguely of rot. There were trees too, but not enough to provide cover.

They split into two squads, each in the charge of a corporal. Kirby, breathing hard, stayed with Blackwood.

The land climbed slowly but steeply and as Blackwood got his bearings and pointed towards the beginning of a ridge he sensed the uneasiness amongst his small party. One hillside had already shut off the river, and he could hear the faint hiss of a breeze as it stirred the dry grass like a hidden army of serpents.

Kirby had already sent two scouts ahead of the others and he could imagine their feelings as they occasionally lost contact with their comrades. Few ever considered men like those, he thought vaguely. The ones who spearheaded an attack, and those who covered a retreat. The lonely ones. The expendable. He stopped his wild thoughts with sudden force. It was like the last time, only the country was different.

Kirby peered at the sky. The rim of hillside was already sharper, or were their eyes getting more used to the gloom?

One of the marines caught his foot in a root and fell on his rifle with a clatter. Everyone froze, barely able to breathe.

Kirby swore obscenely and snarled, 'Take that bugger's name!' But like the rest he was thankful that nothing worse had happened.

'Rest, Sergeant. Ten minutes. Pass the word to the scouts.'

Blackwood threw himself down and saw Swan sitting nearby, cross-legged like an Indian fakir. The sight made him want to laugh out loud. They were creeping towards a hill they knew nothing about, which they would probably find deserted. Whoever had seized Earle possibly thought that was enough. It might have been an accident more than a planned attack. Austad would be raising steam now, he thought. Shortening his cable in readiness to continue upriver. How on earth had a man like him found his way out here, he wondered.

He thought suddenly of the countess. She at least should be safe. The reduced number of marines had nowhere else to go. Even under Bannatyre's hesitant leadership they would give a good account of themselves. Fox would see to that.

Blackwood rolled over on to his elbows and stared at the hillside. What a place to end up. Only the river provided a lifeline and it, like many of the others in China, was dotted with trading missions, which in turn were protected by gunboats from a half a dozen countries. It was a strange impractical arrangement.

It was time to move.

He stood up and stifled a yawn. He could not remember exactly when he had last slept or eaten. 'Check your weapons.' Blackwood walked slowly amongst his men.

Private Kempster who came from Leeds, whose homely Yorkshire voice could usually be heard around the barracks. Trent, a swarthy-faced man who looked more like a Spaniard than anything. Even his friends called him Dago, and yet he came from four generations of marines. Corporal Lyde, who should have been a sergeant but had lost his stripes more times than he could remember for brawling ashore. Roberts, the ex-farm labourer from Sussex, amiable, slow, but probably the best shot in the company. They glanced at him as he passed without recognition. Each one was thinking of himself. If things go badly, how will I behave? Fight? Die?

'All correct, sir.'

Blackwood unclipped his holster and raised his arm to signal the advance. His arm seemed to stiffen in mid-air as if he had been paralysed. Then he heard it again. Surely nothing human could sound like that?

Kirby exclaimed thickly, 'Must be Mr Earle, fer Christ's sake!'

Blackwood wanted to press his hands to his ears. Anything to shut out those terrible agonized screams.

So they *were* there. He had been right. Waiting for the *Bajamar* while they tormented their victim yet denied him death.

Blackwood swallowed hard as somebody retched uncontrollably behind him. He knew that some of them were staring at him, pleading for him to attack and end the terrible cries.

It was too soon. If they ran all the way to the salient without knowing the strength of their enemy or waiting for Austad to appear, they would lose everything. But that would mean little enough to these men.

He said, 'Advance. Extend to right and left.' He heard their feet dragging, a gasp of horror as one terrible shriek scraped their minds like a hot wire. Then like the slamming of a great door it stopped.

Blackwood loosened his revolver and strode steadily through the coarse grass. As he had done before, as his ancestors had done in a hundred places and as many battles. It was what he had wanted, what everyone expected.

He felt the sweat running down his spine. It could have been Ralf up there.

Another half-hour passed and the sky became suddenly clearer. The marines rested amongst some bushes and in a low gully which must have once been cut by torrential rain.

Blackwood looked at them, their set expressions, their uniforms stained and torn as they clutched their rifles and peered at the skyline. The last horizon.

It was hard to picture these same men in scarlet and blue, the wheeling columns and hoarse commands across the barracks square. Even Corporal O'Neil had nothing to offer to break the tension. The screams still lingered in each man's mind.

Blackwood tugged out his watch and flicked open the guard. It had been given to him by his mother on his twenty-first birthday. It was light enough to see its face. He replaced it in his pocket and tried to appear calm. Where the hell was Austad?

A great screech made most of them start with alarm, but Blackwood was too thankful to notice. The Norwegian had kept his word. Right on time, even in the poor light he had picked his way up the river to play his part.

Blackwood said, 'Stand-to.' He glanced at Sergeant Kirby. 'Fix bayonets, if you please.' Then he drew his sword and felt Swan watching him. *His shadow*. Strangely enough it made him feel better. Stronger in some way, although he knew it might not last.

He shut Earle from his thoughts and said, 'Royal Marines will advance!'

The General would have been proud, he thought. Perhaps it would warrant another painting one day, to join all the others at Hawks Hill.

He saw pale sunlight touch the point of Swan's bayonet. It was time.

6

A Walk in the Sun

From one corner of his eye Blackwood saw a swirling plume of dark smoke rise above the salient, proof of Austad's efforts to follow his orders. It was like moving up towards a cliff edge, he thought, the ground so steep that the land beyond as well as the river was completely hidden. To his right he could see a pyramid-shaped hill, still shrouded in early mist, and what looked like tiny dwellings scattered at its foot.

It was hard to imagine that over there people were living peacefully, probably hoping to be left undisturbed by Boxers and foreign troops alike.

It was all completely unreal, the slow-moving smoke, the swish of dry scrub against his feet and legs, and his men fanning out on either side of him in a ragged line, their bayonets glinting to mark their slow advance. *A walk in the sun.*

Blackwood found time to marvel, not for the first time, that training and tradition could hold them all together under any situation.

A figure burst from the ground almost at his feet. There was no place to hide and yet he was there as if he had broken out of hell itself.

Blackwood barely had time to think other than to realize that he was dressed in the same robes as the attackers aboard the *Delhi Star*. He felt the jarring pain in his arm as he parried the man's heavier blade with his own and used the force of his charge to take him off-balance. He heard him scream as he drove his sword under his guard and through his ribs. Swan silenced a last cry with the butt of his rifle.

They stared at each other, barely aware of the sporadic firing which came from the edge of the redoubt. It was the same madness. Blackwood could feel his mouth fixed in a wild grin.

'Together, lads! Charge!'

The marines gathered their strength and blundered up the remaining slope, their eyes slitted against the pungent smoke from the *Bajamar*'s funnel.

There were about twenty of them. Kneeling or lying along the rim of the land as the hidden paddle-wheeler pounded towards them. Some whirled round, eyes staring and wild as Corporal Lyde's squad poured a rapid volley from the right flank, followed instantly by the second party.

Blackwood held his revolver in his left fist although he did not recall drawing it from the holster.

'Advance!'

A wounded Boxer ran and hopped towards a discarded rifle and sprawled gasping as Kirby drove his bayonet through his chest. Not the crazy lunge of a recruit but the cool reaction of the old campaigner.

Blackwood yelled, 'Over there, O'Neil!' He gestured with his sword. 'The *gun!*'

It was carefully hidden in branches and dead leaves but there was no mistaking the ugly revolving snout of an old Hotchkiss cannon. Old perhaps, but if fired directly down on to the *Bajamar*'s helm and bridge it would have a devastating effect.

Blackwood aimed his revolver and saw one man fall, the other turning to cover his face with his arms as he realized for the first time that the marines were amongst them.

'First squad!' That was Lyde again. 'Kneel! Take aim! *Fire!*'

The figures around the Hotchkiss rolled away from the mounting and ammunition like rag puppets.

Kirby was yelling, 'At 'em!' Watch that bugger, Roberts!'

Private Roberts, the farm-boy from Sussex, did not appear to take aim. He waited until the running figure was right on the lip of the salient and then fired from the shoulder. He could have been despatching a rabbit.

Kirby almost kicked Private Trent aside as he gasped, 'No quarter! They'll cut you down, else!' His bayonet lunged and withdrew just as smartly, the blade edged in red.

Blackwood lowered his sword and stood sucking in great gulps of air. He hardly dared to look at his wild, breathless marines. One was staring at the sky, his face stiff with pain as Corporal Lyde expertly knotted a bandage around his arm.

Blackwood saw Kirby watching him and nodded. 'Well done, lads!' He walked slowly to the edge of the land and stood looking down at the curving river. It was yellow like the sun. He could feel his arms shaking, his whole body reacting to the swift attack. Not a man dead. It was still hard to believe. He removed his white helmet and waved it slowly from side to side. Far below Austad responded with another jubilant screech on his siren.

Kirby called, 'No sign of Mr Earle's body, sir.'

Blackwood watched the *Bajamar*'s anchor splash down, the two sampans already lowered to retrieve a landing-party which he doubted if anyone had ever expected to survive.

'Shall we bury this lot, sir?' The sergeant watched him curiously.

'No. Leave them. As a warning.'

He wiped his neck and face with a filthy handkerchief. 'Fall the men in. We'll *march* down to the river.'

He saw his weary, dazed men straighten their backs as if a silent order had been issued.

Corporal O'Neil shouted, 'Come along now, Dago! This is no time at all for slacking!'

Blackwood replaced his helmet and pulled the chinstrap into place. It was not exactly an army. He looked around at the sprawled corpses and an isolated patch of dried blood where they must have tortured Earle before killing him. But he knew he would not have exchanged them at this moment for a whole battalion of his own. Almost to himself he murmured, 'I'm sorry, Charles. I should never have sent you.'

Then he turned on his heel and followed his men down the slope towards the river.

Blackwood stood on the *Bajamar*'s open bridge and trained a borrowed telescope on the slow-moving river-bank and the blue hills beyond. The bridge was little more than a spidery catwalk which linked the two paddle-boxes on either beam together. In the fierce midday sun the rails were too hot to touch. Half of the marines stood guard along the bulwarks, helmets tilted to shield their eyes, their rifles resting on the rails ready for instant use.

But from the moment they had returned aboard and Austad had raised anchor again they had not sighted a living thing. Their return was something Blackwood would not forget. The anxious, grimy faces along the vessel's side, and then, suddenly, the tension had snapped like a taut mooring-wire and the marines had stood to wave and cheer despite every threat which Fox had hurled at them. Even Austad's villainous looking crew had joined in.

'I'm going below.' Blackwood glanced at the big Norwegian. His pipe was going well, and he seemed strangely content after what had happened.

Austad grunted. 'We shall reach the mission soon.' He chuckled. 'That German gunboat captain will be feeling very small, I think!' He was still laughing as Blackwood lowered himself to the deck.

He walked through the saloon his eyes almost blinded by the sun. The marines off-watch made to stand but he waved them down. They were amazing, he thought. In spite of all that had happened, Earle's capture and torture, and the

swift savagery of their fight on the salient, he saw that his
men had managed to shave and fold their blankets as neatly
as in their barracks. There was a smell of coffee, and of
something cooking in the tiny galley.

Swan was waiting for him at the forward end of the
saloon, his rifle slung from one shoulder, his helmet on the
back of his head. 'Beg pardon, sir, but the Countess would
like to see you.'

'Yes.' Blackwood felt suddenly drained, the relief that
they had somehow survived dragging at his last resources
like claws. He wanted to see her, just as he knew he should
stay away. Soon she would be reunited with her husband.
He would become just a part of her memories.

Blackwood walked outside and tapped on her door. He
knew he looked like a vagrant in his filthy uniform, streaks
of dried blood on his sword-arm.

She opened the door and studied him gravely. 'Please
enter, Captain.'

He noticed that the little Chinese maid was not present.
He had barely been alone with her before. How did she
manage to appear so cool, so elegant? She had changed her
clothes again and was dressed in a pale yellow gown with an
Oriental sash that revealed the smallness of her waist. She
was about the same age as himself and yet so different.
Distant in spite of her crowded surroundings. Like Royalty.
It made him feel even less confident. Unclean.

She asked, 'Do you like what you see, Captain?'

He flushed. 'I was staring. I am sorry.'

She gestured to a chair. 'You apologize too much.' She
watched him for several seconds. 'You did not come to see
me when you returned.' It was an accusation. 'I was
anxious. Worried for you.'

He looked at her. 'I am – '

She smiled gently. 'Sorry?'

He grinned. 'I suppose I was too concerned with getting
the ship under way again. It seems quiet enough, but I'm
not sure.'

She walked across the cabin and stared through an open scuttle. 'That poor young man. He died because of me. If I had not insisted on rejoining my husband it would never have happened.'

Blackwood twisted round to look at her but she gripped his shoulder tightly and exclaimed, '*Please*. Do not turn. I do not wish you to see me so.'

He could feel the emotion in her voice just as the strength of her grip told him something new about her.

He said, 'Mr Earle died doing his duty. If anyone is to blame it must be me. Ours can be a dangerous calling. Men die, some for no reason we can understand. We accept it.'

He saw her hand reach round and grope for his. 'You say that to protect me. To help me forget.' She shook her head, the piled crown of hair shining in reflected sunlight from the scuttle. 'I shall *never* forget.'

Blackwood felt the smoothness of her hand and could smell her perfume, her fragrance. What would she do if he took her in his arms here and now?

She turned and looked at him, her face in shadow.

'I know what you are thinking, my gallant young Captain. And I am ashamed of my own feelings towards you.' As he made to rise she pressed him back into the chair. 'But it cannot be. Such a secret is impossible to hide or to share.' She touched his face as she had that other time, as if to memorize every detail. 'Perhaps we shall meet again one day.' She smiled at him but it made her look incredibly sad. 'In the line of duty as you would call it, yes?'

There was a nervous tap at the door. It was Swan.

'Well?' Blackwood tried to sound calm. 'What is it?'

Swan glanced at a point between them.

'The Skipper sends 'is compliments and – '

'Spit it out, man!'

Swan looked at the countess. 'Well, sir – '

Blackwood said quietly, 'It's all right. You can speak in front of our passenger.'

Swan let out a sigh. 'The mission is round the next bend,

sir. But the river's so wide 'ere you can see it already with
the glass.'

Blackwood reached out and took her hand. It seemed
natural and easy in front of Swan.

Swan said wretchedly, 'There's *nothin*', sir. The place is in
ruins. Knocked to bloody hell, beggin' yer pardon, Ma'am.'

'No ship?'

Swan shook his head. 'All gone, sir.'

'Tell Austad I'll come up directly.' As the door shut he
was conscious of the silence which hung over the vessel, so
that the beat of her paddles seemed to intrude like muffled
drums. He needed to think and act quickly.

She stepped closer and placed her hands on his shoulders.
'What will you do?'

He stood up. 'We shall anchor and stand off until I have
gone ashore to investigate. Don't worry, I said I would
protect you. So I shall.' Without realizing it he put his arm
around her shoulders. He felt her stiffen as if about to pull
away. Blackwood said, 'There may have been an attack.' He
dismissed the idea instantly. 'No, the gunboat would not
withdraw. She would be more than a match for a mob of
Boxers.'

He felt her breast touching his tunic, the painful beat of
his heart which she must feel. 'I have to go.' He lowered his
arm. 'You will be safe here.' He was barely aware of what he
was saying. 'Keep away from the ports and scuttles.'

She stayed where she was, watching his mouth as if to
understand what was happening.

Then she said quietly, 'You see, Captain? What you have
done? I am just a woman after all.'

He made to hold her again but she turned away. 'No. Do
what you must but come back. To me.'

He watched her hands opening and closing as if she had
lost control of them.

'You have my word, Countess.'

As he slid back the door she said quietly, 'Friedrike. It is
my name.'

Blackwood barely remembered his climb to the bridge. He was aware of anxious, sun-reddened faces, of Lieutenant Bannatyre's relief as he appeared on the catwalk, of all these things and none of them.

Austad lowered his telescope and handed it to him.

'Burned out.' He watched Blackwood's profile. 'Some parts broken down with gunpowder, I think.'

Blackwood captured the scene of blackened desolation in the powerful lens. Austad was right. It was deliberate, not some frontal attack from outside.

Were they watching him right at this moment? Triumph and hatred, planning their next move against the foreign devils. He thought of her voice her hands in the cabin below. It made it suddenly personal and more dangerous because of it.

'Full landing party, Ian.' He moved the glass slightly. Humps in the rough ground by some trees. Graves. Crudely and hastily done. So there must have been an attack, but not so recently. Bannatyre was calling out his orders to the deck below, then he asked, 'What do you intend, sir?'

Blackwood did not look at him. If that Boxer lookout had been quicker with his great blade he might be lying dead back there. Then Bannatyre would be in command.

He replied, 'First we'll take a look. No chances. And be ready to fall back to the boats if we are attacked.' He lowered his voice and added sharply, 'I don't care if you are scared, Ian. We all get like that. But don't show it in front of the men!' He saw his words strike home and added more gently, 'The Germans may have had to leave overland.' It did not make sense. Where *was* the bloody gunboat?

Bannatyre said, 'Then we shall have to go back down-river, the way we came, sir.'

'It looks that way. At least we tried, eh?' But this time his words left Bannatyre untouched. He was remembering their slow, painful progress, and what the returning marines had told him about the Boxers and those hideous screams.

Blackwood looked past him as the paddles slowed for the final approach.

On the return passage the enemy would have all the time they needed. They would not be caught out again by a handful of marines.

The anchor clattered into shallow water and minutes later the two sampans were being warped alongside.

Blackwood nodded to Austad. 'Keep a close watch, Captain. Your old cannon are going to come in useful, I shouldn't wonder.'

Austad laughed, and the marines who were waiting to enter the boats heard him, and some even grinned as Blackwood strode through them. It couldn't be all that bad if their captain could joke about it. Fox did not smile. He knew the game of old, and understood all the rules better than most.

Blackwood said, 'You will be in charge until we return. Put what few men you have where they can be seen. The one who had his arm cut – '

Fox regarded him patiently. 'Farley, sir.'

'Have him move about the saloon and make it appear we have more men hidden below.'

'Yessir.' Fox shaded his eyes and peered at the shore. 'I'd issue Cap'n Austad with a uniform if I thought 'e could get into it!'

Blackwood eyed him fondly. 'The sooner we leave, the better chance we have of pulling out in daylight. Dawn tomorrow, with any luck.'

Fox stood at the rails and saluted as Blackwood jumped down amongst his men.

To himself he added, 'And we'll have to fight every bloody inch of the way, I shouldn't wonder.'

Blackwood stood quite still, one hand resting on his open holster as his landing party fanned out towards the trees and into the shattered mission. Near to it was even worse. It had been done with great care and deliberation to make certain that nothing of any use remained. There were scars on the burned walls, rifle and some musket fire. The first squad to return reported that there was evidence of shellfire, black holes in the ground to show where the gunboat had hit back from the river.

How many? he wondered. A handful of fanatics, or was the Boxer movement larger than anyone at home really understood. A full-scale rebellion would mark an end to any trade or colonial progress throughout the breadth of China.

Sergeant Kirby hurried down the slope while three of his men followed with what appeared to be some Chinese youths.

Lieutenant Bannatyre exclaimed, 'I'll see if they're armed!'

There were just two of them, both terrified as they were pushed towards Blackwood.

Kirby said dubiously, 'They say they're student interpreters who were employed 'ere by the Germans, sir. Can't be sure o' that neither.' He looked as if he would have killed them without thinking too much about it.

Bannatyre said, 'Could be true, sir. They use a lot of student interpreters at our legation in Peking.'

Blackwood asked quietly, 'What happened here?'

They both stared wild-eyed at him as if they still could not believe what was happening.

Blackwood continued in the same even tone. 'There was an attack.'

One of them nodded violently. 'Many Boxers, sir. Fighting for two days.' He made as if to look at the ruins but seemed to change his mind as if the memory was too vivid and terrible. 'We all ordered to leave in the ship.' He glanced at his friend. 'But we try to find our way across land. No want to go in ship.'

Blackwood could see it in his mind. But he had to know more.

'The German Count von Heiser, did you see him?'

'He go in ship too.'

Kirby muttered, 'Fer Chrissake!'

'D'you know if there are still any Boxers here?'

The youth looked at the ground. 'I think they go.' Once again the quick exchange of glances. 'They nearly found us. We heard them speak of river. They will try to block it.'

Bannatyre stared back at the sluggish current. 'My God, we'll be trapped!'

Blackwood tried to conceal his feelings. It was the only important thing he had discovered. They would know the old *Bajamar* was coming. How they knew was a mystery. But they obviously intended to cut their only line of escape. Perhaps they had forced something out of Earle before they allowed him to die.

He said, 'Send a boat for Austad. I want him here, now.'

He could sense the two Chinese youths shaking with fear. So great was the terror instilled by the Boxers they did not even feel safe with the marines.

The count had of course been under the impression that his wife had gone to Shanghai. They had not seen the gunboat so it seemed likely that the Germans had headed north perhaps with the intention of joining their legation in Peking. It was fast becoming a nightmare.

He said, 'Take these two on board.' In his heart he knew that the interpreters had been sent overland to carry news of the attack to Shanghai. Once they reached a fishing village the rest would have been easy.

Blackwood could find no other solution. One thing stood out above all else. Count von Heiser did not intend to let his wife's safety interfere with his duties.

Austad crunched up the beach and stared at the departing Chinese interpreters.

Blackwood said, 'We must lighten your ship, Captain. When we steer downriver I need you to be able to go as fast as you can.'

Austad removed his pipe and stared. 'Lighten the ship?'

Blackwood nodded. 'I believe the Boxers will try to block

our progress and launch an attack.' He saw his words going home.

Austad said, 'Not a dam, I think. The water would rise, and give my *Bajamar* more speed.'

'A boom then?' Blackwood controlled his impatience. The big Norwegian thought like he spoke, very slowly.

'*Boom?*' He pouted. 'More like.'

Blackwood looked across at the anchored paddle-steamer. She seemed totally at peace against the green backdrop of trees.

He said, 'How many anchors do you carry?'

Austad shrugged. 'Just two, Captain.' He sounded perplexed.

'Then I want one taken aft.' He looked for Kirby. 'Did you hear that? Get a party together and move the spare anchor right aft. Find a hawser of some sort and shackle it on. We may have to use a stream anchor.' The sergeant hurried away calling names. Orders he understood. He would carry them out to the letter.

'You can unload all your coal and burn wood instead. It is much lighter and we can use some of it as barricades.' He glanced at Bannatyre. 'See to it, Ian. I want the helm and Maxim gun protected.'

Austad struggled for words as if his collar was choking him.

'But my coal! I paid much money for it at Shanghai!'

'You'll get it back, Captain.' He eyed him impassively. 'But only if we escape from this bloody river!'

Within an hour the bulk of the marines, stripped and sweating with effort, and almost all of Austad's crew were hard at work. Spare cable, coal, some iron hatch covers, all were dragged or rolled over the side until the top of the pile showed above the surface like a tiny islet.

Blackwood watched from the shore. The waterline was already rising slightly. Just inches, but it would make all the difference. A dash downstream, dodging the worst of the big sandbars, and straight into the ambush. He rubbed

his chin. A boom. It was the most likely. He had heard
stories of such things from the *Arrow* Wars.

It would make even the unmovable Masterman sit up
when the old *Bajamar* came puffing into view. He pictured
Mediator, graceful and sleek as he had last seen her. And yet
in this kind of situation she was as useless as a bow and
arrow. Blackwood walked across to the crude graves. No
name, no markers. They had probably been wondering why
it had happened when death had cut them down.

He saw his pickets moving restlessly by the line of trees,
their rifles and fixed bayonets at the ready. They needed no
reminding now of what could happen.

Blackwood thought of the countess, hiding her feelings,
few would ever guess what she was really enduring. He
hoped that when she realized what had happened she would
be equally strong.

He saw Swan watching him thoughtfully.

'We will ram the boom at full speed.' He found to his
surprise that he could smile even now. The idea of the
Bajamar managing even six knots was hard to believe.

Swan grimaced. 'We might broach-to, sir.' He waited
warily. Blackwood took a few paces this way and that. 'We
shall have to blow it first. The ship can ride on a stream
anchor while we steer one of the sampans into the boom,
barricade or whatever it turns out to be, and explode a
charge against it.'

Swan persisted unhelpfully. 'The sampan might drift into
the bank, sir. Or blow the backside out of our seagoing relic
as we try to get past 'er.' He grinned broadly. 'You may 'ave
to ask for volunteers this time, sir.'

Blackwood was grateful for Swan's trust or indifference,
and not for the first time. He knew exactly how far he could
go, but whatever it was it stayed between them, something
private.

As soon as it was dark they would return aboard. It was
no longer safe to leave isolated pickets on the land. Even
now, no matter what the student interpreters had said,

there might be hundreds of eyes watching them, gauging their readiness to move.

There was another great splash as some iron ballast was tipped into the river. If they ever got to sea the little *Bajamar* would toss about like a leaf on a millrace.

Timber from the burned-out mission was being hoisted from the sampans for Austad's boilers and for use as rough and ready barricades. It could make all the difference when bullets started to fly.

A strange bird squawked in the distance, but Blackwood chilled. It sounded like Earle. He could imagine the letter which the colonel commandant would eventually write to Earle's parents in Surrey. *Died bravely in the Service of his Queen and Country*. His own parents had doubtless had one at Hawks Hill for Neil. His mind shied away from it and he recalled instead a great marble bath he had shared with the army paymaster's young wife at Trincomalee. The thought made him feel even dirtier. Just to sink into a bath again. He touched his tunic beneath which the livid scar was another reminder.

He thought suddenly of the countess. Friedrike. Just to hold her like that, to take her —

Sergeant Kirby interrupted his thoughts. 'Anchor's in position aft, sir. Th' ship's drawin' five inches less as far as I can make out.'

'You've done well.' Blackwood looked away. The sky was changing to deep purple, the shadows from the trees looked like bars across the water.

'Recall all the working parties, Sergeant. See if Austad's cook can produce a good meal as soon as it's dark.'

Kirby understood. 'Long day termorrer.'

He marched off to gather up his sentries. A hard, embittered man, Blackwood thought.

He went over his plan again. It would be a long day right enough. He thought of men like these, Fox and Corporal O'Neil, Dago Trent, Lieutenant Bannatyre. They counted on him. It was no time for mistakes.

He closed his holster and glanced at his hand. He was surprised to discover he was completely unafraid and that unnerved him.

7

Under Fire

In the small cabin the imprisoned air was already hot and humid although it was not yet dawn.

Blackwood watched the countess as she sat on a small canvas chair and waited for her Chinese maid to finish dressing her hair.

Her eyes watched him in the mirror.

'We are leaving soon, Captain?'

Blackwood nodded. It seemed different with the maid here. A sort of formality had come between them.

He replied, 'My men have been fed. They are being mustered at their stations now.' He wished that he felt fresh and alert, but it had been a long night. The sampan to prepare, to transform into a floating bomb. Perhaps the interpreters were wrong, or the Boxers had changed their minds about a boom. But it was very unlikely they would escape downstream without an attack of some kind.

He thought of her face when he had described the scene ashore; he had expected some sign of disappointment, even anger, when he told her about her husband and the gunboat. All she had said was, 'He has a mission in life. Nothing ever obstructs that.'

On deck he heard the scrape of wire and a sudden rumble from the engine room. Soon now.

Blackwood also thought of his men's reactions when he had explained what he intended. They accepted it. The threat of more danger had pushed Earle's capture into the background for the present. They had piled logs and lengths of timber around the gun in the bows to afford some protection to its crew.

Sergeant Kirby had shown some of his own anxiety when he had snapped, 'Bloody Maxim! Trust the Navy to give us one o' them! I'll take the old Nordenfelt any time when it comes to rapid-bloody-fire!'

Captain Masterman had probably offered the Maxim because he thought it would be easier to mount in the ancient *Bajamar*.

Other than that there had been little to reveal what his men really felt.

She said, 'You may tell me, Captain.' Her eyes in the mirror were quite steady. 'What chance do we have?'

Blackwood said, 'I believe we will have to fight our way through.'

She turned on the chair to look at him, her hair gleaming in the lamplight.

It was then that a memory stabbed at Blackwood like a dagger. When he had joined his first ship he had been serving with an old major who had seen a lot of service in China. He had spoken of a hired surveying vessel named *Kite* which had been wrecked on the Chinese mainland. Her captain had been drowned, but his wife who had been on board with him was taken prisoner and dragged by her long red hair from village to village to be humiliated brutally before being put in a small bamboo cage and carried on display to Ningpo. To the Chinese rebels at the time she must have symbolized the foreign invader if only because of her hair. Her captors had carried her for many miles in the cage where she could not sit or lie down. Neither she nor the other survivors from the *Kite* had ever been seen again.

'You are staring, Captain.'

He looked away. 'I am sorry.' He forced a smile but his mouth felt stiff. The Boxers wanted her for an important hostage, but what might they do to her in the meantime?

'I am apologizing again.'

She stood up and faced him.

'I can read it in your eyes. Do not dismay, I will not show fear to *them*.'

He put his hands on her waist. 'In case anything should go wrong.' He hesitated and felt her body tense. 'I just want you to know that I have fallen in love with you.'

Her lips parted as if she would protest and he hurried on, 'I realize it is impossible. I *know* that.' He looked at her for several seconds and added, 'But nothing can change how I feel.'

A fist pounded the door. 'Cap'n Blackwood, *sir!*' It was Fox. Perhaps he knew too. Maybe they all did. It no longer seemed to matter.

'I'm coming right away, Sergeant Major!'

He let his arms drop to his sides. 'I have to go. They are raising the anchor. Time to leave.'

She moved closer, her face uplifted.

Blackwood could feel the maid staring at them, her eyes like saucers.

'May God guard you, my dear Captain.' Then she kissed him on the lips. It was more of a sensation than anything and in the next instant she was standing away from him. Unreachable.

Blackwood walked out to the side-deck and made his way forward to where the capstan clanked round in a cloud of rust.

Lieutenant Bannatyre drew himself to attention and said, 'All in position, sir.' Like the others he was wearing his field-service cap instead of the white helmet with its gleaming spike on the top. The marines might resent the order, but it made them smaller targets. Blackwood knew from bitter experience that a white helmet made a perfect aiming-mark for any marksman. He glanced aft and saw Austad's bulky silhouette on the bridge as he watched the anchor coming inboard. Behind him the smoke rolled downwind from the funnel and sparks too, as the boilers adjusted themselves to freshly cut wood.

Blackwood walked down the sloping deck and felt his

way past one of the great paddles. Figures crouched behind makeshift barricades, their eyes pale in the grey light as they turned to watch him. Corporal O'Neil was right aft by the taffrail, peering down at the sampan which was tied astern. The charge was concealed with canvas and more timber. It would not do to have a stray shot strike that pile of explosive, he thought.

O'Neil said cheerfully, 'Two fuses, sir, in case one misfires.' No questions, no doubts.

Blackwood smiled. 'You've done well.'

O'Neil chuckled. 'Learned a mite from my brother in the RMA, sir. A fine lad even if he is a gunner!'

Blackwood continued on his inspection. Even O'Neil's little joke seemed to symbolize something. The Corps. The *family*.

It was strange to think he had never seen Jonathan in uniform. He like O'Neil's brother was in the Royal Marine Artillery, the first gunner in the Blackwood family. A Blue Marine. That must have given the General a few doubtful moments.

The hull gave a shudder and a man yelled hoarsely from the bows as the anchor rose dripping against the hawsepipe. The great paddle-wheels thrashed round even as the helm went over, and belching more smoke the *Bajamar* pivoted in mid-stream like the old veteran she was.

It was already much lighter, and he could see the river-bank, the indistinct shadow of the ruined mission.

The paddles churned up sand and dirt from the bottom as with a leadsman in the bows she steadied on course. Austad left his little catwalk and stood near the helmsman. Austad looked over at Blackwood without a word and then put a match to his pipe. He reached out for the telegraph and Blackwood heard the bell jangle in the engine room, and the increasing beat of the paddles as they responded.

Corporal Lyde stood near the second anchor and eyed the tackle and slips with obvious contempt. It was a job for sailors, or coolie deckhands. Not Royal Marines.

He patted his ammunition pouches and checked that his Lee-Metford rifle was ready with the safety catch on. But if it had to be done, the Second Platoon would do it best, or he'd want to know why.

Midway between the machine gun and the oblong superstructure, Sergeant Kirby stood with his arms folded, his eyes apparently on the lieutenant in the bows. Bloody Bannatyre was already scared out of his wits and nothing had happened yet. But the thought failed to console him or shift his mind from his terrible secret.

He shouldn't have listened, then he wouldn't have known. Besides which, they could have sorted things out.

A *friend* at Forton Barracks had told him that he had seen Kirby's wife in a London ale house, she had been with a soldier, and they had apparently been aware of nothing but each other. Kirby had considered asking for leave, but with the whole company standing by for overseas he knew it would not be granted. Besides which, he had his pride, both in the Corps which he had entered as a boy, and in what he had achieved to get the chevrons on his sleeve.

He had spent all his money on a train fare to London. He did not really remember planning anything. It had just happened. Kirby could see her face right now, as if she was here on this ruddy steamer. He clutched the guardrail and felt the power running through his fingers.

The way they had stared at him from the bed. His bed. Both naked, and gaping at him in the doorway.

'Oh dear God!' He heard a man shuffle and knew he had spoken aloud.

The soldier had been quick. He had dived from the bed and had run frantically from the room. Kirby did not really care about him anyway. He could have been anyone. She had started to plead, to beg. With the same detached efficiency with which he might examine a recruit's rifle for a speck of dirt, he had strangled her. He could not even remember how long he had sat there after covering her contorted face with a blanket. *All his things*. Pictures of his

past ships, fellow NCOs, even one of himself as a callow
recruit.

Then he had left and had returned to the barracks on a
milk train. Nobody had seen him leave or return. He was
not even a minute adrift for reveille.

When her body was discovered the police would inform
the barracks. Nobody else would care much. And the
soldier? He would be careful to keep his mouth shut. He
might well have been seen with her that night at the pub.

And yet. He felt the anxiety and despair closing round
him like his fingers on her neck. *I know and I care*, his mind
seemed to shout.

And supposing someone had seen him there?

Blackwood stood beside him. Kirby felt ice-cold. How
long had he been watching him?

But Blackwood merely said, 'Ready for Rounds,
Sergeant. Just to make sure we've forgotten nothing.' He
looked at him in the gloom. 'Are you all right?'

Kirby nodded. 'Never better, sir.'

He followed the young captain, glad to be doing
something, grateful to be a part of it all even if he had to die
for it.

Blackwood walked past the saloon. In darkness but with
each port wide open. Here and there a rifle muzzle showed
itself. He pressed the white paintwork. The metal and wood
beneath would not stop a bullet except at long range. But it
was all they had.

He heard Kirby close on his heels. What the hell was the
matter with him? he wondered.

Blackwood paused by the last door and thought of her on
the other side. *Friedrike.* He touched his lips with the back
of his hand and thought of her mouth, her nearness.

Nearby Fox saw his hesitation and allowed his stern
features to relax. Then he glared at the crouching figures by
the bulwark. In their stained whites they looked more like
bloody convicts than marines. He would alter all that when
they reached order and routine again. He looked up at the

masthead, now clearly etched against the sky. Not even a flag. *Gawd*.

There was a sharp crack followed by the thud of a bullet hitting the hull on the port side.

Fox shouted, 'Stand-to! Face yer front but *keep down!*'

He stared at the lieutenant who was standing alone and framed against the sky. It went against Fox's instincts to shout at an officer. But in a few more seconds that marksman would see him and pick him out as a target.

'*Down*, Mr Bannatyre, if you please, sir!'

He sighed as the officer dropped to his knees.

Blackwood crouched beside him. Fox felt the captain's mind going like an engine.

'It's started, sir.'

'Sooner than I expected.' He grimaced as another shot clanged into the low hull. He said, 'No firing until I give the order.'

Fox watched him duck down and move to the opposite side. Sharp as a tack, that one. Blackwood knew that if they were allowed the marines would blaze away and use most of their ammunition before they had got halfway. Nobody liked to sit and take it without shooting back.

He looked at Sergeant Kirby who was kneeling behind a winch.

'All right, Jeff?'

Kirby glared at him. Why don't they all shut up and leave me alone?

But he answered readily, 'Never better, Sar'nt Major!'

The sun's rim shone like a gold halo above one of the pointed hills and with it came the attack.

'Hold yer fire!' Fox's voice carried like a trumpet above the sporadic crack of rifles and muskets which appeared to be coming from either bank.

Blackwood peered over the low bulwark and watched drifting smoke rising from some bushes, but of the marksmen there was no sign at all.

He shouted, 'More speed, Captain Austad!' He guessed the vessel was going as fast as she could, and the spray was flying from the churning paddle wheels like spindrift.

'There's Johnnie Chinaman!'

Blackwood saw the running figures as they broke from cover by some open ground.

'Two 'undred yards! Independent! *Fire!*'

The marines took careful aim and squeezed their triggers. Several of the running men tumbled down the slope, their red ribbons and loose white tunics like untidy bundles amongst the dried scrub.

'Cease firing!' Fox yelled, 'Reload magazines! Watch yer front!'

Blackwood glanced quickly at the nearest marines as they pressed eight more bullets into their rifles. Most of the heavy shooting had come from the port side. They would eventually have to steer closer to the salient where they had fought their swift, decisive battle. Blackwood saw that the dead Boxers had dropped their weapons, not swords this time but great shining blades mounted on staves like pikes. *The Big Knife Society*. It did not seem so bizarre now.

More white-clad figures broke from cover and ran recklessly towards the river, some firing, others brandishing their fearsome-looking blades, apparently oblivious to the danger.

'Commence firing!'

The Maxim gun came to life, *tak-tak-tak*, the ammunition belt jerking through a marine's fingers as the bullets made little spurts in the water, across the bank and then through the mob of yelling figures.

Blackwood recalled what Major Blair had told him in Hong Kong. That the Boxers were so fanatical that they really believed they were invulnerable to sword-cuts, even bullets.

More of them were flung down by the rapid fire, until the

Maxim jerked into silence and Kirby exclaimed, *'Jammed!* Wot did I tell you?'

But nobody listened as the river-bank and shallows swung even closer to the port-side paddle-wheel.

Bullets slammed into the hull and Blackwood heard glass shattering, the cry for assistance as one of his men was hit inside the saloon. The leadsman in the bows rose warily to his feet and flung his line over the side. He seemed to pivot on his heels, his mouth wide in a silent scream as a heavy ball smashed him in the chest and hurled him over the bulwark. Blackwood saw one of the marines shutting his eyes tightly as the leadsman was sucked into the great churning paddle-blades and ground to bloody fragments in seconds. Austad had drawn his old long-barrelled Colt revolver and was firing at some of the Boxers who stood waist-deep in the shallows. One fell, another waded closer, his rifle aimed at the bridge even as the stoppage was cleared from the Maxim and a hail of bullets tossed him aside within yards of the hull.

Blackwood strode to the bows, trying not to duck as several bullets struck sparks from the windlass or ploughed splinters from the deck. They were shooting down into the ship as the *Bajamar* steamed into the narrows at the start of the wide bend. Another marine fell on his back, gasping in agony as a red stain spread across his tunic and one of his comrades ran to drag him to safety.

Lieutenant Bannatyre, his revolver in his fist, stared at Blackwood without recognition.

Blackwood said sharply, 'They'll try and board us in a moment!'

'But – but – ' Bannatyre seemed unable to form his words. 'H-how can they?'

There was no time to explain. It would not help anyway. 'These people don't know what fear is!'

Crack – crack – crack! Shots clattered and ricocheted from the paddle-boxes and superstructure, and holes appeared in the sides of the saloon like brightly edged stars.

Corporal Lyde called hoarsely, 'Two men down, sir! I think Private Elmhirst is done for!'

Blackwood winced as a heavier bang shook the bridge. Probably an ancient Chinese gingall left over from the other wars. Like a giant duck-gun, it needed two men to carry and fire it.

A face intruded into his racing thoughts. Private Elmhirst, Lyde had said. Round and innocent, made more so by his carefully grown moustache. Like Ralf, he thought.

Running and ducking Blackwood hurried into the deeper shadow of a paddle-box and knelt beside the young marine. He looked so pale he could already have been dead. Elmhirst opened his eyes and stared up at him. His eyes seemed unable to focus properly as if he was barely aware of what was happening. More sharp cracks made the deck quiver and Blackwood could hear Fox calling for him. He took Elmhirst's hand in his. 'Easy, lad. Hold on.' Lyde had torn open his white tunic and was trying to staunch the blood with a dressing. It seemed to be everywhere.

'I — I got one of 'em, sir.' Elmhirst's voice was small, almost a whisper.

Lyde said roughly, ''*Course* you did. Two of the buggers more like, eh, sir?' He looked at Blackwood, his face saying it was hopeless.

Blackwood said, 'I'll tell them about it.' He saw the light go out in the youth's eyes and felt the grip on his hand slacken.

Lyde watched him stride forward again, then closed the marine's eyes. 'I hope you heard, that, my son.' Then he picked up his rifle, thumbed off the safety catch and fired over the rail. Lyde had already selected another zig-zagging target even as the first one dropped.

Fox beckoned to Blackwood and pointed at the hillside. 'Smoke, sir! They've got somethin' ready for us!'

A marine pounded the Maxim's breech until blood showed on his knuckles.

'*Bloody bastard!* 'Nother misfire!'

There was a muffled bang and then the early sunlight

vanished completely in a great ball of fire and dense smoke.

Fox rasped, 'Stink-pot, sir. It'll set the ship ablaze if they put one into us!'

Another bang and the hull shook violently as if it had run hard aground. The explosion was deafening, and within seconds the top of the saloon, the catwalk and even the mast flared up like torches.

'Fire party! At the double!'

Water splashed and hissed on the fires but the stink-pot had taken a firm hold. Blackwood could smell the seared paintwork, and heard flames fanning through the cabins, roaring like something alive.

Austad shouted, 'We soon reach the bend!' He stared at the damage with disbelief and anger. 'If we don't sink first!'

Another man dropped as a bullet flung him to the deck. One of Austad's crew this time. The flames licked along the deck and set the man ablaze so that he rolled and kicked while two marines tried to cover him with wet canvas.

Another fireball exploded right alongside, burning a great gash in the paddle-box before striking the river and hurling up a column of smoke and steam.

The Maxim came alive again and raked the nearest bank, back and forth like a reaper in a field. Bodies littered the ground and drifted in the shallows, but nothing stopped them. It was like a tide, Blackwood thought as he fired his revolver into a group behind some bushes, the gun kicking in his hand as if to fight him.

The smoke was thicker, pricking his eyes as it funnelled through the cabins and bridge. If they lost control now and ran into a sandbar they would be butchered without mercy. The lucky ones anyway.

'Put more men on the fires, Sergeant!' Blackwood struggled with his empty revolver then turned as Swan said calmly, 'Let me, sir.' He handed it back and wiped his face with his sleeve, leaving a black mark like a handprint.

Blackwood peered through the smoke and shouted, 'Mr Bannatyre, take charge here!' He did not wait for an answer but thrust his way into the saloon and saw flames darting through the bulkhead, consuming furniture and scattered clothing in an instant. More men followed him with slopping buckets of water, and Blackwood heard somebody screaming through the fires and guessed it was one of the stokers.

He kicked open a door and skidded to a halt as he saw the stooping figure of the countess's brother-in-law carrying a marine to safety behind some chests and upended foot lockers. He was in his shirt-sleeves and was murmuring gently to the sobbing marine who became suddenly quiet as he realized someone was trying to help. Blackwood knew that the marine did not understand a word of German, but the man's soothing voice and almost saintly countenance did more than any surgeon. Blackwood touched his shoulder as he hurried past. It was the first time since his wife had been murdered that he had heard him speak.

He blinked in smoky sunlight as he passed a big hole in the side, the edges bent inwards like wet cardboard. He saw the little Chinese maid crouching in a corner, her head in her hands, and for a moment he thought she had been killed or wounded. But she was sobbing very quietly, her small body rocking to the violent movement of the deck as the *Bajamar* swung on to a new leg of her dash downstream.

'Come along, Anna!' He seized her shoulder and pushed her to the last cabin.

The countess stared at him, her eyes wide and questioning.

Blackwood said, 'Take care of this one!' He ducked as a bullet or metal splinter came through the port and ricocheted across the cabin.

'*Down.*' He took her wrist and pulled her closer to a barricade of luggage which they had heaped against one bulkhead. She crouched beside him without protest as he tried to make her more comfortable. She put her hands over her ears as more crashes and thuds broke against the hull like fiery hammers.

'Sir! Sir! There's a boat ahead!' Swan peered in at them then swung round and fired from the hip as a figure loomed from the water right alongside. Blackwood tried to moisten his lips. God, there must only be a few inches under the keel.

He stood up and peered through the open port. The fires were under control, although he could hear demands for more water coming from aft. They had to keep the flames from reaching the sampan, or from burning the towline. The other sampan had been blasted to pieces by the stink-pots, and in any case time had run out.

She exclaimed suddenly, 'I must help! *Must* do something!' She watched him desperately, 'Dieter, my, my *vollbruder*, is out there, so please let me help him!'

Blackwood smiled. 'I'll send someone.' He heard shouts and the intermittent rattle of the machine-gun. He ran through the smoke catching stark glimpses of grim, determined faces, bolts being jerked, empty cartridge cases rattling in the scuppers to the swish and thunder of the racing paddles.

He found Bannatyre, hatless, with his revolver in his hand, standing beside two wounded marines while the rest of his party fired their rifles over the bulwark as fast as they could aim and reload. One of the wounded men, his head wrapped in a bloody bandage, was also busy reloading the discarded rifles, groaning to himself as he thrust in each new bullet.

Bannatyre looked wild. 'There, *look!*'

It was a large sampan, loaded with Chinese, and being propelled by poles from its stern, so that the men using them were concealed from the marines' rifle fire.

Someone cheered. 'It's aground! The bugger's hit the bottom!'

Fox shouted, 'Hold yer noise, damn you!'

Blackwood turned and looked at Austad's smoke-shrouded figure. The Norwegian made a chopping motion with his fist. The river was too narrow. They would have to keep going. Straight for the big sampan.

Blackwood cupped his hands. 'Stand by to repel boarders! Corporal Lyde, take your squad aft! It's the lowest point!'

The *Bajamar* was moving at full speed and yet it took an eternity to reach the other craft. The men at the poles were trying to thrust the sampan into deeper water, but she was too overloaded, and they were still shouting and screaming like fiends when the end of their boat took the full impact of the *Bajamar*'s blunt stem. Blackwood struggled with his sword hilt and dragged it from the scabbard.

'*Stand fast, Marines!*' The deck swayed over and a whole section of the Boxers' sampan reared up above the bows like something from the depths. Several of the Boxers were sucked bodily into the paddles, others were trapped in their shattered hull as it rolled along the bottom breaking up as it went. But there were many more who managed to climb over the rails unscathed, their teeth bared in unbelievable ferocity.

Blackwood waved his sword. 'At them, lads!'

The marines needed no urging now that the danger was right here, amongst them. Striding shoulder to shoulder, their boots catching and stumbling on fallen gear and ringbolts, they thrust at the Boxers with their bayonets, holding some against the guardrails, driving a few over the side into the frothing water.

Blackwood aimed his revolver as a great blade flashed in the sunshine and struck a marine on the shoulder. It was like an axe driving through a sapling. The revolver recoiled in his hand and he saw the yelling Boxer vanish amongst the gasping, stabbing figures. The marine fell and did not move, nor would he. The blade had all but severed his arm and shoulder from his body.

Bullets cracked amongst the Boxers who found themselves trapped in the narrow confines of the side-deck. Lyde and O'Neil were firing from aft with their men; they took their time to make each shot tell.

Blackwood saw a giant figure in white, his red headcloth

rising above his companions like a banner, hacking and stabbing his way through the marines. There were blood streaks over his clothing, and he must have been dying on his feet.

Kirby shouted, 'Watch out, sir!' Then he had to swing round to parry a blade aside with his bayonet before thrusting it into his attacker's chest.

The tall Boxer did not blink as he kept his eyes fastened on Blackwood. Like an enraged serpent, and making him even more terrible, he was frothing at the mouth.

Blackwood raised his revolver and levelled it on the giant's waist. He felt his heart jump as the hammer clicked on an empty chamber. He had fired every bullet without even noticing.

He saw the long blade glitter as it swung towards him, felt the pain in his wrist as he parried it aside with his sword. There was no change in the Boxer's expression nor did he falter as he pushed a marine aside to give himself space for another, final cut.

Swan darted forward and fired, Blackwood saw the Boxer stagger, the blood glinting like an eye in his shoulder. Then he fell. It was incredible. As he rolled on to his face Blackwood realized he must have been bayoneted or shot several times.

It was like a signal. Chased on by the battle-crazed marines the remaining Boxers were leaping over the bulwarks, floundering or wading in the shallows or falling to the rapid fire from aft. Blackwood dropped his arms to his sides and took several deep breaths.

He saw some of his men tipping the dead and wounded Boxers into the river, others frantically reloading in case of a fresh attack.

But when Blackwood looked at the nearest bank it was deserted. As if the running, chanting figures had been swallowed up. Bannatyre came over to him, his chest heaving as if he was in pain.

'We did it, sir!' He looked about to cheer, or weep.

Sergeant Major Fox joined them. 'Three dead, including young Elmhirst, sir. The others are Munro and Becket.'

Blackwood straightened his aching back. 'Wounded?'

Fox watched him calmly. 'Five, sir. I've 'ad 'em took below.'

Blackwood nodded and looked at the bloodstains on the deck. It was a miracle they had not lost half their number. But it was bad enough.

He tried to think more clearly, but all he could do was marvel they had survived. Behind him Swan was reloading his revolver and whistling quietly to himself. They were still together. He did not seem to need much more than that.

Bannatyre asked in a steadier tone, 'Will they come at us again?'

Blackwood stared past him at the land as it began to climb more steeply. It was not over. Perhaps it had not even begun. There was more smoke above the hill; if they had to anchor the Boxers would try to set the ship alight again with their fireballs and stink-pots.

Down aft he could see Corporal O'Neil and his squad hauling at the towline, making certain that their floating bomb was ready for immediate use. He heard a change in the paddles' beat and knew *Bajamar* was slowing down.

When he shaded his eyes to look for Austad he saw him framed against the sky, he was beckoning urgently with his telescope. Blackwood made himself walk to the bridge ladder. They were all watching him, looking for their fate in his eyes. Dirty, bloodied, ragged and red-eyed, they looked as if they had little more to give him.

He climbed swiftly up the ladder. The handrails were already hot in the sunlight. On the buckled catwalk he saw the extent of their damage, the charred deck and hatchways still smoking from the hastily flung buckets.

But they had done it. In spite of everything.

Even without the telescope he could see the boom. Supported on boats which they must have dragged from some nearby fishing village, the boom consisted of trees, long sharpened stakes of bamboo, the whole roped together from bank to bank. If they attempted to ram it they would lose control or put one of the paddles out of action.

He knew Sergeant Kirby was staring up at him from the foredeck. It was strange he had been so eager to volunteer for the job. Corporal O'Neil had also volunteered, but that made more sense. He was a superb swimmer, and just about mad enough for anything. They would have to swim upstream for about fifty yards after the *Bajamar* had dropped her stream anchor. It was unlikely either of them would survive.

He realized that Austad was staring at him, the telescope held out to him like a baton.

'Here. Look.'

Blackwood raised the glass and saw the crude barrier spring into focus, even a few figures scampering for cover as the vessel pounded towards them.

In the centre of the boom, on a pike, its empty eye-sockets watching their slow approach, was a severed head.

Blackwood handed the telescope back and allowed the hideous spectacle to fall into distance.

'Prepare to anchor. Tell Sergeant Kirby to be ready.'

There was no longer any mystery about Earle's fate. They must have been saving it for this very moment.

'Stop engine.' He felt desperately sick and knew he must not show it. Not now of all times.

'*Let go!*' He heard the anchor clatter down, the hawser just enough to hold them in midstream.

'Silence on deck!' That was Fox. As if he already knew.

It was like a tribute to their first casualty, respect for his final degradation.

8

A Bit of History

Sergeant Jeff Kirby put his shoulder to the long pole and heaved. A few feet away Corporal O'Neil lowered his rifle to watch as the sampan moved slowly away from the *Bajamar*'s bows where it had been hauled by the men on deck.

Kirby said, 'Probably the last time we see that lot, Paddy!'

O'Neil, whose name was Sean, gave a broad grin. Like the sergeant he was stripped to his white trousers and in spite of the tension appeared almost relaxed.

He grinned. 'A good swim will liven things up, eh, Sarge?'

Kirby thrust the pole into the bottom again. When he straightened his back he could see the boom across the river. The cunning bastards. At the narrowest point.

He glanced again at the anchored paddle-steamer. She already looked out of reach and he felt a twinge of panic. It was so deathly quiet after the swift battle, the feeling of hate and madness which had held them together as they had driven the enemy back into the water. He looked at his own rifle where it lay within his reach. There was dried blood on the bayonet, like black paint in the hard sunlight.

O'Neil raised his rifle and lowered it again. 'The buggers can't make us out, Sarge. There's two of 'em on that ridge, see?'

Kirby swallowed as the sweat poured down his body. The boat handled better than he had expected. Maybe there was still a chance. He winced as a sandbar swam to the surface like some sleeping fish. No, there was not a hope in hell. As Captain Blackwood had explained, if abandoned too soon the sampan might run aground or drift into the bank.

He peered at the boom again. It seemed no closer.

O'Neil was humming softly to himself and Kirby was torn between hate and envy.

He said brutally, 'You know what that bloody object is they've stuck on a pike?'

O'Neil regarded him curiously. 'To be sure. The little officer you left on his own, right?'

Kirby felt the blood pound in his veins. 'It wasn't my fault, *you know it!*'

There was a crack and a bullet hit the water several yards abeam. O'Neil lifted his rifle again and readjusted the backsight.

'Now there's a thing.' The rifle sounded twice as loud in the confines of the high banks, and O'Neil jerked open the bolt as a tiny figure rolled down the slope.

Several more shots cracked from the hillside, and from the anchored *Bajamar* came an overwhelming response. Machine-gun and rifle fire, and then one of Austad's little cannons which made the air shake. It probably sounded much more deadly than it was, Kirby thought. Why had he volunteered? To die perhaps in a blaze of glory? And now all he wanted to do was stay alive. It was so unfair.

A heavy shot burst through the side of the boat and made the canvas cover in the bows start to smoulder.

O'Neil was there in a flash and shouted, 'Must have been one o' them big muskets, Sarge!'

He snatched up his rifle and triggered two more shots as some men ran down a cleft in the hillside, firing as they came.

Kirby locked the pole in position and opened fire with his own rifle. He saw one of the bastards drop. But it gave him no satisfaction. Close-quarters, where you could see the enemy's strength or terror as you crossed blades with him, that was more like it. The rifle bucked hard into his bare shoulder and he saw another white-clad figure roll down amongst the scrub, one leg kicking for a full minute as if detached from its dead owner.

As he reloaded his magazine he glanced astern. The *Bajamar* was wreathed in smoke as every man who could pull a trigger laid down a barrage of fire across the salient.

The boom was nearer now, and more figures were thronging the nearest bank, some kneeling to shoot as the little boat drifted towards them.

Bullets slammed into and through the bulwarks, and others spurted water around the two crouching marines with barely a break. Kirby dashed the sweat from his eyes and tried to gauge the distance. He thought briefly of asking O'Neil's opinion but discarded the thought immediately. He was only a corporal and a bloody Irish one at that.

It must be now. Had to be. He felt something like a blow from an iron club and found himself on his back, his head on the bottom boards and one foot dangling from the gunwale.

'Bloody hell!' O'Neil stooped over him and stared at the blood which seemed to be pumping from Kirby's chest in an unstoppable torrent.

Kirby shut his eyes against the agony. He attempted to move but almost lost consciousness as the searing pain drove through him. He tried to speak clearly, but his voice sounded like a sob. 'Fuses! Light 'em now!' When the corporal's shadow remained over him he gasped, 'Do it, you Irish clod! Fer Christ's sake, light 'em!'

O'Neil stumbled towards the bows. He took time to fire and bring down a crouching marksman on the bank before he flung himself beside the fuses, his mind grappling with what he must do. He thought vaguely of Kirby's attempt to frighten and torment him over the severed head. It was just like him. Now he was probably dying. Like they all would unless he could blow the bloody boom. He recoiled, startled almost by the sudden spurt of life from the fuses.

Shots whined and cracked around him but he took time

to reload before struggling aft again to Kirby's sprawled body. It was probably hopeless anyway, he thought. But those fiends would never take him alive. Never.

In a steady voice he barely recognized he said, 'Right, Sarge, we're off then.'

He looked at the river and tried to shut out the sound of those two hissing fuses behind him. It would be a hard swim even without Kirby.

Kirby gasped thickly, 'You go. That's an order, damn you! Leave yer rifle. I'll take a few of the bastards with me!'

O'Neil ignored him. Instead he flung Kirby's rifle over the side and said, 'Give us yer arm. Lively then.' He waited for Kirby to hit the water and submerge, the blood trailing pink around him. Then he fired a full magazine of eight bullets and then with a kind of defiance hurled his own rifle into the river.

The water felt cool after the remorseless sunlight, and with his arm supporting the barely conscious sergeant he began to paddle slowly upstream.

The gunfire seemed to be over and around him as the marines opened rapid fire once again. Through the effort and the pain in his arm O'Neil heard the ship's siren give a loud toot as if to encourage him, to urge him on. He recalled the little pleasure steamers at Galway, on his own Ireland's west coast. Recalled too his dead father who had also been a corporal in the Corps.

'Come on, me boy!' His breath was bursting out in great gulps and once he swallowed some water. It tasted of salt and he thought of the sea. Safety. His pals around him.

Kirby had his eyes closed but knew what was happening. He tried to free himself from O'Neil's iron grip but heard him gasp, *'Together*, Sarge, or not at all!'

The explosion when it came was more of a sensation than a sound. O'Neil felt as if his whole body was being crushed and caressed at the same time as the exploding charge bowled a miniature tidal wave upstream and caught them both in a drunken dance. O'Neil could see it all in his dazed mind, and wanted to laugh, to cheer for what they had done. But his mouth was choked, and his body seemed to be filling with water.

Dying was not so terrible after all.

'Rapid fire!' The remainder of Fox's words were lost as the kneeling and prone marines took aim and squeezed their triggers, oblivious to everything but the distant white figures which were running towards the water.

Blackwood gripped a guardrail until the pain helped to steady him. Set against the land, the sluggish river with the crude boom across it like a gate, the sampan seemed puny. A pointless gesture.

Austad held the telescope to his eye and said, 'The sampan has been hit again, I think.'

Corporal Lyde was yelling, 'Train that gun to port!'

The belt began to jerk in time with the Maxim's laboured stammer and Blackwood thought of Kirby and his sudden anger over the machine-gun. Now he was up there with O'Neil in company with enough explosive to blast them to powder.

'Cease firing! Reload!' Fox strode behind his panting, sweating men. Blackwood wondered how he could do it. Fox's eyes were everywhere, and his voice never let his marines falter or give in. They were hating him, but he got the results he wanted.

Blackwood cupped his hands. 'Stand by to slip!' He saw Austad's big hand close around the telegraph handle and pictured the stokers crouching below in terrible heat, wondering when a shot would burst in amongst them or split open a boiler.

Lyde said harshly, 'One of 'em's down, sir.'

Blackwood nodded. It was obviously Kirby. Even at this distance he could see the boat sway as the other figure scrambled aft to assist him.

Fox muttered, 'Near enough.' He was speaking aloud but

to O'Neil. 'Get out while you can, dammit!'

Another said in a whisper, 'Gawd, Arthur, the mad bugger is bringing the sergeant with 'im!'

Blackwood shaded his eyes as more running figures rose like birds from cover.

'Take aim, rapid fire!'

A puff of smoke and Austad's squat cannon reared inboard on its tackles. Blackwood saw the packed charge scythe above the scrub and bushes, catching one of the Boxers and lifting him several feet in the air.

'Slip the stream anchor!' Blackwood could barely tear his eyes from the two bobbing heads in the water. He felt the deck shiver as the paddles began to churn slowly, almost gently, at the surface.

'All clear aft, sir!'

Blackwood ran to the side and leaned out to watch O'Neil's progress. Over his shoulder and in between sporadic bursts of rifle fire he shouted, 'Corporal Lyde! Warn Mr Bannatyre to stand by in the bows! It will have to be done quickly or we'll lose them in the paddles!'

There was a vivid flash from the boom, followed by a thunderclap of an explosion which seemed to push the *Bajamar* off course for just a few seconds. As a dense pall of smoke lifted and writhed across the river hundreds of fragments splashed down to throw feathers of spray from bank to bank.

Blackwood saw two of Austad's crew and Lieutenant Bannatyre leaning over the bulwark, while two half-naked marines were lowered down the rough plates on bowlines. It was touch and go. O'Neil would be protected by the hull on one side only, but bullets were still striking the rusty plating from the opposite beam.

'Second Section! Rapid fire to starboard!' Fox pushed a young marine with his boot. 'Take aim, you blockhead! Don't just blaze away!'

Austad bit hard on his pipe. 'I stop engine.' The paddles stilled as if seized by a giant's hand.

Through the din and bellowed orders Blackwood heard a wild cheer, and saw the head and shoulders of one of the marines in his bowline as he deftly made a line fast to Kirby's bloodsoaked body.

'Got both of 'em!'

Lyde grinned wildly. 'Deserve Victoria Crosses, th' pair of 'em!' He flushed. 'No disrespect, sir.'

Blackwood swung round as a great groan came from forward.

The smoke was slowly dispersing. Reluctant to go.

It was impossible. The boom was still there.

Fox snapped, 'Get those wounded men under cover.' But his eyes were on Blackwood.

Blackwood wiped his forehead with his sleeve and saw the glances. The utter despair on their faces. After all this. He felt like giving in, he had failed them.

Swan stood by his shoulder, his eyes slitted against the smoky glare.

'A bang like that, sir.' He waited for Blackwood to look at him. 'Chances are it'll 'ave weakened the thing anyway.' He ran his thumb along his rifle's backsight. 'We got nowhere else to go.'

Blackwood reached out and gripped Swan's shoulder. Swan was right. They could not retrace their course upstream. They would be hunted and ambushed at the first opportunity. The ammunition must be getting low anyway. But it was more than that. Certainly more than Swan could ever guess.

He said, 'Thank you.' He turned to Fox. 'Share out the ammunition, Sergeant Major.'

Fox understood. Only one way out. Fight or die. Probably both.

Blackwood glanced at Austad's untidy shape.

'Two minutes. Then full ahead.'

Austad grunted, his eyes fixed professionally beyond the bows, the slow drift as the paddle-wheels barely held the hull steady.

Blackwood raised the telescope and watched the little groups of figures on either bank, many of them struggling out along the boom. At least Earle's grisly remains had been hurled away.

'Nine rounds per man, sir!' That was Lyde.

It was precious little for what they were up against.

Blackwood placed the telescope on its rack by the helmsman.

'How's the sergeant?'

Lyde turned as several marines raised a cheer.

Blackwood stared as O'Neil lurched through a door and picked up one of the spare rifles. He looked dazed, drunk. He saw Blackwood and bared his teeth in a grin.

'I'll not be left out o' this, sir!'

Fox shook his head. 'Hell's bells! I don't bloody well believe it!'

Blackwood drew his revolver.

Here we go. 'Now, Captain Austad. Let us make a bit of history.'

It was soon obvious that Austad had taken Blackwood at his word. The *Bajamar* shook violently from keel to bridge, every plate and plank squeaking and protesting as the twin paddles worked up to full speed.

Blackwood stood on the port side just forward of a paddle-box and watched the boom, the pale figures which stood or crouched along it, and the occasional stab of rifle and musket fire. Someone had even hoisted a banner in the same position where Earle's head had been displayed. It was motionless, as if the air between the banks had been sucked away.

Beyond the high salient the sky was clear, and Blackwood knew that the sea would soon be in view if they managed to break through. When they hit the boom the greatest danger would be if the paddles became entangled, even for a moment. The enemy might try to board them again, and this time they would face less resistance. Nine rounds per head, and the Maxim could not train to the lowest part of *Bajamar*'s freeboard, midships to aft. Bannatyre had taken charge of the opposite side and Blackwood prayed that he would offer the example his weary men needed when the time came.

Shots hammered into the hull and superstructure or whined overhead. Blackwood saw some of the marines' rifles waver as their owners marked down enemy marksmen, and cursed the order not to retaliate.

He tried not to think of the countess as she waited behind the frail barricades with the wounded and the dying. After what she had already experienced it was a wonder she did not break down completely. At the same time he knew she had gained strength in some way. Did she still have her toylike silver pistol, he wondered, and the resolve to use it?

'Here they come!'

Blackwood thumbed back the hammer and stared at the nearest bank. Then he ducked down as the air exploded from another flaming ball hurled from the high bank, and held his breath. As the heat and stench enfolded the deck, he heard men coughing and retching, a solitary shot as one of the marines hit back without waiting for the order.

A tide of running, screaming figures had already reached the waterside and were shooting down at the churning, smoke-enshrouded *Bajamar*, their voices shrill and bonded together like a chorus from hell.

'Be ready! *Easy* there!' Blackwood needed all his strength to hold his voice level and outwardly calm. Like a trainer steadying a frightened horse.

A kneeling marine dropped his rifle and fell on his side, blood running between his fingers as he clutched at his stomach. Blackwood saw the man staring up at him, his eyes outraged and disbelieving even as another fusillade swept over the hull in a hail of splinters. When he looked again the man was dead.

The boom was sweeping towards them now, and he could identify the various figures, the reckless way they stood to fire at the oncoming steamship.

Austad was not even weaving his helm, and Blackwood saw that he had two men on the wheel, while he himself leaned against the binnacle, his long-barrelled Colt levelled towards the shore.

Blackwood watched the barrier rushing towards them and wondered briefly if anyone would ever hear about this day if the worst should happen. His parents, young Jonathan; it might even have some effect on Ralf.

'Stand by to ram!'

The telegraph jangled as Austad cut down the speed. Surely he must have served in the navy, his own country's or somebody else's. He was taking his battered command straight for the boom with all the dash of a torpedo boat destroyer.

Still the Boxers made no attempt to withdraw. Blackwood peered at one of them across the backsight of his revolver and waited for the collision. Maybe that was their only weakness. So fanatical and without fear that they could not recognize the courage of others. The impact was worse than he had expected. The bows seemed to rear right up, as if the hull had broken its back. Men were flung about like dolls, while the remnants of the charred mast plunged amongst them in pieces.

The paddles churned and frothed, forging ahead, catching and grinding at underwater fragments, now barely under control.

Blackwood saw the great pile of blackened timber and splintered fishing boats where the sampan had exploded. The whole boom was bending and lurching under the vessel's iron stem and he saw several Boxers leaping towards the bulwarks, some dropping, others clambering on to the deck to fall and die under the waiting bayonets.

'Take aim! *Fire!*' The rifles cracked out in a ragged volley, cutting down some of the nearest attackers, driving back others from the bows, each bullet aimed with care and desperation.

Blackwood shouted, 'To me, Marines!' Together they charged aft as faces appeared above the bulwark, some within inches of the thrashing paddle-blades.

Blackwood fired his revolver and then drew his sword as feet pounded on the stained planking and a knot of boarders rushed towards him. The hiss and clang of steel as sword met bayonet, the curses and yells of his men matched against the Boxers' blood-chilling screams blotted out all else. Beneath his feet Blackwood felt the deck jerking and sagging as Austad tried to hold her bows-on to the boom. But they were not forging ahead, and he heard one of the paddles grating and ripping at the piled logs like a fractured saw.

'Hold them!' Blackwood drove his blade through one of them, and heard him shriek as Swan, his magazine empty, finished him with his bayonet. But shoulder to shoulder the marines were falling back, pressed together in a tight group as more and more figures clambered over the rails, hampered only by their leaders with their glittering, deadly swords.

Lyde gasped, 'Can't-do-it, sir!' He fired point-blank into a Boxer's face and then lunged at another with his already reddened bayonet. Blackwood was dimly aware that one of the helmsmen was down, his head split open by a single blow, and that Austad, bleeding from a great slash on his cheek, was bellowing like a wild bull, his empty Colt rising and falling like a club.

A sword clattered by his feet and Swan shouted, 'Not this time, Johnnie!' Then he brought down his rifle-butt on the man's neck. His companions, wild-eyed and baring their teeth, stamped over the fallen man in their efforts to hold their advantage and hack down wounded and stragglers alike.

Blackwood felt the deck give one great lurch and saw the nearest barrier of sharpened bamboo stakes begin to fall aside. He heard some of his men cheering like demons, their strength renewed as the boom began to give way under the stem.

They were going through.

Blackwood caught a brief glimpse of a figure framed against the sun and realized he was taking aim. He felt the wind of the bullet and heard it hit the deckhouse beside him. It all took less than a second and he heard himself sob with agony as something like splinters cut into his eye, blinding him instantly. He was aware only that his men were cheering, that screams and splashes told him that most of the boarders were gone. He reeled about, his sense of position gone as the pain left him blinded and gasping. A shadow passed over his face and he heard Swan yell, 'Watch out, sir!'

Something struck him across the neck. He was barely aware that he was falling, or which way he was facing. Perhaps his head had been struck off like Earle's and there was merely a flash of understanding before the darkness came.

And yet he was conscious of a new voice rallying his victorious marines. Clipped and decisive. It was Bannatyre who had found strength through his fear. The hardest kind to discover.

He felt an arm under his shoulder, a shadow across him as the sun was extinguished. Then he seemed to be falling from a great height and tried to tense his limbs against the impact.

But instead there was oblivion.

When Blackwood eventually tried to open his eyes he found nothing but darkness. As his senses reluctantly returned he became aware that there was a cool bandage across his left eye, and that the other one pricked and smarted when he tried to focus it. The deck still swayed, but there was no feeling of movement. The paddles were stilled and for a moment more he imagined they were aground, that the enemy had somehow boarded and seized the ship.

He groped blindly for his holster but it had gone. So too had his tunic, and as his fingers moved across his ribs he felt another bandage although he could not remember being wounded there. In fact the pain in his skull was so intense he could barely think at all. And yet in spite of it his memory was returning. In his mind he could hear the fury of the battle, see the wild eyes, the flash of steel.

He made to move, but the pain held him motionless. Then he heard some empty cartridge cases rolling unheeded on the deck and knew the *Bajamar* was at anchor somewhere. He reached out gingerly and touched the bulkhead. It was cool, the heat of the day had gone. Or had it been more than one day? He felt something like despair while he strained his ears and fought to hold back the terrible throb in his head and neck.

He heard someone cry out. Just one short sound. It was close by, but separated by the bulkhead.

Blackwood moved his head on one side and tried not to catch the bandage on his eye. He was in a bunk and from the faint scent of perfume he knew it was hers.

Where the hell was Swan? He had to know what was happening. He would be needed. But when he tried to call out all he heard was a groan. There was an immediate response and he felt her come out of the darkness and sit beside him on the bunk.

'Rest easy, Captain.'

He felt her hand on his shoulder, her fingers gentle.

She said, 'We are safe. Thanks to you.' Her fingers reached the scar on his shoulder, the one he hated so much. They rested there, soothing him, holding him like someone under a spell.

'My – my men . . .'

The fingers did not move and he could sense that she was sharing his pain.

'Ten wounded.' Again the slight hesitation. 'Five dead.'

'God.' He lay back and peered at the darkness. 'My eyes.'

'You were fortunate. But you must rest.'

Her hand caressed the scar as if she was thinking of something else. Even her voice seemed far away.

'Did you take care of me?'

'Of course. I think your Mr Fox was unwilling to let me attend all the wounded.' He felt her give a little shrug. 'Besides, I wanted to.'

'But – but . . .' He could not form his words. She had undressed him. Washed and tended his injuries.

She said in the same quiet tone, 'Do not worry so much. Would you prefer that I stayed away? Hidden out of danger while you fought for me and nearly died because of it? Is that what you wanted?'

'You know it's not that.' She had stayed with him. Watched over him.

Blackwood struggled on to his elbow, aware of her closeness in spite of the pain, the turmoil in his mind.

'I have to get up. Must, go to them – ' He tried again. 'Could you send someone for Swan, please?' He knew he was pleading, but he had to make her understand.

But she did not argue and Blackwood heard her speaking quietly to her maid outside the door.

She returned and said, 'Close your eyes. I am going to light a lamp.' She stood between him and the small lamp and watched him without speaking as he opened his sound eye and blinked at the cabin. He could see shot and splinter holes in the side, and there were spots of blood on her clothes, his own or one of the wounded's, he did not know.

He peered down at his nakedness. 'Must look a mess.' It was all he could find to say.

Swan entered the cabin, his eyes moving swiftly between them, questioning and understanding.

'Sir?'

'I need to get up.'

Swan regarded him doubtfully. 'You took a real whack on the neck with a pike-'andle, sir. If it 'ad bin a blade – ' He did not finish.

She said, 'If you must, Captain.' She took his tunic from a chair and gently eased one of his arms into it. 'Now the other one.' He winced as the pain shot through him again, but he was very aware of her hair against his face, her breath on his skin.

'Now.' She looked at him gravely. 'Off we go.'

With Swan on one side and the countess on the other Blackwood staggered towards the door.

He gasped, 'Swan, boots and belt.'

Swan sighed. The captain would kill himself if he went on like this, but he knew he would never change, nor would he want him to.

She buttoned his tunic, her eyes averted from his as she said, 'Let me come.'

Swan thrust the door aside and clinging together they moved very slowly towards the saloon. There were several shaded lamps burning here, and the smell of blood and pain.

Those who were not asleep or too faint to care turned towards the trio in the entrance, their eyes flickering in the lamplight.

Blackwood saw it all. Pride, hostility perhaps towards her for throwing them at risk, and something more. They had survived. The victors.

Blackwood moved painfully along the saloon and felt her hand on his back. Somehow his tunic had caught on his belt and he could feel her fingers pressed into his skin like small extensions of her own emotion.

Fox loomed out of the shadows. 'You shouldn't be 'ere, sir.' But from his tone Blackwood knew he had done the right thing.

He paused and looked down at Sergeant Kirby. Even in the poor light he looked old and pale.

Fox said shortly, ''E'll live if we can get 'im to a surgeon in time.' He looked at the countess. 'She done wonders with 'im, sir.' He gave a rare smile. 'With you too, if you don't mind me sayin' so.'

Blackwood felt her fingers biting into his skin as a man cried out and another marine knelt down beside him with a water flask. He knew that some of the sentries were peering through the ports to see what was happening, and could smell the strong aroma of Austad's tobacco. He was glad the Norwegian had survived.

Blackwood said, 'I just want to tell you − ' He hesitated and looked at the deck. Tell them what? They knew well enough what they had achieved. What it had cost them. And this was just a beginning. He tried again. 'I am proud of all of you, grateful that I was given the honour to be with you.' He felt emotion in his unbandaged eye as he remembered the dying marine who had stared up at him. *Why me?* his eyes had asked. Of Corporal O'Neil who had staggered on deck again to fight in spite of everything. Not least of Kirby, so bitter, and yet too much of a marine not to volunteer. Of them all.

'Soon we shall be back aboard ship to await orders. Some of us will be parted.' Her hand stopped moving and lay flat on his spine. As if it, and not she, was listening to the meaning of his words.

Blackwood lifted his chin as he had seen his father do so many times when he had relived one of his experiences aboard ship or in some godforsaken battlefield. How right was the Corps's motto, he thought. *Per Mare, Per Terram.* Do anything, go anywhere. You were never supposed to ask questions.

'And some will never return.' He swayed and might have fallen but for Swan's powerful grip. 'But we shall not forget them. It is not our way.'

He turned with his supports to the door and saw Lieutenant Bannatyre smiling at him, his arms folded as if he hadn't a care in the world.

A voice came from the darkness, 'Good old Blackie, eh lads!' It had to be O'Neil. Nothing could disguise that brogue.

Outside the saloon the three of them stood by the

guardrails and stared abeam. There was no moon, and it was too dark to see how far out Austad had decided to anchor. But Blackwood could smell the land, and feel the power of the swell under the old keel which had somehow carried them to safety.

She said, 'You love those men, don't you?'

He looked at her and then slowly raised his arm around her shoulder. 'I'd never thought of it like that. I just did not know what to say. How to explain.'

He felt her shiver and her fingers bunch tightly against his back. He knew she was crying. Perhaps for all of them.

They returned to the cabin in silence, the ship rolling and creaking around them as if in a restless sleep after her moment of glory. Swan sat him on the bunk, removed his boots but stood aside as she said, 'Thank you, Herr Swan. I can do what is necessary.'

The door closed and Blackwood allowed her to remove his tunic and cradle his shoulders as he lay back on the bunk.

'You sleep now.' She watched him sadly, her cheek marked with tears. 'Tomorrow, who knows?'

He reached out and took her hand. 'I wish – ' Her hand moved in his grasp. In a moment she would pull away.

He persisted, 'If only – '

She grasped his hand in hers and without taking her gaze from his face pressed it beneath her breast and held it there.

'Do you think, my dear David, I am made of ice? That is my heart you can feel.'

He felt her breast against his fingers, the pressure as she leaned over him and kissed him. Not as a countess, but as a young girl.

She stood up, her face flushed, her calm momentarily gone. She said quietly, '*If only*, you said. What words, David. What might have been.'

She reached out suddenly and extinguished the lamp. 'I shall be near if you need me.' Then the door closed behind her.

He stared at the darkness again. She had called him by

name. Even the pain seemed less, the sting in his eyes of no importance. He thought of the way she had looked, the pressure of her breast against his hand.

He was still thinking of her when complete exhaustion carried him into a deep sleep.

9

Divided Loyalty

Captain Vere Masterman watched impassively as *Mediator*'s surgeon completed his examination. Only the fingers of his left hand which plucked at his white drill uniform gave any hint of his impatience and mounting irritation.

Eventually he could stand it no longer.

'Well, Doc, what's the verdict?'

The surgeon straightened his back and wound his hands together as if he was washing them.

'The eyes are excellent, sir. The blow on his head might be described as a serious concussion. There could be some trouble from it unless Captain Blackwood is allowed to rest, or at least undertake light duties.'

Blackwood sat on the edge of the bunk and controlled the desire to laugh. They were discussing him as if he were somewhere else, or did not really exist. Through the door of the sickbay he could see the gently swaying cots, everything spotless, glaring white.

He recalled his return to the *Mediator*, the unreality of it, the tremendous relief hitting him for the first time when he realized he had never expected to see the cruiser again. The poor little *Bajamar* had only just managed it. Even with Austad's skill, his threats and his pleas, they had still had to burn everything movable to get them here to Taku. It had been dusk and the evening air had been torn apart by the wild cheering which had greeted the listing paddle-steamer's arrival.

Now in the cool, ordered world of *Mediator*'s sickbay it

was impossible to accept what they had done. Even the anchorage was a surprise. He had expected to see *Mediator*'s sleek outline, perhaps even a few support ships, but instead there seemed to be a whole fleet. Not just British either. German, Russian, Japanese and American, the vessels ranged from ponderous battleships to low, black-hulled torpedo boat destroyers.

Blackwood touched his head and felt both pairs of eyes turn towards him. If he was not careful he might be sent home to England. He thought of the past few days as the *Bajamar* had puffed and pounded her way north and around the Shantung Peninsula and into the vast Gulf of Chihli, to here off the Peiho River. Friedrike had rarely left his side. She had bathed his injured eye, changed his bandages, and refused to permit even Swan to take care of him. Now it was over and she was somewhere across the anchorage in the German cruiser which had been promised by the official called Westphal in Shanghai. He sighed. A million years ago.

The door slid shut and Masterman said abruptly, 'He's like an old woman.' He smiled, and Blackwood guessed that he probably knew that the surgeon was still listening outside the door. Masterman added, 'I am very glad to have you back aboard, although for how long – '

Blackwood struggled into his white tunic. 'I'm feeling much better, sir.'

Masterman continued wryly, 'I would not release you anyway. We are going to need experienced officers more than ever.' He sounded angry. 'I hate politicians. They seem to believe that a show of force is all that is needed to quell this uprising.' He snorted. 'Uprising? We'll have a full-scale bloody war on our hands if we're not careful!'

Blackwood stood up and glanced through the gleaming scuttle. Concussion, the surgeon had said. He could certainly feel the ache. Like blood pounding. He would have to be careful. He had known of a young lieutenant who had never recovered from a blow on the head. It had made him forgetful, only half aware of what was happening.

'What is the position, sir?'

Masterman shrugged. 'We and our allies have sent more troops by rail to Peking to protect the legations. They are getting very little aid from the Chinese government. Only these damned Boxers seem to have any power. Several outlying missions have been attacked, clergymen and nuns brutally treated. It must be stopped.' He studied Blackwood's grave features. 'It will be stopped. By the way, your new commanding officer has joined us. That chap Blair from Hong Kong.'

'Major Blair?'

Masterman was already thinking of something else. 'Lieutenant Colonel Blair now. That gives you some idea of the urgency. Damned politicians!'

There was a nervous tap at the door and a small midshipman peered at his captain with something like terror.

'Well, boy?' Masterman glared down at him from his great height.

'Th-the Commander sends his respects, sir, and would you repair on board the *Centurion*.'

'Hmm. Call away the pinnace.'

Blackwood pricked up his ears. *Centurion* was a battleship. It was that important.

Masterman saw his expression and nodded. 'Our lord and master, Sir Edward Seymour, is come amongst us.' He snorted again. 'Any captain worth his salt should be able to manage this affair.' Surprisingly he laughed. 'Of course, I won't take that view when *I'm* an admiral, eh?'

Muffled by steel and distance Blackwood heard a boatswain's mate bellow, 'Afternoon watchmen and relief boats' crews to dinner!'

A new anchorage, the very real chance of a war, but nothing changed the Royal Navy.

Masterman said over his shoulder, 'You may return to general duties as far as I'm concerned.' He looked round and added, 'Sorry you had to go through all that other business. You lost some good fellows by all accounts.'

It was the nearest Masterman would ever get to actual praise.

Swan flitted through the door within seconds of the captain's departure. 'I've got your cabin all sorted out, sir.' He bustled about, picking up odd garments and Blackwood's field-service cap, his eyes everywhere. 'You 'eard about 'Tenant Colonel Blair, sir?'

'Yes.' It would be good to see him again, although how Blair would like this sort of situation was something else. 'I'll report to him right away.'

Swan watched him rise to his feet, the way he waited to accustom himself to the gentle roll. This was more like it, he thought.

Swan replied, 'I'm afraid 'e's gone over to *Centurion* too, sir. All captains and senior officers from other ships to repair on board.'

Swan thought of the excitement their return had caused. Slaps on the back, more grog than any man could carry, and the whole ship was still buzzing with what they had done upriver. The German countess put just the right touch to the story, he thought. The beautiful woman in distress, rescued by the gallant Royals. It would read well if it ever reached the papers in Portsmouth.

She was probably over there with Admiral Seymour. Even that made him chuckle. He would never show disrespect for an officer in front of Captain Blackwood, not a senior one anyway, but he knew that right through fleet Admiral Seymour was nicknamed 'See-no-More'.

Blackwood walked slowly through the sickbay, glancing at the various faces as he passed. Most of them were sailors of the ship's company but in the end cots he found familiar ones, some of his own marines who were recovering from their injuries. He paused by one.

'Hello, Erskine, how are you feeling?' God, he thought, he looked such a boy, it was impossible to see him with rifle and fixed bayonet when they had rammed the boom across the Hoshun. He had been badly wounded in the foot and Swan had brought him the news that *Mediator*'s surgeon had amputated it to save his life. Private Erskine peered at him seemingly without recognition. He was drugged but probably still in great pain.

Then he shaded his eyes and said, 'Why did 'e do it, sir?'

Swan tried to move him away but Blackwood was bending over the boy as he whispered, 'I'd rather be dead than like this. I'll be like them others we used to see hangin' around the gates at Forton Barracks.' He turned his face away and said, 'I – I'm sorry, sir, it worn't your fault.' He was sobbing uncontrollably.

Blackwood looked at the other. Sergeant Kirby, pale and tight-lipped, refusing to die. Private Farley who had been the first to be cut down. Now he was trying to play cards with an injured seaman, his arm in a sling. But he was over the worst. He would soon be back with his pals, cursing Fox, and chasing the girls ashore.

Blackwood knew all about Erskine. His father had been in the Corps, but had been drowned seven years ago when his ship the *Victoria* had been accidentally rammed and sunk by the *Camperdown* while on manoeuvres in the Mediterranean. Not only Erskine's father had been killed that day. *Victoria* had been the flagship of Vice-Admiral Sir George Tryon. The admiral and over three hundred others had died because of a stupid miscalculation.

Erskine was the last Royal Marine in the family. Now he was a cripple for the rest of his life.

Why did he do it? he had asked. There was no answer. Men had been asking the same question since the Battle of Hastings.

He touched the boy's shoulder. 'I'll do what I can.'

Swan followed his captain and wondered why he always became so caught up with their affairs. It was the job. You always thought it couldn't happen to you anyway. He shrugged. But if it did, that was it.

Instead of going to the privacy of his cabin Blackwood went on deck, almost blinded by the sun despite the taut awnings above the after guns.

It was more like a fleet review than a preparation for war. He recognized several of the ships at anchor. Like the Corps the Navy was also a family. Ships came and went, old and new, happy ones and those which bred trouble like fever.

'You are looking so much better, sir.'

Blackwood turned and responded to his cousin's salute. Ralf looked wary, as if he expected to be criticized. To Blackwood he was one of the vague faces who had come and gone to visit him in the sick-quarters. The passage to Taku in the little paddle-steamer, to say nothing of the battle, had taken more out of him than he had realized. Even as he returned Ralf's salute he felt the sore tightness across his ribs. The wound he had not even felt in the heat of the fighting. Ralf looked pale. Perhaps he was the sort who never got sunburned.

'It's good to be back.' Was it? He remembered her replacing that dressing within hours of their arrival here. Her hands had been cool against his skin, her eyes downcast to avoid his gaze. He had watched his own hand as if it had belonged to someone else. A stranger. He had touched her shoulder, and as she had worked deftly with the bandage she had bent her head to rest her cheek on his wrist, still without looking at him.

Blackwood had heard some of the *Bajamar*'s crew shouting. They had sighted smoke. Help was close. It would soon all be finished.

Blackwood had raised her chin and had said, 'I love you, Friedrike. You know that — '

She had tried to smile. 'I adore your funny accent. The way you speak my name.' But instead of a smile only tears had come. They hugged each other, murmuring words that neither heard, holding, then touching with a boldness made from desperation.

She had forced herself away, her breasts rising and

falling, her eyes wanting him and yet holding him away.

'Please, David! Please help me! You know I cannot, *must* not!'

He had climbed from the bunk, the dangling bandage forgotten. 'And I love the way you say *my* name.' They had clung together, and she had kissed him again and again while his hand held her breast.

Blackwood looked past his cousin, the ache disturbing him as he knew it would.

'And I was terribly sorry to hear about Charles Earle.' Ralf was almost pleading. 'It should have been me.'

Blackwood smiled. 'It should not have been anyone.' He thought of the young marine with only one foot. 'Have you settled in now?' He almost said 'at last'.

Ralf shrugged easily, glad to be on safer ground.

'They're not a bad crowd. Some of them thought you weren't going to get back. I soon told them to mind their manners!'

A midshipman, the same one who had faced his captain, shouted to the officer-of-the-day, 'Boat coming from the German cruiser, sir! From SMS *Flensburg*, heading this way, sir!'

The lieutenant, who had been melting in the heat and thinking only of a drink before lunch, gripped his sword and snapped, 'Yes, there was a signal about it. Some important German count is coming to pay his respects or something.' He saw Blackwood and added in a calmer voice, 'Inform the Commander, Mr Lacy, and man the side.' He raised his telescope and then exclaimed loudly, 'And clear those idlers off the upper deck! The countess is aboard!'

Blackwood stared at the smart steam pinnace which was pushing up a moustache of foam as it swung in an arc towards the main gangway. He saw the familiar white ensign with its black cross and eagle streaming from the stern, but his eyes fixed on her, holding the brim of her wide hat as she stared up at the anchored cruiser.

Marines were falling into ranks by the gangway, with

Lieutenant de Courcy and Sergeant Greenaway of the Third Platoon making certain that everything was as it should be to receive foreigners.

Swan said quietly, 'I think you should go below an' change, sir.' He saw the curious glance from the second lieutenant. A snotty little bugger, Blackwood or not, Swan decided. It was like talking to a stone wall. His captain did not even hear him.

De Courcy drew his sword with a flourish. 'Royal Marines – '

Blackwood saw them tense, their white gloves gripping their rifles. A few paces inboard from the ship's brass nameplate Commander Wilberforce tipped his hat over his eyes, and dabbed his mouth with the back of his hand.

'Present – *arms!*'

Count Manfred von Heiser stood with his hat in his hand as the small marine band crashed out their version of 'Deutschland über Alles', while the guard of honour, bayonets at the present, and eyes fixed on some far-off point, waited for the din to cease.

Commander Wilberforce said, 'You do us a great honour, Count von Heiser. I regret that the Captain is aboard the flagship and he sends his apology.' He bowed slightly. 'We have of course had the additional honour of carrying the Countess as a passenger.'

The count was a big man, tall and straight-backed like Masterman. It was not difficult to picture him in uniform before he became a respected diplomat.

Blackwood watched and then heard the count reply. He had a deep voice, clear and not at all guttural. Powerful, like the man.

'We all have our duties, Commander. Now, perhaps more than ever.'

Blackwood saw her move slightly away from her husband so that he might see her. Beside him she looked like a very young girl playing a role. She had told Blackwood her husband was forty. He looked a lot older.

Blackwood tried not to think of him holding her, caressing her, wanting an heir. And he could tell from her eyes that she knew it was what he would be thinking.

'I cannot begin to thank you for all you have done, Commander. When I heard what had happened I believed that nothing could save the Countess. I will not waste your time or mine by making speeches. The purpose of my visit is to meet the officer responsible if that is possible?'

Blackwood saw the pain on her face. Perhaps he had brought her here to prove that nothing could ever alter.

'Of course, Count von Heiser.' Wilberforce glanced at a lieutenant and snapped his gloved fingers. 'My compliments to Captain Blackwood, and – '

Blackwood stepped forward and moved hesitatingly towards them. Several tiny images flashed across his mind. Lieutenant de Courcy's eyes filled with horror at the sight of his company commander, hatless and without his proper uniform. Sergeant Greenaway, sucking in his cheeks, but still able to remain motionless beside his men, and as for Wilberforce he seemed to have lost his usual urbane calm.

'So *this* is the man.' Von Heiser gripped his hand, his deep-set eyes exploring Blackwood's face as he continued, 'Blackwood. Victoria Cross. Now I understand.'

He stood aside as she held up her hand to Blackwood. She touched his so lightly with her gloved fingers he could barely feel it.

Blackwood kissed it and it was instantly withdrawn.

Wilberforce said rather too loudly, 'Well, now, we can go aft and take some sherry perhaps.'

Blackwood followed the others like a man in a trance. It would have been better never to see her again. Even as he watched her shoulders as she walked into the shadows of the quartermaster's lobby, he knew it was a lie.

They stood around in Masterman's day cabin like unrehearsed actors. The count's presence amongst them had brought an unnatural stiffness which only made things harder. As the stewards moved around with their trays of sherry Blackwood guessed that the other officers present already had a good idea of what was happening. *Mediator's* own major of marines was here, two or three of the ship's lieutenants and a German officer who had accompanied Von Heiser as his escort.

Von Heiser studied Blackwood and raised his glass in salute. In his powerful hand it looked like a thimble.

'It was pointless to maintain the Hoshun trade mission. The river is too shallow for anything but local craft, and the roads are little better than goat-tracks.' He glanced at his wife. 'So if the Boxers intended to put pressure on my government by capturing the Countess as a hostage it was all to no purpose. Naturally I regret that her sister died in such terrible circumstances.'

It sounded like a carefully prepared speech, Blackwood thought, no matter what the count had said earlier.

He asked, 'What will you do now, sir?' He felt her watching him. It was all he could manage not to return her gaze.

'Proceed as arranged.' Von Heiser sounded mildly surprised at the question. 'Tomorrow we shall start our journey to Peking. By river to begin with, and then by train. The railway is quite safe, and I am assured by Baron von Ketteler in our Peking legation that more soldiers and marines are arriving to protect them. So you see, Captain Blackwood, there is nothing to fear.'

Blackwood stared at him. He knew from the sudden silence that the others were listening.

'I cannot agree, sir. The Boxers are united against all foreigners. There have been several confirmed reports of – '

Von Heiser smiled gently. 'You are a brave man. But you must leave diplomacy to others more experienced.'

The German officer glanced at the bulkhead clock and murmured something across Von Heiser's shoulder.

The count nodded. 'I must leave now.' He turned away to speak with Wilberforce and Blackwood whispered, 'You must not go with him! It is terribly dangerous.'

She flushed. 'Would you have me run away? I have possessions in Peking, and there are also those of my dead sister – ' She faltered and he saw her lip tremble. Although her husband had his back towards them he could sense that he was listening.

Blackwood exclaimed bitterly, 'It is wrong. A new uprising could sweep China from end to end. I may not be a diplomat, but I have seen good men die because of *their* complacency!'

Wilberforce shot him a warning glance but Blackwood could not stop. His head was aching badly, and he knew that he was saying all the wrong things.

She said insistently, 'I have to go, Captain.'

Blackwood could feel the gulf opening between them. What a fool he had been. She at least had tried to warn him. Now the moment was past.

They filed from the cabin, and *Mediator*'s gunnery officer glanced at his watch. 'Time to eat, thank God.' To Blackwood he whispered, 'Steady on, Soldier. It's not worth it.'

Blackwood swung away, blind to everything but his sense of loss. 'What the bloody hell d'you know about it!'

The gunnery officer watched him leave and then said to his companion, 'Well, well. More to him than meets the eye.'

On deck Blackwood stood in the shadows as the pinnace steamed away towards the German cruiser.

Wilberforce strode past and muttered, 'You can thank your lucky stars that I was here and not the Old Man. He'd have roasted you alive!' He paused and looked abeam at the fast-moving boat. 'All the same, I can't say I blame you.'

Swan appeared as if by magic.

God, the captain was taking it bad. Worse than he had ever seen before. Swan waited, gauging the moment. Then as Blackwood turned towards a companionway he said, 'I got somethin' for you, sir.' He held out a small velvet pouch no bigger than a badge. Blackwood opened it and then held the locket in his hand. It contained a perfect miniature of Friedrike, even the hair was exactly as it had been just now in the cabin.

Swan said nothing. It was not the right time. But Swan knew that the locket must have cost a fortune. It was not the kind of thing you handed out as a souvenir.

Blackwood replaced the locket in its velvet pouch and put it carefully in his pocket.

It was not over after all.

Lieutenant Colonel James Blair ran his eyes over a list of names and duties and remarked, 'You've done a good piece of work with your new company, David.' He glanced up from his desk and asked, 'Something wrong, old chap?'

Blackwood tore his eyes from the anchorage and the motionless warships which rested on their reflections like models. In spite of the deckhead fans he could feel the sweltering heat, the sense of apprehension in the ships as they and their companies waited, and waited.

It was a week since the Germans had left for Peking. They had been well supported by troops from several nations and a signal had been received that everyone had arrived safely and unmolested. It had all been too easy.

He replied, 'I wish we could be doing something, sir, and not just swinging round the anchor day after day.'

Blair said, 'It was bad luck about young Earle.' He did not seem to hear what Blackwood had said. As if half of his mind was elsewhere. 'Your Sergeant Kirby must be a strong character. The surgeon tells me he'll be able to walk before much longer.'

Blackwood looked away. In a way it was a miracle. The heavy, old-fashioned bullet which had smashed Kirby down had been deflected by the sampan's gunwale. But for that he would be back there still.

It was maddening the way that the ships were kept in the dark about the true situation ashore. It was said that the various legations, and especially Sir Claude MacDonald, the British minister in Peking, had tried to parley with the Chinese official government without success. But that was all they knew. One ominous note had been the arrival on board *Mediator* of several crates of the new long Lee-Enfield rifles for the marines, and some Nordenfeldt machine guns mounted on wheeled carriages which could only be used ashore.

It was evident that the Boxers were daily getting bolder. Masterman had received some news of a massacre of some seventy Chinese Christians only sixty miles from Peking itself and several savage attacks on foreign properties along the railway line, the last link with the capital.

As if from miles away Blackwood heard Fox drilling a detachment with their newly issued Lee-Enfields. It was a sign that perhaps at long last they were catching up with the army. It was always said by old Royal Marines that the Corps was five years behind the regular army in almost everything from weapons to uniforms. Maybe the necessity of the moment was about to speed the changes.

There was a polite tap at the door and Lieutenant Gravatt, the acting adjutant, stepped into the cabin and handed a piece of paper to the colonel.

Blair read the message slowly. Then he said, 'The Boxers have struck at Peking. They've burned the Racecourse down and sacked all the buildings around it. Our minister, Sir Claude MacDonald, has requested that a strong force of Marines and Bluejackets be sent immediately as reinforcements for the legations.' He looked up sharply. 'When did this signal arrive, Toby?'

'Yesterday, sir.'

'And nothing since?'

Gravatt glanced at Blackwood. 'The telegraph line from Peking has been cut. They're completely on their own.'

Blackwood bit his lip. It was worse even than he had expected.

Blair smoothed out the signal pad, his voice far away as

he said, 'Admiral Seymour will have to send a relief column right away. It'll be very difficult especially if the Boxers have torn up the railway.'

A seaman stood in the open doorway. 'Cap'n Masterman sends 'is compliments, sir. All senior officers to repair on board th' flagship immediately.'

Blair touched his neat moustache with one knuckle.

'It's started, David.' He groped for his cap. 'The bloody fools. They should have listened. Now it will be strength to meet strength. If only they'd *listened!*'

Blackwood wondered momentarily whom he meant by 'they'. The Chinese or the foreigners in their land? He remembered what they had said about Blair's Chinese mistress in Hong Kong and guessed the answer.

They left the small office and walked out into the passageway where some barefooted seamen were polishing the brass handrails.

Blackwood reached up unconsciously and touched the blue ribbon on his chest and remembered the way she had spoken of him to Masterman. How she had demanded his escort upriver.

Was there no end of it for her? He recalled her husband's stern features, the adamant way he had stated his reasons for returning to Peking. Blackwood clenched his fist. Well, he had been wrong about that too, and had put Friedrike directly into the line of fire.

Sergeant Major Fox brought the sweating marines to attention as they walked past to the main gangway. He watched Blackwood's face and understood. He did not need telling. These new rifles had come along at just the right moment.

Later, when the senior officers of the various ships and detachments were assembled in the flagship's spacious wardroom, Admiral Sir Edward Seymour came straight to the point.

'I have received an urgent request from our minister in Peking for us to advance on Peking with reinforcements.'

He was a mildly spoken man with a neat beard who appeared to be completely untroubled by the swift change of events.

The admiral continued, 'I intend to leave for Tientsin tomorrow at dawn and secure several special trains for a force of Royal Marines and Bluejackets. Certain other nations are sending their own support. Overall it will consist of some two thousand men. We shall be in Peking by the end of the day.'

Blackwood darted a quick glance at Blair but the colonel still had the same distant look. Surely Seymour's casual reference was a mistake? It was a hundred miles from Tientsin to Peking through country which was known to be patrolled by parties of Boxers who might even have torn up some of the railway track.

Blackwood had also heard that the Chinese Imperial Army was somewhere between Peking and the sea. When the cards were down it was likely that their general would throw in his hand with the Boxers, especially if he wished to retain the Dowager Empress's favour. She was openly opposed to any further negotiations with the foreigners and although some of her governors were against her alliance she remained firm.

'That is all, gentlemen.' The admiral gave a bleak smile. 'The Royal Marines will be the first to land. As usual.' That brought a few laughs as he had known it would.

Chairs scraped, aides picked up their maps and notebooks and they flowed out into the waiting sunshine to look for their boats.

Blackwood said, 'It's a very tall order, sir.'

Blair shrugged. 'We shall soon know, old chap. *We* are to lead.' He studied Blackwood for the first time since they had boarded the flagship.

'I seem to recall that when you were in Hong Kong you told me that this appointment meant little more than wiping carriage seats for the ladies of our legation, what? It's turning out to be somewhat more complicated, I'd have thought!' He laughed and looked about ten years younger.

Together they joined Captain Masterman by the gangway as the *Mediator*'s boat hooked on to receive them.

Masterman said almost to himself, 'Peking tomorrow, Colonel? That will be *the* day!'

10

No Pity

David Blackwood with Lieutenant Gravatt beside him walked slowly along the side of the railway track. It was a strange sensation, he thought, almost like a school outing. Gone was the apprehension and uncertainty. They had come ashore, ready if ordered to fight, but instead to find something of an anti-climax.

All the way to Tientsin the Royal Marines and Bluejackets had kept good marching distances between each unit, but most of the villages had appeared abandoned, some even derelict, and in the outskirts of the old city itself there had been more Chinese troops in evidence than civilians. Perhaps Von Heiser had been right to scoff at his concern after all.

The railway station to which his special detachment had marched was deserted but for a solitary train. It consisted of a squat, powerful-looking engine, which Private Kempster was quick to point out had been built in his home-town of Leeds.

The engine was to be preceded by a flat car protected by boiler plates, sandbags and heavy timber. This leading car carried a Nordenfeldt machine-gun and Blackwood saw Corporal O'Neil grin down at him as if it was a huge joke. He showed no sign of his ordeal whatsoever. Blackwood recalled his shout, *Good old Blackie.* He had never considered that he had a nickname, even such a mild one.

Gravatt said, 'I've detailed a section of marines for that truck, sir. It'll be a bit unhealthy if we get ambushed.' He dropped his eyes and flushed. 'I – I'm sorry, sir. I forgot.'

Blackwood shook his head. 'Not your fault.' The train's crude defences were typical of those used in Egypt and South Africa. Like the ones Neil had mentioned in his last letter.

Blackwood lifted his chin and walked further along the train. The driver and fireman were obviously Irish. O'Neil would feel quite at-home in the vanguard of their advance.

The coaches behind the engine were for the rest of the detachment, some Bluejackets who would handle the two light field-pieces, and lastly another freight car with rails, ties and tools for making repairs to any damaged sections of the track. The rest of the company waited in the shadow of a sloping roof beside the train, leaning on their rifles, chatting and passing the time with some German sailors from the *Flensburg* who would be taking another train later on.

Blackwood touched his forehead and knew it was irritation which had roused his concussion again.

In spite of everything that had happened Seymour's flag-lieutenant had passed a message to Blair about the state and presentation of this company. 'They are amongst the forces of other foreign governments. The Royal Marines, no matter what might lie ahead, have to be properly turned out in their scarlet kerseys and blue trousers instead of their already crumpled whites.'

Blair had listened to Blackwood's protests and had agreed that as his detachment was to lead he must retain the choice. White uniforms could be boiled in tea if necessary. They had soon discovered that trick when fighting the Boers. Scarlet made a perfect target.

Seymour had apparently accepted this but had snapped back through his aide that the marines would take their proper uniforms with them anyway, so that when they marched through the gates of Peking there could not be a word of criticism aimed at them or their commander.

It was ridiculous, Blackwood thought. Like Seymour's

insistence that the trip would be over by nightfall. For the same reason he had ordered that only three days' rations would be carried.

As Fox had hinted darkly, ''E must 'ave better information than us, sir.'

It had been almost sad to leave the *Mediator*. Masterman's company had made all the extra marines welcome and comfortable in spite of the overcrowding between deck.

As they had been ferried ashore Austad's little *Bajamar* had given a final salute on her siren. She was returning to safer waters and her old habits, but Blackwood doubted if things would ever seem quite the same again for the big Norwegian and his crew.

On the way across the blue water Blackwood had watched the crouching forts which protected the entrance to the Peiho River. Through his powerful binoculars, a present from his mother before he had left England, Blackwood had studied the forts with great care. It was hard to tell where the Taku forts ended and the land began. Ageless. But they could hold back an armada if they fell into the wrong hands.

'Colonel's coming, sir.'

That was Swan, always close by when you needed him. He had already been aboard the train and had doubtless selected a place in the leading compartment for Blackwood and his capacious bag in which he usually carried some whisky for emergencies.

Blair returned their salutes and regarded the train without much enthusiasm.

'Some bloody command, eh?'

Blackwood stared. 'Are you coming with us, sir?'

'Well of course I am, dammit!' He glared along the track towards the sea as if he expected to recognize the admiral amongst the milling troops and sailors.

'I'd not leave it to these – ' he sought for a suitable word, ' – bloody amateurs!'

Blackwood smiled. 'I've brought the two student interpreters we found at the mission, sir. They might try to run, but they'd be invaluable if we meet with an argument.'

Blair nodded. 'Good thinking. Tell them – ' He gave a sad smile. 'No, I shall tell them, that one goes up the front and the other remains in the last carriage with our men. One sign of treachery and I'll blow their heads off! Not that they'll believe it of course.'

He was about to turn away when he added, 'I've detailed Second Lieutenant Blackwood to act as my aide, right? I'll try and keep him out of trouble.'

A runner panted along the track and saluted.

'Signal, sir. Time to move off!'

Blair looked at the engine, shrouded in steam, as if it too was eager to leave.

'Better get them mounted, or whatever you do in a bloody train!' He was desperately worried. You could feel it like a fever.

Blackwood waved to the sergeant major. 'First Platoon!'

Three days' rations, Seymour had decided. It did not seem much. Even when they got to Peking they might find supplies very short. But he would see her again. No matter what she thought, or which way her loyalty directed her, she would know he was there, within call. He found himself smiling as he thought of Hawks Hill, of what his father would say about his lovesick behaviour.

A lot of damned nonsense. A woman is just a woman, boy. Leave it at that. No wonder his mother had aged so noticeably.

It would be high-summer now. The smell of fields and hedgerows, good earth and farmyards. Hampshire.

Blackwood saw Swan swing himself easily into the first compartment, his new rifle already an extension of himself. Did he ever think of home, of the Hampshire they both knew so well?

'Second Platoon?' Fox marched beside the train, his stick at right-angles beneath his arm. He would be missing Sergeant Kirby. They lived only a street apart before they had enlisted. And what of Kirby, still in pain in *Mediator*'s sickbay, but far worse off now that his world had deserted him. Fox paused as someone spoke from one of the windows. It was Private Kempster, telling him about the locomotive.

Fox snarled, '*Leeds?* I thought you all lived in bleedin' caves up there! Now pull yer 'ead inside, man, or they'll be thinkin' it's a cattle truck!'

Ralf Blackwood said quietly, 'I'm glad I'm coming this time, sir.'

Blackwood looked at him and wanted more than anything in the world to like him. Especially now that Neil had gone.

'I am too, Ralf. Keep with the old hands. Don't try to outsmart the NCOs. Most of them have been through it several times.'

'Yes, sir.' Ralf looked up at the leading truck with the machine-gun and jutting rifle muzzles.

O'Neil was standing with his hands on his hips exchanging cheerful insults with the driver and his mate. Ralf tried to hide his contempt. A drunken lout. He had heard Fox telling Gravatt that the Irish corporal was to get his third stripe, a decoration too if he lived through this escapade.

Gravatt had replied seriously, 'A VC I shouldn't wonder. It will look good back at the depot.'

Was that all that mattered to them? He could barely contain his feelings. There was no point to it. He did not belong here. Ralf thought of London, of the girl named Helen. The daughter of a cabinet minister. She understood what he wanted, and taunted him about his family tradition, the Corps, or the Regiment as she called it. Summer balls, bare shoulders and gowns swinging to the orchestra. His stomach contracted. With him overseas she might find someone else. When they had first met her dance-card had always been filled.

Blair snapped, '*Ready*, Mr Blackwood?'

Ralf clambered up the steps, hating Blair for drawing attention to him, for the grins from the marines.

Blackwood watched him and then looked at his colonel.

'Right on the half-hour, sir.' It was strange. The bustle and frantic preparations, and now this station was deserted, all his men and their hopes gathered into carriages like fish in boxes.

Blair still hesitated. 'I expect we shall be too busy to gossip later on, David. I've felt that I can always talk to you.'

Blackwood waited. 'Thank you. Like the day you took it on yourself to tell me about my brother. I appreciated it.'

Blair looked at him searchingly. 'Did you?' He sounded vague. 'Yes, I'm sure.' He turned away so that Blackwood could only see his profile, the neat moustache, a mask for the man behind it.

Blair said, 'I don't have any relatives who count. Not any more. I've left a letter aboard *Mediator* which you can give to a lady in Hong Kong if you would.' His mouth twitched in a smile. 'I'd be grateful.'

Blackwood waited for him to climb aboard. What was there to say? Blackwood was only twenty-seven but he had seen and done enough to know the signs. Blair was old for his rank and he would know too. It was pointless to utter some pretence.

Blackwood hung on the short ladder and waved to the engine driver. The train shuddered and gave a lurch forward as it took the weight of its load.

It was as obvious as a shouted command. Blair was not coming back.

The train rattled along the tracks, the speed held down in case of damage or hidden mines.

Blackwood sat in one corner of the compartment, the window lowered to its full extent to encourage a flow of air. With the sun getting higher above the flat landscape the carriage was already an oven, and he knew they would all have to guard against dozing or falling asleep. *Clack-clack-*

clack-clack, even the wheels on the rails seemed to lull him away from any sort of vigilance.

Occasionally he saw a tiny village or perhaps a farm. Low, yellow buildings almost lost in the heat haze and the train's drifting dust. They always seemed to be a long way from the railway tracks, as if the inhabitants had never really trusted its invasion, another invention of the foreigners.

Private Dago Trent was on the opposite side, his eyes slitted against the glare, his rifle propped on the window ledge. It reminded Blackwood of the youth Erskine who had lost a foot. He and Dago had been friends. The veteran and the wide-eyed recruit. They had been inseparable. Trent was probably thinking of him right now, that he would be better dead than a cripple for all those years to come.

Sergeant Major Fox came through from the rear of the carriage. Blackwood wondered how he always managed to appear neat and tidy no matter what the conditions were like. Even his tunic was whiter than anyone else's.

'All quiet?'

Fox glanced at Blair who was apparently fast asleep, arms folded, his legs thrust out amongst the piled ammunition as if it was the first good rest he had had in weeks.

He replied, 'Corporal Lyde reckons he just spotted some 'orsemen to th' right of us, sir.' He smiled. He had almost said 'starboard'.

Blackwood said, 'Pass the word to the machine-gun section. They might have been some of our people, I suppose.' That was another unsettling thing about the haste of Seymour's actions. There had been no proper information about who was doing what. It was rumoured that the Russians had landed some Cossacks, that the Germans too were to use their cavalry for the relief of Peking. But nobody really knew anything for certain. Corporal Lyde might be a brawler and a natural fighter, but he was a very reliable NCO. If he said he had seen mounted men then there was no doubting him. But if the horsemen stayed out of contact with the slow-moving train it seemed very likely that they were either Chinese regulars or Boxers.

Fox climbed through the little door in the front of the carriage and over a pile of hastily filled sandbags.

Without opening his eyes Blair murmured, 'Boxers. Must be. The whole damned countryside will know we're coming.'

Blackwood grinned. 'Thought you were asleep, sir.'

'Never asleep. Not any more. Getting old. Past it.'

Swan appeared with two steaming mugs. 'Tea, sir.' He saw their surprise. 'One o' th' interpreters 'as brewed up, sir.'

The tea was surprisingly good and refreshing, and once again Blackwood drifted into his thought of Friedrike von Heiser, what she was doing, how she might receive him when they arrived. Her husband would soon suspect something, if he did not already.

Blackwood shook himself. He was deluding himself all over again. The estates in East Prussia, the tradition and the power of the family would not allow such an intrusion. And yet – He touched the locket which hung around his neck, hidden beneath his tunic. Even that made him feel guilty as he glanced quickly at his drowsing companions. Gravatt and de Courcy were too weary to care, but Ralf's eyes were wide open, opaque as he stared through the open window. It must mean something more than a farewell or a paid-off gesture surely?

Blair sat bolt upright. 'Train's slowing down!' He glared at the others. 'Are you all bloody deaf?'

Blackwood leaned out of the window. Here there was a slight curve in the track and he could see the front of the train, the sandbags on the leading car, someone, probably Bannatyre, gesturing with his arm. Blackwood fumbled with his binoculars. Blair's harsh comment had been directed at him also. That made him feel more guilty, as he knew he had earned it.

The train sighed to a halt, steam belching from beneath the engine in a white cloud.

He levelled the binoculars and held his breath. 'The track's been broken, sir.'

Blair grunted testily. 'Didn't imagine we'd stopped to buy souvenirs!'

Blackwood glanced at de Courcy. 'Two sections, Edmund. Tell the others to cover them all the way.' He shaded his eyes. 'At least there's not much shelter. Not enough for an ambush.' He stared beyond the haze to the vague ridge of blue mountains. They never got any nearer. Like the horizon at sea.

Blair said, 'I'm going to take a look. Get the repairs moving. I don't want Admiral Seymour's advance train to catch up with us.' It had obviously become something personal.

Blair strode away from the train, his orderly having to run to keep up with his neat, lithe figure.

Gravatt muttered, 'So much for Peking in a day, sir. I doubt if we've made a good thirty miles.'

Pickets were sent out, rations were served as well as a tot of rum per man to keep up their spirits.

It did not take as long as Blackwood had expected to repair the broken tracks, and much of the credit went to a stoker petty officer from *Mediator*'s engine room. He soon had his working parties sweating back and forth in the boiling heat, laying down rails, and beating them into position.

It was true what they said about sailors, Blackwood thought. They could turn their hands to anything.

In the afternoon the train moved forward again. There was still no sign of an enemy, but all the while Blackwood had the feeling they were being watched by unseen eyes.

Blair unfolded his map and studied it for several minutes as the train clattered unhurriedly through the barren countryside.

'There's this village about ten miles ahead. We'll stop there for the night.' He sounded bitter. 'I shall *have* to wait for Seymour now. Another day at least. But I'm not pushing ahead in the dark.'

Blackwood leaned his back against the worn seat. He felt unusually tense. The feeling he had once had in Africa. It was often like that in the Royal Marines. A river, even a tiny stream, was better than nothing. But here they were cut off from the sea, and each turn of the wheels was carrying them further and further into the unknown.

Blackwood said, 'Tell the Sergeant Major, Toby, half-rations from now on.'

Gravatt grinned. 'They won't like that, sir.'

Blair waited for him to leave and said quietly, 'We may get supplies at the village, but I doubt it.' He ran his finger around his collar. 'I've a nasty intuition about all this. I can see you've got it too.'

Blackwood nodded. The colonel made him feel transparent.

'You're like a naked man out here, sir.'

'Hmm.' He stood up abruptly as a voice shouted, 'Stand-to, lads!' The train rolled to a standstill and while the resting marines snatched up their weapons again, Blackwood climbed through the little hatch and stood on the coal in the tender.

He used levelled binoculars and to his astonishment saw a solitary horseman trotting down the track towards them. He was a white man, and swayed back and forth in the saddle as if he were drunk. The horse too was streaked in sweat and almost done for.

'Go and help him! Corporal Lyde, take six men to that gully, at the double!'

As the marines bounded across the open ground their torpor forgotten, the five-barrelled machine-gun swung round to follow their progress.

There were more shouts as a few shots echoed across the track, but they had been fired at extreme range and whimpered overhead like dying hornets.

The horseman toppled from his saddle even as two marines ran to catch him. They carried him to the train and laid him carefully on one of the seats while Swan moistened his lips with a water flask. Blackwood had expected him to be wounded but he was unhurt. As his strength began to return he stammered out his unbelievable story.

His name was John Twiss and he had been a riding instructor in Peking and used regularly by civilian members of the various legations. He was English, and as he described the realization of the Boxers' intentions and their savage attack on the Peking Racecourse his eyes grew brighter, as if he relived the nightmare.

The legation quarter was surrounded by the Boxers and several large units of the Chinese army who had thrown in their lot with them. Prince Tuan now openly supported the Boxers and held the real power in Peking. It was just a matter of time before a full-scale attack supported by artillery was launched against the legations. Without reinforcements they had no chance of survival.

Blackwood watched as Twiss spoke to the colonel. He seemed to exclude the rest of them. Perhaps even in his distress he had recognized in Blair another old China hand. One whose trust and hope had been hacked aside by the bloody uprising.

The British minister had asked for volunteers to attempt to get through the enemy lines and carry word to Admiral Seymour about the mounting danger. Without telegraph or mail, there was no other way. This man Twiss, and he was nobody you would even notice under ordinary circumstances, had offered to ride along the track until he found help. He had left with two others, both of whom were excellent horsemen. One had been captured when his horse had fallen. The other had been shot dead just this morning near the village up ahead.

Twiss looked at his hands. 'He was the lucky one.'

Blackwood glanced at Swan and saw his grim expression. He too was thinking of Earle's terrible screams.

Blair said, 'Recall the pickets. We'll move on as soon as that horse has been properly watered. Detail someone to ride it beside the train. Might come in handy sooner than we think.' He was scheming ahead, creating obstacles only to find a way around them.

He looked at Twiss. 'You have achieved what you set out to do. You're a brave fellow. I shall tell Admiral Seymour exactly what we all owe to your courage.'

Twiss watched him, his eyes glazed with fatigue. 'He'll never get through, you know. The Boxers will cut the railway ahead of him, and then behind at Tientsin. I heard one of the officers say as much at the legation.'

'Well, we shall have to see about that.' Blair straightened his back and stared through the window at the dust which had begun to settle again. But not before Blackwood had seen the understanding in his eyes. The whole force could be cut off and destroyed piecemeal. It would be Seymour who needed help then.

Eventually the train began to move forward again with many eyes probing the landscape and peering at the glittering rails ahead until they were almost blinded in the glare.

It felt like an age before they sighted the village. Just a few small dwellings on either side of the track, and a water-tower on stilts.

The marines crouched on either side of the train, rifles wavering as they searched for danger.

Private Knowles, who had been raised on a Dorset farm, struggled to control the horse as it reared and kicked when moments earlier it had been trotting quite happily with its new rider.

Blair said quietly, 'Trouble, David. I can smell it. So can the horse.'

The train halted and in sections the first marines fanned out on either side of the train, bayonets fixed in case of a sudden attack.

Lieutenant Gravatt shouted, 'Sar'nt Davis! Use the water-tower to refill all the flasks and canteens!'

Blair snapped, 'Belay that!' He gestured towards a

building beside the track. A marine was leaning against it vomiting helplessly.

Blair said, 'Come on. De Courcy, take charge here!'

You would not really have known they were human, just that they had once been white-skinned. Headless and disembowelled the two corpses hung from a roof like obscene meat.

Fox exclaimed hoarsely, 'An' one of 'em was already dead, yet they still did that to 'im!'

Blair did not sound as if he had heard. 'Send someone to the water-tower. Tell him to watch out for snipers.' He made himself look at the dangling horror. 'Cut those down and bury them.'

It was not then the end of it. The Boxers must have struck the village like a tornado, murdering anyone they could find, men, women, even children in an orgy of horror.

Blackwood walked through the small village, and forced himself to join his men as they searched for any survivors. The village was poor, but with the new railway running right through it, prosperity might one day have been theirs. Perhaps that too was a sin to the puritanical Boxers. A foreign infection which must be stamped out.

He thought of Friedrike that night in her cabin with her little pistol, the terrible scenes of mutilation and death he had seen aboard the *Delhi Star*.

In one dwelling, little more than a hut, he found a young Chinese mother, her eyes wide with terror, but her arms locked protectively around the child which had been feeding at her breast. Mercifully they must both have died together, but what sort of monster could see this young girl with her baby and feel no pity as he swung his great blade.

He leaned against a wall, sick of the stench, the busy murmur of flies. Blair joined him. 'As I thought. The water's poisoned. Full of corpses.' He spoke without any emotion and yet Blackwood imagined he might be near to breaking-point.

He saw some of his men staring around as if shocked out

of their minds. The Boxers had achieved what they had set out to do. These men, even the recruits, would stand and fight, die if need be, if so ordered. But they were no match for such scenes as these, and Blackwood could feel their despair as it moved amongst them like a spectre.

Gravatt crunched across the tracks and asked, 'Orders, sir?' He was as pale as death.

Blackwood looked at the colonel. 'No sense in pushing forward any further, sir.'

'No. Twiss says there could be twenty thousand of the enemy converging on Peking. How many of us?' He looked round at the silent, listless marines. 'A hundred? Even for the Royals I fear we may be outmatched.' He became brisk and businesslike just as quickly. 'There is a siding of some kind here. Change the trucks around, we will reverse the train back to Tientsin, or as near as we can get to it.'

Blackwood passed his orders and then asked, 'What will the admiral do, sir?'

'Do?' Blair's eyes settled on his and Blackwood saw the pain deep inside them for the first time. 'He'll run for the sea. At least I hope he does. If I meet him face to face I shall probably shoot him!'

All that night the train stood beside the poisoned water-tower, surrounded by silence and the smell of death. Nobody slept, not even the sentries when they were relieved.

At first light they found the heads of the two murdered riders, propped on stakes and within yards of where two sentries had been posted. They were as close as that.

The wheels spun, and smoke belched from the funnel and then with the horse trotting beside it the train backed slowly along the tracks.

Blackwood climbed through the carriages, speaking to his men, or just letting them know he was there.

He heard one marine say, 'One thing, Fred, we *are* goin' towards the sea this time, eh?'

Blackwood felt a lump in his throat. Was it that simple?

He thought of the girl with the baby at her breast and pushed the sentiment from his mind.

There was a hell of a lot to do before they found the sea again.

I I

The Hero

Captain Vere Masterman put down his empty teacup and stared impassively through the stern ports of his spacious quarters. Separated from *Mediator*'s busy routine by steel bulkheads he could still hear the shrill of the boatswain's calls, and the cry, 'Hands to breakfast and clean!' Seven in the morning although the light cruiser's people or a large part of them had been up and about for an hour and a half already.

Masterman prepared himself for the many tasks he had to attend to. In another hour the Colours would be hoisted to mark the official start of another day, but to Masterman this was always the best part, the early morning when a man's mind was crisp like the air. He stared at the nearest anchored warships, the German *Flensburg*, and beyond her an elderly French steam sloop. Like some of the other foreign men-of-war they had their guns trained on the shore. Masterman was irritated by what he saw. Things were quite serious enough without this pointless show of force.

Aboard his ship at least things would remain normal until he decided otherwise. When the time came *Mediator* would respond without any fuss or bravado.

He could see two of the Chinese forts through the morning mist, biscuit-coloured in the frail sunlight. There would be another series of useless parleys with the Chinese garrison commanders, but nothing would happen. The Chinese knew that the Allies would not open fire with

Seymour's force still trapped ashore. And every captain knew he would not shoot. So what was the point?

There was a tap at the door. Time to make decisions.

'Come!'

It was Commander Wilberforce as he knew it would be, his arm wrapped around a bundle of lists, requests, and the usual signal pad. Wilberforce took his time as he laid down his papers, it was his usual ploy while he gauged the captain's mood. The signs were not good.

Wilberforce said, 'Signal from Flag, sir. A report has got through to say that Admiral Seymour's force is falling back as planned.'

'Falling back?' He did not hide his anger. 'It's a bloody rout!'

'Yes, sir.'

Masterman glared at the throngs of junks and small Chinese boats which hovered around the anchored warships like moths. Some of them would be pirates, the sweepings of the China Seas, he thought. They probably hated the Boxers more than anyone, as a criminal hates a man who murders a policeman. They knew that while the crime was unavenged they would get no peace to go about their affairs, unlawful or not.

'The sloop *Caistor* has anchored, sir. From Hong Kong with despatches for the flagship.' He held out a signal. 'This came over in the guard-boat, sir.'

Masterman did not look at it immediately. He kept thinking of the Royal Marines he had landed at this godforsaken place. A day to reach Peking the admiral had proclaimed. It was already five days, and Seymour's force was in full retreat, ridding itself of stores and equipment in its haste to reach the sea.

And things were getting steadily worse, backed up by terrible rumours which had spread through the Allied squadron like a forest-fire.

The Boxers had stormed and seized the Native City of Tientsin and were now preparing an attack on the International Settlement there. Word had filtered through that the Japanese Chancellor Sugiyama had been murdered in Peking by Chinese troops, so any hope of some last-minute parley was gone.

He read through the signal and then realized what it said.

'Sergeant Kirby, does he know?'

'No, sir.'

'Well, better get it done as quickly as possible. I'll go and see him myself after Colours.'

As if to measure the time a boatswain's mate called again, 'Guard and Band to muster on the quarterdeck!'

Masterman glanced at the deckhead just inches above him. Some captains hated the tramp of marching above their private quarters, the clatter of weapons and the blare of a Royal Marines band. Not Masterman, he loved every part of it, just as he knew the name and face of every man under his command.

Wilberforce said, 'It's strange you should say that, sir, but Sergeant Kirby has already put in a request to see you. He's walking quite well, considering.'

'Very well. This is bad luck after what he's been through.'

A midshipman tapped on the outer door and Masterman's steward called, 'For the Commander, sir. Two minutes to Colours.'

Wilberforce picked up his cap and withdrew.

The stern swung slightly as the inshore current began to move the anchored warships around their cables. Masterman was glad when that happened, and the land vanished from his vision for a few hours at least.

He picked up the photograph of his wife which stood in a silver frame on a polished cabinet. He was always close to her at this time of the day.

Through the open skylight he heard a voice call, 'Colours, sir!' And Wilberforce's reply, calm, unruffled, 'Make it so!'

'Royal Marines! Pre-*sent arms!*'

The rest was drowned in the blare of bugles and rattle of drums but Masterman did not need to be there. He had seen it in every major harbour around the world, the White Ensign rising in time to the salute. It never failed to move him.

He spoke aloud, 'If only we could get those men off.' Where was Blackwood and his men? Cut off and abandoned by the rest of the landing force. It was unthinkable. Outrageous.

Masterman sat down at his table and contained his sudden rage. It was not the right time.

The outer door opened and he saw Wilberforce again, followed by the wounded sergeant with a sickberth attendant hovering anxiously in the rear.

The sergeant looked very pale, but was moving well, and doing his best not to show the pain he must feel.

Kirby brought his heels together and looked at the captain squarely. He had known it was coming, but the shock seemed somehow worse now that he was away from the company, from his fellow NCOs.

Masterman eyed him gravely, measuring the moment, hating it.

'I have bad news, I'm afraid, Sergeant Kirby.'

'Sir?' He had half expected to be placed under immediate arrest.

'I have just received word from Hong Kong that your wife is dead.'

He snapped his fingers. 'Chair, man!'

The sickberth attendant snatched a chair and held it for Kirby as he slumped down.

'Dead, sir?' Kirby barely recognized his own voice. He was going mad. All the weeks of worrying and tormenting himself and now the captain was acting as if he was sorry for him. Of course she was bloody dead! He felt like screaming, or throwing himself on the deck.

Masterman nodded. 'There was, *is* a street lamp outside your house it seems. There was a gas explosion and I fear that your wife perished in the fire which followed.'

Kirby tried to speak but nothing came. In his reeling thoughts he could see that solitary street lamp. They had often undressed by its glow to save money when they had first got married. An explosion? A fire? Masterman's voice scattered his memories as he continued.

'I have to tell you, Sergeant Kirby, and I hope it may be of some consolation, that I received confirmation from the flagship that your recommendation for an award has been approved. For your gallantry under fire, well over and above the line of duty, you will in due course be decorated with the Victoria Cross, and I am instructed to offer my congratulations.'

Masterman saw the sergeant sway on the chair. He must not prolong it any more.

He said in a gentle voice which Wilberforce would not have recognized had he not been staring at the scene which he would always remember. 'Remember this, Kirby. She would have been proud of you.' He turned away, embarrassed by his own sincerity. 'As we all are.'

Wilberforce gestured to the steward. 'Help the SBA to take Sergeant Kirby down to the sickbay.'

As the door closed behind the two white-coated figures and the tall, bent shape of the sergeant, Masterman said, 'I know how I'd feel.' He glanced at the photograph again, hearing her voice calling the dog, waking him in time to catch the train back to his ship.

'Now, John, about this retreat. What is our state of readiness?'

Wilberforce tried to relax, but he knew that he would never see Masterman as quite the same again.

Safely laid in his cot once more Kirby stared at the revolving deckhead fan and tried to assemble his thoughts. It was hard to believe it had happened. His secret had tortured him for weeks; now because of some impossible act of fate the burden was lifted. He peered over the edge of the cot, but he was alone. Even Private Erskine who had lost a foot had been carried on deck to benefit from the air and the sunshine.

He thought of the medal, of Masterman's words. Of what Fox would say when he heard about it. The Victoria Cross. Just like Captain Blackwood and his father.

Jeff Kirby, born and raised in a London slum, respected and often feared by his men, was suddenly aware of something which had never happened before. He was shocked beyond reason to discover that tears were pouring uncontrollably down his face. He tried to stop, to stifle his terrible sobs in the pillow and to shut out the picture of her terror as she had pleaded with him.

'Oh, Nance!' He crushed the pillow into a ball against his face but he only saw her more clearly. '*Nance!* I – I'm so sorry, love!'

It was worse than any secret.

'Stop the train!' Lieutenant Colonel Blair clambered through the little door at the end of the carriage which was now in the front of the train. 'Quickly.' He blinked at Blackwood, his chest heaving from exertion and the oppressive heat. He had been squatting like a wiry bird on the roof of the carriage for most of the journey. Blackwood heard the warning being shouted from carriage to carriage as the driver applied the brakes.

Blair said, 'They've broken the track again.' He nodded gratefully to Swan as he swallowed a mug of water. 'A mile ahead of us.'

Blackwood wanted to ask why they had stopped here, but knew Blair would have a good reason.

'Not just Boxers this time. Imperial soldiers too.' Blair added quietly, 'I could see the buggers through my glasses. They're waiting for us to stop. They could kill or wound half of our people before we could hit back. They know this territory, we don't.' He unfolded his map and Blackwood saw that his hand was shaking from the strain he was under.

Blair sounded absorbed. 'According to this there's a small river beyond those hills to our right. It joins the Peiho after a mile or so, down to the sea after that, eh?'

Blackwood waited seeing the excitement returning to Blair's thin features.

'If we tried to reach the hills the Boxers would cut us down before we got halfway. I want our men ready to fight, not to die like bloody scavengers!'

Fight? Blackwood pictured their dispirited, weary faces.

Blair glanced up as the lieutenants climbed into the carriage, their faces full of questions.

Blair said, 'We shall detrain here, gentlemen. By platoons as before. Mr Gravatt, go with the Sergeant Major and start the ball rolling.' He spoke lightly, as if it was an exercise rather than a walk into probable death.

Gravatt swallowed hard. 'In the *open*, sir?'

'Yes. There is an army of Boxers and soldiers up there where they've ripped up the tracks. They will expect us to make a stand or break out from there while they shoot us down from cover, right?'

Gravatt nodded. 'I see, sir.'

Blair smiled. 'You don't but never mind. When the Boxers see us leave the train *here* they'll have to leave their cover to cut us off.' He looked at Blackwood. 'The machine-gun sections will remain on the train. We shall have to leave the two field-pieces behind, I'm afraid. Have them spiked before you follow me. Tell the engine driver to go like hell. I want to catch those bastards out in the open with their trousers down for once!'

Blackwood nodded. 'I'll tell him.'

Blair touched his arm. 'It's up to you really. Reverse back here when you're ready and don't leave it too late.' He looked at the others. 'Leave no one behind.' His eyes rested momentarily on Ralf. 'We take care of our own in the Corps.' He nodded curtly. 'So let us be about it, eh?'

Outside Blackwood could hear the bark of commands, the sudden bustle and stamp of feet as the marines jumped

from the train, dragging their packs and ammunition with
them.

'Fall them in, Sergeant Major.'

By the time Blackwood reached the engine the marines
were standing in sections beside the train. He could sense
their sudden reluctance to leave the train's frail protection.

Blair stood in front of them and raised his voice. 'Now
listen to me, all of you. We shall march to those hills, and I
mean *march*. I don't give a damn what you've seen or done in.
the past, this is bloody now! So stop feeling sorry for
yourselves!'

Blackwood saw the hurt and resentment on their faces,
the way they held their rifles as if they wanted to kill the
man who was flaying them with his insults.

'Remember that you are Royal Marines, not a lot of
mummy's boys!'

As Blackwood walked back along the train Blair looked
at him and grinned. 'I'm a real bastard, aren't I?' He
returned Fox's salute and at a shouted command the first
platoon marched away from the train.

Blair's grin widened. 'But it's working.'

Blackwood took a deep breath. The arms were swinging,
the dusty boots moved as one, and the sloped rifles would
have done credit to Forton Barracks.

Blair lifted his glasses and stared along the line. 'It's
working with them too. Now get your men under cover.'

A door squeaked and Blair nodded with satisfaction as the
other Nordenfeldt machine-gun poked through the gap.
Then he strode briskly after the winding column of marines
and did not look back.

Blackwood climbed over the sandbags and boiler plates
on the leading car and knelt down with the small squad of
marines there.

Corporal O'Neil stared at him. 'Is it yourself, sir?'

Blackwood found he could smile in spite of the tension
which held him like claws.

When he trained his binoculars over the barrier he saw

the horde of figures breaking from their hiding places and charging across the flat ground towards the slow-moving column.

Suppose the engine failed to move, or the driver got into a panic and ran for his life?

The men moved around restlessly and dragged up more ammunition to be in easy reach.

O'Neil rested his hand on the machine-gun and murmured, 'And if you jam, me boyo, I'll not forgive you!'

One of the marines said sharply, 'Some of 'em are headin' for the train, sir.'

Blackwood saw Swan nestle his rifle against his cheek while he adjusted his sights with great care. The Boxers on the track were probably coming to loot rather than to fight. They would get a rude surprise.

A few shots cracked across the ground, but the Boxers were too eager to get to grips with the column to take proper aim.

It was almost time. Blackwood felt the sweat trickle down his spine. He made himself count up to twenty and then stood upright on the top of the sandbags so that the driver could see him above the roofs of the carriages.

He yelled, *'Now!'* To his surprise he saw the stoker petty officer and two sailors in their wide-brimmed sennets on the footplate with the driver. He had forgotten all about the stokers. They would make sure that the engine kept going with or without the driver.

The car gave a great lurch and Blackwood almost fell over the side. He looked at O'Neil. *Good old Blackie.* 'Here we go.'

Whatever the Boxers thought was happening they showed no sign of slowing down or changing direction.

Blackwood drew his revolver. 'Open fire!'

The sandbags were rolled aside and the machine-gun clattered into life even as the other one poured a long burst into the charging mob of Boxers and troops. A few rifles joined in, and Blackwood wondered if the marching marines would dare to turn their heads to watch.

Back and forth the five-barrelled gun ripped above the track until the figures which had been running towards the train were either hurled down or had turned to flee.

The train gathered momentum, the bright wheels cutting through the fallen corpses and bringing screams from the wounded before they too were smashed aside.

Blackwood tried to concentrate on the bulk of the attackers. As O'Neil's gun joined forces with the other one, the running figures seemed to become confused, like a sea caught between wind and tide. Many were falling, others ran on, and a few swayed back again against their companions.

'Reload! *Steady*, lads!' A sight like this one was enough to make any man shoot without aiming or caring.

It was unreal and terrible, and Blackwood flinched as two of the marching marines fell from the ranks. They were gathered up into the column as if it was the living being and the marines merely incidental.

We take care of our own, Blair had said. What officers in the Corps had probably said at the Nile and Trafalgar.

Blackwood peered at the torn-up rails. They would never be repaired in time. Blair was right about that also.

'Stop the train! Back up!' It was far enough. The engine shuddered to a halt and Swan vaulted over the side to snatch up a fallen pike with its fearsome blade attached and was back with it even as the wheels spun into reverse.

Blackwood said hoarsely, 'You bloody fool! I should put you on a charge for that!'

Swan hung his head. 'Souvenir, sir.'

They stared at each other, both knowing the real reason for Blackwood's concern.

O'Neil watched impatiently as the gun was reloaded. 'You're a terrible chap, Private Swan, desertin' your train in the face o' the enemy!'

Blackwood stared at his crouching, smoke-grimed men. They were rocking about and laughing as if it was the greatest joke in the world.

'*Open fire!*'

Along the train the few remaining rifles cracked out, while the two machine-guns scythed back and forth with deadly effect.

O'Neil said over his shoulder. 'Nearly out of ammo', sir.' He glanced at his mate. 'Sergeant Kirby wouldn't be happy about that, eh, Willy?'

'They're in full retreat, the bloody hounds!' The man ducked and swore as a stray bullet sang past his head.

The train stopped at the exact spot where Blair had made his brief speech.

It was a strange feeling to climb down without anything happening. There was a slow, hot wind across the open ground and it stirred the white and bloodied garments of the fallen Boxers so that it appeared as if they really were invulnerable and returning to life.

The marching column was completely hidden in dust and haze, as if it too had been swallowed up.

They piled up their spare kit and ammunition on the two Nordenfeldt carriages, and then, pushing and pulling the ungainly wheels, they hurried after the others.

Blackwood saw the engine driver pause to stare back at the abandoned train. Like a master leaving his ship, he thought. The train looked forlorn as it stood with its doors open, and steam still trickling from the boiler.

Blackwood said, 'Come on. There'll be other trains.'

The driver shook his head. Suddenly his whole life was in ruins and he still did not understand why.

'Not like her,' was all he said.

Swan fell into step beside him, his rifle slung, the great blade shining across his other shoulder.

The captain had been afraid for him. It touched Swan more deeply than any bloody medal.

Blackwood lay beside the colonel, his elbows wedged into

some pebbles as they trained their glasses on the scene below. The hill, like the others which rolled away on either side, was not very high, but compared to the flat countryside it still offered a good vantage point.

'There's the river anyway.' Blair moved his glasses with great care. It was sunset and the sky was fiery red, but still strong enough to reflect from a lens if you moved too sharply.

The river was narrow and probably quite shallow like the other one had been. At the point where it joined the Peiho was a long squat building like an ancient fortress. They had seen it earlier when they had been placing the sentries and setting up the machine-guns.

The two marines who had been wounded were only suffering from flesh injuries and with luck would soon recover.

Blair remarked, 'You notice that wide road coming from the rear of the building. Odd, that. It's the end of nowhere, I'd have thought.'

Blair stiffened and readjusted his glasses as a tiny figure appeared on top of the wall.

He said softly, as if the far-off man might hear, 'Soldier, Imperial Army.' He lowered his glasses and studied Blackwood thoughtfully. 'No Boxers in sight. You know what I think, David, this is an arsenal. That would explain the size of the road.' He snapped open his pocket compass. 'Which by my reckoning goes straight into Tientsin.' He nodded to confirm his ideas. 'There are several big arsenals around the city. I was just thinking, it's a pity we had to leave the two field-guns on the train. Still, they'd have slowed us down even more.'

Blackwood waited, it was fascinating just to watch his mind work.

The two little cannon had been rendered useless before they had left, their breech-blocks thrown into the engine's furnace. Even a first-class gun would be so much scrap after that. But surely Blair was not even considering an attack on the arsenal? They would have to cross the river, and even though there did not appear to be any heavy defences it would be an almost impossible task.

Blair twisted on to his side and looked at Swan who lay behind them, his rifle to his shoulder. Just in case.

'How much drinking water have you got, Swan?'

Swan sounded surprised. ''Bout an inch, sir.'

'You see, David? Swan is a veteran and even he's only got a swallow left in his flask. The younger ones will have drunk the lot by now, no matter what threats the NCOs hurl at 'em!' He looked again at the long building which was already falling into deep shadow. 'There's fresh water and rations galore over there, or I'm a Dutchman. The whole countryside is obviously raised against us, so we must act accordingly. They'll need us badly in Tientsin. That's where we'll go.'

'And Admiral Seymour?'

Blair gave his impish grin. 'Who?'

He became serious instantly. 'Fetch the petty officer and one of the student interpreters.' He tapped his teeth with the strap of his binocular case. 'A diversion is what we need.'

He slithered a few yards down the slope. 'I'm going to tell the PO what I want.'

Blackwood peered at the building until his eyes throbbed. They had come all this way and had suffered only two casualties. As far as they could tell there was no pursuit, not yet anyway. Perhaps the other Boxers had changed their minds and had gone to join their army massing in Tientsin as they were in Peking.

He heard Blair say, 'There are several abandoned boats down by the river. Ran like hell when they knew the Boxers were coming, I expect.' His tone sharpened. 'I want you to take one as soon as it's dark and make your way downstream. It shouldn't be difficult. I'll give you a message for Captain Masterman, how about that?'

The petty officer's voice rumbled, 'I'll 'ave a go, sir.' The mention of his captain's name had knocked his defences aside like a battering ram.

'You'll do better than that, Petty Officer.' Blair's voice was incisive. 'We're all depending on you.' He swung round before the man could say anything more. 'David, muster the sailors and see that they're armed.'

As Blackwood walked downhill towards the hidden marines he tried not to think about the beheaded, mutilated corpses. It was lucky that the petty officer had remained inside the train.

Gravatt and the others were waiting for him, while Fox stood just the required number of paces to one side.

Blackwood told them briefly what Blair intended and stressed the vital importance of the food and drink they would find in the arsenal.

Nobody spoke, but their shocked silence made it worse.

Blackwood finished by saying, 'As soon as it's dark I want the men to get as much rest as they can.' He saw them stare as he added, 'The colonel wants the horse led down and watered at the river as soon as we're sure it's safe.'

Gravatt said politely, 'Did he say why, sir?'

Blackwood grinned, the colonel's mood was infectious. 'He's going to ride the bloody thing when he leads us into Tientsin, because *that's* where we're going next!'

Gravatt looked at Lieutenant Bannatyre. ''Pon my soul, Ian, I do believe he means it!'

Blackwood found the colonel sitting alone, his back propped against a huge rock which had been split in equal halves, like an egg. Without the others near him he seemed tense, on edge.

Blair said, 'It's the only way, David. If the trap closes around us this time, it's over.'

'I know.' Blackwood sat down beside him. He found that he was touching the locket beneath his tunic.

Was she safe? he wondered. Did she think of him sometimes?

His head lolled and then he was asleep.

12

The Last Bugle

The silver calls trilled in salute as Captain Masterman stepped on to *Mediator*'s quarterdeck and touched the peak of his cap in acknowledgement to the flag.

Commander Wilberforce hurried forward to greet him but did not get a chance to speak.

Masterman said, 'Bloody hopeless. Allies indeed? You would think we were all on opposite sides!' He glared across at the other warships. 'The Japanese want to go in and attack, the Russians want to wait here off the Taku bar, the Germans are keen to bombard the forts, and the Americans won't do a damn thing. Their Admiral Kempff has his hands tied by a directive from Washington which forbids him from taking part in any hostile acts against the Chinese. The fact that the Americans have their own marines cut off in Peking too, and that we are in a state of war to all intents and purposes with Johnnie Chinaman seems to matter not!' He lowered his voice with an effort. 'I might as well have stayed here. Seymour's second-in-command will do nothing until his master returns. *If* he returns!' He peered over the side. 'And what is that object doing tied to the boom?'

Wilberforce tugged at his collar. It was all going wrong, and Masterman was in no mood for mistakes today.

'I was going to tell you, sir. Stoker Petty Officer Gooch arrived aboard just after you'd gone across to the flagship.'

'*What* did you say?'

Two seamen who were polishing the brass nameplate

stiffened to listen, their cloths motionless.

Wilberforce tried to explain. 'He got downriver in that boat, sir. He has a signal from Lieutenant Colonel Blair.' He wilted under Masterman's angry stare.

Masterman strode to the quarterdeck companionway leaving the officer-of-the-day and his midshipman gaping after him.

The stoker petty officer was found in his mess and bustled aft to the day cabin where his captain was still studying Blair's message. The petty officer had been greeted as something of a conqueror by his messmates, and had even found time to down a large tot of rum after his escape from the river. Masterman soon changed all that.

'How long has *this* man been back aboard, Commander?'

Wilberforce replied unhappily, 'Since eight bells, sir.'

Masterman looked at the petty officer and asked almost gently, 'Why did it take you so long, Gooch? According to this message, you left the others as soon as it was dark.'

'We 'ad trouble, sir. The boat ran aground twice, it were that shallow. Then when we reached the main river we 'ad to 'ide in some rushes. There were Chinese soljers on th' bank. An' further downstream they was layin' mines, least I think they was.'

Masterman frowned. He had heard as much aboard the flagship. If the Chinese succeeded in mining the Peiho's entrance not only would Seymour and his men be done for, but also the last chance of relieving Peking would be gone.

He stared hard at the petty officer. But for him they would know very little. Blackwood and his men were still together, and whereas the petty officer could only thank his lucky stars that he was safely back in his ship, Blair was planning an attack. The Allies would have to act within forty-eight hours at the very latest.

They had to capture the forts, and open a passage for future reinforcements. If they achieved neither they might as well up-anchor and leave the Taku bar for good.

'How were the marines when you left them?'

Petty Officer Gooch tried not to drop his eyes under that remorseless stare.

'Tired, sir, 'ungry too, an' there's no water left.' He flushed. 'They give the last of it to my lads.'

'They would.' Masterman looked away. Over the years he had taught himself to stay calm while he considered his plans, item by item. The poor devils could die out there for nothing.

He said quietly, 'Fetch the Chief Engineer and Gunnery Officer. At once.' To the petty officer he added, 'If by the Grace of God you still have that rank on your sleeve at the end of the day, Gooch, you will know I have intervened with Providence on your behalf. Now get out of my sight!'

Wilberforce was almost knocked over by the petty officer as he ran from the cabin.

'I've sent for them, sir.'

The captain moved to the stern ports and stared across the placid water. The tide had turned again, and the land, apart from some small islets, was hidden.

Wilberforce said carefully, 'I suppose we can't really blame Gooch, sir. It was quite a responsibility for him.'

'I'm not. I blame you for not making a signal directly he came on board.' He relented slightly. 'Now get the chart of the Peiho and those forts.'

The chief engineer entered the cabin and waited, his eyes flitting from one to the other.

'How long to raise steam, Chief?'

The engineer shrugged. 'I'm ready any time, more or less. When you ordered a state of readiness, well, I know your standards by now, sir.'

Masterman smiled. 'So you do, Chief.'

The gunnery officer, some breadcrumbs on his chest, hurried into the cabin.

Masterman eyed him gravely. 'I am going to get under way, Guns. We shall go to the bridge and compare Blair's little map with the chart. As we cross the river-mouth you will have to fire on a difficult bearing, but it must be accurate.'

The gunnery officer glanced at Wilberforce who quickly
shook his head. Masterman added, 'The Royal Marines are
going to attack and capture an arsenal, Guns. We will keep
the enemy occupied, although — ' he glanced at the
bulkhead clock, 'I fear we are already too late.'

He snatched up his cap. 'Clear lower decks, John. Steam
on the capstan and hoist all boats inboard.'

He looked at them and smiled. 'And later, John, you
may clear for action.'

Wilberforce hurried after him beckoning to boatswain's
mates and messengers as he tried to keep up.

'Are you sure, sir? I — I mean, is it our responsibility?'

Masterman paused, framed against the blue sky above the
ladder. The question would ensure that Wilberforce would
never hold any real responsibility.

'It's mine, John. It's called initiative.' He ran up the last
steps. 'Now get the people moving!'

He strode into the wheelhouse and aft to the chartroom.
Men were bustling everywhere, and already he could hear
the dull clank from the capstan as the cable was hove short.

He paused and glanced at the wheel, with the gleaming
binnacle and telegraphs. He really loved this ship more than
any other, and he could remember how proud his wife had
been when he had been given *Mediator*. In a matter of hours
his career could easily be in ruins. Then he thought of
Blackwood, how young he had looked when the German
countess had asked for his escort. When you compared him
with Wilberforce's hesitancy — he shook himself. There was
no comparison.

'Special sea dutymen to your stations! First part o'
starboard watch muster on th' fo'c'sle!'

Mediator seemed to stir beneath his white shoes.

'Signal from flagship, sir.' The lieutenant sounded
confused. '*What do you intend to do?*'

Masterman eyed him thoughtfully. Nelson would have
known what to say. He always did.

'Make to Flag. *My duty.*'

'Aye, sir.' The lieutenant hurried to the flag deck, convinced that the captain was going mad.

The bridge party had closed up now. Quartermaster, telegraphsmen, yeoman of signals. Masterman's tools.

'Anchor's weigh, sir.'

'Slow ahead together.'

The light cruiser moved quietly ahead, her dripping anchor still being hoisted as she turned towards the open water.

The lieutenant was muttering to the yeoman of signals. Then he said uncertainly, 'From flagship, sir. *Your signal not understood.*'

Wilberforce entered the bridge in time to see his captain burst out laughing.

Masterman said, 'The truest words we've heard yet!'

He saw Wilberforce and said more calmly, 'When we pass abeam of the last fort I want you to sound Action Stations.' He walked out on to the sun-blistered wing and stared at the land. 'They might hear it. From one of their own.'

Blackwood scrambled up the slope and dropped beside the colonel. Blair was peering through his binoculars and said, 'Dawn any minute now.' He sounded quite calm again. In control.

Blackwood peered through the rough gorse towards the arsenal. How he had managed to sleep he could not begin to understand. It was behind him now. This was another day. Perhaps the last.

'I've checked with the pickets, sir, and re-sited the machine-gun where it will perform best.' He had ordered all the Nordenfeldt ammunition to be taken to just the one gun. The other one would have to be abandoned like the field-pieces.

Blair never asked him where or what he had been doing,

and he liked him for that. He trusted and he delegated, unlike some field officers Blackwood had known.

He watched the growing light seeping across the top of the arsenal, and wondered if the stoker petty officer and his party had reached safety. What could Masterman do anyway?

Blackwood had spoken to most of the marines while they were munching the last of their meagre rations. Without water or tea to wash it down it was an unhappy way to begin a day like this.

Fox had awakened him during the night after the pickets had found two white-clad sailors stumbling about in the dark. It was a miracle they had not been bayoneted before they had identified themselves. They were both Austro-Hungarian sailors who had become separated and lost from Seymour's column. One spoke a little English, and with the aid of gestures and a crude map they had explained how the column was in full retreat, dropping weapons and equipment to make as much speed as possible. They did not know how far Seymour had reached, but they had told a gruesome story about another massacred village, and about the Boxer flags flying over Tientsin's Native City. The International Settlement there was obviously their goal.

Blair had remarked, 'Well it's two more rifles. That's something, I suppose.'

'Look!' Blair touched his arm. 'Now there's a sight!'

Blackwood imagined he had seen an enemy movement but realized that the sea had suddenly become visible. It was like a dark blue barrier beyond the jutting land which supported the arsenal. Blackwood thought it was the most beautiful thing he had ever seen.

'There's the other fort. Just beyond the bend. Must have been built to command the main river. They have good modern artillery in those forts, I'm told.' He shot Blackwood a grin. 'But they all point out to sea. Bit of luck, eh?'

Blair removed his helmet and crawled to the lip of the hill. 'The boats are still there, and unguarded. We'll have to jump about a bit when we cross the river.' He gauged the distance with his eyes. 'Once across, the machine-gun section can offer covering fire. That'll keep their heads down for a bit.' Surprisingly he rolled on to his back and stared up at the paling sky.

'I've been really happy during my time out here. I suppose I've been getting past it for some time.' He turned his head and looked at Blackwood. 'I'm about twenty years older than you, and I feel it.'

Blackwood watched him in the faint glow. Without his helmet he looked unshaven and tired. For some reason he wanted to talk. To while away the time or to ease the tension, he could not tell.

Blair continued, 'To begin with I was like any other young officer. You learn the jargon and the right postures. The rest comes easily. One ship after the other. Captains with different whims and fancies, and always you're separate from the rest, no matter how crowded the ship might be. I suppose I grew tired of it. Even leave in England had nothing to offer. I've no family to speak of, whereas in Hong Kong . . .' He sighed and rolled over on to his elbows again.

'But all that is far away. We are here.' He became businesslike and brisk once more. 'Order a runner to de Courcy's sector. Tell him to send a squad down to the boats, but keep them hidden.'

Swan said, 'I'll do it, sir.'

Blackwood licked his lips. They were beginning to crack. In an hour the land would start to throw back the heat. They could not go through another day. Even as he thought it, he knew they would if need be. And another, and another until the sun smashed them down.

'Good chap, your man Swan.' Blair yawned hugely. 'A few thousand like him and I could take the whole of China!' But the smile would not come. Blackwood looked at the river as the growing light gave it colour and movement again.

Just to have a drink. Was that all that mattered in the
end?

Hidden in the fold of an adjoining hill Lieutenant
Edmund de Courcy listened to Swan's message and said,
'Right away.' He beckoned to Greenaway, his sergeant. 'Job
for you. Take a squad down to the boats. You should be
hidden from the arsenal, but keep a weather eye on that
bloody fort.'

Sergeant Tom Greenaway was the oldest man in the
whole company and had been in the Corps since he was
fifteen. He had fought in most of the big campaigns in
Africa and Egypt, and several of the little bush wars as well.
He was old enough to be the lieutenant's father and then
some, but he liked de Courcy all the same. He had the
ability to make quick decisions and act on them, unlike
poor young Mr Bannatyre. He came from a good old Royal
Marines family too. That carried more weight than de
Courcy's lack of experience.

Greenaway detailed off his small squad and picked up his
rifle. Some of the youngsters were worried, on edge. But
Greenaway had grown out of all that. Curiously enough he
had never even got a scratch, except once in a brawl with
some soldiers in Southsea.

He heard de Courcy say, 'You go along with them, Ralf.
Get the lie of the land.'

Greenaway dropped his eyes to hide his irritation. The
second lieutenant might be a Blackwood but he was bloody
useless.

He looked up. 'Ready to move off, sir.'

Ralf nodded. 'Very well. Carry on.'

Greenaway gritted his teeth. That was all the little snob
ever said. *Carry on.*

'Poole, take the point. Adams, bring up the rear.'

Ralf said, 'Have them fix bayonets, Sergeant.'

Greenaway pushed his lower lip up into his big, bushy
moustache.

'Too risky. The sun'll be up soon. It'll reflect off 'em.'

De Courcy heard him, but walked away rattling a warm pebble around his tongue and teeth to hold his terrible thirst at bay. Ralf Blackwood would get little change out of Greenaway, he thought.

The squad slithered and crawled amongst some bushes, feeling their way, eyes everywhere as they headed for the river.

How inviting the sea had looked from the hillside, Ralf thought. It was all so unfair. They should have been got out of it at the first sign of danger.

He thought of *Mediator*. Probably lying safe and snug around the next spur of land. Surely they would not be left to die here in a wilderness? The thought unnerved him and for a moment he felt on the verge of panic.

'Far enough, sir.' Greenaway signalled the others to take cover as he flopped down behind a barrier of stones. Perhaps there had once been a terrible flood here, and only the stones remained to mark its passing.

Ralf glared at the sergeant as he studied the boats which had been abandoned on the bank. Big, coarse and ugly, with thick hair on the backs of his hands.

Ralf turned away as the anger swept through him.

The sun touched his face and he dreaded the heat to come. There was a dark patch in the sky which had not been there before. From the direction of Tientsin. Part of it must be on fire. He thought of the mutilated and headless corpses when they had stopped the train and almost vomited.

Here there was no train, no sign of help, and he had heard that only one of the machine-guns was serviceable. Even that fool Blair must see it was hopeless.

An hour dragged past and Ralf's anxiety mounted with each minute. It was as if they had been left behind, that nothing else lived here.

Greenaway sucked on a piece of grass, his rifle pushed through the scrub and resting on the little stones as he watched the opposite bank. After this little lot he would be out of the Corps for good. But it was all he remembered, all he knew. What would he and Beth do when he quit the

barracks for the last time? He had two daughters, but no
son to carry on the tradition. Still, perhaps one of the girls
would give him a grandson.

He heard someone creeping down beside him and tensed
as if he expected a blow from one of those terrible knives.
But it was Corporal Addis from the platoon.

'Gawd, you gave me a start, creepin' up like that, Percy!'

The corporal peered past him at the river. 'We're goin' to
attack. Just 'ad word from Cap'n Blackwood.'

Even with the shock of his announcement Greenaway was
able to hiss, 'Tell the *officer* then!'

Addis glanced contemptuously at the second lieutenant,
'Fifteen minutes, sir. Mr de Courcy's runner 'as reported a
force of Boxers coming from the sou'-west.'

Greenaway grimaced. 'That's torn it. There's only one
way, an' that's through that ruddy arsenal.'

Ralf floundered for words. 'But – but what about the
ship? I thought we were getting support?'

Greenaway frowned. He shouldn't talk like that in front
of a corporal. Percy Addis was well known for his big mouth
and lower-deck gossip.

He growled, 'Tell 'm we're standin' fast until he comes.'
He pulled back his rifle-bolt with extreme care and thrust a
bullet into the breech.

Ralf stood up and stared wildly at the hillside. Addis had
already vanished.

'I'll go and see Mr de Courcy.' He nodded jerkily, only
vaguely aware of the sprawled marines who were staring at
him, their eyes like glass in the sunshine.

Greenaway said, 'It won't do no good, sir.' He reached
out to encourage the young officer back into cover, but as he
touched his sleeve he seemed to trigger off all of his pent-up
fears and emotions.

'Don't you dare to touch me, you – you – ' He ripped
open his holster and made to drag out his revolver. 'You
think you know everything – '

In his agitation Ralf had holstered his revolver while it

was still cocked. Now as he jerked it, his mind blank to everything but their hostility, the hammer caught in his belt and the revolver swung heavily against Greenaway's rifle and exploded.

Nobody saw where the bullet went but the sound of the single shot echoed across the sluggish river like a thunderclap.

Unware of what had provoked someone to open fire Blair jumped to his feet and shouted, 'At the double!' The marines, who had already been mustered in their various sections, came to life like puppets. With grim faces and rifles at the high-port they trotted down the hillside towards the river.

Most of them had no idea of what might be expected of them. And those who had knew they would now do it alone without even the smallest hope of having surprise on their side.

Blackwood waved his arm and saw the men fan out, keeping their proper distance in spite of the swift change of events. He heard the distant sound of a horn, and knew an alarm was being raised.

It was suddenly desperate and they had not even begun.

He yelled, 'Colour Sergeant! The flag!'

Some of the running marines turned to stare as the burly colour sergeant uncased the flag, and swung it through the air to clear its folds.

Blackwood heard Blair panting beside him. It was only a gesture. But battles had been won on less.

Lieutenant de Courcy paused only to stare across at the arsenal's high wall, his eyes blazing as he shouted, 'First Section into the boats!' He pulled out his revolver and waited for the marines to run the last few yards to the water.

A few shots whimpered and cracked around them, some hitting the river, others thudding into the boats.

Sergeant Greenaway waved his men on. 'Pole 'em over,

lads!' One man spun round, his mouth wide in a silent cry as a heavy bullet hit him in the throat.

More marines hurried past, their bodies bent as if carrying great loads, eyes startled at the sight of the dead man in their own uniform.

De Courcy emitted a sigh as the hidden machine-gun clattered into life and cut little spurts of dust from the high parapet where the Chinese bullets had come from.

He glared at Ralf. 'Take charge of the MG section and the wounded!' He seized him and shook his arm. 'Control yourself, man! They'll be looking even to you in a moment.'

Ralf stared at him, his eyes wide. 'But – but the Boxers are coming this way!'

'Second Section!' De Courcy winced as another man cried out in agony. But he had to make Ralf understand. 'I shall signal you to cross the river. Cover us 'til then!' He bounded over the stones and joined the second boat which was already being poled across the river, while some of the marines fired at the heads on the parapet.

Blackwood saw the leading boats grind ashore, their occupants only too glad to leave and run for the hillside which sloped towards the arsenal. But for that single shot they would have had some small benefit. He saw a marine fall, clutching his stomach even as he vaulted from one of the boats. It was all going wrong, but if they stayed here they would be surrounded by the Boxers who were about a mile away and approaching fast.

More men ran for the boats, while Blackwood saw his cousin climbing back up the hill, his revolver still dangling from its lanyard. In his heart he had known it had been Ralf.

Blair joined him and paused to train his binoculars on the arsenal. The whole countryside would have heard the firing by now.

He said, 'Time to go.' He shot him a twisted smile. 'Separate boats, I think.'

Blackwood ran over the last strip of land and saw the

earth spurt beside him as some invisible marksman marked him down. Swan kept pace with him and dropped his rifle only to seize one of the long poles with Corporal Addis.

A snail's pace, Blackwood thought. He cocked his head to listen as the machine-gun fell silent. But it restarted and he pictured the dwindling pile of ammunition beside it.

On, on, on, with the flag adding a touch of vivid colour above their lowered heads and taut faces.

'*Re-form!*' Blair limped up the last few yards and leaned against the rocks below the arsenal. 'Get those wounded off the bank!'

Blackwood glanced along the line of men nearest him. Some were feverishly reloading their magazines from their pouches, others stood with their eyes closed as they sucked in great gulps of air.

Sergeant Major Fox bellowed, 'Remember, lads, there's food and drink over that wall! Come on, smarten yerselves up, goddammit!'

Blackwood saw some of the men glaring at his squared shoulders, loathing him, but still managing to react as Fox knew they would.

Blackwood heard someone give a groan as bullets hammered into one of the crude fishing boats while it was still in mid-stream. He saw several marines fall, one completely out of the boat. Another, probably his friend, tried to reach him but the current carried the dead man away. He looked strangely peaceful.

Blair said sharply, 'Mr Gravatt, have your men fire on the parapet. We shall go around to the gates on the road. It's the weakest point.'

Whistles shrilled and NCOs shouted names. Blair added between his teeth, 'God, what a bloody mess!'

Swan whispered, 'The Colonel's been 'it, sir.'

Blackwood realized that Blair was keeping his left elbow jammed against his side. There were flecks of blood on his sleeve. He seemed to sense Blackwood's concern through his pain and gasped, 'Say nothing, David. Not a bloody thing!'

Blackwood cocked his revolver and saw the bugler watching him, his eyes horrified as a marine bounced from the wall, his face a mass of blood.

He thought suddenly of Ralf, back there with the machine-gun section. It would be too much for him to deal with. The machine-gunners, a riding instructor, the engine driver and his mate, and the horse.

It was not much of a threat to the oncoming Boxers. They were all caught in a trap. There was no way out this time.

He forced his mind to respond. If he showed the slightest hint of anxiety or worse, they might break and run. Back to the boats, anywhere.

He nodded to the bugler and realized he was not afraid, he was not even angry any more.

'Sound the Advance, Oates!' Blackwood's grandfather's old servant had been called Oates, and this callow-looking private was related to him. Nothing changed.

Oates raised his instrument, and Blackwood saw his eyes widen as another bugle call echoed faintly above the firing.

Sergeant Greenaway wiped his streaming face with his forearm and said hoarsely, 'Jesus, will you look at *her!*'

Blackwood swung round and heard the others calling to each other as *Mediator*'s long, graceful hull crossed very slowly from left to right beyond the fort.

Splashes marked the sea around her white sides, but Blackwood saw the guns swinging towards the shore, as if they were pointing directly at him.

He said to the bugler, 'Your turn, Oates.' It was all he could do to keep his voice steady. Masterman had made his gesture too, only he would have kept his bugler for this precise moment.

Blair shouted, 'Now, *at them*, Marines!'

The blare of the bugle, the sudden crash of gunfire from *Mediator*'s six-inch armament were almost drowned by the wild cheers as the marines swept towards the adjoining wall and across the road which Blackwood and the colonel had watched from the hilltop.

Huge gouts of fire and earth shot skywards as the first shell exploded on the land. *Mediator*'s gunnery officer was first-class, Blackwood thought, although through his powerful rangefinder the forts and the arsenal probably looked at arm's length.

The lieutenants shouted wildly to restrain their men from breaking cover until they were ready to attack.

Fox pointed and showed a rare excitement. 'Look, the buggers are comin' out!'

The arsenal's gates were opening even as the marines knelt down to take aim. Just a handful of Imperial soldiers in their strange smocks and dark mandarin hats were crowding each other through the gap, ducking as another salvo blasted into the hillside. Masterman's guns were firing well clear of the arsenal, but these Chinese soldiers were not to know that. One of those six-inch shells exploding inside the ancient arsenal would have blasted them to pieces.

'Take aim!'

Blair gasped, 'Belay that, Gravatt! Let 'em run. There's been enough slaughter.'

Gravatt lowered his revolver, the light of wildness still in his eyes. 'Inside the arsenal, Sergeant! Jump about!'

Blackwood watched the colonel anxiously. He was bleeding badly, but showed no sign of collapse. He heard de Courcy order his runner to recall the machine-gun section, for the Third Platoon to give them covering fire as they crossed the narrow river.

When he turned again most of the others had already vanished through the gates, bayonets ready, nerves brittle in case of a trick or ambush.

A few moments later the Chinese standard above the wall was hauled down and the bright Union Flag appeared in its place. Blackwood stared up at it. But for Masterman he doubted if any of them would have survived to see it.

Swan muttered, 'Close thing.'

There was no more opposition, and while the wounded were carried into the protection of a cool cellar, the dead were dragged to the wall for a hasty burial.

The last boat, with the horse swimming and wading beside it, grated into the bank and Blackwood saw his cousin amongst the small rearguard. They all ducked as another salvo ripped noisily overhead to explode beyond the low hills. The gunnery officer and his spotters could probably see the advancing Boxers. At such range and exposed as they were on open ground, the Boxers would stand no chance at all.

Blair sat down very carefully on an upended ammunition case, his orderly steadying his arm.

Blair asked, 'How are the supplies, David?'

Blackwood began to unbutton Blair's tunic with the aid of his orderly.

'Just as you said, sir. Food, water, ammunition, everything. It must be one of Tientsin's main arsenals.'

Blair nodded dully. 'The road. I knew it was a clue if only we could use it.'

Swan hissed. 'Gawd, sir. That's a bad 'un.'

The bullet had hit Blair in the side and had made a black-rimmed hole which revealed at least one shattered rib. How he had managed to carry on in such terrible agony was beyond understanding.

Blair sat very upright as they tied a thick dressing around his body. Even that was soon sodden with blood. In the shadowy gloom of the building it looked black.

Gravatt whispered, 'We'll get him back to the ship if she comes further inshore, sir.'

Blair heard him despite his low voice. 'No. We keep together. My orders are to reinforce Peking, but first we have to protect our rear and supplies by holding Tientsin, *do you understand?*'

Blackwood nodded sadly. 'Yes, sir.'

Blair peered at him searchingly. 'You're a good chap, David. Now get round the sentries and see that our people are fed.' He seemed to think of something. 'Where's the horse. I want to see it.'

Blackwood climbed some narrow stone stairs, how many he could not guess. When he reached the high parapet he saw the dead soldiers who had been caught by their machine-gun, the exhausted marines leaning behind the wall as they watched the white-hulled cruiser.

Gravatt and the sergeant major had everything in hand; there was even woodsmoke rising from a spindly chimney as they broke open some rations.

Swan handed him a full canteen. ''Ere, sir.'

It was water from an internal well. It tasted like champagne.

There was more gunfire, but intermittent and further along the coast. The Allied admirals had been driven to action at long last against the other fort. But for *Mediator*'s example he doubted if they would have quit the Peiho bar.

Blackwood walked down the stairs again where after the parapet and the river it seemed almost icy.

He saw the horse standing in the centre of the courtyard, drinking from a bucket and apparently unharmed by the battle.

Blackwood crossed to the main building and saw several marines resting on their rifles, and Blair still sitting on the box.

Blackwood said, 'The horse is here, sir.'

Sergeant Greenaway leaned over. ''E don't 'ear you, sir.' He closed Blair's eyes, his big hand surprisingly gentle. ''E won't get no ride after all.'

Blackwood looked at Blair's upright figure. It was as if he was still with them. He felt it like a personal loss, as if they had all been cheated in the face of victory.

They were all watching him. Gravatt and de Courcy, the colour sergeant Nat Chittock, and the bugler whose grandfather had been related to a Blackwood servant.

He heard himself say, 'We'll bury him with the others. Tomorrow we move on. To Tientsin.'

He glanced again at the watching colonel.

I hope you heard that, old friend.

Another salvo shook the hillside. It sounded like a last tribute.

13

Soldiering

As the last notes of the bugle died away Blackwood handed the small prayer book to Lieutenant Gravatt. He looked at the six crude graves and hoped they would be left unmolested. It already seemed strange without Blair. Later it would dim like the other memories. But now ... he sighed and then drove Blair's sword into the head of the grave.

De Courcy said in a hushed tone, 'More firing downriver, sir.' Blackwood nodded. He had already heard it. A machine-gun too. But it seemed excluded from the place, this moment.

He saw his cousin watching him from the far side of the courtyard. So far they had not spoken since the incident. Sergeant Greenaway had said nothing, nor would he unless it was dragged out of him.

A sentry shouted from the ramparts, 'Boat comin', sir!' His voice seemed too bright and cheerful after the burial, and Blackwood guessed that it was one of *Mediator*'s boats.

'Take charge here, Toby. Have the wounded ready to be moved.'

Some of the marines heard what he said, and he saw one of the wounded move into the ranks of the others. He did not want to leave. Blackwood saw it was a private called Carver, the one who had tried to save his friend when he had fallen overboard.

The sentries opened the big gate and Blackwood walked down towards the river. Apart from the abandoned boats and

some blood-stains in the dirt there was nothing to show of
their wild, desperate attack. He shaded his eyes to watch
the boat as it manoeuvred awkwardly amongst the sandbars
and treacherous rushes. Smoke gushed from the brass
funnel, and it appeared to be crammed with men, and there
was a machine-gun in the cockpit.

He recognized the lieutenant in charge of the boat and
saw the man's astonishment as he waded ashore, his eyes
taking in the marines in their crumpled uniforms, the stains
which told their own story.

'My God, David, you are full of surprises!'

Blackwood shook his head. Two Englishmen meeting in
the middle of nowhere. He wanted to laugh, but needed to
cry.

'The Colonel's dead, Harry.' He could feel the naval
officer's concern, his inability to grasp what they had all
endured.

The lieutenant said, 'The Old Man intends to land his
own marines and some Bluejackets as soon as the other
captains agree. They are shelling the other forts, and once
we've driven them back we shall occupy the port.' It
sounded easy. He added, 'We received word that Admiral
Seymour's force have taken another big arsenal, and are
staying put until relief arrives.' It seemed to amuse him.
'The rescuers awaiting rescue, so to speak. The message said
that his men were starving when they took the arsenal.' He
watched Blackwood's strained features and said, 'You must
have been on your last legs too.'

Blackwood said, 'Him and his three days' rations!' He did
not hide his anger and bitterness.

'By the way, I've brought some of your chaps with me.
The Surgeon says they are recovered from their injuries up
to a point. Anyway, they pretty well insisted.' He turned
his head as more shots echoed from the main river. 'We
were fired on by Chinese soldiers on our way here. It's war as
far as they're concerned.'

Blackwood heard the returning marines being greeted by

ironic cheers. With men like these ... Blair had said.

The lieutenant wanted to go. Not because he was afraid, but because it was not his world.

'Tell Captain Masterman, thank you from me. It was a near thing.' He pulled out a hastily written message and handed it to him. 'This will explain about a letter which the Colonel left on board. Perhaps Captain Masterman will deal with it if –' *If* – the word hung between them like a threat.

The lieutenant thrust the message into his pocket and shouted to his coxswain, 'Get those wounded on board, Thomas! Fast as you like.' He turned to Blackwood again. 'There's something else, sir.'

Blackwood saw his eyes move towards the boat and when he looked he saw Sergeant Kirby marching purposefully towards him.

'I don't believe it!'

It was unreal. Even the way Kirby was holding back his shoulders, the set of his jaw, his attempt to conceal his pain and discomfort. The fact that he was dressed from top to toe in clean, fresh whites made it even harder to accept.

Kirby stamped to a halt and saluted. 'The NCOs in *Mediator*'s barracks kitted me out, sir.' He sounded very calm, but his eyes were anxious.

Blackwood knew he should not be here. Men in battle could often stand up to almost anything as Blair had proved. But sooner or later they broke.

He said, 'I'm glad to have you back again.' He held out his hand. 'You're more than welcome.'

Kirby stared at the proffered hand. He must be going mad. Then he seized it and walked up the slope to where Fox was waiting to greet him.

The naval lieutenant said softly, 'We had news. His wife died in a fire.'

Blackwood looked at the marines who were gathered by the gates.

'Poor devil. No wonder he wants to get back with the company. I know I would.'

The lieutenant nodded. 'But he's been put up for the VC I hear.'

Blackwood thought of his dead brother in South Africa, of his frail mother and the pretty girl he had left behind. No decoration on earth could fill that gap.

He walked across to a stretcher as Twiss was carried to the boat.

'Don't worry, I'll take care of the horse.' He had not even seen the riding instructor struck down.

The man grinned up at him, his face pale with pain. '*You* ride him. You're in command now.' He waved to the marines as he was lifted over the gunwale. The engine driver shook Blackwood's hand but said nothing. It was all too much for him.

Corporal Lyde said, 'He misses 'is engine!'

Sergeant Owen Davis of the First Platoon exclaimed, 'Well, there's sorry I am indeed, Corporal, but *he's* still alive, look you!'

The coxswain touched his hat. 'All aboard, sir. The sooner we gets one of 'em to the Surgeon the better, I'm thinkin'.'

'Wait.' Blackwood waded through the yellow water and clung to the gunwale. Without their spiked helmets how young they seemed. The man referred to by the coxswain was a private named Campbell. He looked as if he was dying even while one of the Bluejackets supported his head on his lap.

'Good luck, lads.'

Blackwood heard someone give a weak cheer. 'You too, Blackie!'

Blackwood strode up the bank, afraid they would see his face. *Good God Almighty, what have we done to them?*

The lieutenant held out his hand. 'The Old Man would quite understand if you decide to return to the ship, David. Even if we take the forts we've still got a bloody great army to smash through before we can lift the siege on Tientsin. You'll be stuck there with a mixed garrison, to all intents on your own.'

Return to *Mediator*? It was strange but Blackwood had never even considered it. If the new attacks were repulsed by the Chinese Army, which had obviously joined forces with the Boxers, there was an even greater need for reinforcing the International Settlement in Tientsin.

A small figure dashed past him from the boat and he saw it was the other interpreter who had gone downriver with his message for Masterman. The one who had remained with the marines broke through the group by the gates, his face split in a great grin as his friend ran to meet him and threw his arms around him.

The lieutenant said, 'They must be pretty fond of one another, what?'

Blackwood smiled. 'You must have been at sea a long time, Harry.' No wonder they had not wanted to be separated. 'If you've forgotten what a girl looks like!'

The girl had removed her pointed straw hat and her long hair hung down her back like black silk.

'I stay.' She stepped between Blackwood and her friend. 'We work for you.' She gave Blackwood a coy smile. 'I born in Tientsin. I know secret way through wall.'

Gravatt murmured anxiously, 'It's a big risk, sir. Can she be trusted?'

Blackwood put his fingers under her chin and lifted it gently.

'I believe her.' To the other interpreter, who was also about sixteen, he added, 'Lucky chap.'

He heared the boat churning astern away from the land, and hoped it got back to the cruiser without more pain and damage.

Inside the courtyard it was as if the boat had never been, and the graves were the only reminder of this long day.

A marine was feeding the horse. Blackwood was reminded of its last owner's simple statement. *You're in command now.*

He crossed to the horse and patted it, his eyes distant as

he remembered Blair, his divided affections for the Corps and this mysterious land.

Ralf was waiting by the stairway. He said, 'It wasn't my fault!'

Blackwood studied him calmly. 'What happened exactly?'

Ralf looked startled. 'Did Sergeant Greenaway – '

'Nobody's said anything. What did you expect?'

Ralf replied, 'Greenaway was trying to make me look a fool in front of the men. I am quite capable of doing my job without interference from his sort.'

Blackwood felt sickened by it as he watched the petulant strength returning to Ralf's features. He gestured towards the rough graves, and the one with the sword glittering in the filtered sunlight.

'We lost some good men today. But for your stupid, intolerant behaviour we might have escaped with fewer casualties, so think of that for a change!'

Ralf hung his head. 'I thought you would stand up for me.'

'So I will.' Blackwood knew Fox was waiting for him. There were plans to be made, a route to be discussed with the interpreters. There was not much time to rest. If half of what the naval lieutenant had told him was true most of the Boxers would be rallying to withstand a possible landing. It would be their only chance to get into the city before they too were cut off by the enemy.

He added, 'Even at a court-martial. Now be off to your duties and see that your people eat and rest in turns. Show that you are interested in them, that they can rely on you.' He touched Ralf's shoulder but felt more like hitting him. 'That you've got the gut for it.'

He walked away, knowing that as before Ralf had seen right through him.

Blackwood spread his map carefully on the table while the officers and senior NCOs pressed closer around him. In the light from a solitary lantern the room was spartan like most of the arsenal; there were even some half-consumed dishes of tea left by the small detachment of soldiers when Ralf's revolver had raised the alarm.

It would be dawn again very soon, but it was difficult to believe they had been here since yesterday. Outside the little room he could hear the marines being mustered by their corporals, the horse stamping its newly muffled hooves on the cobbles. Each man would be carrying a full pack which they had recovered from the opposite bank during the night. Blackwood half expected an attack, but Bannatyre's scouting party had found nothing. *Mediator*'s unexpected bombardment had worked. Only corpses lay beyond the humped hill.

Blackwood was sorry they had thrown the second machine-gun into the river. There was three-oh-three ammunition in plenty for it and any other weapon stacked within the arsenal. There was ample food too, but if the marines were required to fight without warning they would have to rid themselves of their overweight packs and equipment.

It was amazing what a good meal and a few gallons of tea had done for his depleted company. In spite of their losses and what still lay ahead they were able to joke about it, to impress the returned wounded who had been the original heroes until now.

Blackwood pointed at the map. 'We shall skirt round the city and make our approach from the south-west. That way we shall avoid the more crowded parts and another big arsenal which will be heavily guarded. It appears that Admiral Seymour's forces have occupied the Hsiku arsenal to the north, that too will be under siege by now. So if our ships are attacking the forts most attention will be concentrated on the places mentioned.' He saw Sergeant Kirby sway forward as if to study the map more closely.

Incredibly brave, foolish too. It was hard to know which he admired most. Kirby knew exactly what he was doing. Reason had flown out of the window.

'I intend to leave at first light, and enter the city at dusk.' He glanced around their intent faces. So much depended on the interpreters' information. He had spent over an hour discussing his tactics with them, and it was remarkable how quickly they had grasped his ideas. The girl, who had been born in Tientsin, had even changed his plan from his original one. She had described a long, empty gully which ran from the south-west wall of the city, intended originally to deal with rare but overwhelming rainfalls in the area.

Madness, just the place the enemy would be guarding? But why should they? The defenders were penned inside the various concessions and could not break out, and the only real danger came from the sea. He half smiled. It was just about the craziest plan he had ever heard, let alone created.

Fox said, 'I laid 'ands on a cart, sir. Useful fer ferryin' wounded an' the like.' He was only concerned with details. The chances of risk and survival were not his to question.

De Courcy remarked, 'We'll need some good scouts for this one.'

He glanced at Sergeant Greenaway who nodded and said, 'Taken care of, sir.'

Chittock, the colour sergeant, said, 'I borrowed a spare flag from the boat, sir. Don't want to damage our own.'

Several of them laughed. They all knew what Chittock meant by 'borrow'.

Blackwood straightened his back and looked at each of them in turn. 'You may think this is a waste of time, perhaps a waste of lives. But think of yourselves under fire in Tientsin, hoping and praying for a relief which never comes. You've all seen what the Boxers are capable of. When we enter the city it will give them new heart.' He had almost said *if* instead of *when*.

'One thing, and it has to be said. There will be no surrender. It would only prolong the agony.' He made himself grin. 'So be prepared to move.'

When the others had left Gravatt said, 'Will we blow the arsenal, sir?'

'No. We would lose any chance of surprise. At the moment the enemy seems to think we left in *Mediator*.'

Gravatt laughed. 'It *would* seem the sensible thing to do!'

Blackwood glanced at the empty room. 'You are second-in-command now, Toby, you may need a plan all of your own!'

'A sobering thought, sir.'

Blackwood clapped him on the shoulder. 'Take my – er, Mr Blackwood with you.' He saw Gravatt's surprise. 'And watch him, for all our sakes.'

Gravatt nodded, his mood changed. He probably guessed what it had cost Blackwood to say it. But there was far more at stake now than family ties.

Gravatt looked down at his uniform and groaned. 'God, look at us!' Like the rest of the men his tunic and trousers had been soaked in a vat of boiled tea, so that they had a dirty mottled appearance. But Blackwood knew from the past it offered some cover and disguise.

Gravatt was unimpressed. 'Lord knows what my chap in Savile Row would say!'

They left the room. Blackwood felt like his adjutant. It was a shame to abandon the arsenal intact. All those weapons and ammunition might one day be used against them. Perhaps Masterman's guns would finish the job once they had moved inland again.

In the courtyard the air still felt cool and damp.

He glanced at the scouting party which Greenaway had hand-picked himself. He thought suddenly of Blair and his trust in others. It worked. They were all there. Corporal O'Neil, Dago Trent, Roberts, the crack shot who said he came from a farm. A poacher more likely. There were a few others too, faces as familiar as his own in a mirror.

Sergeant Greenaway strode towards him, ungainly and heavy.

'Ready, sir.' He hesitated. 'Will an officer be comin' with us?'

'No, Sergeant.' It was painful to see his relief. 'It's up to you.'

O'Neil called to his friend the Nordenfeldt gunner. 'Will you be safe without me, Willy? I'll try not to be too long!'

Kirby's harsh voice echoed from the wall. 'Quiet, you bog-trottin' madman!'

Blackwood looked away. Kirby had changed again in some way. There was no malice in the sergeant's voice. He was glad to be back, more than that, he *needed* to be here.

'Open the gates.'

The scouting party drifted through the gap and vanished into the gloom. From the parapet a sentry called in a hushed voice, 'All's well, sir!'

Blackwood crossed to the graves. What did they always say? No goodbyes, never go back.

'Withdraw the sentries, Mr Bannatyre, and take command of the rearguard.' He stopped him in his tracks. 'No heroics this time, Ian. We'll try and stay together.'

In sections the marines began to move towards the gate, rifles slung, shoulders bowed under their packs, extra ammunition, food and all that went to make them independent of the land.

Swan coughed politely. ''Ere we are, sir.' His teeth were very white in the darkness. ''Is name's Trooper.'

Blackwood smiled. He could almost feel Blair watching and listening. It was what he would have done.

Blackwood raised his foot to the stirrup and heaved himself into the saddle. It reminded him of those keen mornings at Hawks Hill, the copse sweeping past in that first gallop.

Swan stood back and looked at him. 'Wish I 'ad one of them new camera-things, sir. The General'd be right proud of you!'

Blackwood spurred the horse after Fox's handcart. 'Come on then, Trooper, let's see what you can do.'

As he trotted along the lines of marines he saw them glance at him, some to nudge their companions and grin. *A bit of soldiering*, as Fox would put it. What it was all about.

At the rear of the thin column Private Jack Swan placed his captured pike on the cart and fell in step behind the others. His belly was full, his throat was no longer like a kiln, and he had enough ammo to last him quite a while.

When you considered it, he thought, you didn't need much else.

The gully was about ten feet deep and lined with crudely cut stone blocks which looked as old as time.

For most of the day the marines had trudged along the gully's curved base, some gasping for breath as the sun made the airless heat unbearable.

Every so often Blackwood had signalled them to pause and take a rest. Weighed down as they were, they could not be expected to keep up a good pace. And all the time they had heard the distant bark of light artillery, the crack of rifle fire, where or whose it was Blackwood did not know, he was just thankful it was away from their gully. There was smoke too which as dusk closed in looked solid against the sky.

A runner came back along the straggling column, jumping to avoid the cracks between the stones and the great tufts of grass which had somehow survived in the searing heat.

'Beg pardon, sir.' He paused for breath. 'Mr de Courcy's respects, an' we're in sight of the wall.'

'Tell the advance guard to stand-to.'

Sergeant Greenaway would keep his scouts hidden; he always seemed to know what to do.

Blackwood hurried after the runner and heard Swan calling somebody to lead the horse in his place. Even here, Swan trusted nobody to guard him.

He found Gravatt and de Courcy sprawled amongst some stones which had collapsed over the side of the gully.

Neither of them was wearing his helmet as he peered over the side. Another lesson learned, thought Blackwood.

'What is it?' He noticed that Gravatt had Blair's binoculars slung around his neck and saw dried blood on the leather case.

He dragged out his own glasses and wriggled up beside the others. The land was quite flat, and he could see the smouldering buildings of the Native City, and clouds of drifting sparks from the more substantial European houses.

He trained his glasses with great care and saw the wall and sand-bagged defences of the south-west corner. The girl had been right about everything so far.

The gunfire seemed to be coming from the other sector, and he heard someone shouting as more shots cracked amongst the ruins.

He said quietly, 'Most of the fighting seems to be on the far side near the canal. Maybe some of our people are trying to reach the city from the Peiho itself. If so they're getting a hot reception.'

Gravatt pointed at another low wall which crossed diagonally in front of the city. It had obviously been the first line of defence for the various legation guards, but they had been forced back into the city itself. The low wall was pockmarked with white stars where hundreds of bullets had left their mark. In the centre of the wall, almost opposite the barricaded gates, was a great V-shaped gap. A shell must have done it, but it looked as if some giant beast had gnawed it out.

Gravatt waited for him to see the occasional movements where the attackers were now using the same wall for their own cover.

White smocks criss-crossed with bandoliers of ammunition and the now familiar red head scarves.

'No more than a dozen of them, sir.'

Blackwood measured the distance with his eyes. Once they left the gully there was over a hundred yards to the gates. A lot depended on the intelligence of the defenders, and the strength of enemy forces nearby.

They could proceed no further in the gully. Most of the sides had fallen down to block it nearer the city, or had been detonated to prevent a surprise attack.

The sky was getting darker. It was the colour of blood towards the west. He bit his lip. Hopefully not an omen.

'Firing's getting heavier, sir.' De Courcy watched him patiently. 'Another attack before nightfall maybe?'

Gravatt slid down and replaced his helmet. 'We'll not get a better chance, sir.'

'I agree.' Blackwood levelled his glasses again. The Boxers behind the low wall were so confident that only two were watching the city wall, the others had their backs to it, their weapons propped or lying nearby.

One Boxer looked straight at him, his face stark and cruel in the lens. For an instant Blackwood thought he had seen him, but the man's eyes moved on, impassive once again.

'We shall attack in two prongs from left to right. One section only will remain in the centre with the MG carriage and Sergeant Major Fox's cart.' Like the others he always saw the cart as Fox's personal property.

De Courcy eyed him doubtfully. 'They could still pin us down while they call for reinforcements. There are probably others in those ruins over yonder.'

'We must have what our late Colonel would call a *diversion.*' He looked for Swan. 'Lead Trooper up here and fetch the Colour Sergeant and a bugler.'

It was a strange unnerving feeling. As if his whole body had suddenly become weightless. The tension was the biggest drain on men's nerves. It was now or never.

He heard the horse thudding past the crouching marines and saw Chittock with his sheathed flag following close behind.

'Get to your positions.' He glanced at the lieutenants and tried to smile. But his muscles were so hard that he could barely manage it. It was like that other time when he had thought he was about to die. When he had won his VC.

'Good luck. Tell your people to *trot* when they hear the bugle. They'll drop like flies before they've covered half the distance otherwise.'

They nodded, their faces stiff, like strangers.

To Swan he added, 'Take those rags off Trooper's hooves.' He loosened his sword and did the same with his revolver.

Swan stared at him. 'You're not goin' over on '*im*?'

'Watch me.' Blackwood turned to the others. 'When I come past, sound the Charge, and keep on, no matter what.' To Swan he said quietly, 'Listen. The firing is getting less. Soon it will be too late. Try to understand. It's what I'm here for.'

Swan opened his mouth to protest but closed it again. Then he said, 'I'll be with you, sir. All the bloody way.'

Blackwood pulled himself into the saddle and felt the horse flinch nervously, Perhaps it knew, or could smell the blood.

He replied, 'I know that, you rascal.' Then he cantered back down the gully where the NCOs were hissing instructions to their men.

'Fix bayonets!' In the red glow from the sky the blades looked as if they had already been used.

They watched him pass and then Blackwood saw Ralf waiting for him by the cart and the men with the machine-gun carriage. Pity they couldn't use that now, he thought vaguely. But they would need it later on. If they survived.

He wheeled his horse and faced the end of the gully which he had just left. All movement had ceased and the marines crouched or lay along the side, some chewing on their chinstraps, others looking at him as he gauged the moment.

'What is it, Ralf?' It came out sharper than he intended.

'The interpreters, sir. They want to leave.' He sounded on the edge of real fear. 'They'll betray us!'

The two interpreters came and stood beside the horse, the girl soothing the animal with her small hand.

'We leave now.' She was not pleading. 'We go to my home.'

Blackwood thought of the dense smoke and flattened buildings. Home. He tried to control his body. It must be shaking for everyone to see.

He asked, 'Is it safe?'

She touched his stirrup. 'Where is safe?'

Where is safe? Its very simplicity seemed to sum up every campaign he had ever seen.

He tugged down his helmet and then drew his sword. As he bit on his chinstrap he managed to say, 'Pass them through. And good luck.' Then he spurred the horse into a trot, his sword over his shoulder as the waiting marines seemed to flash past him.

Round the long curve and there were the fallen stones, the bugler and the others staring at him as if they would never move again.

'Sound the Charge!' As the bugle blared across the gully Blackwood spurred the horse into a gallop, straight for the fallen barrier. For an instant he thought Trooper was going to rear up and throw him, but he dragged at the reins and felt the powerful body lift beneath him and they were suddenly thundering across open ground. It was all moving like a wild dream, the bugle seemed to go on and on, and in his mind he could see the two halves of his company bursting from cover and pounding along behind him.

And here was the wall, with more gaping faces, and the sudden crack of a rifle. One Boxer ran straight for him but slithered away with a terrible shriek as Blackwood's blade hacked him across the neck. Up again, and through the gap in the wall. There were more shots now, but they were coming from the advancing marines who fired from the hip without even taking aim in the confusion. Pinned against the wall the remaining Boxers stood ready to fight, but those who did not fall reeled before the glittering bayonets as the marines charged through them.

Protected by the centre section the colour sergeant

managed to hold the flag high, his bright scarlet sash at odds with his crumpled tea-stained clothing.

Two marines on the right flank fell in the dust, and as another section opened covering fire they were dragged on to the cart and rushed towards the wall.

Blackwood galloped along the barricades and shell-pitted wall and saw startled faces peering down at him. Their uniforms all seemed to be different, like the flags which flew over Seymour's ships.

'*Open the gate!*' Blackwood waved his sword. 'Move your bloody breeches!'

The gates swung inwards and Blackwood reined back as his breathless wild-eyed men charged through.

A few shots whimpered overhead but Blackwood barely noticed them.

Somewhere a voice shouted, 'The relief's here! My God they've got through! Who are you, lads?'

And Fox's harsh voice as loud as on any parade ground. '*The Royal Marines*, that's who, mate!'

But Blackwood patted the horse and waited for Swan to join him. Only when the gates crashed together behind him did he really understand what they had done.

As he allowed the horse to carry him beneath the overhang of the wall he heard a marine exclaim, 'You should'er seen 'im! Talk abaht the Charge o' the bleedin' Light Brigade!'

Blair would have approved.

14

Love and Hate

Blackwood sat uncomfortably on a straightbacked chair which seemed to have been placed about ten feet from the desk. It made him feel isolated from the man behind it, and he guessed that was probably the intention.

Colonel Sir John Hay of the Foot Guards had sent for him as soon as the Royal Marines had arrived at their temporary quarters, a long stone building which had been stables. At least Trooper would feel at home there.

The thought made him smile. It was like everything else, unreal, larger than life. Sergeant Kirby's return, the mad dash on horseback, the cheers of his men.

It had taken a toll of his own strength. He could feel the hammers beating inside his skull and recalled what the naval surgeon had hinted about concussion.

Colonel Hay was almost the strangest person you might expect to find in this situation, he thought.

He was tall, square-shouldered, with an upturned ginger moustache, and bright, pale eyes which were almost colourless. On the rare occasions Blackwood had seen him smile he changed entirely. His grin, like his voice, was fierce, so that he looked slightly unhinged.

Blackwood recalled Hay's first words as the exhausted marines had waited patiently in a square which was littered with debris from the surrounding buildings, and which stank of corpses still buried under the bricks and charred beams.

After what they had done to reach Tientsin, and the

many pitched battles since their arrival in China, Blackwood had expected a brief speech of welcome at least.

Hay had seemed almost beside himself with disbelief. 'Is this *all*? What happened to the relief?' He had glared at Blackwood accusingly. 'How many have you got, for God's sake?'

Blackwood had answered as calmly as he could. 'Seventy officers and marines, sir.' He had forced a smile. 'And two Austro-Hungarian sailors we gathered on the way.'

Hay had not been amused. 'They promised reinforcements.' He had glared at the marines in their tea-stained uniforms and filthy boots. 'God, they look like – ' He had not said any more. Then as now Hay made a stark contrast in his red tunic and gold shoulder straps. There was not a speck of dust on his uniform in spite of the irregular explosions around the city, the occasional whiplash crack of sniper fire.

Blackwood shifted in the chair. His body felt restricted in his scarlet tunic which Swan had hastily unpacked and brushed for him.

Hay had said hotly, 'We represent the British authorities here. As senior officer in Tientsin I expect, no, demand, a proper turnout at all times. It is the only way to retain these people's respect.'

Blackwood was still not certain whom he had meant by 'these people'. The Chinese, or the Allied troops who made up most of the city's defenders.

Hay turned his head and stared at the heavily shuttered window. 'We've about two thousand soldiers here. Russians, French, Americans, Japanese and of course my own men. We've a perimeter of some five miles to defend, and the barricades make up much of the protection along the river and canal. Some American engineer named Hoover did most of the planning. Quite a fair job.'

It sounded condescending. As if it was of no real importance.

His head was getting worse and he knew he needed sleep

more than anything. It was incredible to accept that they had marched from the arsenal that morning. Now it was midnight or near enough and it was all he could do to concentrate on Hay's sharp, irritated voice.

'Pity you didn't blow up that magazine. The enemy have enough looted weapons as it is. It's been absolute hell here, and we've all the civilians, women and children to care for.'

Blackwood made himself ask, 'How many of the enemy, sir?'

Hay glared at him as if he expected a trap. 'They estimate about ten thousand, with more coming every day. Unless reinforcements can break through there'll soon be nothing to defend. Somebody should try to negotiate again with the Chinese government. This kind of uprising ought to be stamped out immediately.'

There was no point in telling Hay it was no longer just an uprising. At Hawks Hill the General with his maps and his memories would probably agree with him and describe it as a 'skirmish'.

Instead he said, 'The whole countryside is terrified of the Boxers.'

'You would know of course.' Again the fierce grin. 'I've heard about the Royal Marines.'

'I've lost my colonel, another officer and twenty-three others killed and wounded. Some of the latter have voluntarily rejoined the detachment.' He added bitterly, 'They can still give a good account when called for.'

Hay changed tack. 'I shall give your men the south-west sector. Some fortifications, several good strong buildings, and one of the hotels which we use for civilians.' He dropped his pale stare. 'Ours, of course.'

Of course. What was the real cause of his dislike? Blackwood wondered. He thought of the marines' expressions when Hay had criticized their appearance. For an instant he had feared that some wild man might yell something from the safety of the ranks. But as had happened before it had acted as a challenge to the marines.

Within the hour they were paraded again in their scarlet kerseys with buttons as bright as ever.

He had heard Fox saying in a voice just a bit too loud, 'And any Royal Marine who lets me down in front of a bloody Foot Guard will know what my temper can be like!'

Perhaps because of their calling they had hated the dirt, the sweat and torn clothing which they had carried with them all the way from *Mediator*'s gleaming messdecks.

'I've heard that you have seen quite a bit of service, Captain Blackwood.'

Blackwood said nothing. How different from Blair. The day that Hay calls me by my first name will be *the*day.

Hay studied him severely. 'Nowadays I am more used to diplomats than the Brigade.'

A small Chinese girl in a white smock entered the room with a silver tray. On it were two large glasses of whisky.

Blackwood could not remember asking for it, but he was so drained he could hardly recall any sequence of events.

The room gave a shiver as some shells fell somewhere in the city. He saw the servant's eyes widen with alarm and wondered how the two interpreters were getting on, and if they were still alive. The whisky was good and he felt its strength warming him.

Hay said, 'The officers here are a mixed bunch naturally.' He frowned. 'Some of them lost their kit in the first attacks, so there's no need to dress for dinner.'

'I don't have mess kit either, sir.'

'I understand.'

He went off at a tangent again. 'I believe they will mount a big attack tomorrow or the day after. They need to occupy the whole city and destroy the defenders before they can join together at Peking.'

'We are in the same position, sir.'

'Really?' He sounded distant. 'So long as we can hold the perimeter things should get better.'

Blackwood tried not to look at him. At this stage of the game it seemed inconceivable that anyone could ignore the problems of shortages which would soon bear down on them all. Food, ammunition, survival.

Hay said, 'The Boxers never attack at night. Perhaps their invulnerability only works in daylight, eh?' He gave a short laugh, like a dog barking.

He added, 'It was a pity you were not sent directly here in the first place.' Again it sounded like an accusation. 'That business upriver was a waste of time. That's where you lost a subaltern, right?'

'Yes, sir.' Blackwood placed his empty glass on a table and saw that Hay had not drunk any of his. What was the matter with him? One minute he acted towards him with total indifference, and the next he had released some information which he must have gathered from someone else.

'Oh yes, brave enough, no doubt of that, but not thought through.'

Blackwood asked abruptly, 'Who told you about the Hoshun, sir?'

Hay stood up and squared his shoulders. 'I heard something about it when you and Admiral Seymour's advance party went through Tientsin. I also met quite a few of the people who were trying to get back to Peking before you arrived.'

'Did you meet any of the Germans who returned to their Peking legation?' Without noticing it he was leaning forward in the chair.

'Oh yes. Count von Heiser of course.'

Why did he always add *of course*? He tried again, 'I heard they arrived safely.'

'Did you?'

He wants me to beg, but how could he know or guess?

Hay remarked offhandedly, 'They went in separate parties in case the railway was torn up. As it happened, the Chinese closed the city to the Allies the day they arrived. But the second party turned back.' His eyes glittered in the lamplight. 'These Germans don't know everything. It will do them good to have their tails between their legs for a change!' Again the short, humourless laugh.

The colonel pulled a watch from his pocket. 'You'd better get back to your sector. Don't forget, double the sentries. All looters will be shot on sight. Stand-to at first light.' It was dismissal.

Blackwood walked through an outer room where a tired-looking servant was busy polishing the colonel's boots.

Sir John Hay was a strange bird, he thought. Was his comment about dressing for dinner merely to cover something else? He seemed very confident, perhaps too much so.

The warm night air made him yawn. He would have to go round the sentries before speaking to Gravatt.

It was deathly quiet, but in the sky he could still see the reflected fires, drifting smoke.

As he strode towards the sector where they had burst through the gates just a few hours ago he saw Swan's shadow detach itself from the side of a low building.

'You ought to get some rest, Swan. That's one privilege at least your job gives you.'

Swan studied him in the darkness. 'A Chinese girl brought you a letter, sir.' He could not hold the pretence any longer and Blackwood saw his grin splitting his face as he added. 'It was our little Anna.'

Blackwood took the small envelope and turned it over in his hands.

'Tell Mr Gravatt I want him.' He waited for Swan to hurry away and then ducked into the low doorway of the abandoned building. By the light of a shaded lamp he opened the envelope and held a single sheet of notepaper in the glow.

It said, *Please come*, and it was sighed with an *F*.

She is here. Hay had known the reason for his questions, or he soon would. He must be careful for her sake.

Gravatt crunched out of the darkness. 'I've been round our posts, sir. I had the machine-gun mounted on a low building. The men there will be protected by a barricade of sandbags and sacks of grain. Best we can do.'

'Stand-to at first light, Toby.'

'I know, sir.'

Blackwood did not ask him how he knew.

He said, 'Call me if you need me.'

Gravatt watched him go. No wonder the men liked him so much. He had seen Anna give the letter to Swan. The rest was easy to fathom out.

He removed his helmet and dragged his finger around his tunic collar. First light and they would stand and fight. Suddenly he envied Blackwood. Just to hold a woman's hand again, to blurt out your fears, to pretend there was a future.

He sighed and walked around the corner to seek out the last picket.

The hotel which Hay had described in their brief interview was at the rear of the marines' sector, hemmed in on either side by sturdy, barricaded buildings. One of the latter was where Gravatt had sited their only machine-gun. If he lived he would one day make a good field officer Blackwood thought.

If the enemy forced the gates and drove the marines back to their next line of defence, the gun could cover them from the flat roof and still be able to fire above the defences without being moved. The hotel was shuttered and curtained and smelt of musty carpets and decay. The last place on earth where any European might expect to end up.

A British soldier in a white jacket watched Blackwood with obvious suspicion as he explained who he had come to see.

''S like this, sir, we're not supposed to let service people in 'ere after dark. Regulations, sir.'

'Colonel Hay said it was perfectly all right.'

The man looked relieved. 'In that case, sir.' He gestured with his tray. 'Up them stairs, second right.' He hesitated.

'If you're sure, sir?'

Blackwood hurried up the curved staircase. The soldier might call his superior officer, but he doubted it. He guessed that sleep was a bonus around here; it would take a strong heart to wake an officer. He saw a small figure huddled in an armchair outside a door.

'Hello, Anna.'

The girl took his hands in hers and rocked from side to side, as she had aboard the old *Bajamar*, a million years ago.

She whispered, 'Bye um bye we all finish, Sah. Boxer come um choppum head. All gone!'

Blackwood could feel her terror, also the loyalty which held her to her German mistress.

He released his hands and tapped gently on the door.

It opened instantly, as if she had been listening, waiting.

He closed the door quietly and followed her through vague shadow to an adjoining room. There was a small glow from a lamp, but otherwise the place was in darkness, the air humid and without life.

She was wearing the same dark blue robe as when he had burst into her cabin with Swan's shoulder beside him. Her hair too hung down her back, more like gold than honey in the faint glow.

She did not resist as he took her shoulders and pulled her against him.

She said, 'When I heard the excitement and the cheering I knew it was you. It had to be.' She looked up and searched his face. 'You are not hurt? I heard that you had a bad time, that men were killed.'

'Some were. Thank God you are safe, Friedrike.' How easy it was to speak her name. 'When Colonel Hay told me, I could not believe you might be here too.'

Her mouth quivered. 'That man Hay. He is in the wrong army, I think. He should be a Prussian Guard!'

Blackwood held her closer and touched her hair, her soft warmth, and allowed the dream to become reality.

'And you are alone here?'

She rested her head on his shoulder. 'Yes. Manfred had to go to Peking. He will be needed, I think. There is a rumour that Baron von Ketteler has been murdered there by Chinese troops. Nothing is certain.' She looked at him again. 'Except that you came. To me.'

Somewhere in the musty hotel a clock chimed. It sounded doleful, like a dirge. One o'clock.

She said suddenly, 'I need air. I shall open the window. There can be no danger if the light is out.'

He released her reluctantly. Had she done that deliberately but was now once again in control of herself?

He turned off the lamp as she opened the long curtains and pushed the heavy shutters away from the windows.

'Look at the moon, David.' She sounded excited, like a child.

He stood behind her, his hands on her small waist as he stared across the beleaguered city. *Tomorrow*. What was the use of thinking about any tomorrow? It might be pointless.

She asked, 'Will help come, David?'

He felt her shiver, but when he touched her neck it was hot, as if she had a fever.

'They will come. They must.' He thought of Masterman's determination, his example to the others who had waited too long.

'My men are nearest to you. We will protect you, no matter what.'

She spoke with great care and deliberation. 'But if the Boxers come here, David, it will mean – '

'It will mean that we have failed, and have paid for it.' He forced the picture of the murdered Chinese girl and her baby from his mind. 'But we shall make our stand here, you can depend on it.'

She turned easily in his arms and studied him although Blackwood could not see her face in the darkness.

'I feel safe now.'

She did not resist as he lowered his mouth to hers and kissed her very gently. It was like touching something fragile, or saying the wrong word when it counted most. She did not pull away but kissed him in return, her heart pounding to match his own. Only when he slipped his hand through the robe and touched her breast did she exclaim, 'Oh, my God, David, I can't, must not!'

But he held her breast in his hand. It was alive, warm and beating as if it would burst free.

She leaned against him, her hair brushing his mouth as she gasped, 'I can't!' Then she struggled free of his arms and stood a few paces away. 'What am I saying to you, David? We are deluding ourselves, I saw it on your face when you came in. We shall not survive!' She tugged at the cord about her throat and allowed the robe to drop on the floor. Framed against the pale moonlight Blackwood saw her beautiful body as clearly as if she had been naked.

He took her to him again and soothed her sudden despair, the violent trembling which seemed to run right through her.

He said huskily, 'I want you, Friedrike. I want you now. Then tomorrow can do what it will.'

She nodded against his chest. 'I know. But it has been so long for me. I am afraid, just a little bit.'

Blackwood could feel her shivering, and guessed what it was costing her to reveal her feelings to him.

He heard himself murmur, 'I'll lock the outer door.' He saw her watching him as he unbuckled his sword and revolver. The trappings of war which could reach neither of them, until as in the fairy-story the daylight came.

Blackwood placed them carefully on a chair and unbuttoned his tunic. His fingers were all thumbs, his mind blank to the consequences if there was an attack, if the belief that Boxers would not storm the city by night was just a legend.

He turned and for an instant he thought he had imagined all of it. She had gone.

Then he heard her voice from the darkness. 'David.'

He moved into the deeper shadows and saw her arms

rising from the bed to embrace him. His foot caught on the night-dress where she had thrown it, and the next second he was standing over her. In the moonlight, so faint here in one corner of the room, her body stood out like a fallen statue, her hair in disorder around her shoulders. She bunched her hands tightly into fists as he touched her and caressed her breasts, the gentle curve of her stomach and further still. She cried out and shook her head from side to side as if to defy some silent warning.

Blackwood threw his clothes on the floor and sat beside her. It was perfect, and it was torture. He kissed her mouth, and felt her lips part, her tongue on his as he kissed her harder. Only when he knelt above her did she show real fear.

She reached out for him, her hands frantic as they gripped his body.

'Please, be gentle!'

It was like falling, he had known nothing like it. He felt her hand lose its fear as it reached out to guide him. Then she gasped just once as she arched her back to receive and to hold him.

When they had finished it was a long while before they moved. When he made to leave her she seized his hair in both hands and whispered, 'No, stay. I can still feel you. Try to sleep. I will hold you.'

And so it was. When the window became edged with grey they stirred, as did their want of each other. They made love again, with the quiet desperation of wrongdoers.

Blackwood found himself half-running to the staircase, buckling on his weapons as he went. He should be totally exhausted, he could not remember sleeping at all. Only her voice calling his name, and the passion of her body which had been released like a trapped animal.

For a few moments longer he stood outside in the littered street and stared up at the vanishing stars.

He felt as if he could do anything.

Sergeant Tom Greenaway gripped part of the rough
barricade and tried to shake it. It did not budge in spite of
the mixture of things which had gone in to its construction.
Iron rails, boulders, upended waggons and carts and sacks of
grain. It might do the trick. He glanced at the two sentries
who stood together like twins.

'All quiet, Sarge.'

'Good.' Greenaway stood on a cartwheel and peered
across at the shadows. It would be light in no time, he
thought. In these parts the sun came up like a fireball. No
hanging about.

He saw the pale shapes of Boxer corpses lying like
discarded bundles of dhobying. He had laid two of them
low himself on that charge from the gully. Yesterday. Was
that all it had been?

Dago Trent chuckled. 'They brought round some more
grub in the night, Sarge. This billet'll suit me proper!'

The other marine, a new recruit called Vicary, asked,
'You reckon them buggers'll come for us today, Sergeant?'

Greenaway thought about it. 'Likely, I'd say. They've got
everythin' to lose by stayin' put. 'Side which they may be
gettin' short o' rations like we was.' Poor little sod, he
thought. He'd done well this far, but he was still green and
needed more time.

Dago Trent hissed, 'Officer comin'!'

Greenaway tensed. It was the second lieutenant. He
would watch his tongue. Inspect every word before he let it
go.

He said smartly, 'All's well, sir.'

Ralf peered at the sentries. 'Keep your eyes open.' He
turned to the younger man, 'What's your name?'

'V-Vicary, sir.' The young private had a stammer which
showed itself when he was upset.

Greenaway tore his eyes away and stared over at the wall
where Captain Blackwood's horse had made such a fine leap.
How could he and his cousin be so different?

Ralf said, 'Well then, Private V-Vicary, you should

know by now that when you're on sentry-duty you'll – '

Dago Trent said rudely, 'He's not been in the Corps that long, sir.'

'Hold your tongue! Is this what you allow, Sergeant?' He stared at Greenaway who was still standing on the cartwheel and apparently excluding himself completely. 'Pay *attention*, Sergeant!'

Greenaway hissed, 'Quiet, everybody!' He did not hear the officer's furious exclamation. 'Somethin' wrong. I think, no, I'm certain that one o' them corpses 'as moved.'

'Don't be such a blithering idiot, Sergeant!' It suddenly hit him what Greenaway had said. 'It's absurd, you're seeing things!'

Absurd is it, you little maggot. Aloud Greenaway muttered, 'Look, fifty yards. By them torn sandbags.'

Ralf peered blankly into the shadows. 'You must be mistaken!' But his voice lacked conviction this time.

A soft breeze moved one of the corpse's clothing and Ralf added, 'See that? It's what you saw just now, right?'

'*Wrong.*' Greenaway could barely control his breathing. He added, 'Sir.'

'Why don't you go and see?' Ralf was confused.

Dago Trent asked, 'Why don't you, sir?'

Greenaway barked, 'Cut it out, Dago!' Trent usually managed to go just that bit too far.

'I'll see that you regret this, Trent! Don't forget we come under the Army Discipline Act here, a bit of field punishment might teach you to show respect for your betters!'

Greenaway could see the danger. It could go right through his platoon like the pox.

He said heavily, 'You're ordering me to go, sir, is that it?'

Greenaway's sudden challenge took Ralf off-balance, but not for long.

'Yes, I bloody well am!'

'Suits me.' Greenaway picked up his rifle and climbed on

to the barricade. As Trent made to follow he said, 'You stay. Cover me.' He glanced at the youth. 'You come with me, Private Vicary.' He grinned although he knew he was acting foolishly, out of anger. 'An' no stutterin', see?' He did not even glance at the second lieutenant. 'It's not respectful.'

The youth grinned. 'I'm with you, Sarge!' He blushed in the gloom. He was not that much a veteran yet. 'I mean Sergeant.'

Dago Trent threw himself into a niche between the sandbags and levelled his rifle.

Under his breath he murmured softly, 'If they get it, so will you, you little bastard!'

Boots scraped on sand and Blackwood, with Swan behind him, walked along the barricade.

'Where's Vicary?' Blackwood stared at his cousin. 'What the hell's going on here?'

Ralf said, 'He's with Sergeant Greenaway, sir. They're looking at a corpse.' He sounded less sure again. 'Greenaway thought he saw it move.'

'Fetch them back at once.' Blackwood turned to Swan. 'Bugler, *fast!*'

Ralf jumped down from the barricade and hurried after the two marines. For a moment or two he lost his bearings and when he looked back he could not see the point where he had left cover.

'Oh bloody hell!' He drew his revolver carefully, the memory of that moment on the river-bank still painful in his mind.

There they were. That lump Greenaway groping about like an old woman. He shouted, 'Fall back, Sergeant!'

Greenaway turned and stared. 'You'll wake the 'ole of bloody China!' Greenaway swung round and saw Vicary struggling with his rifle as one of the corpses bounded to its feet, and another rolled over before running away at a tangent.

Greenaway almost vomited as the great blade swung

mercilessly across the young marine's neck. Vicary's head seemed to fall to his chest as the force of the blow almost cut it from his body.

Greenaway threw up his rifle and fired. As he jammed home the bolt again he yelled, 'Get the other one! *Shoot*, fer Chrissake!'

Ralf raised his revolver and fired, the flash momentarily blinding him. 'I can't see him!'

He felt the sergeant seize his arm, then as he turned to fire once more Greenaway said harshly, 'Get back! Run while you still can!'

Blackwood saw most of it and guessed the rest. Other pale shapes were emerging from the shadows. Flitting about like spectres on a battlefield.

Swan reappeared on the barricade and threw himself down beside Trent.

The latter was repeating over and over again. 'He's just a kid. A poor bloody kid!'

Blackwood snapped, *'Bugler, sound the Alarm!'*

As the bugle cut through the still air Blackwood heard the bark of orders as the marines ran from their stables where they were being mustered for stand-to.

Blackwood gritted his teeth as more figures darted towards the main wall. 'Send a runner to the colonel's HQ.'

Gravatt stood beside him breathing fast. 'I reckon he'll know, sir.'

'Stand-to! Fix bayonets an' face yer front!'

Blackwood heard Ralf and Greenaway being hoisted over the barricade. Ralf should have known better. So should Greenaway.

As silence settled once again around the crouching marines most of them heard the awful sounds of the long blades hacking at Vicary's corpse.

'Hold yer fire!' That was Fox. 'They *want* you ter get riled up!'

The explosion when it came caught everybody unprepared. It must have been a mine of some kind. To his left

Blackwood saw the high gates through which they had made their entry were blasted completely away. Blackwood's ears rang to the explosion, and all around him men were coughing and spitting out dust and sand.

There was another sound. A great baying noise as if a gigantic throat was making one terrifying chorus of hate.

'*Here they come!*'

'Take aim! Fifty yards!'

Blackwood drew his sword and noticed that it was shining in the frail dawn light.

It was true. The Boxers had kept their word.

15

Stand and Fight

A quick glance to left and right told Blackwood that all of his men were in position at the wall and along the barricades. In the frail sunlight the scene could have been one from the paintings at Hawks Hill. Only the helmets with their glittering spikes were different. The scarlet tunics and the grim faces could be from any of a hundred battles in an expanding Empire.

The noise was deafening and when he looked again he saw the charging mass of Boxers and Imperial soldiers spreading away on either side in a human tide.

Their combined chanting of *Sha! Sha!* was deafening and made any sort of thought or plan impossible. Kill! Kill!

Blackwood raised his sword. 'Ready, lads!' He saw the bayonets waver and then settle as each man selected a target. Not that it mattered, it was impossible to miss.

'*Fire!*'

The rifles stabbed flame along the barricade, but even as they jerked their bolts and reloaded the oncoming horde had already overrun the ones who had fallen.

'Steady!' Gravatt looked at him despairingly. 'We can't stop them!'

Blackwood trained his revolver. 'Rapid fire!'

The rifles cracked out in response, so fast that when the Nordenfeldt gun joined in it sounded slow by comparison.

The Chinese attack wavered as the steady fusillade of bullets tore through their packed ranks. The new bullets cut down two, sometimes three men at a time, and still they came on.

The machine-gun stilled and as Blackwood stared up at the flat roof he saw the gun's five muzzles being depressed towards the broken gates.

The leading Boxers were pouring through them. Blackwood thought suddenly of the hotel somewhere behind him, what the roar of voices and rifle-fire would be doing to those who sheltered there. Her words seemed to murmur inside his reeling mind as the first Boxers to his right reached the barricade, their wild eyes and piercing screams enough to make the strongest heart falter.

Some of the marines had jumped on the barricade to meet the challenge face to face. As swords and axes flashed, the bayonets lunged and withdrew like steel tongues, urged on by Fox and the other NCOs.

A Boxer's head-dress appeared directly opposite Blackwood, but his yell was checked short as the revolver's heavy bullet cracked through his forehead.

The machine-gun rattled into life again and caught the attackers in a tight wedge of struggling bodies inside and beyond the high gateway. Some tried to retreat, but were cut down as the mass behind them continued to press forward.

The machine-gun moved remorselessly back and forth, Corporal O'Neil and his friend Willy Hudson taking their time and fighting their own anxiety while they concentrated on the gates.

'They're pulling back, sir!' Gravatt was frantically reloading his revolver, his eyes almost blinded by the sweat of battle.

The marines fired a last volley and brought down another file of retreating figures before Blackwood signalled to them to cease fire.

Other sounds intruded in the brutal silence. Another bugle in a different part of the city was calling a retreat. Perhaps one of the barricades had collapsed and the defenders were falling back to another line.

'Stretcher bearer!' Blackwood checked his revolver and thrust it into his holster. How familiar was that cry on any battlefield. He heard a man gasping with pain and saw Corporal Lyde trying to staunch the bleeding in a marine's neck.

Along the serried line there were one or two with minor wounds. It was a miracle and nothing less that they had stemmed the first attack.

The sun was already hotter. He wondered if the marines could stand it after their forced march along the gully under full packs. Many had been close to fainting then as the heat had followed them over the hot stones like a fireball.

An army runner came panting along the barricade. He saluted and handed a message to Blackwood.

Blackwood said, 'The French troops have had to pull back from the railway station, Toby. The Boxers are burning some more of the European property, they're killing and looting as they go.' He looked at the young lieutenant. 'We're to hold this sector.' He recalled his words to Friedrike. No matter what.

Gravatt mopped his face and throat with a grubby handkerchief.

'The Japanese infantry and some cavalry are on our left, sir. They'll not give in easily.'

Blackwood scribbled on a pad and handed it to the army runner.

Colonel Sir John Hay needed the marines now all right, he thought bitterly.

He recalled what he had learned about the Boxers and how they hated the Japanese as a race. All foreign devils were inferior, but the land of Nippon was the lowest of all in their beliefs.

'They're gettin' ready to rush us again.'

Blackwood licked his lips. Why did he always get so thirsty? He turned to look at the defences, the corpses scattered untidily below the barricade. The Boxers who had feigned death must have been the ones who had prepared the mine to blow down the gates. Only Greenaway's experience, and some argument which had held him there with the sentries had prevented a much worse disaster.

'We *must* repair the gates, Toby. As soon as it's dark we'll send out a squad.'

'Yes, sir.' Gravatt pulled Blair's binoculars from their case and watched the great pall of dust which swirled above the Chinese soldiers and Boxers. Here and there a Boxer standard waved amidst the shining blades and long bayoneted rifles. If we last that long, he thought.

The defences which had been sited and planned by the American engineer named Herbert Hoover were shaped like a great oblong box. Their strength depended on the tenacity of the defenders in any one sector. With the Japanese on the left, the US Marine Corps somewhere to the south by the old mud wall, and the French to the east by the river, the whole force was extended to its limit. Perhaps beyond it.

Blackwood watched the assembling Chinese. There were no obvious leaders. It was as if the combined army had a mind all of its own.

He saw the marines nearest him pulling in their heads and tucking their Lee-Enfields against their cheeks as the leaderless mob began to sway towards them. He noticed too that the marine who had been wounded in the neck lay behind the barricade, his arms to his side as if on parade, but with his face covered with his helmet.

Sergeant Davis of the First Platoon saw his glance and explained simply, 'Private Frost, sir.' His strong Welsh accent seemed out of place amidst the dust and the scent of death.

Blackwood hardly knew the dead man. He was one of those quiet ones, a countryman like Private Roberts, but whose family connection with the Royals went back further than his own.

Davis added as an afterthought, 'His Da's the Colour Sergeant in the old *Trafalgar*, sir. He'll not take this kindly.'

Blackwood drew his revolver again. The sun was so hot now that the pistol felt as if he had just fired it.

He saw Sergeant Davis wet his thumb and put a clearer edge on his rifle's foresight. He did not miss a trick.

Blackwood said, 'They're coming more slowly this time. Saving their wind for the last few yards.' He saw his words ripple along the tensed shoulders. 'We'll hold our fire to twenty-five yards. Pass the word to the MG.'

It took nerves of steel to stand motionless as a screaming horde came charging towards you. It also required discipline which was every bit as strong as steel.

Once again the rifles steadied along the sand and grain bags, the carts and the pieces of timber.

Blackwood saw a Boxer standard bearer capering from side to side and keeping well ahead of the others. He was a massively built man, like the one who had beaten him unconscious aboard the *Bajamar*.

'Swan, you see him?'

Swan nodded slightly and moved his rifle an inch to his right.

'No one else is to fire.' He counted the seconds. 'Now!'

The rifle bucked into Swan's shoulder and the yellow standard flew through the air like a dying bird.

It seemed to spur the attack forward, with some hanging back as they had been ordered; others maddened by the insult to their standard broke ranks and ran like madmen towards the rifles.

'Take aim! Rapid fire!'

The Nordenfeldt gun sent a hail of bullets through the packed gateway and then swung across to the right where the nearest Boxers were almost at the barricade.

Blackwood squeezed the trigger and felt the recoil jar up his arm. He could have hit several of the enemy, but nothing seemed to make any difference. He found he was pulling in his stomach muscles as if to anticipate a blow or a bullet, but tried to concentrate on his defences, faces and names committed to close-action on the right of the line.

There was a lot of smoke and leaping flames in the next sector, and he wondered if the enemy had already burst through at that point. Once inside both the perimeter defences they would be hard to stop.

The rifles cracked and flashed, and as men reloaded their magazines some of the slightly wounded were dragging up fresh boxes of ammunition.

'*God, here they come!*' Blackwood hauled himself on to the barricade as a mass of Boxers charged into it like a battering ram. He felt it shake as yelling faces and corpses were jammed together below his feet, hacking and stabbing while the marines met them again blade to blade. Further to the left near the gates some Boxers had broken through and were splitting up as they ran towards the next line of obstacles. Rapid fire swept through their flanks and Blackwood realized the Japanese were hurling in a counter-attack with their usual frenzied disregard for casualties.

'Second Platoon extend to the left!' Blackwood parried a bayonet aside with his sword and blasted its owner down with a single bullet. Another marine fell headlong over the barricade. He was hacked to pieces before he hit the ground. The marine nearest him emptied his rifle into the swaying mob and then lunged at a Boxer as he trampled on corpses to cross the barricade. The Boxer slashed out with his blade, his arm scything back and forth even as the marine's bayonet plunged through his bared teeth.

The attack turned to the sound of a horn like the one at the arsenal. As one they surged clear of the barricade, some falling headlong over dead and wounded and pursued by a hail of bullets.

'*Cease firing!*'

Behind him Blackwood heard individual shots as the infiltrators were hunted down in the narrow side-streets. It would be an unenviable task, Blackwood thought. In some of the streets a man could reach out and touch both sides at once.

He turned to see some white-helmeted troops in khaki

uniforms hurrying down the rear of the barricade carrying cases of wine. One of them, an officer, paused and beamed up at him.

'Good morning, Herr Kapitän!' He handed Blackwood a bottle and some goblets. 'We were told you were here.' His grin broadened. 'Royal Marines, ja?'

Blackwood realized that these were German marines of their *Seebataillon*.

Gravatt poured three full goblets, some of the wine slopping over his wrist like blood.

Blackwood smiled, 'Many thanks, Herr Leutnant.' He raised his goblet. He found it strange, unnerving that he could share a joke with this unknown German marine, probably his opposite number in Tientsin, with the enemy only half a cable away and massing again for another attack.

The German glanced at the sweating marines. 'Hot vork, ja?'

Blackwood thought of the discarded white uniforms. They were paying for it now.

He waited for Gravatt to scribble something for his runner and asked quietly, 'You know that the Countess von Heiser is in the hotel?'

The German took the proffered goblet. 'I do. I know all about her, Kapitän.'

Blackwood waited for his goblet to be refilled and saw more wine being handed out to his men. Perhaps all marines were in the same family?

The German asked politely, 'Do you know her?'

'Yes. Quite well.'

'Quite well.' The German repeated the words carefully. He was not fully aware of their use. He nodded. 'I understand.'

Sergeant Major Fox shouted, 'They're comin' back, sir!'

Blackwood wiped his mouth with his wrist. You don't understand at all, my friend. He said, 'If you see her – '

He saw the immediate curiosity in the lieutenant's eyes and added, 'Nothing.'

The German clicked his heels and yelled at his NCO to recall his men.

He smiled. 'I shall tell her, Herr Kapitän.'

The roar of voices intruded and Blackwood drew his revolver and watched as his men gripped their rifles and waited. The wine had been a good gesture. It would be the last drink for some of these same men, he thought.

'Commence firing!' The bugle blared and the machine-gun kicked and clattered from its rooftop. Was it never going to end? There appeared to be thousands of them, but they all had to get through the barricade or the gate if they were to extend their advance.

At a guess there were barely sixty marines still able to fight.

He thought of her in his arms, just hours ago.

Then he fired his revolver at point-blank range at a Chinese soldier who had thrown himself bodily into a gap between some upended carts. We must hold on. We must hold on. The words were like a prayer or an epitaph.

His arms were throbbing with exhaustion, and the revolver was empty. This time they were not falling back, and nothing seemed able to stem the attack.

A hoarse voice boomed from the right. It was Kirby, rallying his men better than any fanfare.

'Come on, you mothers' boys!' He sounded crazy and was obviously in tremendous pain. 'Stand and fight the bas-tards!'

The marines had been falling back but Kirby's strength seemed to spread to them so that they charged at the Boxers in a solid scarlet line.

The horn boomed again and reluctantly the Boxers started to withdraw. They must have lost hundreds, Blackwood thought, and yet they could still advance without hesitation, eyes dilated, teeth bared and with froth on their lips. No wonder the ordinary Chinese people were terrified of them.

Blackwood felt the lanyard on his revolver jerk and knew

Swan was checking it before reloading for him.

His head was beating like iron on an anvil, and his whole body shook as if it would never stop.

Several marines were stretched out on the dirt and having their wounds dressed; another lay as if asleep, his dead eyes watching his friends and comrades as they prepared to meet another assault.

The bugle shattered the stillness. Blackwood heard Gravatt murmur, 'Dear God, don't fail me now!'

He wondered how Ralf was managing, what he would do if anything happened to de Courcy.

Then his thoughts were scattered by that same overwhelming chant. *Sha! Sha!* The urge to kill the foreign devils or drive them out.

'Commence firing!'

This must be what Hell is like, Blackwood thought. Only the dream had been Heaven.

Sergeant Major Arthur Fox ducked through the door of the small airless room and regarded his officers impassively.

Blackwood put down his pen and looked at him. 'All quiet?'

'Sir.' Fox glanced at the others. De Courcy lay on his back on a blanket, his arms across his face as if the tiny lamp was blinding him. Bannatyre sat on an empty box, an untouched glass of whisky gripped in both hands as he stared into nothing. Gravatt looked calm enough, his breathing regular as he made his whisky last. Only his eyes told the truth. He was reliving each terrible minute and hour of the day. The insane charges, the crash and bang of rifle fire, the impartial clatter of the machine-gun.

Now it was dark once again, and the city seemed at peace.

Fox said, 'Three dead, sir, twelve wounded, six badly.' He saw the pain on Blackwood's face. 'It could 'ave bin much worse, sir.'

'I suppose so.' Fox always made it sound like routine. But Blackwood had seen them die, or fall in agony. Some good men, some valuable ones. Corporal Bill Handley had died in the last attack, Corporal Lyde had been bayoneted in the stomach. He would not last out the night. Lyde would be sorely missed. What the General would call a *proper marine*. He could have had Fox's rank if he'd wanted it. But he had been broken to the ranks more times than he could remember, usually for brawling in a foreign port, or smashing up an alehouse in Portsmouth.

I have not slept for days. I am like a machine.

Blackwood said, 'Have you made sure that the rations are getting to them?' It was a pointless question. Fox, for all his threats and fury, always looked after his men before anything else.

'Yessir.' Fox gave a grim smile. 'One good bit er news, sir, I got a Chinese dhobyman to wash out an' repair our whites.'

Blackwood stared at him. Fox was a marvel. Colonel Hay could fume and bluster if he wanted to, but at least the marines would face a new day in clean comfort.

'Have a drink, Mr Fox.'

Fox grinned, 'Ta, sir.' He took the mug in his hand but as always seemed to remain at attention.

'What is our strength?'

Fox pouted. 'Sixty fit men, more or less. Sar'nt Kirby 'as bin an example to the wounded, I must say, sir. They all knows 'ow bad 'e is, so they just carries on like.'

Swan peered through the door and waited for Fox to see him.

'Corporal Lyde's gone, Sar'nt Major.'

Fox sighed. 'A good 'un. The best.'

Blackwood poured some more whisky into Fox's mug. 'You're not too bad yourself, as a matter of fact.'

Gravatt said, 'About tonight, sir.'

Fox said, 'I can muster a squad in a few minutes, sir.'

Blackwood glanced at de Courcy and Bannatyre. They

had done so well, but they were paying for it. That gate had to be blocked. There was no shortage of material. It would have to be soon, before the moon became too strong. He tried not to think of her beautiful body framed in the silver light. She was just yards away and yet it could have been on the other side of the globe.

'I want Mr Blackwood to select his own squad.'

He saw Gravatt start, and even de Courcy dropped his arms to stare at him.

Only Fox seemed to understand. Kill or cure. It was a fair trade. 'I'll see to it, sir. Young Mr Blackwood is doin' Rounds with Sar'nt Davis at the moment.'

'Good. You attend to it. Have the First Platoon stand-to while they're fixing the gates. The remainder are to get some sleep while there's still time. Issue the whites as each post is relieved.'

'Good as done, sir.'

Fox strode away, his mind busy and with no outward sign of fatigue.

Gravatt yawned, 'I sometimes think old Fox must be related to God.'

Blackwood looked at his diary and felt his head loll forward. What was the point anyway? Would anyone ever read his report of their exploits?

He tried again. Supplies, ammunition, fit and wounded marines, those who could still fight or at least assist in loading spare weapons. Those who would never fight again.

Swan stood by the door. 'Second Lieutenant Blackwood to see you, sir.'

Blackwood thrust his weariness aside. 'I'll come.' Ralf obviously wanted to speak to him alone.

He ducked through the door, his eyes instantly adjusting to the darkness, and the high pale stars. He could smell the burned woodwork, the clinging stench of gunsmoke and death.

Ralf was waiting by a barricade and exclaimed, 'I've just heard. You want me to go out with a patrol.'

'That's true.' Blackwood glanced over the barricade. It was easy to see the corpses between it and the gates. Everything was so still. It was impossible to believe that this was the same place where men had fought and died. He said, 'You can select your own men. There should be no danger. If you keep your wits about you, that is.'

Ralf looked away. 'What about you? Will you be in charge here while I'm gone?'

Blackwood answered calmly, 'I shall be here.'

'I mean, that is, I'd not like to think one of the others is left responsible for the safety of my party.'

'What the hell do you mean by that, exactly?'

Ralf shrugged. 'Last night you were at the hotel.' He flinched as Blackwood took half a pace towards him. 'I'm only repeating what someone told me.'

Blackwood replied, 'Tomorrow, the next day, any time I might be killed. So might the others. Then you'll be in command, have you thought about that?'

Ralf faced him with surprising confidence. 'And have you thought what Aunt Deirdre or the General would think if they knew about your affair? I don't suppose that Count von Heiser would be too pleased, either!'

Blackwood clenched his fists but controlled himself with a supreme effort.

'Are you threatening me, Ralf? If so you've picked the wrong chap.'

Ralf sounded as if he was smiling. 'I just wanted you to think about it, *sir*. I'll not face a court-martial because of you. Or anyone else.'

'Have it your way, Ralf. Now go and muster your squad. The Sergeant Major will prepare the necessary gear for you.'

'I don't need him either, thank you.'

Blackwood watched his slim figure melt into the darkness. Fear did strange things to people. Unfortunately in this case Ralf held all the cards. Also he knew he was right. The fact that the General had a wild reputation where women were concerned would not prevent a scandal over Friedrike.

He walked slowly along the battered defence line, pausing occasionally to speak with a sentry, or to peer across at the enemy's campfires which seemed to surround the city like far-off beacons.

If they had more men, preferably cavalry, they could have attacked the Boxers and their comrades in the Imperial Army and cut a corridor right through them.

He thought of Friedrike in her airless room, the little maid combing her hair, or helping her to cleanse her body with the rationed supply of fresh water.

She would be thinking of him. Or was she already regretting her actions, the wanton way she had given herself to him? Someone of her background and breeding might discover how fine the margin between love and disgust could become.

He kicked at a loose stone. No, it was not just an act. The thought gave him strength, and made Ralf's threats seem pathetic and somehow sad.

He found Sergeant Greenaway at the place where the barricade met the old city wall.

The bulky sergeant said, 'All's well, sir. Seems nice an' quiet for the patrol.' He hesitated and added, 'I'm rare sorry about Private Vicary, sir. It weren't 'is fault. It were mine more than anyone's.'

Blackwood nodded. 'Try and forget it. It could have been any one of us.'

'An' about young Mr Blackwood, sir, I'm sure 'e'll be all right given 'alf th' chance.' He fumbled for words. ''E's got the *makin's*, sir.'

Blackwood was glad the darkness hid his face. 'Probably.'

He moved on, knowing that Greenaway was still staring after him. Swan followed at a discreet distance, his rifle in the crook of his arm like a gamekeeper going round his traps.

He had heard most of it. Poor old Greenaway, he thought. Doing his best to spare the captain's feelings. The night-patrol might be very interesting and in a way he wished he was going too.

Sergeant Owen Davis said, 'I've got the men ready, sir.'

Ralf tried to relax as he moved nearer to the small squad of marines by the barricade. He saw the sergeant major's handcart already loaded with ropes and lengths of timber, just enough to block the gateway, to give the rifles and machine-gun a chance to hold back the next attack, and the one after that.

He said, 'Listen to me, all of you. This has to be done quickly.' He turned to the sergeant, 'Where's Corporal Lyde?'

Davis stared at him. 'He died, sir.'

Ralf touched his moustache and tried to remain calm.

Corporal Percy Addis said, 'So *I* stood in for 'im, sir.'

Ralf could sense the sneer in Addis's tone, even though his face was hidden in the darkness. Addis had been there with that ox Greenaway when his revolver had accidentally fired and roused the Chinese garrison at the arsenal. Addis was here for a purpose.

He snapped, 'Very commendable, Corporal. Try not to foul things up this time.'

It was gratifying the way some of the others chuckled. Addis was not from their platoon anyway. It made all the difference.

Davis whispered, 'We'd better leave now, sir.'

'When I'm ready, *Sergeant.*' Ralf fidgeted with his belt and holster. What had happened to him? He felt completely at ease, untroubled even by the task ahead.

'Remove your tunics and leave them behind with your helmets.' He unbuttoned his own and handed it to Davis while he refastened his belt. He had seen his cousin give this kind of order, the way the men always accepted it without question. Now he could sense their resentment, and even that gave him a kind of strength. 'Now, tell the sentry, and we'll move out directly.'

He clambered over the dip in the barricade where a working party had made a space for the handcart.

One officer, a sergeant, a corporal and six privates. They had seemed like a crowd behind the barricade but as soon as they moved beyond it Ralf thought it was like walking naked into a lion's den.

How near the enemy campfires looked, and each sprawled corpse appeared as if it would suddenly leap up and try to hack them to pieces. He heard Sergeant Davis mutter a warning as one of the cartwheels emitted a loud squeak, but they moved on, apparently unheard and undetected.

The gate suddenly towered over them, the ground littered with broken beams across which Boxer corpses lay like exhausted runners.

'Corporal, stand guard.' Ralf walked carefully through the gate and stared over at the twinkling fires. Apart from the flames nothing moved. Probably sleeping after their terrifying charges, he thought.

'Get on with it, Sergeant.' Ralf heard the cautious scrape of timber and fallen stones as the men got to work with ropes and levers. It should not take long. Ralf loosened the revolver and touched its hammer with his thumb. Safe but ready.

He thought of his cousin's quietness when he had attacked him over the German countess, and how it would affect Aunt Deirdre. It had been so easy. Laughable. He recalled when he had joined the countess for tea aboard *Mediator*, and David's pathetic jealousy when he had told him about it.

David was brave and had all the qualities he would have liked. Ralf was surprised to discover he did not mind admitting it, at least to himself. But Victoria Cross or not he was a fool where women were concerned. Surely he did not believe that the German aristocrat would let him touch her; he only made himself ridiculous by deluding his mind with such ideas.

Ralf thought suddenly of the girl in England, Helen.
With her at his side things would be very different. In the
Corps or released from its code and tradition, he would soon
rise to the top. Her father seemed to like him, even if he did
keep going on about the splendid Blackwood heritage.

He felt his lips lift in a smile. That too could be used to
advantage once the old General had passed on.

He started as Addis said, 'Did you 'ear that, sir?'

'What, man?' Ralf hated the corporal. His cocky self-
confidence, the smell of his sweat.

Addis gripped his rifle and peered into the darkness. 'I
dunno, sir.'

Bloody idiot! Why must I be plagued by such mindless
fools? Ralf tensed as he heard the sound himself. It was the
sound of wheels. 'Come with me.' He moved further to the
right with Addis crouching along behind him. Wheels, but
where and what? He continued to move along parallel with
the broken walls and paler-coloured barricades. It would be
just like some nervous sentry to fire on him, he thought
savagely. Soon now. Whatever it was sounded heavy and
should therefore be visible against the lines of campfires.
The simplicity of it made him grin. Bannatyre or de Courcy
would have probably retreated to the defences at the gallop.

'Still.' Ralf groped in his pocket and pulled out a small
collapsible telescope. It only measured five inches but when
extended was still as powerful as some binoculars. He had
never shown it to anyone. It had belonged to his father. The
one he had used in the Crimea. He thought of the great
painting in the General's room. The fire and thunder of the
Russian redoubt. Even the General had admitted that
Philip Blackwood should have been awarded the VC instead
of him.

He opened the small telescope and heard Addis's sharp
breathing. It was not just sweat, he decided. It was the
sweat of fear. Like the others Addis thought him useless. He
would bloody well change his ideas soon.

Addis asked nervously, 'See anythin', sir?'

'Hold your noise.' Ralf moved the telescope slowly and with great care. If some of the corpses were really live Boxers he would be hard put to get back to the barricade before they cut him down. His hand shook slightly as he recalled what they had said about Second Lieutenant Earle's awful screams. When he had been tortured before they had hacked off his head and stuck it on a pole as an obscene trophy. He forgot Earle as he moved the glass back again. Only one figure moved by the nearest fires, a black shadow framed occasionally against the flames as he flung on more wood. But there was nothing else moving between the fires and himself. *There was nobody.* He could feel the hair rising on his neck, as if a chill wind had somehow invaded this desolate place.

He listened, his hair falling across his eyes as he leaned forward. The noise continued as before, a very slow rumbling like iron wheels. He stared round wildly, stunned by his discovery. It was artillery, it had to be.

God, it had been a near thing all the previous day. With heavy guns the Boxers could smash down the defences before attacking at full strength. Nothing would stop them.

Addis watched him, much as a rabbit watches a fox.

'I can't see nothin', sir.'

'It's the gully.' He was startled by his own understanding, his grasp of what was happening. The Boxers must be dragging their guns along that same gully. No wonder they were invisible, just as the marines had been until they had burst from cover to surprise the enemy from their rear.

Sergeant Davis loomed out of the darkness. 'There's done we are, sir.' He looked at the officer and added, 'You heard it too, sir.'

Addis said, 'Artillery, Sarge.'

Davis rubbed his chin. It made a rasping noise. 'We'd better tell the commanding officer.'

Ralf raised his telescope again. No wonder there was no movement around the enemy's fires. They were all hauling the guns. It had to be that.

'We have to be certain. A reconnaissance.'

Addis swallowed hard. 'Who's goin', sir?'

Davis said, 'It'd be a terrible risk, sir.'

Ralf had intended to send Davis and one other while a runner was sent back to alert his cousin.

Addis's dismay that he might be sent because of his insolence by the river, the fact that his was the mouth which was always ready to smear him with gossip was enough. Even the reliable Sergeant Davis was doubtful and would prefer any other officer to be here. Ralf looked at the squad who waited by the barricade, their work done.

There was one marine called Adams, a quiet, modest youth who was often mocked goodheartedly by the seasoned members of his platoon because of his manner. He never swore or complained, and was obviously glad to be in the Corps. Shown on the records as eighteen he seemed nearer to sixteen, he was so keen to better himself. Unlike so many of the others he was a first-time marine, a new recruit with no family connections in the Corps.

'I shall go.' It came out quite easily. 'You too, Adams.'

That would hit Davis and the others where it hurt most. Their pride, and their contempt for any new officer.

By contrast Adams was delighted. Ralf tried not to think of Vicary's pleasure at being selected by Greenaway before he had been killed, beheaded just a few yards from here.

Davis said firmly, 'If you want my advice, sir.'

'I don't.' He thrust the telescope into his pocket and carefully drew his sword. It would make less noise if they stumbled on a Boxer guard. 'You withdraw with the squad, Sergeant. *Try* not to make too much noise about it, eh?'

He trembled with chilled excitement. It was easy. An act, but it worked. Why had he never realized it?

They melted into the shadows and Ralf glanced up as a shaft of moonlight touched the scarred gateway like silver paint.

Adams, his rifle across his body, its bayonet already fixed, trod quietly after the second lieutenant.

Adams's family came from Exeter, where his father was a shoe-maker. His was a large family and times were hard, otherwise his mother would have prevented him from enlisting. Adams had always wanted to join the Corps, and had never lost an opportunity to visit Plymouth to watch the Royal Marines at drill, the men-of-war proud and beflagged in the Sound.

When a recruiting party had visited Exeter Adams had pleaded with his parents and they had reluctantly agreed to his going, and to keeping quiet about his age. He had been just sixteen on that day. The recruiting sergeant had been a jovial fellow, with a big yellow moustache and a breast full of medals.

Adams had never mentioned that his father was also a lay-preacher. That would have got some of the old sweats going, he thought. As it was he still found it difficult not to blush when he heard some of their jokes and stories of past exploits.

Now Private John Adams of the RMLI was here in the middle of danger, fighting his country's enemies just as the recruiting sergeant in his red sash had described in such gory detail.

He was glad to be with the second lieutenant. He too was young, a year or so older than himself, and a Blackwood. It was hard not to hear that family name in Forton Barracks.

He had heard the others saying terrible things about him, but he had ignored it. From his own experience he knew that they always used their brutal humour on new faces, officers and privates alike.

Oblivious to Adams's admiration Ralf glanced at the strengthening moonlight and then paused to listen to the sound of wheels. It was unnerving. As if an enormous underground monster was about to burst from its lair at any moment and devour them.

He gave a thin smile. Goliath.

It was very bright. He looked back at the wall. They had come a long way. His stomach rebelled against the stench of corpses. Why the hell didn't they bury them?

He heard Adams behind him. I must have been mad to bring him. He'd stand no chance at all if things went wrong.

Sergeant Davis would have run to David by now, he thought. All hell would break loose when he found out.

He should go back now. Let the others finish what he alone had begun. He looked at his young companion. 'We shall stroll over and take a look. What d'you say?'

Adams's eyes were like saucers. 'Gosh, sir. Just us two!'

Ralf sighed. If Adams had not been here he knew he would probably have gone back with the others.

'If we see anyone, stand absolutely still.' Ralf eyed him bleakly. 'D'you *understand?*'

Adams bobbed his head, 'Yessir. We'll show 'em, eh, sir?'

Ralf turned and walked slowly towards the noise. It was strangely menacing. He thought only briefly of Adams. For once it seemed he had found someone who looked up to him.

16

Never the Right Words

Second Lieutenant Ralf Blackwood raised himself on his elbows and stared fixedly at the pile of rocks at the end of the gully. The ground was very hard and uncomfortable and he could feel small spiky stones jabbing through his shirt as he tried to discover what was happening.

Once when he looked back over his shoulder he was amazed how far they had come. When they had burst from this same gully for that wild charge towards the old city wall it had seemed to pass in a flash. Now he was very conscious of the gap between him and safety. *Safety*. Even the word was a mockery. He felt his lips twist into a smile.

Private Adams, who was lying nearby, saw the smile in the moonlight and drew comfort from it.

The noise of the wheels had ceased. Maybe they were merely wagons of food or ammunition, Ralf thought. He dismissed it instantly. There would be little need for secrecy with the city surrounded. It had to be something worthwhile, worth this risk of stripping the camp of every available man.

He said quietly, 'You stay here, Adams, and watch the rear. If anyone looks like cutting us off from the main defences *tell me*.'

'What about you, sir?'

'I'm going a bit closer. Have to.' He had a mental picture of their sneers if he failed what he had started out to do. *Show them you've got the gut for it*. He twisted his head to the right. It was a solitary figure crossing the camp fires again.

Even in the strange glacier light he saw the red head-dress and felt his stomach muscles tighten.

He began to crawl forward, rolling from side to side on his elbows as he had been trained to do.

God they were making a din. The wheels had stopped but there were other sounds now. His brain examined them and he realized it was like a ship under sail, the creak of ropes and tackles.

He held his breath as some figures clambered over the gully's lip and scuttled away into the shadows. They appeared to be hauling ropes behind them, and soon he heard the thud of hammers as the Chinese prepared to fasten their blocks and shouted for the others to help them.

Within a couple of minutes there were hundreds of them, ducking and groping through the shadows to take their places along the taut ropes. It was unnerving to see so many. The nearest was about fifty yards away. One, a tall figure with a long halberd, called out an order and the whole column of men threw its weight on the tackles. Ralf wanted to leave but felt mesmerized and unable to move as a gun-muzzle, very slowly at first and then with gathering momentum, lurched out of the gully.

It was a sizeable cannon. Old perhaps but breech-loading. Probably one of the Krupp guns from the forts. It would be able to smash the defenders into oblivion even as they lined the flimsy barricades for the dawn stand-to.

He wriggled backwards, his eyes still fixed on the long human rope.

'I was right, Adams. Time to get out of here.' He almost grinned. 'Not a bloody sentry anywhere.' He rested his hand on the youth's shoulder. 'No chances, all the same. I could be wrong, so take it nice and slowly.'

Adams nodded jerkily and tried to hold his rifle clear of the rough stones. How did the officer behave so calmly? He would never forget it.

Ralf said, 'We'll head for the break in the wall.' Again he fixed a picture in his mind. His cousin flying through the same gap, his sword in the air as the horse lifted him clear.

They reached the wall. The corpses were still where they had fallen. Ralf swallowed hard. He could smell them. Could feel their eyes on him.

He pulled out the little telescope and tried to focus it on the camp, and the edge of the gully. But all of it was lost in shadows, or distorted by silver shafts of moonlight. He could not see the cannon at all. But he heard the tackles squeaking. There must be a second cannon. Not that it mattered. One was all they needed. He closed the telescope and thought of his dead father, how he must have used the telescope in the Crimea.

'Right, Adams, over you go — ' He seized his arm. '*Still!*' Even a whisper sounded too loud.

Adams stared at him but did not move.

Ralf watched the sentry. He must have been resting somewhere, hidden from view.

Now he was walking very slowly towards them, his chin on his chest, asleep on his feet.

'Bloody hell.' Ralf knew there was no chance of not being seen. There were hundreds of armed men near the gully. Neither he nor Adams would make the crossing in time.

'Give me your bayonet.' He kept his hand on Adams's shoulder. Holding him, calming him like a frightened mount.

'Easy now.'

He watched the sentry moving nearer. He was probably grateful to be spared the harder work with the cannon.

'When I drop my hand, Adams.' He spoke very evenly even though every nerve in his body was screaming. 'Stand up. Keep your hands to your sides. All right?'

Adams bobbed his head. 'I think so, sir.'

'You'll do better than that, man.' Ralf gripped the bayonet and tested its weight. Where had he heard those words before?

Then he pressed himself amongst the stones which had been blasted from the wall and as the sentry's shadow flowed across the ground like some black serpent he dropped his hand.

Adams scrambled to his feet, his mind reeling with sudden fear as he saw the sentry stare at him with utter astonishment, then with understanding as he began to unsling his rifle from his shoulder.

Adams did not really know what happened next. The second lieutenant just seemed to appear from the ground a pace behind the Boxer with the levelled rifle.

Ralf wrapped his forearm around the man's throat, tugging him backwards even though he knew the Boxer was taller and far stronger. It had to be quick. With all his strength he drove the bayonet inwards and upwards, the point catching only momentarily on his bandolier before thrusting into his body. Ralf dragged with his forearm and felt the man's strangled cry change to a horrible rattle as he slipped from his grasp and lay between them.

Ralf held his breath. 'Better make certain.' But the corpse did not move as the bayonet found its mark once again.

Ralf handed the blade back to Adams and hoped he had not seen how near he had been to vomiting.

'Right, Adams, off we go. You first.' He drew his revolver and wiped his face with his sleeve. *God Almighty*.

Adams vaulted over the gap and Ralf heard a sharp metallic snap. He clambered into the gap and saw the young marine holding his leg and writhing on the ground in terrible agony. He had trodden on a pile of straw. But beneath it had been a steel-jawed man-trap which he had sprung like a mouse after cheese.

Ralf knelt beside him. It was bad. He felt blood on his fingers as he tested the strength of the trap. But for his boot, it would have taken his foot off.

He groped in his pocket and pulled out a cigar case. 'Here, bite on this.' At any moment Adams would scream. You could hardly blame him.

Ralf tried again, but each time Adams rocked about in

agony, his teeth already half through the case in his jaws.

Ralf wedged a stone into the trap. That would prevent it from closing even tighter. He felt his way to the left and found where the trap was fastened. He could sense Adams terrified eyes watching him. He was almost choking on the gag.

It was no good. The chain was fixed beneath several large stones. It would take a squad to lift them clear.

Ralf peered through the gap to give himself time to think.

Christ in Heaven. There were five figures moving unhurriedly towards the wall. Probably to relieve the other sentries.

One of them called to his companions and Adams must have heard him. He spat out the case and gasped, 'Please, sir! Don't leave me to them!' He was sobbing uncontrollably like a child. 'Kill me, sir, for God's sake, *kill me* first!'

Ralf thumbed back the hammer on his revolver and listened to the distant voices.

'Keep still.' He realized with a start that Adams had closed his eyes. He really expected him to shoot him. One shot. There was no margin for error. He held the muzzle as close as he dared to a link by Adams's foot.

Now or never. He squeezed the trigger and heard Adams cry out as the chain was blasted from the trap.

'Hang on to your rifle!' He did not know why he had said it. Maybe to give Adams something to keep his mind occupied. Thank God he was only a youth. Even so with his rifle and ammunition he was heavy enough.

He hauled him up and over his shoulder, holding him in position with one arm, leaving the other free for his revolver. If he fell he would make sure that neither of them was taken.

Voices yelled, strengthened and faded as the Boxers ran to discover what was happening. A few shots whined dangerously close overhead, and one spat sand against his leg. He felt more blood running from Adams's leg and thought one of the bullets had hit him, that he was carrying a dead man.

He gasped between breaths. 'Hold on, Adams!' His heart must surely burst. 'You must, you're my trophy!'

Adams's voice seemed to come from miles away. 'I – I'm all right, sir.'

They're gaining on me. Ralf tried to blink the sweat from his eyes. Any second now. He saw the gateway where they had built the barricade. So near, so far.

A voice shattered the silence. 'Platoon, *steady!* Take aim, *fire!*'

The bullets tore past Ralf and his sobbing burden like a swarm of hornets. Out of the shadows pale figures ran to lift Adams from his back, others fired into the shadows. At nothing. It was as if the Boxers had never been.

He heard Sergeant Davis exclaim, 'Carry this boy to the Surgeon.'

Adams reached out, his arm flailing about with the pain.

Ralf ran beside him, and seized his hand.

'What's your name?'

'John, sir.'

'Right, John, when you're up and about I'll want you in my platoon.'

The boy nodded, unable to speak as they hustled him away.

Sergeant Davis stared at him, as if he could not believe what he saw.

Ralf said, 'I must see the commanding officer. At once.'

Blackwood walked to meet him. 'I'm here.'

'I saw the guns. One, more likely two.'

'And I saw you, Ralf, just now with that lad.'

Ralf took his tunic and helmet from Davis.

Blackwood said, 'I take back what I said.'

Ralf regarded him calmly. 'Measure up, do I? Good enough at last?'

Blackwood smiled. 'Well let's go and see the Colonel. Together.'

Gravatt said, 'Bloody marvellous.'

Ralf shrugged. 'It won't matter anyway. They'll blow us all to hell. If not today, then tomorrow.'

They found Colonel Sir John Hay wide awake in his small headquarters, roused from his brief rest by the platoon's covering fire. He was wearing his breeches and highly polished boots, doubtless the ones Blackwood had seen being cared for by his servant. But above that he wore only his shirt. It looked almost indecent, Blackwood thought.

Hay listened to his report impassively. Nodding every so often with a grunt. 'Go on then.'

Gravatt said, 'The marine should be all right, sir. He'll not lose a foot, thanks to young Mr Blackwood here.'

'Yes, yes, I daresay,' Hay said impatiently. 'I heard much the same report from the American sector. A withdrawal of Boxers and Imperial troops at dusk. We had no real idea why, of course, but we can't afford to waste chances. An English officer and an escort of two or three Cossacks from the Russian detachment have been sent through the enemy lines. The Chinese will be around us again at dawn. It was a chance which had to be taken. The telegraph has been cut again. We have to let them know at Taku just how serious our position has become.'

Blackwood thought of the English horseman. Another Twiss perhaps? They would need all the luck to reach the Taku forts with their heads on their shoulders. In this strangely mixed assortment of soldiers and sailors from several nations there had already been incredible acts of courage and co-operation, which a few weeks ago would have been thought impossible.

Hay said, 'Even if they get through it will take time. We shall have to withdraw to the second line of barricades. We must.' For the first time he shot Ralf a fierce grin. 'But for you, young fellow, all your people and some of mine would have been on the receiving end of those guns without knowing what had hit them.'

The grin vanished just as quickly. 'We shall evacuate the

hotel immediately. Women, children, and wounded unable
to walk will be moved to the Catholic Mission. I do not
believe in miracles, gentlemen, but I happen to know that
the mission's walls are the thickest in the city.'

Blackwood watched fascinated. After Blair's quiet confidence and occasional uncertainties, Hay was like a tiger. It
was incredible but either he was really looking forward to
the last battle, or he was a damned good actor.

'My men and some of the Germans are evacuating the
hotel and adjoining buildings. I suggest you move your
machine-gun, Captain Blackwood. It's the only one we
have, and I think it will be a prime target where it stands at
present.' His mind veered away. 'I see that you are back in
your white uniforms again.' He allowed his servant to ease
his arms into his perfectly fitting tunic. 'At least they *appear*
cleaner.'

That was probably the nearest he ever got to praise,
Blackwood thought.

'See you all at first light, gentlemen.'

His hard voice held them in the doorway. 'I thought you
might like to know, China has officially declared war on us.'
He smiled at their expressions. 'I know. I thought much the
same!'

Blackwood strode into the shadows and bridges of
moonlight.

'I want the gateway mined right away, Toby. We've no
more fuses, so make sure we have two good marksmen ready
to mark down the charges.' He turned to Ralf. 'Have the
First Platoon relieved and see they're properly fed and have
full canteens. It may be a while before we get another
chance.'

Ralf walked away without even a word or a glance.

Gravatt hurried back, 'Mr de Courcy's dealing with that,
sir.'

They fell in step, Gravatt remaining silent as Blackwood's mind jumped and sidestepped past obstacles he
could only guess at. Somewhere he could hear a baby

crying, and a muffled bang as a Boxer sentry fired his musket towards the city in the hope of a lucky shot. They walked along the deserted barricade which would be their new, and last, line of defence. It was shorter, but that was all you could say for it.

He thought of Ralf. He had certainly shown what he could do. But what had induced him to make such a gesture? But for him the defences would be running with blood when the dawn found them.

He heard someone whistling a cheerful jig and knew it was O'Neil as he supervised the re-siting of his Nordenfeldt.

He said, 'Swan, stay with the adjutant. If I'm needed come at once.'

'Yes, sir.' Swan ignored Gravatt's curious stare. He never needed to be told.

Blackwood closed one of the heavy mission doors behind him and looked at the scene of crowded disorder. Along one wall many children who had arrived earlier were already mercifully asleep, while others clung to their mothers and stared around with obvious anxiety. At the opposite side there were small desks and bench seats, occupied now by weary women and some of the wounded servicemen. In stark contrast along the wall behind them were children's drawings, Chinese characters, and beside a large picture of the Virgin Mary one of a fearsome green dragon.

The nuns who served the mission moved sedately amongst the new arrivals, ready to share their sparse rations or to answer the many questions which were fired at them.

It was a cruel twist of fate, Blackwood thought, that these same gentle nuns were one of the main targets for Boxer hatred. Foreign missionaries of any kind represented a threat to their beliefs, to the very roots of their religion. Missionaries, men and women, had been among the first to fall victim to the long knives of the Righteous Harmonious Fists.

Above the head and shoulders of a nun who was kneeling

to placate a small sobbing girl Blackwood suddenly saw
Friedrike. She looked very calm or would appear so to
anyone who did not know her, and seemed withdrawn from
the bustle around her.

She looked straight at him, and as Blackwood pushed his
way across the room he marvelled at the way she managed to
appear so unafraid. He made to seize her hands but
something in her violet eyes signalled a caution. He realized
that several women were standing nearby, and although
they were apparently speaking to each other, he had the
feeling they were watching and listening.

Blackwood said awkwardly, 'I'm so sorry about this – '
He faltered. 'Countess.'

He saw the pain and the relief in her eyes. She understood
what it was costing him. Both of them.

She said, 'You must not always apologize, Captain. I
think the war is *not* of your doing.' She tried to smile, but it
only made her look more sad.

It was like saying goodbye minutes before a troopship
casts off, and the thin path of water widens to an impossible
gulf. Never the right words when you needed them most. It
was always too late.

Blackwood said quietly, 'You look wonderful. I want to
hold you, to touch you – '

She dropped her eyes and he saw her breasts moving
quickly despite her guard, her pretence.

'Please, David. I cannot bear it. To have you so close, and
yet – '

He said, 'I am wearing the locket.' He looked round at
the milling figures, his voice despairing. 'I love you.'

She forgot her caution and reached up to touch his
mouth. 'Shh. Do not torture yourself.' She could barely
hold back the tears.

'I have to go, Friedrike.' He could smell perfume or soap
on her fingers and wanted all the more to hold her, to shut
out the others, the war, everything.

She glanced quickly at the other women, probably the

wives of German officials and traders.

'Together yet so apart, David.' She looked up, startled as a stray bullet cracked amongst the buildings. 'I must be strong.'

Blackwood knew he had to leave but found it almost impossible.

She whispered, 'Our night together, my dearest. I shall never, *never* forget no matter what happens.'

He started to protest. 'It's not over, Friedrike!'

She smiled at him but did not speak as she studied his face. As if they would never see each other again.

A solider stood beside them, his arm in a sling. 'Pardon, sir, but one of your men is here.'

Blackwood turned towards the door, knowing it would be Swan.

Swan was wearing his blue field-service cap. Blackwood had ordered his men to discard their helmets. It was just possible that the enemy might think there were fresh, unused troops on the barricade, but now as Swan looked across at him it seemed a pitiful deception. Against the cannon they would need more than party-tricks.

He said, 'I'm needed.' He moved slightly towards her so that her back was towards the other women. 'I hate to go. I want you so much.'

Her eyes glistened in the full lamplight. 'I *know*.' She bit her lip to hold back the emotion. 'I *know*.'

Blackwood took her hand and kissed it. Then he released it and looked at her. 'Until we meet — '

She lifted her chin as he had seen her do many times. 'Take care, David.'

Oblivious to the watching eyes Blackwood hurried from the room. He did not look back. He did not dare.

Swan held the door for him and shot the countess a quick glance. Had they? he wondered. God she was a fair treat to look at.

'Mr Gravatt's musterin' the men now, sir.'

He glanced at Blackwood's stern profile.

'Think we'll 'old the buggers off, sir?'

Blackwood tried not to think of her at the mercy of the Boxers.

'Of course.' It was what Hay would have said.

Blackwood paused by the machine-gun and lowered his head to peer along its five barrels. The old Nordenfeldt might be hand-operated but a good gun-layer like Private Hudson could still get off some three-hundred and-fifty rounds a minute.

Corporal O'Neil followed his glance and said, 'When they come over the outer barricade we'll give them a right welcome, sir.' His face was blistered from the sun after all his hours on the flat roof which he had now abandoned.

Blackwood looked at the gates, the rough and ready defences. De Courcy had used his common sense again and had painted two large aiming marks so that the marksmen could fire off the explosion.

He saw the two sharpshooters, Roberts and Dago Trent, in their sandbagged positions, each with extra ammunition pouches opened and within reach. Colour Sergeant Chittock had unrolled his Colours although in the morning gloom the red looked black. Before they had fallen back to the second defence line Chittock had hoisted his borrowed Union Jack above the gateway. That more than anything would attract the enemy's anger and attention.

Blackwood walked slowly down the line. He saw Sergeant Kirby leaning on some old steel plates and gripping them with both hands. It looked as if he was taking slow, deep breaths, but before he saw Blackwood's approach and straightened his back, the pain on his heavy face was only too apparent.

'Morning, Sergeant.'

'Sir.'

'How's the wound?' Blackwood watched the sudden wariness in Kirby's eyes. What was the matter with him? If he was afraid of being sent back to the *Mediator* or a field dressing station he could put it from his mind. Nobody would leave Tientsin until the battle was fought and won, or the city was relieved.

'Never better, sir.' Kirby stared at a point above Blackwood's shoulder.

'Good, I'm glad to hear it.' He saw the relief on the sergeant's face. What did he expect him to say?

The sergeant major stood near the colour sergeant, his features calm, as if he had accepted the reality of defeat.

Blackwood said, 'Have you spoken to Mr Bannatyre?'

'Yessir.' Fox looked at him squarely and added, ''E'll be a good 'un, after this, sir.'

It was the worse part of it. But they had to make a show of defending the outer barricades until the last moment. Twenty men including Bannatyre and the sergeant major, and that was more than they could really spare.

Somewhere a voice yelled a command. The Japanese were preparing for their own dawn. Blackwood had met their major only briefly, a stocky little man in blue cap and tunic, with a sword which seemed far too large for him. A dangerous adversary to meet in battle.

He found Gravatt with de Courcy and a runner, drinking tea from giant mugs which they had carried from their quarters.

Gravatt put down his mug. 'Sorry to call you so soon, sir. It's all quiet now, but the pickets saw some movement on our left front. It could be they're moving a cannon, and making sure we can't see where it's hidden.' He peered forward. 'Have you had any sleep, sir?' He sounded concerned.

Blackwood climbed over the barricade and walked across the open ground to the outer defence line.

'I don't need sleep.'

He found the same box he had used before and stood on it to peer towards the enemy's camp. Most of the fires were out now, and even the stars had almost faded away. He shivered in spite of the fact he knew he was prepared for what must come. He did not feel afraid, at least he did not recognize it. Committed, resigned, it was an empty ache like hunger.

It would soon be dawn. He glanced at the gateway's battered silhouette. It would serve him right if the enemy fired first because they already knew the packed charges were there. He would be blown to pieces in the blink of an eye.

Lieutenant Bannatyre turned to face him. He had removed his field-service cap and had tucked it in his belt.

Blackwood said, 'They may gather behind the old wall where Adams was caught in the trap. It would give them cover until the gun is brought to bear.' He recalled Ralf's description, the hostility in his voice, Blackwood could almost see the gun for himself.

He heard the careful tread of feet as the marines who were to man these defences approached from the rear.

He said, 'God, Ian, you've not brought Sergeant Kirby here with you?'

Bannatyre shrugged. 'I tried to dissuade him, sir. But he *is* my platoon sergeant, and sick or not the men respect him.'

'I see.' Blackwood thought of Kirby's anxious eyes. It was like the last time when he had volunteered to go with O'Neil to blow up the boom across the river. He had been eager then. It had been far more than bravado. Kirby was too professional a Royal Marine for that.

'In position, sir.'

'Very well, Sergeant.' Bannatyre sounded as if he wanted to yawn. A bad sign. Men who were afraid often needed to yawn; Blackwood had known the feeling but had never understood it.

A marine who stood with his back to the enemy said, 'Looks good, dunnit, sir?'

Blackwood followed his gaze and saw Chittock's borrowed flag lift lazily in a tiny breeze above the gateway. The red no longer looked black, and the white crosses were as clear as a marine's belts.

'Permission to sound Stand-To, sir?'

'Not yet. I want every man under cover first. Tell Mr Gravatt to pass the word.' He knew that Fox was standing nearby although he had not heard his approach.

'It's time, Sergeant Major.' Blackwood looked at his tall figure with affection, and recalled his words about Neil when he had received the news of his death. At times like these Fox was like a rock, and yet Blackwood felt he knew as little about him as when they had first met.

Swan glanced up at the gateway. The whole of the Union Jack and its staff were now clearly visible. But the small breeze had expended itself, and the flag had no movement. It was as if the whole area including the scattered corpses was holding its breath.

Bannatyre said, 'Good luck, sir.'

Blackwood nodded as he glanced at the extended line of pale uniforms. 'You too. Keep those men down and out of the way until the signal.'

He walked slowly across the open stretch of churned-up ground and thought of the injured marine with the vicious trap still clamped to his leg, of Ralf, aloof, defiant, but changed for all that. The General might approve now, he decided.

Gravatt reached down to assist him over the barricade. He saw the nearest marines looking at him. They trusted him, and yet he had nothing to offer. They needed him more than ever, and would never understand that he needed them more.

Sergeant Greenaway, his rifle like a stick in his massive fists. Private Kempster, the lad from Leeds who had been so excited at seeing the engine from his home-town. Oates, the bugler, Corporal Addis, the barrack-room lawyer who had been strangely subdued since Ralf's return with the injured marine. But there were too many missing faces. There would be more.

He took out his handkerchief and unbuttoned his collar

to wipe his throat. He felt the locket-chain warm against his skin and thought of that one night when they had loved so fiercely and with such need.

He heard a man whisper, ''Ere comes 'is lordship!'

Blackwood pretended he had not heard and turned to greet Colonel Hay who was to his surprise riding the horse Trooper.

Hay looked along the defences. 'All ready, I see.' The horse sidestepped but Hay brought it instantly under control. 'These animals need exercise. I hope you don't object to my borrowing him, what?'

'Not at all, sir. He doesn't belong to me either.'

'I see.' Hay made even trivialities sound important. 'I shall visit you later on.' He looked at Blackwood and lowered his voice. 'This line will be held, d'you understand?'

'I do, sir.'

'Good.' Hay nodded to Gravatt and spurred the horse on towards the other sector beyond the mission.

Gravatt emitted a deep sigh. 'I was just thinking, sir. Summer in England. It's hard to believe, isn't it? I don't suppose anyones knows about Tientsin, or cares for that matter.'

Blackwood smiled grimly. 'Well I care and so must you.' He tugged out his watch and held it up to his eyes. He saw Gravatt and Swan watching him, and pictured de Courcy and Ralf at the other end of the line which would act as a hinge if the defences were forced back.

This line will be held, Hay had said. The *buts* and the *if onlys* no longer counted for anything.

Blackwood licked his lips and tried to shut out the memories and the hopes. They never helped.

'Bugler! Sound off!'

He stepped down from the barricade and watched the retreating shadows as the bugle's clear notes put an end to the night and its protection.

Along the outer line of barricades he heard the hoarse

shouts from Bannatyre's small detachment, calling along the line as if it were fully manned as usual, so that it would sound more like a battalion than a mere handful of men.

Blackwood watched the sky and remembered how he had torn himself from her when dawn had been near. The heat of her body, the curve of her breasts in his hands. Everything.

There was a violent bang, very loud and without an echo, and seconds later the shell landed inside the defences with a deafening explosion.

'*Keep down!*' Not that they needed telling. The aiming shot. The next would be more accurate. Blackwood saw a young marine press his face against some sandbags, his fingers locked into them like claws.

Crash. The next shell hit the centre of the open space where Blackwood had just been walking. He felt the air sucked from his lungs, the hiss and crack of steel splinters as they scythed wall and barricade alike. But for Ralf's unexpected act of courage that one shell alone would have killed and wounded a third of their strength.

Gravatt muttered, 'Here comes another bastard!'

Blackwood turned his face away. He wanted to yawn, and the discovery was worse than any wound.

17

Roll-Call

The bombardment of the south-western defences continued
for an hour. Each explosion was deafening to the men
crouching and hiding behind their barricades or inside
collapsed buildings, but by some miracle none of the
marines had been seriously hurt.

Lieutenant Ian Bannatyre counted each shot. The bang,
the abbreviated whistle followed instantly by the crash of an
exploding shell seemed to scrape the inside of his skull like
hot claws. There was a ten-minute interval between each
shot. Either the Boxers were short of ammunition, which
seemed unlikely, or they were having to carry it some
distance to the gun, probably from that same gully, he
thought despairingly.

When he looked back at the nearest buildings there was
smoke everywhere. A few reluctant coolies had been ordered
to douse the fires, and to carry more material to the
barricades, but they were more afraid of the Boxers than of
the marines.

Sergeant Major Fox peered over the sandbags as the dust
swirled overhead from the last shell.

'They're massin' for a charge, sir.'

Bannatyre raised his head and saw the vague groups of
Boxers and troops beginning to merge into a solid wedge of
men and weapons. Like that last time. He shuddered.

Fox watched him grimly. 'We just makes a show, then
we falls back to the second line, sir. We should catch a few
'undred of 'em 'til they catches on wot we're up to.'

Bannatyre worried him. For one who had never seen any real combat before, the young lieutenant had done fairly well, he thought. But his strength was running away like sand.

Bannatyre gripped his revolver until his fingers ached. 'God, how long can we hold out?'

Fox thought, as long as it bloody well takes. He said, 'They've only got one gun anyway. The other wheels must 'ave been a limber for the ammo.'

Bannatyre looked along his stretched line of men. He could only see the occasional cap, or the gleam of a bayonet.

There was a dull roar of voices which rose to a terrifying crescendo as the enemy began to lope forward. They were moving more slowly than before. It only added to the menace. Bannatyre tried to moisten his lips but they were hard and dry like leather.

Fox snapped, 'They can't understand.' What was the use. Bannatyre was too frightened to give the order.

'Open fire!' He snatched up a rifle and poked it through the sandbags. *'Rapid fire*, damn you!'

Along the barricade the rifles cracked and spat flame at the oncoming horde. Some of the enemy must have fallen but they were trampled underfoot so that it appeared as if the yelling, screaming ranks were unstoppable.

Fox felt the butt kick into his shoulder and jerked the bolt even as he took aim on one of the leaders. He groped for fresh bullets before his target had hit the ground.

He thought of Blackwood and all the others watching and waiting. It would have to be perfectly timed. He thought too of Blackwood's behaviour in the past, his ability to think of everyone but himself.

Fox took careful aim and fired again.

Bannatyre emptied his revolver over the barricade, his breath rasping aloud like an old man's.

Some of the Boxers were almost at the barricade where it joined the broken wall. Above the old gateway the Union Jack moved only occasionally as a bullet or musket ball cut it into defiant ribbons. It seemed to draw the enemy like a magnet, a symbol of all they hated.

The bugle bleated above the crackle of rifles and the roar of voices. 'Retreat! Fall back!'

Bannatyre was trying to reload his revolver, his mind reeling to the din. More than anything he wanted to run with his men as they scrambled or fell from the barricades and pelted for the second line.

Fox shouted, 'Come on, sir!' He gave a mad grin. 'No time for a picnic!'

The surging mass of Boxers and Imperial soldiers seemed to sway as one and change direction towards the gates as they realized that the defenders were running for their lives.

A bullet slammed into the barricade and Bannatyre clapped his hand to his eye as some grit spurted into it. He tried to climb down to the ground but stumbled over a corpse and pitched headlong.

Fox believed that Bannatyre was behind him and only realized what had happened when he turned and saw some jubilant Boxers on top of the abandoned barricade.

Two figures charged from the right, one was Private Carver, the other was Sergeant Kirby. As one of the Boxers jumped down towards Bannatyre, his bayoneted rifle ready to pin him to the ground, Kirby gave a great, inhuman bellow.

In those split seconds Fox saw it all, the veins bulging from Kirby's head and neck, the great bloody patch on his tunic where his terrible wound had burst open. Kirby swung his rifle and caught the Boxer off-balance with the heel-plate then as the man toppled sideways he drove his bayonet into his side, almost to the hilt.

Fox ran towards them, firing from his hip as more of the enemy bobbed over the barricade. The main force of attackers were at the gates now and he could hear them tearing the makeshift defences apart with their bare hands.

Bullets whistled across the clearing, and Private Carver fell dead, blood pouring from his mouth. Another Boxer dropped to the ground as lightly as a cat. Fox saw the blade swing in his hands and retched as it cleaved Bannatyre across the neck and shoulder.

Fox's last bullet brought the Boxer down. He did not wait any longer but thrust his arm about Kirby's waist and together they ran and staggered towards the next barricade.

Fox was only vaguely aware of some shouted commands, the heads and levelled rifles rising above the defences as the marines poured a devastating volley into the men below the wall. Two other shots were aimed at the packed explosives in the gateway, and even as the barricade there collapsed under the weight of bodies and the enemy surged through the air was rent apart by one thunderous explosion.

Fox heard Kirby gasping in agony. Nothing could save him now. Hands reached out to haul him to safety and Fox shouted, 'Easy! Carry 'im to the army dressin' station!'

Some last reserve of strength seemed to rouse Kirby from his terrible pain.

'*No!* Just put me down!'

Fox reloaded his rifle and nodded to the grim faces around him.

'All right, Jeff. You'll be good as new soon.'

Surprisingly Kirby managed a weak grin. 'You always was a bloody good liar!' Then his face twisted in agony again and he fell silent.

Corporal O'Neil waited until the Boxers already inside the defences were trapped by the gateway which was choked with corpses and the remains of a stone arch which had crossed above the original gates. The machine-gun rattled into life, the bullets knocking the confused Boxers from their feet like an invisible arm.

'They're running!'

Blackwood strode along the barricade, the bugler hurrying behind him.

'Cease firing!' He saw Kirby lying on his back, a blanket folded beneath his head.

Fox said heavily. ''E tried to save Mr Bannatyre, sir.'

Blackwood watched him gravely. 'I know. I saw it. I saw what you did too.' He knelt down beside the dying sergeant, knowing in his heart he should not be wasting time. He was needed everywhere. His mind still quaked from the roar of firing and the crash of those great shells. Bannatyre was dead, and for what? He was wrong to let his mind drift like this. Bannatyre had been doing his job. Because of his desperate rearguard action at least two hundred Boxers had been killed or badly wounded. It might blunt the edge of their next attack. It was all they could hope for.

Kirby opened his eyes and peered up at him. 'Sorry 'bout this, sir.'

'Don't talk.'

Kirby tried to shake his head but the pain made him whimper like a child.

'Must talk. 'Ave to.'

Fox said uneasily, 'Stow it, Jeff.'

Kirby glared at him. 'I bin in the Corps almost as long as you. I knows me rights. Dyin' declaration, that's wot.'

Fox knelt beside Blackwood. ''E's goin' fast, sir. Losin' 'is mind.'

Kirby gritted his teeth. 'My wife,' he groaned. 'Nance, she's dead.'

Blackwood said gently, 'I know.'

'I killed 'er! The fire was later. Oh, Nance, forgive me!'

He opened his mouth wide as if to shout, but it remained open, and his eyes were fixed and without understanding.

Fox stood up. 'Wot's he talking about, sir?' He shook his head. 'Poor sod. 'E was a good mate.'

Blackwood walked along his men, and waited for de Courcy to lead a party of marines to the outer defences again. There was no point in trying to barricade the gate. If they did, the Boxers would use their gun to blow it down. He saw a wounded Boxer rise up on his elbow and aim a musket at a passing marine. Sergeant Greenaway kicked the weapon aside and brought his bayonet down in a straight lunge.

'No you don't, matey.'

He found Gravatt and Ralf in the centre of the line staring after the retreating enemy.

Gravatt said, 'They'll be back.' He saw Blackwood. 'I heard about Ian, sir. Bad luck.'

They looked at each other. It was always the way. Any one of them could have been killed. As it was they had hardly lost a man. Poor Bannatyre and Private Carver. And now Kirby who had acted like a lion right to the end.

Had he been delirious, or did he really murder his wife?

Blackwood discovered he did not care. Kirby had shown remarkable courage. As if, like the time on the river, he had wanted to die. But who would ever know for certain? Even fewer would care.

Gravatt watched his face and said, 'I wonder if Colonel Hay's messenger got through the Chinese lines, sir.'

Blackwood winced as the cannon fired again, then ducked as a shell exploded on the top of a nearby building. Where O'Neil and his machine-gun would have been. Maybe the Boxers did not realize it had been moved. Not yet.

He said, 'I think we have to assume he didn't get through, Toby. So until a relief does reach us we must hold on.' He stared bitterly at the dust above the enemy camp. 'But for that damned gun – '

Ralf said, 'Is there no way of destroying it, or knocking it out of action?'

Blackwood studied him thoughtfully. Ralf had certainly changed since he had carried the injured Private Adams to safety.

'Impossible.' He saw the shutter drop instantly behind Ralf's opaque stare. He added, 'The gun will be in the centre of their camp. There are thousands of the enemy out there, night or day. It would be suicide.' He saw Swan leaning on his rifle, his eyes closed as if he was asleep on his feet. 'But I agree with you, Ralf. It's the *only* way.'

They ducked again as another explosion made the ground jump beneath them and pebbles and broken beams were

flung into the air almost where the previous shell had
landed.

'Ten minutes between each shot or near enough. They
must be frightened we'll produce some artillery of our own
and blow up their ammunition store.'

Gravatt grimaced. 'Some hopes.'

Blackwood tried not to measure their limit of existence.
Two more days? At the most. But not with the shells
crashing down every few minutes. It seemed likely that even
if the Boxers did not attack at night, they would keep up a
bombardment around the clock. Then even rest would be
denied to his men.

He tried to think it out, but his head was aching
unmercifully.

Gravatt lowered his binoculars. 'They don't look as if
they're going to attack for a while, sir.'

'No. They'll try to soften us with shellfire first.' He
looked at the scattered corpses, some already grotesque in
the strong sunlight. 'Have that lot cleared away from our
lines, Toby. Things are bad enough without the stench.'

Gravatt nodded. 'I'll get Ian Bannatyre to – ' Their eyes
met and he left the rest unsaid. It was often impossible to
accept the loss of a man in such a close-knit body.

Blackwood nudged Swan. 'Come on, man, I have to see
the Colonel.'

Ralf blocked his way. 'I want to do it.' He dropped his
eyes. 'Sir.'

They ducked as another shell ploughed amongst some
hovels near the mission. Somewhere a voice shouted,
'Stretcher bearer, this way!'

Blackwood eyed his cousin and said, 'It would mean
blowing up their supply of shells. Without them, the gun is
just scrap-iron.'

Ralf fell in step beside him, his hands moving jerkily as
he said, 'The General told me often enough about my father
in the Crimea, and the way they blew up the Russian guns.'

Blackwood replied, 'I'll speak with Sir John Hay. Then

we'll see.' He smiled sadly. 'I'm supposed to be looking after you, remember?'

Ralf shrugged. 'I can manage.'

Blackwood found Hay in his battered command post, sitting on a canvas chair and sipping a glass of wine. He was studying a map and looked up when he saw Blackwood's shadow.

'Holding out?'

Blackwood sighed. There was no wastage with Hay. Not even with words.

'We're under heavy fire, sir.'

'I know that, dammit. But can you hold?'

'No, sir. Not with that gun out there.'

Hay glared at him. 'If we try to attack it, they'll cut us into pieces! Dammit, Blackwood, they outnumber us twenty times over. I've heard that Chinese resistance is stiffening, by the way. So it may take even longer to force a relief column through to us.'

Blackwood gauged the moment. It was not easy for Hay. No amount of bluster could change the cruel facts.

Blackwood said, 'I think we should try to blow up the enemy's magazine or limber, sir. It's in the gully, I'm certain of it.'

A shell exploded somewhere, the sound muffled here. Blackwood saw dust fall from the roof and sprinkle Hay's immaculate red tunic. He did not appear to notice. 'It sounds like madness.' For the first time he gave his maniac grin. 'But I suppose if you've earned the VC you must be crazy enough for anything, what?' He shook with soundless laughter.

He became suddenly serious. 'Volunteers of course.'

'Of course, sir.'

'And you can forget any idea of going yourself. You're here to *command*, not to lead some death-or-glory escapade, see?'

Blackwood smiled. What did Hay expect? Whoever volunteered would be unlikely to return. This was not the Crimea as described by the General at Hawks Hill. No great armies this time. A handful of men against an unknown force of fanatics. Surrounded, and probably already listed as missing, it was a terrible responsibility to ask men to throw away their lives because of some hazy idea.

Hay added. 'I'll try to get some support for you of course.'

Blackwood walked out into the sunlight and saw Swan waiting for him.

'Tonight, sir?'

'It has to be.'

Swan slung his rifle and waited for the dust to settle from the last shellburst. 'Rather them than me.'

Blackwood found Gravatt at his post and told him. The adjutant listened without comment then said quietly, 'I'll go.'

He saw the colour sergeant standing back from the ruined gateway staring up at the bullet-riddled flag which he had obviously replaced in spite of the bursting shells.

Sergeant Greenaway shouted, 'I think they're coming at us again, sir!'

Blackwood looked at Gravatt. 'I shall decide later, Toby.' *You may be in command by then.*

Gravatt bit his lip. 'Very well, sir.' He drew his revolver and examined it automatically.

'Until then, Toby, we must hold this line.'

'Stand-to!' Fox came striding along the barricade, Kirby momentarily forgotten. 'Face yer front! Give the bastards 'ell!'

Blackwood walked away from Gravatt. They were too few in number now to be caught together.

He leaned on the rough parapet and levelled his revolver with both hands.

She would be listening. Packed in the mission with all those women and children. He shivered in spite of his taut nerves.

'Fifty yards! Independent! *Fire!*'

It was never-ending.

Inside the stone-built stables where the marines were housed, where they rested or fretted with anxiety while they waited for daylight, it was almost dark.

Ralf Blackwood glanced around the spartan surroundings where some marines were lying exhausted beside their kit and was amazed that he felt so self-controlled.

It had been a terrible day. The bombardment, then the wild charges to the barricades. It had sounded as if the Japanese troops were under equal pressure too. It could not last. The realization gave him a strange sensation of power and inner strength.

They had lost three more marines killed, and several wounded; Ralf was not certain how many. Or maybe he did not really care. It could not help to dwell on weakness, he thought.

And soon he would be going out into the darkness. It was sheer, utter madness.

But when the fighting had died down, and they had stood gasping at their posts like stricken animals, his cousin David had told them about the proposed raid into the enemy's territory. The others had volunteered, and Ralf had seen from the pain in his cousin's eyes that he wanted to go himself.

Ralf had watched their faces when he had said, 'I'm the one. I've been out there in the dark before, remember?'

He had expected an argument and he had been surprised by their acceptance. Perhaps they believed his simple explanation. Unlikely. They needed to keep together when the end came, it was obvious.

By contrast Ralf hated the stand-and-die sentiment. But he needed two volunteers to accompany him. He could see them now watching him from the shadows.

His cousin had asked if they were genuine volunteers. Ralf almost smiled. How could they refuse in front of their *mates*?

Corporal Addis was one. It would be interesting to discover if he could still sneer behind his back on this impossible mission. And Private Roberts, the Sussex countryman who never missed with any sort of rifle. He had been brought up in the fields and hedgerows, and could move like a ghost when need be. He would have detailed Sergeant Greenaway but his size and age would only jeopardize the raid. It would have taught him a lesson too.

The sergeant major was already present, as Ralf knew he would be.

'Six grenades, sir, two each.'

'I can count, Sergeant Major.' It was easy when you knew how. Fox was no better than a hotel porter when you learned his weakness, his instant obedience.

There was an uncomfortable silence, broken only by the horse Trooper who was munching contentedly from a feed-bag. Trooper was apparently untroubled by the stench of death and charred buildings, the day's chorus of gunfire and yells.

Ralf said, 'Now, you two, pay attention.' He saw some of the resting marines propping themselves on their elbows, hating him for disturbing them rather than for what he was saying.

'I want you to strip to your trousers.' He gestured towards an old unused fireplace, perhaps where a blacksmith had worked in safer times. 'Rub yourselves all over with soot. I want you as black as boots.' David would have made a joke about it, even though his mind told him otherwise. There was no point in it, any more than there was with Fox.

I don't need them. I don't need anyone.

He thought momentarily of the German countess and wondered if they had made love. He had watched his cousin since that night, but if he had acted with dishonour he was hiding it well.

He recalled that afternoon, during an attack when the centre of the line had almost collapsed. There had been Chinese everywhere, and the marines' bayonets had shone with blood.

In the weakest part of the line he had seen David waving

his sword, his teeth white in the smoky sunshine as he had urged, encouraged, and forced his men back and the enemy with them.

Once as David had turned towards him he had seen the real man, spent, sickened at what was happening, knowing he had to keep them all going. Like a state of shock, Ralf thought, he had looked right through him.

Enough of this. It was time to make a move.

He unbuttoned his tunic and threw it with his shirt on the ground. He saw the youthful Private Adams staring at him from a rough stretcher, his injured foot a mass of bandages.

'Here, sir, let me.'

Ralf smiled and sat beside the youth as he leaned over to slap the wet soot all over his naked back. It was wet because at one stage of the battle the roof of the stable had taken fire. Several buildings were still blazing but to the marines this wretched slum was a temporary barracks and they had quickly doused the flames.

They stood and looked at each other. Roberts was unconcerned about going on the raid. For, apart from his genuine pride in the Corps and its comradeship, he was in fact a loner. On leave in Portsmouth, or runs ashore from one ship or another, he always went by himself.

Corporal Addis on the other hand was almost shaking with anxiety and worse. He still could not really believe it. When the second lieutenant had put the idea of volunteering to him it had been in earshot of several other marines. Men he had known and had often dominated with his apparent knowledge of the law and his inside-information about their officers.

Fox said, 'Cap'n Blackwood is comin', sir.' He sounded wary, which was unusual.

Ralf faced the doorway as Blackwood and Private Swan ducked through a rough sacking curtain.

'Good luck, all of you. If you get sighted before you reach an objective return immediately. There's been enough waste of life already.'

Ralf watched him. That was what Blair might have said.

Ralf said, 'I intend to make a wide detour. Longer but safer.'

Blackwood nodded. He felt like dropping, and every nerve and muscle screamed out for sleep. He tried not to think of that afternoon. The relentless attacks, his men fighting them back again and again. He thought of the faces which had fallen. Private Knowles, the one who had ridden Trooper. Hacked to death as a shot had brought him down. Davis, the Welsh sergeant, killed while fighting three Boxers single-handed, and Private McCulloch, whose father was a sergeant major at Forton Barracks. So many faces that they became mixed up in his aching mind.

There seemed to be no more cannon-fire. The enemy were probably saving their strength for the next morning. Perhaps the last one. He watched his young cousin and wanted to say something which might bridge the gulf. At the same time he knew Ralf would resent it. Perhaps his total independence was all he had to sustain him.

Blackwood said simply, 'I shall miss you.' It came out unintentionally. Just like that. He was surprised to discover that he meant it.

Ralf looked up, his eyes very pale in his nigger-black face.

'Don't. It'll be over for all of us soon.' He tightened his belt and waited for the others to pick up the grenades. Then he said, 'I hope the General will be satisfied.' Then he turned on his heel and walked out. He did not even look back to see if Addis and Roberts were following.

At the outer barricade de Courcy and the colour sergeant waited to see them through the shattered gateway.

Ralf noticed that many of the corpses had been dragged away. As if a dead army had risen and marched from the killing-ground.

The night breeze was warm on his bare shoulders and he was grateful for the cup of whisky which Swan had got for him.

Ralf touched his trousers pocket and felt the brass telescope hot against his thigh.

He wished he had really known his father. From the portrait which hung at Hawks Hill he had looked more like David, he thought. He tightened his jaw. Maybe it was David he was really trying to impress.

Ralf glanced angrily at the first pale stars.

'This way. Follow me.'

He thought suddenly of the boy Adams, the way he wanted to help and serve him.

The realization hit him like a fist. It was not just Adams. Like it or not they all depended on him now.

'Wake up, sir. It's time.'

Blackwood rolled over and groaned as Swan released his grip on his shoulder. As his senses returned he wished he had not given in to sleep. It made him feel weak, vulnerable, his whole body protesting. It was very dark. Not for long.

Swan held out a mug of tea. 'Best I could do, sir.'

Blackwood nodded thankfully. 'Any news of my cousin?'

Swan eyed him steadily. 'No. Probably too early.'

Blackwood said, 'I'd like to have a shave.' Swan got to his feet. The request did not surprise him. It was odd the way blokes made the effort before a last battle. He had already seen some of the marines rolling and packing their kit, their faces strangely dedicated, as if nothing else mattered.

He had heard that it had been common enough in the great days of sail. Clean shirt and a good meal before hell broke loose.

Blackwood stared up at the sky as he sipped the scalding tea. There was more hot water than tea leaves, he thought. Everything was suddenly in short supply.

He wondered if Ralf was still safe or out there unable to move in either direction. A wide detour, he had said. If he

was too long he and his two volunteers might be the only
survivors.

He looked round as Swan returned with his shaving kit.
Ralf might already be a prisoner, gasping out his life,
praying for death. He heard a dog barking somewhere, a
few hasty footsteps as the remaining coolies were released
from their work removing enemy corpses. What did they
think about it? They surely could not believe the Boxers to
be invulnerable to foreign bullets any more?

He thought too of Friedrike at the mission building.
Gravatt had told him that it was now being defended by the
German marines, the *Seebataillon*. It might comfort her to
hear her own language around her.

Swan handed him a towel and he cleaned his face, the
skin tender after a quick shave. Bravado, another gesture,
what did it matter? He got to his feet and stared at the
horizon. There was still smoke and a few sparks across the
sky, but he could see the outline of the buildings, a gradual
lightening which meant an early dawn.

'I want you to go to Mr Gravatt.'

Swan checked his rifle. 'No bother, sir. 'E's taken care of
everythin'.'

Blackwood ran his fingers through his hair. It felt full of
grit, dirtied by gunsmoke and sweat.

He heard Gravatt approaching and straightened his back.

Swan saw his composure return, the outer confidence
which the other took for granted. He felt moved by what he
saw, to know he had always shared it.

Gravatt reported, 'All available men are in position, sir.
Some of the wounded have joined them. They can keep the
spare rifles loaded.' He added with sudden bitterness,
'There are enough of them!'

Blackwood climbed on to a slab of stone and lifted his
glasses. It was still too dark to see much. If he was wrong
about the Boxers they might rush the outer wall and use it
as a defence while they fired directly on to the inner
barricades.

There was a sudden bang and seconds later the first shell exploded at the foot of the wall. Blackwood did not need to see it; he could hear the worn stones crashing down, splinters whining overhead or cracking into the barricades.

He had been right. The enemy intended to make so many breaks in the wall that they could attack several places at once.

Crash.

Blackwood said, 'Tell them to keep down. The Boxers are firing more often this time.'

A gold rim of sunlight touched one of the tallest buildings then vanished momentarily in a cloud of smoke and fragments as another shell exploded.

He felt Swan remove his revolver and then murmur, 'Only three shots left in it, sir.'

Blackwood loosened his sword and said nothing. He no longer trusted his voice. He would feel better when action was joined. It was always like that. The madness. The wild excitement which could preserve or kill with equal indifference.

He heard O'Neil dragging an ammunition box beside the machine-gun, and Sergeant Chittock unsheathing the Colours. Individual acts of defiance but with little hope left.

The cannon fired once again and Blackwood felt the ground vibrate as more stones and bricks rained down. The wall had been built a long time ago, strong enough to withstand muskets and pikes. It was no match for shellfire.

The sunlight continued remorselessly to lay bare the battlefield, the other lower wall where they had made their first appearance at Tientsin. Blackwood thought of Admiral Seymour's anticipated arrival in Peking in a single day. That was two weeks ago, a century.

He levelled his glasses. 'Bugler, sound the alarm!'

On either side of him he heard the marines preparing themselves. The click of rifle-bolts, the nervous movements along the sandbags as each man tried to find the best vantage point.

He heard the Boxers' horn, mournful but threatening, and pictured the mass of men beginning to form up, to move towards the hated foreigners with gathering momentum.

'*Stand-to!*' Fox was everywhere as usual. Eventually he planted his boots at the place where the barricade had almost collapsed. He would not move unless he fell dead.

Sergeant Greenaway was on the left of the line, and Blackwood found time to notice he had chosen a position amongst some of the youngest marines, new recruits such a short while ago. An ancient warrior to most of them, but he could give them strength when they most needed it. That was now.

Blackwood shouted, 'Hold your fire until I give the order!'

If they fired too soon the first wave of attackers would take cover behind the wall. As the light continued to strengthen he saw the great holes and gaps in the outer wall. Impossible to defend, but still good cover for the advancing enemy.

Hidden on the other side of some sand and grain bags he heard someone repeating over and over again, 'Oh God, oh God' – like that time on the mad dash downriver.

He balanced his revolver in his left hand and drew his sword with the other. Three bullets Swan had said.

He wiped his face with his sleeve.

Come on, you bastards! He glanced quickly at Swan. He had imagined he had shouted the words aloud. But Swan was concentrating on a gap in the wall directly opposite the barricade. There were lots of fallen stones on the inside. The enemy might stumble, others would certainly be thrusting them from the rear. It would give him time to bring several of them down, he thought.

The noise was deafening, and dust from thousands of running feet drove towards the waiting marines like a desert sandstorm.

'*Ready!*'

The rifles moved slightly and then settled on their selected targets.

'*Fire!*'

The charging figures were pouring through the shattered gateway and the gaps along the wall, others knelt on the outer barricade and fired across the shell-pitted ground.

Blackwood waved his sword. 'Again, lads!' He yelled at the nearest marine, the one who had been sobbing prayers. 'Take aim, man, don't waste them!'

'*Fire!*' The order was almost lost in the lethal clatter of the machine-gun. The front ranks seemed to bend and fall or were stamped underfoot by the press of figures behind.

It was hopeless. They were almost here. Blackwood saw two marines step back from the barricade, as if unable to face the onslaught.

It was now or never.

He climbed on to the barricade and shouted above the din, 'Meet them! Come on, the Royals!'

The madness gripped all of them as they leapt from their hiding places and met the oncoming mob out in the open.

Blackwood parried a pike to one side and drove his blade through an Imperial soldier's neck. As he tore the sword free he swung it across the front of a marine who had dropped to one knee, his fingers locked around his thigh as the blood shone to match his fallen bayonet.

Oates sounded his bugle again and again, it was the only sound to carry from one end of the embattled line to the other. The Boxers surged against the barricade, and tried to pull the marines down amongst them. The bayonets darted and lunged, and here and there a marine found time to reload his rifle and fire into the screaming mass of faces which could not move forward or back.

Corporal O'Neil yelled, 'Quick, me boy! Put your weight on this wheel, we'll give the gateway a burst.' He stared horrified as his friend the gun-layer fell backwards, a gaping hole punched between his eyes. O'Neil sobbed, 'Oh, Willy! Not you too!'

Then he dragged his friend aside and threw himself at the machine-gun yelling curses and obscenities as he worked the firing-handle until his hand seemed blurred. Once a bullet cut across his forearm and left a livid, black scar, but O'Neil barely noticed.

At the centre of the line some of the Boxers, one carrying a yellow standard, hurled themselves over the top. Some were impaled on bayonets, another shot down by one of the marines who had been wounded earlier.

Lieutenant de Courcy shouted, 'Can't hold 'em, sir!' He fired his revolver until it was empty and then charged into the fight with only his sword.

Blackwood saw the colour sergeant clinging to his staff, his eyes squinting with pain as blood ran from two wounds in his shoulder. But he clung to the flag, for it was what he had always done. When the truth came to him at last he managed to pass the flag to a wild-eyed marine and gasp, 'Don't let go, Dago! Not fer nothing!' Then he died.

The explosion when it came felt like an earthquake, as if it was many miles away and did not concern them at all.

Blackwood locked swords with a yelling Chinese officer, pushed him against the barricade and then drove the blade into his stomach. The dying officer was still shouting as he dropped. Hate, surrender, Blackwood did not care which. In his mind all he could recognize was the gigantic explosion. Ralf and his men had done it. It must have taken more than mere courage to wait for daylight and the first shots from the cannon. Every available Boxer and soldier must have gathered for the attack after the shells had done their work.

'*Cease firing!*' That was Gravatt, instantly supported by the bugler.

Blackwood stared dazedly as the enemy melted back towards the wall, over the dead and dying and through the gaps without firing another shot.

Blackwood sheathed his sword. It clung to the scabbard, sticky with blood.

Gravatt shouted wildly, 'They're on the run!' He waved his cap in the air. 'Look at 'em go!'

The explosion must have caught the enemy completely off-balance, Blackwood thought. Then he looked along his line of breathless, bleeding marines. Fox still a ramrod amidst chaos and horror. De Courcy gritting his teeth as a marine bandaged his wounded hand. He had seized a Chinese blade to push it away and might lose all his fingers. But his face said it all. *I am alive.*

Blackwood walked slowly amongst his men. Several were dead, and more wounded than otherwise.

The Boxers would come back. They had to. Without Tientsin in their hands they would be in the same position as Seymour.

Blackwood saw O'Neil carrying Private Willy Hudson away from the machine-gun. He glanced briefly at Blackwood who was moved by the tears on his battered face. He carried his friend to the nearest building and laid him to rest there. Then he snatched up a rifle and said brokenly. 'No more ammo for th' Nordenfeldt, sir. I'll stand with you.'

Sergeant Greenaway yelled, ''Ere come three o' th' bastards!'

A few rifles lifted and steadied as the figures tumbled through a smashed barricade.

Blackwood held up his hand. 'Belay that!'

In their stolen clothing, their faces still liberally smeared with soot, Ralf and his two marines walked slowly through the dead Boxers. They stopped at the barricade where the battle-shocked marines peered despairingly at the rising dust above the enemy camp.

Ralf said huskily, 'I thought we were too late.' He looked across at Colour Sergeant Nat Chittock who lay with one arm outflung, unwilling to the last to release his precious flag.

Blackwood grasped his cousin by the shoulders. 'You were bloody marvellous, Ralf. It knocked the stuffing out of them.'

Ralf studied him emptily. 'They'll be back.' He tore off the Boxer smock and threw it to one side. 'We laid all night with the other corpses.' It seemed to amuse him. 'I stink.'

Blackwood dropped his arms to his sides. They were like lead. But Ralf was right. Gun or no gun they would be back. He looked at the marines who stood along the barricade. There were great gaps between them. He doubted if there were more than thirty who were still able to fight. But at least Ralf's action had given them time to regroup, then to fall back to the city-centre, or wherever Hay intended to see it through to a bloody conclusion.

'Get the wounded under cover, Toby.' He nodded gratefully as Swan handed him a canteen of water. It was like wine. Perhaps it was; Swan could do anything.

Blackwood took another grip on himself. If he cracked now – He swung round and said, 'Share out the ammunition.' He realized he had spoken sharply and saw Gravatt watching him.

Ralf said, 'I'll see to it.' He looked at him and added, 'Then I'll be back.'

Blackwood walked to the barricade. They would be together when it happened.

Sergeant Greenaway said, 'Private Smith is signallin', sir!'

Blackwood wanted to weep. So soon? The enemy were wasting no time to take their revenge on the ragged flag and those who continued to defend it.

'*Up, lads!*' Fox picked up a rifle. 'Move yerselves!' But when his eyes met Blackwood's they told the truth. It was already finished.

Blackwood raised his glasses and saw the solid mass of Chinese surging about in the dusty sunlight, a few banners still waving here and there; it was like something from a nightmare.

The sun touched on gleaming sabres and suddenly as he watched spellbound Blackwood saw the horses for the first time. Cavalry, a solid wedge of them charging straight for the stampeding mass of Boxers and troops.

I must be going mad. Blackwood recognized the tall headgear of the riders, Cossacks, their heavy sabres slashing a path right through the enemy. He blinked to clear the mist from his eyes. Troops too. Bayonets fixed. He could even hear the raucous call of a bugle.

Gravatt whispered, 'Dear God, it's the relief!'

Blackwood lowered his binoculars and pressed his hands on the empty machine-gun. The enemy was in full retreat. First their shells had been destroyed, and now they were caught between two fires.

It seemed to take an eternity for the first of the relief force to reach them. The Cossacks remained at a distance, or galloped after a few groups of Boxers, their sabres more than a match for the Long Knives.

Fox bellowed, 'Fall in there! Smarten yerselves up!' He sounded angry that soldiers should see them like this.

The first to arrive in the gateway was an army lieutenant colonel mounted on a fine grey stallion. He reined up just a few yards from the Royal Marines and looked at them for what seemed like an age before he said anything. Then he dismounted and returned Blackwood's salute.

He said quietly, 'I've seen a lot of battles in my service, Captain Blackwood.' He glanced along the swaying line of filthy marines, and saw their determination to hold on. 'But never anything like this. We thought you were already dead.' He faced the marines and saluted them stiffly. 'Now I must find Colonel Hay.' He seemed strangely unwilling to leave a scene which he knew he could never forget.

Blackwood said, 'Then on to Peking, sir.'

The officer eyed him sadly. 'You are relieved, Captain Blackwood. You and your men have done more than enough.' He glanced towards the drifting smoke. 'Where are the rest of your company?'

Blackwood bunched his hands into fists to control his sudden emotion.

'These are all of them, sir.'

The lieutenant colonel looked at Sergeant Major Fox, at Ralf, his young features a mask of disapproval even now, at Swan, and Oates, and all the survivors.

He said half to himself. 'What do they say about your Corps? *The first to land*, right?'

Blackwood thought of the others who were not there. Of Bannatyre and young Earle, Sergeants Kirby and Davis, Corporals Lyde and Handley, Chittock, the colour sergeant. And all the other rough graves which had marked their course to this place.

He heard himself say, 'And the last to leave.'

Epilogue

Captain David Blackwood leaned back in a comfortable leather chair and stared through the open French windows. Inside the great house nothing seemed to have changed, he thought. Only when the carriage had carried him through the high gates of Hawks Hill three days ago had he noticed any difference. The big gates needed painting badly, and the lodge-house looked unkempt.

Later after an emotional welcome, Trent, the estate steward, had told him that two of the small farms had been sold off in an effort to pay for some of the General's extravagances.

But that could wait. It was good to be back in England and in time for another summer. Through the windows he could see the neatly trimmed bushes, the swaying masses of colour from the well-tended flower-beds.

Upon his return to Portsmouth in a slow troopship he had heard the news of the Allies finally lifting the siege of Peking, and the end of the Boxers' Society. The damage to Chinese trade and finances was almost crippling with millions of pounds' indemnity to be paid to the European powers and their allies.

Now, looking at the gardens and the green Hampshire countryside beyond, it was hard to believe that it was exactly a year since he and his men had stood together for the final attack which never came.

Most of the survivors of his company had also returned to England, some to their homes, others to the naval hospital at Haslar. Blackwood had made a point of visiting the wounded before he had left Portsmouth for Hawks Hill. They had seemed cheerful enough, but Blackwood doubted if their nights were so peaceful. But now that he was home again perhaps the nightmares would leave him alone. The distorted, screaming faces, the terrible chant *Sha! Sha!* Even in the troopship he had awakened in a cold sweat night after night.

He thought of the General and his mother. They seemed to have got over Neil's death, or at least they were able to accept it. His return and Ralf's impulsive gallantry in that final battle had made up for a lot.

Blackwood often recalled the last time he had seen Friedrike. Almost as soon as the relief force had occupied the city, and the weary defenders relieved, he had hurried to the mission to see her. He had been in time to see her being assisted to a carriage with a full escort of German marines.

They had touched hands and he had seen the tears in her eyes before a black-coated official had coughed politely and guided her into the carriage. It all seemed like a dream. Something which had happened and which he could not accept or understand.

Like the news which had greeted his return to home waters. The Queen was dead. The end of an era. A personality they had all come to take for granted. Perhaps the affairs of state, the wars in China and South Africa, Egypt and the Crimea during her long reign had finally been too much for her.

But the memory of Friedrike and their one night of love together rarely left his thoughts. When he walked round the estate to meet new faces and renew old acquaintances he had touched the locket around his neck, and had wondered about her.

He saw Trooper, the ubiquitous horse, being led by Swan towards the stables. A very adaptable animal, he thought, who seemed as much at home here as in Tientsin. How much younger Swan looked out of uniform. If he was surprised to have survived he kept it a secret.

He heard a door open and watched his father settle himself in one of the big chairs. If he had changed at all it was only that he no longer bothered about the servants seeing him wearing spectacles in the house.

He would want to hear it all over again. The events which had led up to the battle, pieced together with names and faces, strength and weakness.

When Blackwood had told him about Ralf he had chuckled. 'Young puppy. Up in London now chasin' some filly or other.' His severe features had relaxed. 'God, Philip would have been *proud* of him. I am.'

There was to be a special dinner in David Blackwood's honour tonight. He hoped his stomach could cope after all the bad food and coarse rations of the campaign.

And there was Sarah, the girl Neil had hoped to marry. *A nice sensible girl*, as his mother had described her. But there was a lot more to her than that. She would be here too. She had seemed pleased to meet him, with a sort of questioning shyness. Perhaps she was searching for Neil in him?

He smiled to himself. His mother had taken the girl with her to Alresford, their nearest village. Perhaps she was match-making in her quiet way.

He glanced at the headlines on his father's newspaper. *The Kaiser demands massive rearmament. German Fleet to be reinforced.*

His father looked over his glasses.

'There was a piece about your German countess in the paper a few weeks back. I meant to mention it, but what with your return and the news about – '

'What was it?' He found himself on the edge of his chair.

The General eyed him curiously. 'On the society page. The Countess von Heiser had a baby, a boy as it turns out. So the old family line will continue after all. Strange, I heard at the Club that the Count was supposed to be impotent.'

He went back to his newspaper.

Blackwood stood up and walked slowly into the clean June air.

They had both wanted an heir more than anything. They would tell nobody. Only he knew the truth. He touched the locket beneath his shirt. *Our son.*

The old General looked up and watched him cross the terrace to speak with Swan.

Then he gave a slow smile. He had not yet forgotten what it was like to be young.